100

Wicked Little

Witch

Stories

W9-BMO-880

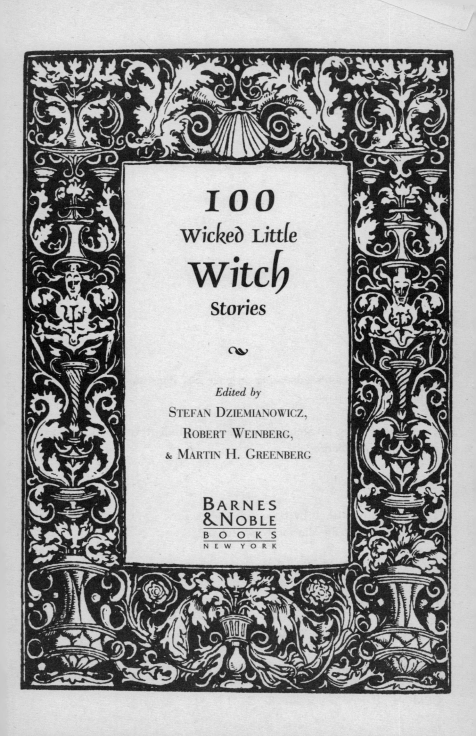

100
Wicked Little
Witch
Stories

❧

Edited by
STEFAN DZIEMIANOWICZ,
ROBERT WEINBERG,
& MARTIN H. GREENBERG

BARNES
&NOBLE
BOOKS
NEW YORK

This edition published by Barnes & Noble, Inc.,
by arrangement with Martin H. Greenberg.

1995 Barnes & Noble Books

ISBN 0-76070-208-X

Book design by Mario A. Moreno

Printed and bound in the United States of America

OPM 9 8 7 6 5 4 3 2 1

Contents

Introduction

Witches are among the most familiar beings in all fantastic fiction. They are as well-known to readers as ghosts and vampires, and are invariably mentioned in the same alliterative breath as warlocks and werewolves. Their ability to cast spells, conjure the infernal, and traffick with the unholy ranks them among the most formidable and fearsome agents of supernatural dread.

Yet witches differ from their weird brethren in one important respect: their fundamental humanity. Unlike ghosts, they have not undergone a transformation that has rendered them something less than human, and unlike vampires and werewolves they are not restricted from the daylit or moonlit paths trod by mortals. For all their remarkable powers, they are as accessible as a next-door neighbor, and sometimes as vulnerable. It is this dual nature that makes witches so fascinating—and frightening.

Historical treatment of witches bears this out. The thousands of victims of witch hunts in medieval Europe and the scores of so-called witches persecuted in the American colonies all shared one common stigma: the perception that they differed in subtle and insidious ways from their fellow men and women. Though the scale of those differences could vary from simple physical anomalies to unusual skills that belied their otherwise normal appearances, their greatest transgression was their simple nonconformity.

So it was that witches came to be seen as pariahs on the periphery of the human race. So it was, too, that in their deviations from others, witches provided those they differed from with a yardstick for measuring the norm.

In the stories that follow, you will encounter good witches and bad witches, practitioners of white witchcraft and devotees of black magic. Most are female, but some are male and others completely unclassifiable within traditional gender and biological categories. Several were to their dark heritage born, yet many deliberately chose the path they walk. A few mix simple love potions, and a few more volatile concoctions that threaten the viability of all we hold dear. Some resent their treatment by those with lesser powers than they, others are unaware that they have any special influence at all. A number are presented as outcasts from their societies, and a different number as inextricably integrated into the fabric of their environments. Some can't be taken too seriously; others it would not be too wise to cross.

Although each of these stories is unique in its particular approach to the witch theme, all have one thing in common: distilled through the alembics of their creators' imaginations into essences of only several thousand words, they have the power to make us reflect on how we define our own humanity.

That's the real magic at work here.

Stefan Dziemianowicz
New York, 1995

Gramma Grunt

Donald R. Burleson

Like Jason Mitchell's childhood itself, the apartment building was a bygone structure now, a relic, fallen away like a half-forgotten dream. Ah, but only half forgotten. He remembered many things about his far-off early years here, and like his memories, the old building itself was not gone beyond recall. Portions still stood, their ragged outlines marking the night sky like the battlements of some time-lost castle noble even in its ruin. Whether the place had ever really been noble, he couldn't say, but it had been home.

Strange, to be back here, back on the corner of Jespersen Avenue and Third Street, after all these years. Back here old and half-lame and wheezing from the walk across town. How long had it been since he cavorted, all bright young eyes and lusty lungs, with his friends on these streets, in this city? Sixty years? No—longer, oh God, appallingly long ago. The dirty sidewalk was empty now, yet the very air seemed charged with restless ghosts writhing awake in the echoes of his mind, a diaphanous crowd of milling reminiscences.

He'd been a "tough guy" then, an impoverished, street-wise kid feeling all the seasoning of his ten years. The gang that he'd hung out with had never gotten into any serious trouble; they had only presented, to the world, a face of impudence mirrored by kindred faces in ten thousand such bleak streets in a hundred such tired old cities, a collective face of prematurely world-weary urban youth with nothing in life's colorless, seemingly endless span to do.

1

Well—they did used to have *some* things to do, especially in those sultry days of summer when the schools disgorged them upon the streets. They had managed to keep busy enough.

They had tormented *her,* for one thing. Sometimes mercilessly.

Right down there, in that old alleyway between this building and the next (itself in ruins now too), to the left as you went away from the street corner—that old alleyway whose yawning entrance now the wan light of a rising late-October moon only half-heartedly tried to illumine. The old alley, where now a breath of night wind moaned through the crevices making a sound like a low, lonesome flute note. In there, that's where she used to sit, a sorry mess of rags on a rotting wooden chair.

Gramma Grunt, they had called her, among themselves, and Gramma Grunt they had often called her, tauntingly, even to her face.

She was a witch.

Or so the smaller children had always said. Of course, the smaller children, younger brothers and sisters of Jason's and Hank's and Billy's and Tommy's and Lester's, would believe anything—that the Tooth Fairy really came in the night, that a grasshopper could spit tobacco in your eye, that if you went all the way up over the bar on the swings in the playground you would come back around turned inside out with all your tubes and shiny-wet organs hanging out for all to see. So no wonder they believed in witches, and believed they knew one. Gramma Grunt—no one knew, no one had ever known, her real name. No one knew where she slept—probably in some dank cellar. She was a rich vein of folklore around the neighborhood, to the little children and to some of the adults alike; seemingly, only Jason's own age group, stridently all-wise and pubescent, were indifferent, unmoved, skeptical of the things said about the old woman.

Such as Jason's own mother's remark, one night, that she had seen her raise a thunderstorm by elevating her rag-tattered bony old arms and muttering, reaching for the scattered clouds and snorting like a pig and mouthing unintelligible imprecations at the sky. His mother and his Aunt Lucille had really believed that—that Gramma Grunt could raise a storm, and could do heaven only knew what else.

It was because she did grunt like a pig, anyway, that the kids called her Gramma Grunt, sometimes even prancing around her in the grimy alley and chanting *Gramma Grunt, Gramma Grunt, witchy-witchy Gramma Grunt.* Even though this would sound childish in the extreme to a passerby, Jason and his friends had been just big enough to make the shameful ritual a little threatening, something a little more than the cruel but harmless foolishness and caprice of children. When one of them would veer too close to the old woman where she sat in her incredibly filthy jumble of rags, or when one of them would venture to poke her in the arm, she would actually grunt like a wild boar: *Khhhnok*! *Khhhnok*! Her ancient lizard face, an incomprehensible nest of wrinkles, would contort like some nameless thing disturbed under a rock, and her arms in their mad fluttering tatters would flail like bird wings, and a vile yellow spittle would overflow her mouth, and she would curse the offender in hissing, gurgling syllables that no one could quite understand.

Tommy Fenton, nine years old and quarrelsome, had shoved her down in a puddle of rainwater in the alley one day, and she cursed him, and three days later Tommy Fenton, coming out of Fletcher's Market and dashing across Eighth Street, was run over by a garbage truck. It was a coincidence, of course, Jason knew, but it was the talk of the neighborhood for quite some time, and people didn't quickly forget the old woman's behavior toward the boy, provoked or not. Some heads nodded, some tongues clucked: yes, she *was* a witch.

Jason had had reason to ponder the question of witchcraft, if only to reject it, because shortly after Tommy's death, the boys were hounding Gramma Grunt one day and suddenly decided, like blackbirds taking to flight in unison, to leave her and scamper away on some other errand. Jason had been the last to turn away, and in that instant the old woman's eyes had met his, arresting his gaze with their feverish glow, and she had snorted: *Khhhnok, I'll—khhhnok—I'll get you someday.* That was ages ago, but he had never forgotten; she had clearly meant for him never to forget.

Pulling his coat collar tighter against the chill breeze that had come up, he hobbled now toward the old opening to the alley. Long ago, long ago, those memories, seen through the prism of so many intervening years. His father had gotten a better job and the family had moved away when Jason was barely eleven, and everything had changed: there were new friends; a suburban neighborhood; suburban schools; and later college; graduate school; a family; a career teaching English at the state college; retirement; his wife Nancy's death; the encroachment, on his own fragile being, of illness, purposelessness, and a lonely old age in which he felt, recently, more nearly able to trust his memory of the distant past than his memory, his fumbling grasp, of yesterday or last week. He didn't really have any clear recollection, for example, of get-

3

ting the sudden urge he must have gotten to come here—here, the old neighborhood, the remembered street corner, the alleyway. What had he been doing when he felt that urge? He couldn't remember.

Over the years he had thought of Gramma Grunt from time to time, but had never, so far as he could recall, wanted to return to the place where he remembered her, and time had replaced his tough ten-year-old bravado, that audacious bravado anxious to repudiate all adult understanding and all folklore of younger sisters and brothers, replaced it with a more worldly and sophisticated skepticism.

In his youth there had been no witches because people younger or older believed there *were*; now there were no witches because—because there just *weren't*; any educated person knew that.

He stepped into the entrance to the alley, where just enough of the surrounding brick walls remained to make it still an alleyway, but where the pallid play of moonlight, though finding a path here and there through the crumbling walls, largely had to give way to a maw of darkness. But just within sight, at the edge of the pale reach of light, he saw —something.

A mound of rags.

And he smelled something in here, in the closer air of the passage, something undefinable but distinctly unpleasant.

He looked at the formless pile of dirty rags, and in some crazy way half expected it to move.

And it did.

It seemed to shudder and shift a little—on its own? Or had the wind subtly touched it?

He stepped closer, peered at the cloth tatters, and began to pull at them, near the top, with his fingers, shredding them away like the layers of an onion, until at length he thought, in the uncertain light, that the rags had begun to look different. He only slowly realized, then, that he was looking at an astonishingly ancient and wrinkled face, whose folds of sickly skin could scarcely be distinguished from the filth-choked tatters in which they were embedded. He thought it must be an illusion, this face, but an illusion would not have opened two baleful yellow eyes to stare at him.

It was unthinkable, preposterous—why, she had been exceedingly old *then*, when he was a boy! As if in sardonic response to this thought, a confusion of wrinkles beneath the eyes widened into a cruel smile, in which a crusty tongue ran snakelike over a staggered row of rotten teeth.

4

"You!" He was shocked at the horror in his own voice.

The smile creased out wider still. *Khhhnok*! In a way loathsome to see, the whole mass of rags convulsed with the piglike snort. When the voice came out, it was like the dry scuttering of spiders.

"I told you I'd get you someday."

He choked and spluttered, suddenly intensely angry. "You? Get me? I'm not a boy of ten anymore, you know."

Khhhnnnnnnok! With the grunt, this time a sickeningly protracted sound from deep in the well of her throat, the creature lifted her arms, bony arms feathered in dirty rags, and in the same instant the sky rumbled with thunder.

"Huh!" He was furious now, though he had the feeling, in some corner of his mind, that his anger was an avoidance of some other emotion. "Don't give me that nonsense about raising a storm. You're not a witch. I never believed you were, even when I was a child."

"Then," the old woman croaked, "you were a fool. And are." She clenched her fingers, thin and angular like talons at the ends of her outstretched arms, and the thunder grumbled in the sky once more, longer and louder this time.

He laughed, though it sounded hollow to his ears. "Save your antics for someone more credulous. You can't raise a storm. You can't raise anything."

She drew her arms back in and glared at him, her face gloating and horrible with a smile that had nothing in it of mirth, and she spoke one more time.

"I raised *you*, didn't I?"

In that awful moment he remembered, he understood everything. He had only a few seconds to reflect, but in those fleeting seconds, with a black veil of clouds drawing across the face of the moon and with thunder reverberating through the alley and a cold rain beginning to fall, he remembered the *beginning* of his walk across town, and he also pictured in his mind the scene that the police would find, if they ever entered this forgotten place: they would find an untenanted mound of dirt-encrusted rags and, in front of it, a fallen pile of less accountable debris. He was almost savoring the irony of it, the humor residing in the realization of where it was that she had raised him *from*, when—her spell no doubt having released him—his consciousness faded into grainy dissolution and the very contours of his face and limbs began to slide, amidst an exhalation of steam and an odor like rotten meat, cascading into a nightmare of bone and sinew and grave-sod on the rain-dampened ground.

By the Hair of the Head

JOE R. LANSDALE

The lighthouse was gray and brutally weathered, kissed each morning by a cold, salt spray. Perched there among the rocks and sand, it seemed a last, weak sentinel against an encroaching sea; a relentless, pounding surf that had slowly swallowed up the shoreline and deposited it in the all-consuming belly of the ocean.

Once the lighthouse had been bright-colored, candy-striped like a barber's pole, with a high beacon light and a horn that honked out to the ships on the sea. No more. The lighthouse director, the last of a long line of sea watchers, had cashed in the job ten years back when the need died, but the lighthouse was now his and he lived there alone, bunked down nightly to the tune of the wind and the raging sea.

Below he had renovated the bottom of the tower and built rooms, and one of these he had locked away from all persons, from all eyes but his own.

I came there fresh from college to write my novel, dreams of being the new Norman Mailer dancing in my head. I rented in with him, as he needed a boarder to help him pay for the place, for he no longer worked and his pension was as meager as stale bread.

High up in the top was where we lived, a bamboo partition drawn between our cots each night, giving us some semblance of privacy, and dark curtains were pulled round the thick, foggy windows that traveled the tower completely around.

By day the curtains were drawn and the partition was pulled and I sat at my typewriter, and he, Howard Machen, sat with his book and his pipe, swelled the room full of gray smoke the thickness of his beard. Sometimes he rose and went below, but he was always quiet and never disturbed my work.

It was a pleasant life. Agreeable to both of us. Mornings we had

6

coffee outside on the little railed walkway and had a word or two as well, then I went to my work and he to his book, and at dinner we had food and talk and brandies; sometimes one, sometimes two, depending on mood and the content of our chatter.

We sometimes spoke of the lighthouse and he told me of the old days, of how he had shone that light out many times on the sea. Out like a great, bright fishing line to snag the ships and guide them in; let them follow the light in the manner that Theseus followed Ariadne's thread.

"Was fine," he'd say. "That pretty old light flashing out there. Best job I had in all my born days. Just couldn't leave her when she shut down, so I bought her."

"It is beautiful up here, but lonely at times."

"I have my company."

I took that as a compliment, and we tossed off another brandy. Any idea of my writing later I cast aside. I had done four good pages and was content to spit the rest of the day away in talk and dreams.

"You say this was your best job," I said as a way of conversation. "What did you do before this?"

He lifted his head and looked at me over the briar and its smoke. His eyes squinted against the tinge of the tobacco. "A good many things. I was born in Wales. Moved to Ireland with my family, was brought up there, and went to work there. Learned the carpentry trade from my father. Later I was a tailor. I've also been a mason—note the rooms I built below with my own two hands—and I've been a boat builder and a ventriloquist in a magician's show."

"A ventriloquist?"

"Correct," he said, and his voice danced around me and seemed not to come from where he sat.

"Hey, that's good."

"Not so good really. I was never good, just sort of fell into it. I'm worse now. No practice, but I've no urge to take it up again."

"I've an interest in such things."

"Have you now?"

"Yes."

"Ever tried a bit of voice throwing?"

"No. But it interests me. The magic stuff interests me more. You said you worked in a magician's show?"

"That I did. I was the lead-up act."

"Learn any of the magic tricks, being an insider and all?"

7

"That I did, but that's not something I'm interested in," he said flatly.

"Was the magician you worked for good?"

"Damn good, m'boy. But his wife was better."

"His wife?"

"Marilyn was her name. A beautiful woman." He winked at me. "Claimed to be a witch."

"You don't say?"

"I do, I do. Said her father was a witch and she learned it and inherited it from him."

"Her father?"

"That's right. Not just women can be witches. Men too."

We poured ourselves another and exchanged sloppy grins, hooked elbows, and tossed it down.

"And another to meet the first," the old man said and poured. Then: "Here's to company." We tossed it off.

"She taught me the ventriloquism, you know," the old man said, relighting his pipe.

"Marilyn?"

"Right, Marilyn."

"She seems to have been a rather all-round lady."

"She was at that. And pretty as an Irish morning."

"I thought witches were all old crones, or young crones. Hook noses, warts . . ."

"Not Marilyn. She was a fine-looking woman. Fine bones, agate eyes that clouded in mystery, and hair the color of a fresh-robbed hive."

"Odd she didn't do the magic herself. I mean, if she was the better magician, why was her husband the star attraction?"

"Oh, but she did do magic. Or rather she helped McDonald to look better than he was, and he was some good. But Marilyn was better.

"Those days were different, m'boy. Women weren't the ones to take the initiative, least not openly. Kept to themselves. Was a sad thing. Back then it wasn't thought fittin' for a woman to be about such business. Wasn't ladylike. Oh, she could get sawed in half, or disappear in a wooden crate, priss and look pretty, but take the lead? Not on your life!"

I fumbled myself another brandy. "A pretty witch, huh?"

"Ummmm."

"Had the old pointed hat and broom passed down, so to speak?" My voice was becoming slightly slurred.

"It's not a laughin' matter, m'boy." Machen clenched the pipe in his teeth.

"I've touched a nerve, have I not? I apologize. Too much sauce." Machen smiled. "Not at all. It's a silly thing, you're right. To hell with it."

"No, no, I'm the one who spoiled the fun. You were telling me she claimed to be the descendant of a long line of witches."

Machen smiled. It did not remind me of other smiles he had worn. This one seemed to come from a borrowed collection.

"Just some silly tattle is all. Don't really know much about it, just worked for her, m'boy." That was the end of that. Standing, he knocked out his pipe on the concrete floor and went to his cot.

For a moment I sat there, the last breath of Machen's pipe still in the air, the brandy still warm in my throat and stomach. I looked at the windows that surrounded the lighthouse, and everywhere I looked was my own ghostly reflection. It was like looking out through the compound eyes of an insect, seeing a multiple image.

I turned out the lights, pulled the curtains and drew the partition between our beds, wrapped myself in my blanket, and soon washed up on the distant shore of a recurring dream. A dream not quite in grasp, but heard like the far, fuzzy cry of a gull out from land.

It had been with me almost since moving into the tower. Sounds, voices . . .

A clunking noise like peg legs on stone . . .

. . . a voice, fading in, fading out . . . Machen's voice, the words not quite clear, but soft and coaxing . . . then solid and firm: "Then be a beast. Have your own way. Look away from me with your mother's eyes."

". . . your fault," came a child's voice, followed by other words that were chopped out by the howl of the sea wind, the roar of the waves.

". . . getting too loud. He'll hear. . . ." came Machen's voice.

"Don't care . . . I . . ." lost voices now.

I tried to stir, but then the tube of sleep, nourished by the brandy, came unclogged, and I descended down into richer blackness.

Was a bright morning full of sun, and no fog for a change. Cool clear out there on the landing, and the sea even seemed to roll in soft and bounce against the rocks and lighthouse like puffy cotton balls blown on the wind.

9

I was out there with my morning coffee, holding the cup in one hand and grasping the railing with the other. It was a narrow area but safe enough, provided you didn't lean too far out or run along the walk when it was slick with rain. Machen told me of a man who had done just that and found himself plummeting over to be shattered like a dropped melon on the rocks below.

Machen came out with a cup of coffee in one hand, his unlit pipe in the other. He looked haggard this morning, as if a bit of old age had crept upon him in the night, fastened a straw to his face, and sucked out part of his substance.

"Morning," I said.

"Morning." He emptied his cup in one long draft. He balanced the cup on the metal railing and began to pack his pipe.

"Sleep bad?" I asked.

He looked at me, then at his pipe, finished his packing, and put the pouch away in his coat pocket. He took a long match from the same pocket, gave it fire with his thumbnail, lit the pipe. He puffed quite awhile before he answered me. "Not too well. Not too well."

"We drank too much."

"We did at that."

I sipped my coffee and looked at the sky, watched a snowy gull dive down and peck at the foam, rise up with a wriggling fish in its beak. It climbed high in the sky, became a speck of froth on crystal blue.

"I had funny dreams," I said. "I think I've had them all along, since I came here. But last night they were stronger than ever."

"Oh?"

"Thought I heard your voice speaking to someone. Thought I heard steps on the stairs, or more like the plunking of peg legs, like those old sea captains have."

"You don't say?"

"And another voice, a child's."

"That right? Well . . . maybe you did hear me speakin'. I wasn't entirely straight with you last night. I do have quite an interest in the voice throwing, and I practice it from time to time on my dummy. Last night must have been louder than usual, being drunk and all."

"Dummy?"

"My old dummy from the act. Keep it in the room below."

"Could I see it?"

He grimaced. "Maybe another time. It's kind of a private thing with me. Only bring her out when we're alone."

"Her?"

"Right. Name's Caroline, a right smart-looking girl dummy, rosy cheeked with blonde pigtails."

"Well, maybe someday I can look at her."

"Maybe someday." He stood up, popped the contents of the pipe out over the railing, and started inside. Then he turned: "I talk too much. Pay no mind to an old, crazy man."

Then he was gone, and I was there with a hot cup of coffee, a bright, warm day, and an odd, unexplained chill at the base of my bones.

Two days later we got on witches again, and I guess it was my fault. We hit the brandy hard that night. I had sold a short story for a goodly sum—my largest check to date—and we were celebrating and talking and saying how my fame would be as high as the stars. We got pretty sicky there, and to hear Machen tell it, and to hear me agree—no matter he hadn't read the story—I was another Hemingway, Wolfe, and Fitzgerald all balled into one.

"If Marilyn were here," I said thoughtlessly, drunk, "why we could get her to consult her crystal and tell us my literary future."

"Why that's nonsense, she used no crystal."

"No crystal, broom, or pointed hat? No eerie evil deeds for her? A white magician no doubt?"

"Magic is magic, m'boy. And even good intentions can backfire."

"Whatever happened to her, Marilyn I mean?"

"Dead."

"Old age?"

"Died young and beautiful, m'boy. Grief killed her."

"I see," I said, as you'll do to show attentiveness.

Suddenly, it was as if the memories were a balloon overloaded with air, about to burst if pressure were not taken off. So, he let loose the pressure and began to talk.

"She took her a lover, Marilyn did. Taught him many a thing, about love, magic, what have you. Lost her husband on account of it, the magician, I mean. Lost respect for herself in time.

"You see, there was this little girl she had, by her lover. A fine-looking sprite, lived until she was three. Had no proper father. He had taken to the sea and had never much entertained the idea of marryin'

11

Marilyn. Keep them stringing was his motto then, damn his eyes. So he left them to fend for themselves."

"What happened to the child?"

"She died. Some childhood disease."

"That's sad," I said, "a little girl gone and having only sipped at life."

"Gone? Oh no. There's the soul, you know."

I wasn't much of a believer in the soul and I said so.

"Oh, but there is a soul. The body perishes but the soul lives on."

"I've seen no evidence of it."

"But I have," Machen said solemnly. "Marilyn was determined that the girl would live on, if not in her own form, then in another."

"Hogwash!"

Machen looked at me sternly. "Maybe. You see, there is a part of witchcraft that deals with the soul, a part that believes the soul can be trapped and held, kept from escaping this earth and into the beyond. That's why a lot of natives are superstitious about having their picture taken. They believe once their image is captured, through magic, their soul can be contained.

"Voodoo works much the same. It's nothing but another form of witchcraft. Practitioners of that art believe their souls can be held to this earth by means of someone collecting nail parin's or hair from them while they're still alive.

"That's what Marilyn had in mind. When she saw the girl was fadin', she snipped one of the girl's long pigtails and kept it to herself. Cast spells on it while the child lay dyin', and again after life had left the child."

"The soul was supposed to be contained within the hair?"

"That's right. It can be restored, in a sense, to some other object through the hair. It's like those voodoo dolls. A bit of hair or nail parin' is collected from the person you want to control, or if not control, maintain the presence of their soul, and it's sewn into those dolls. That way, when the pins are stuck into the doll, the living suffer, and when they die their soul is trapped in the doll for all eternity, or rather as long as the doll with its hair or nail parin's exists."

"So she preserved the hair so she could make a doll and have the little girl live on, in a sense?"

"Something like that."

"Sounds crazy."

"I suppose."

"And what of the little girl's father?"

"Ah, that sonofabitch! He came home to find the little girl dead and buried and the mother mad. But there was that little gold lock of hair, and knowing Marilyn, he figured her intentions."

"Machen," I said slowly. "It was you, was it not? You were the father?"

"I was."

"I'm sorry."

"Don't be. We were both foolish. I was the more foolish. She left her husband for me and I cast her aside. Ignored my own child. I was the fool, a great fool."

"Do you really believe in that stuff about the soul? About the hair and what Marilyn was doing?"

"Better I didn't. A soul once lost from the body would best prefer to be departed I think . . . but love is sometimes a brutal thing."

We just sat there after that. We drank more. Machen smoked his pipe, and about an hour later we went to bed.

There were sounds again, gnawing at the edge of my sleep. The sounds that had always been there, but now, since we had talked of Marilyn, I was less able to drift off into blissful slumber. I kept thinking of those crazy things Machen had said. I remembered, too, those voices I had heard, and the fact that Machen was a ventriloquist, and perhaps, not altogether stable.

But those sounds.

I sat up and opened my eyes. They were coming from below. Voices. Machen's first. ". . . not be the death of you, girl, not at all . . . my only reminder of Marilyn . . ."

And then to my horror. "Let me be, Papa. Let it end." The last had been a little girl's voice, but the words had been bitter and wise beyond the youngness of tone.

I stepped out of bed and into my trousers, crept to the curtain, and looked on Machen's side.

Nothing, just a lonely cot. I wasn't dreaming. I had heard him all right, and the other voice . . . it had to be that Machen, grieved over what he had done in the past, over Marilyn's death, had taken to speaking to himself in the little girl's voice. All that stuff Marilyn had told him about the soul, it had gotten to him, cracked his stability.

13

I climbed down the cold metal stairs, listening. Below I heard the old, weathered door that led outside slam. Heard the thud of boots going down the outside steps.

I went back up, went to the windows, and pulling back the curtains section by section, finally saw the old man. He was carrying something wrapped in a black cloth and he had a shovel in his hand. I watched as, out there by the shore, he dug a shallow grave and placed the cloth-wrapped object within, placed a rock over it, and left it to the night and the incoming tide.

I pretended to be asleep when he returned, and later, when I felt certain he was well visited by Morpheus, I went downstairs and retrieved the shovel from the tool room. I went out to where I had seen him dig and went to work, first turning over the large stone and shoveling down into the pebbly dirt. Due to the freshness of the hole, it was easy digging.

I found the cloth and what was inside. It made me flinch at first, it looked so real. I thought it was a little rosy-cheeked girl buried alive, for it looked alive . . . but it was a dummy. A ventriloquist dummy. It had aged badly, as if water had gotten to it. In some ways it looked as if it were rotting from the inside out. My finger went easily and deeply into the wood of one of the legs.

Out of some odd curiosity, I reached up and pushed back the wooden eyelids. There were no wooden painted eyes, just darkness, empty sockets that uncomfortably reminded me of looking down into the black hollows of a human skull. And the hair. On one side of the head was a yellow pigtail, but where the other should have been was a bare spot, as if the hair had been ripped away from the wooden skull.

With a trembling hand I closed the lids down over those empty eyes, put the dirt back in place, the rock, and returned to bed. But I did not sleep well. I dreamed of a grown man talking to a wooden doll and using another voice to answer back, pretending that the doll lived and loved him too.

But the water had gotten to it, and the sight of those rotting legs had snapped him back to reality, dashed his insane hopes of containing a soul by magic, shocked him brutally from foolish dreams. Dead is dead.

The next day, Machen was silent and had little to say. I suspected the events of last night weighed on his mind. Our conversation must have returned to him this morning in sober memory, and he, somewhat embarrassed, was reluctant to recall it. He kept to himself down below in the locked room, and I busied myself with my work.

It was night when he came up, and there was a smug look about him, as if he had accomplished some great deed. We spoke a bit, but not of witches, of past times and the sea. Then he pulled back the curtains and looked at the moon rise above the water like a cold fish eye.

"Machen," I said, "maybe I shouldn't say anything, but if you should ever have something bothering you. If you should ever want to talk about it . . . Well, feel free to come to me."

He smiled at me. "Thank you. But any problem that might have been bothering me is . . . shall we say, all sewn up."

We said little more and soon went to bed.

I slept sounder that night, but again I was rousted from my dreams by voices. Machen's voice again, and then the poor man speaking in that little child's voice.

"It's a fine home for you," Machen said in his own voice.

"I want no home," came the little girl's voice. "I want to be free."

"You want to stay with me, with the living. You're just not thinking. There's only darkness beyond the veil."

The voices were very clear and loud. I sat up in bed and strained my ears.

"It's where I belong," the little girl's voice again, but it spoke not in a little girl manner. There was only the tone.

"Things have been bad lately," Machen said. "And you're not yourself."

Laughter, horrible little girl laughter.

"I haven't been myself for years."

"Now, Caroline . . . play your piano. You used to play it so well. Why, you haven't touched it in years."

"Play. Play. With these!"

"You're too loud."

"I don't care. Let him hear, let him . . ."

A door closed sharply and the sound died off to a mumble, a word caught here and there was scattered and confused by the throb of the sea.

Next morning Machen had nothing for me, not even a smile from his borrowed collection. Nothing but coldness, his back, and a frown.

I saw little of him after coffee, and once, from below—for he stayed down there the whole day through—I thought I heard him cry in a loud voice, "Have it your way then," and then there was the sound of a slamming door and some other sort of commotion below.

After a while I looked out at the land and the sea, and down there, striding back and forth, hands behind his back, went Machen, like some great confused penguin contemplating the far shore.

I like to think there was something more than curiosity in what I did next. Like to think I was looking for the source of my friend's agony; looking for some way to help him find peace.

I went downstairs and pulled at the door he kept locked, hoping that, in his anguish, he had forgotten to lock it back. He had not forgotten.

I pressed my ear against the door and listened. Was that crying I heard?

No. I was being susceptible, caught up in Machen's fantasy. It was merely the wind whipping about the tower.

I went back upstairs, had coffee, and wrote not a line.

So day fell into night, and I could not sleep but finally got the strange business out of my mind by reading a novel. A rollicking good sea story of daring men and bloody battles, great ships clashing in a merciless sea.

And then, from his side of the curtain, I heard Machen creak off his cot and take to the stairs. One flight below was the door that led to the railing round about the tower, and I heard that open and close.

I rose, folded a small piece of paper into my book for a marker, and pulled back one of the window curtains. I walked around pulling curtains and looking until I could see him below.

He stood with his hands behind his back, looking out at the sea like a stern father keeping an eye on his children. Then, calmly, he mounted the railing and leaped out into the air.

I ran. Not that it mattered, but I ran, out to the railing . . . and looked down. His body looked like a rag doll splayed on the rocks.

There was no question in my mind that he was dead, but slowly I wound my way down the steps . . . and was distracted by the room. The door stood wide open.

I don't know what compelled me to look in, but I was drawn to it. It was a small room with a desk and a lot of shelves filled with books, mostly occult and black magic. There were carpentry tools on the wall, and all manner of needles and devices that might be used by a tailor. The air was filled with an odd odor I could not place, and on Machen's desk, something that was definitely not tobacco smoldered away.

There was another room beyond the one in which I stood. The door to it was cracked open. I pushed it back and stepped inside. It was a little child's room filled thick with toys and such: jack-in-the-boxes, dolls, kid books, and a toy piano. All were covered in dust.

On the bed lay a teddy bear. It was ripped open and the stuffing was pulled out. There was one long strand of hair hanging out of that gutted belly, just one, as if it were the last morsel of a greater whole. It was the color of honey from a fresh-robbed hive. I knew what the smell in the ashtray was now.

I took the hair and put a match to it, just in case.

The Hunt

JAMES S. DORR

She rode like the wind. Like she used to ride on her grandparents' farm. She rode—what was the name her grandmother used when the winter winds blew around the chimney? She rode like Frau Berchta, the Devil's huntress.

Except . . . how had she found a horse in the city?

She'd loved to ride horses when she was little. Before her grandparents had sold the farm. She'd loved to listen to Grandmother's stories, about the country that *she* had grown up in, and then Grandfather's explanations of how, in Bavaria, long ago, people gave names to the forces of nature.

How they made stories up, hoping in that way that they'd understand them. For instance, in winter, when storm winds blew at night, they said the noise was the sound of the Witches' Hunt, led by Frau Berchta, seeking the souls of those who'd done evil.

She'd loved to ride horses, so much so in fact that sometimes, joking, Grandmother would say that *she* was Frau Berchta. "You see," the old woman would tell her, "not always is Frau Berchta evil. In

17

winter, even, she just seeks out bad men to take them to hell. But also she makes the snow, making it lie like a blanket on top of the burrows of small creatures, keeping them warm so they'll sleep until springtime. So, even though she hunts, she still loves animals."

And so she grew up, sometimes called "Berchta," although her real name was Elizabeth—Betty. She didn't like "Betty." It sounded old-fashioned. But she did love animals too, like Berchta.

Then later her grandparents sold the farm, and she grew up and went to college. And later still, she had married Ernest.

Ernest, she thought. Ernest didn't like horses. She looked around her, saw buildings flash past her. The hooves of the horse she rode striking sparks against the pavement.

Why was she riding?

He didn't like horses or any animals much, she thought now, but they were in love then. And so they had married.

Their first real argument came, she remembered, when she'd lost her baby. Her gynecologist had told her it might be dangerous to try again—that any new baby might be stillborn too—and then, to console her, her mother's sister had brought her a kitten. "I know it's not much," the aunt had said, "but you have so much love, Betty. Love needs an object—something to nurture, however small."

Her aunt had meant well, she'd thought at the time, and in time she *had* come to love it. She'd named the kitten Tamisina right at the start, after her grandmother, and, as she fed it and brushed it and took it to the vet for its shots, she thought more and more of it as a kind of replacement baby.

But Ernest, as soon as he saw it, disliked it. "Cats scratch people," he'd said. "They're filthy. They make people sick. There's a guy at work who got bit by a cat once and had to take shots. . . ."

"Ernest," she'd answered. "Not Tamisina! She won't scratch any-one if you love her, and I'll take care of her. You won't even have to touch her if you don't want to. And anyway"—she remembered now how her voice had lowered and taken a hard edge—"anyway Tamisina's *mine.*"

Her husband had grumbled, but let her keep it. He'd never come to accept the cat, though. He'd always hated it, up until . . .

Her horse bucked, suddenly, jarring her thoughts. Up until *what?* She leaned to its crest, caressing its mane, calming the horse down.

Then looked down. Below her.

Below was the city. Her horse was *flying*. Around her the wind blew, rattling second- and third-story windows as she rose higher. Around her snow swirled, starting to course from the clouds way above her. Clouds moving nearer.

Somewhere, she heard thunder.

Then she realized. Of course—she was dead. Somehow it didn't bother her though. An automobile crash, just that evening. But where was Ernest?

And why had she come back to be Frau Berchta?

Because . . . she *was* Frau Berchta, wasn't she? She gripped her horse's reins, looked down again at the animal's sides. As black as midnight. She looked at her horse's hooves, still striking sparks even though they clawed air now as it galloped higher.

She looked, as it turned its head, once, to stare back at her—eyes bright as headlights, glowing orange like hell's own fire. Seeking, with her, to find . . .

Was Ernest dead too?

She thought . . . it was something about Tamisina. The kitten had long since grown to be a cat, but Ernest's hatred had grown along with it. And not just for Tamisina either.

Their marriage had died a long time ago, she realized now, although, in fairness, it wasn't all Ernest's fault. Job pressures didn't help. Her losing her job. His in trouble because of cutbacks. Money was short for them.

"Damn good thing you couldn't have a kid," he'd said once to her. That was after he'd taken to drinking. Not very much—just on Fridays and weekends. And she would drink with him. But sometimes it made him mean.

"Damn good thing. And that cat of yours—you ought to get rid of it. Eats like a damn horse."

"*Not* Tamisina!"

They argued more now. Sometimes she'd even thought of divorce, but the way she'd been brought up—and Ernest as well—people were not supposed to try to get out of marriages. They were supposed to try to make them work. Except that, after the arguments grew louder and more frequent, she'd given up trying.

She would just retreat into her bedroom with Tamisina and think about childhood. About how it had been with her grandparents, after her parents had died and she'd gone to live with them year round. How they had spoiled her. Those were the happy times—after she'd gotten over the loss. Her times on the farm.

She'd had her own horse. She remembered riding—riding like she was now. Riding like wildfire. Like wind in the trees.

Her grandfather chiding her when once, without thinking, she'd ridden into a not yet harvested field of snap beans.

"Just like Frau Berchta," he had told her. Angry, not joking now. "Riding like storm wind, just like the Witches' Hunt. Not looking. Not caring. Flattening peasants' crops—anything in their way."

Flattening. Driving. Alone, in her husband's car, driving too fast. A bridge abutment . . .

And then, on horseback, like back on the farm when winter winds blew. They'd sit around the fireplace then and Grandmother would remember the "smoke days," just after Christmas, when in the old country they burned special, aromatic wood so the smoke would rise up and appease the Hunt. Because who knew whose soul Frau Berchta would seek next?

Like Ernest's, the bastard.

Why had she thought that?

If she was Frau Berchta. And Ernest . . .

She knew now. She knew what had killed her. Not just a car accident. Rather, when Ernest had driven home late from work. Since it was Friday, as usual drinking . . .

And when Tamisina ran into the driveway, playing with something she'd found in the snow.

She screamed. She remembered. Her voice rose up, above the wind that whistled around her.

The blood in the tire track.

She'd seen it all from the kitchen window. And then she had taken the knife she'd been using and held it behind her, waiting until he came in through the back door.

She saw he was crying, as if he realized what he had just done. And yet she enticed him. Smiling up at him as he approached her. Holding her face up, just so, for him to kiss.

He didn't kiss her. He only hugged her. Held her gently.

As if he realized.

She stabbed. Once. Twice. In the side, then the back as he sagged to the floor.

She remembered shrieking. Fumbling the car keys from his still clutching hand. Dropping the knife into her handbag, then putting her coat on.

She knew she had to leave. Get away somewhere. Go out the front door, so neighbors would see her. Vouch for her later when she would say her husband came home, then she'd gone out shopping. Returned to find the back door open. Her husband's body . . .

She rode with the wind. Up. Into the lightning of the winter's storm. Searching for Ernest—perhaps not dead yet?

Around her she saw the first shadowy forms—the wild witch-riders joining her. Heard the hounds baying.

Perhaps Ernest still lived, and that was her mission. To gather his soul up herself for the Devil.

She thought of the darkness of night. Her car speeding. Her thinking—it was a good thing she'd thought to keep the knife with her. That way, if someone—if someone came by before she could clear her head—could come back home herself—*they* found the body. At least they wouldn't find a weapon with fingerprints on it.

But what of the front door? Her thoughts had been racing. Her hands were still stained with blood. Had she remembered to wipe off the doorknob?

And what about Tamisina's body?—she hadn't removed it. Everyone knew how much she loved her kitten. . . .

She'd swerved. She remembered. Speeding, she'd lost control. Battled to stop the skid.

The bridge abutment.

And found herself riding, the wind in her hair. Wind-fast through the city.

Above the city, her horse's sides straining. The screams of the Witches' Hunt now all around her. She saw, through the snow swirls, more wild riders joining her. One with a bundle draped over its saddlebow.

Nearer—she saw now—the bundle was *Ernest.*

Then why was she riding?

She'd loved to ride horses. Before she was married. She wheeled, enjoying the wind in her hair. The sound. The hoofbeats. The horses' neighing.

Except . . . then she realized.

The real Frau Berchta, hair unbound, streaming blood-caked behind her, loomed suddenly down on her.

She was the quarry.

The Fit

RAMSEY CAMPBELL

I must have passed the end of the path a hundred times before I saw it. Walking into Keswick, I always gazed at the distant fells, mossed by fields and gorse and woods. On cloudy days shadows rode the fells; the figures tramping the ridges looked as though they could steady themselves with one hand on the clouds. On clear days I would marvel at the multitude of shades of green and yellow, a spectrum in themselves, and notice nothing else.

But this was a dull day. The landscape looked dusty, as though from the lorries that pulverized the roads. I might have stayed in the house, but my Aunt Naomi was fitting; the sight of people turning like inexperienced models before the full-length mirror made me feel out of place. I'd exhausted Keswick—games of Crazy Golf, boats on the lake or strolls round it, narrow streets clogged with cars and people scaffolded with rucksacks—and I didn't feel like toiling up the fells today, even for the vistas of the lakes.

If I hadn't been watching my feet trudging I would have missed the path. It led away from the road a mile or so outside Keswick, through a gap in the hedges and across a field overgrown with grass and wildflowers. Solitude appealed to me, and I squeezed through the gap, which was hardly large enough for a sheep.

As soon as I stepped on the path I felt the breeze. That raised my spirits; the lorries had half-deafened me, the grubby light and the clouds of dust had made me feel grimy. Though the grass was waist high I strode forward, determined to follow the path.

Grass blurred its meanderings, but I managed to trace it to the far side of the field, only to find that it gave out entirely. I peered about, blinded by smouldering green. Elusive grasshoppers chirred, regular as telephones. Eventually I made my way to the corner where the field met

22

two others. Here the path sneaked through the hedge, almost invisibly. Had it been made difficult to follow?

Beyond the hedge it passed close to a pond, whose surface was green as the fields; I slithered on the brink. A dragonfly, its wings wafers of stained glass, skimmed the pond. The breeze coaxed me along the path, until I reached what I'd thought was the edge of the field, but which proved to be a trough in the ground, about fifteen feet deep.

It wasn't a valley, though its stony floor sloped towards a dark hole ragged with grass. Its banks were a mass of gorse and herbs; gorse obscured a dark green mound low down on the far bank. Except that the breeze was urging me, I wouldn't have gone close enough to realize that the mound was a cottage.

It was hardly larger than a room. Moss had blurred its outlines, so that it resembled the banks of the trough; it was impossible to tell where the roof ended and the walls began. Now I could see a window, and I was eager to look in. The breeze guided me forwards, caressing and soothing, and I saw where the path led down to the cottage.

I had just climbed down below the edge when the breeze turned cold. Was it the damp, striking upwards from the crack in the earth? The crack was narrower than it had looked, which must be why I was all at once much closer to the cottage—close enough to realize that the cottage must be decaying, eaten away by moss; perhaps that was what I could smell. Inside the cottage a light crept towards the window, a light pale as marsh gas, pale as the face that loomed behind it.

Someone was in there, and I was trespassing. When I tried to struggle out of the trough, my feet slipped on the path; the breeze was a huge cushion, a softness that forced me backwards. Clutching at gorse, I dragged myself over the edge. Nobody followed, and by the time I'd fled past the pond I couldn't distinguish the crack in the earth.

I didn't tell my aunt about the incident. Though she insisted I call her Naomi, and let me stay up at night far later than my parents did, I felt she might disapprove. I didn't want her to think that I was still a child. If I hadn't stopped myself brooding about it, I might have realized that I felt guiltier than the incident warranted; after all, I had done nothing.

Before long she touched on the subject herself. One night we sat sipping more of the wine we'd had with dinner, something else my parents would have frowned upon if they'd known. Mellowed by wine, I said, "That was a nice meal." Without warning, to my dismay which I concealed with a laugh, my voice fell an octave.

"You're growing up." As though that had reminded her, she said, "See what you make of this."

From a drawer she produced two small grey dresses, too smartly cut for school. One of her clients had brought them for alteration, her two small daughters clutching each other and giggling at me. Aunt Naomi handed me the dresses. "Look at them closely," she said.

Handling them made me uneasy. As they drooped emptily over my lap they looked unnervingly minute. Strands of a different grey were woven into the material. Somehow I didn't like to touch those strands.

"I know how you feel," my aunt said. "It's the material."

"What about it?"

"The strands of lighter grey—I think they're hair."

I handed back the dresses hastily, pinching them by one corner of the shoulders. "Old Fanny Cave made them," she said as though that explained everything.

"Who's Fanny Cave?"

"Maybe she's just an old woman who isn't quite right in the head. I wouldn't trust some of the tales I've heard about her. Mind you, I'd trust her even less."

I must have looked intrigued, for she said: "She's just an unpleasant old woman, Peter. Take my advice and stay away from her."

"I can't stay away from her if I don't know where she lives," I said slyly.

"In a hole in the ground near a pond, so they tell me. You can't even see it from the road, so don't bother trying."

She took my sudden nervousness for assent. "I wish Mrs. Gibson hadn't accepted those dresses," she mused. "She couldn't bring herself to refuse, she said, when Fanny Cave had gone to so much trouble. Well, she said the children felt uncomfortable in them. I'm going to tell her the material isn't good for their skin."

I should have liked more chance to decide whether I wanted to confess to having gone near Fanny Cave's. Still, I felt too guilty to revive the subject or even to show too much interest in the old woman. Two days later I had the chance to see her for myself.

I was mooching about the house, trying to keep out of my aunt's way. There was nowhere downstairs I felt comfortable; her sewing machine chattered in the dining room, by the table spread with cut-out

24

patterns; dress forms stood in the lounge, waiting for clothes or limbs. From my bedroom window I watched the rain stir the fields into mud, dissolve the fells into mounds of mist. I was glad when the doorbell rang; at least it gave me something to do.

As soon as I opened the door the old woman pushed in. I thought she was impatient for shelter; she wore only a grey dress. Parts of it glistened with rain—or were they patterns of a different grey, symbols of some kind? I found myself squinting at them, trying to make them out, before I looked up at her face.

She was over six feet tall. Her grey hair dangled to her waist. Presumably it smelled of earth; certainly she did. Her leathery face was too small for her body. As it stooped, peering through grey strands at me as though I was merchandise, I thought of a rodent peering from its lair.

She strode into the dining room. "You've been saying things about me. You've been telling them not to wear my clothes."

"I'm sure nobody told you that," my aunt said.

"Nobody had to." Her voice sounded stiff and rusty, as if she wasn't used to talking to people. "I know when anyone meddles in my affairs."

How could she fit into that dwarfish cottage? I stood in the hall, wondering if my aunt needed help and if I would have the courage to provide it. But now the old woman sounded less threatening than peevish. "I'm getting old. I need someone to look after me sometimes. I've no children of my own."

"But giving them clothes won't make them your children."

Through the doorway I saw the old woman glaring as though she had been found out. "Don't you meddle in my affairs or I'll meddle in yours," she said, and stalked away. It must have been the draught of her movements that made the dress patterns fly off the table, some of them into the fire.

For the rest of the day I felt uneasy, almost glad to be going home tomorrow. Clouds oozed down the fells; swaying curtains of rain enclosed the house, beneath the looming sky. The grey had seeped into the house. Together with the lingering smell of earth it made me feel buried alive.

I roamed the house as though it was a cage. Once, as I wandered into the lounge, I thought two figures were waiting in the dimness, arms outstretched to grab me. They were dress forms, and the arms of their dresses hung limp at their sides; I couldn't see how I had made the mistake.

My aunt did most of the chatting at dinner. I kept imagining Fanny Cave in her cottage, her long limbs folded up like a spider's in hiding. The cottage must be larger than it looked, but she certainly lived in a lair in the earth—in the mud, on a day like this.

After dinner we played cards. When I began to nod sleepily my aunt continued playing, though she knew I had a long coach journey in the morning; perhaps she wanted company. By the time I went to bed the rain had stopped; a cheesy moon hung in a rainbow. As I undressed I heard her pegging clothes on the line below my window.

When I'd packed my case I parted the curtains for a last drowsy look at the view. The fells were a moonlit patchwork, black and white. Why was my aunt taking so long to hang out the clothes? I peered down more sharply. There was no sign of her. The clothes were moving by themselves, dancing and swaying in the moonlight, inching along the line towards the house.

When I raised the sash of the window the night seemed perfectly still, no sign of a breeze. Nothing moved on the lawn except the shadows of the clothes, advancing a little and retreating, almost ritualistically. Hovering dresses waved holes where hands should be, nodded the sockets of their necks.

Were they really moving towards the house? Before I could tell, the line gave way, dropping them into the mud of the lawn. When I heard my aunt's vexed cry I slipped the window shut and retreated into bed; somehow I didn't want to admit what I'd seen, whatever it was. Sleep came so quickly that next day I could believe I'd been dreaming.

I didn't tell my parents; I'd learned to suppress details that they might find worrying. They were uneasy with my aunt—she was too careless of propriety, the time she had taken them tramping the fells she'd mocked them for dressing as though they were going out for dinner. I think the only reason they let me stay with her was to get me out of the polluted Birmingham air.

By the time I was due for my next visit I was more than ready. My voice had broken, my body had grown unfamiliar, I felt clumsy, ungainly, neither a man nor myself. My parents didn't help. They'd turned wistful as soon as my voice began to change; my mother treated visitors to photographs of me as a baby. She and my father kept telling me to concentrate on my studies and examining my school books as if pornography might lurk behind the covers. They seemed relieved that I attended a boys' school, until my father started wondering nervously if I was "particularly fond" of any of the boys. After nine months of this sort of thing I was glad to get away at Easter.

As soon as the coach moved off I felt better. In half an hour it left behind the Midlands hills, reefs built of red brick terraces. Lancashire seemed so flat that the glimpses of distant hills might have been mirages. After a couple of hours the fells began, great deceptively gentle monsters that slept at the edges of lakes blue as ice, two sorts of stillness. At least I would be free for a week.

But I was not, for I'd brought my new feelings with me. I knew that as soon as I saw my aunt walking upstairs. She had always seemed much younger than my mother, though there were only two years between them, and I'd been vaguely aware that she often wore tight jeans; now I saw how round her bottom was. I felt breathless with guilt in case she guessed what I was thinking, yet I couldn't look away.

At dinner, whenever she touched me I felt a shock of excitement, too strange and uncontrollable to be pleasant. Her skirts were considerably shorter than my mother's. My feelings crept up on me like the wine, which seemed to be urging them on. Half my conversation seemed fraught with double meanings. At last I found what I thought was a neutral subject. "Have you seen Fanny Cave again?" I said.

"Only once." My aunt seemed reluctant to talk about her. "She'd given away some more dresses, and Mrs. Gibson referred the mother to me. They were nastier than the others—I'm sure she would have thrown them away even if I hadn't said anything. But old Fanny came storming up here, just a few weeks ago. When I wouldn't let her in she stood out there in the pouring rain, threatening all sorts of things."

"What sort of things?"

"Oh, just unpleasant things. In the old days they would have burned her at the stake, if that's what they used to do. Anyway," she said with a frown to close the subject, "she's gone now."

"Dead you mean?" I was impatient with euphemisms.

"Nobody knows for sure. Most people think she's in the pond. To tell you the truth, I don't think anyone's anxious to look."

Of course I was. I lay in bed and imagined probing the pond that nobody else dared search, a dream that seemed preferable to the thoughts that had been tormenting me recently as I tried to sleep. Next day, as I walked to the path, I peeled myself a fallen branch.

Bypassing the pond, I went first to the cottage. I could hear what sounded like a multitude of flies down in the trough. Was the cottage more overgrown than when I'd last seen it? Was that why it looked shrunken by decay, near to collapse? The single dusty window made me think of a dulling eye, half engulfed by moss; the facade might have been a dead face that was falling inwards. Surely the flies were attracted by wildflowers—but I didn't want to go down into the crack; I hurried back to the pond.

Flies swarmed there too, bumbling above the scum. As I approached they turned on me. They made the air in front of my face seem dark, oppressive, infected. Nevertheless I poked my stick through the green skin and tried to sound the pond while keeping back from the slippery edge.

The depths felt muddy, soft and clinging. I poked for a while, until I began to imagine what I sought to touch. All at once I was afraid that something might grab the branch, overbalance me, drag me into the opaque depths. Was it a rush of sweat that made my clothes feel heavy and obstructive? As I shoved myself back, a breeze clutched them, hindering my retreat. I fled, skidding on mud, and saw the branch sink lethargically. A moment after it vanished the slime was unbroken.

That night I told Aunt Naomi where I'd been. I didn't think she would mind; after all, Fanny Cave was supposed to be out of the way. But she bent lower over her sewing, as if she didn't want to hear. "Please don't go there again," she said. "Now let's talk about something else."

"Why?" At that age I had no tact at all.

"Oh, for heaven's sake. Because I think she probably died on her way home from coming here. That's the last time anyone saw her. She must have been in such a rage that she slipped at the edge of the pond —I told you it was pouring with rain. Well, how was I to know what had happened?"

Perhaps her resentment concealed a need for reassurance, but I was unable to help, for I was struggling with the idea that she had been partly responsible for someone's death. Was nothing in my life to be trusted? I was so deep in brooding that I was hardly able to look at her when she cried out.

Presumably her needle had slipped on the thimble; she'd driven the point beneath one of her nails. Yet as she hurried out, furiously sucking her finger, I found that my gaze was drawn to the dress she had

28

been sewing. As she'd cried out—of course it must have been then, not before—the dress had seemed to twist in her hands, jerking the needle.

When I went to bed I couldn't sleep. The room smelled faintly of earth; was that something to do with spring? The wardrobe door kept opening, though it had never behaved like that before, and displaying my clothes suspended batlike in the dark. Each time I got up to close the door their shapes looked less familiar, more unpleasant. Eventually I managed to sleep, only to dream that dresses were waddling limblessly through the doorway of my room, towards the bed.

The next day, Sunday, my aunt suggested a walk on the fells. I would have settled for Skiddaw, the easiest of them, but it was already swarming with walkers like fleas. "Let's go somewhere we'll be alone," Aunt Naomi said, which excited me in ways I'd begun to enjoy but preferred not to define, in case that scared the excitement away.

We climbed Grisedale Pike. Most of it was gentle, until just below the summit we reached an almost vertical scramble up a narrow spiky ridge. I clung there with all my limbs, trapped thousands of feet above the countryside, afraid to go up or down. I was almost hysterical with self-disgust; I'd let my half-admitted fantasies lure me up here, when all my aunt had wanted was to enjoy the walk without being crowded by tourists. Eventually I managed to clamber to the summit, my face blazing.

As we descended, it began to rain. By the time we reached home we were soaked. I felt suffocated by the smell of wet earth, the water flooding down my face, the dangling locks of sodden hair that wouldn't go away. I hurried upstairs to change.

I had just about finished—undressing had felt like peeling wall-paper, except that I was the wall—when my aunt called out. Though she was in the next room, her voice sounded muffled. Before I could go to her she called again, nearer to panic. I hurried across the landing, into her room.

The walls were streaming with shadows. The air was dark as mud, in which she was struggling wildly. A shapeless thing was swallowing her head and arms. When I switched on the light I saw it was nothing; she'd become entangled in the jumper she was trying to remove, that was all.

"Help me," she cried. She sounded as if she was choking, yet I didn't like to touch her; apart from a bra, her torso was naked. What was wrong with her, for God's sake? Couldn't she take off her jumper by herself? Eventually I helped her as best I could without touching her. It seemed glued to her, by the rain, I assumed. At last she emerged, red faced and panting.

Neither of us said much at dinner. I thought her unease was directed at me, at the way I'd let her struggle. Or was she growing aware of my new feelings? That night, as I drifted into sleep, I thought I heard a jangling of hangers in the wardrobe. Perhaps it was just the start of a dream.

The morning was dull. Clouds swallowed the tops of the fells. My aunt lit fires in the downstairs rooms. I loitered about the house for a while, hoping for a glimpse of customers undressing, until the dimness made me claustrophobic. Firelight set the shadows of dress forms dancing spastically on the walls; when I stood with my back to the forms their shadows seemed to raise their arms.

I caught a bus to Keswick, for want of something to do. The bus had passed Fanny Cave's path before I thought of looking. I glanced back sharply, but a bend in the road intervened. Had I glimpsed a scarecrow by the pond, its sleeves fluttering? But it had seemed to rear up: it must have been a bird.

In Keswick I followed leggy girls up the narrow hilly streets, dawdled nervously outside pubs and wondered if I looked old enough to risk buying a drink. When I found myself in the library, leafing desultorily through broken paperbacks, I went home. There was nothing by the pond that I could see, though closer to Aunt Naomi's house something grey was flapping in the grass—litter, I supposed.

The house seemed more oppressive than ever. Though my aunt tended to use whichever room she was in for sewing, she was generally tidy; now the house was crowded with half-finished clothes, lolling on chairs, their necks yawning. When I tried to chat at dinner my voice sounded muffled by the presence of so much cloth.

My aunt drank more than usual, and seemed not to care if I did too. My drinking made the light seem yellowish, suffocated. Soon I felt very sleepy. "Stay down a little longer," my aunt mumbled, jerking herself awake, when I made to go to bed. I couldn't understand why she didn't go herself. I chatted mechanically, about anything except what might be wrong. Firelight brought clothes nodding forward to listen.

At last she muttered, "Let's go to bed." Of course she meant that unambiguously, yet it made me nervous. As I undressed hastily I heard her below me in the kitchen, opening the window a notch for air. A moment later the patch of light from the kitchen went out. I wished it had stayed lit for just another moment, for I'd glimpsed something lying beneath the empty clothesline.

Was it a nightdress? But I'd never seen my aunt hang out a nightdress, nor pyjamas either. It occurred to me that she must sleep naked. That disturbed me so much that I crawled into bed and tried to sleep at once, without thinking.

I dreamed I was buried, unable to breathe, and when I awoke I was. Blankets, which I felt heavy as collapsed earth, had settled over my face. I heaved them off me and lay trying to calm myself, so that I would sink back into sleep—but by the time my breathing slowed I realized I was listening.

The room felt padded with silence. Dimness draped the chair and dressing table, blurring their shapes; perhaps the wardrobe door was ajar, for I thought I saw vague forms hanging ominously still. Now I was struggling to fall asleep before I could realize what was keeping me awake. I drew long slow breaths to lull myself, but it was no use. In the silence between them I heard something sodden creeping upstairs.

I lay determined not to hear. Perhaps it was the wind or the creaking of the house, not the sound of a wet thing slopping stealthily upstairs at all. Perhaps if I didn't move, didn't make a noise, I would hear what it really was—but in any case I was incapable of moving, for I'd heard the wet thing flop on the landing outside my door.

For an interminable pause there was silence, thicker than ever, then I heard my aunt's door open next to mine. I braced myself for her scream. If she screamed I would go to her. I would have to. But the scream never came; there was only the sound of her pulling something sodden off the floor. Soon I heard her padding downstairs barefoot, and the click of a lock.

Everything was all right now. Whatever it had been, she'd dealt with it. Perhaps wallpaper had fallen on the stairs, and she'd gone down to throw it out. Now I could sleep—so why couldn't I? Several minutes passed before I was conscious of wondering why she hadn't come back upstairs.

I forced myself to move. There was nothing to fear, nothing now outside my door—but I got dressed to delay going out on the landing. The landing proved to be empty, and so did the house. Beyond the open front door the prints of Aunt Naomi's bare feet led over the moist lawn towards the road.

The moon was doused by clouds. Once I reached the road I couldn't see my aunt's tracks, but I knew instinctively which way she'd gone. I ran wildly towards Fanny Cave's path. Hedges, mounds of congealed night, boxed me in. The only sound I could hear was the ringing of my heels on the asphalt.

I had just reached the gap in the hedge when the moon swam free. A woman was following the path towards the pond, but was it my aunt? Even with the field between us I recognized the grey dress she wore. It was Fanny Cave's.

I was terrified to set foot on the path until the figure turned a bend and I saw my aunt's profile. I plunged across the field, tearing my way through the grass. It might have been quicker to follow the path, for by the time I reached the gap into the second field she was nearly at the pond.

In the moonlight the surface of the pond looked milky, fungoid. The scum was broken by a rock, plastered with strands of grass, close to the edge towards which my aunt was walking. I threw myself forwards, grass slashing my legs.

When I came abreast of her I saw her eyes, empty except for two shrunken reflections of the moon. I knew not to wake a sleepwalker, and so I caught her gently by the shoulders, though my hands wanted to shake, and tried to turn her away from the pond.

She wouldn't turn. She was pulling towards the scummy water, or Fanny Cave's dress was, for the drowned material seemed to writhe beneath my hands. It was pulling towards the rock whose eyes glared just above the scum, through glistening strands which were not grass but hair.

It seemed there was only one thing to do. I grabbed the neck of the dress and tore it down. The material was rotten, and tore easily. I dragged it from my aunt's body and flung it towards the pond. Did it land near the edge then slither into the water? All I knew was that when I dared to look the scum was unbroken.

My aunt stood there naked and unaware until I draped my anorak around her. That seemed to rouse her. She stared about for a moment, then down at herself. "It's all right, Naomi," I said awkwardly.

She sobbed only once before she controlled herself, but I could see that the effort was cruel. "Come on, quickly," she said in a voice older and harsher than I'd ever heard her use, and strode home without looking at me.

Next day we didn't refer to the events of the night; in fact, we hardly spoke. No doubt she had lain awake all night as I had, as uncomfortably aware of me as I was of her. After breakfast she said that she wanted to be left alone, and asked me to go home early. I never visited her again; she always found a reason why I couldn't stay. I suspect the reasons served only to prevent my parents from questioning me.

Before I went home I found a long branch and went to the pond. It didn't take much probing for me to find something solid but repulsively soft. I drove the branch into it again and again, until I felt things break. My disgust was so violent it was beyond defining. Perhaps I already knew deep in myself that since the night I undressed my aunt I would never be able to touch a woman.

Witches in the Cornfield

CARL JACOBI

oth Mr. Maudsley and Mr. Trask were resplendent that October evening. Mr. Maudsley stood deep in the cornfield, overall trousers ballooning in the wind, one hand nailed to a pie-tin that caught the moonlight and reflected it like a mirror. While across the road the hat of Mr. Trask was bright with the strip of foil Jimmy had fastened to it that morning.

From the rear seat of the car Jimmy looked down upon the two figures as the road wound between the shocked fields.

Next to him his sister, Stella, said, "Mr. Trask looks fine tonight. I think he likes the silver ribbon you gave him."

Jimmy nodded. "Mr. Maudsley looks good too. See the way his hand shines?"

In the driver's seat as he twisted the wheel to avoid a rut in the road, gray-haired Mr. Tapping coughed and glanced at his wife.

"What are those kids whispering about?"

The whispers died abruptly, and the car rattled over Goose Creek bridge and began the long climb to the Tapping farm.

They stopped at the roadside mailbox, but there was no mail; then they were rolling up the cedar-lined lane, past the silo, past the barn, into the farmyard.

Stella went into the house with her mother, but Jimmy remained with his father to open the garage doors. He snapped the big padlock shut after the car was put away, made a vain attempt to catch Higgins, the cat, and followed Mr. Tapping up the porch steps into the house. Upstairs in his room half an hour later, he undressed reluctantly and climbed into bed, wide awake. He lay there listening to the old house creak and groan in the night wind.

From the distance came the mournful wail of a train whistle.

Presently Jimmy got out of bed, crossed to the window and stood looking out into the moonlight. Below him he could see his ball bat leaning against the shadows. Beyond was the outline of a mounted horseman, the pump, and beyond that the gray circular walls of the silo pointed upward like a castle tower. Something caught Jimmy's eye, made him look to the east. He looked again, then moved to the table and rummaged through the drawer until he found the silver spyglass his father had given him last Christmas. He carried the glass back to the window, pushed the window open and peered out.

In the bright moonlight he could see Mr. Maudsley clearly. And a little farther on he could see Mr. Trask. Two silent figures alone in the cornfields.

The boy lowered the glass, wiped the lens on his sleeve, and carefully focused again. A puzzled frown furrowed his face. Save for the flapping of his trousers in the wind, Mr. Maudsley stood motionless, as of course he should. But, Mr. Trask . . . A passing cloud slid over the moon, darkening the landscape. In the few seconds before it brought complete blackness Jimmy thought he saw Mr. Trask kick up his heels, leap high in the air and begin to dance a rigadoon over the shocked corn.

At breakfast next morning Jimmy waited impatiently for his sister to come downstairs. He hoped she would get to the table before his father because with Papa present he couldn't talk, and he wanted to talk. When at last Stella took her chair, he stretched his foot under the table and kicked her slightly.

"I've got a secret," he whispered.

"Tell it to me," said Stella.

"It's a big secret."

"If you won't tell, I won't give you any of my Flinch candy."

Jimmy was silent a moment as he gave this thought. Then he leaned forward and whispered.

"Mr. Trask moved last night."

"He always moves," replied Stella, unimpressed.

"I mean really moved. Toward Mr. Maudsley."

Stella choked on her porridge and the spoon all but slipped from her hand. She stared with wide open eyes. "He didn't."

Their whispers broke off as Mr. Tapping strode across the kitchen and took his place at the head of the table. A heavy-set unimaginative man who seldom entered into conversation with the children, he eyed them speculatively. But he said nothing and began to eat his eggs and thick strips of bacon. He ate slowly and methodically, keeping his eyes to the table. When he had finished his coffee, he settled back to light his pipe. He passed the match back and forth across the bowl with quiet deliberation.

"Who's Mr. Maudsley and who's Mr. Trask?"

His wife smiled. "Those are just the names the children have given the scarecrows."

"What scarecrows?"

"The one in our field and the one on Edmund's land."

Mr. Tapping considered this while strong curls of strong tobacco smoke rose about him.

"Why those names? Why not Brown and Smith?"

"Because those are their names," explained Stella patiently.

Mr. Tapping cogitated on the mysteries of the juvenile mind. Abruptly he rememberd the section of pasture fence that needed repairing and got to his feet.

But it was nearly noon before he got around to fence fixing, and then he had but one wire stapled when he heard a "halloo" and, turning, saw old Jason Southby hobbling across the field toward him.

Jimmy, who was holding the wire for his father, let go the pliers and joined Stella who was trying to capture a bumblebee in a fruit jar.

"Howdy," said old Jason, reaching the fence. "Got a couple of helpers, I see."

Mr. Tapping smiled and nodded his greeting.

"I came over to ask if you're goin' to post your property for no huntin' this year."

"Don't think so," replied Mr. Tapping. "Aren't many grouse, and I don't expect there'll be many hunters."

"No," agreed old Jason, "the birds are dyin' out. It ain't like the old days."

Mr. Tapping nodded.

"Remember when Maudsley was here. Things was different then."

"Who did you say?" said Mr. Tapping.

"Maudsley," repeated old Jason. "He owned your farm twenty . . . thirty years ago."

Mr. Tapping shook his head. Maudsley, eh? Jimmy and Stella must have heard the name from one of the neighbors' children.

"Yep," continued old Jason. "Maudsley had this place, and Trask rented the strip across the road."

"So?"

"Quite a story about them two."

Mr. Tapping said nothing. There would be no hurrying old Jason; and no stopping him either. The man obviously had a tale to tell, and he was enjoying every moment of this prelude. He bit off a piece of plug tobacco, chewed a moment and spat.

"It was corn that started it," he said. "Maudsley was a great one to fool around with hybrids, and he worked out an early variety he called Maudsley Number Two. That ain't bein' planted anymore, but in those days it was well thought of."

"Then Trask moved into the farm across the road. Trask was from down south, from around New Orleans way, and he was fired up with all sorts of backwoods stuff. Pretty soon he began to fight with Maudsley about how good his hybrid corn was. Seems Trask believed the only way to grow good crops was by usin' voodoo spells. Got so them two couldn't come into sight of each other without startin' an argument. One day Trask got so mad he let his cattle loose in Maudsley's cornfield. That settled it. Maudsley headed for Trask's place, armed with a double-barreled shotgun. But before he got there, Trask made himself invisible."

"He did what?" demanded Mr. Tapping.

"Well, anyway, that's the story Maudsley spread around. Funny thing is, folks believed him. He said Trask, bein' from New Orleans country, knew all sorts of voodoo spells, and he said that Trask, bein' afraid, had cast a spell over himself to make himself vanish. 'Course some persons were suspicious and the sheriff asked Maudsley some questions. But Maudsley proved his shotgun hadn't been fired, and no one had seen him commit any crime. Trask was never seen around these parts again. After that Maudsley got to actin' sorta queer: lookin' over his shoulder, talkin' to himself. Then one day he up and cleared out, and the next anything was heard of him he had moved south to New Orleans, the very place Trask had come from. Maudsley is still down there; he wouldn't come back even long enough to complete the sale of his farm." Jason's voice died off as he reached the end of his story.

"Did you hear what he said?" said Jimmy in a low voice.

"Sure." Stella rose triumphant from capturing her bumblebee. "I knew it all the time."

It rained the next night and even with the spyglass Jimmy could see nothing in the cornfields. But he knew the two scarecrows were out there, and he could imagine them standing in the rain with beads of water dripping from their hats. The muddy water would be running in rivulets between the rows of shocked corn and when the lightning flashed the shocks would gleam dully like so many stacked guns at an army encampment.

Next day after lunch Jimmy drew his sister aside.

"If you don't tell anybody I'll show you the present I've got for Mr. Maudsley. Promise?"

"I promise," said Stella.

Jimmy led the way into the barn and in the rear near one of the horse stalls, swept aside a covering of hay. He picked up a long rusty knife and displayed it with an air of pride. Stella was disappointed.

"Just an old knife."

"It's a voodoo knife, that's what it is. See the way the handle is carved."

Stella looked and saw a yellowed handle of what once might have been ivory, carved in the shape of a running goat with several quasi-human faces low down near the hilt.

"What are you going to do with it?" she said.

"I told you. Give it to Mr. Maudsley. It's his."

"How do you know it's his?"

"This is Mr. Maudsley's barn, isn't it? Besides, it was near his other stuff."

Stella was not enthusiastic. "Papa won't like it. He got mad when you nailed that pie-tin to Mr. Maudsley's hand."

"Papa won't know a thing about it. Come on."

It was hot in the cornfield. The morning sun beat down fiercely and the air smelled of damp earth. The ground between the rows of stubble was marked with tiny channels that running water had cut the night before. But the shocks were dry again and in the slight breeze they whispered and rustled gently. The two children made a bee-line for the center of the field until they came to the two cross boards that served as a framework for the scarecrow.

The scarecrow was fashioned of some old clothing which had once belonged to a fat man—overalls, a coat that might have been a Sunday suit at one time, and an ancient felt hat—castaways which the children had found in the barn. The cardboard face, marked in black crayon, a little blurred now from the rain, had been copied by Jimmy from an old photograph the boy had come upon among some old papers when he had cleaned out the attic. Jimmy had decided that even a crow wouldn't be fooled by a faceless scarecrow.

Jimmy was about to climb the upright shaft when Stella stopped him.

"Wait," she said. "Let's not give Mr. Maudsley the knife."

"Why not? It's his."

"Let's give it to Mr. Trask."

The boy's jaw dropped as the enormity of the idea grew upon him. Then he uttered a squeal of delight.

Laughing and giggling, the two children turned and ran down the aisle of shocks to the road and vaulted the fence that enclosed the adjacent field.

Five minutes later the second scarecrow brandished a knife at the end of one of its handless sleeves.

But as Jimmy came out on the road again, he looked across at Mr. Maudsley. In full view in the sunlight, it wasn't a cardboard face now; it was a round full face, with great folds of fat, and it was twisted in an expression of stark fear.

For three nights the skies over the Tapping farm were black, and a cold wind huffing down from the north kept the children indoors where they played Parcheesi. On the fourth night the moon broke through the clouds.

Jimmy, squatting by the window, the spyglass to his eye, stared out at the two scarecrows. At intervals he thought he saw Mr. Trask descend from the mounting pole, leap up over the shocks and begin his strange dance. But at the instant those capers began, the clouds always managed to blot out the light, and the boy never could be sure if it was a trick of his eye or the glass.

And then Jimmy observed two things. With him in his gyrations Mr. Trask carried the knife, and as he darted back and forth, he edged almost imperceptibly toward Mr. Maudsley.

The boy watched a long time to confirm his fears. Then he turned and ran to his sister's room.

"Mr. Trask is getting closer," he said. "You'd better come see."

At the window Stella spent several moments focusing the glass. Slowly her body went rigid, and she uttered a hoarse exclamation.

"He's going to kill Mr. Maudsley."

The boy nodded, his eyes shining with terror.

"We've got to try and stop him!"

She turned and ran down the stairs and through the lower floor rooms to the back door. Jimmy ran after her. Crossing the yard, they sped halfway down the lane, then pushed through the cedar windbreak and veered toward the cornfield. Pumpkins, golden in the moonlight, rose up on either side as they raced up the incline.

Suddenly Stella drew up short. "Look!"

Mr. Trask had crossed the road and now was coming full tilt through the row of shocks. Jimmy, arms spread wide, threw himself forward to block the onrushing figure's path. He had a brief impression of a blurred shadow bowling toward him and passing through him while he struck out with his small fists ineffectually. Behind there was a ripping of cloth and a hoarse scream.

Stella came running to where Jimmy stood. Together they saw two shadows locked in an incredible embrace. Like a scythe raised aloft, Mr. Trask's knife swept downward in a wide arc and with a quick stroke cut off Mr. Maudsley's head. Mr. Maudsley's hat flew up, Mr. Maudsley's head rolled off, and a thin cry of triumph welled up and faded.

And then there was nothing, except that Mr. Trask was back on one side of the fence, and Mr. Maudsley was on the other, minus his head, of course.

"Gee!" said Stella.

"Golly!" said Jimmy. He ran over to pick up Mr. Maudsley's hat; Jimmy tried to put Mr. Maudsley's head back but somehow it wouldn't stick.

"We'll fix it in the morning," said Jimmy.

At the edge of the field Jimmy paused and caught his sister's arm anxiously. "You won't tell, Stella?"

"No, of course not."

"Cross your heart . . . ?"

"Cross my heart and hope to die."

It was night of the next day and the children sat playing Parcheesi. Mrs. Tapping was knitting. Mr. Tapping, settled back in the platform rocker, was reading the newspaper aloud, as was his custom. Outside, Mr. Trask was in one field, and Mr. Maudsley was in the other; his head was back in place, but only tied on—it was not the same; it looked very dead, even though Jimmy and Stella had done their best.

"Any news?" asked Mrs. Tapping.

"Same old stuff. New taxes, one of them foreign countries talkin' big and threatenin' war," said Mr. Tapping. "One thing here, though—they found a fellow with his head cut off right in the middle of a city street."

"My land! Not here in Akerstown?"

Mr. Tapping laughed. "Lord, no! Happened way down in New Orleans."

Somewhere My Love

STEPHEN MARK RAINEY

She lived in the only run-down house in the neighborhood: a two-story Victorian with a pepperbox turret and windows of leaded glass, a sagging roof with missing shingles and a number of blackened brick chimneys. What little paint remained was no longer white but crusty gray, its walls barely seen through the dense cedar trees that surrounded the property. Weeds sprouted from the unkempt, split-rail fenced yard, and rather than a nice paved driveway like all the others in the community, she had only a short gravel apron for her car. The man of the house had died before I was born, leaving her alone in the old place for all those years. At night, not a light ever shone in any of the windows.

And sometimes after dark, I'd hear her voice echoing out of that old house, raised in songs that seemed to me unearthly.

Of course she was a witch.

Her name was Jeanne Weiler, and she was my music teacher when I was in elementary school.

Looking back now, I'd have to say she was quite an attractive woman, though at the time, she presented such an imposing image that just being in the same room with her intimidated me to the edge of fright. She stood almost six feet (which when I was just over four feet tall seemed so very high indeed), had long, wavy black hair that she often wore stacked atop her head, and possessed the most piercing green eyes I think I've ever seen even to this day. She virtually always wore a severe, tight-fitting black outfit that showed off a fine figure unappreciated by my youthful eyes, but which spoke of no impropriety—only of dignity.

And despite my fear of Mrs. Weiler, I loved her so. While I couldn't begin to have sexual thoughts about her in those days, I reacted physically to her presence by having chills and almost uncontrollable trembling. I recall many a time when, had she but asked it, I would have fallen to my knees and kissed her feet and been so excited by the prospect that I might have wet my drawers.

All the more reason to be assured that she was a witch, for this was power—the purest power ever exerted upon me, miles and leagues beyond any held by my parents, or any other teachers, or the minister at church, or any of my fellow fourth graders. I was afraid of her because she could have made me do things. Anything.

But she always spoke kindly to me, treated me with the same respect with which she treated all the kids. All the parents liked her. I know she was aware of the effect she had on me because often I would catch her glancing at me with appraisal in her cool eyes, one hand curled beneath her chin as if she contemplated things held in store for me that I could not imagine.

And oh, her voice! She would sing so many songs to us as she attempted to teach us music, and that sweet alto would weave its way through my mind down to my deepest core, tugging at my soul with sorrow or joy, whatever emotion to which the song was tuned. I remember she would sing "A Time for Us," the theme to *Romeo and Juliet,* with such passion that the whole class would be in tears.

No one else could have ever done that to me, or to any of my friends.

She was a witch.

Some of the songs we had to learn were stupid, and she took great

41

pleasure in watching us humiliate ourselves by singing them—badly, at that—and I loved her all the more for it. Things like "Morning Comes Bringing" and "Dreidle" and "Cherry Ripe" made my teeth grind, but because she desired it, we'd sing our little hearts out, and she would smile with such joy. She was our mistress and could not be refused. She would reward us sometimes with milk and cookies or even let us out five minutes before the bell rang in the afternoon, for hers was the last class of the day.

Late in the school year came the day that I learned what she'd had in store for me from the beginning. Not only for me, I might add, but for Johnny McCrickard and Tina Truman as well. The horror of it all nearly destroyed me, and I think the time she announced it was the first and only time I ever hyperventilated uncontrollably. Johnny and Tina didn't have such strong reactions, but the dread showed just as plainly in their eyes, and in their chalky faces. The rest of the class, of course, cheered and sang their praises to Mrs. Weiler, no doubt relieved that none of them had been similarly singled out.

Johnny, Tina, and I were to sing. Solos. Not only in front of the class, but in front of the school. We had shown such superior achievement that Mrs. Weiler was certain we would shine, and make her—and our parents, and everyone—so proud.

Johnny would sing "The Impossible Dream." Tina would sing "Love Is Blue." And I—I would sing "Somewhere My Love," Lara's theme from *Dr. Zhivago,* the big blockbuster of the day.

Mrs. Weiler looked pained and fearful when I began breathing and sobbing so hard—and came immediately to me and stroked my hand, and gazed at me with such sadness in her green eyes. And almost immediately the paroxysm passed. Kneeling before me, she looked truly beautiful, and I wanted to kiss her. But she said, "Warren, you can do it, I know. Won't you sing for us? Won't you please?"

And taking a deep breath, I said, "Yes," because I could not refuse her.

The big event would happen two weeks later, at a special assembly held in the evening so the parents could come. There was plenty of other programming: scholastic awards, athletic awards, a farewell presentation for Mrs. Clairmont, who would be retiring at the end of the term. The music event would not occur until almost the end of the assembly, which gave the three unlucky participants all the more time in which to sweat and fidget.

And through it all, Mrs. Weiler stayed by me, whispered little encouragements in my ear, ran her fingers affectionately through my hair —making me melt as her power coursed through my body like an electrical current. She was kind enough to Johnny and Tina, but her attentions were focused on me; an attempt, I suppose, to cast a spell upon me like none she'd ever conjured before. It must have worked, for by the time I was to sing my song, my heart was thumping and my knees were weak, yet I went out on stage after Tina and Johnny had done their numbers with only the desire to please Mrs. Weiler in my heart. The multitudes of eyes on me, and all those expectant faces, including my mom's and dad's, meant nothing. Only the green eyes behind the stage curtain gazing at me with such tenderness had any influence on me whatsoever.

The record began playing over the loudspeakers, an instrumental version that left the vocals to be provided entirely by me. I glanced at my teacher, who nodded at just the right moment, giving me the cue to begin. I stepped up to the microphone and the voice that came out was no longer mine. It was a rich, hearty stranger's voice, entirely on-key and without a trace of quaver. "Somewhere my love," I sang, surprised and shocked by the entity that must have entered me for the sole purpose of releasing its voice via my mouth. I saw my teacher leave her place behind the curtain and make her way down the stage steps, coming slowly to stand at the edge of the platform before me. Her eyes flashed, and this thing of Mrs. Weiler's making, it seized my lungs and my vocal cords, and it had its way with me until the music ended, and I stood there alone in a vacuum, without so much as a whisper of breath to break the silence.

Until I looked down at the green eyes, and saw them smiling. And then a single pair of hands came together, cracking in the air like a gunshot, and a moment later a thunder erupted in the auditorium, a monstrous peal of applause joined by the crying out of hundreds of voices. I nearly swooned, for it seemed that a cold wind swept past my body, threatening to topple me as my adrenaline high faded, leaving me unsteady and on the verge of hyperventilating again.

I was upheld by Mrs. Weiler's strong hands though, for in an instant she was beside me, and for the first time I looked into my parents' eyes and saw them beaming with pride. I smiled, probably for the first time since the news of my "performance" had been broken to me. And without looking at her, I knew Mrs. Weiler's eyes were focused on me, perhaps in attempt to take back the thing she'd released to take possession of my body. Was it a kind thing? I wondered. A dangerous thing? All I knew was that for a time it had been mine, and Mrs. Weiler had made it so.

Because she was a witch.

That night became something special in my memory. Afterwards, I sang and I enjoyed the sound of my voice, but it was always *my* voice. The sounds I had let fall from my lips at that assembly surely had come from something apart from me, and try as I might, I could not regain it. Only Mrs. Weiler knew the secret.

And shortly after school ended for that summer, Mrs. Weiler died. I do not know how or why, only that I never saw her again. And I cried, harder than I cried when my grandparents died, more bitterly than when my father passed away a couple of years later. My mother is still alive, and I love her dearly, yet I cannot imagine shedding tears more meaningful when her time comes than those I shed for Mrs. Weiler.

One day when I was eighteen, I went to the house where she had lived, which remains today as something of a monument in this old town. On that day, though, remembering so well the effect she'd had on my life, I wandered around the place, taken by a feeling of melancholy. I stepped up to the rickety front porch and tried the front door, not expecting it to be unlocked.

But it was. As if I were expected.

So I went inside and as soon as I stepped over the darkened threshold, the scent of her rushed into my nostrils, undiluted after nearly nine years. Dust-shrouded furniture remained in place, as if nothing had been touched since she'd died. A grand piano occupied one corner of the large living room, and stepping up to it, I touched a key. A clear note rang out, and so I played a few chords, to my surprise finding each key in perfect tune. I had learned how to play piano over the course of several years, though never as well as I would have, had Mrs. Weiler been there to guide my hand and attune my senses to the music.

But what came out in that dusty old chamber was a clear melody— "Somewhere My Love"—a song I had never played myself, now played as perfectly as I had sung it on that night in fourth grade. I felt the same current in my soul that I had the night she'd released her power into me, and I would have sworn for a time that I heard her voice singing the words in accompaniment.

I suddenly stopped, and the notes echoed into the darkened halls of that house, stirring something. Something that whispered my name and touched my cheek and brushed my lips with a sweet caress.

I left there knowing I would return. Soon.

And I did.

Once I'd graduated college, I disavowed the ritual practiced by my friends and virtually all the rest of the town's youth—leaving home for greener pastures, never to return, or if so, only for brief family visits. Instead, I managed to place myself as music teacher in the local school system.

And I moved into the old Weiler place, which is where I still reside. I often wish I had been able to know her as an adult, for I had come to understand her power and her love of music. I came to feel what she must have felt when a beautiful melody played and touched her heart. I still feel her and hear her and smell her in the halls of this house, and within these walls, I feel the magic she once gave to me on the stage of our little elementary school.

I take that magic with me every day, and when I encounter a little one who shares, however vaguely, the power that Mrs. Weiler bestowed upon me, I give to that child all I can spare, conjuring up that *thing* that once took me and that still lives within the walls of my old house. It doesn't like light, but favors the dark, so in the evenings, I walk with it and sing, or play the piano or the guitar, or whichever instrument that brings it pleasure. It prefers the old things, so I don't change the furniture, or otherwise renovate the place any more than necessary to keep it habitable. And I remember those times when I was a child and heard Mrs. Weiler's voice in the night, but didn't understand.

Of course I am older now, and understand so much more. And though most of the children don't understand, there are those few who one day *will*. Those are the ones upon whom I focus—to perpetuate the spirit that Mrs. Weiler passed on to me. I can do this; I have that power.

Because I am a witch.

Of course.

Burning in the Light

JULEEN BRANTINGHAM

All the way home from the hospital I kept thinking, he won't be there; I've lost him; I've lost everything that matters. When the cab stopped I turned too quickly, looking for him, and was overcome by dizziness. The rods of the fence, an army of spears, broke ranks and milled about. The porch was a ship that had come loose from its moorings, looming over me. My heart was pounding.

Then Paul was there, though I was too dizzy to see him.

"Why are you crying?"

I wiped away the tears, smiling, relieved. "I'm not. I'm just dizzy."

Getting out of the cab was difficult. My body was unresponsive, quick to kindle into pain. I couldn't have made it up the steps if the driver hadn't helped me. Where had Paul gone?

As I fumbled my key into the lock I remembered this was Marlene's day off. In the living room I eased into a chair with a sigh of relief. I tried to touch the wounds near my eyes but my hand flinched away before completing the gesture. Where was Paul? Wasn't he glad to have me back?

The living room was dim. In the shadows near the fireplace, in the alcove by the bay window I heard him whisper. I couldn't make out what he was saying.

Then Marlene was there, her iron-gray hair pulled back in a knot, her housedress so stiff with starch it crackled. "I had a feeling you'd be home today. I've got your bed turned down, everything just the way you like it."

When I got up, leaning on her arm, the whispering started again, fast, urgent. I took a breath, pushed the pain away.

"Wait. Something I have to do. In the studio."

"You're worn out, child. Come and rest now."

When she used that tone I couldn't argue.

* * *

Drifting on a pill haze to the borders of sleep, I heard a radio playing, an appliance whirring in the kitchen, a bird singing. Comforting sounds of home. I didn't hear Paul come in.

"Still awake?"

"Not really," I said. Eyes closed, I reached for him. He cradled me in an embrace I could almost feel.

"Missed you," I said.

"Me too, you."

"I was afraid you'd be gone."

"Yeah, lunch with the president, stockholders' meetings. So many demands on my time."

I ached to feel his touch.

"I'll never forgive myself."

I opened my eyes but the sun had found a gap in the shade. It blinded me with its glare.

"Why? You had nothing to do with the accident." Marlene said I was alone in the studio when it happened. She had been working in the kitchen or she couldn't have heard the glass shatter when I fell. If not for her I would have bled to death.

Thoughts of blood and death made me uneasy.

"You still don't remember how it happened?"

I shook my head.

"It was hot. You must have been trying to open the window, the one that sticks. You pushed too hard and fell through. It's a wonder you weren't killed."

The lower floor of my studio was a garage; beneath that window was a concrete parking apron. Marlene said when she found me there were shards of glass sticking out so close to my eyes she'd thought I would be blind.

"If I'd fixed it when you asked me—"

"It was an accident. You know how impatient I am. It was my own fault."

"You must be anxious to get out there, make sure everything's all right. Feel up to a walk?"

I rolled away. "Not now."

"Sweetheart, you're not nervous about the studio, are you? You could develop a phobia about that place, like that problem I had last spring."

Last spring we'd argued constantly. He accused me of being obsessed with my work, said I only wanted him around when I was tired, when I had nothing left to give. He wouldn't understand that was when I needed him most.

Several times he came to the door to tell me he was going out, to see if I needed anything. Once he had his tools and I thought he was going to fix the window. Each time he left, making excuses. I thought he was being childish, making a point about work taking all my time. Finally he said he couldn't cross the threshold. When he tried he'd break out in a sweat, feel sick to his stomach. I had a talk with Marlene and his problem went away.

Shortly after that he left me.

"I'm tired. I'll go later."

He started to leave.

"Paul, what was I painting that day?"

"What else? The river."

I was born beside the river. As a child I'd played on its banks. As an artist I found inspiration in its moods, its lights, its seasons.

Sometimes I get lost in my work. Another part of me takes over and the hours pass, shapes take form, colors flow. I've been very successful. A few years ago I bought the house where Marlene and my mother used to work.

One morning I set up my easel on the deck overlooking the river. I lost myself in trying to capture a hazy golden light that's visible only at certain times of the year. I wasn't aware of the lateness of the hour until I looked up and found the sun had dropped behind the trees.

I looked at the canvas. From one angle the painting was a pattern of light and shadow but when I tilted my head, the figure of a man coalesced from seemingly random details. He was sitting on the bank, his back toward the viewer. When I moved my head he disappeared, becoming a reflection, a ripple of light, a few sticks, a scattering of leaves.

I glanced over the rail of the deck, catching my breath when I saw the man. It was as if I had brought him into being with my brush and the magic of the river.

He turned and raised his hand in greeting.

Maybe I'd had too much sun.

He crossed the yard toward me. His shirt was open and his trousers rode low on his hips. As he climbed the steps I watched the play of muscles beneath his skin. I didn't believe he was real until I smelled his sweat, felt his heat.

He studied the painting. I can't remember what he said, something about my having captured a mood, a moment.

Then he turned to study me as closely as he had my work. I wished I could disappear. My hair was stringy, my shirt stained, my face tight with sunburn.

"Mary Swan," I blurted, holding out my hand.

"Paul," he said.

Does a river need a last name? Does a perfect day?

"Where are you going?"

"To the studio."

She was a heavy woman but she moved with the grace of a dancer. I'd thought I could get out before she heard me.

"Doctor said you was to rest."

"I'm not planning to work."

"Then for pity's sake, why?"

Paul wanted to show me something. He'd promised he would be waiting. I couldn't tell Marlene that.

She steered me into the kitchen. "Your pictures will still be there next week. Now. I'm fixing a nice shrimp salad for your lunch. Sit and keep me company."

The iron Dutch oven presided over the range as it had for as long as I could remember, like a goddess presiding over her altar. Rag rugs covered the floor; bundles of herbs dangled from the ceiling. Dark, roughly woven curtains shaded the windows. Marlene's cat looked up from the seat of the rocker and blinked at me.

After I bought the house, before Paul came, I always took my meals here with her. In this room I always felt I was her guest.

She poured me a cup of coffee. "Seen Mr. Paul lately?"

I dropped the cup, scalding myself.

"Now why would I do a thing like that?"

I had planned my speech word for word. I'd never given Marlene an order before. Paul's problem had to be her doing. "I know you don't like him—"

She snorted. "Don't like what he does to you, upsetting you so you can't use your goddess-given talent."

"—but I love him. You must accept that. I *like* having him there, even when he interrupts my work. Whatever you did to keep him out of the studio, undo it."

"I don't know nothing about it."

"He says it feels like someone died there."

She caught her breath, then tried to pretend it meant nothing.

I could never get enough of looking at him, his smile, the way his eyes changed color. I could never get enough of waking in the morning to find him next to me. Now I had only his voice.

"What did you do yesterday?"

"Talked to Marlene. Took a nap." I ached to touch him, to see him. Outside, the wind gusted at the approach of a storm; in my room the shadows danced. Now and then I glimpsed an eye, a chin, the curve of his neck.

"I waited for you at the studio."

I hugged myself. It wasn't the touch I craved. "Let's go for a walk by the river, the way we used to."

"It's going to rain."

We had been fighting again. We had problems but I was sure we could work them out. I came back from the studio and found his closet empty. I didn't make a sound but inside I was screaming. As always when I needed her, Marlene was there. She put her arms around me but offered cold comfort.

"You know it's for the best. The fighting was making you sick, getting in the way of your work. You said so yourself."

"Bring him back."

She drew away. "You don't know what you're asking."

"When my bike was stolen, when my puppy ran away, you brought them back. You have the power. Use it. I can't live without him."

"It wouldn't be right."

I kept after her day and night. I threatened never to pick up a brush again. I wasn't proud of myself but I had to do it.

"Mary, what I do, I do *with* the goddess, not against her."

"I need him."

"Wanting and needing is two different things."

"I can make things right," I promised. "I can make him happy. I need another chance."

With a snapshot and hair from his pillow, with fire and words, she cast her spell. The stench of burning still lingered in the air when I heard his step and ran to the door. He looked as if he'd been dragged backward through a barbed wire fence. I wondered for a moment if my love was strong enough.

"I couldn't stay away, couldn't stop thinking about you. I guess I love you too much," he said, defeated.

When I put my arms around him, my doubts vanished. I would never let anything part us again. He would forget he'd ever wanted to leave me.

The storm passed without giving any relief from the heat. Marlene's cat, prowling under the hedge, arched her back and hissed, then raced toward the house. When I opened the studio door I was assaulted by a dark, musty smell. Paul wasn't there, though the room was full of shadows, whispers, the electricity of his presence.

The broken window had been replaced.

My easel stood in front of the door that opened onto the deck. The canvas showed an unfinished scene of the river. Paul said I had been painting the river that day. He was wrong.

For a moment I thought I saw his face shimmering in the shadows. I couldn't catch my breath. The musty smell made me gag, a smell like old blood.

Blood and death.

After he came back I tried to make things right. He kept saying I was obsessed with my work, that I had no time for him.

Behind me the door opened. I forgot for a moment and turned, smiling.

"You expecting someone else?"

"N-no."

"Have you see him?"

To distract her I gestured toward the canvas. "This isn't what I was working on the day of the accident. Where is that one?"

"You remember what you were working on?"

I started to laugh, choked off the sound when I thought I heard Paul whisper my name. "Isn't it silly? I remember the heat, the feel of the brush in my hand. I was trying . . ." No, I couldn't remember.

She held my hands. "Don't be afraid. I'm here now."

The light was too strong, as it had been that day. It burned through the glass, sizzled the air.

Marlene went to the wall where I'd stacked several finished canvases. She picked one up and held it facing toward her.

I looked away. Darkness caught my eye and I made a sound of annoyance. It was a stain on the floor. How had it gotten there? Splinters of wood showed through. Someone had tried to scrape the floor clean.

"He must have hated me," I said.

She put the painting on the easel. It was meant to be a portrait of Paul.

When I found him I couldn't stop screaming. My throat was raw by the time Marlene reached me.

"He can't— This isn't— Marlene, I tried. He didn't give me a chance."

"Whatever was wrong, you can't help him now."

He sprawled on the floor, the ghastly wound gaping in his neck. The blood was fresh. A palette knife had fallen from his hand. My studio. My knife. So much hate.

"Bring him back."

Her expression turned cold. "I'll call the police."

I screamed. I pleaded. I fell to my knees and clutched at her hands but she turned her back and left me, for the first time in my life.

I don't know how long I crouched there, whimpering. Finally I staggered to my feet and began to pace, stepping over the blood without looking at it. I cursed Paul. I cursed Marlene and her goddess. I thought I saw him lurking in the shadows. I thought I heard the echo of his laughter—laughter because he had won, he'd gotten away. Then I noticed the spray of blood on a canvas I'd prepared the day before.

Fresh canvas. Fresh blood.

Blood was . . . the essence of life.

I had no magic, didn't know what words to speak. I had only my talent, my special vision. And I had his blood.

Dipping my fingers into the thick pool I called upon whatever powers might be listening. Before Marlene returned with the police, my hastily done sketch had dried enough that I could hide it from their prying eyes.

"You ought to be ashamed, making him suffer."

After the funeral I locked myself into the studio and took the

52

sketch from its hiding place. I applied paint with a loving touch, adding layer after layer, building up depth and detail over tracings of blood.

"I think I caught him in time. I can hear him. Sometimes I can almost see him. But he won't touch me."

If I could make his portrait true, he would never, ever leave me again. But the blood, through some mysterious alchemy, changed what I had painted. Each morning when I lifted the damp cloth from the canvas I found the blood had seeped through, distorting my beloved's features. I would scrape it down carefully and start again.

Again and again and again.

"It's not his face!" I cried, knocking it from Marlene's hands. I had been away too long. The paint had hardened. If I scraped it down again the blood, his essence, would be lost.

"No, child, this is what you did to him. Blood is true."

I picked up the canvas and embraced it as I would have embraced him. Marlene tried to take it from me. I fended her off.

"What happened the day of the accident?" Her voice was as soft as a whisper in the shadows.

I touched the half-healed scars around my eyes. I remembered the plunge through the glass, felt the shards stab at my eyes.

Sunlight burned through the window as it had that day, so bright it brought tears to my eyes. Before I could blink them away, something moved out there. A figure coalesced from the glare, burning in the light.

He promised he would be waiting.

Marlene was wrong. The image on the canvas wasn't Paul. He was out there in the light. He was real and he wanted us to be together.

"Yes!" I cried, starting toward him.

Marlene held me back. She was strong but not as strong as my love for Paul. She thought I wanted to kill myself.

It was life I wanted, not death. Life with Paul. If I gave him what he asked for— He only wanted to take what had always kept us apart.

Marlene wasn't quick enough to stop me from snatching up the palette knife.

"Take them!" I cried joyfully. "Only *touch* me!"

The Scream

MIKE ASHLEY

It was a spider-web morning. The gossamer threads shimmered with the dew, creating a passageway of silver along the hedge-rows. Along the passage in the cold mists of morning came the small procession. First an altar boy holding high a golden crucifix. Then the priest, his eyes all but closed, reciting passages from the Book of Life. Then a young girl, scarcely fifteen, clad in torn and filthy rags. Her hands were tightly bound behind her, and it was all she could do to walk. Her feet were blistered and bruised. Her face showed signs of violence. And where once had been long, dark, shining hair, was now a shaven and scarred scalp. She was accompanied on either side by her jailers, two young squires who looked the worse for making the girl's last night a hell on earth.

Behind her came the executioners, the village elders, carrying aloft their burning torches, themselves led by Wilfred, the sheriff of the county, who was there to ensure all went according to law.

A few villagers straggled behind them, but most were already gathered at the crossroads where the pyre had been constructed. They looked on in fear as the procession approached. They had never known a witch before and most had never seen an execution. They had known Sarah all her short life and knew her as a kind and gentle girl, always helpful and willing to please—until this last year when the village was beset by problems. A harsh winter had led to floods followed by drought and for the first time the well dried up. The summer brought illness and all of the townsfolk suffered, all except Sarah. Many had died. Then fire swept through the village. It was almost wholly destroyed, except for the church and a few stone houses. And then came the poor harvest. The villagers, having survived the plague and fire, were now starving. And through all this Sarah had passed unscathed, always present, always seeking to please.

It was then the rumours had started. How could Sarah always look so healthy and unperturbed. The villagers knew. *The devil protects his own.*

The procession turned the final corner towards the crossroads and as Sarah came in view the gathered townsfolk were audibly shocked at how she looked and their fear turned to pity. Others, though, remembered their dead and began to jeer and shout.

Other eyes watched the procession. Unseen, unnoticed, two bright green eyes peered through the gossamer hedge, watching her mistress stumbling the final steps to her fate. The cat flicked its tail in fear but it stayed its ground, huddling under the hedgerow, waiting for the moment.

The procession stopped. The elders moved toward the pyre, their firebrands casting black smoke into the misty sky. The priest took the crucifix from the altar boy, kissed it and held it before him, as he chanted the final passages. A hush came over the assembly.

The priest now, for the first time, turned his eyes to the girl. He was an old man. He had known Sarah since the day she was born, and had always loved her bright smile, her sparkling eyes, her joy of life. He barely stifled a wince as he saw her battered and bruised body. The girl, like any wayward human, should have one final chance to repent.

"Sarah, child, do you commit your soul to your Father in heaven or to your Master in eternal damnation?"

The girl scarcely moved. A slight flicker of the eyelids suggested she may have heard the priest, but there was no other recognition.

"Sarah, these folk who were once your friends have had to suffer your torment and vengeance for a twelve-month. Do you wish to go to hell with all their hatred at your heels, or will you beseech their love and repent your sins?"

The girl's head shifted and for the first time her eyes met those of the priest. For some moments their eyes locked, and it was the priest whose gaze finally faltered. There was something in those eyes that made him shiver. He sighed. The girl was clearly a daughter of the devil. Her soul was lost. It was time to send her to hell. If only they had found her familiar, it too would be despatched in the flames.

The priest signalled to the two squires, who dragged Sarah toward the makeshift pyre. A space at the front had been left clear to allow them to strap her to the stake, but once she was secure the final logs and branches, all covered in pitch and animal grease, were piled around her.

Sarah took one final look at the crowd. Somewhere amongst these she must seek her salvation. But who? Few could look her in the eye.

Her gaze passed from one to another, and eyes looked down under her stare. Only three returned her gaze. The priest, the altar boy, and the sheriff. One bore sorrow, one bore sympathy, and one saw only a job to be done.

And so she decided. Now she must concentrate. She forced her mind inward. As an expectant hush settled over the villagers and the priest intoned his final chant, Sarah began to refocus her will. She had never sky-walked but had been told the way. The voices in the woods had assured her it was easy, but the only other time she had tried she had fainted. But now, if her spirit was to escape the final agony, she had to leave her body and find a new home.

But her body and senses had been weakened by the night's endurance. She needed strength. She looked beyond the villagers, her sixth sense seeking a friend. She found it. Although she could not see the penetrating green gaze from beyond the crowd, she knew that Toby was there, and if ever his healing spirit were needed, it was now. She sensed his will coursing toward her and together their minds locked. At last she began to feel some strength.

The priest stopped. In the silence, somewhere in the distance, a cock crowed. As if it were a signal, the priest nodded and the elders lowered their brands. Never before had they been called upon to burn a witch, and they were hesitant. They had all known and loved Sarah as a child. But they could not suffer a witch to live in their midst. It was God's will that they must do. But still they hesitated, until the sheriff thrust his torch at the outer branches. They soon crackled into flame and within moments the outer ring of the pyre was alight, belching black smoke into the misty morning.

Their deed done, the elders hurried back into the crowd. Aware that the priest had hung his head in prayer, the elders and the townsfolk did the same. This way they would not have to witness the terror of the girl's death and could pray for their own souls.

To Sarah the sudden strength of the villagers' prayers uplifted her. She could feel their plea for their own forgiveness. Waves of goodwill began to charge her soul. Although the flames had still not harmed her, the black smoke was filling her lungs and smarting her eyes, and she believed she would be asphyxiated before ever she burned to death. There were clearly only moments to go.

Sarah now blanked out all thoughts of the world about her, even as the flames began to lick around her feet, the heat singe her rags and the smoke clog her nose and lungs. She focussed on the power of the prayers from the townsfolk and on the healing energy from Toby. She remembered what the spirit-voices had told her and she withdrew into herself. Her mind channelled down into the void of plenty where in the distance a light began to shine. She drove toward that light. The dark mists about it began to swirl and tumble, but the light now began to glow and strengthen and with increasing speed she moved toward it. Suddenly it was all about her, a glow of light and life.

It was then it began.

The altar boy, whose curiosity was greater than the others, looked up at a slight sound. He could just see the girl through the smoke and noticed her head and body slump. Was she dead? As her full weight pulled on the stake, it shifted, its base probably already weakened by fire. The sticks and logs settled, resulting in a gush of sparks and smoke into the air. The movement allowed more air to circulate and suddenly the pyre erupted into flame. In the depths of the roar he sensed a sound. His body felt it before his ears. A slight shiver ran down his back, like ice. Even with the heat from the fire his arms bristled with goose bumps. And so began the scream.

It was faint and distant like the wind in the trees, but then it began to build. It passed from a whisper to a low hum, which steadily became sharper and more shrill. Now all the townsfolk heard it and they lifted their heads. Surely it was not the girl screaming. They could scarcely see her through the smoke and flames but she was slumped, mercifully dead. But the sound seemed to come from the pyre. Now it was rising in pitch. The faces of the crowd showed how their thoughts changed from curiosity to fear and apprehension. *What was this sound?*

It was now dominating the roar of the flames. It sounded like all the souls of hell in torment. A sharp, high-pitched wailing that turned the strength of the villagers to jelly. They began to quail, even the priest, who clung to his crucifix, chanting in Latin, shouting in an effort to outcry the scream.

But still it rose. The sound of hell set free.

And now another sound joined it—a shriller, more defiant scream. The howling of a cat. It began as a distant cry that rapidly rose in pitch and then united in resonance with the all-pervading wail. It was this sound that made the villagers drop to their knees, crossing themselves as they fell, holding their heads in their arms, trying to sink into the earth.

What had they done?

The wailing and howling was contained by the mists and did not echo but droned around them. It began to swirl in a gathering vortex. The sound dropped and rose again, a siren of death screaming around the flames. The villagers could feel it drive past them, rustling their hair and clothes before passing on, and then returning within moments. The very hedgerows began to buzz with the sound, the spider webs shimmering and vibrating. The world was a cacophony of torment.

Then, as the villagers felt their ears about to burst, they sensed the scream lifting. The sound rose above them, and one or two villagers dared look up toward the pyre.

The flames seemed to have united with the scream. As it rose and fell so did the fire, and as the scream became higher the flames started to drive upward. Taller and thinner became the pyre until it became a single vibrant pillar of flame and within that pillar the scream began to echo. The howling and caterwauling rose to its most painful and the pillar of flame flickered with the sound as if it were striving to speak.

Could the altar boy hear a whisper within the crescendo of howls? He felt as if a curtain of sound had parted and within was another, softer, deeper sound. He strained to listen whilst seeking to shield himself from the scream.

Thank . . . you, he seemed to hear.

He strained again.

Your love has saved me.

The scream began to fade, rising and swirling within the pillar of fire.

And I . . .

He shut his eyes trying to hear the distant whisper.

. . . shall never leave you. . . .

The final word faded into the distance as the scream rose in crescendo, the sound gaining a higher and higher pitch rising further into the sky. The pillar of flame seemed to stretch to heaven and those who dared to watch believed they could see something within rising from the pyre. Something white and serene. It glowed and rose as if with wings. Was it an angel? They cast down their eyes for fear they were looking upon the glory of the Lord, and so none saw whom the spirit sought, though one sensed it.

The villagers cowered.

What had they done? Had they destroyed a child of God instead of the daughter of the Devil?

The priest had closed his eyes, and clenched the crucifix so tight that his hands were white. But now he opened them and looked at the pillar of fire. The coruscations of sound and light battled against his senses. He shouted to the Lord for forgiveness for the village and for the love of Sarah. The sheriff was stunned at the events and struggled to come to terms with what was happening. He looked around him for something to grasp as reality, but could only see the terror-struck villagers. Only the altar boy seemed in awe, looking like a soul blessed toward the pillar of fire.

And so at last the scream began to subside. It seemed to fold into the sky, and many who remembered the day and told of it to their children said that the scream softened and became like a heavenly choir. The flames began to fade. The silver glow of the pillar of fire turned yellow . . . then red . . . then transparent . . .

. . . and stopped.

The silence was like a pit, dragging the villagers into the depths. Not a soul moved, not even the priest, who had collapsed to the ground. It was the sheriff who was the first to rise. Stunned, bewildered, he straightened himself and looked about him.

The fire was out, with only a few wisps of smoke rising from the remains. Of the girl there was nothing to be seen. Even her bones must have turned to ash and risen on the pillar of fire to be scattered across the world.

The sheriff turned to the priest, who was struggling to rise, and helped him to his feet. Gradually the other villagers rose. No one dared speak. What had happened here was a sign from God that the village had sinned. Whether the future held retribution or salvation they did not know, but many were already convinced that Sarah was a saint and were making plans to remember her all of their days.

The priest had his own plans. Only the sheriff had noticed the strange look in his eyes, distant and unfocussed, but as he rose and regained his composure they became twinkling and lively. A slight smile broke across his face.

"Are you all right, Father?" the sheriff asked, concerned.

"Thank you, Wilfred, I am fine. We have witnessed a miracle, Wilfred, a miracle, and one that is proof of God's will."

"What do you mean?"

The priest did not answer, but smiled. He knew that the village would remember Sarah for a long time, longer than many would dare to dream. And he would make them remember her. All of their lives.

The priest helped others rise and bring themselves back to reality. He was astonished at the sight of the altar boy with a beatific smile on his face, looking for all as if he had seen Paradise. The priest lay his hand upon the boy's head, and with that the boy seemed to pass out of a trance. He looked up into the priest's face and for a moment their eyes locked. A look passed between them that was more than recognition. The sheriff looked on, aware of something strange but too bewildered to know. It was down to him to ensure this moment did not lead to the glorification of the girl. Justice had been done here, and the villagers must remember the pain of the past. Still, as he turned to the elders and prepared to return to the village, he remained unsettled and uncertain.

The villagers began to shift back to their homes, still stunned and overwhelmed by the morning's events, but all determined to make their amends.

As the last of them left the scene, a shape moved out from the hedgerow. Toby sniffed the air and began to trot along the side of the road ready to find a new master. He was satisfied with a job well done, and hoped his mistress had been pleased with him, and would know him again.

He rounded the corner and his eyes focussed on the group returning to the village. An expression crept across his face, and he smiled as only cats can smile. He looked in particular at a small group of three that sought to stride authoritatively back to the village. Yes, there was his new master. He must bide his time but would make himself known to him at the right moment.

Ready to serve, Toby set off down the road.

The Mandrakes

CLARK ASHTON SMITH

Gilles Grenier the sorcerer and his wife, Sabine, coming into lower Averoigne from parts unknown or at least unverified, had selected the location of their hut with a careful forethought.

The hut was close to those marshes through which the slackening waters of the river Isoile, after leaving the great forest, had overflowed in sluggish, reed-clogged channels and sedge-hidden pools mantled with scum like witches' oils. It stood among osiers and alders on a low, mound-shaped elevation; and in front, toward the marshes, there was a loamy meadow-bottom where the short fat stems and tufted leaves of the mandrake grew in lush abundance, being more plentiful and of greater size than elsewhere through all that sorcery-ridden province. The fleshly, bifurcated roots of this plant, held by many to resemble the human body, were used by Gilles and Sabine in the brewing of love-philtres. Their potions, being compounded with much care and cunning, soon acquired a marvelous renown among the peasants and villagers, and were even in request among people of a loftier station, who came privily to the wizard's hut. They would rouse, people said, a kindly warmth in the coldest and most prudent bosom, would melt the armor of the most obdurate virtue. As a result, the demand for these sovereign magistrals became enormous.

The couple dealt also in other drugs and simples, in charms and divination; and Gilles, according to common belief, could read infallibly the dictates of the stars. Oddly enough, considering the temper of the fifteenth century, when magic and witchcraft were still so widely reprobated, he and his wife enjoyed a repute by no means ill or unsavory. No charges of malefice were brought against them; and because of the number of honest marriages promoted by the philtres, the local clergy were content to disregard the many illicit amours that had come to a successful issue through the same agency.

It is true, there were those who looked askance at Gilles in the beginning, and who whispered fearfully that he had been driven out of Blois, where all persons bearing the name Grenier were popularly believed to be werewolves. They called attention to the excessive hairiness of the wizard, whose hands were black with bristles and whose beard grew almost to his eyes. Such insinuations, however, were generally considered as lacking proof, insomuch as no other signs or marks of lycanthropy were ever displayed by Gilles. And in time, for reasons that have been sufficiently indicated, the few detractors of Gilles were wholly overborne by a secret but widespread sentiment of public favor.

Even by their patrons, very little was known regarding the strange couple, who maintained the reserve proper to those who dealt in mystery and enchantment. Sabine, a comely women with blue-gray eyes and wheat-colored hair, and no trace of the traditional witch in her appearance, was obviously much younger than Gilles, whose sable mane and beard were already touched with the white warp of time. It was rumored by visitors that she had oftentimes been overheard in sharp dispute with her husband; and people soon made a jest of this, remarking that the philtres might well be put to a domestic use by those who purveyed them. But aside from such rumors and ribaldries, little was thought of the matter. The connubial infelicities of Gilles and his wife, whether grave or trivial, in no wise impaired the renown of their love-potions.

Also, little was thought of Sabine's presence, when, five years after the coming of the pair into Averoigne, it became remarked by neighbors and customers that Gilles was alone. In reply to queries, the sorcerer merely said that his spouse had departed on a long journey, to visit relatives in a remote province. The explanation was accepted without debate, and it did not occur to any one that there had been no eyewitnesses of Sabine's departure.

It was then mid-autumn; and Gilles told the inquirers, in a somewhat vague and indirect fashion, that his wife would not return before spring. Winter came early that year and tarried late, with deeply crusted snows in the forest and on the uplands, and a heavy armor of fretted ice on the marshes. It was a winter of much hardship and privation. When the tardy spring had broken the silver buds of the willows and covered the alders with a foliage of chrysolite, few thought to ask Gilles regarding Sabine's return. And later, when the purple bells of the mandrake were succeeded by small orange-colored apples, her prolonged absence was taken for granted.

Gilles, living tranquilly with his books and cauldrons, and gathering the roots and herbs for his magical medicaments, was well enough pleased to have it taken for granted. He did not believe that Sabine would ever return; and his unbelief, it would seem, was far from irrational. He had killed her one evening in autumn, during a dispute of unbearable acrimony, slitting her soft, pale throat in self-defense with a knife which he had wrested from her fingers when she lifted it against him. Afterward he had buried her by the late rays of a gibbous moon beneath the mandrakes in the meadow-bottom, replacing the leafy sods with much care, so that there was no evidence of their having been disturbed other than by the digging of a few roots in the way of daily business.

After the melting of the long snows from the meadow, he himself could scarcely have been altogether sure of the spot in which he had interred her body. He noticed, however, as the season drew on, that there was a place where the mandrakes grew with even more than their wonted exuberance; and this place, he believed, was the very site of her grave. Visiting it often, he smiled with a secret irony, and was pleased rather than troubled by the thought of that charnel nourishment which might have contributed to the lushness of the dark, glossy leaves. In fact, it may well have been a similar irony that had led him to choose the mandrake meadow as a place of burial for the murdered witch-wife.

Gilles Grenier was not sorry that he had killed Sabine. They had been ill-mated from the beginning, and the woman had shown toward him in their quotidian quarrels the venomous spitefulness of a very hellcat. He had not loved the vixen; and it was far pleasanter to be alone, with his somewhat somber temper unruffled by her acrid speeches, and his sallow face and grizzling beard untorn by her sharp fingernails.

With the renewal of spring, as the sorcerer had expected, there was much demand for his love-philtres among the smitten swains and lasses of the neighborhood. There came to him, also, the gallants who sought to overcome a stubborn chastity, and the wives who wished to recall a wandering fancy or allure the forbidden desires of young men. Anon, it became necessary for Gilles to replenish his stock of mandrake potions; and with this purpose in mind, he went forth at midnight beneath the full May moon, to dig the newly grown roots from which he would brew his amatory enchantments.

Smiling darkly beneath his beard, he began to cull the great, moon-pale plants which flourished on Sabine's grave, digging out the homunculuslike taproots very carefully with a curious trowel made from the femur of a witch.

Though he was well used to the weird and often vaguely human forms assumed by the mandrake, Gilles was somewhat surprised by the appearance of the first root. It seemed inordinately large, unnaturally white; and, eyeing it more closely, he saw that it bore the exact likeness of a woman's body and lower limbs, being cloven to the middle and clearly formed even to the ten toes! There were no arms, however, and the bosom ended in the large tuft of ovate leaves.

Gilles was more than startled by the fashion in which the root seemed to turn and writhe when he lifted it from the ground. He dropped it hastily, and the minikin limbs lay quivering on the grass. But, after a little reflection, he took the prodigy as a possible mark of Satanic favor, and continued his digging. To his amazement, the next root was formed in much the same manner as the first. A half-dozen more, which he proceeded to dig, were shaped in miniature mockery of a woman from breasts to heels; and amid the superstituous awe and wonder with which he regarded them, he became aware of their singularly intimate resemblance to Sabine.

At this discovery, Gilles was deeply perturbed, for the thing was beyond his comprehension. The miracle, whether divine or demoniac, began to assume a sinister and doubtful aspect. It was as if the slain woman herself had returned, or had somehow wrought her unholy silmulacrum in the mandrakes.

His hand trembled as he started to dig up another plant; and working with less than his usual care, he failed to remove the whole of the bifurcated root, cutting into it clumsily with the trowel of sharp bone.

He saw that he had severed one of the tiny ankles. At the same instant, a shrill, reproachful cry, like the voice of Sabine herself in mingled pain and anger, seemed to pierce his ears with intolerable acuity, though the volume was strangely lessened, as if the voice had come from a distance. The cry ceased, and was not repeated. Gilles, sorely terrified, found himself staring at the trowel, on which there was a dark, bloodlike stain. Trembling, he pulled out the severed root, and saw that it was dripping with a sanguine fluid.

At first, in his dark fear and half-guilty apprehension he thought of burying the roots which lay palely before him with their eldritch and obscene similitude to the dead sorceress. He would hide them deeply from his own sight and the ken of others, lest the murder he had done should somehow be suspected.

Presently, however, his alarm began to lessen. It occurred to him that, even if seen by others, the roots would be looked upon merely as a freak of nature and would in no manner serve to betray his crime, since their actual resemblance to the person of Sabine was a thing which none but he could rightfully know.

Also, he thought, the roots might well possess an extraordinary virtue, and from them, perhaps, he would brew philtres of never-equalled power and efficacy. Overcoming entirely his initial dread and repulsion, he filled a small osier basket with the quivering, leaf-headed figurines. Then he went back to his hut, seeing in the bizarre phenomenon merely the curious advantage to which it might be turned, and wholly oblivious to any darker meaning, such as might have been read by others in his place.

In his callous hardihood, he was not disquieted overmuch by the profuse bleeding of a sanguine matter from the mandrakes when he came to prepare them for his cauldron. The ungodly, furious hissing, the mad foaming and boiling of the brew, like a devil's broth, he ascribed to the unique potency of its ingredients. He even dared to choose the most shapely and perfect of the womanlike plants, and hung it up in his hut amid other roots and dried herbs and simples, intending to consult it as an oracle in future, according to the custom of wizards.

The new philtres which he had concocted were bought by eager customers, and Gilles ventured to recommend them for their surpassing virtue, which would kindle amorous warmth in a bosom of marble or enflame the very dead.

Now, in the old legend of Averoigne which I recount herewith, it is told that the impious and audacious wizard, fearing neither God nor devil nor witch-woman, dared to dig again in the earth of Sabine's grave, removing many more of the white, female-shapen roots, which cried aloud in shrill complaint to the waning moon or turned like living limbs at his violence. And all those which he dug were formed alike, in the miniature image of the dead Sabine from breasts to toes. And from them, it is said, he compounded other philtres, which he meant to sell in time when such should be requested.

As it happened, however, these latter potions were never dispensed; and only a few of the first were sold, owing to the frightful and calamitous consequences that followed their use. For those to whom the potions had been administered privily, whether men or women, were not moved by the genial fury of desire, as was the wonted result, but were driven by a darker rage, by a woful and Satanic madness, irresistibly impelling them to harm or even slay the persons who had sought to attract their love.

Husbands were turned against wives, lasses against their lovers, with speeches of bitter hate and scatheful deeds. A certain young gallant who had gone to the promised rendezvous was met by a vengeful madwoman, who tore his face into bleeding shreds with her nails. A mistress who had thought to win back her recreant knight was mistreated foully and done to death by him who had hitherto been impeccably gentle, even if faithless.

The scandal of these untoward happenings was such as would attend an invasion of demons. The crazed men and women, it was thought at first, were veritably possessed by devils. But when the use of the potions became rumored, and their provenance was clearly established, the burden of the blame fell upon Gilles Grenier, who, by the law of both church and state, was now charged with sorcery.

The constables who went to arrest Gilles found him at evening in his hut of raddled osiers, stooping and muttering above a cauldron that foamed and hissed and boiled as if it had been filled with the spate of Phlegethon. They entered and took him unaware. He submitted calmly, but expressed surprise when told of the lamentable effect of the love-philtres; and he neither affirmed nor denied the charge of wizardry.

As they were about to leave with their prisoner, the officers heard a shrill, tiny, shrewish voice that cried from the shadows of the hut, where bunches of dried simples and other sorcerous ingredients were hanging. It appeared to issue from a strange, half-withered root, cloven in the very likeness of a woman's body and legs—a root that was partly pale, and partly black with cauldron-smoke. One of the constables thought that he recognized the voice as being that of Sabine, the sorcerer's wife. All swore that they heard the voice clearly, and were able to distinguish these words:

"Dig deeply in the meadow, where the mandrakes grow the thickliest."

The officers were sorely frightened, both by this uncanny voice and the obscene likeness of the root, which they regarded as a work of Satan. Also, there was much doubt anent the wisdom of obeying the oracular injunction. Gilles, who was questioned narrowly as to its meaning, refused to offer any interpretation; but certain marks of perturbation in his manner finally led the officers to examine the mandrake meadow below the hut.

Digging by lantern-light in the specified spot, they found many more of the roots, which seemed to crowd the ground; and beneath, they came to the rotting corpse of a woman, which was still recognizable as that of Sabine. As a result of this discovery, Gilles Grenier was arraigned not only for sorcery but also for the murder of his wife. He was readily convicted of both crimes, though he denied stoutly the imputation of intentional malefice, and claimed to the very last that he had killed Sabine only in defense of his own life against her termagant fury. He was hanged on the gibbet in company with other murderers, and his dead body was then burned at the stake.

Next-Door Neighbor

Don D'Ammassa

She's put a curse on my dad and I've got to make her stop!"

Kevin rolled his eyes dramatically and shook his head. "Give it a rest, Luce. There's no such thing as witches. And what are you going to do, burn her at the stake?"

The thirteen-year-old dropped her eyes, but her voice was just as firm as ever. "I don't know exactly, but I have to do something. And I need you to help."

"Whoa!" Kevin backed away from the couch with his hands raised protectively. "No way I'm getting mixed up in this. You want to sneak into Old Lady Brackford's house, then go right ahead. I won't tell anyone, but I'm not going with you."

Lucy unfolded her legs and stood up, meeting her friend's eyes steadily. "I'm not asking you to go with me. All I want you to do is call the next time she comes into your father's store. That way I'll know she's going to be out of the house long enough for me to look around without getting caught."

Kevin bit his lip, dubious but unable to find a good reason to refuse. "If Dad finds out . . ."

"He won't. I promise."

The phone rang while she was eating lunch with her mother the following Saturday.

"I'll get it." Lucy pushed back from the table and snagged the phone off the wall before her mother could react. Her father was upstairs in bed, still suffering from the mysterious illness that had bothered him ever since he had argued with Mrs. Brackford about the condition of her yard. The neighbors had never been on good terms; Mrs. Brackford rarely came outside, left the house only once a week to do her shopping, and hadn't spoken a hundred words to Lucy's parents during the three years they'd lived in Managansett.

"Luce? It's Kevin. She's here."

Lucy blinked, glanced nervously toward her mother, who was staring out the kitchen window, face drawn with tension. "In the store?"

"Yes, of course in the store. What do you think, we invited her over for tea?"

Lucy cupped her hand around the mouthpiece, forced herself to speak casually. "Okay, thanks a lot. I'm on my way." She hung up.

"That was Kevin," she volunteered. "He wants to know if I can help him with some deliveries."

Her mother glanced up, her expression puzzled for the few seconds it took her to replay the words in her mind. "If you want. Finish your lunch first."

"I'll take it with me." Lucy snatched the remains of her sandwich from the table, but her appetite had vanished.

There was a crumbling stone wall surrounding Mrs. Brackford's property, but Lucy knew half a dozen places where she could climb over without difficulty. She chose one as far from the road as possible. It wouldn't do to be seen; Mrs. Brackford didn't tolerate children on her property. Three years earlier, Kevin's parents had been forced to retrieve him from the police after he'd indulged a ten-year-old's curiosity and dropped down inside the wall from an overhanging branch.

The yard was so thickly overgrown that Lucy barely had to crouch to remain concealed as she made her way to the back porch. The grass was up to her waist, and a riot of mock orange, forsythia, and lilac, all tied together with tethers of wisteria and bullbriar, screened her from the street. Beyond the rear wall was the dirt access road to the reservoir, and on the opposite side, the Nettletons had put up a ten-foot stockade fence to cut off all sight of their reclusive neighbor's property.

The back door was latched, but the adjacent window was wide open, lacked a screen, and was just the right size for climbing through.

Lucy found herself in a pantry. The room was long and narrow, dimly illuminated, and lined with shelves. Most of the items stored there were recognizable, familiar brands of canned goods, bags of flour and salt, boxes of cereal, bottles of fruit juice and soda. There were also two rows of mason jars with handwritten labels, but the scrawl was illegible and the contents amorphous and unidentifiable.

A door at one end opened into the kitchen.

Kevin hung up the phone and hurried back out to the store. There were still two more aisles of groceries to restock before his father would let him go for the day, and he wanted to take the bus to Providence with some of his friends. The surreptitious phone call was no big deal, but he felt nervous anyway. What if Lucy was right? What if Old Lady Brackford really was a witch and somehow knew magically what he'd done?

He looked around nervously. There weren't many people in the store; business had been bad ever since the big shopping plaza had opened just outside of town. Kevin walked to the front, crossed the head of each aisle, puzzled at first, then mildly alarmed.

"Are you lost, young man?"

Startled, Kevin looked behind him. His father was standing there with his hands on his hips.

"Hi, Dad. Just needed a stretch. Almost done."

"Well hurry it up. People can't buy what they can't see."

"Yeah. Hey, Dad, didn't I just see Old L— Mrs. Brackford come in?"

His father frowned. "Came and went. Spent three bucks. I think she's taking her trade over to Foodworld now. That's one customer I don't mind losing. Now get cracking if you want the afternoon off."

Kevin went back to work, briefly considered trying to call Lucy. "Too late for that," he whispered.

* * *

The kitchen was worse than the yard outside. The sink was filled with dirty dishes and pans, which spilled over onto the counters. There were so many piles of them on the floor, Lucy had to pick her way carefully. Open packages of food were interspersed with the crockery, many of them sporting thick coats of fuzzy green mold.

The smell was so overwhelming that Lucy's eyes stung, and she almost turned around and fled back the way she'd come. Instead she passed through to the door beyond.

The front room was less repulsive, though just as neglected. A layer of dust covered most of the visible surfaces, and small clouds plumed from the rug with each step. There was very little light; heavy drapes cloaked the windows.

A narrow staircase led to the second floor. Lucy licked her lips, aware that her heart was beating frantically, but refused to turn back now. Her father's life might be at stake.

There was a narrow hall at the top, with two doors on either side. The first two rooms were cluttered with old furniture, piles of clothing and blankets, and other household odds and ends. It looked as though neither had been disturbed for years. The third was quite obviously where Mrs. Brackford slept. It was marginally cleaner than the rest of the house, but piles of dirty clothing had accumulated in every corner and under the bed, which was not made, and even in the dim light Lucy could tell that the sheets were heavily stained. There was a small adjoining bathroom, similarly cluttered and unsanitary, the counter and floor littered with a forest of broken gray hairs. She poked around briefly, opening each of the bureau drawers, but found nothing of interest.

The last room was very different.

Margery Dodge extracted four envelopes from the mailbox, three of them bills. She sighed. If Ed didn't get better soon and go back to work, they were going to be in serious difficulties. The doctors were hinting that it was psychological, but she knew better than that. Ed had always been so enthusiastic about life, it was hard to recognize him in the tired, dispirited, weak-willed body that lay upstairs.

She glanced up to see their neighbor, Mrs. Brackford, unlocking her front gate, a small paper bag tucked under one arm. Margery grimaced with distaste. The kids called her a witch, and she figured they were only one letter wrong.

* * *

Amazingly enough, the last room was immaculate. The walls were clean and bare except for a pair of woven tapestries whose subject matter seemed to be the sufferings of the damned in the nethermost regions of hell. There was a worktable in the center of the room and a curtained alcove at the far end. When Lucy brushed the curtains aside, she found herself facing what appeared to be a small altar, flanked by two elaborate pewter candelabras fitted with black candles. There was a reddish brown stain covering parts of the altar and such a rancid, unpleasant smell, she backed away, letting the curtains fall back into place.

There was a doll on the table.

It was Ken, Barbie's companion, twin to the one now tucked at the very back of Lucy's closet, wearing a poorly cut shirt and no pants. She picked the doll up tentatively, then dropped it when something pricked her fingers. More cautiously, she turned it over, saw that the buttocks were coated with grime of some sort. She squinted and raised it close to her face. Hair, lots of short hairs like those her father left on the sink when he shaved in the morning. And little semicircles that must be nail clippings.

Lucy gasped. She recognized the shirt as well; it was cut from the same material as one of her father's favorites—the one he had reluctantly thrown away two weeks past when he wore through one elbow. This was it; this was her proof that Old Lady Brackford was a witch. Clutching the doll tightly, she turned to leave.

That's when she heard the front door open and shut downstairs.

Ruth Brackford carried her small package through to the kitchen, removed the syrup of ipecac and tossed the bag aside without looking to see where it fell. There were a few other things she needed and she began gathering them from where they lay within the chaos.

She shivered slightly. The afternoon was growing chill and she was more sensitive to the cold lately. The pantry window was broken and wouldn't close properly, and she'd been putting off getting it fixed, so she simply closed the pantry door, cutting off the draft.

The lock clicked as it engaged.

Lucy's first thought was to escape and she was actually halfway to the stairs before she hesitated. To have come this far without accomplishing anything was unbearable. She stopped, thinking furiously. She

71

would have the doll, of course, but no one would believe her, or if they did, would dismiss it as an old woman's self-delusion. And it would only provide her father a brief respite; Old Lady Brackford would not admit defeat so easily.

Lucy turned and quietly walked back down the hall, then slipped into the bedroom and bathroom beyond. She had to hurry.

Ruth Brackford started the laborious journey upstairs. The climb seemed to require more effort every day. She thought idly of having her bed moved downstairs. There was an oubliette off the kitchen that would serve as a bathroom, and the pantry could be redone to meet her other, more special needs. But that would involve bringing strangers into her house; she couldn't possibly move the furniture herself. No, she thought, I'll just have to make do.

Edward Dodge's effigy lay where she had left it. She set down the small bowl she was carrying and leaned forward, regaining her breath. "No hurry is there, neighbor? You'll be happy to wait for me."

When the stitch in her side subsided, she used a spoon to move a dollop of the noxious brew she'd concocted to the doll's face, smearing the plastic lips. "Tastes wonderful, doesn't it?" Her laugh was a thin crackle. "Ipecac and sour cream, mashed maggot and rotting meat, everything needed for a healthy lad like you."

Lucy watched from where she hid concealed by the altar curtain, terrified but elated when Old Lady Brackford's thin, ugly laughter changed tone. She began to gasp and raised one hand to her throat. Lucy hadn't been able to remove all the residue of her father's body from the doll, but she had managed to add a good number of discarded gray hairs to the sticky patch. Enough of them, it appeared.

Ruth Brackford gasped and bent forward, shoulders heaving as her stomach abruptly tried to empty itself. She maintained control, but swayed as she turned, lurching toward the door. When she was out of sight, Lucy emerged from her hiding place, snatched up the doll, and headed for the door.

"Clever girl, aren't you?" Mrs. Brackford was standing just out of reach, leaning against the wall. Lucy had expected her to go directly to the bathroom. She froze in the doorway, clutching the doll to her chest.

"Give that here, you little thief!" She held out a none too steady hand and Lucy realized she was still suffering the effects of the potion she'd inadvertently administered to herself as well as Edward Dodge.

"All right, take it." She held the doll out, just a few inches beyond the woman's reach. Old Lady Brackford's eyes glittered with hatred, but she pushed away from the wall, took an unsteady step forward.

And Lucy bolted past her, shuddering as she brushed against the woman's thigh. She almost fell in her haste to get downstairs, recovered and continued at no less hectic a pace.

The front door had an old-fashioned key lock and wouldn't budge. Lucy glanced up toward the head of the stairs. Ruth Brackford was leaning on the rail, her face split into an unpleasant smile. "Leaving so soon, child? I won't hear of it."

Lucy didn't even notice the kitchen's odor this time, masked as it was by the smell of her own fear, a fear that grew to absolute terror when she found the pantry exit also locked. There were no other kitchen windows big enough for her to escape through, so she ran back to the front of the house.

Old Lady Brackford had moved to the head of the stairs but hadn't descended yet. She had both hands pressed tightly against her stomach and her face was, if possible, even paler than it had been before. No wonder her father was so sick, Lucy realized, if even a small portion of the vile concoction could so affect someone.

"You've been a bad girl, you know." The voice was a bit less ragged and Mrs. Brackford descended a single step. The windows were larger in the front room, but multipaned, held together by a latticework of wood. She could smash one, given time, but there wasn't that much time left.

"I haven't had visitors in ever so long."

Lucy glanced up the staircase. Mrs. Brackford was three steps down now, one hand holding the rail. Desperately, Lucy held the doll out with one extended arm, closed her eyes, and began to turn in place.

She spun desperately, moving her feet as quickly as possible, trying to stay in the same spot. Twice she bumped into the back of a chair and once into an end table, but she kept her eyes shut, afraid to see how close her enemy might have come. But eventually she was overcome with dizziness and staggered to a stop, out of breath, leaned against an overstuffed chair while her breathing returned to normal.

There was no one on the staircase. Ruth Brackford lay crumpled at its foot.

* * *

Lucy found the keyring on the kitchen table and let herself out. She scrubbed the doll clean in a stream that ran through the woodlot separating the development from the reservoir, then buried it under a pine tree.

When she got home, her father was sitting in a chair in the living room, his color better than it had been for over a month.

"How are you feeling, Daddy?"

He smiled with considerable animation. "A lot better, squirt. Gave your mother quite a fright though."

Margery Dodge walked in from the kitchen. "Your father fell down in the bathroom. I thought he'd had a heart attack."

"Just dizzy for a minute or two," he said quietly. "But I feel a lot better now. As good as new, in fact."

Witch Hunt

CHRISTIE GOLDEN

Jason stopped just a half a block down the street from the witch's house, breathing heavily. He couldn't believe he was doing this. He was the one who had come up with the idea; he was *not* supposed to be the one to have to execute it. But the straw he had drawn had been the short one, and now he was stuck with it.

He glanced down at the bucket he carried, filled with a dozen grade A eggs he had "borrowed" from the refrigerator. He hoped he wasn't around next time his mom wanted to bake anything.

Catching his breath, he peered cautiously ahead to where the witch lived.

It looked like an ordinary house: small, two-story, with a neatly kept front lawn and a fenced backyard. Only the black cat, sitting in the window and gazing out at the world with speculative yellow eyes, gave any hint as to the inhabitant's real identity.

He'd watched her leave an hour ago, then hurried home to get the weapon of choice he and the other kids had decided on. Glancing quickly around, Jason ascertained that he was indeed alone on the quiet suburban street . . . for the moment.

Jason squeezed his eyes shut. He was scared, and he was embarrassed that he was scared. After all, he was the one who put the other guys up to it. He was the one who made clucking noises and flapped his arms when little Warren Campbell, spooked by the stories they had told about Old Lady Barrett, had burst into tears. Now he was the one who desperately wanted to cry and run home.

But he couldn't. Because the other guys would know if he didn't egg Old Lady Barrett's house like he said he would. Because they would then know that he, Jason Clark, was just as chicken as little Warren Campbell.

Jason opened his eyes. They were bright blue and enormous with fright. He pursed his soft, eight-year-old mouth closed in an imitation of an adult's grim line and stepped forward.

It was four-thirty. The other kids were home, washing up for dinner. Stay-at-home moms were supervising the washing-up process, and the parents who worked hadn't arrived yet. Old Lady Barrett had gone to the grocery store and shouldn't be home for at least another few minutes.

The coast was clear. It was safe.

Quickly, Jason ran past the Smith's house and the Davis's house and stood in the front yard of the Barrett place. The cat in the window lost its languid air and sat up. Its eyes met Jason's, and it meowed, silent behind the pane of glass.

That was exactly what Jason needed: a target, something real and solid to pitch the eggs at. And pitch he did, smiling ferociously as the egg splattered right in front of the cat's startled face. The animal arched its back and hissed soundlessly. Another egg hit the pane, and another. The cat decided that it had had enough and disappeared, vanishing behind the curtains.

Jason laughed aloud. He had completely lost his fear, forgotten it in the heat of excitement at doing something forbidden. There were lots of eggs left. He reached down, seized a white oval, and hurled this one at the front door. It landed smack in the center of a wreath, its yellow and clear gooey contents oozing down to forever ruin the wreath's dried flowers. He whooped happily, and reached down for another one.

A hand closed on his right shoulder.

Jason shrieked. He dropped the bucket and whirled around, knowing without having to look who it was.

Old Lady Barrett towered over him. One bony arm cradled a brown paper sack. The other hand was clamped down on Jason's shoulder.

He knew what to expect: piercing green eyes, sharp teeth, hook nose, evil cackle. He was shaking badly. Jason couldn't help himself; his blue eyes traveled inexorably upward to meet the commanding gaze of the witch.

The face, while gaunt, wasn't filled with either malicious glee or fury. The expression on the wrinkled face was sorrow. Her eyes weren't green, they were brown, and kind of sad-looking. The nose, while sharp, was more patrician than cronelike.

She had no wart at all.

"I didn't think it would be you, Jason Clark. You seemed to be a good boy. I didn't think you'd be the one to stoop to egging an old woman's house."

Jason couldn't reply. He was too busy trying not to wet himself.

"Well, come on in, then," said the witch, with a heavy sigh. Her voice wasn't the high, sharp cackle he'd expected. It was low, and raspy, and tired-sounding. "I've got something I want to show you."

That sparked the boy into new life. He began to struggle, but stopped, shocked, when the witch let him go.

"I'm going to call your mother when you leave. If you come inside with me for a few moments, and let me explain some things to you, I'll just forget about the whole thing."

Jason was beginning to wonder if he and the guys hadn't pegged Old Lady Barrett all wrong. Up close, she didn't really look like a witch in the slightest. Suddenly he thought that she wasn't going to pop him in the oven and serve him up with gravy and potatoes after all. And not having Mom find out about this was something to think about.

He was still scared, but now he was more scared of his mom's angry lectures than he was of this old, sad-looking woman.

"Okay," he agreed reluctantly.

Old Lady Barrett walked, slowly, to the house and ascended the sagging porch steps. She fumbled for the key and opened the door. The cat was there to greet her, meowing and weaving through her legs, purring just like any ordinary cat.

"This, Jason, is Cuddles." She walked into the foyer and past a winding stairway whose faded-carpet steps sagged almost as much as those on the porch. Old Lady Barrett set the bag down on a table in a perfectly normal-looking kitchen. The walls of the hallway were covered with photographs, but Jason paid them little heed.

"Cuddles?" Jason repeated, shocked. Surely the cat would be named Devil or Satan or Lucifer or—

"When she was a kitten, she loved to cuddle in my lap. Still does." Old Lady Barrett began to empty the grocery bag. Terribly mundane items appeared: celery, cans of soup, oatmeal, cat food, milk, apples.

Jason began to feel something akin to disappointment.

"Would you like a cookie, son? There's one in the jar on the counter." She pointed to a round little ceramic bear with a cookie in its paws.

Aha! thought Jason. She's going to poison me!

"While you're at it, get me one, too."

I guess poisoning's out, Jason thought as he went to the jar and opened it. Perfectly ordinary chocolate chip cookies met his gaze. They smelled wonderful.

"Do you always have cookies on hand for kids who egg your house?" he asked daringly.

The woman smiled a little. "Heavens, no. *I* like chocolate chip cookies myself. And at my age, well, I feel that I deserve a treat now and then."

She extended a gnarled hand for the sweet. Jason observed that she wore a wedding ring on her fourth finger. Tentatively, he placed the cookie in her palm and watched her bring it to her withered lips. She took a bite, chewed, swallowed, took a second one. He bit into his own cookie; it tasted just like the ones his mom made. He finished it slowly, watching as Old Lady Barrett put the perishables away in the fridge.

"Would you like some milk?" she asked.

Jason shook his tousled head. "No thanks. Mrs. Barrett—what did you want to show me?"

The woman turned and met his gaze with a sharp look from behind her glasses. She was wearing sensible shoes, support hose, a plain dress, and an old gray sweater. She looked like someone's grandmother. With a sudden horrible thought, Jason realized that the pictures in the hall *were* grandchildren.

"I wanted to show you the *inside* of my house," she said quietly.

Jason blushed suddenly as shame overwhelmed him. This woman wasn't a witch. She was just a simple old grandmother. Any magic that surrounded her was the horrible, malicious magic of fear and rumors concocted by a group of school kids who had nothing better to do with their time than to harass an old woman. Jason was only eight, but he knew better than that. At least, the better part of him did.

"Mrs. Barrett," he said, swallowing hard, "I'm really sorry. I—I don't know what to say. I'm sorry I egged your house, and I won't do it again. It was mean, and I can see that now."

Again, Old Lady Barrett smiled, and there was a grandmotherly twinkle in her eyes. "Why, Mr. Clark, I do believe that you mean that. In that case, help yourself to a handful of cookies, and we'll just forget about this, all right?"

Feeling terribly embarrassed, Jason took two more cookies, mumbled another apology, and ran for the door.

The old woman heard it bang shut, and went to the door to watch the boy run home. The black cat sat at her feet for a moment, then peered up at the old woman.

"*Cuddles?*" meowed the cat indignantly.

The witch shrugged, her eyes still on the form of the retreating youth. "I had to think of something that sounded appropriately harmless."

"But Cuddles . . ." The cat sighed. "Well, do you think he swallowed it?"

The witch chuckled. "Hook, line, and sinker. The chocolate chip cookies work every time." She closed the door securely, and with a wave of her hand dispelled the illusion she had created. In the place of an old woman stood a slim, lithe young blonde.

The witch stooped, and picked up her familiar, scratching its ears affectionately. "Come on, Isis," she said. "We're missing Oprah."

The Laurel Lake Laser

AIMEE KRATTS

Dear departed Grandmother Goldpenny's tiresome refrain ran through Penny Goldpenny's mind as she wound the split oak twine around the birch twigs, binding them to the broomstick in the vise. *Every witch must have a craft.* Penny answered the voice in her head, *and the Goldpenny craft is making magic brooms.*

Wistfully, Penny looked out the porch window to the lake. The retired man and wife who lived two cottages down the shore were trolling for bass in a canoe powered by an electric motor. Penny, too, wanted to be outside in the early September sunshine. Fishing like the neighbors sounded nice, or better yet, racing across the sky getting windburn on her cheeks. She knew she looked wild and witchy when she had a flush on her fair-skinned face.

Besides broom-making, Penny's looks were the other family trait Penny had in common with her grandmother. She had the dark hair and fair skin of the black Irish, and a short, wiry body and tough hands that were perfect for making brooms, Grandmother had said. It had been so long since she had had the time to ride her own broom in the sky.

A cool breeze ran through the cottage coming in the screened-in front porch and going out through the open window in the back. It brought the sounds of gulls screeching at some imagined threat. The ropes that secured the boat at the boathouse creaked from the strain as the waves bounced the hull up and down.

Penny sighed and continued with her binding. *And you dasn't break a single twig,* the voice in her mind continued in her grand-mother's Irish-Canadian brogue. *Goldpenny brooms are like Waterford crystal. We don't sell seconds.*

Marion, Penny's weremink, squeaked as someone rapped on the kitchen door at the side of the cabin. Once, twice, thrice, a fourth time. *One too many,* thought Penny. *It's a stranger.*

She tied off the twine in a half hitch and looked around the cottage. Dirty frying pan in the sink smelling of bacon and eggs. Newfound poles in a pile waiting to be sized. Two half-finished brooms hanging on the gun rack over the fireplace. A spray of ashes on the floor near the woodstove from the last time her weremink turned into a nasty little girl during a full moon and tipped the ash bucket over just for spite.

Penny glanced through the window next to the door and saw only the edge of a white fog surrounding the visitor. "A flipping white witch dressing the part?" she asked Marion. Penny shrugged and opened the door. A heavenly light dazzled her eyes. "Come on now, eh?" she said, covering her eyes with her forearm.

"Sorry, Miss Goldpenny," said a man's voice. "I'll turn it down. There."

Penny lowered her arm and saw a young man with precisely

trimmed blond hair. He wore a blue suit and tie; his white shirt threw its own light. So did his feathery wings.

Narrowing her eyes, Penny asked, "How can I help you?" The sweet stink of angelic goodness was pungent to her.

The weremink circled around Penny's ankles, sniffing at the man and growling.

"I'm an angel," he said. When Penny looked at him skeptically, he fluffed the feathers on his wings to make the point. "I've come to buy a Goldpenny broom." The young man smiled, his white teeth gleaming.

"Goldpennys are for witches, not angels. Why do you need one, anyway? You have wings."

Penny watched the angel debate about something in his mind before he spoke. "May I come in?" he asked finally. "I'll explain my situation."

The young witch gestured him in. "All right, but don't you go blessing my home. It wasn't built to take that kind of magic. The roof will cave in."

"I understand." The angel spread his wing tips slightly and sat on an old orange vinyl chair. He arranged his wings behind the chair and leaned back. Penny untied the half-hitch knot and continued her work on the broom in the vise.

"The long and short of it, Miss Goldpenny, is that I'm a guardian angel. I watch over someone and protect him from harm—or rather, from making bad mistakes. I guess you could say I'm an adviser of sorts. Unfortunately, when my charge travels in Air Force One, I can't keep up. I don't have the wing power. I heard that owning a Goldpenny would solve my problem. Do they really travel at the speed of light?"

Penny flipped her black hair over her shoulder. *I'm sorry I let this nutty bird in,* she thought. "Mister Angel, Goldpenny brooms do not go the speed of light. Only light goes the speed of light."

"Then the Santa rumor isn't true?"

Penny ground her teeth. The St. Nicholas incident was a black spot on the family's reputation and someone was speaking out of turn about it. Of course, the angel could be fishing for information.

"What Santa rumor?" she asked.

"About the reindeer being for show," said the angel. "What dear old St. Nicholas is really using for speed are two custom Goldpennys bolted to the bottom of his sleigh."

His earnestness irritated her. "Those stinking elves stole them from my great-grandmother! We didn't make them for St. Nicholas. We don't sell to saints." She spat on her hands and tied off the twine. "It's against family policy."

The angel's forehead creased in sympathy. "I am so sorry to hear that. But I do hope you'll consider selling me one of your brooms."

"We don't—"

The angel held up his hand against her protest. "Why don't we discuss the actual selling later, Miss Goldpenny. Right now, I'd like to see your famous brooms. Maybe even watch you ride one."

Penny took the broom out of the vise and lifted it to the gun rack. *I haven't had a break in a while,* she told herself. *This bird is as good a reason as any to go outside.* She rubbed her raw palms on her jeans. "Look, Mr. Angel, if I show you my Goldpennys and maybe"—the angel smiled—"I said maybe, even ride one, will you go away?"

"I promise."

It was expressly against the rules to show any witch the broom curing shed. No one was supposed to see it for fear she would grab more than her broom and run off with it. But angels, Penny had heard, were bound by their word. Poor things.

"Humph. Come with me, then. I'll show you where the brooms are cured after they've been finished and spelled."

The shed was up the hill behind Penny's cabin. It was a plain-looking building about the size of a garage, covered with aluminum siding painted green. The door was locked with a black, bulletproof padlock that Penny unlocked with a key on a string around her neck. She turned to the angel. "A broom should only be touched by the owner or the maker before its spells have set and it's been reasonably broken in. Promise you won't touch a single one. And as long as you stay within the circle in the middle of the room, you won't sour any of the spells."

"I promise, Miss Goldpenny."

As the door opened, Penny's heart could not help but come near to bursting with pride. Thirteen custom-made Goldpennys leaned against the walls curing, waiting for their owners. It was obvious the angel was impressed. Penny could see that he wanted very badly to step outside the circle and pick one up.

"A standing tour, please, Miss Goldpenny," he said softly.

As Penny spoke, raindrops started to patter on the tin roof. She picked up the switch leaning against the door to use as a pointer. "The varieties of Goldpennys are almost as endless as the witches who ride them. They do break out into categories, though." She pointed to the broom at the immediate left of the door. "This one's a regular saw-grass broom with a beaver-chewed broomstick of pine. Southerners order this quite often. We call it the 'Confederate Belle.' Here's a Douglas fir broom on a willow broomstick. It's soft on your bottom. Old ladies like it. We call it the 'Granny.' The one over in the corner is the model most often ordered by your full-bodied witch. It's got a thick broomstick of oak and a broom of maple leaves. We call it the 'Hefty Hag.' Next to it you've got an unfinished beaver-gnawed ash broomstick with a broom of long cedar twigs. That's the 'Laurel Lake Laser.' It's the fastest model we've got, eh? We sell chaps with it if you don't like to ride sidesaddle. It chafes a bit on take-off because of the pickup. This one's got one more night of curing left."

"Can that keep up with Air Force One?" The angel looked at her with such hope in his eyes, it made her stomach queasy.

"Does Air Force One go Mach four?"

"No."

"Then, yes."

"Can I ride it, please?" The angel reached out, almost breaking the invisible barrier of the circle. Penny smacked the back of his hand hard with the switch. Drops of sunshine came from his hand before the wound closed.

"You got a death wish, eh? Cover that hand before you bleed good-will on something and ruin it. Now, get out of my shed and off my property. I don't have time for your kind."

The angel nodded, acknowledging his transgression, and backed out of the shed. The rain was coming down harder as Penny locked up. It pounded warm drops on her head. She liked storms. It made an equilibrium between the inside of her head and the outside world. She felt the angel waiting patiently for her to turn around. He bowed. "Good-bye, Miss Goldpenny. Thank you for your time."

He spread his wings and lifted himself into the air. One stroke.

Is that a hole in his right wing? Penny asked herself. The angel listed to the side and corrected himself with the second stroke. *It is a hole. A hole the size of a shotgun blast. That flipping bird took a shot for somebody.* He rose above the lake with his third stroke, listed again and corrected with the fourth.

"For the love of moose piss," Penny said aloud. "Come back here, you stupid sack of feathers!" The wind was blowing toward her and the angel did not hear her. He continued his flight over the lake. Penny ran inside the porch and grabbed her Goldpenny Goldenrod from its rack above the windows. In five strides across the lawn, she took to the rain-filled sky. "It's an ill wind that blows from the east bringing angels," she muttered to herself. She followed the angel through the storm and caught up with him above the clouds.

Pulling up beside him, she shouted over the wind, "Hey, you! Why didn't you tell me about your injured wing, eh?"

"You would have thought I was lying, Miss Goldpenny! Besides, using sympathy to get what you need is against the Code of Angels!"

"Why can't you just heal it like your hand?"

"We only get one set of wings and they're not really part of us any more than that broom is a part of you. Once they're damaged . . . well, we just have to keep being angels the best we can."

The sun made the tops of the clouds below look like rosy cotton. Penny shook her wet hair and smoothed it out of her face. She sighed. "Well, I'm up here now, eh, and you wanted to see me on a Goldpenny. I loathe wasting a trip. This model's a Goldenrod. She's one of my favorites. She's not as fast as a Laser but she's still pretty quick. She's dependable and she doesn't leave a witch trail. I can't be seen leaving trails in the sky. Someone could follow me home."

Penny stopped lecturing for a moment when a particularly large pillar of clouds at the end of the lake caught her eye. She got an idea. "See that humpy puff cloud in the distance?"

The angel nodded.

"Race me to it."

"What?"

Penny did not give him time to think. "Ready, set, go!"

The witch and the angel sped along the length of Laurel Lake, the angel always behind and slowly losing distance. Penny's hair waved in the wind behind her in black streamers. Giggles burbled up from inside her. *I'm flying again! And a race is a race, even if it is with a handicapped angel.*

She came to a break in the storm clouds just before Stoeckel's Cove. After that, she saw Campbell's Island below her. It looked like a lizard floating on the lake. There was Preacher White's cottage on the left. Then came Moffit's Island to the right and Moffit's Pond.

The storm clouds came together again by the time Penny got to the end of the lake. She swung wide around the pillar in the cloud bank and was on her way back to meet the angel. He looked tired and breathless but happy. The excitement of the race sparkled in his eyes. His pleasantly angelic smile was replaced by a hearty grin. Penny did a loop-de-loop around him and shouted, "Get on board!"

The angel hesitated and cupped his hands around his mouth. "But I promised not to sour any brooms!"

"Her spell was set years ago! Besides, she's so seasoned, you couldn't possibly spoil her!"

The angel nodded and wheeled backward to slow himself. Penny pulled up beside him. She edged the Goldenrod under the angel's wings and the angel sat sidesaddle. They were back to Penny's cottage in the flicker of a northern light. Penny sat them down gently on the front lawn. The gap in the storm clouds was now overhead.

Penny leaned the broom against the porch. "Racing makes you thirsty, eh? Would you like a beer? It's a home brew."

"I'm sure it is, but no, thank you, Miss Goldpenny. I really must be going." He looked longingly at the Goldenrod.

Penny pursed her lips. Anyone who would race with her for the fun of it was all right. She wished she could do something for him. The weremink wound its lithe body around the Goldenrod and sniffed at the broom. Penny got a wicked notion that her Grandmother Goldpenny would have hated. "Don't leave just yet. As you can see, I'm going into the cottage right now to get us some beers. I'm leaving my Goldpenny Goldenrod right here against the porch with nothing to guard it." She gave the angel an exaggerated wink and went into the cottage. "Gee, I guess it's time to trim the grass on the lawn behind the cabin! Do you know, from here I can't see the lake at all! It'll only take me a moment! I'll get the beer now, eh! What shall I see in the sky when I return?"

When she came back with the beer, the angel was still there. So was the broom. "What are doing here?" asked Penny, exasperated. "You were supposed to take the broom and fly away."

The angel raised his hands, palms up, in a gesture of helplessness. "I can't steal," he said. "It's against the Code."

Penny opened her beer and took a drink. She swallowed and sighed. "Well, I can't sell it to you. It's against Goldpenny policy. I don't suppose you know any dirty little thieving elves who would—"

The angel shook his head, a sorrowful expression on his face.

The wind blew in gusts, bringing the rest of the storm along, the afternoon gone. Through the last break in the gathering clouds, Penny saw an almost-full moon sitting on the tops of the trees across the lake. She got another idea.

"Look, angel, I can't sell you my Goldenrod and I can't give you my Goldenrod, but tomorrow night's a full moon, eh? That's when my weremink Marion turns into a hateful little girl. I can't help what she does with my brooms when I go up to the reservation to play bingo, which I plan on doing tomorrow night. So, if you're smart, you might come flying by tomorrow evening at moonrise, eh?"

The angel smiled. He spread his wings and lifted himself off the grass. Marion squeaked and jumped up to bite his toes. "Not that angels know anything about bingo, but I'm feeling something about extra jackpot money being found tomorrow night for a second round. The thirteenth person in line might get a card with the numbers B-3, I-28, N-32, G-45, O-60. I think that second jackpot will be five-hundred and fifty-dollars."

"Hey, that's the price of the new Coleman generator I've been saving for," said Penny.

"It is? What a coincidence," said the angel.

Penny watched him fly away, always listing to one side and correcting himself. She noticed that he kept his word and didn't wave goodbye. A stray blessing might have escaped his fingers and damaged her roof.

"Marion," Penny said to the weremink, "I'm going to leave the shed key on the table tomorrow. The Laurel Lake Laser is the one just inside the door on the right."

The Only Way to Fly

NANCY HOLDER

Jessamyne was either gazing out the window or dozing when Drucilla's scratchy Cockney twang pierced her right eardrum.

"Blimey!" Drucilla cried. "The movie's *Bell, Book, and Candle*. Oh, isn't that just too right?"

"How nice," Jessamyne said mildly. Her own accent, very Re-

85

ceived Standard, very prim and proper, rang as condescending, though she didn't mean it to be.

"Oh, and we're 'aving eye of newt for tea!"

That got Jessamyne's interest. How many years since she'd tasted that delicacy? Of course she knew the answer: Since she had married Michael Wood. From that point on, everything had fallen away, everything had changed, more drastically than she could have imagined.

"'Course it's airline food," Drucilla said speculatively. There seemed to be a bit of the old Romany line in her high cheekbones and hooked nose, the wart on the end of her chin. She gave a tug on the brim of her steepled hat (Jessamyne had put her own, newly purchased, in the overhead bin shortly after takeoff, finding the size and weight of it uncomfortable) and looked every part the witch she was.

Jessamyne was not so lucky. After all the time she had lived undercover, it was difficult to "let it all hang out," as the kids used to say. The kids of this century, at any rate. If one looked into a mirror—or, in this case, the window over the ice-coated wing of a large silver jetliner —one saw a rather pleasant, plump old lady with a dumpling face, square glasses perched on the tip of her nose, and gray hair pulled back in a bun. Not the stuff of nightmares.

She sighed wistfully. Not even the stuff of a second, startled glance.

"I wonder if it's fresh," Drucilla went on. She wrinkled up her fabulous nose and pulled back her lips, showing awe-inspiring jagged yellow teeth. "No doubt they'll zap it." She laughed at her double entendre and pantomimed enchanting an object with a magic wand. "Not 'abracadabra' zap, I mean. Microwave."

"Yes." Jessamyne settled back in her seat and thought about taking out her knitting. Michael had loved to watch her knit as they sat by the fire. But everyone else here would probably cackle at her; witches did not knit, not even those on the brink of retirement.

She surveyed the others. Pointed hats, a few white ruffled bonnets on the really old witches. Some wore buttons they had purchased at the airport gift shop: I SURVIVED THE INQUISITION. OLD WITCHES NEVER DIE, THEY JUST LOST THEIR MAGIC. I ♥ BLACK CATS. They were chatting and laughing, milling in the aisles, waving at ancient friends now reunited with them—in short, having a high old time.

Jessamyne only dimly remembered a few of their faces. Along with everything else, she had given up attending Sabbats and Samhains. All

Hallows' Eve found her handing out candy to little mortals. And how many times had she hidden her tears from Michael on the various Friday the Thirteenths, remembering all the fun she used to have? Curdling milk, backing up chimneys—ah, those had been good days!

And now those days were nothing more than memories. Michael was gone the way of all mortal men, and she, old before her time, was on her way to the Royal Home for English Witches in Kent. Gathered with some other British war brides—those wars ranging from the French and Indian War, the Revolutionary War, the War Between the States, and so forth—she was going home.

But could it be that she and she alone was the only witch who had stopped using her powers to please her husband? Surely not; there had been an American television series about that very thing. *Bewitched.* She had watched it not so much for amusement as for instruction, and had found it soothing on those days when it just didn't make much sense not to launch her husband to the top of his profession, conjure up expensive cars and beautiful clothes and gems for herself, and keep them both young-looking as long as possible. *No, no, no,* he had insisted. And, because she loved him, she had obeyed him.

Now, her powers fading both with disuse and with age—though she was only three hundred and twelve years old—she wondered if she had done the right thing.

"Miss, miss!" Drucilla cried, waving her hand in the air. "Miss!"

"Yes, ma'am?" A stewardess bustled over. Oh, fabulous creature. She wore a short, tight black dress draped over her bosom and a heavy necklace of jet shaped into a bat. Her black hair fell to the small of her back. Jessamyne's hair had been black. At first she had had to bleach it gray to match Michael's as he aged (so rapidly!) but very quickly it began to lighten and to dull. It would take powerful restorative magic to blacken it now. That, or a visit to a beauty parlor. How they would laugh at her for that.

"The newt, is it fresh?"

The stewardess smiled kindly. "I'm afraid not, ma'am. But we do have a nice dessert of floating toad."

"Oh, bloody good!" Drucilla clapped her hands together. "Jessamyne, isn't that wonderful?"

Jessamyne winced. She had never fallen into the American habit of calling perfect strangers by their first names. But they were all wearing name tags emblazoned with HELLO, MY NAME IS and their names printed in thick red ink. (It was supposed to look like blood, but it didn't. It didn't smell like blood, either, so what was the point?)

"Oh, yes, yummy toads for all you nice ladies," the beautiful young stewardess went on, including Jessamyne in her smile. Jessamyne had a dismal image of someone in a nurse's cap and dress saying exactly the same thing in one or two days' time.

She shifted uncomfortably. Perhaps this was all a big mistake. She had thought that returning to the Sisterhood would be a wonderful thing. Her thirst for coven life had gone unquenched for over sixty years, and the idea of spending her last century or so with rooms and rooms of other aged witches had been nothing less than an oasis to her. But was it a mirage? As she looked around at the humped old ladies, she thought, *Am I like that? How did it happen so soon?*

As the kids of today also said: *Use it or lose it.*

"More bloody Marys!" an old crone shouted three rows away.

The stewardess smiled again at them both and said, "Anything you ladies need, y'all just let me know." She had a slight Texas twang. Michael had had relatives in Texas.

Oh, Michael. She pushed the recline button on her chair and closed her eyes, allowing his image to enter her mind's eye even though it still hurt. She remembered when she had first seen him, fresh from battle—he had conquered the beach in Normandy! She was visiting a cousin in the London hospital, a warlock once removed who had insisted on doing his bit for Britain, and had actually been wounded. (No one knew how *that* had happened! There had been a few jokes about his patrimony—the milkman, the mailman, the Grand Inquisitor, and so on, but he had taken them all with good grace.)

Michael had lain in his hospital cot, so dashing and heroic, his arm in a sling, his vivid blue eyes shining from beneath his bandaged forehead. The attraction had been so intense, so complete, that Jessamyne simply assumed he was a warlock friend of her cousin out to enchant her. Imagine her dismay when she learned that he was mortal. Her family's fury when she had married him and announced they were moving back to America. How it had hurt to leave them all!

The homesickness. And then, Michael's edict: No Witchcraft. None. Not even for protection. He would not have it. And if she would not agree to it, he would send her flying back to England.

"In an airplane," he had added firmly.

Alone, perplexed, homesick, and desperately in love, she had agreed.

At first, it had been terrible for her. The laborious chores, done by her instead of familiars and enchanted household appliances, the endless sameness of mortal life. Watching herself age, and doing nothing about it. But worst of all, feeling her powers weaken from lack of use.

But what could she do? If she did otherwise, she would lose Michael's love. And that was a power she had no ability to withstand. So perhaps he had been a warlock after all. At the least, a demon lover.

She managed a wistful smile. Drucilla misread it, saying, "Isn't it wonderful, how they're taking care of us?"

"Oh, yes, quite," Jessamyne said. *Taking care of us.* That's what Michael had said when he had laid down the law: *I want to take care of you, Jessie. It makes me feel like a man.*

How puzzled she had been, and how confused. But she had permitted it, even perhaps growing to like it.

She thought of the brochure for the Home: *Three meals a day to tuck into! Your own room with a lovely view of the Kentish countryside. Our staff on hand twenty-four hours a day to anticipate your every need.*

Her every need. She didn't suppose they would let her fly Aphrodite, her trusty broom, but she had brought her nonetheless. She barely knew how to ride anymore, had fallen off last night when she'd tried to take one last turn around the small Connecticut village where she had lived with Michael. They would probably pack Aphrodite away somewhere where she would be "safe."

"No!" she cried. She clapped her hands. "This is a terrible mistake! What are we doing?"

Drucilla stared at her goggle-eyed. "Jessamyne?"

"You've forgotten," Jessamyne said. "You don't remember the glory. The wonder. Think for a moment. Think of riding the moon! Riding the night wind! Think how splendid! How free, how marvelous!" She squeezed Drucilla's biceps. "Remember it!"

"What?"

"Or will you go off to the airy coffin in Kent with everyone waiting on you?"

"Coffin? Coffin?" Drucilla echoed, distressed. "I thought we were going to a pensioners' home!"

"Let's get out, go, before it's too late," Jessamyne told her fiercely. She raised her voice and called, "Aphrodite!"

There was a rumbling beneath their feet.

Then parts of the the floor whooshed up toward the ceiling, as Aphrodite flew into the compartment and hovered beside Jessamyne. The stewardess hurried toward the broom, repairing the floor with a wave of her hand as she said, "I'm sorry, ma'am, but all brooms must be safely stowed in the baggage compartment."

"Move, *move*," Jessamyne hissed at Drucilla, who got out of her seat and took a few steps down the aisle, out of the way.

Jessamyne grabbed Aphrodite by the handle. The broom nickered in her grasp. "Gone!" she shouted, pointing at the nearest window. It shattered instantly. Wind howled around them, the suction pulled at everything in the plane.

"Madam!" the stewardess remonstrated, raising her hands to repair the damage.

Jessamyne hopped on Aphrodite and shot through the window. A few loose pieces of straw were caught in the window as it sealed up again.

And then she was outside the plane in the icy night, the howling blackness, with a half-moon overhead. At first she faltered, plummeting a thousand feet downward, but she felt the blood move in her veins again, felt the magic circulating again.

"Aieee, hee-hee-hee-hee!" she shrieked, speeding to catch up with the plane. She flew, she soared, she turned in huge circles. Aphrodite reared and pranced beneath her hands. The old broom was overjoyed to be back among the stars.

Through ice clouds she flew until she was beside the large jet. Hundreds of witches peering at her, some in shock, some with tears in their eyes. A few were cheering. To those she called, "Come on!"

Suddenly a dozen windows popped and a dozen witches flew out. A dozen more, and more. Soon there were a hundred. They coursed behind Jessamyne, shrieking and cackling, calling to the others in the plane.

"Freedom!" shouted an aged witch with wispy green hair.

"A new coven!" another cried.

"A new queen!"

They looked admiringly at Jessamyne. "Let's ride, sisters!" she cried, with her fist above her head. "And as the Dark Brother is my witness, we'll never eat oatmeal *ever*!"

"Aye!" they all cried as one, all the very old witches who could barely stay astride their brooms.

"To England. And Spain! And Japan! To curdle milk and make two-headed calves." Jessamyne grinned and jerked her head toward the jet. "And to terrify old ladies who have forgotten how to live."

"Aye!" came the shout all around her like a thunderclap. With Jessamyne at their head, they screamed into the night, flying as witches were meant to fly to their dying day . . . and as all wise witches do.

The Princess and the Frog

Tina L. Jens

Once upon a time, a long time ago (the 1920s), in a land reasonably far away (Paris, France, to be exact), there was a beautiful young girl named Cindy. Her hair shone like polished gold, her eyes sparkled like sapphires, and her lips were the color of rubies. She wasn't really a princess (unless you count her mother's half-brother's sister-in-law, Gladys, who was a great-grandniece-in-law to Louis Philippe, Duke of Orleans).

"Cindy was a talented, career-minded, young girl, who kept a busy professional schedule and didn't want to be bothered with dating. But in those days, a girl's reputation was judged by the quality of her date at the season's social functions."

Serena the witch paused in her tale and pulled her shawl more tightly around her shoulders. She wasn't really cold. Any witch worth her snuff could control her own body temperature, otherwise she'd freeze her bum off dancing naked in the forest on Halloween.

No, she paused and adjusted her shawl because the break created tension. And in storytelling, as in witchcraft, timing is everything.

"Did she fall in love with a prince and live happily ever after?" Jenna, Serena's granddaughter, asked hopefully.

"Bet you turned her boyfriend into a frog!" Jenna's older brother, Jason, said, upsetting his sister.

"Cindy was my client. Back in the olden days they would have called me a fairy godmother. But I've never gone in for any of that highfalutin stuff. I'm a witch plain and simple."

"Whenever one of the palaces held a royal ball, Cindy always showed up with the most dashing, handsome, mysterious prince in all the land.

"The other girls wondered how Cindy could attract such fine men, coming from a respectable but middle-class background as she did. But Cindy had inherited brains from her mother—and that's far more important than inheriting wealth.

"I had a little shop on the south end. We had a good business relationship for years, until that one time. . . ."

Serena let her voice trail off. The children crowded closer.

"The twenties were a crazy time all over the world, but nowhere more than in the Parisian circles of magic. There was a sudden reversal in the magic polarity and everything was backward. Some say a shift in the magnetic poles brought it all about. Some say the kids started it as a prank and it just kept building till it was out of control.

"All I know is, the magic was backward. You couldn't blight a crop with all the amulets in Europe. Black cats had lost their power. Some say the political assassination of Jean Jaures was really just a love potion that worked in reverse.

"It took folks a while to figure out what was going on. But you should have seen the run on white cats when they did. Instead of blighting your enemy's crops, you had to cast fertile spells. The fields overran the roads.

"You couldn't cast an effective spell for warts or aging, so you plagued your romantic rivals with Beautiful Hair—that grew up to a foot a day—or shackled them with a Glamour spell that had every man within a quarter mile lusting after them. It was easy to tell who had been hit with that one—as they walked down the street you could see the bulges in the men's—" Serena looked at the upturned faces of her young audience.

"Perhaps I'll tell you that bit when you're older," she said quickly.

The bell jingled over the door of the shoppe. Serena looked up from the green powder she was crushing in a wooden mortar, to wave hello at the girl. The tiny shoppe was buzzing with people, but Cindy was a steady customer who paid her bills on time and followed magical instructions to the letter.

With the coming of the backward time, magic was a much more

time-consuming, difficult task. The spell books had to be put aside and new incantations and methods developed.

Serena added a drop of deer musk to the green powder. The solution fizzed and crackled before bursting briefly into flame. Serena coughed and fanned the noxious yellow smoke out of her face.

The concoction was now a dark amber, the consistency of lumpy mashed potatoes. She dumped the contents into the trash. When henbane and orris root no longer worked to break the attention of an unwanted suitor, what was a witch to do?

She motioned Cindy over and called to her new assistant.

"This is my apprentice, Jeannie. Just tell her what you want."

Serena would have preferred to take care of Cindy herself. She knew the proper height to prevent Cindy from getting a crick in her neck looking up, the proper leg length so they could dance well together, the hundred little physical details that make a couple compatible. But the shoppe was busy and Cindy's request was simple compared to the complex, highly experimental spells the other customers wanted.

"Remember, use a bullfrog instead of a tree frog or horny toad," she told her assistant. "They're a little more expensive, but the results are worth it."

Jeannie led Cindy through a curtain of beads, into the private workshop. The sound of jazz playing on the phonograph was softer here, and the buzzing of customers not so distracting.

Jeannie sighed with relief. Her apprenticeship had been rushed along. Serena desperately needed help, and Jeannie, even more desperately, needed a job. Her knowledge of the fundamentals had been shaky to start with. With the backward time, Jeannie suffered a panic attack whenever she cast a spell. A simple cure for warts could wind up as a bad case of Elephant Man disease.

But the workshop always calmed her nerves. It reminded her of a forest, with the scent of herbs and mosses blending together and the sounds of the mice quietly tittering to themselves while the frogs and toads croaked and chirped in a pleasing, if cacophonous, chorus.

Jeannie removed the screen from the top of the large wooden tub that held the bullfrogs. The tub was half-filled with gently moving marsh water (circulated by a low-powered nature spell) and lily pads. Jeannie gently scooped one off a floating log and held it out for Cindy's inspection.

Then she looked over Cindy's file, while Cindy did her best to keep the frog's wanderings confined to the workbench.

"Any special requests?"

"What?" Cindy asked, distracted. The bullfrog had taken a liking to her nail color. He had wrapped his tongue around its tip, and was sucking on her finger.

"Green eyes would be nice. Not too tall. Chocolate-colored hair, better give him a range of dancing skills, there's no telling what music they'll be playing. Slightly less muscle than last time—the guy squeezed me so hard, he bruised my ribs. Conversant on jazz and modern art, skip the politics. Oh, Scott and Zelda will probably be there, so he should be familiar with Fitzgerald's work. And make him a wine drinker. The combination of whiskey and French onion soup last time is not a bad-breath experience I want to repeat."

Jeannie took careful notes, consulting several reference books on the appropriate incantations for the variables. She jotted down the words of power, mumbling them to herself, as if rehearsing for a speech, erased a bit, rewrote a line here. Finally, she nodded to herself.

The apprentice still looked a tad too uncertain for Cindy's comfort, but Serena's shoppe offered a money-back guarantee.

Jeannie took her magic wand, borrowed from Serena, out of the glass display case that protected it. She glanced nervously at her client.

The wand was made of a short length of pine sapling, stripped of the bark, with a star, cut out of cardboard and decorated with silver glitter, glued on the end. It was all rather embarrassing to Jeannie, but Serena had assured her that it was the only appropriate wand for the job.

Peeking once more at her notes, Jeannie closed her eyes and began to recite the incantation. Her voice wavered at first, but steadied as she progressed through the spell. Even so, Cindy could not make out all the words.

". . . Sancto Sanctorum . . . by the power vested in . . . Abracadabra!"

Jeannie gave the star wand one firm shake, winced, and waited for the "poof" and the smoke to clear. She opened one eye cautiously. The results looked humanoid. She opened both eyes and fanned the smoke away.

It was a man. He was perhaps a little too tall, and a bit gangly. His hair had a reddish cast, but his eyes would be green—if viewed in the right light. Jeannie snuck a peek at her client to gauge her reaction.

He wasn't exactly to spec, Cindy thought. But she could only blame herself. She couldn't place her order at the last minute and expect perfection. And this was only a minor ball for one of the newer branches of the many houses of Louises. She nodded.

"He'll do."

Jeannie gave an audible sigh of relief.

"Um, pardon me," said the newly created man, holding up one hand to get their attention. He was awkwardly bent forward, the other hand, and most of that same arm, trying desperately to cover up parts of his anatomy he was sure shouldn't be on view.

"Sorry," Jeannie said, quickly grabbing a towel from the workbench and tossing it to him. "Guess I should have done the clothing first."

Leaving the man behind, Cindy followed Jeannie out the back door to a sheep pen. The young witch "baaaed" soothingly until she lured two young ewes to the front of the pen, where she tethered them. She cast her hands out in front of her and recited another spell.

"Baabaablacksheep . . ."

To Cindy's ears the words sounded suspiciously like the Mother Goose nursery rhyme repeated three times, very, very, fast. Whatever the young witch said, it worked. In moments, wool sprouted in two great clouds from the sheep. Jeannie picked up a pair of shears, clipped it off, and stuffed it into a bag.

Then she walked to a small shed and threw open the door.

Cindy gasped. The wall was covered by a sparkling web.

"Silkworms," Jeannie said.

Once more, she threw out her hands and cast an accelerated growing spell, her voice sounding like a phonograph spinning out of control.

"Silkwormsilkwormspinyourlittleweb . . ."

When the worms were done, Jeannie pulled the cloud of dainty filaments down, stuffed it in another bag and went back inside.

The man leapt behind a cabinet, clutching modestly at his towel.

Jeannie opened a large black trunk and tossed in the bundles of wool and silk. Dipping into a glass canister labeled "Crushed Poppy," she scattered a handful of red dust over the wool. She ladled a glop of axle grease on the silk. On top of that sticky mess, she tossed in a needle, thread, thimble, and pair of sewing shears. Finally, she dropped in Serena's favorite pair of mice, Walter and Dysne.

"Size eight," she said, and slammed the trunk shut. She sank down on the lid with a sigh of relief.

"This'll take a few minutes."

Cindy was speechless. This was her first peek behind the scenes of witchcraft. Serena just seated her in the fortune-telling alcove with a cup of tea and dashed off. When everything was done, Cindy would use the alcove as a dressing room and meet her escort in the coach parked out front.

The apprentice cleared her throat.

"About the transportation details—the pumpkin into a carriage thing isn't working right now. If you want a carriage turned into a pumpkin—no problem." Jeannie shrugged.

"We've experimented with cucumbers, squash, gourds, mushrooms. Rocks give us a nice shape, but they need a team of horses or they're too heavy to pull. We've gotten some nice designs from onions, but we can't get rid of the smell. We've done some experimenting with logs, but there's still a bad splinter problem."

"That won't do," Cindy said.

"Frankly, I'd recommend you go next door to Ralph's stable and rent a horse and carriage. It'll be cheaper. Tell him Serena sent you, and don't let him give you Nellie the Nag. We've been running a life-support spell on that beast for a month. It'll drop dead any day now."

They heard three tiny knocks from inside the chest. Jeannie slid off the top, opened it, and pulled out a ball gown.

It was a stunning little number, exactly the color of poppy blossoms. It was cut off the shoulder, with black satin bows, fastened with rhinestones, adorning the sleeve puffs, waist, and hem.

Next out of the trunk came a black tux and white ruffled shirt with a red satin cummerbund and bow tie.

Serena came into the room just as the couple finished dressing. She handed Cindy a gold foil-wrapped box.

"You look absolutely stunning, dear."

Cindy blushed, then opened her present. Inside was an elegant rhinestone tiara and dainty glass slippers.

"Just a little gift, dear, since I didn't have time to help you."

"Jeannie did a wonderful job," Cindy assured the older witch.

"Now remember the rules . . ."

"Twelve o'clock, sharp," Cindy said.

"Have fun!"

The two witches waved the young couple out the door and locked it behind them.

"What a night!" Serena said, sinking into a chair in the now empty shoppe.

"I'm very proud of you, Jeannie. You did a top-notch job."

Jeannie beamed at the praise.

"Just out of curiosity, what did you use for the change-back trigger?"

The smile dripped slowly off the young witch's face.

"What's a change-back trigger?"

"Oh dear."

In the backward time, enchantments wore off at noon and spells were cast when the sun was at its zenith. Because so much of society relied on magic, and because it was never safe to be milling about when witches were at work, polite society had adjusted its schedule. Thus, the ball started at eight A.M.

Large black tapestries hung over the windows, blocking out the rising sun. The better to hide the greenish cast to her escort's skin, Cindy thought. He was not quite up to Serena's standards. He didn't walk so much as hop, Cindy noticed, as he went to get them some punch. Bending it at the knee, he lifted his leg high up in the air, drawing it closer to his body until, all at once, he thrust it out in front of him. Then the other leg would begin the slow process.

He had a disconcerting habit of sticking his tongue out, as if tasting the air. And he would sit, staring at you, in rapt attention. Cindy found her eyes aching in sympathy, until she wanted to urge him to blink.

Still, he was handsome in an odd way. Cindy called him Jeremiah.

They strolled, arm in arm, around the edge of the dance floor, chatting with the other guests.

"Political affiliations," Cindy told Jeremiah, "can be discerned by the person's dress."

"Monarchist?" he whispered, as they greeted Lady Eleanore and her nephew.

Lady Eleanore wore an ivory lace dress with an immense bustle. Her hair was done up in an elaborately sculptured birdcage with two live canaries inside.

Jeremiah's eyes popped.

"Wire framework and hair extensions," Cindy explained.

The nephew sported a black velvet suit, shoulders dusted white by the flakes of powder fallen from his wig.

The monarchy believed it was only proper for them to remain a century behind the times. They worked hard to ensure that their fashion and viewpoints reflected that belief.

Cindy and Jeremiah giggled together as Lady Eleanore encountered their hostess, Vicky, Prince Louis's great-granddaughter twice removed. She was a loyal supporter of the Popular Front, a flapper, and terribly fond of cheap gin.

It had been her idea to have a jazz quartet alternate sets with a trio of classical harpsichords, thus annoying everyone equally.

"Gosh, she's something," Jeremiah said, hypnotized by the swinging beads on the tight sheath dress.

"Bloop!" Jeremiah said, as Cindy dragged him across the room.

Cindy's arch-rival, Jeannette, stopped by to check out her date.

"Well, he's a different look for you," she said cattily. But Cindy could tell she was jealous.

The dinner was uneventful, except for the third course, where Jeremiah made an unnecessary fuss and refused to eat the Grenouilles Valeuris. (They tasted suspiciously like chicken.)

The only serious disagreement between the couple arose late in the evening (at 10:30 A.M.), when Vicky lured Jeremiah on top of the dinner table and taught him to Charleston. Cindy had to grudgingly admit Jeremiah was a natural at it.

She was actually disappointed when it was time to leave. But she'd learned the hard way to be prompt where magic was concerned. At twenty minutes to noon she instructed their driver to take them to the woods. He parked beside a pond and left them, discreetly alone.

There the couple waited.

And waited.

And waited.

By one thirty, Cindy was hot and cross and ready to launch into a proper cussing regarding a certain apprentice witch. Jeremiah sat on the running board of the carriage and blooped, confused and miserable.

Cindy was not a cruel girl, but she'd lost her patience, and was about to call to the driver to abandon Jeremiah by the side of the road.

Jeremiah didn't really need her to sit and hold his hand while he metamorphosed back into his rightful form.

She didn't notice the sky very suddenly cloud over. A downpour began. (Even an apprentice witch can call forth a decent storm.) Jeremiah's blooping changed tone—he sounded happy.

"Finally!" Cindy thought, opening the carriage door to check on him.

But he was still in human form, leap-frogging through the rain and splashing in all the puddles. He hopped over to her and gave her a wet, froggy kiss.

"You see, rain makes frogs amorous," Serena explained.

"What's that, Grandma?"

Serena pondered the question. "Loving," she said, finally.

"I expected her to bring him back in for a refund, but something happened out there in the rain. Cindy and Jeremiah fell in love. I guess there's no accounting for taste."

"So they lived happily ever after?" Jenna asked.

Serena nodded.

Jason said, "Ugh!"

There'll Be Witches

JOE MENO

As soon as my mom turned off my bedroom light, I buried myself under my sheets and blankets, careful to leave a small hole for peeking.

"Spitter?" I called out anxiously.

"Shh!" he yelled back.

"Spitter, you've got the first shift, okay?"

"All right, but you better keep quiet or you'll wake 'em up anyway." I closed my eyes and dozed off to sleep uncomfortably. A few minutes later, I awoke, suddenly seized by fear and doubt.

"Spitter!" I whispered. No reply.

"Spitter!" Again, no reply. From under the blankets and out of my peekhole, I saw him, fast asleep on his guard shift.

"Spitter!" I yelled, this time sure to wake the goof.

"What?" he answered groggily.

"You were sleeping!"

"No, I wasn't," he replied. "I was only resting my eyes." He smiled stupidly, wiping the sleep away.

"Did you see any?" I asked nervously.

"No, stupid. If I did, I would have woke you up!" he said snottily.

"Good." I fell back asleep. I woke up again, some time later, and I really had to pee. "Spitter, I gotta pee," I said loudly, sure to wake him on the first try. "Spitter, look under the bed."

Spitter got up, and leaned over the side of the bed slowly. "OH MY GOD!" he yelled, diving under the covers I had been hiding under.

"What is it?" I asked, horrified to hear his answer.

"WITCHES!!!" he squeaked, "WITCHES!!!"

Sure as Spitter said, they came out from under the bed, a dozen or so witches, dressed in black cloaks and long black hats, carrying knives and brooms. Their queen stepped forward, her green face stern and ugly.

"Hello, Little Danny Bed Wetter!" she said, grimacing at her own cruel joke. Her teeth were rotten and yellow and looked as if she hadn't brushed them for some time.

"What do you want?" I asked, already knowing the answer.

"I think you know, Danny," she said grimly. The queen motioned to a short witch with a large silver knife. The short witch pulled the covers off me, and pressed the knife's blade against my throat. "Do it!" the queen ordered. I closed my eyes and began to pee on myself, soiling my Superman pajamas and Star Wars sheets. The whole coven laughed and then slipped back beneath the bed. Spitter crawled out from under the covers and looked at me sadly. We both fell asleep quickly, too afraid to see if they would return.

"Goddamnit, Danny! You wet the bed again?" my mom screamed the next morning. This had been going on for almost two weeks now. "You're in the second grade, Danny. You're not a baby anymore," she said, full of frustration. "Now get ready for school!"

She dropped me off and I met my friend Sean in the schoolyard.

"My mom says you still wet the bed. My mom says only retards still wet the bed in the second grade," he said plaintively. "Are you a retard?" he asked.

"Shut up!" I said, walking away. Leave it to my mother to discuss my problems with the whole world. I sat down on a curb and rested my chin on my knees.

"DANNY'S A BED WETTER! DANNY'S A BED WETTER!" I heard chorused by every second grader on the schoolyard. I hid my head in my arms and waited until the schoolbell rang. I rushed into my classroom and put my head down on my desk. Within minutes, I was asleep.

After school, I walked home alone, sure to avoid contact with anyone from my class.

"So, everybody knows, huh?" Spitter asked sympathetically.

"Yeah, I guess so." I looked down at my feet as we walked, afraid to look Spitter in the eye. I opened my back door, walked into the kitchen, and saw my mom talking on the telephone. She made several attempts to communicate, using some weird telephone sign language, but seeing this as a reprieve from another discussion on bed-wetting, I darted upstairs, and changed from my clothes. I sat on my bed, hoping my mom would forget about the incident or just be too frustrated to talk about it anymore.

"She's not gonna forget," Spitter announced, destroying any sense of hope I had. "Maybe if you blocked the door with something," he offered, grinning mischievously.

Maybe if you block the door with something. "That's it!" I yelled. I dove into my closet, pulling out every toy and game I had.

"What are you doing?" Spitter asked, perplexed. I began stuffing the toys beneath my bed, filling the gaps with books and clothes. I finished the barricade off with an old stuffed animal from my teething days, maybe a bear or a dog, which was too mangled and tattered to really tell.

"No witch could get through there!" I announced, satisfied.

"I guess not," Spitter agreed. I lay on my bed and fell asleep, proud of my own ingenuity.

I woke for dinner and afterwards did my spelling homework, watched some TV, and ate a bowl of ice cream. Nobody remembered! They all forgot about last night! I smiled as I took another spoonful of chocolate chip.

"DANNY!" my dad called from upstairs, the anger apparent in his intonation. "Danny, get your butt up here right now!" I climbed the stairs slowly, as if I were walking my last steps, and met my father at the top of the stairs. He grabbed me by the arm. "Your teacher called and talked to your mother today, Danny. You're failing all your subjects. She says all you do is daydream and draw pictures. She says you don't know how to listen to directions. She says maybe if you spent less time daydreaming, you'd be a better student." He dragged me into my bedroom and pushed me down. He walked out, and fearing he'd return with the belt, I began to cry. Merely as a self-defense. The belt was my father's instrument of retribution and deterrence, a thick leather belt that had met with my backside on more than one occasion. Instead, he returned with a large cardboard box and tossed it at me angrily. "I want all your toys in this box. Then bring it downstairs when you're done."

"But, Dad," I begged. "Dad, there'll be witches."

"WHAT!!?" he yelled. "Goddamnit, Danny, don't even start your talk about witches. There's no such thing as goddamn witches! How many times do I have to tell you? Fifty? A hundred?"

"No," I replied sheepishly. I pulled the toys from beneath my bed, hoping the queen herself would jump out and gobble up my father. But I knew she wouldn't. The queen was too smart for that. She'd never come out when my parents were around.

I took a bath and hopped into bed, resigned to the fact that I would be dead as soon as the lights went out. My mother, still frustrated, didn't even bother to kiss me goodnight, and turned off the light, sealing my doom.

I was right. They didn't even wait for me to hide beneath my blankets. The witches jumped out from beneath my bed and surrounded me, grinning hungrily, awaiting the queen's orders before they tore me to ribbons. The queen stepped forward, her face green and gnarled; her stringy black hair hung like cobwebs, a large curved blade in her twisted hands. She smiled a massive smile, which seemed to stretch her skin to the corners around her mouth. Slowly, she reached under the covers, pulling Spitter from his refuge under the comforter.

"So, Danny, you tried to block us out?" she asked, the smile grotesquely wide on her face. "That's not very nice, Danny." She lifted Spitter by his hair and stabbed him, spraying imaginary blood everywhere. The whole coven burst into laughter. Spitter fell to the floor, limp and dead. I dove under the covers, so upset the urine flooded the bed quickly and without any hesitation. The coven laughed again. "Tomorrow night, Danny," the queen promised. "Tomorrow night, Danny, it'll be your turn." Again she smiled, disappearing into the darkness under the bed.

The next day was Wednesday, and as usual, we went to dinner at my grandparents' house. My grandma was a soft, gentle woman, who smiled all the time and listened to every word I said attentively. My grandpa, on the other hand, was quite different. He had emphysema, and sat in the back room all day, watching TV and waiting to die. He was withered and bony, and behind his horn-rimmed spectacles, there was no warmth, only beady eyes. He refused to talk to anyone usually, and only spoke when he wanted something. "Loretta," he'd yell. "Get me some water." Or "Loretta, get the damn dog out of here." He smelled funny, and quite frankly, I didn't like him at all. As soon as we arrived, my mother ordered me to go say hello to him. I crept into the back room, which was wallpapered pea green, the only light the sinister flicker and buzz of the TV.

"Hi, Grandpa," I said, trying to sound as unexcited as possible. He broke his gaze with the TV and looked at me, squinting his eyes to focus.

"C'mere," he said in a throaty voice. I was horrified. I crept into the back room slowly. "Your mother says you've been wetting yourself every night." Again, my mother had been so gracious to tell everyone she knew about my predicament.

"Something about witches," he mumbled. I nodded my head yes. "Witches, huh?" He stood up slowly, and closed the back room door. He reached into a desk drawer and pulled out something shiny.

It was a small knife.

"This'll take care of those damn witches!!" he insisted. "Just stab 'em once with this baby, and they'll never bother you again. Just don't show your mother." Finally, some adult saw what was going on. And now, I was ready to do battle with the queen herself.

I ate dinner happily, and during the meal, I dislodged a loose tooth, drooling blood onto my grandma's good china, smiling happily all the while. I didn't care about the tooth. I was worried about the queen.

We went home, and I went to bed, holding the knife under my pillow. My mom shut off the light, and I grasped the knife, ready to run the queen through. I heard something move about suddenly, creeping about in the darkness. Buried beneath my blanket barricade, I felt her next to me, ready to strike. I was also ready. I sprang up and ran my knife into the figureless form, sending my attacker to the floor. I squinted my eyes, which hadn't adjusted to the darkness yet, ready to see the queen writhing about in pain.

It wasn't the queen. It was the tooth fairy.

She fluttered about the floor like a fallen angel, her wings glowing dimly, spilling quarters and teeth about as she choked on her fairy dust and died.

I stood above her in horror. *Oh, my God, I just killed the tooth fairy!* I thought, shocked and terrified, knowing my parents would surely scold me something awful. I sat on my bed, wondering what punishment I would receive for this. I began to cry, knowing it would be something severe, suddenly startled by the motion from beneath my bed. Out the witches came, this time two dozen or so. They all gathered around the tooth fairy, shocked and horrified by my deed.

"You killed the tooth fairy?" the queen asked nervously.

"I guess so," I said, wiping the tears from my eyes.

"You can't kill the tooth fairy," she said repulsed. "You can't kill the tooth fairy."

"Well, she's dead, and I did it," I said almost proudly.

"Well, ah, we didn't know . . . I mean you, you would do something like this . . . we were just fooling around . . . and umm." The queen hung her head low and crept back beneath the bed, never to return.

The next day, I had a funeral for Spitter and buried him under my bed, with the rest of my dead imaginary friends, right next to Spaceman Stan, who got hit by a car last year.

Alan's Mother

STEVE RASNIC TEM

He had just turned ten before the summer began that year, and for the fourth summer in a row he had left his father's home in the city to stay with his mother in a cottage by the dark green pond.

Years later he would doubt his memories of that time, and would wonder, after all, what had really occurred. This was the last summer Alan would believe his mother to be magical.

He did not understand his parents' divorce; when he was six his mother had come to him one day and explained it all, but he hadn't really understood what she was saying. He did remember that she had said his father did not like the things she wanted to do, and that this made her very unhappy. She said people owed it to themselves to do the things that made them happiest. That had made a lot of sense to him at the time, and when his father or others had criticized his mother for it, he had objected strongly. But then he couldn't understand why she didn't take him along with her, and he was always a little angry with her for that.

His mother's cottage was a beautiful place, with many flowers and animals and, of course, the dark green pond, which always seemed to hold your reflection a moment—an image clearer than any mirror's—before drawing it into the deep dark green of itself. As he stared into the water, Alan always felt that he was drowning, but for some reason it was a nice feeling, as if the pond were delivering him to some other, more beautiful world beneath the surface.

Sometimes the image of himself seemed older than he was by a week, by a year, by decades. The clothes would be different, or the willow tree hanging over him in the reflection would be showing signs of a different season from the one on his side of the reflecting surface. And one time the willow tree wasn't there at all, and the image in the water was that of an old, old man.

It had seemed, then, without a doubt, that his mother was magical. Each summer when she greeted him at the crossroads beyond her cottage, she had presented him with a gift, and it was always the gift he had secretly wished for: a teddy bear, or a spin top, or the comic book he'd begged his father to buy him the previous week, only to see the last copy sold when he ran to the drugstore out of breath, the dime clutched in his anxious fist.

When he asked his mother how she knew, she always replied the same: "Mothers know everything." She'd laugh and he'd laugh too, but always a little more puzzled than before.

Another time she showed her magical powers was when he was sick or injured. There seemed to be nothing she couldn't cure. Her neighbors in this part of the country seemed to think this, too, and were always bringing rashes and bellyaches and broken bones for her to mend. She'd send them away with mixtures of herbs, homemade ointments, or sometimes even water from the dark green pond. And he never heard any of them say she hadn't cured them; all praised her abilities.

He remembered the day he had cut his hand badly on a piece of broken glass out by the crossroads. He knew he wasn't supposed to be playing out there—she'd always warned him against it—so he didn't want to come to her at first, afraid she'd punish him. Or perhaps she wouldn't cure it at all because he'd disobeyed her. Perhaps she'd even make it hurt worse. But it bled a great deal, all over his new blue shirt, and he was afraid he would die if he did not go to his mother.

He'd raced into the cottage crying hysterically, bare-chested, his bleeding hand wrapped in his new shirt. His mother had cried out in alarm and embraced him, stroked him, cooed to him—all this, even though he was bleeding over her. Her reaction pleased him and made him uneasy at the same time; she'd always seemed so calm and controlled about everything else.

After she had comforted him she'd taken him into her sitting room, and showed him a small, shiny wood table covered with a piece of red velvet. He was to lay the back of his hand on the velvet.

She took a jar of ground herbs off one of her shelves and sprinkled the powder over his hand. Then she added a few drops of a blue liquid. Then she wrapped the velvet up around his hand and led him out by the pond, where she dipped his hand for several minutes.

Later he would try to understand exactly what had happened next. He remembered her taking the velvet and his bloodied bandage off immediately after pulling it out of the water. But it had to have been a period of weeks, he was sure, for the skin was completely healed. There wasn't even a scab.

His mother always seemed to know what he had been thinking back then. Later he would wonder if perhaps all little boys thought that of their mothers. He would always remember the day he had been so disappointed that he wouldn't be in the city for a friend's party, and how his mother had surprised him with a big party in her cottage, with all the neighboring kids and some kids he couldn't recognize. It was funny, because he had thought he knew all the kids around there, and he never saw those other kids again. But they had been especially nice to him.

And then his eleventh summer came, and everything was different after that.

The first thing he noticed was in the taxi on the way to the crossroads. He suddenly realized he wasn't all that excited about seeing his mother that year. It was his first year of eligibility for the baseball league at the city park, and he had to admit he'd really rather be playing baseball that summer. All the other boys had even made fun of him when he'd told them how he was spending the summer.

"Well, I don't *really* want to go. But my dad says I have to . . ." he'd told them, and his face had suddenly gone hot with shame. What if his mother knew *then*, what he had been thinking and saying? A chill played with his fingers, and he imagined her invisible form standing beside him, looking sadly down at him as a cold wind lifted her hair.

There was a lot to do in the city that summer, he had suddenly realized, and for the life of him he couldn't remember doing anything those summers at his mother's that had been fun at all.

But he was proud of his new jeans, his baseball cap, the tennis shoes the big boys wore. He wasn't a little kid anymore; he wanted his mother to see that.

His mother was there at the crossroads to greet him, her tall dark gray form standing by the high embankment covered with dead weeds. He was almost startled to see her; she looked old, and he could not remember her looking old before. Her hair was gray, her face starkly shadowed, and as the cab pulled up beside her he could see lines in the shadows. Her once-smooth face was lined. And her characteristically stoic expression seemed one of sadness this time, as if a thin line of mood had been crossed in her advancing age.

He got out of the cab, and it sped off. He watched it leave, purposefully delaying the moment he must look her in the face. When he did turn and look up at his mother, she was holding something out to him. He had almost forgotten. It was his yearly gift.

"A slingshot?" he asked in surprise. She did not answer him, just slipped it into his hands. He stroked the hardwood handle. "How did you—" But something about her expression stopped his question.

It wasn't a toy, nothing like the ones he'd had before. He'd seen one just like it in one of his father's sporting goods catalogs. He'd wanted it badly ever since then: something he could show the other kids down at the park.

But his father had said it wasn't a toy; it was a hunting weapon. It wasn't for him. How did she know that was what he wanted? And moreover, why was she giving him this? He would have expected her not to approve.

His mother was looking at him sadly. And unlike any summer before, she did not take his hand when they left the crossroads for her cottage. But he was a big boy now; she must have seen that.

The cottage seemed much as he had remembered it: the lace table-cloth on the small table in her alcove she used for dining, the kitchen with its natural woods and cast iron, the fireplace of gray stone. But it was all smaller and older than it had been before, and there seemed nothing there that might interest him.

For the first time she fixed a dinner he did not enjoy. Why didn't she know he didn't like fish anymore?

And the story she read him that evening was one he'd become bored with a long time ago.

He could tell she was feeling the difference, too. All her smiles were sad ones this summer.

All summer he waited for his mother to do something special, magical. Neighbors still came to her for aid, and she gave them herbs and ointments as before, but never did he see the miracles he remembered. How could he know if the people had been cured? They seemed satisfied with her help; people came back to her and no one ever appeared to complain. But he was losing confidence in her this year. Alan wanted proof.

Then one cool summer's morning Alan received his opportunity. He had been sitting down by the pond, picking up small pebbles and seeing how far he could shoot them. After weeks of practice he had gotten good enough to get them across the pond, where they landed on a large moss-covered rock with a satisfying thump. When that no longer was a challenge, he started aiming at the large and small trees which bordered the other side of the pond.

Suddenly he stopped; he thought he'd seen something in the weeds covering one small section of the far bank.

There it was again! Alan sat up on his heels. By squinting carefully he was able to focus in on one particular spot. It was a rabbit, brown with patches of gray.

Alan held his breath. He could not remember ever having seen a creature so beautiful. It was just like the rabbits in stores. In fact, he had a stuffed toy at home that looked much like it—though he didn't play with it very much anymore, because he was a big boy now, too big for that kind of toy.

He wanted it to come to him. He wanted it very badly.

The next thing he would remember was running around the edge of the pond, staring straight ahead at the clump of weeds where the rabbit had been. Then staring down at the still form, the mouth open over the teeth, the eyes glassy.

He'd scooped it up even though it smelled, and had raced all the way to his mother's cottage.

But she'd only looked at him in sadness, and at his precious slingshot he'd not forgotten even in his haste, stuffed into his front pocket. She shook her head slowly. "I cannot," she'd said. "I'm sorry, Alan."

"But you have to, you have to!" he'd cried, his face wet with tears. He wanted to stop his crying; how could he be a big boy and cry? But he couldn't stop. "You've always been able to fix things. Always."

"Do you still believe in my magic, Alan? Do you still believe those things?"

Dumbly he stared at her. And finally shook his head. "No . . ."

Alan never paid attention to the people visiting his mother for cures after that. Sometimes when a storekeeper in the nearby town would say, "Oh, you're the conjure woman's boy," he'd merely laugh, wondering how those grown-ups could be so gullible.

Blood Mary

SIMON McCAFFERY

Karen Harmon sat waiting in the family's minivan outside Emerson Elementary when the scream rose up from the schoolyard—a shrill, panicked cry that instantly raised the skin and baby-fine hair along her arms and neck in cold, bumpy goose flesh.

The effect was the same across the crowded, puddle-dotted parking lot; every mother within earshot shrank back or flinched at the sound. Karen actually dropped the paperback she had been resting against the steering wheel (she was reading, somewhat guiltily, the latest Danielle Steele), and stared fearfully through the rain-dotted windshield. For a moment she fully expected to see the small crumpled body of a child that had hurried into the path of an arriving or departing car—the scream had been that bright and wrenching.

Eight-year-old children are always in a hurry and they forget to look both ways. They forget, no matter how many times the mantra of safe street-crossing is drilled into them. *Allison* did it all the time—stepped carelessly off street curbs or wandered too close to traffic hurrying to claim empty parking spots at the mall. Karen had to watch her like a hawk. For a moment she tasted sharp metallic panic. What if she looked out now and saw *Allison* lying there, bloody and broken on the wet pavement?

Karen leaned forward and saw a girl—not her daughter, thank God, but a smaller classmate named Holly Burke—running across the schoolyard, her blue and yellow raincoat flapping. The girl's hands were outstretched, her large brown eyes bright with terror. She looked like a frightened sparrow in flight.

Karen watched the girl run, nearly stumbling, toward a familiar cinnamon-colored Jeep Cherokee parked two cars away. When the girl's pallid, tear-streaked face glanced briefly over her shoulder, Karen followed her gaze to the open doors of the school. A small cluster of girls stood silently at one side of the doorway. Karen recognized some of them: Pam Wilson, Diane Lester, and Mina Phipps. And Allison. They looked odd standing there, like sisters in a precocious clique or secret club. All of their eyes seemed fixed on the fleeing girl.

When Karen looked back at the Cherokee she saw a flustered Barbara Burke trying to soothe her sobbing daughter.

"Wasn't that your friend Holly I saw?" Karen asked Allison as they turned out of the school's gravel exit. "She looked very upset."

Allison sat buckled into the center of the benchseat directly behind the van's driver's seat, absorbed in a library book. She shrugged.

"Did someone say something mean to her?"

Allison shook her head and absently stuck a strand of blonde hair in the corner of her mouth.

"Don't chew on your hair, Allison," Karen said automatically, "or we'll have to trim it back."

Allison frowned and smoothed her hair.

"Well," Karen said, trying to keep the exasperation from her voice, "what did you do in school today?"

"*Mother* . . ." Allison whined, rolling her eyes. In kindergarten Allison had always been ready to burst with the details of her day. Now, Karen thought sadly, these mother-daughter conversations seemed more like daily interrogations. Children seemed to grow up so much sooner in this age of classroom PCs, cable TV, and Super Nintendo.

A shadow suddenly passed over Karen's thoughts like a cloud, eclipsing her musings.

"Allison, you girls didn't say something to frighten Holly, did you?"

Allison dipped her nose back in *Jumanji*—the boy and girl in the story were trying to deal with the veldt lion they had conjured up—but not before she smiled a tiny, secret smile, which Karen happened to glimpse in the rearview mirror.

"No, Mom."

"Blood Mary," Barbara Burke's voice said in her ear three hours later. "Isn't that a horrible name? A *dreadful* name."

Karen gripped the phone tighter and glanced at the clock above the kitchen bar. It was a quarter past seven. Gary had called from work —he wrote software for a marine electronics manufacturer—at 5:30 to say he'd be working late again on some indecipherable project that was overdue. Dinner plates and glasses rattled inside the churning dishwasher; she and Allison had dined alone again. Allison had retreated upstairs to finish her schoolwork in her room, and then the phone had rung. A snakelike coil of dread uncurled in Karen's stomach even before she lifted the receiver and recognized Barbara's voice on the other end.

"Holly was scared half out of her mind," Barbara said. "She could hardly get the words out. I'm still not sure *what* that girl told her—I'm not sure I *want* to know—but someone needs to have a serious talk with her parents—"

"What girl?"

"Well, that's why I called *you*." Barbara's buzzing voice, honed in innumerable PTA meetings, rose a notch. The slight slurring of her words suggested that she might have had a glass or two of wine, not that the spectacle in the schoolyard that afternoon wouldn't warrant it. "Allison was standing right next to her. Red hair and a houndstooth outfit. I didn't recognize her. I started to walk over there, but Holly was . . . hysterical. Allison *must* know her."

"Is Holly all right now?"

There was a steady intake of breath on the other end of the line. "She's asleep, the poor dear. I gave her some liquid Tylenol and tucked her in early. I just hope she doesn't have nightmares."

Karen assured her she would speak with Allison and hung up.

Blood Mary. A grisly name, like something sinister served up across a crackling autumn campfire. Karen left the kitchen and walked toward the stairs. . . .

A fragment of a long, long buried memory made her pause at the bottom of the staircase. Blood Mary? Did the name mean something to her? Some ancient playground game or initiation?

Something about a mirror. Turning. And that fearful name, repeated aloud.

Before it could fully surface the memory sank, grew more opaque, and vanished. The air kicked on and Karen shivered. She couldn't quite remember. She stalked up the stairs, determined to have an earnest talk with Allison.

Twenty minutes later it was Karen who wanted a glassful of wine. A bottle of it. Badly. Gary still hadn't made it home and a headache had begun to tap dully at the back of her skull.

"Honey, I don't care *what* Janice Orcutt says, there are no such things as witches."

"Yes there *are*," Allison said calmly. "Janice showed us a book about them."

"In stories, yes," Karen amended, fighting to keep her temper in check. *Janice Orcutt.* A tall, thin girl with fiery hair, deep-socketed green eyes, and expensive designer clothes.

"*Not* in stories," Allison insisted. "They had witches in olden times. And in America. People did bad things to them if they caught 'em."

Karen's stomach sank as if she were riding a falling elevator car. *Dear lord, what book had that evil little girl shown them?* Karen had taken only a survey course of history in college before meeting and marrying Gary Harmon. She could dimly recall recoiling from fiendish illustrations of the dark underground chambers of the Inquisition; women and men undergoing the rack, pulleys, water torture, and other inhuman engines of torment.

"Did Janice show this . . . book . . . to Holly? Is that what scared her so badly?"

Allison shook her head in disgust. "She wouldn't even *look* at it. She said she didn't believe in witches. She said she didn't believe in Blood Mary."

Karen gripped her daughter's shoulders. "Allison! *Who* is Blood Mary"—she *hated* the way the words tasted on her lips—"and what did Janice say to Holly?"

Allison raised her chin and said without batting an eye, "She said Blood Mary *is* real, and she told Holly how to call her up."

Something about a mirror. Turning as you chant. Something with outstretched hands rising up behind your reflection—

"Why do witches wear name tags?" Gary said nearly an hour later as they sat on the living room couch. His rumpled shirtsleeves were rolled up and he held a sweating bottle of beer. His grin was maddening.

"Give up? So they can tell which witch is which." Gary grinned, then chuckled, then leaned back on their faux-leather sectional couch and *laughed* until his blossoming, thirtysomething beer belly shook underneath his white dress shirt.

Karen blinked in confusion and came within a hair's width of doing something she had never done in eleven years of marriage: slapping her husband as hard as she could.

"Gary, I can't imagine what you think is so funny. Besides spreading God knows what kinds of horror stories to our daughter and her friends, that malicious little *bitch* was terrorizing Barbara Burke's girl."

Gary sat forward, a grin still twitching at the corners of his thin mouth. "Come *on*, Karen. Kids that age are cruel. Honestly, this Blood Mary business is nothing more than a spook story. It's an urban legend."

Karen frowned. Her right palm still itched to erase the smug look off her husband's face.

"*Urban legend*? Since when did you become a pocket sociologist, Gary?"

"Sure it's an urban legend. A myth. A story that gets passed down from generation to generation. The minor details change, but the basic story stays the same through a thousand retellings. Ten thousand. The Hook, the Killer in the Back Seat, Alligators in the Sewers, that sort of thing. You're telling me you never heard any of those?"

"I really don't remember." For a second the cloudy image of that schoolyard memory tried unsuccessfully to re-form in her mind's eye. "The point is, the damned *point* is . . ."

"I'll go talk to her," Gary said, setting his empty bottle on the coasterless coffee table and heaving himself up. "Why don't you pop my dinner in the microwave? This won't take long."

Karen stared at the ring of water seeping out from the beer bottle and kept her jaw clenched shut. Hadn't she once found Gary's self-assured, take-charge mannerisms attractive? Hadn't she?

Karen rose and walked into the kitchen. While she placed two cold pork chops, a dab of stiff mashed potatoes, and a roll onto a microwave-safe plate, she listened to the sound of Gary's footsteps ascending the carpeted stairs. Heard him open Allison's bedroom door. Heard the door shut.

She was removing Gary's steaming plate from the microwave when she heard their voices begin to chant in unison. That was the catalyst that unlocked everything. For a split second the memory Karen had successfully blocked for thirty years unfolded and she was back on that long-ago March recess playground. *(Damp, cool air . . . a hint of excitement and fear as she huddles closer to the other pig-tailed girls . . . a classmate's low, conspiratorial voice whispering that dread name and how to call it up as a dare from some ancient, sacrificial pyre . . .)*

A chilling gust of pure superstitious dread brushed Karen's heart. Gary's plate slipped from her fingers as she turned and ran for the stairs.

Upstairs, the chanting grew louder, and she realized what Gary was doing, how he planned to convince Allison.

Oh my God, the mirror above Allison's vanity!

Karen could see them turning slowly in the darkened room, hands clasped, moonlight sliding across their closed eyes and moving lips. That condescending parental look on Gary's face. *Blood Mary . . . Blood Mary . . . Blood—*

A black shape rising up like smoke from behind them, half-charred arms outstretched, the hands hooked in claws, the wild, rolling eyes gleaming—

Karen reached the first landing when the screams began to slice the air behind the door. She was lunging down the hallway when the rending sounds of butchery began. Something heavy slammed against the door hard enough to make it buckle against its frame. Then there was only the sound a leaky kitchen-sink faucet makes and the quiet sobbing of her daughter.

Karen reached for the doorknob with numb fingers, knowing that opening it would probably blast away what remained of her sanity. She stood panting and swaying for a moment, her hair hanging in her face, and the word she had sought as she watched Janice Orcutt and her freckled disciples track the wailing girl's flight across the schoolyard popped effortlessly into her head.

Coven.

Mobile Home

MICHAEL SKEET

"This one will be big enough," Brad said, holding the rock up so they could all see it. "Find a bunch more like this one, and we can start."

The day was hot, and Tommy could taste it in the dust that made his teeth feel gritty. He sat down on the slope of the huge, flat rock from which they sometimes launched their bicycles on brief flights into space. He did not want to be here; even sitting at home reading a book would be better than this. "Couldn't we play War instead?" he asked. "You could use my Uzi, Brad."

"We can play War later," Brad said. "I want to do this first. Pick up a rock, Tommy. Everybody else is ready."

I hate this game, Tommy thought. He picked up a rock that he knew was too heavy to throw accurately.

"Okay," said Brad, "I've changed the rules a little. You still get the same points for hitting a gopher and for killing it. But now"—he paused, grinning diabolically—"the loser has to spend the night in Old Lady Fedoruk's yard."

A moan went up from the gang. Everyone knew that Mrs. Fedoruk was a witch. She was the old lady who managed the trailer camp, and all of the kids were terrified of her. No one had ever seen her—and lived, anyway.

Tommy hated hurting animals, hated even more the fact that it didn't seem to bother any of his friends—and that Brad even seemed to like it. But he was just as scared of Mrs. Fedoruk as any of the others. He could always run away, of course, and tell his mother. But that wouldn't help him. You couldn't tell grown-ups how scary Mrs. Fedoruk was; they just looked at you like you were mental. Once, Ms. Miller the teacher had caught a bunch of them chasing each other around pretend-

115

ing to be Mrs. Fedoruk, and she'd threatened to make them all take something called Ritalin.

And it wouldn't save him from Brad. Brad, the strongest of them all, unscrewed the tops of two big plastic jugs and began pouring water into a gopher hole. Tommy wished that the gophers would all be away, sunning themselves on rocks far from here, but as soon as he'd wished it, a gopher popped out of a hole right in front of him.

Get away! Tommy screamed inside himself. "There it is!" shouted Brad.

"C'mon, Tommy! Get it!" shouted the gang, rushing toward Tommy, screaming and yelling. Tommy backed up, looking at the gopher and then at the others, wanting to be anywhere but here.

"You *weenie!*" Brad shouted at him, throwing his rock. The stone hit the gopher on its back; the animal rolled in a cloud of dust. The boys shouted, and a flurry of stones poured down as the animal tried to drag itself to safety. Tommy turned away, unable to watch, and began walking back across the empty field toward the line of poplars that marked the boundary of the trailer park.

That night, when the kids from the park gathered in the playground for their nightly game of Rumble, Tommy tried to stay away. But his mom made him go outside, and the sound of kids having fun drew him toward the park in spite of himself. He was just standing on the pathway beside the park when Brad saw him.

"There's our loser!" Brad shouted, and jumped Tommy before he could get away. "Why'd you run away this aft, baby?" Brad asked as Tommy's breath burst from him. "You didn't get to see that gopher's head squashed flat."

Tommy shut his eyes and sucked as much air as he could into his lungs. His voice still came out as a strangled croak. "I think killing gophers is stupid," he said.

"You're a sucky little fag, Oleschuk," Brad said. He hocked up and spat a thick, wet wad into Tommy's ear. The other guys were gathered around them now. Over by the swings, a girl screamed. "Tommy's got a date," Brad chanted. "A date with *Mrs. Fedoruk!*" While Brad held Tommy down, the others tied his hands and legs with jump ropes. Then they picked him up and, jeering, carried him away.

Mrs. Fedoruk lived in a tiny clearing in the middle of a dense stand of trees at the northern edge of the park; the trees were all that was left of a big forest that the other kids said had been here from the time the world began until Mrs. Fedoruk set up the trailer park hundreds of years ago. The trees certainly looked old; and, from Tommy's perspective—bound, on his back and staring up at the darkening sky framed by dark, looming, leaf-clouded branches—they didn't look very friendly, either. The world spun crazily for a second as the gang dumped Tommy onto cool, damp grass. When he looked up, he was alone in Mrs. Fedoruk's yard.

Tommy's mom insisted on calling their house a "modular home," but Mrs. Fedoruk lived in a trailer, plain and simple. It wasn't boxy like most trailers Tommy had seen; it was sort of round and made of shiny metal. It didn't look dangerous, but Tommy was frightened anyway.

Tommy struggled with the ropes that bound him. Fortunately, they hadn't been tied very tightly and he was soon able to work his hands free. The darkness was held at bay by small lights on poles, and Tommy was able to see enough by that light to free his legs as well. He got to his feet—and came face-to-face with the source of the light. Those weren't cheap garden lights on top of the little plastic lampposts around Mrs. Fedoruk's trailer. They were skulls. The light was coming from the holes where the eyes, nose, and mouth should have been. "Mom . . ." he said softly.

"Who's out there?" Tommy had never actually heard Mrs. Fedoruk speak, but that sound could only be her voice. It was the sound of the rusty wheels on his old toy wagon turning. "Tell me who you are," Mrs. Fedoruk said, "or you'll be sorry."

"To—Tommy Oleschuk," Tommy said. "And I'm already sorry."

"What are you doing here?" Mrs. Fedoruk asked.

"They made me come," Tommy said.

"Who made you come? I think you'd better talk to me inside," Mrs. Fedoruk said. *No!* Tommy screamed to himself. If he went into that trailer, he didn't think he'd come out again. Then the door to her trailer opened, seemingly by itself. A strange, lemony-yellow light spilled through the open doorway. "Don't just stand there," Mrs. Fedoruk said. "The mosquitoes are getting in." He shook his head, puzzled. Mrs. Fedoruk's voice had grown softer and sweeter. How did she do that? He wanted to go home, but instead found himself stepping up and into the trailer.

Mrs. Fedoruk's trailer was smaller on the inside than it looked on the outside. Tommy found himself standing in a tiny little kitchen, with barely enough room to turn around in. A pot of some kind of soup simmered on a stove small enough to be part of a pretend-kitchen; the soup smelled wonderful, with spices that tickled his nose. To his right hung a thousand beads on strings, dangling down like a shimmering curtain. From behind the beads, Mrs. Fedoruk's voice told him to come in and sit down.

She was sitting at a small table. Looking at her, Tommy was astonished: Mrs. Fedoruk looked younger than his mom, and prettier even than Wayne Grace's older sister Betty. Her eyes were bright green, with thick lashes and thin, curved brows. Her hair was the colour of new pennies. Her teeth, when she smiled, were whiter than fresh snow. Mrs. Fedoruk let him stare for a minute, then laughed lightly and told him to sit down. "Would you like some tea?" she asked. Tommy nodded.

A second later, a cup of hot, sweet tea was steaming in front of him. Tommy was not aware of Mrs. Fedoruk's having left her chair. "Now, then," she said. "Suppose you tell me how you came to be here."

The story of the day's events burst out of him. By the time he had finished the telling, he was weeping hot tears of anger and shame. "I wish I could leave this stupid trailer park," he said, snuffling. "Or that Brad would."

Mrs. Fedoruk handed him a tissue. "Do you mean you wish that Brad was dead?" she asked as he blew his nose.

Tommy was startled. He was pretty sure he hated Brad, but . . . "No," he said. "He's a creep, but—no."

"You have to wish it," Mrs. Fedoruk said softly, "before I can do anything to help you."

Tommy didn't recall asking her for help. "I don't want to kill him," Tommy said.

"Very well," Mrs. Fedoruk said. "You have no real grievance against this boy, then. But I may." She leaned forward, and stared Tommy straight in the eye. There was something orange and swirling, like fire, in the centres of her eyes. "You say this Brad kills gophers. Does he like to kill other animals, too?" Tommy squirmed in his seat, unable to get away from her eyes. "Does he kill cats, too?"

Tommy couldn't breathe. He twisted in the seat, trying to get away, but movement was impossible. He would have to open his mouth to breathe, and when he opened his mouth the words would come out. "He killed a black cat," Tommy gasped. "A week ago." He gulped more air into his lungs. "He showed us the body. He made me look at it. I threw up." He was crying again. Without touching him, Mrs. Fedoruk was hurting him.

Suddenly he could look away from her eyes, and the pain began to subside. "I didn't do anything," he cried. "It's not my fault."

"Of course not," Mrs. Fedoruk said. Her voice was sharpening, returning to the rusty sounds she had first made. "You don't have to worry, but with Bradley Hinton I have a bone to pick. Maybe it'll be one of his own." She laughed, and Tommy was horrified to realize that her teeth were no longer snow-white and even. Now they came to jagged points, and they were as shiny and metallic as the outside of her trailer.

"What are you?" Tommy stuttered. Mrs. Fedoruk's face, without actually changing, had become all angles and sharp edges. Her eyes— he could not make himself look at her eyes anymore.

"I'm just a cat-lover who doesn't like to see small animals being tortured and killed," Mrs. Fedoruk said. "You may not wish any harm to come to that loathsome boy, but if he isn't taught a lesson, he's going to continue torturing the helpless. Today it's gophers and cats. Tomorrow— well, you might not want to think too much about tomorrow. Do you understand me?"

Tommy nodded. Then his eyes were drawn to his teacup: the rust-coloured liquid was sloshing back and forth against the stained china. He looked out the window: The stars were gently bobbing up and down. They were moving.

"What are you doing?" he cried. "I want to go home. I want to go home now!"

"If you're a good boy and don't make too much of a fuss, you can go home when I'm finished," Mrs. Fedoruk said. "For now, keep quiet and see what happens to boys who pick on the weak."

Mrs. Fedoruk poured some tea from her cup onto the table in front of her, shaping the liquid with her finger into a rough circle. Then she passed her open hands, palms down, over the tea while muttering to herself. The circle of liquid began to glow and shimmer, and suddenly Tommy could see a tiny picture of Brad, standing in the field outside the trailer park where the gopher-killing had happened. The picture was all bent and shivery, so that it was less like watching Brad on TV and more like seeing him in a nightmare. Tommy was sure now that everything that he had heard about Mrs. Fedoruk was true; he was never going to disbelieve anything the other kids told him, ever again. If there was an ever again.

119

"I see you, brat," Mrs. Fedoruk said, peering down at the circle of tea. "Time to learn your lesson." The trailer was now bobbing more vigorously, the stars dancing past. Then the trailer stopped moving and Mrs. Fedoruk got out of her chair. "You stay here," she said to Tommy. "If I see you outside, I'll teach you a lesson, too."

Tommy was so frightened his teeth were chattering, but nothing Mrs. Fedoruk could say was going to make him stay in this trailer. He was convinced that he was going to end up inside the tiny oven as soon as Mrs. Fedoruk had finished doing whatever awful thing she was going to do to Brad, and he didn't intend to give her the opportunity if he could avoid it. He knew the field the trailer was in, knew from countless summer days spent running back and forth between here and the trailer park just exactly how long it would take him to reach the safety of home. When Mrs. Fedoruk closed the door behind her, Tommy counted to ten. Then he made himself count again, just to be safe, before carefully turning the handle on the trailer door. He looked around; Mrs. Fedoruk had vanished, and if he couldn't see her then there was a chance she couldn't see him. He jumped down from the trailer; it was further off the ground than he remembered it, and he stumbled when he hit the ground.

The moon was fat and orange, hovering just above the trees. He ran toward it as quietly as he could: home was just beyond those trees. Then a thin, terrified scream from behind brought him to a halt. He turned around.

In the pale light cast by the moon, Tommy could see almost as clearly as if it had been morning. Beyond the trailer, Mrs. Fedoruk stood over Brad, who lay screaming on the ground. Hovering high over his head was the big rock they used as a bicycle launch ramp. Mrs. Fedoruk's magic had pulled it from the ground and lifted it up high. Tommy suddenly knew what lesson she planned to teach Brad.

Before he realized what he was doing, he was running, not homeward, but back toward Mrs. Fedoruk. *This is crazy*, he thought when he was finally capable of thought; he did not stop running.

Then he looked at the trailer again. Where wheels had been earlier in the evening, the trailer now stood on two gigantic chicken legs. It should have seemed funny, but the feet were tipped by gigantic claws and Tommy didn't feel like laughing. The picture was made even worse by the *way* the trailer stood: it tilted down at the front and a little to one side, as if it was watching Mrs. Fedoruk and listening carefully to Brad's screams. Tommy continued to run until Mrs. Fedoruk saw him. Her green eyes glowed with amber fire that stopped Tommy so abruptly his head snapped backwards. "I told you to stay in the trailer," she said in a voice like a railroad train.

"You can't do this," Tommy cried. Now the trailer turned to look at him. He hadn't had the courage this afternoon to save the gopher; somehow, he had to find that courage tonight, even if it was only for Brad.

"Why can't I do this?" Mrs. Fedoruk asked. She smiled her cruel metal smile. "He has offended me, and offended nature. Besides, I have the power to deal with him. Are you going to stop me?" The air seemed to crackle with danger, the way it felt just before Tommy touched a metal doorknob on a dry winter day.

"I can't stop you," Tommy whispered. "And your cat and that gopher couldn't stop Brad, either. He had power over them, didn't he?"

Mrs. Fedoruk stared at Tommy for the longest second of his life. Then the fire in her eyes died down, and the cool night breeze began to tickle his neck as the magic in the air leaked away. "Congratulations," she said to him. "You've learned something tonight after all." She gestured with her fingers and the giant stone fell back into its place in the ground, silent as snow coming down.

Then she turned back to Brad. "This boy still has to learn his lesson, though. What can I do to teach him to respect all of nature's creatures—and most of all, not to anger a witch?"

From his hiding place at the edge of the clearing, Tommy watched as Mrs. Fedoruk's trailer returned to its daytime resting place. It was a week after his late-night ride with Mrs. Fedoruk, who had turned out to be a very active witch; in that time, Tommy had seen the trailer either leave the park to walk the countryside or returning home from such a journey at least three times.

Nobody but he seemed to have noticed what had happened to Brad, but Tommy was pretty sure that that was more of Mrs. Fedoruk's doing. And she had said that it wouldn't last forever, so Tommy had taken it on himself to look after Brad, and bring him to the clearing whenever there was a chance of seeing Mrs. Fedoruk, in the hope that she'd relent sooner rather than later.

The trailer found what must have been the right spot, because it shivered just a little bit before scratching a couple of times at the dirt and settling itself back down to being a regular trailer again. "Wow," Tommy breathed.

The lid of the shoebox beside him popped up, and a gopher emerged to wrinkle its nose in distaste. "Well, I don't care what you think, Brad," Tommy said to the animal. "I think it's a cool way to move around."

Of Time and Space

HUGH B. CAVE

I'll be downstairs if you need me," Victor Dalbin said to his wife that Sunday afternoon in the living room of their New England home. "I want to look at those photos Dan sent."

"All right."

"Well, you're reading."

She glanced up from her book and moved her pretty shoulders in a shrug. "Is there some reason why I shouldn't be?"

Victor shrugged in reply. He had glanced at the book's dust jacket earlier, while she was doing the dishes after the noon meal. It was another novel of the kind she seemed to find so compelling lately, aimed at relieving the boredom of love-starved women. With no further comment other than a glance of contempt, he left her sitting there and went down to his basement study.

The photographs he had mentioned had been in the house a week now, and were still in the carton in which his younger brother, Dan, had mailed them from Florida. On the phone before their arrival Dan had said simply, "You're in a lot of them, so I thought you'd like to have them. I'm moving to a smaller apartment and won't have room for them. Okay?"

"Well, sure, if you say so. Thanks."

"Have fun with them," Dan said, and hung up.

Opening the box now, Victor lifted the first of the heavy albums onto his desk. There were three and they were numbered. He might as well begin at the beginning.

Photography had been Dan's hobby since his college days, when he had paid most of his school expenses with his cameras. All these pictures had been taken by him, developed by him, printed by him. Most were black-and-white eight-by-tens.

They were put in with some kind of adhesive, Victor discovered now when he lifted an overlay of plastic and tried to straighten one that was a trifle crooked. As an engineer he was a stickler for having things precise, which was one of the many things he and Anne often quarreled about. She, for God's sake, had even wanted to hang a primitive painting that dear brother Dan had bought in Haiti while doing a picture story of that Caribbean country for some magazine and given them for a wedding present.

Well, anyway . . .

The first half-dozen photos were of himself, marching with his trombone in the college band. Handsome Victor Dalbin in a blue and white uniform, taller than most of the others, proudly strutting and enjoying it. Then there was a shot (he remembered this one, taken with a self-timer that enabled the photographer himself to get into the picture) of the two of them, him and Danny, with their arms around each other on the pier at the college lake. Dad had been a professor then at the same college.

The next dozen photos were of himself and Dan and Anne, when Anne and Danny had been sophs and he, Victor, a senior. Again taken with a self-timer, these showed the three of them on the beach at Narragansett Pier—what a beauty Anne was in that bikini!—but as he looked at them more closely, they began to blur.

He shook his head and rubbed his eyes with the heels of his hands because for the past week his vision had been doing this: misting over, blurring, worrying him with little floating black specks when he tried to concentrate on any kind of fine print. Then he got a very real, wholly alive feeling that he and Anne and Danny were actually there—there at Narragansett—and the time was now, right now, this minute.

"Hey," Danny said. "Are we going to swim or just stand here looking stupid in front of a camera on a tripod with nobody behind it?"

"Why don't we get dressed, and eat, and then head for the Casino?" Victor said. He never had been the swimmer Dan was, but he could dance like a fool, and that was one thing Dan couldn't do. Dan had inherited two left feet from Dad while Victor took after Mom, who had been a professional dancer at one point in her life.

So he, Danny, and Anne had gone to the Casino that evening, dancing—because Anne loved to dance almost as much as she loved

Danny—and that was when he had first got the idea of taking her away from Danny. Dancing with her that evening, he'd sown the first seeds in her mind, how she really deserved someone better. Then a month or so later when the three of them and a second girl, his date, had gone up to Lake Pearl in Wrentham to dance, he had sensed a little flame there and taken step number two.

The orchestra that night was somebody special—Claude Hopkins and his great little gang, with Claude at the piano and Orlando Robeson singing those high tenor vocals. Yes, it was Hopkins, because he, Victor, had used the words of their theme song, "I Would Do Anything for You," to lead into what he wanted to tell her. And what he told her was that she and Danny would never be right for each other; they were too different in every way; but he, Victor, was going places and would make her happy.

"I love you, Anne," he told her that night while holding her in his arms on the dance floor. "We've got a real problem here, and we've got to work it out. Start thinking about it, will you?"

Well, it went on and on. He and whatever girl he happened to be dating at the moment would go out with Anne and Danny, and whenever he and Anne danced together or were able to get off by themselves for a few minutes, he kept up the pressure. "Anne, you can't throw your life away just because he's my brother. You have to think of *your* future and *mine.*"

He meant it too. Maybe his first stab at taking her away from Dan had just been for the hell of it, to see if he could do it, but the more he kept at it, the more convinced he became that he actually had to have her.

So she gradually cooled it with Danny, though still dating him now and then so as to let him down gently. Then when Victor got his degree and went to work for an engineering firm in Providence, she told Dan the facts of life. And Dan confronted him.

He was reliving that scene this minute, this very minute, even though physically he was seated at the desk in his basement study poring over an album of photographs.

It was a Saturday evening. He and Dan were still living at home, but the folks had gone to a show in Boston. Danny was out with Anne. He, Victor, sat at the dining room table, doing some work brought home from the office.

The front door opened so quietly he would not have known it

opened but for the sudden intrusion of wind that fluttered his papers. It closed the same way. He might have heard footsteps or he might not. He did sense a presence behind him and swung about on his chair.

Motionless, but with a strange burning in his eyes, brother Danny stood there gazing at him.

For a long ten seconds neither spoke. Then Danny said in a terribly calm, low voice, "You knew she meant everything in the world to me. Still you did it."

"Danny, it wasn't anything *I* did. She fell in love with me, that's all."

"Are you going to marry her?"

"Of course I'm going to marry her! What do you think I am?"

"I don't know. Perhaps it's too early to tell. But I'll find out, brother. Be sure of that. I'll find out." Turning on his heel, Danny went slowly to his room and shut the door.

With the door's closing, the scene faded from the mist of Victor Dalbin's memory. Once more he was in the present, seated at his desk in his study, with an album of photos open under his hands and his wife Anne upstairs struggling to lose herself in a book.

Album number two, which Victor looked at a few nights later, contained pictures of the wedding. Returning from a second photo trip to Haiti in time to attend, Dan had asked if they would like a photographic record of the event, and Anne was delighted. As before, Victor experienced a blurring of his vision while looking at the pictures.

He should see an eye doctor, he supposed. Probably he had been using his eyes too much at work. That the trouble had not begun until the photographs arrived from Miami was only coincidental, of course. How could there be a connection?

He was alone in the house this Wednesday evening. Anne had gone to her mother's and, if the visit followed the usual pattern, would not be back until eleven or so. It was now nine. Wanting to watch a program on TV at ten, he had carried album number two up from the study and was seated with it on the living room sofa.

Pictures of the wedding, yes. And the reception, of course. Danny had done a terrific job, as usual. Some of them Victor had seen before, for Danny had mounted the best ones in a wedding book for Anne. Where was that book now, by the way? Anne must have put it away somewhere. Or had she thrown it away?

Not too interested in such pictures, even in those he hadn't seen before, Victor went through them indifferently. But the blurring of his vision worsened even so, and suddenly, on coming to a photo of Danny's wedding present—this one in color—he again felt he had slipped out of the present into the past.

He was, in short, looking at the painting itself, not at a photograph of it. And as he stared at it in disbelief, he could have sworn he was hearing things.

Yes, hearing things.

The scene was a Haitian peasant yard at night. Crooked poles held up a roof of old, ragged thatch. Lanterns suspended under the thatch cast an eerie yellow glow over a handful of people seated there on crude, homemade chairs. The creature before whom they sat, and at whom they stared as though hypnotized, was an old woman in a black dress seated on a somewhat larger chair that had flat wooden arms. A *very* old woman with a face impossibly full of wrinkles. On her lap she held a small white goat, cradling it in one bony arm. Her other hand held a long, gleaming knife.

In the background a man in blue denim pants, otherwise naked, crouched over a drum. And the picture had a title, "The Sorceress," lettered in English above the name of the primitive artist who obviously had created it to sell to tourists.

And he, Victor Dalbin, was there. He has hearing the throb of the drum and the murmuring of the assembled people. He could even hear the bleating of the goat that was seemingly about to be sacrificed.

Something fell from his face onto the photograph, and it was a drop of his own sweat. He realized he was trembling uncontrollably. In near panic he turned the page in an effort to break the spell. Then his eyes stopped playing their tricks and the blurring of his vision ceased, and he felt he had snatched himself back from something too real and frightening to be dismissed as a mere illusion.

He was still seated on the sofa when Anne returned. He had not watched the TV program after all, but was simply staring into space with the album on his knees.

"Is something wrong?" Anne asked. Standing there before him, she was still a beautiful woman despite the sadness that was almost always to be seen on her face now. One of these days, Victor supposed, she would want a divorce.

126

"Where is that Haitian painting Dan gave us when we were married?" he demanded.

"In the attic. Why?"

"I just wondered."

"Have you finally decided we ought to hang it somewhere?"

"God, no!"

"I wish you would. Miss Perkins, at the library, told me some of those Haitian primitive artists are famous."

"I don't want to talk about it," Victor snapped. And after returning the album to his study, he went to his bedroom. But two evenings later, when Anne left him alone again for a while, he retrieved the painting from the attic, took it to the trash-burner in the backyard, and set fire to it.

Soon after the wedding, Danny had gone to Miami to work as a photographer on a newspaper. A note in album three said that the first dozen pictures therein were some he had taken for a feature story about that section of the city known as Little Haiti.

"Hope you find them interesting," the note said.

"Why should I?" Victor muttered.

He was in his basement study again, wondering why he even wanted to look at the pictures in this last album. He did want to, though. He felt he was committed to an unpleasant or even dangerous task that he must finish before he could be free again. This evening, a week after his burning the witch-woman painting, he would shut the final door. Anne was in her room, writing letters.

So all right, these were pictures taken in a Miami slum occupied by refugees from a land of sorcery and witchcraft. He was definitely not interested. Yet when he started looking at them he found himself *there*. Not here in his study but there in Little Haiti, in a shabby room filled with a sound of drumming. Another witchcraft session, apparently.

Frightened, he squeezed his eyes shut in hope of causing the scene to vanish.

It didn't.

There was a black-garbed sorceress again, with a goat on her knees and a knife in her hand. And two drummers this time. And in the light of a single bare bulb that hung from the ceiling, half a dozen seated people stared at the sorceress as though mesmerized.

But wait. Something else was happening this time. A white man

127

had entered the room from a doorway behind the seated witch-woman and was approaching her. He was falling to his knees in front of her, with his back to her, and bending backward so that his head took the place of the goat on her lap. The goat, displaced, leaped to the floor and slowly walked away. Wide-eyed, the man gazed up at the woman in seeming helplessness as she leaned over him with the knife upraised.

The man was himself, Victor Dalbin.

"Oh my God," Victor moaned. *"Why?"*

Then the scene began to dissolve. The light dimmed and went out. The players in the drama disappeared in darkness. Victor, the real Victor, realized with a moan of relief that he was back at his desk, merely looking at an album of photographs.

Recovering, he savagely cursed the album and the brother who had sent it to him. Now, of course, he understood what was behind the gift. And to hell with it. He would look at the few remaining photos—because if he didn't he would never know peace of mind again—and then burn all three albums and be free.

There was only one more picture, he discovered to his surprise. On the next to last page, it was a photo of a coffin. Nothing more—just a plain wooden coffin with a closed lid.

But as he fought, quaking with terror, against the dreaded mist that now began to warp his vision again, he saw that Danny had written something on the book's final page. And as he began still another journey through time and space, he saw what it was.

"Goodbye, Victor. Pleasant dreams."

A Matter of Honor

R. K. PARTAIN

Albert knew something was wrong the moment he noticed his feet had been turned into green flappers. He released a long sigh and elbowed his wife, Marilyn, who lay sleeping like a baby next to him.

"Wha . . . ?" she mumbled.

"Your mother's been fooling around again. Look what she did!"

Marilyn didn't bother to turn and look at his newest addition. "She'll fix it back. She always does, you know. Now go back to sleep."

Yeah, that was easy for her to say. She wasn't the one who had frog feet this morning. He swung his legs over the side of the bed and stood up. Oh, this is just peachy, he thought, as he stared at the huge webbed toes and slimy flesh that were now his sole means of locomotion.

Marilyn rolled over and cracked open sleepy eyes. She peeked over the side of the bed and looked at his green feet. "Oh, god," she muttered, but not nearly as loud as the occasion warranted. He, on the other hand, felt like screaming. "You shouldn't have called her a wicked old witch, Al. You know she hates it when you do that." Marilyn glanced up at him, her eyes narrowed with suspicion. "And I'm not sure you said 'witch' and not bit—"

"I was joking with her! How come she can't take a joke?"

"How come you have to keep on taunting her?" Marilyn flopped back on the mattress and covered her face with an arm. "I wish you two could get along."

Albert took a few steps around the bedroom. It was like walking with scuba flippers on his feet. "Can't you do something about this?" he whined.

"I can turn the rest of you into a frog to match it, if you like. But, otherwise, no. You know the rules. I can't break another witch's spell."

"Well, I've had all I can take," Albert said, pressing his hands on his hips in defiance. "You get her over here and make her fix me. And I mean right now." He turned too quickly, one pancake-shaped foot trapping the other, and fell headlong toward the hardwood floor. In a split second, he saw Marilyn move her hands in one of her secret glyphs, and his fall stopped abruptly. As if invisible hands had come to his rescue, he hung in midair at an impossible angle. "Thank you," he said with more dignity than he felt as she magically stood him back up. "I'm going to the shower. When I get out, I expect Ann Marie to be here." With head held high, he left the bedroom, and flip-flopped down the hall.

Albert learned long ago to never get into the shower before turning on the spigots and examining what came out of them. To date, he'd been washed with sand, blood, worms, and motor oil. Today, it looked like water.

Relieved that something was going his way, he pulled down his cotton pajama bottoms and nearly crashed into the tub when his big, rubbery feet refused to go through the small openings at the cuffs. Stumbling and muttering, he hopped over to the toilet and sat down.

"Count to ten," he told himself.

He counted to ten and, then, using both hands, he grabbed the material and tore it to shreds.

For ten years now he had put up with this crap. Ten looong years, and still he could not—would not—bring himself to leave Marilyn. That's what Ann Marie wanted. Albert had known from the very beginning that his mother-in-law hated his guts, but he'd be damned if he would cave in to her wishes. Besides, he just so happened to love Marilyn, and from where he came from—which was not some boiling cauldron of snake parts, which was surely where Ann Marie had been spawned—that meant something. No, Ann Marie would have to do a lot more than this to get him to leave Marilyn.

Albert tossed the ruined pajama bottoms into the corner and padded to the tub. Holding on to the wall, he slapped one ugly foot into the tub and then the other. He drew the plastic curtain shut and lifted his face to the hot, steamy water. A few moments later, he felt the water level rising up to his ankles. He glanced down. His frog feet covered the drain.

It's going to be one of those days, he thought sullenly.

"You really should mind what you say about me," Ann Marie said as she flung the curtain open.

Albert yelped, startled by her sudden appearance. He tried to cover himself. "What the hell are you doing in here?"

Ann Marie smiled at him. Albert had no idea how old Ann Marie was. Marilyn was 117 years old, but looked as if she were in her early thirties; Ann Marie, who looked to be in her late fifties, must certainly be older than dirt.

"You sent for me, Albert. Or has that little mind of yours forgotten about that?"

Albert tried to gain some composure. "Would you please leave? We can talk when I'm finished."

"First you want me, then you don't. I wish you'd make up your mind." Ann Marie's gaze traveled down his body, lingering too long at the spot he was trying desperately to conceal. "I can fix that," she said, pointing to his manhood. "Make it bigger. More manly, so to speak."

Albert actually found himself considering her offer. He shook his head. "No! Thank you."

Ann Marie shrugged lightly. "As you wish." She whirled around to gaze in the mirror above the sink. The long red robe she wore swirled in her wake. Albert snatched a towel from the hook next to the tub and wrapped himself in it. "I want my feet back," he said as he turned off the water and stepped out of the tub and sat on the rim.

"Say you're sorry," she cooed.

"I will not. If anyone owes apologies here, it's you."

"I hardly think so," she replied.

Albert knew from long experience that this sort of sparring could go on for hours. He didn't have the energy for it today. Perhaps her incessant torments really were getting to him. Just last week he'd lost his job when, unbeknownst to him, she had written "Kiss My Butt" on his forehead. Most of his co-workers at the bank had thought it rather funny. Jeffrey Perkins, the bank president, had seen absolutely no humor at all in the little message. Perkins had given Albert five minutes to "get that filth" off his head; Albert had nearly rubbed a hole in his skull, but the letters remained intact. Four years at the bank, down the drain.

And now he had frog feet.

"All right, Ann Marie. I know it bothers you that your daughter married a mere mortal. I suppose if I were a wizard or a warlock or whatever it is you call worthy males, I wouldn't have to go through all this craziness. So why don't you just tell me how we can come to an agreement?"

She glanced down at him, and he thought he saw something like respect on her face. "An agreement?" she asked.

He nodded slowly. "Yes. Tell me what I can do and I'll do it."

"Well, now that you mention it, there is something."

"What?"

"In the old days, when a man wanted to wed a woman he had to prove himself. It was such a romantic time, Albert." Her eyes sort of glassed over as if she were remembering some far-off memory. "Oh, the men back then. So strong and brave. I can't tell you how many of them came back maimed and mauled. It was wonderful."

"Maimed and mauled?" He didn't like the sound of this.

Ann Marie smiled and nodded. "Only those that came back."

"And the others? The ones who didn't come back?"

"Oh, they were killed. But killed with such honor."

Albert shook his head. "I don't like this."

"What? Wouldn't you fight for your wife?"

"Of course, I would. That's not what I meant."

"So you would fight for her?"

"Yes, I said that already! But not . . ."

"That's all I wanted to hear."

The next thing Albert knew he was gone.

"Damnit, Ann Marie!" he shouted as he tumbled into what looked like a cave filled with fog. It was dark and cold and the ground that met him was hard and rocky. He made it to his feet and looked around. He was in a large cavern, rough-hewn walls of stone ran the length of the place. A dim red light filtered out from a hole in the rock, some twenty feet ahead of him. Wishing she had at least given him some clothes to wear, Albert started toward the light, mindful of where he put his feet, which were still as big as gunboats.

Albert peeked into the room and then slowly withdrew his head. He was a dead man, of that he was certain.

"No sense hiding in the hall, young sire," a loud, booming voice said from within the chamber. "Enter and let us have a look at you."

There was nowhere to run, and with feet as big as couch cushions, he wasn't sure he *could* run. Swallowing hard, he stepped into the room.

A giant sat upon a wooden throne. The man had to be eight feet tall, and was as broad as the front end of a car. A long gray beard hung down over his barrel chest, which was covered in a brown leather vest. His hands were the size of picnic hams, and when he smiled, Albert saw the man had all of three teeth, none of which were close neighbors.

"Hello." Albert realized as soon as he'd said it that it sounded more like a squeal than a word.

The monster-man glared down at him. His bushy eyebrows furrowed as if he were wondering what manner of creature stood in front of him. Suddenly, the giant cleared his throat. "It has been a long time since someone has come to fight for the hand of a fair maiden. I have fought thousands of men. Bested many of them. But never, in all my long years, have I seen anything as pitiful as you. What is your name?"

"Albert."

"Albert." The giant nodded slowly. "That is a fine name. Tell me, Albert, what demon have you insulted to earn such hideous feet?"

"My mother-in-law."

"Mother-in-law? Methinks you are in the wrong place, Albert. The Battle of Honor is to take place *before* you take the maiden's hand. Not afterwards."

"Yes, sir. I understand that. But you see, my mother-in-law is a witch and she's sort of old-fashioned and, well, to make a long story short, I didn't know about this little battle thingie until just a few minutes ago."

"Judging from your lack of attire, I must think you were eager to get here."

"Well, no. Not really. I was having a shower when she sent me here."

The giant's eyes narrowed as he scratched his rough cheek. "This is some mother-in-law you have, Albert. What did she tell you you were supposed to do here?"

Albert shrugged and shook his head. "I guess, from what I've heard, and I'm no expert on this, believe me, I'm supposed to kill you or something. Or you'll kill me, which, I'm sure, would please her to no end."

"Yes," the giant said slowly. "That's the usual routine. Mayhap I am mistaken, but I do not see that you carry a weapon. How would you battle me when you have no weapon?"

Hmmmm, now that was a good question. Albert gave it some thought and decided to say the only thing that came to his mind. "Could I borrow yours?"

The giant roared with laughter. "I think not. Tell me, young warrior, what sort of things has this wicked woman done to you?"

"You name it, and she's probably done it. Once she turned my ears into nickels. Then there was the time she locked the doors on my car and filled it up with snakes. That wouldn't have been too bad, except I was in it at the time, and driving down the interstate. She put a wild boar in my closet once. And there was that time she made my elbows disappear. You ever try eating without elbows?"

The giant acknowledged that he had not.

"Well, it's impossible!"

"Young Albert, far be it for me to tell you your business, but are you sure you want to go back to this torment?"

"Yes! I love my wife. If her mother would just leave us alone, we'd be happy."

"I was only asking," the giant said patiently. "There is a way for you not to return."

"I know. She told me about those who don't come back from here."

"Yes, well, women have often imagined things that are not so. Did this woman tell you where these brave men go?"

"No. I just assumed that you killed them."

"That is what we like the women to think."

"I don't get it."

"Many a fine young man has come to me with stories much like yours, in that their future mothers-in-law were terrors far too wicked to be endured until the customary 'death do us part.' Most of these men were the victims of arranged marriages. I don't see much of that anymore, but that is beside the point. The point is, these men needed an escape. A way of saving themselves from a lifetime of horror, while at the same time upholding the honor of their families. Tricky business, this honor thing. Anyway, I offer them the chance to leave their fate behind and start over in some new place."

Albert smiled widely. "No kidding?"

"No kidding."

"But I don't want to vanish. I want to be with my wife. How can I do that?"

"You must take home the Sword of Honor."

"And how do I do that?"

The giant's voice deepened. "You must take it from me, for I am the rightful owner of it."

"I was afraid you'd say that," Albert replied. This was awful. The giant wasn't such a bad fellow and Albert had no desire to harm the man, if, indeed, he even got close enough to harm him.

"Do you want to take the sword?" the giant asked.

"I guess so."

"Then go get one," the giant said and pointed toward a far corner.

Albert looked to where the man pointed and saw a huge stash of swords leaning against the wall.

His mouth dropped open. "You mean I can just take one and that's it?"

"That's it. It's rather idiotic for two men to hack each other up over a woman, is it not?"

"Yeah, you can say that again."

"I'm glad you agree. I'd hate to cut you into little pieces."

Albert grinned. "I'd hate that, too." He hurried over to the corner and picked out one of the long swords. It was heavy and cold and sent shivers down his naked spine.

"Thank you," Albert said.

The giant stood up and came toward him. "My pleasure. There is one small detail we have to conclude before you can leave, my friend."

"What's that?"

"I have to beat you up a little so it looks as if we fought."

The next thing he saw was a fist the size of a tree stump coming for his head.

"Albert! Albert! Wake up!"

Albert opened sore eyes and saw Marilyn kneeling over his prone body. Ann Marie stood behind Marilyn, a frown etched across her thin lips.

"Whahappend?" He tried to sit up, but Marilyn pushed him back to the floor.

"You beat the giant!" she said, her eyes glowing with admiration. "God, I love you." She wrapped her arms around him and nearly crushed his ribs as she hugged him.

"I guess you're a better man than I thought," Ann Marie said.

"What about our deal?" he asked.

Ann Marie glanced down at the sword lying at his side. "You win." And with that she waved her hands in some complex fashion and vanished.

"You didn't have to do that," Marilyn said. "You never have to prove that you love me, Albert. I *know* you do."

Albert was pleased to hear that, but even more pleased to see that his frog feet were gone. "I guess we know who's the man of this house now, don't we?"

Marilyn kissed his mouth, ravished it, in fact. "Oh, yes."

Albert sighed deeply, thinking this hero stuff wasn't half bad.

Hair Apparent

Don D'Ammassa

Melanie read the framed certificate for the fourth time since seating herself in Madame Estelle's waiting room:

ESTELLE BARON IS DULY CERTIFIED
TO PRACTICE WITCHCRAFT IN ACCORDANCE WITH
ALL LOCAL LAWS AND REGULATIONS.

It bore the imprimatur of the American Wiccan Association.

"It'll be all right," she whispered to herself. "She's a professional. It's just like going to a doctor."

Indeed, it had been her regular physician, Dr. Chalmers, who had sent her here.

"I've made an appointment for you with a specialist, Ms. Rule. I've referred several other patients to her in the past and they've all been completely satisfied."

But a witch? Melanie shook her head. She knew intellectually that the AWA had scientifically proven the efficacy of its treatment, but it had always seemed remote and inapplicable to herself, like acupuncture.

She grabbed a magazine from the table, paged past an editorial condemning the life insurance industry's adamant refusal to pay for the lifting of curses. A sidebar proclaimed in bold print that "the contention that curses are criminal acts and therefore not health issues is specious at best."

"Ms. Rule?"

Melanie glanced up. The apprentice who had taken her name when she first arrived had returned. A patch bearing a pair of stylized snakes coiled around a broomstick was sewed on one shoulder and over the breast pocket.

"Yes?"

"Madame Estelle will see you now. This way please."

The moment had come. Melanie felt a sudden thrust of nausea, suppressed it. She needed help, after all, and this might be the only place she could get it.

"So what seems to be the problem?"

Madame Estelle was not at all what Melanie had expected. No exotic clothing, for example. She wore a tailored business suit and her pepper-gray hair was neat and attractive. The office could have been that of a lawyer if it hadn't been for the crystal ball bookends, the elaborate zodiac tapestry adorning one wall, and the beautifully constructed replica of Stonehenge set in a glass case beside the desk.

Melanie tried to speak, couldn't get the words out.

"Your first time seeing a Wiccan?" Madame Estelle smiled and turned away, giving Melanie time to recover her composure. "I imagine I'm not at all what you expected, either. Hollywood still insists on the old familiar caricature despite the efforts of the Wiccan Defense League."

"I'm sorry. I didn't mean to be rude. Dr. Chalmers referred me to you because he couldn't find a physical cause for my illness and it's clearly not psychosomatic."

"And just what exactly is wrong with you?" Melanie hesitated and Madame Estelle made an impatient sound. "Out with it, girl. I don't read minds, you know. Not my specialty."

With a conscious effort to keep her voice level, Melanie explained her problem. "My hair won't stop growing. I mean, it won't grow at a normal rate. Two or three inches a day, usually, sometimes even more."

The witch raised her eyebrows but her expression was otherwise neutral. "An unusual curse, if that's what it is. Some might find it a blessing."

Melanie shook her head vigorously. "Surely you know how long it takes to wash and dry that much hair. And I can't afford to see the hairdresser every three or four days. Can you help me?"

Madame Estelle nodded. "I think so. But first we'll need to do some tests. My apprentice will take an auragram and we'll need an ectoplasmic sample for testing." She paused thoughtfully. "And I'll want you to give some thought to what might have happened in the weeks preceding the onset of this condition. Any change in your living habits, new job, new lover, new enemies, that sort of thing. The curse is a symptom, you realize? The root cause must be addressed or you'll simply find yourself with a new disorder, hives, a wen, or something even less pleasant."

"I can't imagine . . ."

Madame Estelle raised a hand. "Don't think about it just now. You'll need to be calm for the auragram."

Melanie left the office in a state of some confusion. On the one hand, the brisk professional manner with which she'd been treated was reassuring, as was Madame Estelle's evident self-confidence. On the other hand, neither having her picture taken with a peculiar-looking camera using a blacklight flashbulb nor watching the apprentice painlessly sample a wispy white substance that seemed to seep from the palm of Melanie's hand had seemed quite normal.

But neither was waking up with hair down to her shoulder blades every morning.

She reached into her pocket, checked to be certain the small pamphlet was still there. Madame Estelle had handed it to her just before she'd left the office.

"It's a book of charms," she'd explained. "Just before bed I want you to chant three mantras, and call me in the morning."

Melanie spent the evening lying on her couch, trying to think of anyone she might have annoyed recently. The curse had only been active for four weeks, and little in her life had changed in the period immediately preceding. She'd finished the preliminary engineering for the new distillation column at Vesuvius Chemical, but that was only one of several routine projects she'd been dealing with for months. There'd been no arguments, her staff seemed happy, and there hadn't been anyserious rivalries at the firm in over a year.

There was a new CAD operator, Peter Reynolds, unusually shy but friendly. At first she'd thought he was interested in Carla, the purchasing manager, but now she was pretty certain he was working up his courage to ask her out instead, and Melanie had already decided to say yes. But she hadn't rejected him and couldn't believe he bore her any malice.

"This is ridiculous." She tossed aside the legal pad on which she'd been making notes. "I'm not mad at anyone and I can't imagine why anyone would be mad at me."

But in the morning, her hair had grown another four inches.

"The results of your tests were quite interesting. Could you come in to see me this afternoon at, say, three o'clock?"

Melanie nodded, then spoke aloud into the phone. "Sure, I'll be there. Thank you, Madame Estelle." So far, no one at work knew of her problem, and she didn't plan to explain her absence except in the vaguest of terms. She had sick leave coming, and if Vesuvius balked at that, she'd take some of her accumulated vacation.

Melanie left at lunch, which provided enough time for another trim.

"I've never seen anything exactly like this." Madame Estelle pointed at the silhouette mounted on her wall. It was a human form, the outline filled with swirling greens and yellows, except for the head, which displayed a faint superimposed latticework of red and a cap of vivid blue.

"Is that me?"

"That's your auragram, yes. By interpreting the colors and patterns, we can often determine where the imbalances lie. The normal colors of life are hues of green and yellow, as you see. Anger, distress, hatred, any strong negative emotion shows up as red."

"Is that the curse then?" Melanie pointed to the lightning shaped red lines.

"I think not. It is too fragile and undirected. What you see there is probably your own fear and concern. No, this is the interesting feature." And she pointed to the blue spot, which covered the top of the skull. "Curses are, generally, manifestations of black magic, and therefore show up as black spots, much as cancer might in an X-ray. Considering the location, which I suspect we will find entirely covers the scalp, I feel certain this is the source of your problem."

"Can you get rid of it?"

"Yes, I believe so. But as I told you before, we must cure the disease rather than treat a symptom. Have you thought of anything that might have led to this situation?"

She shook her head. "Nothing at all. I can't imagine why anyone would dislike me so much. . . ."

Madame Estelle shook her head. "It is not, perhaps, that they dislike you. This coloration is all wrong for a vengeful curse. I think you've encountered a latent."

"A latent? I don't understand."

The witch paused a moment, then pointed to the encased Stonehenge. "There was and is no magic in these stones, Ms. Rule. Nor is there anything magical in crystal balls, Tarot cards, or most of the other paraphernalia of Wicca. Witchcraft is the power of the will, and the instruments we use are merely symbols that help us to concentrate and achieve our purpose. But it is possible to achieve the same thing without any of the ritual, even without knowing what one is doing, if the ability lies within."

Melanie thought about that. "You mean, someone might have cursed me by accident?"

"That's exactly what I think. There was no evil intent here, or the aura would show black. Instead, it is blue."

"And what does blue signify?"

"Friendship, admiration, love." Madame Estelle sighed. "So I ask you again, has anything happened recently that might have changed the way someone thinks about you?"

Realization came suddenly. "Peter!"

Madame Estelle was thoughtfully silent after Melanie finished describing her relationship, such as it was, with Peter Reynolds. Melanie waited for as long as she could, then blurted out her concern. "Are you saying Peter is some kind of witch?"

"Not in the ordinary sense, perhaps, though with the proper training, he could probably become a master warlock. This much power from someone unskilled in the Arts is quite rare."

"But I still don't understand why he'd do this to me, even unconsciously. I thought he liked me."

"He undoubtedly does. I told you, the aura would be black if it were otherwise, conscious act or not. I believe his unacknowledged motives are . . . well . . . benevolent."

"Benevolent?" Melanie reached up to touch her hair, which was already perceptibly longer than when she'd left the Clipjoint an hour before.

"Yes. I suspect your admiring friend thinks you'd be more attractive if you let your hair grow longer. And his unconscious mind is trying to help."

Melanie digested that, nodded. "All right, this all sounds crazy to me, but I'm obviously out of my depth. What do I do?"

"Nothing for the moment. Come back Friday afternoon. I'll have the answer for you then."

* * *

Wednesday her hair grew three inches, Thursday only two, but Friday morning it regained lost ground and gained five inches in six hours. Melanie showed up for her appointment forty-five minutes early.

"So can you help me?"

"As I said I would. Take these." Melanie accepted two vials.

"What do I do with them?"

"The orange is a shampoo. Use it all up in a single washing, as many rinses as it takes. Work the solution into your scalp vigorously and let it stand for a full minute before each rinse. That should return the growth rate to normal. I warn you the odor is quite unpleasant. But wait for at least an hour afterward before shampooing it normally."

"And this?" Melanie held up the blue vial.

"That's the true cure. There are two tablets in it. You must get your admirer to consume them both entirely, as they are precisely measured. It will reverse his fondness for long hair and prevent any recurrence of your condition."

Melanie twisted off the cap, sniffed a mildly repugnant odor. "What is it?"

"You don't really want to know. Finely ground rat hair is its most savory component. There's a bit of an unpleasant taste, but it should be masked by, say, dissolving them in a strong cup of coffee."

Peter positively blushed when she offered to bring him coffee from the canteen, and he asked her to dinner while he was drinking it. Melanie accepted, but watched carefully to be certain he drained his cup. She was smiling when she returned to her office.

Madame Estelle looked forward to her Coven's bowling night avidly, even more so this month because she wanted to tell Simone about the strange case she'd treated this past week. But to her surprise, and growing alarm, it turned out Simone had dealt with the identical complaint a day earlier. And had treated it in the same fashion.

Peter Reynolds felt wonderful. For weeks he'd been trying to gather the nerve to ask either Melanie Rule or Carla Henderson out on a date, and today they'd both approached him. He hadn't really wanted a second cup of coffee, but Carla had been so insistent.

* * *

Melanie woke up feeling wonderful. The dinner had been superb, both the food and the company. Peter was really clever and funny once he'd relaxed. This could be the one, she thought, then dismissed it as more than slightly premature. We hardly know each other, she thought.

It was Saturday so she didn't have to get up, but her bladder demanded attention. She rolled out of bed, fumbled her way into slippers, and staggered to the bathroom.

She didn't start screaming until she looked into the mirror and discovered she was completely bald.

A Good Witch Is Hard to Find

Dawn Dunn

Calvin Cleaver stared at the hideous, cauliflower-shaped wart on the end of his recently enlarged nose and cringed. What in God's name was he to do? But it wasn't God; it was that rotten witch, Delilah Pritchard, who had done this to him. And a week before his wedding!

He'd been warned, but he hadn't believed it. *I mean, it had to be some kind of joke, didn't it?* he thought as he faced himself in the mirror.

But it wasn't.

How could he show his face at work? Everybody would know. Even his boss had said, "Stay away from her. You don't know what kind of fire you're playing with." Calvin had called in sick for today, but that didn't solve his problem. Amanda would never marry him, not looking like this, even if she never found out how it had happened.

One last fling, one quick roll in the sack, and he had a nose that would put Cyrano de Bergerac to shame.

Delilah had looked so hot in her skin-tight black jeans and stiletto heels, a cashmere sweater pulled low over her shoulders. "Got a light?" she'd purred.

What a line! She didn't even smoke, but he'd fallen for it, head over heels. Maybe that wasn't quite the part of his anatomy that had been affected, but the result was the same. She'd needed a match to light the endless row of candles on her desk, and like the stupid chump he was, he'd given her one. The next thing he'd known, he was asking her for a date. Wouldn't any man have, any man about to be married?

It wasn't anything serious. Just a movie and a candlelight dinner back at her place. A little romantic music, a glass of wine or two, a slippery hand, a few promises of love he didn't mean. What woman in the nineties believed anything a man said?

Well, apparently Delilah did. When he got ready to leave, she'd suddenly turned into an innocent schoolgirl. "When will I see you again?" she'd asked, batting her eyes.

He'd grinned a little, hemmed and hawed, then told her the truth. He was expecting a slap in the face or a few tears, maybe not even that. She waved her hand over her head, and it was as though he'd been struck by lightning. He'd staggered back in the doorway and felt this awful burning sensation in his nose.

She'd laughed as he'd run down the sidewalk to his car and looked in the rearview mirror—

Oh, hell, he was just wasting time. Calvin picked up the phone book and flipped through the yellow pages, not really sure what he was looking for. He could go to a surgeon to have the wart removed, but that wouldn't shorten his nose. It was six inches long, for God's sake! He looked like a freak.

His finger stopped at the top of the page. There it was in bold black print: WITCHES AND WARLOCKS. *Pagan ceremonies and rituals.* He read through the ads. There were only a couple: Shelly's Love Potions for the Romance Challenged; The Coven of Six, Weddings and Burials; Pagan Blessings. None of them sounded exactly like what he needed, but he decided to give Shelly a call, hoping she'd at least be able to point him in the right direction.

"An eye of newt. A pinch of grave mold." The chubby, middle-aged blonde giggled and winked at him. "I haven't used this recipe in years, but don't you worry. Nothing works like an old spell. My mother left me a whole cookbook full."

Shelly laughed again, but Calvin wasn't feeling amused. He'd caught a cold on the subway to match his enormous proboscis. "I could cure that, too," she said as he sneezed.

"Just shrink it back down to size," he muttered. "That's all I want."

"Another ten minutes. It's got to come to a full boil. You don't want it to be too weak. There, that looks about right." She carried the kettle over to the sink and poured the mixture into a strainer. "It's just about ready, Mr. Cleaver. You know, I usually get twenty-five dollars in advance, and another fifty when the potion brings results, which in your case should be fairly quick."

Calvin reached into his wallet and laid the money on the counter. "There's the whole seventy-five."

She pulled the grounds from the strainer and dropped them onto a saucer. "Here you go, Mr. Cleaver. Be sure to eat the entire amount."

She slid the money into her ample brassiere as he placed the first pinch in his mouth. "It's not the taste that counts," she said as he grimaced. She stood back to watch the results.

Calvin shuddered and chewed, then licked the plate clean. "How's that? Is it shrinking?" He could feel a definite burning as he had before, but this time it was in his cheeks.

"Oh, my," the plump witch gasped. "I'm not sure. Something's not right."

Calvin panicked. "What do you mean?" He leapt to his feet and grabbed the mirror she had placed on the counter. Shelly wrung her hands and jumped out of his reach.

"I'm sure it will be all right. It just takes a little time—"

"You said it would be immediate. You promised . . . look at my face. It's turning green."

"Just a little green."

"Why, you rotten quack!" He threw the mirror onto the floor, shattering it.

"That's seven years' bad luck," she said as he raised his fist. "I think you'd better leave."

He was going to hit her, then remembered what had happened the last time he'd crossed a witch. "I'll be back!" he shouted. "You'll pay. I'll see you run out of business. I'll call the police."

Calvin paced the street in a heavy downpour with an oversized handkerchief stuffed in his pocket, looking for 616 West Hickory Lane. He had no choice except to try again. The wedding was in three days. He'd used up half the vacation time he'd planned on for his honeymoon. This witch had better know what she was doing. But what kind of guarantee could he get? Could he ask to see her diploma? Her witches' license?

He stopped before an old Victorian mansion that had been divided into four apartments. A sign in the lower window read THE COVEN OF SIX.

What the devil was a coven of six?

He knocked and was greeted by a woman, who at least looked the part. Her wrinkled, octogenarian face twisted into a hag's toothless grin. "Mr. Cleaver?" she lisped.

"Who else?" he demanded. Who could mistake a beak like his?

The old woman nodded. "Come in. I have the incense ready."

"Incense, not a potion, huh? The last one told me she had a potion."

The old woman led him into an old-fashioned parlor. "Potions are often helpful, but given the extreme nature of your problem"—he was now the color of an avocado—"I thought this would be more useful. Take off your coat. You'll need to relax. Sit here in this chair." She patted the arm of an overstuffed recliner.

"Sure. Whatever you say." Incense didn't sound as likely to produce harmful side effects as something he had to swallow, and what did he have to lose? "You're sure this is going to work?"

"If the original spell is not too powerful. Some spells are more powerful than others, but it's unlikely you've run across one of those. Here, put your feet up. Breathe deeply through your nose, and try to relax. Think of something pleasant."

Calvin tipped back his head as the old woman lit the tall incense in the brass holder beside him.

"I'll come back when it's finished. It works better if you're completely at ease."

"You don't need any money up front?" he asked, not intending to give it to her even if she did.

"I never deal in money, Mr. Cleaver."

He was about to ask what she did deal in, but she'd already left. Well, whatever the price, he'd pay it if the incense worked. He could feel it taking effect. The smoke itself was relaxing him. He lay back in the chair and tried to think about Amanda, the night they'd spent in the hot tub, but images of Delilah kept distracting him. Delilah in her stiletto heels between black satin sheets . . .

He woke to find himself soaked in sweat. The room was filled with smoke, more than any stick of incense could give off. He covered his face with his sleeve and bounded out of the chair. "Old woman!" he croaked, unable to remember her name, not sure she'd even told him. "Old woman!"

A cat leapt from the piano against the opposite wall and ran toward the kitchen. The smoke was too thick for him to follow. Groping his way toward the front, he managed to get out onto the porch. There was no sign of the old woman. One of the other tenants screamed at him, and he asked her to call the fire department.

He forgot all about his nose and the color of his skin till he saw two firemen laughing at him. He slipped into his car and checked the mirror. His nose was still the size and hue of a cucumber, and his ears were now brilliant red. He beat on the steering wheel, calling the old woman every foul name he could think of.

The firemen searched the house, but the old woman was gone.

Pagan Blessings. It had taken him two days to screw up his courage to try again. This was his last chance. The wedding was tomorrow. He would never see Amanda again if he showed up looking like this. And what would his boss say? Sooner or later, he would have to go back to work.

He had no choice, really. He pushed the small black button that took him to the thirteenth floor of the Cartwright Building. A black alley cat, or should he say office cat, greeted him at the elevator.

Nice touch, he thought. At least, this place had class. A woman in a gray business suit sat behind a stylish desk polishing her nails. They were painted black, of course. "May I help you?" she asked.

"I have an appointment to see . . . Miss Bountiful," he said, embarrassed to repeat the name.

The woman smiled casually. "Right this way."

He was led through a vintage wooden door with an etched glass inset and Miss Bountiful's name printed in gold. Miss Bountiful looked nothing like what her name implied. She was dressed in a black business suit and wore heavy red lipstick and nails, but no other makeup. Her face was almost deathly pale, by contrast, and her plain dark hair was pulled back in a chignon.

"I can see your problem," she said, as he was sure everyone could.

"Can you fix it?" he asked and began to tremble. He was running out of time. He couldn't afford any more inept witches.

Miss Bountiful moved from behind her desk in a rather seductive manner, after all, and waved her hand at him in almost the same way

Delilah had. He'd already given them his credit card number over the phone. She chanted a few Latin-sounding words, and his skin tingled. The spell was working. His nose tightened and throbbed, then grew out another inch. He couldn't believe his eyes, but it was easy to see at this length.

"My God!" he cried.

Miss Bountiful took a step backward. "It isn't supposed to work like that. I don't understand."

Something was growing out of the pores in his ears. "What've you done to me! This is horrible! It's the end of my life!"

Miss Bountiful's face flushed. "You'll be entitled to a full refund, of course."

"I'll sue!" he shouted, feeling hair beginning to grow on the soles of his feet as well. "I'll sue every one of you!"

As music played in the chapel beyond the hall, Calvin's green nose and red ears paled, though they could scarcely be seen through the hair. He was doomed, doomed, doomed. He had tried to shave, but the magical hair had resisted an ordinary razor. And what good would it have done? It was too late for any more remedies, good or bad. The groomsmen stared at him in awe, unable to believe what had happened.

The minister came and gasped in shock. There was no time to explain. The assembly was waiting. "My son," he muttered briefly, then led them forth from the rectory.

Calvin felt his ears glow. Perhaps he should run. Maybe Amanda would think it was only grease paint, a poor joke on the part of a nervous groom.

His friends and relatives whispered in surprise as he made his appearance. The stunned organist faltered in her rendition of *Amazing Grace,* then immediately proceeded into the *Wedding March.* Calvin turned. The bridesmaids giggled and blushed, but Calvin hardly noticed them. Neither did he notice the flowers nor the flowing white dresses. All he could see was the huge cauliflower wart on the end of Amanda's incredible elongated nose.

Psychomildew Love

LOIS H. GRESH

Cora Cromley scratched the fungus pinwheels from her window. It was a shame to destroy such perfect mold, but to get a good look at her neighbor, Warren Truckenmiller, she had to clear some space.

Ah, there he was, muscles bulging beneath the frayed cutoffs, square face grim under the frayed blond hair. A shaggy mutt of a man, playing with his machines: bug zapper, weed whacker, four-wheel muscle bike. Half Cora's age. And a newlywed. His wife, Maralee, clung to him and whispered in his ear.

Oh, what Cora would give to be Maralee; so young, so lithe, with the streaming black hair and the eyes of melted ice.

Warren lifted what looked like an oxygen tank with gas mask and suction tubes—oh, yes, the leaf blower—and strapped it to his back. He put on the mask, then a helmet, and grasped the blower's nozzle. In the death of day, under a half-mast sun, he looked like a rocketman.

Maralee crunched over dead autumn leaves and perched on the edge of a lawn chair. She rubbed their dog, Yapper, under the ears.

The blower *vroomed* to life, and Yapper howled.

Fingernails scraped down Cora's back. That noise again; that noise! The dog, the machines—

Cora screeched.

The newlyweds turned and squinted in Cora's direction. Cora ducked beneath the windowsill. The blower died, and she heard muffled laughs.

"What an old bat," said Maralee.

"Leave her be," said Warren, "she's just a lonely old maid."

Cora's eyes misted. Yes, she was lonely, so lonely that she talked to the psychomildew that stretched like soft sealskins across the walls. But an old maid? Never. "It's not too late for me. I'll get a husband. I'll get kids."

She wiped her tears on her hot-pink negligee, swept gray wisps

148

from her forehead, and peeked from the window. Maralee was wrapped around Warren, kissing his neck, his cheeks, his hair. "Turn it back on, Warren baby, it gives me such a thrill. Who cares about that old witch anyway?"

Indeed, Cora was a witch, descended from a long line of inbreeding and proud of it. She cranked open her window and hollered, "So what if I'm a witch? What are you gonna do about it, eh?"

Warren leered at his wife. The leaf blower *vroomed* back to life.

Cora screamed and clutched at her chest, her legs, her back. The blower was a drill bit down her spine: grinding, blasting.

Now Maralee was on Warren's back, hugging the blower, the two of them vibrating and writhing. Warren with the weed whacker, zapping the dandelion tendrils and the hollyhocks off Cora's lawn. He kicked on the four-wheeler, hopped on with Maralee, and they rode it like a bucking bronco. Around them danced Yapper, barking and leaping, a black jot on a dying sun.

Cora retreated into the pit of her house. Her mind steamed with thoughts as black and foaming as the psychomildew rotting in her walls. She would have Warren Truckenmiller. She would tear him from his wifey; she would force him to love her. She would force him to give her children.

She cradled her cheek on the green mold by the fireplace. Cool, slimy, it calmed her, cleared her thoughts. On the mantle were photos of her ancestors, witches and warlocks with eyes like boils erupted from pus-pocked skin. But Cora was the most beautiful of all. On her chin, the warts grew in concentric circles. On her lip, a hairy mole dangled like a cherry from her brown lips.

How could Warren resist?

She ran her fingertips over the velvet walls. Green fungus by the scalpel cabinet, good for thunder and rain. Brown and black by the poison flask hutch, perfect for love spells.

She fingered the flasks of toad throat peelings and bat claw clippings. She would cast a love spell on Warren Truckenmiller. She pressed her palms against the brown and black mildew. Her fingers tingled, her hands; then the tingle flew up her arms, shot straight to her brain. She said, "Psychomildew pions. Boson bombs. Make Maralee flee, and make Warren love *me*."

But something was wrong. Her mind wasn't floating in ecstasy. She pressed against the wall, this time harder. The wall sank beneath her hands, fell in wet slabs to the floor. She peered into the crumbled ruins. Egg yolk mold. Fungi ropes looped in nooses around flabby necks of mildew. The smell so sweet, a thousand dead bodies stewing for a thousand years.

Cora's head swam in the perfume. She felt the glow hit her cheeks. Why hadn't the love spell worked? What was wrong?

She poked her head through the vast hole, found that the entire inside of the wall had been eaten away as if by moths.

Well, what would she do? Without the pion boson psychomildew wall, she couldn't cast a love spell on Warren.

Scampering. Chittering. Gnawing. It was the roach pack again, the roaches that fed on the soul of her organic house. She slammed her fist into the wall. A large chunk of dripping splotch splashed onto her head. She flung it down and stomped on it.

Had to fix the wall. Had to nourish it with flesh and make the psychomildew grow.

She stumbled back to the window. Outside, Warren was alone, tinkering with an air compressor. Maralee must have gone inside to take a fragrant bath and slip into something sexy.

"Hey, Warren, you wanna come over for some . . . cookies?" called Cora.

He looked up and laughed. "You gotta be kidding."

"No kidding. I have some real delicious cookies here. And . . . doughnuts, too."

He pointed a finger at her. "I'm not coming in *your* house, lady, not for a million bucks."

From afar, Maralee sang, "Oh, Warren, come and get it."

"Look, I gotta go now." Warren was an excited little boy, packing his toys into his mower bins, gunning the motor, kicking into high gear. Yapper barked and leapt aboard.

"I want you *now*," screamed Cora over the noise.

But Warren didn't hear her.

She thrust her hands against the sides of the window and inched them slowly across the psychomildew walls. Here, where the spells transformed people into—

she couldn't remember—

people into—

"Do it, fungus, do it now. Make Warren into a gorgeous cow."

Was it a cow? Had she spoken the right words, the ones that the wall would transform into vibration balls of bosons and pions?

The mower hiccuped. The dog yowled and ran toward Warren's house.

Cora heard a snort.

In the dusk, it was hard to be certain, but as the creature crept closer, she knew: Cora Cromley had turned Warren Truckenmiller into an anteater. Powerful sexy legs, claws longer than Cora's, and a snout that would drive any woman mad.

Cora raced from the kitchen, slammed the back door, and hurried over to Warren. His snout was stuck in an anthill. She grabbed his fur by the neck and yanked up his head. It came up coated with ants and termites. His long tongue flapped.

"Listen here," she said, "you're comin' into the house with me. And I mean now."

Maralee was running across the lawn wearing next to nothing. The moon glowed against a red-chiseled sky. Maralee's black hair singed with red. Her eyes singed with fear. "Warren! Warren, where are you, baby?"

Cora cackled. "He's nowhere to be found, dear. Now go on home and leave me in peace, would you?" She looped her arms around Warren's neck and hauled him toward the house.

Maralee stopped by the hollyhock bed, crushed dandelions curling over her toes. "But I . . . but I know he's out here, I left him here. Where would he be?" She was crying, her tears splashing like blood from a great wound.

"Come on, Warren." Cora shoved his fat, furry tail into her kitchen. Beady eyes looked up at her; termites dropped from his tongue. She rummaged in the refrigerator. "Now you be good. I'll be back soon. I have to go out and find something to feed to the wall." She plopped the box of chocolate-covered locusts on the floor and left him there.

It was black outside. She was in night's cup, where she belonged. She slipped by the side of her house between the poison oak and the splintered board. In Warren's bedroom window, Maralee's black profile heaved and sobbed against a backdrop of white light.

Cora crouched behind the towering juniper. Crickets chirruped. A frog croaked. She heard herself breathing.

Then something growled. Right behind her, something growled. She whirled and saw it: the dog, Yapper, food for the wall. She screeched and dove at the beast, and it lunged for her throat, but she squeezed the neck tightly and snapped it back, and as quickly as the dog had attacked, she claimed its life and it groaned and whimpered and then lay limp at her feet.

She dragged it into the house.

A half-eaten locust dangled from Warren's snout. His little eyes filmed with tears, and he fell crying into his box of goodies.

Cora stroked Warren's black and gray fur and then stuffed the dog into the collapsed wall. A loud suck and slurp, and she knew that the psychomildew was devouring Yapper's flesh and replenishing itself.

She turned back to Warren. "If you promise to be good, I'll turn you back into a man," she said.

He whimpered and nodded his snout.

She stroked the wall again, this time uttered the spell that turned beasts back into people. Warren popped into human form. He dove for the door. She flew at him, knocked him to the floor. They rolled in the locusts and termites and mold. He was slapping her and bellowing, and she was plunging her claws into his ears and his cheeks and screaming, "You said you'd be good! You said you'd be good!" And he couldn't fight her, for she was a witch, born from generations of inbreeding, and she could pin down any mortal, and she was proud of it.

She slammed him against the wall, said, "Do it, fungus, do it now. Turn Warren into a gorgeous cow."

Her spell disintegrated into particles, coalesced into boson bombs and psychomildew pions that penetrated the wall, massaged its growths, and then surged in a streak of silver and struck Warren like lightning; he fell back against the scalpel cabinet, then slumped to the floor.

Warren was an anteater again. "And you shall stay that way, you naughty, naughty boy," said Cora.

She stalked into the living room and propped her elbow on the mantle. He trundled behind her and grunted. He squatted at her feet and whimpered. He rose on his hind legs, put his front paws on her knees. He mewed like a sick cat.

"Honestly, you're pathetic, Warren Truckenmiller. I give you all my love, and what do you do? You try to escape. I should lock *you* in the psychomildew wall with the dog."

Warren snuffled at her black boots. She kicked his snout. She remembered his cruel words: Leave her be, she's just a lonely old maid.

It's not too late for me, Warren. I'll get a husband. I'll get kids.

She looked at the slender snout. The toothless mouth slit. The sticky, flicking tongue.

As a man, Warren would always run from her, hate her, laugh at her.

As an anteater, did he have any choice but to love her?

She sank to her knees. "Would you like me to be an anteater, too?"

He whimpered, snuffled close.

She thought of the children they would have together, of the happy family life. And she muttered the spell that would cast her forever into the world of anthills and thrusting snouts and termite tunnels, and never-ending love.

The Career Witch

THOMAS M. SIPOS

Alex was alone in the darkened room, seated in front of the Ouija board.

"Oh spirits! Can anyone hear my voice? Give me a sign so that I may speak to Cassandra. Give me a sign!"

There came three loud raps!

He became tense. "Cassandra, is that you? Have you returned to me as promised?"

More raps, then shouting. "Alex! Can you hear me?"

Alex opened his eyes, sadly realizing that both the raps and the shouts came from outside. Adjusting his tie, he opened the front door to his empty house.

Outside in the dark stood a thirtysomething flower child in a granny dress. "Alex, I was so worried something had happened." Kissing his cheek, Meg entered. "You sounded so anxious over the phone. Is everything all right?"

"My wife is dead."

"I'm sorry. I know how much you loved my sister. But Alex, it's been nearly a year. Isn't it time you started . . . seeing other people?"

"I'll never find anyone like Cassie. Besides, her death is only temporary. She promised she'd return."

"But you've tried tarot cards, crystal balls, séances. You still haven't reached her."

"But I haven't tried the Ouija yet!"

Meg saw the Ouija board, its wooden surface shimmering from the glow of the red candles burning in the candelabra.

"Meg, darling," he said, "you have to understand, my skills are nowhere near as powerful as Cassie's. She was the witch in the family. Whenever I needed supernatural help in business, she handled it."

"If she was so powerful, *she* would have contacted you by now." Meg held him. "Alex, I think it's very noble of you to keep a torch lit for Cassandra. But look what it's doing to you. You're wasting away. You've got to get out. If only for one night."

"But I feel so close. As if at any moment, she'll break on through from the other side."

"Maybe she doesn't *want* to break on through. Death can be a powerful trip. Maybe she's changed."

Alex scowled.

"Not that she no longer loves you," Meg added. "But maybe she's happy in her new scene."

"I could never be happy without *her*."

"And I'm sure she'd *prefer* to have you with her. But as you said, she loved you, so she wouldn't want you to destroy yourself over her. Let me take you out tonight. Dinner's on me."

"I don't know. Cassie was very wise about metaphysics. If she preferred death, she would have known that before she died. She knew more about death than you or I."

"But not as much as she knows now."

Alex shook his head.

"Oh, Alex! I wish I could help you."

"You can! That's why I called you here."

Meg brightened. "Name it! Anything you want."

"You're Cassie's closest living relative. She told me you two were quite close growing up together."

"About six feet. We shared the same bedroom."

"I was thinking, if we merge our efforts to reach Cassie, we'd double our chances of succeeding."

Meg played with her mood ring. "It's not that I don't want to help. But there's a time for everything. A time to live. A time to love. A time

154

to die. A cosmic harmony. Cassandra is dead. You have to accept it or you'll keep getting bummed out."

"I'll get a nervous breakdown if we don't reach her. At the very least we should *ask* Cassie if she's happy where she is. I owe her that much."

Meg sighed. "All right, Alex. For your sake, I'll try it this once. But you have to promise. If we don't reach Cassandra within the next half hour, you're going out with me tonight. And this way, you pay for dinner!"

Alex gave her a quick kiss. "I knew I could depend on you."

"You'll always be able to."

The two of them sat down at the Ouija, placing their fingers on the pointer.

"Like this?" Meg asked.

"That's right. Lightly, so it's free to move."

"I'll try my best."

"I'm surprised you asked. I thought you and Cassie were part of the same coven."

"Long ago."

Alex stared at the Ouija. "Beloved wife. Wherever you are. Your husband and sister eagerly await your return."

Meg looked askance before adding, "I sense she's in heaven right now. Happy and wanting you to live your own life."

"Then I want to hear her say it."

"Maybe she can't. Maybe it's against the rules."

"Wait a minute! It's moving!"

Astonished, they watched the pointer spell: HELP ME.

"Cassie's in trouble!" Alex exclaimed.

"Maybe it isn't Cassandra."

The pointer continued to spell: USE THE BOOK OF REMAKING.

"It doesn't make any sense!" cried Meg. "We'd better stop."

"Cassie! Is that you?" asked Alex. "Where are you?"

The pointer spelled its answer: HELL.

Meg sighed. "It's her."

Alex flipped through the book. "One of Cassie's most prized possessions."

Meg paced the living room, arms folded nervously. *The Book of ReMaking?* That's a book of alchemy. Transmuting reality by summoning demons. You can't get Cassandra out of hell with that. You don't know *what* you'll pull from hell with those spells."

"Cassie wouldn't have asked for the book if she didn't know its powers."

"If she knows what she's talking about, how did she get *downstairs* in the first place?"

"Obviously, a cosmic error." Book cradled in his arms, Alex pushed aside furniture, clearing a space in the middle of the room. "You knew Cassie. A good witch. A kind and loving wife. I always felt her death was a mistake."

"Even if it was, you're going about this the wrong way."

Chalk in hand, Alex drew a pentagram on the parquet floor, then a circle around it, careful so it matched the diagram in the book.

"Has it occurred to you," Meg asked, "that it might be her occult stuff that got Cassandra into the mess she's in? Maybe if we prayed for her? Catholics say enough prayers can free a soul from purgatory and send them to heaven."

"Cassie isn't *in* purgatory. And I don't want her in heaven. I want her with me!"

"You're playing with fire. Whatever your goals are, *The Book of ReMaking* is not the right path. If you insist on fooling around with magic, there is some positive magic I can use."

"Positive magic? That sounds like something discussed on talk radio. Along with fad diets and pop psychology." Alex put away his chalk. "Meg, you're a sweet girl, but you always were a flake. Cassie was different. A professional. A career witch."

"Cassandra was greedy. I know we belonged to the same coven long ago, but we went two separate ways."

"Now she needs your help."

"I'm trying to tell you, I gave up that dark stuff. I *can't* help her. I don't know how."

"It's in the book. We just follow instructions."

"Dammit, I wouldn't help Cassandra even if I could! It's no mistake her being down there. She sold her soul to the devil!"

Alex paused, then continued searching for candles. "That's absurd. Her powers were pure. They came from within herself."

"They came from hell! Long ago my sister wanted something that belonged to me. And when she couldn't get it honestly, she had Satan stack the deck." Meg collapsed into an armchair. "Not that it was the end of it. Black magic is a heavy trip. You get addicted. You can't stop once you're hooked."

"My wife was ambitious. And why not? She was smart, talented, beautiful. She *deserved* the best."

"And she got it. Then her credit statement came due."

"No one has the right to imprison my wife in hell!"

"Her Master does. And you're wrong. They don't make errors like that down there. Hell can't stomach good people. It's like indigestion. They'd be . . . vomited out."

"She's my wife!" He placed candles at each pentagram tip. "If need be, I'll break open the gates of hell and yank her from Satan myself."

Meg sighed. "Alex, you're an amateur. You don't know what *The Book of ReMaking* is capable of."

"I have faith in my wife and her guidance. Whatever she may have done to others, I know she loved me, and I intend to aid her in her hour of need." He lit each candle. "Ready."

As Alex read from the book, a gentle breeze blew through the enclosed room, building into a gust, then a gale. "Hear me, king of the dead! Obey my commands, ruler of the underworld! By the strength of my will, throw open the gates of inferno! Let free the sorceress Cassandra, whom you have unjustly enslaved!"

Pulling her wind-whipped hair away from her eyes, Meg stared at the circle. The wood within it melted away. But instead of a hole, there was a cauldron of reddish-yellow light. A portal to another dimension. Two female hands pressed against an invisible barrier separating her world from the living room. The rest of her was shrouded in a glowing reddish-yellow mist.

Alex saw the hands. "She's alive! My Cassie has returned!"

Meg trembled from cold and fear. "How do you know it's her? It could be anybody! It could be any*thing!*"

Alex watched her fingers frantically scratching against the invisible barrier. "Something's wrong! She can't get through!"

Meg grabbed him, shouting to be heard over the howling wind. "Alex, I'm scared. I don't know who or what is down there and I don't want to find out. Let's run as far as possible and forget tonight ever happened."

"How can I run now? I've waited a year to get my wife back. To hold her in my arms. To gaze into her eyes." His face glowed red from the portal fire. "And there she is. So near . . ." He reached down, as if to place his hands against the woman's.

"No!" Meg grabbed him, they struggled, she scratched his wrists. Tiny blood droplets struck the barrier, dissolving it.

A finger slipped through.

"Blood! That's the key!" Alex clawed at his wrists. New droplets created new holes. Tiny but expanding.

Meg realized what was happening.

Long fingernails pressed through the new holes.

Alex glanced about the room. "Too slow. I need a knife."

Meg swept her arm across the candles, knocking them down. Thunder shook the room, a tornado wrecked brief havoc, the magic force was sucked down whirlwindlike into the portal.

Within seconds the wind was gone. So was the portal.

"The problem lies in drawing sufficient blood to let Cassie in, while ensuring I don't bleed to death." Alex chuckled as he studied the diagram of human blood vessels in the medical book. "If I'm not careful, I'll end up trading places with Cassie, and then she'll have to rescue me."

"If you really think she would." Meg mumbled, then said, "If you're going to cut yourself, you should minimize the risks."

"Why do you think I'm wasting time with this book, when just by slashing my wrists I could have my arms around my beloved wife at this very moment?"

"So have a nurse at the blood bank do it."

"Blood banks don't let you take blood home. Even if they did, it would mean an extra day. I've waited long enough."

"You could buy blood. People go there to sell. All you'd have to do is outbid the blood bank. Or bribe somebody who works there. It would be smart trading. Cassie would like that."

He shook his head. "Not as romantic as slashing open my own flesh. There's something special about spilling your own blood to rescue your wife. Besides, I want Cassie rescued by clean blood. So many blood donors are disease-ridden addicts or back-street winos."

"Cassandra talked the same way about blood. Always speaking of blood mysticism and blood oaths and pacts written in blood."

"Blood is the stuff of life. A vital element in all magic."

"Only in black magic. Good witches don't use blood."

"Can *you* rescue Cassie without it?"

"No, if she *deserves* to be where she is, white magic won't save her."

"Why do you say *if* when you have no doubt?" Alex snapped. "Are you trying to spare my feelings?"

"Yes, I'm trying to spare your feelings! I'm trying harder than you ever tried with me when . . . when I loved you, long before you even met Cassandra."

Alex nearly popped his button-down. "You loved me?"

"And you loved me! We were both very much in love, until I introduced you to Cassandra. Until she sold her soul to the devil for the power to steal you from me. She couldn't have done that with white magic. A good witch can only make people aware of something they already feel. Only black magic can create an illusion of false love, which is what you feel for Cassandra." Meg was near tears. "My sister *deserves* to burn in hell!"

Alex turned away uneasily. "I've heard younger sisters are often jealous of their older siblings."

Meg slumped into the armchair. "If only you could remember. When you asked me here tonight, I thought her power over you had finally been severed. Ever since Cassandra died, I was waiting for you to feel again what you once felt so strongly. But I should have known my sister would do her best to pull you down into hell with her."

Alex ran the dagger's blade over a candle flame. "The lower forearm should do." He collected his blood in a chalice.

"Look what Cassandra's making you do! At all of this." Meg indicated the dim room. "Does it seem natural to you? Or healthy or normal? Ten years ago you wouldn't have fooled around with demonology and bizarre blood rituals."

Alex bound his arm with a strip of cloth.

"We used to believe in good magic," Meg continued. "You and I together. In a path of peaceful nirvana."

"You're sweet. But you're not Cassie. She was strong and exciting. The only woman I could *ever* love." Alex cradled *The Book of ReMaking* in one arm, approached the magic circle with the chalice. The candles were already lit. "If you won't help, then please don't interfere. I'll just cut myself once again. And you won't be welcome here anymore."

"Tell me one thing, Alex. Since Cassandra died, have you ever felt anything at all for me?"

"Always. You're my sister-in-law. I care a great deal for you. But I love Cassie."

"Good." Then Meg said to herself, "Before she died, you stopped caring completely. Her power into this world *is* weaker. I just have to cut her off for good."

Again, Alex read from *The Book of ReMaking*. The wind began. The portal appeared. Meg glanced nervously into the mist and light, saw the hands against the barrier.

Alex raised the chalice over the portal, began tilting, but before a single drop spilled, Meg knocked the chalice out of his hand, sent it flying past the circle, striking and splashing its blood against the wall.

"Just what do you think that accomplishes?" Alex demanded. "I just have to draw more blood from myself." He set the book down, went to his dagger, undid the cloth around his forearm.

Meg grabbed *The Book of Remaking*, tore out some pages, held them over a candle. "Don't waste your blood, Alex. You'll never open the gates to hell without these pages." Disembodied screams hollered from the portal as paper caught fire.

Alex was stopped by Meg's raised arm. "I dump these candles now, the door to hell slams shut forever!"

"Meg! If you ever cared for me . . ."

"I loved you. I still do. That's why I have no choice."

Fingers were still scratching the barrier when Meg swept the candles. As before, a whirlwind blew through the room, sucking itself through the portal. The hands spun within the circle, as if the woman were caught in a whirlpool.

Still clutching the dagger, Alex rushed Meg, they struggled, she stumbled onto the blade. Her blood spilled and spiraled into the portal, melting through the barrier as lava through a frozen lake. Enraged at losing his wife, Alex stabbed Meg repeatedly, her blood reacting as gasoline to fire, until the light from the gaping hole was too bright for Alex. He stepped back. Meg's body crumpled and disappeared down the hole.

Cassandra spun up the whirlpool, her swirling body halting at floor level. The wind ceased. The portal vanished. Complete silence.

Cassandra stood on the pentagram, wearing a ceremonial robe, her hair golden against its crimson cloth, her arms outstretched to Alex. "Faithful husband. I *knew* I could depend on you."

Alex rushed into her arms. "My beloved wife!"

"Now we'll be together forever. Just as I promised."

"I knew you would defeat death."

She became hesitant. "Now, darling. I only promised death would not separate us. I never claimed I could *defeat* it."

"Nevertheless, whatever you've done, someone else needs your help. It's your sister. I've—" he broke into tears. "I've killed her."

"Of course you did. And I'm glad you did. Her blood opened the door for us. Now we are together again."

"*My* blood could have done that. She didn't have to die."

"Yes she did. Your blood was by choice. That was enough to open the door. But not enough to allow me to take you back. But with her blood on your hands, we'll always be together. You see, my Master won't let me stay up here. And so I came to get you!"

She grabbed him just as the floor crashed open beneath them, sending them into the fires below.

Soon, Alex's screams were heard no more.

The hole coughed. Meg's bloody body flew through the hole. The hole sealed itself before she crashed down on the pentagram.

She awoke dazed and confused. She saw blood on herself, but found no wounds. She glanced about the room.

"Alex? Alex, where are you?"

Retrocurses

TERRY CAMPBELL

Amanda Collins peered through the rusted wrought-iron fence that surrounded the centuries-old Massachusetts cemetery, past the scraggly tree limbs that cut through the chilled October air, breaking up the crisp blue sky like cracks in an old oil painting. From her vantage point, Amanda could not see the six new graves, but she could detect the acrid odor of freshly turned soil over the clinging aroma of the moist, rotting leaves that covered the grounds. Amanda moved closer, toward the front gate, and when she spotted the large piles of upturned earth near the rear of the cemetery, she knew the rumors were true.

Amanda frowned. The cemetery had been a place of solitude for her at one time; now, it seemed only cold and forsaken, as cemeteries often are. Was it the encroaching winter, the bitter nip in the air that clawed at her clothing no matter how valiantly the sun fought? Was it the dark cloud of her recent problems that hovered over her and cast a pall over Amanda's presence?

Or was it the idea of the six soon-to-be new inhabitants that had turned her sanctuary from the cruel taunts of her classmates into a dismal setting with all the charm of a prison cell?

Amanda slid the latch back and pushed the front gate open. She had always enjoyed the grating sound the hinges made, but now the noise seemed excessively loud, as if an alarm sounded at her intrusion. Amanda apprehensively entered the graveyard, trying with no success to soften the crunch of the freshly fallen leaves that covered the wet layer on the ground.

She moved deliberately past all the familiar old tombstones inscribed with the names of faceless people she had learned to call friends, until she stood before six sparkling white granite markers—new markers all bearing the same date of death: OCTOBER 16, 1692.

These names were forever etched in the memories of the residents of Downer's Grove, the names of six young women tried and convicted of witchcraft and hanged during a dark time in the town's history.

Amanda paused and reflected on each grave, wondering why the arrival of these poor, unfortunate girls was making her so uneasy. They were probably a lot like her, perhaps misunderstood by the adults who governed their world. But when Amanda reached the last stone, she stepped back, suddenly startled for reasons she could not understand.

ABIGAIL MARTIN. BORN OCTOBER 16, 1676. DIED OCTOBER 16, 1692.

A noise erupted from somewhere behind Amanda, like the unison fluttering of many small birds. She turned, her eyes wide.

A horned owl sat solemnly atop one of the rusted spikes that adorned the fence. Its round, yellow eyes locked onto Amanda's; tiny ear tufts rose slowly from above its eyes, making it look like a small feathered demon.

Amanda's gaze drifted from the new arrival to Abigail Martin's grave, then back to the owl.

Do you know who I am?

Amanda turned in circles, trying to locate the owner of this voice.

Do you know who I am?

Until she realized the voice was in her head. *No, not again,* Amanda moaned to herself. *Go away. Just leave me alone.*

I'm the devil.

Amanda stood breathless, staring at the owl through watery eyes, her body shaking uncontrollably.

Sounding distant, yet very near, just behind her, yet all around her, encircling her, cloaking the cemetery with its pitiful mewling, a baby wailed.

Amanda turned and bolted for the entrance, oblivious to the noise the dry, brittle autumn leaves made under her feet.

"Loyal denizens of Downer's Grove, Massachusetts," Reverend Denny Brown said. "We have gathered here today outside our humble church, a church that was built over three hundred years ago with the blood, tears, and sweat of our forefathers, for a sort of spiritual healing."

Amanda stared through the crowd of people gathered at the back of Downer's Grove Cemetery, catching momentary glimpses of the six black holes cut into the moist, cool earth, her attention focused on the crude yellow pine boxes at the foot of each grave.

"We all know, even the relative newcomers to our tiny community, what happened on this day in the year of our Lord 1692. A gross atrocity was carried out that day. Six beautiful young women, Sarah Lawson, Rebecca Giles, Abigail Martin, Mary Elizabeth Hawthorne, Patricia Goode, and Susan Winthrop were sentenced to death by hanging. In a time of ignorance and uncertainty, when the well-meaning yet gravely mistaken town elders were searching for solutions to problems they couldn't quite understand, these victims were singled out and accused of bringing about the troubled times through the devil's magic."

Amanda's mother noticed her daughter's distraction from the proceedings and nudged her. Amanda turned her thoughts back to Reverend Brown, but her attention was soon on what lay within the wooden boxes.

Bones, Amanda. Bones and insects and worms.

"These poor women have lain at the foot of the tree from which they were hanged for 302 years, almost forgotten, their souls in turmoil and bitter unrest. Excommunicated from their church, this church of Downer's Grove, they have waited these many, many years for retribution.

"What happened to these girls has been a dark cloud hanging over our community ever since. Today we correct that shameful wrong by readmitting their names into the church records and giving these poor souls a proper burial in our own Downer's Grove Cemetery."

The congregation applauded the minister's words, and the appointed pallbearers moved to the foot of each makeshift coffin. The crowd fell silent as the first box was lifted to the edge of the waiting hole.

"Oh, look," Mrs. Spencer said, pointing to the bare tree limbs. "It's an owl."

"Oh, how beautiful," old Mrs. Syler said.

"You don't see many owls in daylight."

Do you know who I am?

Amanda began to shake, her teeth began to chatter, but not as a result of the chill in the air.

I'm the devil.

"I've heard that an owl appearing during the day is a sign of good fortune to come," someone said.

Reverend Brown stood before the six new graves. "Then it is truly a time of healing. Let us remember this blessed day."

Amanda watched as the pine boxes were gently lowered into the ground. Inside, bones that had remained undisturbed for over three hundred years rolled restlessly with the motions.

Bones and insects and maggots.

As the last box, the one holding the remains of Abigail Martin, was placed in the earth, the owl screeched loudly once and flew away.

Amanda closed her eyes tightly and wished she was somewhere far, far away. She could hear the thumping of clods of dirt hitting thin wood as the homemade coffins were covered.

Amanda felt something bump the tip of her nose.

It was a feather.

Don't worry, Amanda. I'll never go away.

Amanda awoke from a restless sleep to the sound of tapping at her bedroom window. She sat up in bed, her eyes heavy with sleep, trying to decide if she had dreamed the noise. Another soft rapping confirmed she had not. She pushed the blanket back and slid from the bed.

The tapping continued as Amanda cautiously approached the window. Her heart beat rapidly; her nightgown stuck to her body from cold sweat. Amanda peered around the edges of the sheer curtain covering the window.

A girl stood outside motioning for Amanda to open the window. Her ash-blonde hair floated on the cold, night breeze. An old tattered dress made of heavy material hung loosely to her pale body, but the girl did not seem to be affected by the chill. Amanda did not know this girl, but something inside her commanded her to open the window.

"Who are you?" Amanda whispered.

"You must not let them keep Abigail Martin in the church," the girl finally said. Her speech was slow, monotonous. "She does not belong.

"She is a witch."

Amanda could feel her pulse increasing. The cold air had dried her lips, and her tongue held no moisture with which to wet them.

"They . . . they were all witches," Amanda stammered. "According to legend."

"No," the girl said. "Only Abigail. It was she who cursed the town, she who brought the famine. Only she got caught up in her own little game, and she was convicted as well. The curse ended with her death. But she has been given new life now."

The girl looked back nervously over her shoulder. It was then that Amanda noticed she could see right through the girl.

"You must remove her. If she stays on church grounds, her curse will return."

Suddenly, the wind began to intensify. The girl's dress whipped against her thin, white legs; her hair slapped against her soiled face. The spectral visitor's eyes turned skyward, and Amanda saw only a quick flash as the owl descended, its gnarled, yellow talons ripping into the girl's face.

Amanda stepped quietly from the porch, pausing to listen at the front door for any indication that she had awakened her parents. When she did not hear them stir, she started, flashlight in one hand and shovel in the other, toward the cemetery.

She could not go to the townspeople. She had told her parents earlier about the ghost's visit. They thought she was going crazy again, had probably even called Dr. Prescott already. If her parents didn't believe her, what made Amanda think anyone else would? The townspeople would tell her parents for sure, and then she would have to go back to that horrible place where she had spent six long, agonizing months. It was up to her to correct what had been done.

She couldn't blame the townspeople. They had no reason to believe in witches, just as their forefathers had no reason not to believe in them. But the forefathers had been right. They had succeeded in removing the town's curse by disposing of the instigator of the curse. But now, the modern town officials were unwittingly bringing the curse back.

Amanda stopped. She had reached her destination. She placed the flashlight on the ground, aiming it toward Abigail Martin's tombstone. Cold dew clung to the neatly cropped graveyard grass, shining silver in the beam of the flashlight.

The first bite of the shovel dug into the ground, surprising Amanda with the ease with which it slid into the freshly turned earth. Amanda's heavily booted foot pushed it further into the black soil. The damp odor of soured earth wafted to her nose as the shovel repeatedly uncovered more earth. Soon, Amanda found herself at eye level with Abigail Martin's tombstone.

At long last, the shovel made a thumping sound as it struck something solid. Amanda laughed out loud.

She stopped when she heard the cry of the owl.

Amanda looked around, but she could not locate the owl in the dark. Working frantically, attempting to ignore the hooting, she dropped to her knees, clawing at the remaining layer of dirt covering the casket until the tips of her fingers were raw and bloody.

They'll put you away forever this time.

Amanda looked up from the grave.

She had never seen a girl so beautiful. The ghostly arrival had pale smooth skin that seemed to glow, framed by long dark hair that almost disappeared in the surrounding blackness of the night. Her lovely white eighteenth-century gown floated in the brisk wind; the bottom hem kissed the pile of earth Amanda had removed.

Poor little Amanda. All that abuse and all those mental problems have finally taken their toll on her. You'll never come back this time.

Amanda felt panic rising in her throat, and she looked over at the other fresh graves. Against each tombstone, curled in a fetal position and weeping uncontrollably, was a girl clad in a knee-length dress of dirty coarse fabric. Amanda recognized one of them as the girl who had visited her.

The girl looked up from the tombstone. "You can't fight her," she cried. "They won't listen to you, just as they wouldn't listen to us. She'll always win."

"What the hell's going on here?" a man's voice cried out in the darkness.

Amanda turned and was blinded by the high beam of a flashlight. The beam shifted momentarily, allowing Amanda to see it was old Barney Wilson, the cemetery's caretaker.

"Amanda Collins?" he said, surprised. "Is that you?"

Wilson shined the light into the grave.

"Lord a'mighty, girl. What've you done this time?"

They'll put you away forever. You'll never see the sun again. Abigail Martin stood next to Barney Wilson, staring down at Amanda.

The staccato flapping of wings sounded from overhead, and an owl lit on Abigail's shoulders.

Do you know who I am?

"You crazy dumb girl," Wilson said. "Ain't no one ever gonna believe another word you say, you know that?"

Do you know who I am?

Amanda's eyes grew wide as she watched Barney Wilson unhook his belt, letting his oversized work trousers fall around his knees.

"Ain't nobody gonna believe *nothin'* you tell them, girl."

There was a loud thump as Wilson landed beside Amanda on top of Abigail Martin's casket. He smiled, revealing blackened nubs of teeth, and his breath smelled of alcohol.

I'm the devil.

It was a sunny but chilly Sunday morning when the Downer's Grove Church held its first Sunday service since reinstating the victims of the 1692 witch hunt and placing their remains on hallowed grounds.

Reverend Brown's sermon was sincere and passionate, calling for forgiveness and mercy on all lost souls. There were more than a few tears shed.

As the sermon ended and the congregation began to filter slowly from the church, some stopping to pay respect to the hapless victims, Mrs. Abercrombie approached Mrs. Collins.

"Becky, I'm so sorry about Amanda. How is she doing?"

"Well, they're going to keep her indefinitely. I suppose it will be a month-to-month thing from here on out."

"It's sad it had to come to this. She's been through so much. It's the way the world is today. Kids just have too much to deal with. My daughter Tammy has been acting strange lately. Staying out late, coming home smelling of alcohol. It's a troubling time."

"Well, I look at it this way. Amanda was at the end of her rope and we had to make a decision. Things can only get better from here."

Amanda's mother pulled her coat tighter around herself as they stepped outside. The sun was still low on the horizon, and the stiff cool breeze chased brittle, autumn leaves around the dozens of tombstones that dotted Downer's Grove Cemetery.

"Oh, look," Mrs. Abercrombie said, pointing toward the back of the cemetery at the last tombstone. "There's our good luck symbol again."

The owl landed elegantly on the crest of Abigail Martin's white granite tombstone and spread its great wings, the long shadows thrown by the early morning sun stretching across the other tombstones, cloaking the church grounds in a shroud of darkness.

Daughters

JULEEN BRANTINGHAM

It begins with a dream. It ends with a dream. My mother's people say a dream is the shadow of something real. For all their wisdom, I think they may be wrong about this, and what we think of as real is merely the shadow of a dream.

The First Dream

I open the front door of my house and step inside. The carpet has turned to moss. Where I step, then lift my foot, my footprint fills with water. The walls are dark and rough as bark. The smell of blood is in the air. Ahead and to my left is the staircase. The stairs have become a muddy hill. Vines hang down from the second floor.

I hear a distant piping. The music is as familiar to me as the beating of my heart.

The air is thick and hard to breathe.

To my right is the doorway to the living room. I notice in passing that an oak tree, its roots buried in the hearth, is growing from the fireplace opening. It is an ancient oak, gnarled, its bark green with algae. Its branches and leaves form a ceiling beneath the ceiling.

Close to the walls, half-hidden by leaves and shadows, are strangers who watch me pass. The lust for burning is in their eyes. I know their faces, though not their names. I acquired their portraits after years of searching through museum shops and antique stores.

I walk down the hall to the kitchen, pass through it seeing nothing, aware only of the aroma of ripe fruit, which, strong as it is, does not blot out the smell of blood. I reach for the door to the cellar but it yawns open before I can turn the knob. The hinges groan in protest. My steps are sure and I do not stumble.

The piping music follows me.

Seven steps descend to the landing where a ground-level window looks out on what should be the backyard. Earth fills the window. I see the lacework of roots, a worm twining among them, a splinter of bone.

I turn on the landing and go down seven more steps. Another turn, another landing, another seven steps.

In my house in the world there is no second landing, no third flight of steps.

At the bottom of the steps my bare feet are immersed in air so cold that I have to look down to be certain I am not standing in a stream of water. I find myself facing an arch carved from living rock. Water trickles down the chipped surface. I pass through the arch into a room little bigger than a table. It is dark when I enter but a moment later, candles spring to life all around me, tens of them. The flames waver in the air, refusing to illuminate those who stand behind them.

Centered on the wall in front of me is an alcove, also carved from the rock. Lying on the waist-high ledge of that alcove, like a sleeper in a bed, is a skeleton dressed in a long gown of white linen. The stems of roses, fresh as though they had been plucked only moments ago, are twined around and through the skeleton's finger bones.

I touch the skull as if to bless it, and all the bones collapse to dust. I wet the tips of the fingers of my left hand, dip them in the skull dust. With those fingers I trace a symbol on my forehead.

I take up the dress and slip it on, scarcely noticing that somewhere between the front door and this niche I have shed my clothing. I pick up the roses, twine their stems around my hands. I lie down on the pile of scattered dust.

I wait.

There the dream ends.

I shivered for hours after I woke. Nothing could warm me, not the blankets Carl piled around me, not the tea he prepared for me, not his arms nor his naked body. It wasn't until dawn began to lighten the sky that I could bring myself to tell him.

"I have to find her, Carl." As soon as I said it I began to feel warmer.

"That's what this is all about? Finding your mother?" Carl considers himself a rational, practical man. He does not remember his dreams.

I smiled at him, a tremulous smile but the best I could manage. He was very dear to me. My failure was not his and we both knew it, yet he never blamed me.

"She needs me. I need her. Then, I'm sure, there will be no more problems."

"I never heard such nonsense."

As I drove to school I found myself humming the music from my dream. It made me uneasy so I turned on the radio. The same music was playing on every station.

I was supposed to have lunchroom duty that day but I pleaded headache and a friend took my place. I called the agency that had tracked down my mother for me and I told them, yes, I was sure, and would they please arrange the meeting. Afterward I sat at my desk, sipping a cup of cold water, trying to pretend I was not scared to death. I had always known that I was adopted. My mother told me that my birth mother was her sister and she had died when I was six months old.

I was in high school when I decided that I needed to know more than Mother was willing to tell me. By chance I found someone who had known her before she was married. She said both my parents were only children.

Mother found out what I was doing and there was a terrible scene. The thing that persuaded me to stop searching was not Mother's anger. It was the fear I saw behind that anger.

Mother had died a year ago. By then I had become upset by my inability to conceive and I think I would have started the search again even if she were alive, in spite of her fear.

As I sat at my desk the classroom door banged open and a cold breeze swirled into the room. It carried the scent of blood and the sound of rustling leaves.

"A dream is the shadow of something real."

It was dismissal time and the corridor was a confusion of scampering feet, slamming doors, shouts, and laughter. The person who spoke was on the other side of the corridor but I heard her words as clearly as if she were standing next to me. She was small and dark skinned, with straight black hair that hung to her waist. Her silver earrings were in the shape of crescent moons. She was dressed in black.

"Excuse me, what did you say?" I made my way over to her, wading through a flood of children.

She held out her hand. "My name is Dori Ashe."

Mother's friend. I had been told to expect her. For some reason my mother would not come to me, nor would she allow a stranger to take me to her.

The other teachers were staring at us. Their looks were disapproving.

Dori—"Please don't call me Miss Ashe"—drove me to a part of town I had never seen before, a street of row houses, bleak and shabby like decades-old government housing. There was no grass, no trees, no shrubbery or flowers. Poorly dressed children with red hands and dripping noses played listlessly in the street. They turned to watch as Dori led me to a door with peeling green paint. The door was unlocked.

The interior of the house was strangely like my own, but bare, dark, and dirty, as if the inhabitants were staying here temporarily and did not plan to make it their home. To my left a flight of stairs led to the second floor. To my right was an arched doorway into a room with a fireplace and no furniture except for a vinyl-covered hassock, coming apart at the seams. A fire smoldered in the fireplace, giving off an acrid stench.

"Wait here, dear," Dori said. "I will go and prepare her."

"Prepare her? What—"

I was alone.

I walked over to the fireplace, holding out my hands. I couldn't feel any heat. Then I saw what was burning. Shreds of the doll's white dress remained unburned, though most of her body had melted to a gooey puddle. It was her head that was burning. It must have been made of wood. Where her eyes should have been were two red embers.

"She's ready for you now, dear," Dori said from the hall.

She led me to the back, toward what would have been the kitchen in my house. She opened a door into a small dark room and politely stood back for me to enter. To my left was a single window covered by a torn black shade. In front of me was a cot.

There was no one lying on the cot, only a white dress and a scattering of red roses.

"There's no one—"

Dori was closing the door. "She'll be right with you, dear. Please put on the dress. You want to look pretty for her, don't you?"

"No! What *is* this? Come back!" The words were right but they lacked force. I'm sure Dori couldn't have heard me on the other side of that closed door.

What I did may seem foolish. I only know it was not. No matter what happened, I was prepared to accept the consequences. I cannot explain my state of mind any better than that.

I put on the dress. I lay down on the cot, holding the roses in my hands.

Carl had to come to the emergency room to fetch me. The police had found me wandering in the street near the school. The doctor said I was not sick, not injured. I was simply too dazed to speak or to follow what others said to me. Later I told Carl I had been too excited to eat breakfast and I had skipped lunch. He soon forgot the incident.

Six months after my daughter was born, Carl left us, for reasons having nothing to do with those few missing hours.

Two days later Dori came for the child.

The Last Dream

I am walking down the street, my shoes clacking on the cobblestones. Townspeople nod to me but behind my back they glare for I am the wife of the witch finder, a person they hate but dare not offend.

I leave the last townhouse behind me, skirting a man driving three pigs to market. I pass down a country road to a dark wood. I slip into the shadows and watch the road for a while but no one has followed me.

The ground underfoot is wet. Where I step, then lift my foot, my footprint fills with water. The trees grow so close together that I almost feel I am surrounded by walls. I hurry because I know I haven't much time. My husband will expect to find me at home when he returns from administering the strappado and the Spanish boot. The smell of blood is in the air.

Beneath an ancient oak is a cottage made of sticks and mud. Dead vines form a curtain over the doorway. I brush them aside and enter. It is dark inside. I hear a breathy piping, the music as familiar to me as the beating of my own heart, but so soft it cannot be heard outside the cottage.

Candles spring to life all around me. Behind the flames are the faces of women I have never seen before, my sisters. No one speaks as I disrobe.

A girl lies on a pallet against the far wall. She is wearing a white dress. There is a symbol sketched on her forehead, and in her hands she holds red roses. Her eyes are closed.

I go to her and kiss her eyelids, her throat, her hands. Then I part her lips and breathe my soul into her. Life quickens in her womb. I dress again and return home to the witch finder.

Thus we survive, one generation after another, living among you, unseen.

Beware of That for Which You Wish

LINDA J. DUNN

Moria gasped for breath as she collapsed onto the boulder. This was it. The place no woman went twice.

She kicked off her shoes and hobbled over to the nearby stream. The cold water felt good on her feet.

You are an old fool, she told herself. *This place is for young girls. A place for wishes of romance.*

Go home. Tend the children. Forget Ronan's dreams.

She rubbed her feet and smiled at her own foolishness. *What would the other villagers say if they saw me climbing the path to cast a wish?*

Best get back before I'm missed.

"And who will miss you, Moria?"

She jumped up and bit back a scream. The woman standing before her looked far too young to be the one all the townspeople whispered about.

Moria stepped backwards slightly, lost her footing, and nearly fell into the stream. The woman grabbed her and pulled her forward with a strength that seemed oddly out of place with her slender body and silky white hands.

"Are you Eithne?" Moria asked.

The woman smiled. "Is that old story still making the rounds? Eithne is my name, true. But if you're looking for magic you best go elsewhere, as true magic asks a cruel price. Besides, aren't you a little —shall we say mature—to be looking for romance?"

Moria felt her cheeks growing hot. "I didn't come seeking romance. Found that when I was young. Married and six children now."

Eithne tightened her grip on Moria's arm and turned her hand palm up. "You've health and wealth. A good man and fine, strong children." She let go. "So why did you brave the steep path to seek a gift? You have everything for which a woman could wish."

"Almost."

Their eyes met and the Eithne shook her head sadly. "Ah, so it's like that, is it?"

"I don't understand." She tried to look away but she couldn't. Eithne nodded.

"You're approaching that age and you feel the lack."

"What?"

"Your children all be girls."

Moria turned away. "Is it that obvious?"

Eithne laughed. "Why a boy? There are many who would envy your healthy girls. Can't you be content with that?"

Moria turned her head slightly. "Ronan is happy with his houseful of girls, but I feel a failure. Why can't I give the man I love the same thing that many a woman has given her husband?"

She stared as the woman brushed her long blonde hair back from her face. The ears were almost pointed and the face a little too pale.

"You *are* one, aren't you? The fairy-witch who haunts this stream?"

Eithne smiled and folded her arms across her chest. "Some like to believe so and it does me no harm to humor them.

"The young ones, they want love potions. I give them some lotions I make from flowers and they go away happy. The smell attracts the young men. The girls' self-confidence keeps them. It's a simple matter, really. There's no magic here."

"Oh." Moria took a deep breath and looked back the way she came. "I best return. Someone will notice my absence soon."

Eithne stooped down and picked a small purple flower. "Wait. Stay a while please. I have few visitors and those are usually empty-headed girls. Tell me the gossip in the village."

Moria looked into the woman's sea-blue eyes and felt sorry for her. Just for today, the chores could wait. She picked up her shoes and turned to Eithne. "How much do you know about the families below?"

Eithne smiled. "I was born in that village and once knew every adult and child. But time passes differently in the valley than it does in this place."

Moria stopped walking and looked over her shoulder.

"Fear not. You are safe for today. Tell me, did the smith's daughter ever marry?"

Moria paused for a moment. "The smith's daughter? Why, she's but a child."

Eithne sighed and looked across the stream. "And the smith's daughter before her?"

Moria thought a moment. "He had only sons."

Eithne shook her head. "Surely there was a smith's daughter who was proud of her looks and refused each man in turn as unworthy of her—"

"Old Annie? But she—"

"Ah. Anna was her name. A truly beautiful lass who led all the men on a merry chase.

Moria stared for a moment. "Annie died when I was a mere child. I remember the story only because my mother went on and on after her funeral about how she always said no man was good enough for her and then died alone."

Eithne nodded. "I warned her that beauty had its price but she would hear none of it."

"You knew her?"

"She's the reason I'm here."

Moria stopped walking and looked around her. Never had she seen such a beautiful garden. "What are you, Eithne?"

"Sometimes I ask myself that question." She sighed and handed Moria a bitter-smelling plant. "If you're set upon a son, place this under your pillow tonight. But I warn you, wanting something and actually having what you desire are two different things."

Moria's fingers shook as she took the offered gift. "I don't know how to thank you."

Eithne shook her head. "In a few years you'll probably curse me. Go home. Time will change soon."

Three months passed before Moria was sure. Ronan, as expected, was delighted with the news and even more excited when the child she bore proved to be the long-awaited boy.

Ronan changed after their son was born. Oh, how he changed. A stern and caring father with the girls, he indulged his son's every whim. The boy grew older and crueler, and the day came when Moria knew there was only one thing to do.

The girls accompanied her this time.

"I expected you back," Eithne said, turning to look at each girl fully in turn. "My, but you look a sorry bunch. Didn't your wish bring you happiness?"

"I think you know it did not."

"That's the problem with wishes. Sometimes what we want most isn't good for us. What wish you now?"

Moria's voice was a mere whisper. "My son will marry soon."

"Most sons usually do."

"Ronan intends to give him everything. The house. The farm. The girls will be beggars. No one wants to marry someone who brings nothing but trouble into their home."

Eithne shook her head. "Old fools are the biggest fools. And what would you do about this?"

Moria's voice broke as she worded her request carefully. "I seek your wisdom this time, not my own foolishness."

"Ah. The years have taught you well." Eithne looked upward for a moment, almost as though searching the clouds for an answer.

"Your son should be decked out as finely as possible for a wedding, should he not?"

Moria nodded.

"Then take him to the tailor whose shop is near the sea. He is expensive but I assure you it will be worth every penny of it."

"Nothing bad will happen to him?"

Eithne shook her head. "You ask for a solution and you want it without cost. Yes. A few bad things will happen to him. But he will not die from them. Now go."

Moria and her daughters left and did as she said. Ronan not only agreed to the most expensive tailor around, he also suggested the girls also have new clothing so they would not disgrace their brother by their appearances.

Thus, everyone was there when it happened.

No monsters appeared and took him away. No siren from the sea called him to drown. Nothing like that at all occurred.

Instead, the tailor's brother stopped by for a quite unexpected visit.

Erin had left years ago to seek his fortune and found it. While the tailor took measurements, Erin told him and everyone around about a land where the streets were paved with gold and everyone was rich.

Moria's son disappeared the next morning and has not been seen since. Ronan died the following spring. Some say he died of grief but others said it was from relief of not needing to chase after his ill-begotten son anymore.

Mourning lasted but a short time as the girls were quickly married off with good dowries.

When the last was gone, Moria left the house and made the long walk again to the place where no other one but her had ever ventured twice, let alone three times.

"You've come again?" Eithne asked. "I recognize your walk."

Moria answered softly. "Yes. It's me. I know the price now."

"You may have to wait a long time," Eithne warned.

"I know. But I've learned the value of patience and to be satisfied with simple pleasures."

"Ah. Then it's with happiness that I leave this place. Farewell."

Moria blinked her eyes as the old woman vanished without even telling her where she might find her new home. She found such advice unnecessary as her mind suddenly filled with everything she needed to know. At last, she understood how fairy time differed from mortal time.

It was, to the best she could determine, only a few days before footsteps pounded on the trail.

"Eithne?" A young girl called.

"My sister has gone on," Moria answered. "I answer your needs now. My name is Moria. What be your wish here?"

The girl's face blushed bright red. "There's a man I like. He just returned from a long journey and bought back his father's farm from his sister's husbands. I want to marry him."

Moria smiled. "I know the lad of which you speak. He was a wild one but I trust his travels have taught him well. Come with me and we will talk of the gossip in the village while I work the spell."

And after she left, Moria settled in for a long wait. For now she understood the old saying "What goes around, comes around."

Cerile and the Journeyer

ADAM-TROY CASTRO

The journeyer was still a young man when he embarked on his search for the all-powerful witch Cerile.

He was gray-haired and stooped a lifetime later when he found a map to her home in the tomb of the forgotten kings.

The map directed him halfway across the world, over the Soul-Eater Mountains, through the Curtains of Night, past the scars of the Eternal War, and across a great grassy plain, to the outskirts of Cerile's desert.

The desert was an ocean of luminescent white sand, which even in the dead of night still radiated the killing heat it swallowed during the day; he knew at once that it could broil the blood in his veins before he traveled even half the distance to the horizon. It even warned him: "Turn back, journeyer. I am as sharp as broken glass, and as hot as open flame; I am filled with soft shifting places that can open up and swallow you without warning; I can drive you mad and leave you to wander in circles until your strength sinks into the earth; and when you die of thirst, as you surely shall if you attempt to pass, I can ride the winds to flay the skin from your burnt and blistered bones."

He proceeded across the dunes, stumbling as his feet sank ankle-deep into the sand, gasping as the furnace heat turned his breath to a dry rasp, but hesitating not at all, merely continuing his march toward the destiny that could mean either death or Cerile.

When the desert saw it couldn't stop him, the ground burst open in a million places, pierced by a great forest that with the speed known only by miracles shot up to scrape the sky. The trees were all hundreds of arm-lengths across, the spaces between them so narrow that even an uncommonly thin man would have had to hold his breath to pass. It was a forest that could exhaust him utterly before he traveled even halfway to the horizon. It even warned him: "Turn back, journeyer. I am as dark as the night itself, and as threatening as your worst dreams; I am rich with thorns sharp enough to rip the skin from your arms; and if you die lost and alone, as you surely shall if you attempt to pass, I can dig roots into your flesh and grow more trees on your bones."

He entered the woods anyway, crying out as thorns drew blood from his arms and legs, gasping as the trees drew close and threatened to imprison him, but hesitating not at all: merely continuing to march west, toward the destiny that could be either death or Cerile.

When the forest saw that it couldn't stop him, then the trees all around him merely withered away, and the ground ahead of him rose up, like a thing on hinges, to form a right angle with the ground at his feet. The resulting wall stretched from one horizon to the other, rising straight up into the sky to disappear ominously in the clouds. He knew at once that he did not have the skill or the strength to climb even halfway to the unseen summit. It even warned him: "Turn back, journeyer. I am as smooth as glass and as treacherous as an enemy; I am poor with hand-holds and impossible to climb; and if you fall, as you surely will if you attempt to pass, then the ground where I stand will be the resting place of your shattered corpse."

He proceeded to climb anyway, moaning as his arms and legs turned to lead from exhaustion, gasping as the temperature around him turned chilly and then frigid, but hesitating not at all, merely continuing to climb upward, toward the destiny that could be either death or Cerile.

When the cliff saw that it couldn't stop him, the warm winds came and gently lifted him into the sky, over the top of the wall, and down into a lush green valley on the other side, where a frail, white-haired old woman sat beside a still and mirrored pond.

The winds deposited him on his feet on the opposite side of the pond, allowing him to see himself in the water: how he was bent, and stooped, and white-haired, and old, with skin the texture of leather, and eyes that had suffered too much for too long.

He looked away from his reflection, and faced the crone across the water. "You are Cerile?"

"I am," she croaked, in a voice ancient and filled with dust.

"I have heard of you," he said, with the last of his battered strength. "How you have mastered all the secrets of the heavens and the earth, and can make the world itself do its bidding for you. How you've hidden yourself in this place at the edge of the world, and sworn to grant the fondest Wish of any soul clever and brave enough to find you. I have spent my entire life journeying here, Cerile, just to ask this of you. I wish—"

The old woman shushed him, softly but emphatically, and painfully pulled herself to her feet, her bent back forcing her to face the ground as she spoke to him again. "Never mind your Wish. Meet me in the water, journeyer."

And with that she doffed her clothes and lowered her withered, emaciated frame in the pond, disturbing its mirrored surface not at all. By the time she was knee-deep, her white hair darkened, turning raven black; by the time she was hip-deep, the wrinkles in her face had smoothed out, becoming perfect, unblemished skin; by the time she was shoulder-deep, her rheumy, unfocused eyes had unclouded, revealing a shade of green as brilliant and as beautiful as the most precious emerald.

By then, of course, the journeyer had also descended naked into the magical pond, to feel the weight of years lifted from his flesh; to feel his weathered skin smooth out, growing strong and supple again; to feel his spine grow straight and his eyes grow clear and his shoulders grow broad, as they had been before he started his quest, more years ago than he could count.

When they met, at the deepest part of the pond, she surprised him with an embrace.

"I am Cerile," she said. "I have been awaiting your arrival for longer than you can possibly know."

He couldn't speak. He knew only that she was right, that he had known her for an age far beyond the limited reach of his memory, that they had loved each other once, and would now love each other again.

They kissed, and she led him from the water, to a small cottage that hadn't been standing on the spot a heartbeat before. There were fine clothes waiting for him, to replace those torn to rags by his long journey. There was a feast, too, to fill the yawning void in his belly. There were other wonders too, things that could only exist in the home of a miracle-worker like Cerile: things he had not the wit to name, that glittered and whirred in odd corners, spinning soft music unlike any he had ever heard. He would have been dazzled by them had Cerile not also been there, to dazzle him even more.

But still, something gnawed at him.

It wasn't the Wish, which seemed such a trivial little thing, now, a trifle not even worth mentioning, because Cerile in her love gave him everything any man could possibly want . . . and yet, yes, damn him, it was the Wish, the miracle he'd waited his entire life to see, and had marched across kingdoms to find.

It had something to do with all those oceans he'd crossed, all those monsters he'd fought, all the winters he'd endured.

It was pride.

He stayed with her for a year and a day, in that little valley where the days themselves seemed written for them, where the gardens changed colors daily to fit their moods, and the stars danced whimsical little jigs to accompany the musical way she laughed at night. Even troubled as he was, he knew a happiness that he hadn't known for a long time, maybe not ever, certainly not for as far back as his limited memory recorded: not since sometime before the day, a lifetime before, when he'd found himself a stranger in a small fishing village, wholly unable to remember who he was or how he'd come to that place.

Then, late one night, at the end of their year together, he awoke tormented by the strange restlessness in his heart, and rose from their bed to walk alone by the edge of her private fountain of youth. The water had always reflected the stars, every other night he'd looked upon it; it had always seemed to contain an entirely self-contained universe, as filled with endless possibility as the one where he and Cerile lived and walked and breathed. But tonight, though there were plenty of stars in the sky, none were reflected on the pond surface; the water showed only a dark, inky blackness that reflected not possibility but the cold finality of a prison.

Cerile's beautiful voice rang out from somewhere in the darkness that suddenly surrounded him: "What is wrong, my love?"

"I was thinking," he said, without turning to face her, "that I journeyed all this distance and spent all this time here and never got around to asking you to grant my Wish."

"Is there any point?" she asked—and for the first time since he arrived, he heard in her voice an unsettling note of despair. "What could you possibly wish for that would be of any value to you here? Health? Strength? Eternal youth and beauty? You already have that, here. Love? Happiness? I've given you those, too. Riches? Power? Stay here and you can have as much of either as any man could possibly want."

"I know," he said. "They were all things I once thought I'd wish for when I found you. You gave them to me without waiting for me to wish for them. But my Wish is still hanging over my head, demanding to be used."

"You don't have to listen to it."

"I do. It's the only thing I own that I earned myself, that I can truly say you didn't give me. And if I don't use it, then everything I've done means nothing."

"Why don't you just wish that you can be content to always stay here with me, and love me forever, as I'll love you forever?"

He turned and faced her, seeing her forlorn and lost by the door of their cottage, wanting her more than everything he'd ever wanted before, feeling his own heart break at the knowledge that he'd caused the sorrow welling in her eyes. And for the first time he understood that they'd endured this moment hundreds or even thousands of times before, for as long as the sun had been a fire in the sky.

He said, "I'm sorry. I can't wish for that. I wish for the one thing I lost when I came here. A purpose. Something to struggle for. A reason to deserve everything you give me, whenever I manage to find my way back."

She granted his Wish, then fell to her knees and sobbed: not the tears of an omnipotent creature who controlled the earth and the stars, and could have had everything she ever wanted, but the tears of a lonely little girl who couldn't.

When she rose again, she approached the waters of eternal youth and sat down beside them, knowing that she wouldn't feel their touch again until the inevitable day, still a lifetime away, when he would, all too briefly, return to her.

Someday, she swore, she'd make him so happy that he'd never wish to leave.

Until then—

The journeyer was still a young man when he embarked upon his search for the great witch Cerile.

He was gray-haired and stooped a lifetime later when he found a map to her home in the tomb of the forgotten kings. . . .

The Witch of the World's End

DARRELL SCHWEITZER

The Witch of the World's End dwelt alone in a tower of glass, at the Earth's uttermost rim. For attendants, she had only spirits, figures of light that flickered like flame. Whirling columns of dust came and went as she bade them; and brilliantly plumed metallic birds sang for her, animated by the captive souls of the dead. At night, stone soldiers guarded her battlements, the statues of her garden stirred to life, eyes hollow and darkly gleaming, animated by the strength of her dreams.

She wanted no other company, for all her waking hours she spent at her loom, weaving a tapestry of shadow and starlight and something infinitely finer than spider's silk; and in that tapestry were depicted all the lives of men, their deeds and their glories, their sins and their sufferings, and, most especially, their manifold but ultimately monotonous deaths.

All these things she shaped with her delicate hands, and whether they were true because she wove them, or she wove them because they were true, not even the Witch of the World's End knew for certain.

Once she glanced up, noticing the Moon as it came drifting through her great hall, high up near the ceiling, entering by the east window and leaving by the west, like a pigeon fluttering under the eaves.

Her hand slipped. A thread tangled, distorting the pattern she had intended. She paused to study this new thing, then sighed softly and continued her work, embroidering around the tangled thread, naming the new figure she created Antharic. She wrought him as a splendid knight, astride a black war-steed, his silver armor gleaming in the moonlight, his spearhead like the flash of an enormous jewel suddenly revealed in the dark, the emblem on his shield that of a charging bull.

That same bull that is sacred to Vastorion, who ranks in Hell as Lord of Vengeance.

Antharic was coming to kill the Witch of the World's End.

She wove the outline of him, humming softly the litanies of Vengeance, and of Satan.

The long hangings in her chamber rippled in some secret draught.

When Antharic was small, he stood ragged and barefoot on a little mound, waving a stick and shouting, "Look! I'm a giant-killer! I am Caesar! I am Alexander! I am braver than all the knights in the world!"

His father laughed bitterly and swatted him with the back of a huge hand, sending the boy tumbling into a puddle.

"You're just a dirty boy. You'll grow up to be a dirty man. Now get to work and forget your silly dreams."

And Antharic labored in the fields beside his father and his brothers, knee-deep in mud. Even his grandfather was there for a time, until the work broke him and the old man died. The sun rose and set, rose and set; the stars turned in their courses and the seasons passed in turn. At each harvest, the King's men came to collect their share, and everyone went hungry.

That was all anyone knew. In the winter, the family sat in the cold and the dark, telling stories no one believed, or singing songs that had no life in them.

"I will be a great hero one day," Antharic said. "You will be amazed."

Often his father was too weary even to laugh.

But Antharic dreamed his dreams, and in them he beheld the witch in her chamber, weaving. She was young and slender, as exquisite as anything she wove. Sometimes she spoke to him in a soft voice, and sometimes the weaving seemed to pass through his own hands. He saw the figure of the knight clearly, its visor raised to reveal a broad face with pale, passionless eyes. He admired the strong form of the hero, the massive shoulders and thighs, like those of Hercules in the old stories.

"Antharic," the witch said to him. "This knight is named Antharic."

But Antharic was a dirty boy, famine-thin, with a gaping, round face, like a pumpkin atop a stick, people always said.

In his dreams, too, in the witch's weaving, Antharic saw a second figure, that of Pestilence, a skeleton in a black shroud, sowing seeds of death like dragon's teeth, out of a pouch worn at the hip.

When he awoke, his mother and his sisters were already dying, shivering and coughing up blood. Only he and his father survived. They had to burn the house to get the contagion out, then bury their dead, and when these things were done, his father looked very old and very tired.

Soon after the King's men came for the crops, but there were no crops, because no one had been able to harvest them.

That day, for the first time in his life, Antharic beheld a genuine knight, a mighty man of war in tarnished armor, seated on a war-horse, pointing and giving orders to the others.

"Where is your fee?" asked the knight, leaning down from his saddle.

Antharic's father could only show his empty hands.

"My lord must be paid," said the knight.

Without further words, he struck off the old man's head. His men stuck it on a post, as a warning, then all of them rode away, laughing.

Antharic hated that knight at once, and resolved to slay him, but he knew that first, in madness or guile, he would have to become like him; and his hatred was as for one who had stolen what was rightfully his own.

Antharic ran after them, waving his arms and shouting. "Take me with you! I will be a knight too!"

"The child is crazed," someone said. The men rode on at their own pace.

When he was still following them on the second day, the knight said, "No, I think he is some demon, sent to hound us into sin." So the others crossed themselves fearfully, and spread out, to find and slay Antharic. But they couldn't find him, and told their master so. "He has gone back to Hell then," said the knight.

The others laughed, uneasily.

Antharic, meanwhile, had fallen down in exhaustion and grief, dreaming fierce dreams. In those dreams, he paced back and forth in the chamber of the Witch of the World's End, ashamed of the rags he wore and his muddy, bare feet shuffling on the witch's polished floor. But still she wove. The needle in her hand was like a silver fish, leaping from wave to wave, appearing and reappearing, sparkling as it moved. And she sang her soft song; and once she paused to take his hand in hers, and even to place the needle in his hand, though he didn't know what to do with it.

"What I have made, will be," she said. "Therefore be comforted."

He gave the needle back to her, but as he did, he pricked his finger. A droplet of his blood stained the tapestry, and the witch went on with her work, as he shuffled away from her, then back again, then away, glancing fearfully at her handiwork, as his own tale within it grew and changed.

And once he fell down faint from hunger and seemed to awaken into another, different dream, where a holy anchorite had carried him to his cell deep in a forest. There, in the quiet darkness, the holy man healed him; and Antharic confided all he had experienced in his other dream. He spoke of the Witch of the World's End.

"These are Satan's tricks," said the anchorite. "Snares and devouring mouths. If you let them, they will indeed devour you."

When Antharic at last rose to leave, his host bade him tarry and pray a while, and turn from the path he had already begun to follow. Antharic prayed, but uncertainly, and finally said, "No, Brother. I must be going. I have to be glorious."

He described again what he had seen in the witch's tapestry, and told some of the stories of the hero-knight, Antharic.

"Is this what you really want?" said the anchorite.

"Yes. More than anything."

"Then I weep for you."

Antharic walked through the forest a little ways, where ghosts of armored men stirred in the darkness and whispered to him of glory, and of destiny. After a while, he awoke from his second dream, back into his first, and he stood once more in the weaving chamber of the Witch of the World's End.

She held up a section of her work, showing him the tiny figure of the anchorite, his cell enclosed by a circle of thread, and hundreds of warrior figures swirling around and past it like a stream rushing past a rock.

"Go now," she told him. "Be what you are to be."

He bowed low to her, as a knight must to his lady. He kissed her hand, his heart racing, shocked that he should be so bold. But the witch merely smiled, and turned back to her weaving. So he left her, and journeyed for a time in the forest among the ghosts; their armor creaked and clanked faintly in the cold wind.

Once he heard the anchorite's voice, far away and very faint, like the voice of a dove in the morning, calling out to God. But he kept on walking, and after a while he heard it no longer.

Later, came shouts and screams, the thud of hooves, and the clangor of arms.

He began to run, and suddenly the forest around him was filled with rushing figures on horseback, and with fire; and the air filled with arrows rattling through the branches like hail. He leapt over corpses and the writhing wounded, and emerged into a field beneath a wintry evening sky, where a castle burned and ash and snow swirled.

The rout of battle raged around him, mounted knights riding down footmen whose lines had broken, knights clashing with other knights, their horses rearing and shrieking. The dead lay in heaps beneath their shields, snow on their faces.

And suddenly, it seemed to Antharic that his eyes were opened for the first time, and he saw no glory in any of this, only horror. He turned and tried to flee, to find his way back to the anchorite's cell, or back home, somewhere, anywhere; but he heard the Witch of the World's End singing her song, and in his mind's eye he saw her hands working at her loom, faster and faster.

A huge knight with a helmet horned like a charging bull bore down on him. He yelped and tried to duck, but the great sweep of the knight's sword clipped him on the side of the head and he tumbled head over heels through the air, like a leaf in a whirlwind.

There was no sound at all then, nothing in the world but for the song of the Witch of the World's End, and no other motion but for the silver flicker of her needle, rising and falling from a sea of thread. Dully, far away, someone else, not Antharic, felt the terrible, burning cold, and the dull throb of his wound, and the warmth on one cheek where blood poured over it.

All around him, shadow-men fought and fell in utter silence. He walked among them, and their spears did not touch him.

The drawbridge stretched over the moat of the burning castle. A single armored figure lay there.

"I know you," said Antharic, kneeling down.

"And I, you," said the other.

It was that same knight who had killed Antharic's father.

"I have seen you in my dreams," this knight said, "and I know you to be some evil spirit, who brings my death."

"I have seen you in mine, too," said Antharic, who drew a dagger from the fallen knight's belt and slit the knight's throat with it. "My lady must be paid."

The knight coughed, then wept softly, his eyes wide, as if he were looking far away and he too beheld the Witch of the World's End and heard her song. But no, Antharic thought, this man was a simple brute, a coarse butcher who defiled the form of a true knight. Such a one could not possibly share his vision.

Therefore he raised the dagger to drive it through the dying man's heart, but then he saw there was no need, stripped him of his armor and clothes, and rolled the naked corpse into the moat.

He armed himself then, in the manner of a knight, as best he could manage, though his fingers were numb with cold and the armor was far heavier than he had ever imagined it would be. Nothing fit. The metal pinched and cut. Staggering, rattling, he made his way to the end of the drawbridge, only to confront that same huge, bull-horned warrior who had struck him down before.

"Stand and draw your sword," said the other, in a voice like thunder rumbling behind hills. "Be not craven."

"But . . . but . . ." Antharic staggered back, tripped over his own scabbard, and fell in a clanking heap. He struggled desperately to all fours, but could not rise. With sweeping strides, the bull-headed knight crossed the drawbridge. Boards trembled.

"Get up and draw your sword."

Antharic called out then to the Witch of the World's End, and he heard her song. He saw her needle rising, falling, flickering like a silver fish. She worked faster, faster. Antharic knew that his own story could not end here, on this bridge.

Therefore he rose, and dead men whispered in his ears; ghosts gathered around him, thick as smoke, screaming ever so softly how they too had risen and fought and suffered and died for the weaving of the Witch of the World's End, how she gave them strength when it pleased her to, and all of them, too, had performed great deeds for her, even miracles.

Antharic rose, and though he had no skill at arms, he somehow fought. The battle went on for hours in the darkness, across the frozen field, into the forest, amid the heaps of the slain; for thus the Witch of the World's End wove the tale of Antharic. He bore the fallen knight's shield, which was marked with an hourglass and a horn. His foeman's shield was that of the Lord of Vengeance, but Vengeance drove Antharic now. He lusted after it, hating and sorrowing as he did; his mind filled with remorse and joy together, with a sense of loss and of dawning glory.

This was what it meant to become a knight. Sparks flew. Metal clanged. The bull-man charged again and again, but Antharic turned him away with blows and with his stolen shield. Sometimes it seemed that the two of them fought amid vast armies, that some greater conflict rushed around them like a swollen stream around two rocks. But always they found one another again, cutting their way through the armies like reapers through wheat.

"What *are* you?" asked the bull-headed knight, gasping, as he paused to rest on his shield.

"I am Antharic, a knight of great worship and renown. Isn't that obvious?"

"Is it?"

"*Yes!*"

Their swords contended.

The Witch of the World's End wove and sang at her weaving.

From far, far away came the voice of the holy anchorite, mourning for the boy Antharic who had been lost.

"And what are *you*?" Antharic asked of his foe.

The other, raising his visor, revealed only flames, as if he had opened the door of a furnace. "Don't you recognize me?"

At that instant, the sun rose; and the flames beneath the visor burst out and became the blinding face of the sun. Antharic fell to his knees, covering his face, and he heard his enemy's battle-shout of triumph. But Antharic leapt to his feet again, blind as he was, and thrust upward with his sword.

The foeman's battle-shout became a death-cry.

When his sight returned, Antharic stood alone amid frozen corpses on the battlefield. It was dawn. The ruined castle smoldered. Crows perched on helms, pecking for difficult meat. A heap of empty, charred armor lay at Antharic's feet. He knelt down, painfully, and exchanged his own shield for the one emblazoned with the sign of the charging bull.

Now came the most terrible part of that dream which was the boy Antharic's life.

(The Witch of the World's End wove, hands like fluttering moths.)

He galloped on a mighty steed, through many lands, through many wars, contending with giants, with many knights, all of whom he overthrew and slew without mercy, until the hideous glory of his name spread before him and all men fled at his approach. He rode past crows pecking at corpses. Towns and castles smoldered, ravaged. Deeper, deeper, into the darkness, into forests he plunged; and metal-clad things with the faces of wolves swarmed from beneath the trees, calling him to battle; and he fought with them, and slew them all.

He never paused to rest within this dream, this dream within another dream; but sometimes he didn't seem to be a knight at all, but the boy Antharic who lay in a ditch, cold and muddy and weeping. That boy, lying there, dreamed impossible fantasies of vengeance, and his mind was filled with monsters and battles and fiery knights with heads like bulls.

He thought he heard the anchorite calling out once, but could not find him.

(And the Witch of the World's End wove, her needle leaping like a fish.)

He rode. Fires roared around him. Ghosts screamed amid the burning, and all the pain of the world was his, to cause and to suffer, and he was filled to overflowing with it as he crossed into Hell itself and the damned cursed the Witch of the World's End; and Satan loomed high amid swirling, blood-red clouds, like a dark mountain, impassive, silent, brooding.

Once more, even there, Antharic heard the voice of the anchorite, calling out to him.

"Turn from this path."

"But where?"

"Merely turn away."

"Am I not glorious?"

The anchorite cried out in despair, and was gone.

Devils raced alongside Antharic, and he conversed long with bull-headed Vengeance, and he came to understand that the Witch of the World's End wove mankind's sorrows into her tapestry merely to amuse herself, as a child might arrange a course for ants to follow, then smash them all when tired of the game.

Therefore Antharic swore a quest against the Witch of the World's End, in the name of Vengeance.

(And she wove. She sang. Her needle leapt.)

He rose from out of the low plains of Hell, out of fire and swirling ash, up, across a dead sea's bottom filled with dust, up, through a forest of white bone, where harpies with needle-claws tried to tear out his eyes. But his sword swept them aside, and the shield of Vengeance protected him.

He galloped toward the purple evening, and saw the Moon emerge from the window of a glass tower; and he knew he had come at last to the Earth's very rim, where the Witch of the World's End had always waited for him.

He heard her song in his mind, and he saw her needle flickering in his fevered, waking dreams.

She spoke to him, inside his mind.

"Do you remember Antharic, who was a tangled knot in my weaving?"

"I am Antharic."

"I think Antharic died long ago. Maybe he froze in a ditch. Behold, I have woven the shape of someone else entirely."

He shouted his war-cry, screaming his hatred, lusting for glory, as he thundered onto the witch's drawbridge. The glass bridge shattered, but his steed leapt clear across, trailing gleaming shards, landing with an explosion of sparks in the courtyard. Still mounted, he forced his way into the tower. Stone automatons opposed him, but he broke them to pieces with his sword. Up and up, around and around, spiraling along a glass staircase that splintered as he passed; up, as metal birds came against him in a shrieking mass, but the shield of Vengeance brushed them aside; up he climbed on horseback.

A serpent with a woman's head wriggled out of a side chamber and called out to him, beseeching him merely to stop, and lie with her forever, for the sake of pleasure.

He shouted and cut the serpent in twain with a single stroke of his sword.

At the top, he paused in just an instant of silence. Already the tower was beginning to crumble, bits of glass tinkling down like ice rattling out of trees in a sudden winter wind.

He stood before the witch as she worked at her weaving, very still, his drawn sword like a motionless thunderbolt, waiting.

And he saw that she had come to the end of her tapestry, that there was very little thread left. He noticed the colors of her weaving: black and grey, darkness and smoke; the white of bones; the brown of earth;

red for blood and for fire; the silver of swords; and many others. There were only a few golden threads, which stood for hope and happiness; indeed they were the scarcest of all.

"Why didn't you make it otherwise?" said Antharic in a voice like the stilled thunderbolt, trembling with barely restrained violence.

The witch merely held up a fold of the cloth, and there was the figure of the monk in his cell, outlined in gold amid the dark colors.

In his rage, Antharic smashed her loom with his sword, tearing the tapestry into a million drifting motes.

Far below, at the base of the tower, a monster shrieked. Glass poured down, rattling. The floor shifted beneath Antharic's feet.

"You are a vile thing," he said. "Now has vengeance come."

The witch held up a handful of loose thread. "I can't finish. Look what you've done."

She held black strands and red strands, but also, even yet, a single golden one.

Antharic raised his sword to strike once more.

"Monster," he said.

"You are the dreamer and I am the dream," she said, "and yet I have seen you in my own dreams and I knew what I must do. Each of us is the mirror held up to the other, and by the other are we defined. You *needed* me. How else could you have become a hero at the completion of a fantastic quest . . . so why are you angry at me, at this very last? Ask yourself. Does it make any sense?"

Antharic struck off her head, cursing, weeping, unable to make any sense of it at all, out of his dreams, out of the memories of the boy who lay shivering in a ditch raving of impossible revenge.

The Witch of the World's End disintegrated like her own tapestry, into something like smoke dispersed by a sudden wind.

He couldn't—

Nothing—

He leapt for a golden strand that floated on the air like spider's silk—

And in the end he found himself falling forever amid the stars beyond the World's rim, beyond even the reach of dreams, for there was no one left to dream him. He had lived for this purpose only: to uncreate himself.

He hadn't entirely succeeded.

It was a cessation of pain, at least.

* * *

Later, another hero came to seek the Witch of the World's End, a plain, broad-shouldered man armed only with a staff. He found her as he had expected her from his dreams, a bent crone stirring her cauldron on the edge of a cliff, while behind her dragons rose up out of the abyss like dark, threatening clouds.

Inyanga

JANET BERLINER GLUCKMAN AND GEORGE GUTHRIDGE

With the approach of evening, the *inyanga* padded flat-footed toward the town of Lüderitz. Because the sun lay low in the sky, her bare breasts and protruding buttocks cast long shadows across the hard-packed south West African desert sand.

Slowing down, she scanned the distant sail-dotted waters of Walvis Bay and cursed her aching feet, her sweating body, and the indignity of aging. She was sorcerer, witch, inyanga, but even she could not alter the fact that she was growing old, and that the times themselves were changing. Why else would she walk ten miles across the Kalahari to prove in public that she could do what the new German doctor and the Zana Malata intruder inyanga from Madagascar could not do?

Cure the boy.

She closed in on town and stopped beneath an acacia tree to take stock. Directly ahead of her, down a slight hill, the Zana Malata reclined like an odalisque across the dirty glass counter of the only bar in town, posing for the tourists. Cameras clicked. He was disgusting, the inyanga thought, his face eaten away by the congenital syphilis with which Europeans had endowed so many of his people, and hers.

She turned her attention to her other rival, the German doctor they called Heinz. He sat at a rickety table, sucking at a beer and listening to a diminutive woman who held firmly onto a complicated-looking camera. They said she had come across the sea from Germany to film the Bushman.

The German woman had come to the right place at the right time.

193

Normally she would have had to go out into the desert, first to find the little ones and then to convince them that the camera would not take their souls. Today, thanks to the fact that the sick boy was Bushman, she would find them right here, in town.

Hands on hips, the inyanga looked down the line of tall blacks, Hereros, who waited at the side of the dirt street, and a crowd of smaller blacks who had gathered at the far end of the town square. Her people. Bushmen. She did not move until the sun dropped toward the horizon, tinting the sky with variegated shades of pinks and reds and oranges.

"I have come," she called out then.

Fingers interlocked, she began a slow, shuffling dance, weaving in and out of the lacy shadows of the acacia. The people surged forward, gawking, murmuring. A gray-haired black threw a smoldering stick onto the ground; others added twigs, small branches . . . the beginnings of a fire.

Hereros and Bushmen who did not usually dance together gathered around her and began to clap and sway. Head uptilted, knowing only the whites of her eyes were visible, she stamped her feet against the dust. She was chanting softly, jiggling her buttocks beneath her loincloth.

"Janha Janha Jan-ha!" the crowd chanted.

She snaked her hands over her breasts, neck, face. Her fingers gripped her peppercorn hair, released it, started again: breasts, neck, hair.

Linking arms, the crowd moved in a circle, clockwise first, counterclockwise, clockwise. . . .

She glanced around quickly to see if the Zana Malata was attempting to join them. She saw him crouching at the edge of the mob like a beggar, trying to see between the legs. Then a Herero looked down at him and anxiously leaned away to let him by. Soon the rest were nudging each other, intent on letting him through without touching him. As a Malagasy, he was as foreign to them as the Europeans. He was part African, but he was also part Javanese, part English pirate—product, it was said, of the union two hundred years before between a white devil and a Betsimisaraka woman.

The tall, very black Hereros gave way to the inner group—the tiny brown Bushmen with thick, flattened noses and perforated gourd-rattles around their calves.

Four Bushmen, imitating young gazelles by holding gemsbok horns against their foreheads, jumped through the inner ring and into the center of the circle. Gyrating, they approached and retreated, approached and retreated. Pelvises pulsing and shoulders rolling, they yowled and grunted and gesticulated in time to the pounding hands and feet of the Hereros, who rushed from the outer edges of the crowd to the inner circle to throw imaginary spears at the dancers.

"*Watubai na! Ha! Watubai na!*"

She stood in the center. She could feel the heat rising beneath her skin. Breasts bouncing, head rolling, she patted herself as if cooling her burning flesh. She made a nasal sound and clicked her tongue. *N/um.* Calling out to the fire-hot power that she could bring up boiling from her belly to fill her head like steam and help her talk with gods . . . enable her to perform *kai*-healings. Spirit healings.

The Zana Malata closed in on her. Deep down in his throat, he unsuccessfully attempted to duplicate the glottal click. She might have laughed at his childish efforts had not two men emerged right then from the direction of the sand spit that formed Lüderitz's western edge. They were carrying a makeshift stretcher. On it lay a small naked boy.

The crowd parted. The bearers passed between the Hereros and moved into the inner ring of Bushmen, who threw dried crushed leaves mixed with dust onto the prostrate figure. Then, gently, they placed the stretcher upon the ground, beside the fire.

While the Hereros continued their spear-throwing motions, the Bushmen leapt high into the air and fell on their knees. Twitching, trembling, rolling their eyes upward, they fell into a more rhythmic chanting. The occasional wail ascended into the branches of the acacia tree.

She edged forward to look more closely at the patient. The boy's belly was distended, his arms and legs thin as a grasshopper's, his face so gaunt it seemed to contain nothing but eyes.

"*Kai!*" she screamed, toppling to her knees.

She wrapped her arms around herself and tilted toward the flames, leaning forward until her nose and forehead were among the embers. When she lifted her head, smoke plumed from her hair.

The stretcher was withdrawn. She touched her face to make sure it was unscathed by the fire. Then she lay down beside the boy, and put her arms around his shoulders and cradled his head against her chest, not only to comfort him, but to still the spastic movements of her own limbs. She knew enough not to give her audience time to grow restive, and allowed herself only a moment of quiet before continuing the performance.

I'm too old for this, she thought again, as she took a deep breath and began groaning and wailing.

Four squatting male dancers surrounded her. One massaged her with dust. The second rubbed ointment, which he kept stored in his armpits, onto her body until her face and shoulders gleamed. The third dipped into a small tortoise shell held by the fourth and rubbed herbs into her hair.

When they stepped away, a hush came over the crowd. The circle tightened. The inyanga opened her eyes and raised her head. All this time there had been no sign of life from the boy; now she could see tears emerging from the outside corners of the child's eyes and rolling down the sides of his face.

Leaning over her patient, she scraped his cheeks with her fingernails—a town cat sharpening its nails against a piece of bark. She was purring softly, pleased that her trembling had become less violent.

The boy's head moved slowly from side to side. When it was stilled, he opened his mouth. Even in the semidarkness, she saw the white thing twitching inside his throat.

Shuddering, she seized it and, with a milking motion, drew the two-meter-long tapeworm slowly from between the boy's lips.

She held it on high like a trophy. At once, the four males removed knives from the sheaths attached to their legs and hacked at the worm, cutting it into a dozen pieces. The crowd opened like a small sea as the men, collecting the pieces of tapeworm, crossed the street and pitched them onto the harbor's dirty flats. Two gulls wheeled. What they might not consume the incoming tide would claim.

As the men returned, two women appeared, one elderly and one in her late twenties. They lifted the boy to his feet and, with their help, he walked away.

One of the men kicked apart the tiny fire. Lifting a stick on which a flame continued to burn, he glanced at the inyanga. She bucked her hips once and lay still, one arm crooked beneath her cheek, the other stretched out above her head. Wordlessly he handed her the burning stick and turned away.

Gradually the crowd departed, whispering among themselves, until only she herself, the Zana Malata sorceror, and the two Germans—the doctor and the photographer—remained, squatting beside the embers.

"I am Leni Riefenstahl," the white woman said. She pointed at her camera. "I will show this film to the Führer and to the world. You will be famous."

Since she did not know what the small white woman had said, for the language was not of her tribe, the inyanga merely gestured. Whatever it was, it did not matter, for she did not share the common people's fear of the mechanical eye, which could not capture or claim her soul. As for her likeness, no matter what the white woman's skill, the picture would be dark and without form.

Having not yet fully regained her strength, she remained on the ground. From her prone position, she watched the tourists reenter the bar to relive the experience over toasts and nervous jokes. She saw the Zana Malata cross the street, to sit with his legs dangling down the wooden seawall. The gulls rose slightly in the air, circled, and alighted to reclaim their places. He stared at them and, squawking, they took flight once more.

She felt a wave of compassion for the Zana Malata, whose own people shied from his ugliness. Having done what she had set out to do, she had no real reason to shun the Malagasy sorcerer. She stood, brushed herself off, and walked slowly over to the hideous man-creature. Her hand was hot when she touched his shoulder, yet he shivered.

"*Hamba Gashle,*" she said, handing him the flame-stick the man had given her—smoldering now. "*Hamba Gashle.*" Go softly.

He took the stick from her and answered in courtesy. "*Salamba Gashle.*" Return softly. Keeping his gaze fixed on the gulls, he vaulted over the wall onto the muddy flats below.

"*Salamba Gashle,*" she repeated against the susurrus of the waves.

She turned from the water and padded past the bar. Heinz had returned to his table. Several empty shot glasses reflected in the light of an old hurricane lamp on the bar. The German doctor rose unsteadily to his feet and lifted his arm in a salute. She nodded, grinned, and started to ascend the slight incline that led to the flat desert entry.

The talk in the bar faded behind her. Evening had come on suddenly, as it did in Africa. Now the acacia's shadows ribbed the street by moonlight like the cicatrization with which her face had been marked when she became inyanga.

She fingered the raised weals and looked to the east where, as though rising out of the Zana Malata's homeland, Madagascar, two thousand miles away, hung a silver moon. A hollow moon, which her people believed held a place for their souls. Thanks to her skill, she thought, the place being held there for the boy she had cured would stay empty for a while longer.

The Malagasy's soul would enter a crocodile, the boy's would fly from south West Africa to the moon. What the German doctor believed about *his* soul, or whether or not he even believed he had one, was something she could not know. As for her own soul, she had no idea what she truly believed. She knew only that suddenly, despite her triumph, she felt frail and cold.

She stared ahead into the silence of the Kalahari.

N/um, she clicked, taking comfort in the familiar sound and in the warmth that rose to protect her against the desert night.

N/um.

Requiem for a Witch

DAN PEREZ

The snow swirled down, and a few stray flakes settled on Winnie's eyelashes like frozen tears. She wiped her eyes with the bony knuckles of one hand, and a shiver rocked through her body. Winnie was miserably cold, for to broom-fly meant that she could wear only her gray spidersilk dress, and the garment was nothing against winter's cold breath. She could warm herself, she knew, but she would not use that spell. It was held in reserve for another.

To take her mind off the cold, she tried to concentrate on other things: the wild broom-flight she had taken over these mountains only a few months ago on Halloween night, when the conifer-scented breeze had caught in her hair and the custard-colored moon had risen full over the mountaintops and valleys. Winnie was ill then, of course; indeed she knew that it would be her last Halloween. But the rush of excitement and joy she felt as she swooped down through the valleys—chasing the ghostly will-o'-the-wisps across rushing water and between the lichen-splotched tree trunks—all that had washed the sickness from her bones for a little while.

She smiled, remembering the dizzy, roller-coaster feel of her flight, the cries of ravens and screech owls, the sharp ozone-smelling crackle of the flickering will-o'-the-wisps as they fled before her. Oh, for one more October night!

A bitter spasm shook her, and she clutched the broom tightly. It was insane to be flying now, as her craft-mother and -sisters would say if they knew. Flying at the lowest ebb of power, when stars and moon cloaked themselves with wintry floss, and the land itself slumbered beneath its snowy blanket—perhaps it was insane. But there was need.

Below her, yellow and red lights flashed dimly through the snow-haze. The searchers, Winnie knew. Their vehicles were trapped on the mountain road by a fallen fir tree. She glimpsed a cluster of figures and heard the whine of a chainsaw. Further down the slope, shrouded from sight by the snowfall, Winnie heard a muffled crack, followed by a crashing, tumbling sound. Another fir tree had collapsed under its burden of snow.

Winnie shook almost constantly now, teeth rattling in her jaws. The cold wind had turned torturer now, plucking at her fingers and toes, at her nipples and nose and ears with icy pincers. *Uta, craft-mother, what do I do now?* she wondered, following the winding road higher and higher. It was a curse to be so young, Winnie thought—to command power but not know the right thing to do!

"A difficult time, yes indeed," Uta had said to her, shrewd green eyes gleaming beneath iron-gray brows and a lined, freckled forehead. "But we've all been through it, dear. Girl grows into woman, and the swollen bud of craft breaks into glorious bloom, both nearly before you know it. In Goddess's good time, both woman and craft become firm in themselves, as new growth hardens on the tree. In Goddess's good time."

Winnie remembered those words, spoken in Uta's brightly lit kitchen, warm and fragrant with the smell of cinnamon bread in the oven. And yet they had been spoken before anyone knew, before Winnie had fallen ill and the diagnosis had been myelogenous leukemia. Maybe that was why people feared skeletons. Because sometimes your bones turn against you.

Uta had asked Winnie to consider leaving the coven for treatment, or at least to consult with her mother before making a decision. But Winnie's mind had been made up. Witches didn't undergo chemotherapy or bone marrow transplants. Or at least they didn't do it and retain the power of the craft. And to lose your powers was to be shut out of a much larger and marvelous world forever.

199

Still, Winnie had flown to see her mother in Seattle and they had cried together and agreed that for her to give up her powers would be too much of a sacrifice. Mother had told her there were spells that would slow the cancer in Winnie's bones and others to lessen her suffering, but that ultimately nature would win. Winnie had decided that she wanted to remain a witch for whatever time she had left, and they had embraced and cried again.

So Winnie had returned to the huge, rambling house in Pinetop, Montana, and her training with Uta and her craft-sisters. Things had gone well for a number of months; there had been little discomfort—nosebleeds and weakness, mostly—and her powers grew. But then Winnie had succumbed to curiosity and cast the spell of portent late one night, aided by her sisters. The portent came to her as she slept, and when she awakened, she knew that she had only four months to live the rest of her life. She hadn't said anything to Uta and her sisters.

That had been in September, and now it was December. "Today might be the last day," she had told herself this morning, in the comfort of the living room, curled up by the fireplace. Then the news had come on the television, and with it the report that had sent her on this journey.

The swirling, snowy wind turned from torturer to seducer now, as Winnie felt a dreamy, sleepy sensation overtaking her. She felt numb and it was strangely luxurious, like falling asleep in a heap of eider-down—

"NO!" she snarled, and a lightning tracery of pain flared across her face. She quickly intoned the spell of warmth and it crackled like fire through her. She gasped in sudden agony, lost control of her flight, and spiraled down, thudding painfully into a snowbank. Shuddering, she lay there for a moment, but soon the needlelike pain gave way to a dull ache in her hands and bare feet. And she was warm—the snow was melting as it struck her.

"Damn!" she said, sitting up. She'd had no choice but to cast the warmth spell. She'd never find the boy if she froze to death out here first.

The boy. What did she know about him? His name was Jimmy Branton and he was seven years old and he'd had the bad luck to go hiking up the mountain road a few hours before the snowstorm of the decade had hit. His parents were frantic, and rescue efforts had been delayed because Pinetop didn't have the equipment—it had to be brought in from Harlowton. Winnie had seen Jimmy's mother and father fighting back tears on the news, and her breath had caught in her throat.

She knew then that she'd never have children, never watch them grow, never pass along her powers to a daughter. Wiping tears from her eyes, she had realized that if she'd never have the chance to bring a child into the world, maybe she could give this boy back to his parents.

Winnie stood up and retrieved her broom. She paused, concentrating, attuning herself to her surroundings. She felt the subtle shift as her awareness sharpened. There were the natural things: wind, snow, rocks, frozen earth, dormant plants and trees. And there were the man-made things: the road cut into the mountainside, a metal sign, and long spikes that environmentalists had driven into some of the trees.

She breathed deeply, listening now to the sound of her breath, to the hidden sounds of animals hibernating in their dens or sitting out the snowfall. *There!* It was a boy's breathing, rasping gently in and out of his nostrils—the rhythm drawing out as though he were falling asleep. Winnie knew that that was very bad.

Something else! A dry, electric humming—patient somehow in its aspect, but with anticipation behind the patience. This thing was not natural. *Supernatural.*

Winnie snapped alert. "Jimmy!" she shouted, climbing astride her broom. "Jimmy, wake up!"

She flew around a bend in the road and zoomed up to the spot she had been searching for. She hopped off the broomstick and sank to her knees in the fine, powdery snow. A large drift had piled up against a rock outcropping, leaving only a tiny space between the overhang of rock and the top of the drift.

"Jimmy!" she called out again as she began to dig. "Fight it! Wake up!"

She frantically scooped away the snow, digging hand over hand like a dog. Snow kept sliding down from the drift, ruining her work, but she kept at it, and the gap at the top of the drift widened until she was sure she could get through it. She clambered up and over, sliding down into the dim space beyond. She collided with Jimmy at the bottom. He was crouched up against a hollow in the rock, his legs drawn up and his arms wrapped tightly around them. He wore a light jacket and gloves, but his face was ghastly pale and his eyes were closed. Winnie's heart sank.

She started at the electrical crackle and the stinging sensation on her left arm. Then she saw the glowing, pale green orb flickering next to the snowbank a few feet away. Tiny blue veins of electricity arced over its surface, and it buzzed softly like a neon sign. She'd never seen a will-o'-the-wisp so close.

There was a flash of light, and a thick streamer of blue-white electricity shot out to her, lancing into her cheek. She crawled up to Jimmy and said, "You can't have him!"

The will-o'-the-wisp buzzed like a swarm of bees and emitted another long spark, striking Winnie's foot.

She launched herself at it then, angry tears in her eyes. It slipped out of her grasp, if ever she had it, and a blinding series of flashes went off like a strobe light. She felt hot little stabs on her face, neck, and arms, as though someone were touching her with dozens of lit cigarettes. She cried out and lunged blindly, flailing with her arms. There was a rushing sound like television static and then all was quiet.

Winnie pushed herself up in time to see the will-o'-the-wisp sweeping out of the opening of the chamber. Breathing hard and trembling all over, she crawled to Jimmy, who still looked dead as he sat there. "It's gone now," she said softly, putting her arms around him. She touched her lips to his skin, which was so, so cold.

Witches aid an ailing sister by gathering close to her and lending their life energy to her, each literally pushing a bit of it from their bodies into her. Uta and Winnie's sisters had done it for her, to subdue the effects of the cancer, and now Winnie did it for Jimmy. She hugged against him, wrapped her arms and legs about him, concentrating hard. She pushed what remained in her out and into the boy, never sure if it would even be enough to save him. All the while, she whispered close to his ear: "Crawl out. Go back down the road."

Winnie felt cold again, a freezing, soul-cracking cold that no wind could conjure. *Too far!* her craft-sense screamed. *You're pushing too far!*

"Crawl out," she whispered into his ear, her stiff lips barely moving, "Go back down the road."

Everything spun now, a hurricane in Winnie's mind. She thought she saw glimpses of Jimmy, his blue eyes open, his lips intoning her words, and there came a dizzy sense of disentangling arms and legs, as though she were losing her grip on something or someone.

Words that might have been composed of pure will boomed out against the raucous tumult. *Crawl out. Go back down the road.* Even those faded and nothing remained but a tumbling flight through darkness and unimaginably awful cold. And through it, somehow, the distant thought remained that as nature now triumphed, so had Winnie. Goddess's will . . .

James Branton woke from a troubled sleep. Wind whistled around the house, and there was a steady pattering of rain on the roof. Marla stirred next to him and he murmured softly in her ear until she stilled. He eased out of bed, the floor painfully chilly against his frostbite-scarred feet. He got his slippers on and went across the room to the crib. Staring down at his daughter, a strange, dreamy welter of emotion swirled in his heart. Happiness mostly, but mingled with a strange, faraway sense of sadness and loss. It seemed a strange combination to James.

The wind blew up strong again and the timbers of the house groaned. The baby's tiny eyelids fluttered. James reached down to her and stroked her head gently. "Sleepytime," he cooed to her. "Go back to sleep now, Winnie."

Crone Woman Gandy

RICHARD GILLIAM

On the morning that Rachel Elizabeth Colton was born, she was taken to Crone Woman Gandy for a blessing.

"My, my. What a child," said the old woman upon seeing the infant. "This one's very special, yes she be."

This blessing brought much pride into the heart of Jeremiah Colton, the child's father. Never before had he heard the crone woman to proclaim any newborn child to be special, nor had he heard of any other person who knew of such an event.

"Born at the dawn just like you predicted," said Jeremiah, his smile evident of his pride. "Still a surprise though you told us what to expect." Jeremiah had much wanted a son, but if the child was to be a girl, then to have one named special by someone so powerful and wise was perhaps even better.

Crone Woman Gandy returned the smile of Jeremiah, then looked to the sky. "Shortest day of the year," she said. "It'll soon be midday. You did well to hurry."

"Margaret is resting. She said to apologize, but she is still too sore from giving birth to travel, even the small ride to the meadow."

"Would have been foolish to have endangered your wife's health for her to be here," said the old woman. "All that's needed is the child. It's fine you brought so much of your family along to share the celebration, but it's the child that is needed. Were I younger I would have been at Margaret's side when the child was born."

"You helped birth me, Crone Woman, and my father before that. Most of us in Jefferson Valley can trace ourselves by you. Most of the old families, anyway."

Crone Woman Gandy smiled again. "The others are at the meadow?"

"Yes. Just as always."

"Then we best be going. Could you hand me the child after we get into your buckboard? Wouldn't want to risk hurting a child born at the dawn of the last winter solstice of the eighteen hundreds."

The morning frost had melted from the meadow long before the sun neared midday, creating a muddy slush as the wagon wheels rolled along the more traveled parts of the path. The heal stone was in clear view, surrounded by a broad expanse of winter-browned grass leading to the circle of trees that defined the clearing. The air was cold but pleasant, and the wind still, as though in respect for the occasion.

As was tradition, the family had gathered along the sides of the pathway, leaving a clear trail to the heal stone. Jeremiah counted twenty-four, including toddlers, twelve to each side, with Margaret's family to the right and his kinfolk to the left. His sister, Jessica, was not among those gathered, and for this he was thankful, relieved that she and her husband Tom had stayed away. Time enough soon to baptize Rachel at Tom's church, well after Crone Woman delivered the blessings on her day of birth.

Jeremiah guided the buckboard to within ten feet of the heal stone, then carefully helped his passenger and the infant she held out onto the field. Mark and Mitchell, two of the younger men of the Haggerty clan, helped steady the old woman, while Jeremiah moved the wagon back to the edge of the clearing, so as to make unbroken room around the stone.

The families joined hands in a circle, alternating Colton and Haggerty in a union of joy. Jeremiah took his place near the center, just to the west of the stone. Rachel, warmly wrapped in a shawl from her mother, rested easily on the stone's top surface, her face turned to the sky and the nearing sun. Crone Woman turned the child so that Rachel's head pointed north, then took her place to the side of the child.

"We're early, yes we are," said the old woman, as she leaned against the stone. "Sun keeps its own pace. Not our place to hurry it."

Chuckles and smiles filled the circle. "It's a great day for a blessing, Crone Woman!" came a voice from behind Jeremiah, which he recognized as that of his brother.

"Rained a lot at your blessing, Walter," replied the old woman. "Rained a nice warm rain. That's why you got a way with crops. Why your lands don't fall parched so much as others."

"What was my blessing, Crone Woman?" asked Lenny, a younger member of the Haggerty clan.

"Your blessing was that we didn't leave you on this rock," cackled the old woman. "Never heard a baby squall so much in all my years. And you cried just as much on the way back to your mama. You might ought to think of something you can do with that voice other than annoy people."

The crowd laughed, and it was a good-natured laugh. "Lenny sings in the choir, Crone Woman. He sings real good." It was young Lucy Colton speaking this time. She had tried to position herself next to Lenny for the hand joining, and had been disappointed when she found herself next to his mother, Dorothy.

Lucy Colton, the Elder, stood at the southernmost point of the circle, somewhat saddened as she often was at these occasions. She alone had not received a birth blessing—her stern father having forbid it. She had always promised that her children would be blessed, but alas, though having had three husbands and several lovers, she had proven barren and without issue.

She had been fifty at the birth of her namesake, a kind gift of remembrance from her cousin, Rachel Haggerty, after whom Jeremiah and Margaret had named their newest born. The family trees of the Haggertys and the Coltons were much intermixed and few members could keep all the branches in order. Lucy acted as the keeper of her father's Bible, into which the name of each member was written. No kin closer than second cousin had married, however, and the lines were not so recursive as to stain the Good Book with their recording.

In the distance, the crack of the whip against horses split the air, and Jeremiah knew without looking that Jessica and her husband had come.

The sound of the carriage sloshing through the muddy path came though even yet deep within the forest. Jeremiah looked to the sky, and knew that the sun lay too low for the ceremony to commence before their arrival. A somber quiet came over those joined, while the wind began to cut through the valley.

The yet unmarried of the Lucy Coltons looked to her feet, and realized that she and Dorothy were the ones whose linked hands blocked the pathway between the carriage and the stone. Dorothy squeezed the younger woman's hand as if to reassure her, then broke the grasp.

"Let them pass," she said, looking toward Crone Woman.

The old woman nodded her approval and stepped toward the path. "They will do what they must do," she said. "Let us deal with them quickly before the sun takes its zenith."

The carriage was upon them now, and the circle now stood as one family. They stood facing the carriage, Jeremiah and Crone Woman to the front, behind them the stone and the infant.

"Jessica, you shouldn't have come," said Jeremiah as his sister and her husband stepped from the wagon.

"Hush, Jeremiah!" came the reply. "Do you want to send this infant to perdition before she lives her first day?"

"Jesse . . ."

"This woman is a witch, and I will not stand to see my niece be the object of her accursed black arts."

Crone Woman smiled. "I'm a witch, all right," she cackled. "And a right good one, too."

The families laughed, breaking the spirit of the momentum set against them by Jessica's arrival.

A redness rose into Jessica's face, her cheeks puffed and indignant. She paused for a moment, allowing the chuckles to fade. Her composure having returned, she spoke again. "God's righteous justice will be upon you, Jeremiah. And upon this bride of Satan whom you serve. May hell await all those who rebuke the Lord."

"Serve Satan?" said the old woman, barely attempting to submerge her amusement. "Did you not just invoke damnation upon us all? Who serves Satan more, the gentle people who come here to bless this child, or you who would fill Satan's realm with those whom you judge unholy?"

"Wicked witch!" shouted Jessica.

"A witch, yes," said the old woman. "Wicked, no. In my many years of practicing these arts, never have I asked for there to be harm to another, neither to their person nor to their spirit. The wicked one here is you, Jessica Haggerty."

"Blasphemy! Blasphemy! May you suffer forever for your words," said Jessica, her face livid with rage.

"In all the magic arts, there is none darker than that by which one person asks that the spirit of another be sent into eternal torment," said the old woman. "Do you not even wear your somber black while at your worship rituals?"

"What say you to this, Tom?" Jeremiah interjected, stepping between the two women.

"I don't rightly know, Jeremiah," said the preacher. "I didn't want Jessica to come, told her that it were your business and not hers. Couldn't not stand by her side, though, and as an ordained minister, I must tell you I'm none pleased with what you're doing. I know you intend for Rachel to be baptized in the church, but how can she be a Christian if you raise her to be a heathen, too?"

"She needs a choice," said the old woman.

"A choice?" said Jessica, somewhat more calmly.

"She needs to know much before she makes her choices," said the old woman.

"There are only those who serve the Lord," said Jessica. "All others are against Him."

"Hush, Jessica," said Tom. "I'll hear this woman out."

"There are choices," said Crone Woman, pausing to look toward Tom and toward the crowd, but not toward Jessica.

"There are choices," she continued, "choices that are made whether we want them to be made or not. Every moment is a choice, whether we speak, what we speak, whom we speak to, and how much we listen to what is said in return. Same for other doings. Lots of choices. The more a person knows about choices, the more they can be secure in what choices they make. My gift to this child is that I shall live a few more years yet to teach her the ways I understand. Your gift, Tom, should be to help her learn the goodness that is taught in your Holy

Bible. Same for each of you. We each understand a little something that everyone else needs to know. Even you, Jessica, though it's my short-coming that I haven't figured out what yours is yet."

"The words of Satan are clever. Don't let her distract you from her evil," Jessica pleaded, to little effect.

The old woman looked to the sky. "Almost time, now. Be a shame to waste such a pretty setting for a blessing. I make you this promise, Jessica Haggerty. Little Rachel here is a most special child, more special than you might know. I can't teach her everything, particularly things about the dark arts that you seem so at home with. I want you to teach her about damnation, and about hell, and how people get sent there. I want her to learn from you, and from me, and from Tom, and from her parents, and from everyone else. If her powers are to be as great as I suspect, she'll need to know what's out there to be chosen. Jeremiah? Do you and Margaret promise that Jessica shall be allowed to teach Rachel how to be a good church woman? And that you'll help Rachel find her own path, whatever that may be?"

"You know we do, Crone Woman," said Jeremiah.

"Jessica? How about you? You promise to teach her your choices?"

"I'll do all I can to stop her from learning your ways of evil, Crone Woman."

"You do that, Jessica. I suspect Rachel will probably want other-wise, but then that'll be Rachel's choice," said the old woman.

"Evil witch!" shouted Jessica, her voice shrill against the gaining wind.

An unsettled murmur arose from those gathered, and above that, the crying of a child, loud and clear and unhappy. The elder Lucy Colton, who had stayed by the stone, took Rachel in her arms, and softly began to sing. She was joined by the younger Lucy, and then by Lenny, who stood between them, placing his arms around each. Though Rachel no longer cried, soon the entire circle was gathered, and the sound of their voices lifted through the once again calm and peaceful air.

> *"Amazing grace, how sweet the sound,*
> *that saved a wretch like me.*
> *I once was lost, but now am found.*
> *Was blind but now can see."*

"You're welcome to stay, Jessica and Tom. You should see what blessings it is that we ask," said Crone Woman, looking her accuser in the eye not as an adversary, but with an invitation of friendship.

"It's not over, Crone Woman. You win today, but I'll fight you for the soul of that child, and anyone else taken in by your heresy." With that said Jessica turned, stepped onto the carriage alongside Tom, neither of them looking back toward the heal stone nor listening to the singing, though the sound of the joy they had left behind remained with them well into the woods.

On the morning that Rachel Elizabeth Colton turned twelve years old, she was taken to the funeral of Crone Woman Gandy, where she said a blessing for the old woman, and then made the choice that she could not avoid making, deciding what it was she would do with the rest of her life.

The Devil's Men

BRIAN STABLEFORD

When they came to apprehend him, he knew that it must be a mistake, and told them so: that he was naught but a schoolmaster, and a respectable man, and that his name was not Fian at all but only John Cunningham, and that he did not know Geillis Duncan—who had named him a witch—at all. When they threw him into prison, he was certain in his own mind that they would quickly discover their mistake and release him.

When rumour was carried to him that the king himself had taken an interest in those whom Geillis Duncan had accused, he felt certain that justice would soon be done and that all would be well. When further rumour reached him that one Agnes Thompson had told the king that Satan himself had appeared at North Berwick kirk in order to instruct the witches gathered there to make stormy mischief against the king, he declared that the king could not possibly believe such mad fancies. Even when they told him, gloatingly, that the king himself had said as much, but that Agnes Thompson had then offered firm proof, he could not credit it.

"The witch took the king aside," his jailer explained, "and whispered in his ear the very words that passed between his majesty and his queen on the night of their marriage. The king swore by the living God that all the devils in hell could not have discovered as much."

"Nor could they," he replied, contemptuously. "But a king is surrounded by servants even on his wedding night, expert eavesdroppers all; they might easily do what no demon ever could."

"But the king's servants are very loyal," the jailer told him, "for this same witch confessed that she had been intimately acquainted with one of them, John Kerr, and had tried to persuade him to obtain an item of the king's linen, which she might anoint with the venom of a toad, thus to place a curse—and he would not do it!"

"Would that Master Kerr had kept such discretion with his flapping tongue," he remarked, not knowing how utterly the irony would be lost.

First of all, they questioned him as they had earlier questioned Geillis Duncan, by knotting a rope tight about his head and wrenching it back and forth, tearing the skin from his temples.

He gave them no answer save to protest his innocence of all wrongdoing.

After that they talked to him softly and persuasively, telling him that he must see how things would go henceforth, and that he ought to save himself further agony by a confession that would justify their efforts.

Still he could not believe that an innocent and respectable man could be condemned on the word of a tortured servant, and he refused.

Then they put his feet into the iron boots, and struck the wedges three times with a sledgehammer, the awful agony of which rendered him unconscious.

When they had brought him round they told him that he must see by now how things were, and explained again that once they had begun such treatment they could not possibly end it without obtaining the result that they desired. Because he was a man and not a hagwife, they said, and a man of good standing too, they would make a compromise with him. They would say, if he consented, that he had not spoken before because his tongue had been held fast to his palate by two great pins put there by the magic of the old hags, thus making him as much a victim as a criminal. Nor would they require him to confess that he had tried to kill the king by magic, but only that he was guilty of the acts specified in the rumour that was commonly told against him, which everyone had heard.

"What is it that everyone has heard?" he wailed, quite mystified.

"That you required one of your scholars to obtain hair from his sister's private parts," they said, "in order that you might possess the gentlewoman by magic, having earlier cursed her husband so that he was overtaken by a fit in the king's presence. When the mother of the gentlewoman, seeing what was afoot, plucked hairs from the udder of a heifer and told the scholar to bring them to you instead, the heifer came to the door of the school, and followed you therefrom to church, revealing to the world your pact with Satan."

He began to understand, then, what must have happened. Some aggrieved schoolboy had invented a wild tale, so amusing that it had been repeated and repeated, eventually passing for news instead of malice, travelling so fast and so far that Geillis Duncan, asked to name witches, had drawn on it for inspiration. But he understood also that what his inquisitors said to him was true, and that matters had now developed to the point that such ludicrous tales could no longer be seen for what they really were.

The master of the prison promised him that if he confessed to the lesser crime, he might be excused as an unlucky dupe of those witches who had confessed to far more heinous crimes—but that if he did not, the wedges placed in his iron clogs would be driven further and further, until his feet were crushed to pulp.

He signed the paper they offered him, admitting the crime laid against him by rumour and conceding that he had been seduced by Satan—but declaring withal that he now renounced Satan and all his wicked works, and would henceforth lead the blameless life of a pious Christian.

That night, he was released from the prison and he returned to Saltpans, where he lived and worked.

The next day, they came for him again, and brought him back to his cell. The jailer explained to him that the king's men had waxed indignant when told of his release by the master of the prison, and had ordered that it be put about that he had escaped, for they were not prepared to have any man set free who had been implicated in the affairs said to have taken place at North Berwick Kirk.

"I was never at North Berwick Kirk!" he protested. "Nor were those who claim that they were, for their tales are all wild fantasy!"

"It matters not," the jailer said. "They are determined to place you there, and they will do whatever may be necessary to make you say so."

"God will not allow it!" he said, although he knew in his heart that if God were disposed to prevent such things the world would be a very different place.

On the next day they twisted his fingernails with pincers, and drove needles under them, and finally tore them away, asking him all the while to confess that he had been won back to Satan's cause after signing the paper they had first given him, and that Satan had in consequence set him free.

He would not own to it, saying over and over again that *they* were the Devil's men, and that *their* work was the Devil's work, and that they knew full well that they themselves had set him free—but the greater his wrath became against them, the greater theirs became against him.

They brought out the boots again, and this time did not hesitate to drive the wedges in to their extremest limit, crushing the flesh and the bones within the flesh until the blood and the marrow flooded out.

They demanded, meanwhile, that he confess that he had betrayed their kindness by returning to the Devil's cause after his apparent repentance—but he would not do that, insisting that they had betrayed him, and that no power on earth could make him declare that he had been fairly treated, and that his first confession had been wrung from him by means of lies and false promises of exactly the kind that Satan might design.

When there was no more that could be done to his hands or feet, the master of the prison accepted that no confession would be forthcoming, and berated him for his stubbornness.

"We cannot let you make liars of us," the master said, "and you are exceedingly unkind to try. If you were a good Christian, and a loyal subject of your king, you would understand that the king's peace and the Almighty's authority must be preserved at all costs, against all manner of treasons. You should do your part, as even the witches Geillis Duncan and Agnes Thompson consented to do. What manner of man are you, to be so resolute in foolishness?"

Had he been capable of clear speech, he would have answered, but the pain was too great. Indeed, the pain was so great as almost to deny him further thought—but while he lay sleepless all night on the cold stone floor of his cell, trying with all his might not to move a muscle lest he destroy his mind with pain, he made the most strenuous efforts to understand exactly what had been done to him, so that he might make his reply when the occasion presented itself again. He knew now that he was doomed to die, and that the only consolation or achievement left to him would be to tell the truth to anyone who might hear him.

Item by item, harried all the while by terrible pains, he put together his indictment:

> *There are no witches save those made by malicious rumour and vicious torture. Were men not so ready to listen to malicious rumours, and repeat them laughing, there would be no accusations of witchcraft. Were men not so ready to take savage delight in torture, there would be no proof of it.*
>
> *You, not I, are the Devil's men.*
>
> *Yet the danger is that in treating their fellows thus—in being led by malice and tyranny to call their fellows servants of Satan—men will soon create witches where none exist: witches who will say, "If these are men of God, then Satan must be far the better master," and will gladly embrace any and all causes that set themselves against cruel authority. For this reason, all who are complicit in doing to any man what has been done to me are doing the work of Satan, recruiting armies to his cause.*
>
> *You, in sober truth, are the Devil's men.*
>
> *And who shall say that the witches thus created have not justice on their side? For who among the servants of God, the servants of the king, and the servants of the law, have ever endured what witches are forced to endure in the cause of preserving innocence? We who are called witches are surely to be reckoned martyrs, as true to our cause as any listed in the Golden Legend.*
>
> *You, not we, are the Devil's men.*
>
> *By the treatment you mete out to us, you damn yourselves; in using us as scapegoats, you increase the burden of your sin.*
>
> *You, and you alone, are the Devil's men.*

Before his ordeal, it would have been easy enough for him to formulate a speech like that; he was, after all, a schoolmaster. As things were, it was a very remarkable achievement.

The next day, they took him to be burned on Castle Hill in Edinburgh—but first they strangled him, so that he would not be able to speak to anyone about what had been done to him and why. Then they caused his story to be published, offering the extent of the tortures he had endured without confessing as firm proof of his commitment to Satan, and representing the fact that they had strangled him before putting him into the fire as incontrovertible evidence of their merciful disposition.

The Caress of Ash and Cinder

CINDIE GEDDES

The cell was cold and barren, its stained stone walls muting the screams from the pyres outside. The guards bragged that the skies had been filled with smoke for nearly a month now, and the shiny buckles of their boots, the cut of their clothes, their soft round bellies attested to the payments that were forced from the families of those turned to ash. Torture and death were looked upon by the righteous as privilege—a chance to redeem oneself. And privilege, even if edifying, had to be paid for.

As the smoke filled Sarei's nostrils and added to the chills that racked her weak body, she wondered how many of the condemned were people she knew, people from the farms and woods surrounding the town. What body once laid claim to the bits of ash that came in through the one high window and now covered her skin? Was her mother among the smoke and cinder? Were those horrible screams her dying words? Sarei had called to her nearly constantly the first few days, but got no recognizable answer. None of those with whom she'd been brought in were anywhere near, and after four days with nothing but a little water and old, dry, salted bread, she stopped calling.

The lack of food and drink were simple tortures meant to weaken the mind and the body. The proximity of the pyres and the lack of heat in the cold chambers, as well as the spacing of prisoners who could feed off one another's fear, were to confuse and scare. No other tortures would be applied until the questioning began.

So far no one had questioned Sarei at all. But an old woman in the cell next to her had been beaten so badly (ostensibly for refusing to tell the truth) that she had not even awakened when the fire was lit beneath her naked, outstretched body. The woman had denied any hint of heresy throughout. Bent and withered like a crone from the woodsmen's tales, she tried to explain how she had gone to the ceremonies, learned the proper incantations, performed the rites, all as the law required. It made no difference to her accusers.

On the seventh day Sarei was told of her mother's death. Weakened by hunger and thirst, frightened of having her clothes removed, her body shaved in an attempt to find the mark of the man-god, Sarei had forgotten her mother's face. Now, whenever she tried to think of the kind woman who had nurtured and loved her all her young life, she only saw the crone. The old woman, shivering in the corner, standing against the inquisitors, falling under their blows, naked above the flames. Only the crone.

She began to pray that they would come soon and deliver her from her fear.

As of the ninth day there was no more daylight. The sun, blotted by ash and smoke, was no more than a cold, orange glow that cast shadows and deepened every crevice but illuminated nothing. It began to snow late the day the sun was snuffed out, and Sarei could only laugh hysterically.

The snow was gray from the ash.

She could no longer feel her toes, didn't dare look at the stumps that had burned with an inner fire before going numb. It was the cold, she knew. Killing her off piece by piece. Slow, almost painless, shearing away her toes first, now beginning to blacken her fingers, turning her nose and lips to useless stubs.

Frostbite.

And it was like mercy.

If she were to die before they came, die before they forced some horrible false accusation, she could die with her soul clean. But torture

—the screams, the sounds of the chains, the rack and the spikes, the strappado and the vise, crushing skin and bone again and again and again. How could anyone withstand the pain? Why not just give them what they wanted? The names. Names that would perpetuate the abomination of torture and death. And condemn others to the same horrors she experienced?

But how could anyone endure it?

Ah, but the crone had, hadn't she?

They came for Sarei on the eleventh day: three finely dressed men from town. One she recognized from political campaigns, the other two she could only think of as thugs—large, brutish men whose obvious predisposition to violence could not be masked by fine clothes or perfumed soaps.

The cell door closing behind them woke her from a fitful dream, dragging a pitiful yelp out of her that angered her with its show of weakness. She was determined to be strong. Like the crone.

"Sarei," the politician said with his voice filled with dismay. "What has happened to you? I knew you as a child. At the ceremonies. You had such potential. Your gift for glyphs was unprecedented. And your talents for divination amazed even the Hall of Mothers. We all thought someday you might even join the Hall."

"I've done nothing wrong," she squeaked, surprised she could still form words past the dryness of her throat and the ruin of her lips.

"Now, Sarei, you know I would love to believe that, but we have proof. We have witnesses. We even have a confession from your mother."

"You have no proof. Only the conjecture of your sick, twisted minds. You see only what you want."

"Your mother admitted . . ."

"You tortured my mother. She would have told you anything you told her to."

"In matters of the spirit, only extraordinary measures can assure honesty."

"My mother was always honest."

"So you admit to being a heretic?"

"No."

"Then what do you wish to tell us?"

"I am dying," she said simply, truthfully. "You have starved me and left me here to rot. You have denounced the Mother in your treatment of my mother and me. You are condemned to eternal bleakness just as surely as I am condemned to the pyres."

"Now you admit to being a heretic," the politician said, his eyes bright, his mind paying no heed to that which did not make his case.

"I am not a heretic," she said, but unconsciously backed away as the two thugs stepped forward. Silently, she prayed that they would not remove her clothes, that they would leave her some dignity.

"Your mother confessed. She was a heretic, but at least she made her peace with the Mother before her death. Her confession freed her."

"You murdered her. The Mother does not tolerate murder."

"No, your mother was killed by your false god. He didn't want her to find the truth and come back to righteousness, so he broke her neck."

"You murdered an innocent woman. My mother," she said, trying to keep her voice controlled, "did more for your Mother-forsaken town than any of you ever even thought of doing. She led the ceremonies; she was the strongest charmer in the valley; her incantations could not be reversed save by the Mother herself!"

"Yes, she was powerful. But in the end, maybe it was her lust for power that turned her to other gods."

"There is only one God," Sarei said.

"Yes, but she no longer worshipped the Mother. We have witnesses. We know of the idol in your mother's attic. We know of the altar."

"You know nothing."

Then a fist, harder than the stone wall she was thrown against, knocked the world out from under her. It took all her effort to simply remain conscious on the dirty, cold floor of the cell. She tried not to shiver, tried to keep the tears at bay, knowing it was only the beginning. "I will not confess."

"Everyone confesses in the end."

But they didn't and she knew it. She'd listened to the crone, waiting, wondering if she would break down. Almost hoping she would. But she hadn't. She'd proved it could be done. "I will not betray my friends."

"So you do confess."

"No. I confess nothing."

One of the brutes lunged forward, a sticky grin showing brown teeth and white gums. He grabbed her arms and tied them behind her back as the other one slung a rope over the rafter above. She prayed they were going to hang her and be done with it, but knew it was not their way.

"Confess, Sarei, and we will not hurt you. Confess and let the Mother cleanse you."

"I won't."

"You know the only way for a heretic to return to the Mother is through the absolutions of confession or fire."

"Then burn me," she spat as the brute yanked her by the hair over to the dangling rope. Already she could feel the blood welling up around the coarse fibers that bound her, turning them red, staining them with her courage.

"I offer you salvation."

"And what of those I name? You offer them condemnation and torture."

The brute tied her hands to the hanging rope. The other began to pull it tight.

"I offer them what they are too ignorant to find themselves."

Sarei's feet were lifted from the ground, and she screamed as she felt the delicate balls of her shoulders begin to slip from their sockets with excruciating creaking. While she dangled, heavy weights were tied to her ankles, adding to the pain that turned the world a sour gray before her.

"Confess!" the politician yelled at her as she was lifted all the way to the rafter. "Confess!"

She was suspended, vision blurred by tears, the scent of the moldy wood of the rafter strong in her nose, for long minutes. Out the one window, she could finally see. Fires dotted the distance and the foreground like a pox. Smoke rose in lazy, unhurried columns from piles of wood and cinder, straight into the sky, untouched by wind or breeze. Bones littered the woodpiles, charred black, almost indistinguishable from the fuel itself. Only the rounded curve of a hip, the gloss of a skull, brought the distinction clear.

"Confess!" the politician yelled again, the reserve completely gone from his voice. Then, when she did not answer: "Now!" and she plummeted down for a heartbeat and was pulled up short just before her feet could hit the ground. The momentum tore the ball and socket construction of her joints apart, ripping muscles and tendons in one hideously painful jerk, and for a moment the world went black.

*   *   *

Cold water in her face, and the pain was back in an immediate rending of all she was. Like nothing she had ever felt before. She could not even think straight. "Why are you torturing me?" was all she could force herself to say.

"You're a heretic," the politician said with righteous indignation, once again controlling his voice. "A worshipper of blood and pain. And you speak to me of torture? You, a woman who idolizes the unnatural image of a man as creator. Blasphemy! A man! To claim to be God, that which She created, which cannot create in or of itself, usurping Her power for his own glory. And you are worshipping death, for your god is, by his own admission, dead!" With a wave of his hand, she was being lifted again and was introduced to yet another level of pain. Still, she thought, I am being strong. And there was hope in that.

The crone had not confessed.

The brutes still had not removed Sarei's clothes. She'd heard the sounds from other cells, knew that there was many a woman who had had her honor defiled as well as her physical being. But she was being spared that torture. Spared, most likely by this politician who knew her family name would carry weight even after her death.

The torture continued in some space that existed between the blink of an eye and eternity. Concepts such as time, guilt, and redemption were wiped away by the all-consuming red haze of brutal pain. Burned, whipped, flayed, crushed, Sarei could remember nothing that existed before the pain. Nothing except the face of the crone and the need to be silent. There were times, when one torture was being ended while another was being prepared, that she would wish with all her heart that the magic worked on the men. But no, the laws of nature could not be changed now. The brutes, the politician, like all others of their kind, could neither make magic nor be affected by it. But if those laws could be suspended for only a moment . . . Better to wish for the seasons to halt their change, the tides to still their motion.

What kind of God did this to Her creatures? Sarei knew. And so was silent.

At last. Twigs and logs piled high, townsfolk assembled to see the pathetic creature she had become. Arms—bloody, blackened husks— useless at her side, face so swollen she could hardly see, legs crushed beyond recognition so that she must be carried to the pyre. And in every face, every eye, the look of hatred, of horror, and not one of them offering the healing that any could administer. Rather, she felt the curses land on her brittle skin, pass into her broken bones, and it would have made her laugh, had she had a tongue left. Curses. Now. As if there were anything left that could bring her harm.

In silence, they placed Sarei on the mound of dry wood. The splinters and jagged edges poked through her worn frock, drawing blood, opening wounds that had only just begun to heal. Sarei lay upon them gratefully, ready for this, wanting it. A woman from the Hall of Mothers came forward, bearing a torch. She was solemn and appeared calm, but Sarei could sense the fear lying just below the surface. Fear of the men who had learned how to use the belief in the Mother against Her chosen. The older woman, bedecked in her ceremonial finery, gently, reverently touched the torch to the hungry, dry kindling at the bottom of the pile.

Heat. Warm for a moment below her back. Then burning, igniting her clothes in an instant. Blisters, popping, drying, burning away, layer after layer, upward, ever upward.

Sarei closed her eyes as the flames licked high around her, burning, yes, but no worse than any other pain. Burning, heating, the icon around her neck coloring the skin momentarily before fire engorged all. And in those last moments, Sarei had to smile. She could see her bones in the pile of ash and cinder. Brittle, broken bones surrounded by remnants of the woods and fields, denuded of trees, like stripping the Mother, as they gathered more and more fuel for the fires. And among the ash, embraced by cinders, shining in the muted orange glow of yet another cruel day, the thing that had brought her through it all.

Revenge.

Sweet revenge as they looked down and saw it among the ashes— the tiny silver cross her mother had given her.

I Feel My Body Grow

Del Stone, Jr.

She touches them, and I feel my body grow.

A man with eyes like polished knobs of bone, who stands behind a counter, trembling, the exertion of life a tension ringing through him. A hairless pupa of a child, wrapped in hospital sheets, quietly and almost lovingly feeding on itself to death. A woman dressed in white, starched and straight and sure of most things, the way women who know the tides of emotion are sure of most things.

She touches them all, and I feel my body grow.

But somehow, over the lifetimes, I still ache at the thought of her. I see my thoughts of her rising above the black chasm of all evil things that have come to pass, and somehow, I still ache at the thought of her. It is a thrall of some kind, I am sure, as sure of it as the woman in starched white is sure of most things, and I pray to be released from this thrall of sickness.

A thrall. That is what this is. Surely, it is not—

She touches a young man who is bright with life and love, and I feel my body growing, cell by twisted cell. I feel it growing through the man, a sharp angle of darkness, and soon he too will feel it, awakening one night in an astonished sweat, a dream of sickness spinning out of his mind that does not evaporate in the light of day.

A sickness. Inflicted by her, from the moment I saw her those lifetimes ago, a shy young woman dressed in simple black and white, her hair a primal darkness wrapped about her head like a coiled snake, her eyes without depth, her cheekbones and the ridge of her jawline smoothed to soft yet strong angles. Her beauty suggested intelligence and spirit, and I could not help but notice . . . and admire. Inflicted by her, surely. Inflicted, inflicted, inflicted—

She touches the frail hand of an elderly woman who is lying in a plump bed, surrounded by cats and photographs of loved ones and lilac sachets.

I feel my body growing. Horribly, I feel it.

221

Everything about her, magical. Her laughter, like wind blowing through the strings of a musical instrument; her manner, so comfortably alluring . . . I could not help myself.

Inflicted, and afflicted. My wife's gaze lingering a moment too long, I sensed she heard my thoughts the way a woman who has lived with a man for many years can sense the drift of his heart. And I, too, could feel the anger growing within my wife, could feel the coolness of her shadow falling over me as I sought through prayer and meditation to rid myself of the growing sickness within.

She touches a little girl, and I feel my body growing.

Inflicted, inflicted, inflicted—through the fields I tended and the drawing of water from the stream and the recitations of prayer at Sabbath services. Everywhere and everything, I saw her face and heard her laughter and wondered and worried and prayed.

She touches and touches and touches and my body grows, bloated and monstrous and twisted, my body grows.

A thrall, then. It had to be. Nothing else could have brought me to such spiritual ruin. Nothing else could have forced me to forsake my teachings, my faith, my devotion to the laws by which we all lived. Nothing else could have driven me to follow her into the field that final night, to . . . to take her, her coy overtures giving way to a pretense of terror as I ripped at her clothes . . . my God, how could I have done it?

A thrall. It had to be. A thrall of sickness.

She touches a woman dark of hair and thin of face, a woman so much like herself, laughing and beautiful and innocent—no, it cannot be innocence!—and I feel my body grow. Against my will, it grows, and it grows to disfigure and kill. The idea of innocence sends a special knife through me, and everything that has happened before and since focuses into sharp relief, as one of the photographs people frame and hang on their walls in this lifetime, and I feel my body twisting and hurting and the unmerciful evidence of memory.

My wife. It was she who said the word.

Witch.

She touches every child in a classroom, where outside, men wearing masks are ripping fibers from a wall.

And it was I who stood before her as she coughed amid the stinking, pitch-soaked timbers, her hands and feet bound to the stake, her terrified eyes darting from mine to the men who held the torches. It was I who pronounced the sentence, choking the words out, my throat so tight I could barely breathe but a greater terror falling upon me from the angry stares of the townspeople gathered around for the coming spectacle.

It was I who told her that by the laws of our community, she might have one question answered before the sentence was carried out.

And so she asked me, in a voice so small I leaned closer to hear her.

She asked me how I wanted to die.

Within the Lord's embrace, I told her, speaking in a powerful and righteous voice, despite my fear. My fear. She sensed it, and she asked me again. How did I want to die?

I felt myself frowning at her, unprepared and apprehensive, and then I answered again: within the Lord's embrace.

She stared at me a long moment, her gaze clear and strong. And then she asked me again, the tone of her voice insisting I tell the truth: How did I want to die?

Her words seemed to reach within, to grasp my heart and squeeze it, as if she were testing for ripeness, and in a moment that arrived and departed so quickly I could not be certain it had even come at all, I felt nothing but black, rancid loathing for myself, because for that sliver of a moment I asked myself: What if this disease of lust that had afflicted me were nothing more than a weakness of my conviction? What if this woman stood wrongly accused?

And I could not help but whisper:

If you are innocent, then let me live in misery for all eternity.

She touched me.

Somehow, she slipped her hand from the bindings and touched me, in the center of my chest, a touch as feathery and insubstantial as a dream of a touch. And as I staggered back, a warmth spreading along the curves of my ribs and sinking into all the secret places inside me, the men shouted angrily and hurled their torches into the timbers, drowning everything in a sudden roar of combustion.

She did not scream.

Afterwards, I could not remain for the reconsecration of the soil. I could not bear my wife's smirking glances. I could not perform my devotions or say a prayer. Something had fallen over me, the sudden idea of innocence a black film that covered my skin and poisoned my blood and sank into my dreams, and it stained everything I believed in with a mark of hypocrisy, murder, and despair.

Lurking beneath this, I would not admit at the time, was a memory of her, the eyes, the sharp cheekbones, the spirit. The memory always brought with it a wrenching of the heart, a sinking of the gut, a bonfire of hatred for myself and my glaring wife and the good people who somehow, some way, had forced me to do this thing.

Inflicted, inflicted, inflicted . . . yes. But now I was no longer sure. Had it been by my own hand?

I fell ill. A physical sickness, to match the infection that had claimed my soul. The warmth in my chest became a fire, and lesions ate my flesh. I did not seek relief through poultices or ecclesiastical ministrations. I did not do anything but wait.

Until she came for me. In the night, when I knew she would come, her dark, dark hair a penumbra of shadow floating around the sharp curve of her face, her body unmarked by fire or any other flaw. She came to me and took my hand and we left, floating through walls and trees and finally the sky itself.

She said to me: You will live forever.

Ah, my heart soared. I could not believe there was room within her for mercy, or forgiveness, but she spoke the words with such conviction and compassion that I believed her. I let go of the constraints that had held me, and I told her I loved her, and I would stay with her forever.

She did not reply.

But she led me to a village, much like my own, and she took me into a cottage where a family slept around the banked embers of a fire.

We watched them a moment. Then she whispered: Goodness, and evil, exist in every act. Only truth never changes.

And then she touched the father. She touched the mother. She touched the sleeping children.

I felt my body grow.

Horribly. I felt my body grow.

And it has grown. All the years, all the lifetimes, all the ages that have passed, my body has grown.

The world is different now, a loveless place that glitters with machines and science and godlessness. My body grows quickly now, metastasizing despite the radiation and chemotherapy these people use to kill it, the tumors an ever-ripening harvest of sickness and pain that will never know end.

But somehow, I still ache at the thought of her. Rising above everything else, I still do.

A thrall, yes. But by my own hand? I will never know the truth.

As she touches them, and I feel my body grow.

The Conversion of St. Monocarp

BRIAN McNAUGHTON

hy are you doing this to me?" Twisting by his heels on a chain, the dwarf addressed the vaulting orgy of shadows and firelight on stone walls until he revolved toward Friedegunde. With her face upside down, she looked unfamiliar; but, oddly, less unusual. He cried: "I love you!"

"That's why." She sliced into his spine with her father's second-favorite sword, reserved for those he didn't dislike.

What had she done? Tender-heartedness had always been her worst fault, she believed, and a wish to shorten the little man's suffering had impelled a butcher's cut. His lifeblood should have dribbled into the brazier of aromatic herbs while she completed the enchantment. But he was jerking, gurgling, spraying blood everywhere—even on her gown, the horrid freak!—and within an inch of death. Was there time?

She dropped the sword clanging and hurled herself at the stairs. She pounded upward on legs as strong, and on ankles a good deal thicker, than those of her father the graf's staunchest warriors. Fumbling among the weighty keys at the girdle often compared in length and strength to a catapult-sling, she alternately beseeched the Blessed Virgin and damned her for an obstinate Jewess until she found the right one and burst into the room, blasting out most of the tallow candles around the still form of Brother Monocarp.

In dizzying contrast to the coarse brutes whose red faces forever puked and guffawed around her, he was smooth and white as a peeled willow. His hair was not yellow straw, it was the silk of the barley; his eyes were not blue stones at the bottom of a cold brook, they were the sky on that one summer day she recalled from her fifth year when she had lisped, "Mummy, where is the fog?"

She kissed his lips. Still warm, they recalled her to her purpose. She recited the words that the wise woman of the woods had taught her.

Through an embrasure, she fixed her eyes on the moon that oozed light onto the pine-tops like juice from a squashed toadstool. She thought of Willi, dangling in the room below. Did his lifeblood still flow? If he knew what was good for him, it had damned well better!

Little Willi was the only man who had ever loved her. She knew the fine shades that debarred her from beauty. Her jaw was her least attractive feature, for it had never stopped growing. It had spread her large, square teeth until anyone foolhardy enough to try it could have inserted the tip of an index finger between any two of them. This drew attention to her second-least attractive feature, narrow temples that squeezed her tiny eyes together in a squint.

She hoarded slights and could sob bitterly over any one of them. Poor Siegfried, for instance, later felled by food-poisoning, had remarked that she had less nose than an old corpse. And Gunther, cut down by some coward who had stamped his spine to the consistency of fingernail-parings, had compared her generous mouth to an old sow's rump, bristles and all.

Even her good points were blessings of an evil fairy. Her hair was unparalleled in its golden voluminousness, and it served to conceal less attractive features (including ears like the lids of the castle's cisterns, to quote Adolf, later waylaid by a werewolf who had induced him to strip to his skin and put his arms aside before tearing him limb from limb); but she would sometimes trip over this glorious hair, forcing her to show the temper that admittedly was more pungent than sweet.

Her eyebrows were fine as spiderwebs, and this drew notice from their thickness, their union over her nominal nose, and the fact that they writhed like a convulsing caterpillar when anger blotched her face red. Remarked upon with favor were her bulging breasts and yard-wide buttocks, and in their cups the warriors would sometimes grope for them. Her tutors of love had been men too drunk to teach her anything beyond the variety of snores a sot can trumpet. Some never gave any woman this lesson again, for she would exact justice from inept teachers with the selfsame scissors that Delilah had used to shear Samson, purchased from and blessed by Pope John XII on her late mother's pilgrimage to Rome.

But Little Willi, dying in the room below—common, yes; crook-backed, yes; ugly, yes; no taller than her knees, yes, yes, *yes*! But he had loved her, he had worshipped her, and even when sober, he had lusted for her. *Willi!*

She forced her mind back to the incantation. The moon had risen a full handspan above the forest. It appeared green, and the chorus of shrieks and howls that hailed it could not be ascribed to wolves alone.

Willi had his faults. Foremost was his hideous ugliness. Although her nausea was intensified by the quantities of beer she put away each night, she would sometimes vomit at the sight and feel of him clinging to her like an enormous spider when she woke, nor were his charms enhanced by his daily being hurled to the stone floor beside her bed. But unlike other lovers, he was eager to please her, and he often did.

Monocarp, the holy hermit, could not have spurned her more vehemently if she were a toad he had discovered in his penitential meals of thistles mashed with charcoal and horse-dung. The Christ-crazed cockroach had denounced her as a monster of carnality, another Jezebel, a second Salome. Those ladies had been burning in hell for a long time now, but they'd gotten some fun out of their wickedness. Friedegunde's sins were a frumpish gown whose train of punishments was borne along behind her by capering imps of loathing and regret.

She lowered her eyes from the disconcerting moon, lapping her tower with lurid tongues of fire, to gaze upon the holy man. Once he had succumbed to the potion, accepted in its foulness as the special penance he constantly sought, she had stripped him of his horsehair shirt and girdle of briers and bathed him lovingly. She had found nothing to displease her except his filth; even by the exacting standards of the day, it was heroic. Such desperate excess abounded as the Millennium impended. Her father had taken a twittering pubescent called Flosshilde to wife, and his mighty men were so quick to reach for their weapons nowadays that they hardly dared speak to one another.

She recited with passion, for she had seen no effect beyond the curious behavior of the moon and of the putative wolves. But now a wind rose below her, although it sounded more as if all the dead of her glorious tribe had arisen to groan hollowly of those few sins they had neglected to commit or failed to imagine. The remaining candles streamed in the breeze like banners, and those that had died spontaneously ignited. As the last word was spoken, the eyes of the saintly eremite snapped open.

"Friede," he breathed. "I had a horrible dream. . . ."

"That I killed you . . . Willi?"

He turned his translucent face and his beautiful blue eyes toward her. "How did you know, my dearest darling?"

It was a long time before the long-repressed young man remembered to ask any more vexing questions, and by that time she could respond only with murmurous vaporings.

His trull perched on his mailed knee, Graf Heinrich von der Hiedlerheim strafed the table with his solitary eye. He had the look of a man who has misplaced something—his wits, Friedegunde believed— but cannot recall what.

"My *dwarf*!" he cried at last.

"You mustn't call it that, Papa," Flosshilde chirped as she shifted her weight obligingly. "It's really quite—"

"Shut up, moron. My dwarf! Where is he, that Willi? I haven't laughed in days. Remember"—he could scarcely continue, he was laughing so hard—"remember how we used to toss him from the battlements and catch him? Remember the look on his horrible face when we failed?"

"I—" Brother Monocarp began, but Friedegunde jerked him down.

"What is your confessor doing here?" her father demanded. "Priests should slither among the women without besmearing my sight. Someone seize that eunuch and castrate him!"

"No, Father!" Friedegunde hammered the table with her huge fist, and those who had jumped to obey their lord quickly sat down. She improvised: "The Apostle Hermann said that he who harms a priest shall be beloved of the Bulgars. At least twenty of them, he said."

"Some wishful priest made that up." Heinrich canceled his order with a wave. "But where is Willi, my dwarf?"

Many a steely eye locked on Friedegunde. Brother Monocarp's lip trembled, but he said no word. Under the table, her fingers gripped him in an intimate threat.

"Search our domains for the malingering ingrate," the graf ordered, "and when you find him, feed him to the dogs."

His hounds frisked to their feet with a great clanking of chains and stared speculatively at the knights and ladies, the squires and singers and slaves, for they knew what those last words meant.

"May I have a confessor, Papa?" the baggage squeaked.

"What sins could you possibly confess, pet?"

"Oh, nothing really, but last week a girl snagged a knot in my hair.

While she was combing it. And when I held her down in the coals of the hearth-fire she bit my foot. I fear I took Our Blessed Savior's name in vain."

When he could control his indulgent chuckling, Heinrich said, "My dear, you may share that weasely manling with my daughter."

Christ could come tomorrow, for Friedegunde had known heaven. The seepage of Willi's mind had boiled against his twisted little body; the juices of Brother Monocarp's body had boiled against his twisted little mind. Both brews now combined in one glorious bath for her senses. She grew slim enough to squeeze frontward through some doors. Her blotches glowed.

"You've done something to me, haven't you?" her lover asked.

"Why, what do you mean?"

"My body." Willi gazed down in anguish at his straight limbs.

"Don't you like it?" To distract him, she dropped to her massive knees and did that which he liked best.

"Yes, but . . . It's not mine, do you understand? I feel like a fish playing at bird."

"So, swim and chirp."

Willi pondered. At length he said, "It's odd, isn't it? That Flosshilde should be so slender, and yet have breasts as large as yours?"

As the slaves were now afraid to do it, Friedegunde had volunteered to plait the horror's hair. On an ancient crone this *silver* hair would have been acceptable, but on a child whose skin was luminously smooth, it was grotesque. Those breasts, too, that Willi had dared to praise were indeed large as her own, but they flaunted themselves brazenly upright.

"Where is Brother Monocarp?" the slut piped.

"He wanted to mortify his most sinful part, and somehow he managed to bite it."

The thing had the audacity to titter. "I wouldn't bite it."

"The Apostle Horst said that she who even *thinks* of lying with a priest shall be ravished by scaly serpents for all eternity."

"That sounds like fun. Ow, you filthy fat swine, you've pulled my hair!"

* * *

229

"Drink this, dear Stepmother," Friedegunde said when Flosshilde revived the next day.

"What . . . ? Did I faint? My chin hurts!"

"This will help." She had some of the wise woman's black potion left, and she tilted the chalice against those foul, flower-petal lips.

Not even the ghastliest of grimaces could wrench the beauty from her face, Friedegunde grudgingly admitted. As might have been expected, her last words were a stupid question: "Oh, Daughter, have you stolen my life?"

"Look on it from your vantage point in the lowest pit of hell, when your eyelashes turn to wasp-stings, when your hair becomes wires that grow inward, when you give birth to myriad vipers every hour, when Satan himself gags at the sight of you and slams the lid on your pit, look on it then, dear Stepmother, as a loan."

Having wiped the chalice clean, disordered her hair and gown, and taken the poppet's tears to streak her own cheeks, Friedegunde dashed from the room, howling: "Horror! Madness! Joy—I mean, despair!"

"She looks more beautiful than ever," Willi said when he had pried up the coffin-lid.

"You mustn't say things like that, not with a pathetic catch in your voice, not when you are standing in a grave and I am standing over you with"—she tapped his tonsure—"a shovel."

Willi staggered to his feet and wiped the blood from his eyes. "Can't I even admire her as one would admire a—a beautiful tree?"

"Only as a dog would. But take heart, dear Willi. She will be yours, all yours, but burning with the same love I bear for you."

Willi lifted Flosshilde from the coffin and laid her at the graveside with such reverence that Friedegunde's eyeballs seemed about to burst. She restrained an itch to kick the thing back into the grave, dead or not, and shovel the dirt over it.

She dropped to her knees beside it. No: despite all appearances, despite the opinion of her distracted father's physician (whose flayed body, hanging from the highest rampart, seemed to twitch when the ravens tore it), the detestable object was warm. Every few minutes, the ghost of a breath crept from its sickeningly pert nose. Left to itself, the creature would bounce back to the state it fancied to be consciousness before the cock crowed.

She was tempted to bury it again and let that happen, to sit at breakfast and savor the picture of her stepmother shredding her fingers to the bone against splintery planks as she shrieked beneath the muffling tonnage of the earth; but one couldn't have everything. A glimpse of the longing in Willi's newly beautiful eyes as he lifted the body convinced her that she had no other choice. Willi wanted the wanton who wanted Willi, and she would be blown aside by the power of that rune. She must sacrifice her sturdy and comfortable body to her lover's whim. Since Flosshilde's was younger, and hers was becoming very sore indeed, it seemed a small sacrifice.

"Do you remember the incantation?" she demanded.

"Yes, but how will I . . . *explain* her?"

"You're a holy man, clown! You raised her from the dead by prayer. My father will buy you a bishopric, and all good Christians will wade through one another's blood to pay for the privilege of kissing your saintly foot. While I, in my new body, as bishop's mistress—"

"You'll have to sleep with your father, won't you?"

"Willi, that prosing ancient fought beside the great Otto at Augsberg, and he has crept a good five years beyond the half-century mark. A pillow can now do what a dozen Wendish lances once couldn't. Will it be a sin to help him totter to his eternal reward?"

She made no comment at the tender care with which he arranged Flosshilde over his shoulder. She showed saintly restraint in saying nothing when she caught him fondling her buttocks, which would presently be her own. But she could no longer contain herself when he revealed the emptiness of the head that crowned his glorious body by asking, "How can I explain your death? They'll blame me, they'll put me to torture—"

"Whoever heard of anyone being murdered inside a locked room?"

"Yes. I'll show them the key—"

"No, Willi, *I'll* have the key."

"Are you sure that's how it works?"

"Willi . . . My body will rot in unhallowed ground. I will break my dear father's heart by taking my life in the prime of my youth and beauty. I dare all this for you, for you, dear dwarf. All you have to do is what I tell you to do."

"And if something should go wrong," he mused, "I can say that I was only following orders."

She said nothing, but she was awed by his originality. She knew she had seen something greater in him than wormish lust.

Hanging above the brazier, Friedegunde thought she might linger awhile and recall the treasures of her life: the beloved doll whose arms and legs she had pulled off when she understood that it was prettier than she would ever be; the look on her mother's face when she had tripped her off the parapet, her mother's evil mind having misconstrued the innocent game that she played with her father. But the smoke made her sneeze, and she cut short her reminiscences with a stroke of the sword. The smoke became more acrid as the herbs fizzed in the drizzle of her blood.

The cut was more painful than she had imagined, and blood blurred her vision. Blinking and shaking her head whenever the window swung into view, she saw nothing odd about the moon. She heard no howling of wolves, only the dull croaking and chirping of lesser creatures and the song of drunken warriors in the great hall.

Further straining her ears, she heard no recitation of witchly runes —and why were her father's heroes singing about all men being brothers, when not one of them believed that for a minute? But she had often noticed that music made more sense than words, and the tune was lovely. She nearly forgot pain as she drifted on the virile chorus.

Twisting in the steam of her dripping blood, she forced herself to concentrate hard on the room upstairs. She heard a thumping sound, as of someone pounding a straw mattress. Try as she would, she couldn't shake the image this evoked of a nasty dwarf using his fine new body to have his way with a drugged and defenseless nitwit.

She thought of screaming a protest, but it was so much easier to revolve on a stately axis and enjoy the music.

She found herself humming along.

Garage Sale

JANET FOX

They were driving around the city on a steamy late-summer afternoon, two secretaries beating the heat of their inner-city walkup by cruising through suburbia. Here lawns lay crisp and green under a mist from sprinkler systems, the houses hermetically sealed to hold in the coolness breathed by air conditioners. Stella clacked as she drove, but only because she was addicted to plastic bracelets. She also liked to dye her hair different colors—though mercifully just one color at a time.

Jen was to Stella as the wren is to the cardinal, not noticeable beside the more flamboyant display, yet having a quiet style all her own.

"They got it made, huh?" said Stella. "Not having to bust their buns in a dumb office every day. House, hubby, and kids—the American dream, right?"

"I think you made a wrong turn."

"Where?"

"Back there. Some of these residential streets end in a cul-de-sac, and—"

"A cool de *what?*"

Jen subsided since it was too late to get Stella going in the right direction. Shadows of low-hanging foliage immersed the car, but only served to intensify the heat. The neat cookie-cutter ranches had given way to older residences in a variety of styles, most of them pretentious, spread more widely apart and set well back from the street.

"Or how about these? Woo-eee!"

As they passed a neo-Victorian horror, rife with gingerbread and flanked about with fountains and marble statues, both of them saw at once the hand-lettered sign poked into the funeral-grass lawn:

GARAGE SALE
TODAY ONLY

233

"Do you believe that?" giggled Stella, putting on the brakes so suddenly that Jen had to steady herself with a hand on the dash.

"What do you suppose they're selling, the Crown Jewels?" asked Jen.

"As long as it's a bargain," said Stella, her bracelets rattling as she climbed out of the car.

The house awed Jen a little as she walked toward it. Stella giggled and pointed as she passed a marble Cupid relieving himself into an ornamental pool.

"I know you love these sales," said Jen, "but every time I go to one, I get talked into buying some worthless junk."

"Never can tell. Today may be your day to find a treasure."

Jen looked furtively at the cupolas and the stained glass windows. "A place like this—it could just be some kind of joke."

Stella gestured toward a cardboard sign tacked to the porch railing: GARAGE SALE IN BACK, with a scarlet arrow pointing the way.

There was a garage in back, though the builders had evidently not felt called upon to give it the ornateness they'd showered upon the house itself. Though the place was large inside, almost barnlike, they saw to their wonder that it was stacked wall to wall with a jumble of artifacts, furniture of all kinds and periods, clothing of several different eras, tools, household gadgets, and things that defied description.

"I think I just died and went to heaven," said Stella. She began to root contentedly about among the merchandise.

Jen nodded a greeting to the woman who seemed to be in charge of the sale. She sat behind a card table on a tattered chaise longue of violet brocade, most of her attention claimed by a cheap paperback romance. There was something odd about her, something Jen couldn't quite put her finger on, though certainly she might have been any housewife in faded jeans and a checkered shirt rolled to the elbows, a bandanna covering her head, the fat coils of hair rollers distending it.

"There's something funny about this place," she told Stella, who ignored her, rummaging through a trunk of musty-smelling garments, a moth-eaten feather boa draped about her shoulders. "Something funny," she muttered to herself, and began to move desultorily around the place, seeing an enormous moose head, the bottom half of a store-window mannikin, and the photographs of generals Grant and Lee framed in what looked like the seat of a privy. "What an incredible collection of junk!" she said under her breath. Yet despite her incredulity, she began to be carried away by the sheer volume. What had Stella been saying about finding treasure?

She was poking about in a dim corner when she moved aside a Chinese silk screen patterned with tigers. As she did, she drew in her breath and hastily began to apologize. A man sat before her in a thread-bare recliner, seemingly staring out at her, though with the reflection on his glasses she couldn't quite be sure. Her apology trailed off as she realized he wasn't moving.

"My God! Stella, he's dead! Stel—"

As she turned to run, she collided with someone she at first thought was her friend. It was the woman in charge of the sale; she smiled a small, secretive smile that made her angular, high-cheekboned face seem anything but ordinary, and she gripped Jen's arms to keep her from falling.

Jen opened her mouth to scream to Stella, but as she looked, by some trick of vision, her friend seemed small and far away, waltzing dreamily, a gown of blue voile held up before her.

"She can't hear you—not from here," said the woman calmly. Released from her grasp, Jen stood unsteadily before the strangely immobile man in the chair.

"Here? Where's here?"

"A juncture. A pivotal moment outside of time. Do you like him?" The woman removed the man's glasses with a proprietary gesture and cleaned them on the tail of her shirt. Jen saw that he had gentle myopic blue eyes.

"Do I like him?"

"I won't pretend he's like new. The hair's thinning on top, and he could lose a bit down here." She patted the obvious paunch beneath his white shirt. "But in many ways he was a good husband."

"He's your— No, you couldn't be selling—"

"Well, a person gets tired of things sometimes before they're quite worn out. You know how it is." A tiny dark questing head peeped from beneath the bandanna and slowly oozed its length down the woman's face: a snake as big around as a pencil with a minuscule tongue that darted out to taste the woman's cheek. Almost before the image registered, certainly before it was believed, the woman had swept it back under the bandanna with a casual gesture. Up close Jen could see the bulges beneath the cloth move, coiling and sliding.

"I guess so," said Jen, licking her lips and looking back toward the man in the chair. "He looks nice, but—" She hadn't noticed before, but there was a price written in grease pencil on his forehead. *$10.* "But why does he just sit there like that?"

"Since it's getting late," said the woman, lowering her voice conspiratorially, "and no one else has been interested, I'll let him go for half price."

"Is he dead or—"

"He's fully functional. I'll reanimate him when the time comes."

"Are you telling me you're some kind of . . . witch?"

"That's just a word, but I guess it'll do."

"They used to catch witches and burn them!"

The woman laughed, shaking her head until a darkly patterned tail slipped out onto her forehead and quickly slithered back under cover. "Not real witches, they didn't," she said.

"You must be crazy, and—" Jen looked desperately for Stella, but she was no longer there. A yellow plastic bracelet lay on the floor in a prosaic patch of sunlight.

"Don't expect corroboration from your friend. She was never here. Neither were you, if I don't make the sale."

"What if you do? Make the sale."

The woman smiled. "Yeah, I kind of thought you were interested. Well, you'll have a husband, that's all. Say you met him right after you finished business school."

"That's what I'll think?"

"That's what will have happened," said the woman, looking at her fingernails. They were very long fingernails, polished black, and the tips curved inward.

"Do we have . . . children?"

"For five dollars?"

Jen's fingers moved numbly, opening the catch of her purse. She didn't think she could just leave him there like that, staring into space and sitting in that ratty recliner for all eternity. And then, she hadn't had much luck getting a husband the usual way, so . . .

As she handed over the bill, the woman's eyes caught hers, cool amber eyes, steady-burning as lamps, the pupils a horizontal bar of darkness. Her whisper, grown low and sinister, hung in the air. "Tell you what, I'll even throw in the chair."

* * *

"Just look at me, Ben. Sometimes I think you're *glued* in that goddamned chair!"

Ben blinked up at her, his blue eyes so innocent, so vulnerable behind their panes of glass that she felt she could gladly throttle him. It was so predictable, so irritating. Screwing up his face with concentration, he did something to the TV's remote control, and the volume of the football game rose imperceptibly. "Really, Jen, I don't suppose you could come up with this overpowering desire to go out on any night except Monday? A man works hard; he deserves a chance to sit down once in a while." He twitched like a rabbit. "So what's for supper?"

"Oh, God!" A wisp of smoke curled through the kitchen door, and Jen ran to remove the smoking pan from the stove. She turned the water on it, half choking on the smell. Then she stood at the sink, looking at the charred and drowned remains. "If I had it all to do over again," she said quietly, drawing a hand across her face and leaving a black smear. She sighed inaudibly, thinking that no one ever had a chance to do it over, no one.

Never.

She busied herself in the kitchen for a few minutes, then returned to the living room, automatically picking up newspapers from the floor and an empty beer can that had left a ring on the coffee table.

"I burned the chops, so I put in a couple of TV dinners. I figured you'd like that, you like the damn TV so much anyway." For a moment she thought he hadn't heard her; he sat there immobile, like a graven idol, blue images from the screen flickering on his glasses.

At last he grunted. "That's just great," he said. "A man works hard all day and comes home to TV dinners. Some wife I found for myself."

"Listen," she said, interposing herself between him and the set. "You're not that big a bargain yourself, mister." For some reason even she could not fathom, she found that vastly amusing, and repeated it. "No bargain," she said, and laughed until tears came to her eyes.

Buyer Beware

TIM WAGGONER

how we doing today?"

Isobel didn't turn at the salesman's approach. She wanted to say, "*I* am doing just fine, thank you," but instead she hoped—vainly, she knew—that he'd go away. She continued examining the '85 Cutlass Ciera that had caught her eye. She liked its color. She thought the blue rather matched her familiar's eyes.

"That's a beauty, isn't it?" the salesman said as he sidled up next to her, smelling of too much aftershave and a recently ingested breath mint. "The body's in great shape, not too many miles on it. Runs great too."

Despite herself, Isobel looked at the Ciera with heightened interest. Then, when she realized what had happened, she chided herself mentally and shook her head, setting her tiny bell earrings to tinkling. They had been spelled to help the wearer resist sales pitches, and as their soft, pure tones echoed in her ears, she felt her interest in the car flagging and gave a little sigh of relief.

She turned toward the salesman. He was handsome enough, in a boyish sort of way, in his early to mid-thirties. He had short black hair, sincere brown eyes, and an open, friendly smile. He was tall, too, six feet, perhaps a bit more. He wore a white shirt with the sleeves rolled up, navy pants, and a maroon tie. He looked professional, but not stuffy. Just a regular guy at work on a regular day, doing a job he loved.

Isobel didn't buy it for a minute.

"Hi, my name's Dan, Dan Mulroy." He stuck out his hand for her to shake.

Isobel looked at it suspiciously, as if it might be some sort of trap. She didn't want to shake, but on the other hand, she didn't want to appear rude, either. So she shook, and immediately after stuck her hand in her right skirt pocket and hurriedly rubbed it in the mixture of grave mold—gathered at midnight, naturally—and powdered dragon's blood to counter any undue influence the salesman's touch might have had on her.

She then gave him her name. "Isobel Washburn." It wasn't her *true* name, of course, not the name she was known by to her sisters. She wasn't that foolish.

The salesman, Dan, grinned. "Pleased to meet you, Isobel."

His gaze roamed up and down her body quickly and Isobel felt suddenly self-conscious. She was a small, thin woman who could pull off looking late-thirtyish when the light was right, but the unforgiving August sun revealed her to be in her mid-forties. She had simple, plain features that weren't helped by her washed-out complexion. Her short blonde hair was the color of wet straw and always hung limply no matter how many hair-care products—both mundane and esoteric—she tried. She wore a black blouse and skirt, even though it was summertime. Black was de rigueur for a witch, no matter the season. Hot as it was, though, she would have loved to have been wearing a white T-shirt and shorts.

A number of accessories completed her ensemble: a pair of ruby-framed glasses, her bell earrings, a gold locket that hung down between her small breasts, and several bracelets on each wrist. She carried a small red purse tucked beneath her arm that, like most women's purses, was full to bulging. But unlike other women, her purse contained a rather out-of-the-ordinary assortment of possessions that would have been more at home in a biology lab.

Dan nodded toward the Ciera. "How about it, Isobel? Like to take her for a test drive?"

Isobel glanced at the price painted on the car's windshield in day-glo green. $3,700. Quite a bit more than she wanted to spend. Still, she did like that blue. . . .

With a start, she realized what was happening and reached into her left skirt pocket and fingered the nail that was there. The nail was enchanted to fix her to her course and help keep her from being distracted. As she rubbed the nail, she felt her interest in the Ciera fading, not as quickly as she would have liked, but fading.

"No," she said finally. "Not today." She turned and walked away from Dan, hoping that he wouldn't follow, knowing that he would.

"Well, how about this '86 Thunderbird over here?" He took her elbow and steered her over to the car in question. "This is a great deal.

It's got a completely rebuilt engine. That makes it practically a new car."

That sounded good to Isobel. She was absolutely terrible with mechanical things, and a practically new engine would be less liable to break down, wouldn't it? The price was even higher than the Ciera's, but that was only to be expected given the fact that it had an almost new engine. She was actually reaching for the door handle so she could take a look inside when a breeze came along and set her earrings to tinkling.

She suddenly felt as if she had woken up from a trance. She shook her head as much to clear it as to indicate her disinterest in the Thunderbird and moved off, Dan following close behind.

This was going even more poorly than she had feared.

Isobel belonged to the East Brunswick coven. It wasn't much of a name, and they'd been trying to come up with a better one for years. Half the membership wanted to call themselves the Daughters of Darkness but the other half favored the Sisters of Sin. They'd been fighting about it for years without coming to any sort of consensus, leaving the coven no choice but to keep its dull name for the foreseeable future.

Like the other witches in the coven, Isobel normally traveled by broom. But she was rather absent-minded when it came to having the motive spells maintained, and thus her broom's enchantments had fallen into such a sorry state that it was no longer able to fly. Embarrassed, she took her broom to Magister Joachim, who said he could repair it, but that given the amount of damage done thanks to Isobel's neglect, it would take some time.

So Isobel found herself bereft of transportation. She couldn't just borrow a broom. A witch's broom was attuned to each individual as intimately as was her familiar. No other would work for her. And she was too proud to go about constantly begging rides from her sisters.

Autumn was fast approaching, the busiest time of year for a witch, and Isobel couldn't afford to be without transport. There was just too much to do. So she had had no choice but to consider purchasing a car. She didn't need anything fancy, just something that would get her around until the Magister had finished repairing her broom.

Isobel, however, had a slight problem: she was completely unresistant to sales pressure.

Once, a witch from a neighboring coven, the Servants of Circe—now there was a name!—talked Isobel into trading five centimeters of hangman's rope, which was quite rare these days, for what she claimed was dust from Nostradamus's coffin, but which in truth was nothing but flour mixed with a little bit of Drāno. Isobel had nearly killed herself when she used the "dust" in an attempt to summon a wind elemental. The mystic explosion blew out all the windows of her house and reduced most of her furniture to kindling. On the bright side, however, her drains had never been so clean.

And then there was the time Isobel cast a spell to hook her television up to cable illegally. She flipped through the channels until she came to QVC, and within an hour she had spent over six thousand dollars. It had taken the entire coven working in unison to magically remove Isobel's order from the network's computers. Afterwards, her sisters took her TV away.

So it was with full self-knowledge of her weakness that Isobel began her car search. She examined animal entrails, cast bones, drew up astrological charts, all in order to determine the most advantageous day for her to go shopping. She then summoned and consulted a half-dozen spirits as to which was the best dealership to visit. But since spirits weren't very knowledgeable about such real-world matters, she had ended up choosing a car place at random out of the phone book—Priced Rite Auto Sales.

And so she had engaged a cab and come here. But she hadn't come unwarded, oh no! She had loaded herself down with the most powerful protective charms she could devise, charms designed to compensate for her weakness and help her resist the inevitable sales pressure.

And they were working. But the question was, for how long? She had fashioned the charms as well as she was able, had labored day and night to get the spells just right. Perhaps she hadn't done as good a job as she'd thought. She had already shown signs of weakening.

Well, she was just going to have to forge ahead and hope the charms' magic would last long enough for her to get the very best deal on the very best car—without being cheated.

"Okay, so you're not interested in the T-bird," Dan said. "I don't blame you; they can be real gas guzzlers." He thought for a moment. "How about this Chevette?" He pointed to a drab little brown car at the end of the row. The price on the window was $2,500. "It's an '84. I took a guy for a test drive in it the other day, and it runs real well."

The price was nearer to what she wanted to spend, but still high. Without thinking, she said, "How many miles on it?"

Dan grinned and escorted her over to the car.

"What'd I tell you? Drives like a dream, doesn't it?"

Isobel put the car in park and turned off the ignition.

"It . . . drove well enough." She wiggled her head, but the tinkling of the bells didn't drive the thought away. She reached into her pocket and clutched the nail, but still the impression remained. Either it was true and the drive had gone well, or her charm was malfunctioning. She wished she had some way to know which was the case.

They got out of the car and while Dan stood back, Isobel walked around slowly, squinting through her glasses as she examined the Chevette. There was nothing wrong with her vision; these were glasses of Trueseeing. If there were any flaws with the car, they would make her aware of them.

She inspected the body for rust—a little, not much—and checked the tires. All four looked good. Now for the real test. She had Dan pop the hood and she peered at the cooling engine. Not that she would know exactly what to look for, but her glasses would. For a moment she thought she saw the engine as an ancient grimy thing with hoses on the verge of cracking, but then her vision cleared and what she saw was an old engine, yes, but one reasonably well maintained with solid hoses and little dirt.

Must've been a glitch in the spell, she thought.

She stepped back and Dan lowered the hood for her.

"So, what do you think? Are we ready to talk money?"

Isobel hesitated before finally saying, "Yes, I think we are."

Inside the small, air-conditioned building that housed Priced Rite's offices, they sat at Dan's desk and got down to business.

Twenty-five hundred was simply too much for Isobel's budget. She offered fifteen hundred. Dan made doubtful noises but said he'd take her offer back to his manager.

He wasn't long in returning.

"Sorry, Isobel, no can do. That's less than the car cost us in the first place. We want to come to an agreement with you, but we have to make a little money, too, you know. I'm sure you understand."

"Yes, of course." Isobel reached up and clasped the locket, her most powerful charm. Inside was a mixture of a number of nasty ingredients, the most potent of which were three strands of pubic hair from a mummy. The charm was designed to make an opponent in business dealings lose his good judgment and become overly generous.

She smiled, willing her charm to work. "How about eighteen hundred?"

Dan sighed. "I don't know. Let me go ask."

He left once more and when he returned, he said, "My manager says he'll come down to twenty three hundred."

Isobel shook her head. "Nineteen hundred. And that's my final offer."

"All right. I'll be back."

Isobel chortled inwardly. If her locket worked as it was supposed to, she would soon be the proud owner of a new—well, new to her—car.

Dan reappeared and he didn't look happy. "I'm real sorry, but my manager says he can get two thousand easy if he sends it to auction."

"Auction?"

"We auction off the cars we haven't been able to sell at the price we want. That way we get the most money we can out of them. Next auction's tomorrow. If you decide to pass on that little beauty, my manager'll send it on over."

Isobel reached into her skirt pocket and gripped her nail so hard she bent it. She knew Dan was probably just lying to her to get her to buy the car, but what if it was true, what if they did send the car away tomorrow? Sent *her* car away?

"Nineteen ninety nine?" she said hopefully.

Dan gave her a great big smile. "Isobel, you drive a hard bargain."

Isobel waved back at Dan as she pulled out of the lot. She had spent more money than she'd wanted to, but she had talked them down five hundred dollars—five hundred and one to be precise—and she felt pretty good about herself.

As she drove down the road, she thought she heard a suspicious knocking coming from the engine. And when she pulled up to a stoplight, she realized that the brakes seemed much more squeaky than they had during the test drive. And had the seat been this uncomfortable?

She decided that like most people, she was probably just second-guessing herself after a major purchase. The car was fine.

When the light turned green, she pressed the accelerator and the

Chevette moved sluggishly forward. But Isobel didn't notice the car's lack of pick-up. She was too busy composing a mental shopping list for the black mass this evening.

Dan watched Isobel drive off and when she was gone, he returned to the office. He went into the back room, and there was his manager, dressed in a crimson robe, standing before a stone altar upon which rested the severed head of a goat. In his hand was a crude wax figure from which protruded dozens of silvery quills.

"You can relax now, Jim. She's gone."

"Thank Satan!" his manager exclaimed. "I was running out of pins!"

On the Wings of the Wind

LILLIAN CSERNICA

Luisa stood in the empty silence of her studio and glared at her sculpture. The harsh morning light showed her a female figure that could have been an embryo for all the shape it had. She could do nothing with it.

She held up her hands, studying them. Like the rest of her body the fingers were long and thin, seemingly fragile but containing a hidden strength. She'd been sculpting for five years, nurturing her skill into success steady enough to live on. Now the hands that had done all that work were as unfeeling and lifeless as the clay she tried to shape. Two weeks ago her skills had failed her. Nothing she touched came out the way it should. Her house plants were dead. Her cooking had suffered. Worst of all was the last time David tried to make love to her. She'd felt cold and hard as fired ceramic.

Luisa closed her eyes and pictured a rod extending from the base of her spine deep into the earth below her. There churned all the natural energies she needed to create. She concentrated on drawing the energies up the rod and into her hands. The effort of concentration made her clench her teeth. The energies rose a little way, then fell back. A sudden pain between her eyes made her lose concentration altogether. New panic filled her. The raising of power was one of the first magical exercises she'd been taught. Even that small talent had deserted her.

She fled to the kitchen for comfort. In the center of the kitchen table her statue of the goddess Gaia rested on a woven mat. She'd sculpted the statue as part of her training for the Oakleaf Coven. The lesson was to seek out her own element, to find the one that spoke to her deepest self. That was easy. Her career had begun at age six when she started making mud babies in her mother's flower garden. Maybe the key to regaining her skills lay in going back to that beginning.

She examined the statue, noting every detail. What was it inside her that had given her the vision to create such beauty? Hair the color of wheat, a gown of autumn colors, feet resting on a rich loamy base; the Goddess radiated life. It was one of her best, calling on clays of different color and texture instead of paints. The eyes made alive by her skill would not look at her, no matter how she moved around the statue. If the element she called home had closed itself to her—her heart began to pound. This meant far more than just a loss of income. To be cut off from her art was to be cut off from life itself.

Luisa marched to the phone and took it off the hook, then drew the drapes and locked the front door. If she couldn't get the physical world to respond, she'd search for the answer elsewhere. As above, so below!

In the east corner of her studio, her altar stood behind the folding screen that separated her sacred space from the everyday world. Before entering that special realm she kicked off her slippers, shed her jeans and clay-smeared sweatshirt, then dropped her bra and panties on top of them. Naked as the Goddess when She entered the Underworld, Luisa stepped up to her altar. The small rosewood table sat against the wall. On it stood three plaster figurines, representing Athena, Brigit, and Cerridwen. They were her Trinity, of handicrafts, the fire that baked her sculptures, and the cauldron that symbolized her intangible ideas being brought forth into form. She lit a charcoal disk and sprinkled Dragon's Blood incense over it. The red smoke coiled around the figurines.

She picked up the athame that sat on the altar, and faced east, south, west, and north in turn, using the dagger to draw the blazing pentacles that would protect her while she walked between the worlds. Her priestess had warned her that the beings who dwelled there loved to play tricks.

She settled herself on a floor cushion and shook out her dark hair. Her breathing slowed. She cleared her mind of all anxiety and concentrated on visualizing herself standing in the dream-meadow where her magical work took place. Again it was a strain. Images flickered past her inner eye, refusing to come into focus. She forced herself to relax, to stop insisting on the image she wanted. The muddle of images settled. She found herself standing on a flat, bare plain under a cold sun. Jagged mountains sat on the horizon. A fierce wind whipped at her. She stared in every direction, praying for something she could recognize.

"Holy Gaia, I call you here." The wind beat at her. She crouched down to keep it from knocking her over. "Have I done something wrong?"

Luisa listened, her whole being alert. Shadows ghosted over the plain. Clouds veiled the sun. She shivered.

"Not here too. *Please!*" she cried. "Give me an answer!"

No response. Just like the energies she'd tried to raise, what she needed here was beyond her grasp. Far back where she'd left her body, her breath hitched with sobs.

The clouds massed, dense and threatening. Despite the fear clawing at her, she was reluctant to rush back to the safety of her studio. That would gain her nothing but more anguish. A movement to the east drew her eye. Something was coming. It rode the winds of the storm front, racing the lightning toward her. No sun burned brighter than its wings like feathered golden mirrors. No night matched its darkness.

"Do you know me, lady?" a deep male voice cried through the sighing wind. "Know you my name?"

Luisa stared at him, her fright mixed with fascination. She couldn't remember anything like him from her lessons.

"I called for the Goddess! Who are you?"

His laughter buffeted the scudding clouds. "Perhaps I am your answer!" He hovered above her with slight fanning beats of his lustrous wings. Eyes of silvered fire burned down at her. "Are you so afraid of the answers within you? Name me!"

She made her four protective pentacles blaze against him. He laughed and plucked them out of the air, juggling them high over his head. She fought back her panic. She had to solve this here and now. If she didn't, she'd carry the spiritual conflict back into her physical life.

"I don't know you! Go away before I call Nemesis!"

"You dare threaten me? And in my own domain?"

Lightning flashed. He snatched a bolt out of the air and hurled it like a silver spear of rage. It struck the ground near her, spraying her with clods of dirt.

"Have you been a creature of the clay so long you burrow blindly in your fear? Earth child, it's time you knew the sky!"

His strong arms seized her and his wide wings flared. They shot up into the turbulent sky. Luisa screamed and clung to the arm around her waist.

"Lady, ease your grip. It is your fear you clutch, not me."

In his voice was the patter of first raindrops. His wings beat a rhythm through the storm. Lightning lit their way as the clouds frowned darker. Luisa felt their heaviness within her, their roiling and churning. When the storm broke, would she break as well?

"Behold the Air!" he cried. "Behold the power of the wild wind!"

His laughter bellowed forth and knocked the lightning from its path. Luisa looked up to see his mad eyes aglow with that icy fire. For a moment the artist in her marveled. The mightiest eagle was a sparrow to his majesty.

"Would you know me, lady? Would you know the very core of your darkness and the answer you seek?"

Thunder swallowed her denial. The fear of falling nearly paralyzed her. That which hurt the image of her body here could damage her real body also. One thing was sure. She had to escape him, escape whatever the destination of this terrifying flight. She willed herself out of his grip. Down she fell, hurtling into the belly of the storm.

"Mother!" she screamed. *"Help me!"*

The heavy dampness of the black clouds smothered her. The lightning strobed on all sides, blinding her. She fought her way past the panic to that quiet place where her ideas were born. Wings! Wings would save her.

She held her hands out before her and visualized a lump of clay between them. She worked at it, exploring the airy texture of the clay, opening her mind to the creative urge. Her hands took over, once again sure as they shaped the clay into a growing form. Rainbows flashed and bent beneath her fingers. Something like thickened fire hardened into lines of structure. The radiant colors swirled and fell into place across her shoulders. She glanced back. Her mouth fell open in wonder.

There, arching high and blushing all the gentle colors of sunrise, were a pair of wings to rival those of Pegasus. She flexed her shoulders and shot up into the sky, rising above the storm into the starry night. Her heart swelled with unbearable joy.

"Holy Gaia, thank you!"

At last the voice of the Goddess answered her. "Look elsewhere for this gift."

Luisa looked around. Her escort to the airy regions had vanished.

"There can be no creation without inspiration," he said. "I am Master of that in-drawn breath."

She whirled. He hovered behind her.

"The Earth is but one element of the Four, lady. Do not neglect the others."

His great sun-feathered wings fanned out to surround her. Bright as mirrors, they reflected her on all sides. Luisa saw the colors of her wings glowing in her eyes as well. She laughed, whirling round and round in his embrace. He smiled.

"Go home, lady. You have your answer."

Her eyes opened. Luisa stood and stretched, then walked naked to her supply of clay. Humming, she buried her hands in it and dragged forth a good-sized lump. She closed her eyes and let the vision in her spirit guide her hands. They wandered over the clay, pushing and stroking it. The man shape grew. Wings rose from his back. She smiled on her work. The blood sang in her limber fingers.

Alexa, Skyclad

BENJAMIN ADAMS

—the flash of light—

Alexa Grant woke from a nightmare of startled fright and violation, momentarily disoriented by the strange room. Then memory flooded back and she remembered where she was—the family cabin in the Sierra Nevada, just a quarter mile up the road from Lake Tahoe. Her husband, Rick, lay snoring in the bed next to her, and all was right with the world.

Except the nightmare was not a dream at all, but had actually happened.

Alexa temporarily blotted the experience from her mind. The new morning was cool and brisk, a breeze carrying in fresh air from the slightly opened bedroom window. Careful not to disturb Rick, she slipped out of bed, put on her old brick-red Oklahoma State sweatshirt and a pair of jeans, and wandered into the kitchen, yawning. This was their second day of vacation, and she wanted her husband to enjoy the rare pleasure of sleeping in. She broke up some stale bread and took it outside, putting the crumbs in the battered green birdfeeder in the small garden off the front porch.

She took a deep breath of the crisp mountain air. The delightful scent of the Ponderosa pines always appealed to her. She'd fallen in love with this place the first year Rick had brought her here, before they got married. His parents had still been alive then, and had retired to the mountain house from Reno. They'd made her sleep on the foldout couch downstairs, just outside the master bedroom, while Rick stayed upstairs in the "kids' room." How proper Mrs. Grant was, trying to maintain some level of decorum even though Alexa and her son had already been living together in Sacramento for six months.

And now here they were, ten years later. The elder Grants had passed away, leaving the mountain home to Rick and Alexa. Yet she still felt awkward making love to him here, as if her mother-in-law still inhabited the place, watching them with disapproval. That thought and what had happened last night threatened to turn this vacation into a disaster.

What would Mrs. Grant have done if she'd known her daughter-in-law was a witch?

—the flash of light—

Never had Alexa felt so violated. The circle and pentagram had always been a place of safety for her before. On her visits here, she always slipped away from the cabin, worshiping privately in the thick woods at the rear of the Grants' property—it felt good being on her own, without the coven back in Sacramento, every now and then. Last night had been *Litha,* the summer solstice. Inside the circle, she'd doffed her robe and become one with nature—skyclad—communing with the Goddess and the God at the turn of the year; the longest day, yet the point at which begins the decline into the darkness of winter.

—the flash of light—

Suddenly she was no longer skyclad. Just a naked woman, alone in the woods, all dignity and illusions of safety stolen. She'd grabbed her robe and hurriedly slipped it back on, glancing around wildly. Someone was out there—

—*footsteps running away, crunching across the dry pine needles*—

A squirrel ran across the sandy driveway, chased by a scolding bluejay. Alexa stopped to watch in amusement, trying to forget the humiliation of the previous night. The squirrel darted under Rick's black Isuzu Trooper and the jay pulled up to avoid a collision. Temporarily foiled, the bird took up watch on a low pine branch overhanging the Trooper and continued loudly nattering away.

"Mommy!" called Charlie. He stood on the outside landing on the second floor, clad in a T-shirt and Toughskin jeans. The dogs, a young black Labrador named Kip and an older golden retriever, Dora, stood panting happily at the boy's side. "I dressed myself, Mommy!"

Alexa clapped her hands together. "Oh, that's so good, honey!"

A solemn look crossed Charlie's face. "I can't come down yet, though, 'cos I can't get my shoes tied."

"That's okay, sweetie. I'll be right up to help you."

The squirrel chose this moment to dart from under the Trooper despite the bluejay's angry protests. On the landing, Kip saw the sudden movement and barked.

"Oh, hell," murmured Alexa.

Kip tensed and launched himself down the steps, a sleek black missile directly on target for the squirrel.

Caught on the sandy driveway between the jay and Kip, the squirrel froze momentarily, glancing quickly to the left and right.

The squirrel evidently made a decision at that point, because it turned and ran back for the cover of the Trooper. Kip arrived directly behind it and hunched down, crawling under the car.

"Get 'im, Kip!" encouraged Charlie, avidly watching the whole scene from his second-floor vantage. Dora remained by his side, above such things as chasing squirrels.

A low growling came from Kip. All Alexa could see of him was his black tail wagging back and forth in the sand, almost looking like a furry extension of the Trooper's paint job. "Dammit, Kip, get out from there!" she ordered. "I *don't* want to wash you today!"

Kip's growling became more pronounced. The squirrel emerged from the other side and ran up the nearest pine, the bluejay resuming its raucous pursuit. The dog burst from beneath the car and slammed head-first into the base of the pine.

Alexa's clenched fist flew to her mouth. She didn't know whether to laugh at Kip's stupidity or comfort the poor beast. "Oh, Goddess."

"Is he okay, Mommy?" called Charlie.

Kip sat by the pine and looked back toward Alexa, eyebrows twitching in doggy bemusement. Then a nearby pinecone caught his attention and he began sniffing at it.

"He's fine, honey," she replied distractedly. Something large, square, and brownish was on the windshield of the Trooper, stuck underneath the wiper blade like an oversized parking ticket. She walked to the car and carefully pulled it out. A manila envelope, its gummed flap loosely folded inside. Frowning, she opened it and pulled out its contents.

Goddess preserve me, she thought.

A note, scrawled in a childish hand:

I CAN MAKE COPIES OF THIS
LEAVE MONEY IN THE CIRCLE UNDER A ROCK OR ELSE.

And attached to the note, a photograph of a red-haired woman in her early thirties, still attractive. Nude, kneeling in the center of a stone circle, flanked by Ponderosa pines. Alexa clasped the photo to her chest, her lower lip trembling with anger.

—*the flash of light*—

A flashbulb.

"You don't tug on Superman's cape—"

Jim Croce crooned "You Don't Mess Around with Jim" on the portable compact disc boombox set on the mantel, while Charlie rolled a toy car around on the soft plush carpet of the living room floor. "Vrooommmm," he said softly. Alexa smiled. He was such a good boy; sometimes he seemed like more of an adult than his father.

As if on cue, Rick Grant swept into the room, all brown beard and blue eyes, and started tickling Charlie. The six-year-old collapsed in helpless giggles on the floor, his Hot Wheel temporarily abandoned. "Who's Daddy's boy?" Rick demanded, a smile in his voice.

Between squeals of laughter, Charlie attempted responding. "Da— Don't! Hee hee hee! Da, stoppit!"

Alexa laid her novel—something about a pair of truckers cursed never to stop moving—on the couch cushion beside her. "Rick, don't get him worked up. It's almost his bedtime."

Her husband, oblivious, kept tickling Charlie. "Are you my boy? Huh?"

A tear worked its way from the corner of Charlie's eye. His giggles had taken on an edge now, no longer joyful. "Da! Da, stop! *Stop!*"

"That's enough!" Alexa said. "Rick, he doesn't like it!"

Chastened, Rick pulled away from Charlie, who lay gasping on the floor, still convulsed by an occasional giggle. "Sorry, Charlie. Give your old man a hug, okay?"

The little boy unsteadily got to his feet and solemnly hugged Rick.

"Okay. You go get ready for bed now," said Alexa.

Charlie pattered out of the living room, headed for the stairway off the kitchen.

"You are so terrible," Alexa said to Rick, shaking her head.

"Daddy's prerogative," he grinned.

"And Mommy's headache." She paused and gave Rick a close look. He had that studiously nonchalant expression he liked using before springing an unwelcome surprise on her.

Sure enough, he dropped the bomb. "Um . . . honey, I invited the Trammelhorns over for dinner tomorrow night. Is that okay by you?"

"Is this a rhetorical question?" Alexa felt a wave of fury at Rick's boneheadedness. *The Trammelhorns! Goddess help me!*

Visions of the uncouth family swam through her mind. The Trammelhorns from Yuba City had bought the summer house on the lot across Bristlecone Way from the Grant cabin about five years previously, and the neighborhood was never the same again. Alexa made a point of being open-minded about people; it was an integral part of her Wiccan beliefs. But the Trammelhorns seemed designed for testing those beliefs to their limits—and beyond. The fat, rude slob of a father, Vince, who always called her "Allie" instead of Alexa; Frankie, the obnoxious, hyperactive little boy. And then there was Desirée Trammelhorn, the honking, screeching mother in her tie-dyed muu-muus. Try as she might, Alexa could find no redeeming qualities in the Trammelhorn clan. Goddess be praised, she only saw them for a few days every year.

Rick shrugged. "I'm sorry, honey—"

"Sorry? *Sorry?* You know how I feel about that woman—"

He held up his hands, palms out. "Hold on a sec, okay? Desirée died a few months back. Car wreck."

Alexa's jaw snapped shut. "What about Vince?" she finally managed.

"He's all alone over there with Frankie. I was out for a walk and started chatting with Vince, and the poor guy was just aching for some company. So, I thought, what the hell—may as well do a good deed."

Her heart softening, Alexa pondered the situation. *Without Desirée around, this may not be such a bad thing.* A terrible thought, but true. "Okay," she said finally. "It's not a big deal."

Rick beamed. "Great!" He leaned forward and kissed her. "You know, you won't even recognize Frankie. He's really grown. I guess he's around thirteen now. A lot more mature. The kid was walking around with this brand new Minolta setup, taking pictures of *everything.* Vince got it for him after the divorce. Telephoto zoom, the works. Even develops his own pictures."

"His own—*pictures,*" said Alexa. She winced, gritting her teeth. "I bet he's getting some nice nighttime shots."

"What do you mean?"

Alexa took a deep breath. Although Rick knew of and supported her Wiccan religion, he'd flip if he knew she'd been worshiping in the nude. He had a huge problem with her being skyclad. This was something she'd have to handle by herself, with the prudence and wisdom passed down by generations of witches in her family. "Nothing," she said. "Nothing at all. . . ."

"Mmmmm," Vince Trammelhorn breathed around a mouthful of steaming food. "Allie . . . whatchoo say this is?"

"Alexa," she corrected automatically. "It's a North African couscous paella."

"Kooskoos," said Vince. He smacked his lips. "Desirée . . . sure never fixed anything like this. I sure like the . . . um, shrimp in it." He was dressed in true suburban sportsman's fashion, with a glowing neon blue plaid shirt and stiff new jeans that looked like they hadn't been through a washer yet.

Across the table, fat Frankie Trammelhorn made a face. "Uh—I don't know if I can finish this," he said, his pubescent voice cracking.

"Well, you don't have to eat it," Alexa said sweetly. "Would you like something else?"

Charlie glanced toward his mother, then at Frankie—sullenly clad in a black T-shirt emblazoned with the logo of the band Metallica—and finally at the couscous on his own plate. "Mommy, is there something wrong with him?"

"Hey, shut up, you little—" began Frankie.

"Well, hey!" jumped in Rick. "It sure is great to have you guys over."

His look toward Alexa suggested *great* was the last word he felt like using; as the dinner had approached, Rick's enthusiasm for the concept of the Trammelhorns' visit waned almost exponentially. She shrugged back at Rick. *Hey, this was YOUR idea,* her eyes told him.

As for herself, Alexa had no intent of letting the Trammelhorn men spoil her dinner. She took another bite and chewed slowly, almost sensually.

Uncomfortably, she noticed Vince's eyes on her as she chewed. The poor man had lost his wife, but yet . . . there was something about him that made Alexa feel odd.

She glanced at Frankie again. The fat youth managed to make the act of drinking his milk look sullen, but there was nothing else about him that seemed strange.

Suspicion, slowly dawning, began crossing Alexa's mind.

Without much more conflict, the supper ended. Charlie, Rick, and Frankie had wandered outside to the patio, sitting on plastic lawn chairs under the yellow bug light. The dogs, Kip and Dora, joined them there. Vince Trammelhorn took it upon himself to help Alexa take the empty plates into the kitchen.

"That . . . sure was a great dinner, Allie," said Vince, handing her the casserole dish.

She replied without thinking, "Alexa. And thanks."

"So . . . um . . . what are you guys gonna do for the rest of the evenin'?"

"Oh, I don't know," Alexa said vaguely. *Nothing with you,* she thought. "Probably read a book or listen to some music."

Vince ran a hamlike hand through his greasy crew cut. "Aw . . . is that all? Night like this, it'd be perfect for gettin' outside . . . walkin' through the forest . . . gettin' close to nature. . . ."

Alexa paused in the middle of putting a couple of glasses in the dishwasher, her hackles raised. The strange feeling she'd had at supper was correct.

—the flash of light—

It hadn't been Frankie Trammelhorn with his new photo outfit at all.

It was Vince, out there in the woods, who had spied on her while she was skyclad; reduced her religion to a one-handed spectator sport.

She grinned widely as she took the next plate from Vince. "Oh, no. I'm not really in the mood for a walk tonight."

Vince seemed startled by her grin, but smiled back, a little warily.

Got you, she exulted silently. *Thank the Goddess, I got you, you creep!*

Once again Alexa stood among the thick firs, not far beyond the family cabin. Inside, both Charlie and Rick were sound asleep, ready for whatever adventures tomorrow would bring.

She checked her Timex. A minute to twelve, by the glowing hands. The Witching Hour.

Just beyond her lay the stone circle and pentagram. Useless to her now; she'd have to reconsecrate it once this foolishness was ended.

In the very center of the circle, a large, smooth rock barely covered a manila envelope.

Goddess preserve me, she thought, and drew back slightly, out of sight. *I hear him coming.*

Heavy footfalls crunched through fallen pine needles, and Vince Trammelhorn came stumbling into the stone circle, breathing heavily. With a quick glance around, he knelt and grasped the rock in the center of the pentagram. "Uhhh!" he grunted.

He managed to hoist it out of the circle; it bashed against the trunk of a nearby Ponderosa pine and softly thudded to the forest floor.

"Damn heavy thing—how'd the hell a little babe like that move a rock like that?" Vince muttered.

Nearby, Alexa nearly snorted with laughter, but kept quiet with great effort. *Typical male!* she thought, biting her tongue. *Just typical!*

Vince knelt and lifted the manila envelope, brushing it free of soft, powdery earth. He ripped it open with a paw of a hand and reached inside eagerly.

"What the hell—"

There was no money inside the envelope. He shook it violently, but only a scrap of paper fluttered out.

Printed on the scrap was:

"Vince Trammelhorn, you no good goddamn son-of-a-bitch deluxe!" roared a voice like an entire flock of Canadian geese, startling the suddenly horrified would-be blackmailer.

"De—Desirée?" stammered Vince, stepping backward and dropping the piece of paper.

Desirée Trammelhorn stepped out of the trees directly opposite Alexa, blue ectoplasmic mist curling around her ankles. If anything, the woman had grown larger since Alexa had last seen her. Her glowing purple muu-muu billowed off her imposing form like an exterminator's tent. Thick wads of spit flew from her lips as she approached Vince, fury in her shining red eyes.

Alexa grinned widely.

Raising Desirée's shade hadn't been easy—Alexa hadn't been sure the ancient incantation, passed down by generations of witches in her family, would work—but it had been worth it. Just a few words: *Your rotten husband is trying to blackmail me with some nudie shots,* and Desirée had agreed to "take care of the problem," as she put it.

In fact, she'd seemed quite enthusiastic.

There was no love lost between Alexa and Desirée, but certain bonds of sisterhood still existed, even after death.

"You blackmailing scumbag!"

"But—but, Desirée, I can *explain*—" stammered Vince.

"Explain *what?*" bellowed the natural fury that was Desirée Trammelhorn. "*EXPLAIN WHAT?*"

"I—um . . . that is, I—"

"*That's it, Vince!*" railed Desirée. "We're going right back over to that cabin. And you're going to give that Grant woman back any photos or negatives you have of her. D'you hear me?"

"But I—"

"*DO YOU HEAR ME?*"

"I—" Vince Trammelhorn suddenly collapsed in on himself, like a deflating balloon. "Yes, Desirée."

"That's better. I can see I'm going to have to keep an eye on you for a *very* long time."

As the implications of "a *very* long time" sank in on Vince, his broad face looked drawn, haggard. For a moment Alexa almost felt sorry for him. Almost, but not quite.

Vince stumbled away toward his cabin, accompanied by Desirée's vengeful shade.

After a moment, Alexa crossed to the stone circle and pentangle, preparing to reconsecrate the spot to the Goddess and offering a prayer skyward as she worked.

Thank you, O Goddess, for the wisdom and prudence You granted me in dealing with my small problem here tonight.

You are wise and good in Your ways.

A bit of that old Jim Croce song ran through her head as she replaced the final stone knocked loose by Vince Trammelhorn's invading feet, and she hummed softly.

You don't tug on Superman's cape—

And you never, ever blackmail a witch—or a mother.

Skyclad and smiling, Alexa opened her arms in worship.

Angel of the Eleventh Hour

JOEL S. ROSS

Andromeda leaped up beside Mara, receiving a scratch behind the ears as her mistress sipped at her chilled tea of elder bark, catnip, and valerian root. Mara grimaced as the different flavors played on various parts of her tongue, but everything had its price and this was a small one.

The tea's formula, one of Tom's legacies before he moved out, was as bitter as the memory of their last night. . . .

Never mind that. Business before pleasure. Right now she needed to invest her all energies to ensure complete merger with her familiar.

There was a hiss and flare as she lit the fluted candles. Andromeda, her midnight-colored fur soft and thick as whipped cream, her eyes the color of a cloudless sky, purred her anticipation.

Mara hefted her bronze athame and studied its edge in the flickering candlelight. It seemed sharp enough. She extended it to Andromeda for approval, took a deep breath, then drew it across her hand. She winced as a wet line welled up to pool in her palm. She placed her hand over the brass bowl on the table for thirteen heartbeats before withdrawing it to stanch the wound.

It stung a bit, but that also was part of the cost.

Andromeda purred louder as she lapped up the coagulating liquid.

All was prepared, except her courage. What was she afraid of? She had studied for this moment for ten years and despite Tom's derision about her ability, she was skilled.

Still, though her instruments were ready, was she?

Mara knelt besides the candles—green, for envy—and recited the prayer.

> *"Powers of night, grant thy servant on this most sacred and revered Sabbat of Lugnasad, the strength to carry out thy bidding from this Eleventh Hour. . . ."*

Concentrate.

The runes had indicated only three Wiccan Adepts competing with her. If—correction, when—she eliminated them, nothing could stop her from becoming the next Magus.

Nothing.

When Mara next opened her eyes, the candles had melted an inch. She stared into their flame, focusing her mind like sunlight through a magnifying glass, until . . .

With Andromeda leading the way, Mara lurched over the threshold of consciousness into . . . a subway.

The few passengers swayed back and forth in time to the rocking of the car. No one looked at the cat, or gaped at the naked woman in their midst. There was nothing for them to see.

To them it was just zone-out time on the "A" train.

Cathedral Parkway flashed by.

As the car's lights flickered, Andromeda strutted up to a swarthy man cradling the old leather-bound book on his lap and curled her spirit in front of him. When the cat glanced back at her, Mara's mind drifted forward, her voice silken, urging Andromeda on: ". . . by the throat. Squeeze. So easy. He's earned it. NOW!"

Mara visualized her polished nails sinking into soft flesh and made it so.

The man's eyes grew wide as his hands flew to his neck.

Hollow, choking sounds filled the car.

The others stared. A stout woman sitting opposite crossed herself repeatedly as a skinny teen in jeans and muscle-tee rushed forward. The gasping man dropped his book and fell across the seat. The gagging sounds continued as he rolled off the molded plastic onto the grime-coated floor and thrashed like a freshly caught fish on the bottom of the boat.

Only two left.

Mara's dream self closed its eyes as her physical one's flew open a moment later.

Andromeda stretched out full length and rolled against her bare leg. When Mara sat up she felt her gorge rise. What had she done, throttling a stranger . . . ?

"Not a stranger, Mara. A rival. An enemy."

She dashed to the bathroom, knelt by the toilet, and retched. There went the tea. The nausea ebbed, like a receding wave, and the sweat dried on her brow and bare chest. As she crouched there, she ran her fingers through Andromeda's warm fur as the animal did figure-eights between her legs.

She'd killed someone—a man she didn't even know—solely to attain a rank never before held by someone her age. Murdered another human, just for . . .

When she opened her eyes again, the candles had shrunk another half-inch. She felt much better, like a young tree on a bright spring day.

A whisper tickled her brain—urging her on.

Andromeda opened her bewhiskered muzzle in a silent meow. Mara took another deep breath and shuddered.

"Nerves," she said aloud, not really believing herself. She couldn't indulge in that now, with this her only chance to eliminate her remaining rivals. She envisioned the story on tomorrow's *Eyewitness News*.

". . . died mysteriously on the IND line, between Cathedral Parkway and . . ."—showing the shadowy face with the caption of VICTIM under it—". . . the Coroner's Office theorizing that a seizure may have caused the neck muscles to spasm and contract to the point of crushing his windpipe. Witnesses said . . ."

What could they say? Or how would Tom react if he knew?

He was always claiming Mara couldn't control a familiar or project her essence. Always saying she could never surpass his own powers. Boasting about how his family had been Adepts since before the Great Suppression of the Seventeenth Century.

Next case. She closed her eyes and opened her mind to another headline.

"Elsewhere in the news, in Queens, a young woman will be mangled almost beyond recognit . . ."

There, the next patient of her Lugnasad operation, chosen. Mara almost chuckled at the thought when Andromeda's scream filled the living room. The cat was perched on the sill, her normally perked ears angled back flat against her skull as a rumble grew in her throat. She stared at the steamy street four stories below, the muscles in her back and haunches bunching up, rear legs doing a little cha-cha-cha as if getting ready to . . .

"Andromeda—no! Wait!"

Too late. Too late!

Andromeda leaped just as Mara dashed to the window, lunged and found herself sailing through that same space.

Space, but not air. Empty. So empty, feeling nothing, not even the stomach-churning sensation of tumbling, swooping, borne along the currents of something powerful, omnipotent.

In the palm of a giant's hand.

Andromeda led as they soared between concrete canyons, streets teeming with people seeking respite from the torrid temperature. For Mara there was no feeling, no sound. The only sense was sight and even that blurred in dizzy acceleration. She had a fleeting impression of water, a steamy labyrinth of brick boxes. Andromeda alighted on a terrace.

Mara peered in.

A woman, perhaps thirty-five, knelt before five candles laid out at the apexes of a pentacle. Inside these was a tall, slender carving of a female in a gown.

The Goddess! Let her try evoking her protection. . . .

The woman sprinkled laurel and anise into five ivory bowls and gestured toward . . .

Mara took a "step" to one side—to get a better look—and watched the woman's head snap toward the picture window.

Andromeda's hackles rose as the woman uncurled and got to her feet, hissed when she walked onto the terrace and looked out.

She was so close Mara could see the thin wrinkles on her otherwise smooth forehead, could see her eyes narrow in question before turning to slide the glass door shut.

Mara felt a thin smile blossom on her lips. The woman hadn't seen her . . . couldn't have seen her, because there was nothing to see; her body was still in Manhattan.

Number two was ready for surgery.

The woman cast a last furtive glance toward the terrace, shrugged, and went back to her own Lugnasad ritual.

Do unto others before they do it to you.

Mara's smile grew until the silken voice brushed it aside.

"She deserves it, Mara. She blocks your future, holds you back. She needs to be punished. IT was decreed, decided. DO it! It will feel so good. Tear! Rip! Claw! Pull! Sooo good . . ."

The woman scrambled to a table and grabbed a salt shaker, twisting its head off to spill a clockwise arc about her.

NOW! QUICKLY! Before she evokes the protective circle!

Andromeda passed through the window as if it were air, Mara at her heels, before the ring of white crystals was completed and screened her out.

The woman's head jerked toward the window just as the candles flickered and the front of her thin summer dress turned scarlet. Huge dark eyes bulged as her mouth dropped open, but instead of a scream there was only a hiss of air, as from an overheated radiator.

Crimson gouts of liquid spurted up to and beyond the edges of the chalk star.

"Good, Mara, sooo good. There's but one remaining."

Mara stretched and glanced to her right, peering through sleep-pasted eyes at the clock announcing four A.M. Barely an hour before dawn and already she felt the curtains of humid air drift up to her apartment.

She'd have to hurry this last one.

Wouldn't she?

Mara's eyes narrowed (like the woman in her vision).

Andromeda pawed at her, reminding her of their mission, which overrode even the need for sleep. She could rest later, for as long as she wished.

Levering herself off the floor, Mara wondered if there would be enough time for the final transformation. She staggered toward the small dinette table where the green candles flickered, guttering down to their final inch of wax. A tall glass and pitcher sat next to them, their frosted sides etched by crystal drops of condensation.

Teatime.

Mara ran her tongue across suddenly dry lips and reached for the cool glass, Andromeda curling around her feet like a silken shadow, purring softly.

Her hand paused an inch from the dripping glass. The ice cubes caught the soft light and froze it in place. What the hell was she doing? Was it worth taking yet another life, whoever it might be?

She backstepped onto Andromeda and heard her hiss.

No!

The satiny voice—harsh this time—bore into her brain. Mara felt a shiver zip down her spine and she whimpered.

"You know you want it, Mara. . . . Do it now. Otherwise the other two will have died for nothing. Besides, you deserve it."

The voice softened, but there was still the hint of steel within fur. Mara shuddered again as Andromeda leaped onto the table next to the pitcher, her eyes glowing in the candlelight.

Hot tears slalomed down Mara's cheeks. "The tea, Mara . . . drink and you'll have what you most desire."

Her fingers traced random patterns on the icy glass. Everything she desired? And what would that be? The ability to sleep soundly again, never knowing when someone else down the road, younger and stronger, would plot to unseat her as Magus?

Three wishes? A good headshrinker? Something like a chuckle, or was it a sob, escaped her lips.

"All I want is to get Tom. . . ."

"Done! Drink, Mara, and Tom you will get. Tom it will be."

Andromeda purr-retted as Mara lifted the glass to her lips and downed it in one parched gulp. She felt its calm wash over her. Just what the hell had she been worried about?

Letting the glass fall—and shatter—to the floor, Mara tipped forward and rubbed her chin against the top of the cat's head. Andromeda nudged back, then leaped off the table, heading for the bedroom.

Mara followed, the distance seeming farther this time, and then— felt concrete against the souls of her bare feet.

A man strolled ahead of her, shoulders hunched, hands slowly being pulled from the pockets of his jeans.

He paused outside a yellow pool of sodium vapor light, then broke into a trot, then a canter down the empty streets, his footfalls echoing off the husks of burnt-out and abandoned buildings.

Mara swooped after him, his panting, sobbing—like the sound of a straining lover—exciting her. Growling deep in her throat, Mara reached out and swiped at his back.

The white T-shirt parted in four dark, glistening furrows as he fell, knees and hands striking the sidewalk . . . flipping him onto his back. When he raised his arms across his face, Mara saw bloodied scrapes on his palms.

Tom's hands!

NO!

Gasping, she leaned forward to caress his face and saw long parallel slits gush, erupting gore across his forehead. A scream started, was stillborn, like the needle jerked from the phonograph. She watched the face, Tom's face . . . the face she had so often studied as he slept . . . dissolve under a bloody wave!

"Good, Mara. Sooo good. You got Tom, as promised."

She bolted upright in bed, her naked body damp despite the air conditioning. From her place on the bureau, bathed in young sunlight leaking through the blinds, Andromeda opened one hooded eye and licked her lips.

"Sooo good."

A thin scream rushed from Mara's lungs when the phone rang.

"Mara?" Her friend Carol's voice, stressed out, strained . . . light years away. "I just heard it on the news. I feel awful. Mara . . . ?"

"Huh?" Mara pressed the receiver closer to her ear—heard her blood pounding—closed her eyes.

"Mara?"

"It's Tom," she heard herself say. "Isn't it?"

"I really feel terrible."

Mara's eyes sprang open. Andromeda was still sitting in the patch of rising sun, delicately licking the red off her right front paw. "Sooo good." In the background, like an ignored news program, Carol's voice droned on and on and on and . . .

". . . figured a gang or an escaped psycho or some wild dog. I still can't figure what Tom was doing out so late. I can't believe this, Mara. Can I help . . . ?"

". . . am sooo sorry . . ." Andromeda winked.

The receiver slipped from Mara's fingers and dangled over the edge. Andromeda stared down at her and yawned.

"Why the hell did you . . . ?"

The cat blinked, then stood to stretch, her dark fur shimmering in the sunlight.

"I asked you why the hell you did it? Why to me?"

The cat stared into Mara's eyes without blinking. "Sooo good, Mara . . . perfect souls—greedy souls on which to feed—'unknown victims of an unknown killer.' But we know the true killer, don't we, Mara? And thanks to you helping us eliminate those other Adepts last night, there will be no one left able to stop us now. It will be OUR time. At last. For we know what patient predators cats can be."

Mara's scream rose to a shriek as she threw herself at Andromeda, who leaped aside at the last moment, hit the floor, then sprang onto the quivering air-conditioning unit.

Her back bristling like a cardboard Halloween silhouette, the cat glared at Mara and hissed. "Sooo good . . ."

"BITCH!"

Grabbing the gilt-handled hairbrush that Tom—he's dead, butchered—had given her, Mara lunged at her demon in black fur—her betraying familiar.

And felt something rake the side of her face, felt blood and corneal tissue weep from her left eye.

The last thing Mara saw with her remaining eye as she hit the air conditioner and felt it break free . . . felt it carry her out into the already hot sunlight . . . was the blood on her nails.

Long nails—hooked at the ends and sinking into the silky pads of her fingers . . .

A flash, the sensation of being ripped from her body.

Shrinking, being crushed and twisted, compressing into . . .

Mara's howl was cut short as she slammed into the sidewalk. Far above, a woman with midnight-black hair and eyes the color of a cloudless sky covered her naked breast with one arm as she leaned out the broken window.

"Is she all right?" asked an almost familiar voice. "She leaped up on the air conditioner before I could do anything!"

A sneaker nudged Mara in the ribs. She winced, tried to pull away, but felt things give way deep within her.

"Afraid not, lady. You'll have to get yourself another cat."

"Oh, no more cats," said the silken voice from above as blackness came. "They're so destructive. And they just can't be trusted."

Overdue Fines

Edo van Belkom

The library was quiet, all except for the *zip!*

Zip! Zip! Zip!

The fleshy inside thighs of the librarian's pantyhose rubbed together as she walked. She was on her way to the study area where some smart-assed teenagers were acting up. Their whispers could be heard clear across the library and loud whispering was strictly forbidden in Gale Hardcastle's library.

Zip! Zip! Zip!

"What's going on here?" she said, casting an icy stare at the blonde-haired girl sitting at one of the heavy oak tables.

"Nuthin'," the teen said. She gestured to the boy sitting at the table with her. "We're just doing our homework."

Gale continued to glare at the girl, resting her palms on the edge of the table. She leaned forward until her huge body blocked out the overhead light and cast a dark shadow upon the no-longer-smiling teen.

"Nothing . . . ma'am," said the boy meekly.

"This isn't the mall!" she said. "This is a library. So you'd better keep it down, or I'll have you out of here so fast you'll wonder if you were ever inside to begin with."

The teens looked away and Gale knew she'd won. No one could stand that look of hers for long, least of all two punk kids. Satisfied with herself, Gale rolled her body back until all of her weight was safely loaded onto her feet. Then she turned and headed back to her post at the information desk.

Zip! Zip! Zip!

Gale was head librarian at Burlington Memorial Library. The library was built in 1920 and a lot of people joked that Gale had worked at the library ever since it had opened. Truth was, her twenty-seven years there had only seemed like forever. She started out as a teenager shelving books after school. Then, after she received her M.L.S.—third in her class—in 1967, she was hired on full-time.

Among other things, patrons called her the Dragonlady, a nickname that, like the library itself, had staying power. For one thing, people said they could feel the heat of her breath whenever she got riled. Then there was her strange fascination with anything to do with magic, witchcraft, wizards, and lizards. It was unnatural the way Gale always had her nose buried in books that had a dragon on its cover. And finally, the library's noncirculating reference collection was supposedly filled with all sorts of medieval histories and books on torture and swordsmithing, black magic, and spellcasting. There were even rumors that Gale was a witch herself, but no one had ever been curious enough—or brave enough—to ask her face-to-face.

"Where d'ya keep the Danielle Steeles?" asked a patron.

Gale lifted her head out of her book, *Dragonsbane* by Barbara Hambly, and looked up at the woman standing before her. "Pardon me?"

"I said, where d'ya keep the Danielle Steeles?"

The woman was Mrs. Arlo Whitehead, wife of the new bank president. Gale had overheard others talk about Mrs. Whitehead and her pink and blue two-tone BMW, her ranch house on the outskirts of town, and her attitude. Needless to say, she hadn't been impressed.

Gale stared up at Mrs. Whitehead a moment. The woman was blonde, but not naturally so. The black roots close to her skull shouted too darkly from beneath the yellow-white strands—*lookitme! lookitme!* —for the color to be real. She was tanned, but that too, thought Gale, was surely also the result of a technological manipulation.

"Which title did you have in mind?" Gale said, putting her book down and swiveling the computer terminal so she could view the screen.

"Wad'ya mean?" Mrs. Whitehead said.

"Which title are you looking for?" Gale asked again, her patient tone of voice rapidly draining away.

"I don't know the name of it. I saw it in the store yesterday. I think it had a green cover."

"That's not a lot to go on, but if you're looking for Danielle Steele books you can find them on the bottom shelf on the third aisle from this wall."

"Thank you *very* much," Mrs. Whitehead said in a huff.

Fifteen minutes later, the woman was standing at the circulation desk waiting for someone to wand her books into the computer. "Ex-cuse me," she called over to Gale. "Can I get some service? I've been standing here for more than half an hour."

Gale looked up from her book, *Dragonslayer* by Wayland Drew, and turned to Mrs. Whitehead. "The circulation person has just stepped into the bathroom. She'll be with you in a minute."

"I don't care if she's gone and left the country. I want some service here." Her eyes narrowed into two tiny slits. "Why don't *you* get up and help me?"

For one brief but wild moment Gale thought about throwing her book at the woman, but decided it wouldn't do nearly as much damage as she'd like. Instead, she got up to try and hasten the woman's departure.

Zip! Zip! Zip!

In silence, Gale took the woman's library card and wanded its bar code into the computer. After a brief wait, a long list of book titles rolled up on the screen, many of them—including four by Danielle Steele— way overdue. Gale looked up from the screen and gave the woman a long cold stare. "You've got several books overdue."

"I know."

"Aren't you going to pay the fines?"

"No."

Gale glared at the woman. The look was similar to the one she'd used on the teens but a little colder and slightly more penetrating. It was the most powerful stare in her arsenal, but it wasn't having any effect at all.

"I don't have to pay any fines," Mrs. Whitehead said. "In addition to being the new bank president, my husband just happens to be the newest member of the library board. He told me he can have my fines waived whenever they get too high. Now, can I get some service? Or would you like me to ask my husband to look into your job status as well?"

The blood throbbed at Gale's temples and she wanted nothing more than to give the woman a severe tongue lashing to show her who was really in charge at Burlington Memorial. But . . . she breathed deeply and steeled herself against taking action; there were better times and better ways of getting even. Without another word, she wanded the books into the computer and watched the woman leave the library.

* * *

"You run along, I'll close up myself," Gale said as she ushered the part-time staff out of the library. "I've got some work that needs doing anyway."

With the last of the staff gone, Gale locked the door and turned off all the inside lights except for the few that were necessary for her to find her way. With a flick of a switch the library was transformed into a labyrinth of shadows, but she had no trouble weaving through the maze to the door that led down into the basement and the noncirculating reference collection there.

Zip! Zip! Zip!

The wooden steps creaked wearily under Gale's considerable weight and for a moment the *zip!* was drowned out by the sound of moaning wood. At the bottom of the stairs she took the fob of keys from her skirt pocket and shook it until she found the right one. The lock snicked open and Gale placed a hand on the brass knob and pushed against the solid oak door.

The room was lit only by what light trickled down from the top of the stairs, but Gale instinctively knew her way around. She switched on the lamps, and the room slowly brightened as the gas in the old-fashioned arc lights began warming.

The room was furnished with antique bookshelves and chairs, each a work of art with intricate hand-carved designs that created a dark atmosphere of magic and endless possibilities.

At last the lamp lights were fully illuminated and the room was bathed in a soft warm glow. Gale took a dusty leather-bound book from the middle of a bookshelf and pulled a heavy leather chair close to the lamps.

She sat down and began to read. The book was entitled *The Spell of Seven,* and tooled into the leather cover was a black-cloaked skeleton standing in the middle of hell's fire. The skeleton's bony hands held a burning cup and inside the cup a bearded older man was impaling a fully armored knight on the end of his pike.

The spells in the book were designed to exact revenge against those who had wronged the spellcaster. Gale had read the book before, but only for the simple pleasure of reading it. This time was different, however. She felt drawn to the book, like a child drawn to an older brother after receiving a punch from the neighborhood bully. She leafed through the book gently, turning over the thick decorative pages as if they were as fine as tissue.

Finally, she stopped on the third spell. Although the type was Latin, Gale had no trouble understanding the words of the text.

> Come to Life, Inanimate Object,
> Destroy All in Your Path
> Who Have Abused Privilege,
> And Return What I Seek
> To Its Rightful Place. . . .

She laughed at the thought of it. If the spell worked the way it was supposed to, she could call to life the stone lions that stood guard at the top of the library steps. If the spell worked, she could send the creatures out on nightly hunts for overdue books. With the spell, she could teach a lasting lesson to all the people who'd taken advantage of the loopholes in library policy.

It's perfect, she thought.

She'd cast spells before, but never anything so daring. She'd given co-workers and patrons colds and other minor maladies over the years, but there was always some doubt in her mind about whether the illnesses had been caused by her spells or simply by the changing of the seasons. If this spell worked, there would be no such doubt. . . .

She shook her head, dismissed the thought from her mind as being just too crazy, and continued reading. At eleven o'clock, she switched off the lights and headed upstairs with a stack of books from the noncirculating reference collection under one arm. The books really weren't supposed to leave the library, but an honor system for staff allowed them to take the books out overnight as long as they were returned first thing in the morning.

The cool night air felt refreshing against her cheeks as she locked the front doors of the library behind her. "Good night, Lionel," she said to the stone lion on the left of the library steps. "Keep an eye out for those nasty book bandits," she giggled. Then she noticed a bird stain on the tip of Lionel's nose and took a handkerchief from her purse to wipe it clean. She spit into the hankie and began to wipe. As she did this, the thought of the spell leaped into her mind. She stopped wiping and stood motionless for a moment, considering the magnitude of what she proposed to do. And then, without another moment's thought she began the Latin chant—

Come to Life, Inanimate Object,
Destroy All in Your Path . . .

She said the chant solemnly all the way to the end. She remained there for a minute or so, but it was obvious that the spell wasn't working. Her shoulders sagged in disappointment as she lumbered down the steps toward Main Street.

By the time she was on the sidewalk the only sound that could be heard was the hard click of her heels and the *zip!* of her pantyhose slowly fading in the distance as she headed for home.

And then silence . . .

Except for the deep throaty growl, like that of an angry animal awakened from a long and peaceful sleep.

The long day had exhausted Gale and she moved slowly through her modest apartment.

In the kitchen, her thoughts turned to a soothing, hot cup of tea. She set her books down on top of the refrigerator and reached for the kettle. She filled it with water and plugged it into the outlet on the stove. That done, she took off her coat and hung it on the hook on the back of the kitchen door. When the kettle came to a boil, she went to the refrigerator for some cream. As she opened the refrigerator, the movement of the swinging door jostled the pile of books on top and one slid between the refrigerator and wall.

Just then the kettle whistled shrilly, demanding to be unplugged. Gale shut the refrigerator, unplugged the kettle, and poured the boiling water into her cup.

Hmm? she thought. *Now what was I doing? Ah, yes, the cream.* She went back to the refrigerator and took out the cream for her tea. It billowed into her dark cup like a storm cloud.

A few minutes later she was under the covers and tucked snugly into the middle of her sagging mattress. The cup of hot tea steamed on her bed table and a book, *Tea with the Black Dragon* by R. A. MacAvoy, rested in her lap.

And all was right with the world.

Gale took her time getting up the forty-seven steps that led to the library's front doors. When she got to the top of the steps she noticed a pile of books waiting for her. "No matter how many times I tell people not to, they still insist on dropping their books off after-hours," she said, kneeling heavily on one knee to pick up one of the books. "Danielle Steele," she said. "Huh." She picked up a second book, also by Danielle Steele. There were several more books in the pile, including two more by Danielle Steele. She held the books under one arm and fished through her coat pockets for her keys.

It was then that she noticed the lion. There were red stains around the maw of the stone giant and long reddish streaks running down its chin all the way to its front paws. Looking at the paws, Gale saw a tuft of hair seemingly embedded in the stone.

She pulled the hair out with a yank and examined it closely. It was blonde hair for the most part, but turned black about a half inch from one of the ends. The black end also seemed to be held together by a crusty flap of leather.

All of a sudden she was overcome by a chill. Quickly, she unlocked the library doors and took the books inside. She booted the computer system and immediately checked the titles. Each of them had been taken out by Mrs. Whitehead, and each of them was long overdue.

A cold sweat broke out across Gale's forehead as she imagined where the hair and skin and . . . *blood* had come from. But, she thought a moment later when the dark flash of horror had brightened in her mind, the spell had worked and . . . I've got my books back. That's the important thing, right?

With that thought, she went to the library's staff room and prepared herself a cup of tea. As her tea cooled, she went back outside and hosed Mrs. Whitehead's blood from the lion. "Out, damn spot!" she giggled.

Later that morning, the library was all abuzz.

"Did you hear?"

"Yes. Isn't it just awful. They say it looked like she was mauled by a bear, only worse. Like she'd been eaten alive. Can you imagine?"

"No, I can't."

"Me neither."

Gale listened closely to the talk, smiling all the while. In fact, she was smiling almost all the time these days.

Each morning she'd pick up the books on the front steps, hose down Lionel, and have the books on the shelves with plenty of time left for a nice hot cup of tea.

The library's shelves had never been fuller.

The system was flawless.

She was in bed, but she wasn't asleep.

Gale lay on her back, wide awake. Everything was as it usually was: eleven-thirty P.M., a hot cup of tea on the bed table, a book on her lap, *The White Dragon* by Anne McCaffery, sheets and blankets pulled neatly up to her armpits, the lights off, the curtains drawn, and the room shrouded in darkness. . . .

Still, something was wrong. She closed her eyes and thought about it for a moment. The alarm. Yes, that was it. She hadn't set the alarm. She reached over and pressed the two buttons on the side of the clock. Then she lay back and closed her eyes.

Still, sleep would not come. Even though nothing was wrong, something seemed to be *not* right. What is it? she sighed and went through a mental checklist of things that had to be done and things that had been done.

But she stopped herself when she heard a sound at her door.

It was a gentle sound, a pawing sound, the kind of sound the neighbor's cat sometimes made when its owners went away for the weekend, leaving the poor thing out in the rain.

But this was Monday. . . .

The sound gathered strength. Scratch became screech, like fingernails against a chalkboard.

. . . and that doesn't sound much like a cat.

The roar was deep and throaty. It was obvious that the beast was hungry.

And then she remembered. . . .

The book behind the refrigerator was long overdue.

1-900-Witches

NANCY HOLDER AND WAYNE HOLDER

Seated at the far end of the polished mahogany table, Mr. Francis Bell, C.E.O. and founding partner of the firm, folded his long, spindly fingers and smiled. Jay sat up a little straighter. Here it came. After all the years of overtime, the skipped vacations, the days he was so sick he could barely drag himself from his bed to his car, he was getting his due.

He could see his name on the door now: Bell, Lighthart, Wood, and last (and least for just a little while, he hoped) Jameson. Jay Jameson, *Partner*.

"And now, something I have wanted to do for a long, long time," said Bell. (He would have to get used to calling him Frank, Jay supposed excitedly.) "Ladies and gentlemen, I'm most happy to present to you our newest partner."

Jay adjusted his tie.

Bell gestured toward him with his hand.

Jay prepared to acknowledge the applause.

Bell said, "Mr. Aaron Spivak."

Everyone applauded happily.

Jay's mouth dropped open. It continued to hang there when the founder adjourned the meeting and asked everyone to reconvene in the office courtyard, where champagne and caviar would welcome the newest member of "the team."

Stumbling like a zombie, Jay followed the happy group. There must be a mistake. Bell had already promised him the partnership. It was already a done deal. It was a fait accompli.

The courtyard was brimming with his colleagues: the lawyers in their pricey suits, the paralegals in their midrange suits, the secretaries in flowery but tasteful dresses and gold jewelry. Champagne corks popped; forks tinked against plates of hors d'oeuvres.

Near a potted palm, Aaron Spivak stared straight at Jay and smiled. Smiled wickedly. Smiled as if he had pulled off the impossible.

In a fury, Jay balled his fists and headed toward him, only to be halted in his tracks by none other than Bell himself.

"Good day, my boy," Bell said.

"Good *day*? Mr. Bell, are you *serious*?" Jay shouted at him. Heads swiveled. He fought for control. In a lower voice, he said, "What have you done to me?"

"Done to you?" The older man looked puzzled.

"That partnership was mine! You promised it to me!"

The man's confusion grew. "I'm sorry? I don't recall any such thing."

In his amazement, Jay took a step backward. "Mr. Bell, don't you remember?" Was the old man senile? "I brought in my brief on executive privilege and legal immunity and you told me it was brilliant. You said it cinched the partnership for me!"

Bell cocked his head and put a hand on Jay's shoulder. "I did receive a brief on executive immunity."

"There!" Jay said, vindicated.

"And it was brilliant."

Jay waited. When Bell said nothing more, he pressed, "Yes, and you said—"

"But Aaron Spivak wrote that brief." He frowned at Jay. "I'm surprised at you, Jameson. Trying to take credit when—"

"I wrote it," Jay insisted. "You know I did. My name's right on it."

"No, son, no it's not." Now Bell was talking to Jay as if he were crazy. He waved a finger and his assistant—a bright young man in a baggy suit—hustled over to him with a beautifully worn briefcase. "Open it, Friedman."

"Yes, sir." The man flicked the latches and the case popped open. Bell reached in and extracted a brief bound in a red cover. Jay recognized it immediately and almost grabbed for it. *Easy, easy,* he told himself. This would soon be set to rights.

"There, you see?" The older man opened the brief and pointed to the first page.

EXECUTIVE PRIVILEGE VS. LEGAL IMMUNITY
BY
AARON SPIVAK

"Mr. Bell, you *know* I wrote that!" Jay said. He flipped open the brief. "Look! On page twelve, I said that . . . I said . . ." He frowned. There was no page twelve. The brief ended on page eleven.

"Mr. Jameson, I think you'd better go home," Bell said icily, whipping the brief out of Jay's hand. "Clearly, you aren't feeling well."

"But . . . but . . ." Jay stammered.

Bell turned his back on him. "Good day, sir."

Jay couldn't remember how he got home. He couldn't remember feeding Clancy, his dog. He couldn't remember turning on the TV. But hour after hour he sat numb before the screen, not even channel surfing, surely not watching.

Show after show came and went; he didn't move. His mind wrestled with what had happened. Impossible. Was this some kind of joke? Something they did to every new partner?

His head drooped forward. He caught himself and blinked his bleary eyes. He was exhausted. Maybe he could try to get some rest.

He pointed the remote at his wide-screen to turn it off and started to get out of his chair.

"Had a bad day? Had a fight? Don't get mad, get even!" crooned a voice on the screen. His lips parted. A stunning, pale-skinned woman with long black hair and huge dark eyes pouted at him. Her lips were moist and crimson. She wore a tight black dress that made his eyes pop.

"Our professional staff of accredited witches is standing by to help you with your needs," she went on in her sultry voice. She smiled and took a step back. Smoke billowed, then cleared, revealing several more women—a blonde, four redheads, a brunette, and two with blue-black hair like hers—all in equally tight, eye-popping gowns. Some of them held black cats. Some of them wore pointy hats. One of them picked up a broom and leaned it against her cheek.

"Call. We want to help you. We really, really do."

A number flashed on the screen: 1-900-WITCHES.

"Yeah, right," Jay snickered.

She seemed to look straight at him. "Call *right now*."

Before he realized what he was doing, his portable was in his hands and he was dialing the number. "What?" he said, and then, "Hello?" as the same voice as had been on the screen—there was an old *Bewitched* episode on now—murmured, "Good evening, 1-900-WITCHES. What spell may I cast for you?"

"Oh." He almost dropped the phone. This must be another gag. It must be part of the *Bewitched* episode. "I'm sorry." He started to hang up.

"We can do hexes, curses, and there's a special on toadings tonight, just for you." Toadings? What on earth was a toading? "What can I do for you?"

"Oh." He laughed nervously. "I, uh, nothi—" And then he remembered Aaron Spivak's nasty smile. His air of triumph. He said, "Put a curse on someone for me. Make him lose his job. Yeah. Fix his wagon!"

"You really might try a toading," she said.

"No, no toading. Just curse him!"

"All right. Victim's name?"

"Aaron Spivak. S-P-I-V-A-K."

"Very good. VISA," she said cheerfully, "or MasterCard?"

As soon as he hung up, Jay felt ridiculous. He called the number right back to cancel but the line was busy. And busy. And busy. Everyone in America must be calling.

What the heck. It had been fun to vent. And it would be even more fun to take credit for the fall Spivak would inevitably take—you didn't get far on someone else's efforts. Sooner or later Bell would see Spivak for what he was: a cheat and a liar.

Jay went up to bed with a somewhat lighter heart—but only *somewhat* lighter. After all, Bell had taken Spivak's side. He had lied, too. Well, if he didn't come clean, Jay would call up the witches and put a curse on him, too.

Ha ha.

It took every effort of will for Jay to get up the next morning. He couldn't stand the thought of going into work and watching Spivak throw his weight around, having to endure Spivak's lording it over him. If it got too bad, he promised himself, he would quit.

He put on his suit, drank his orange juice, and picked up his briefcase. Beside it lay his portable phone. With a silent chuckle at himself, he hung it back on the wall charger and left for work.

When he got there, things were in turmoil. A police car was parked out front beside a Chevy Caprice with a man in it who wore silvered sunglasses and was talking on a car phone. Inside the building, secretaries were huddled together and attorneys peered ashen-faced from half-closed doors.

In the distance he heard someone shouting, "This is nuts! I've been framed! I'm innocent!"

It was Aaron Spivak.

"What's going on?" Jay asked a paralegal as she hurried past.

"Oh, it's so awful!" she cried. "Mr. Spivak is being arrested for treason!"

"*What*?"

"He's been passing secrets to the Chinese! It's awful!" she said again, and hurried on. "I have to give a deposition to the authorities right now!"

Jay stared after her. Then he made a right toward his office, only to find workmen inside painting the walls.

"Jameson," Bell said, approaching. He looked shaken but determinedly pleasant. "I'm sorry this had to happen on your big day. I knew that man was trouble. I never wanted to hire him in the first place." Shaking his head, he continued, "I'll see you through the questioning, my boy." At Jay's bewildered expression, he went on, "It was your immunity brief that did him in. He photocopied it and passed it to his contact. He didn't know the man was an undercover FBI agent."

"My . . . ?" Jay stared at him. The man had no idea that that didn't make any sense. Then he realized what Bell had said: *Your* brief. "Mr. Bell, which brief?" he asked cautiously.

"Which brief? Zounds, man, have you written two of them?" He clapped Jay on the back. "I told the youngsters at your party yesterday that if you want to swim with the fishes, you'll have to jump into the deep waters just like Jay Jameson!"

"Oh, thank you, sir." His head spun. The phone call. The curse. It had worked.

A fly buzzed above Bell's head. Jay watched it circling. Just then Friedman came down the hall with a burly-looking man in a trench coat. The man was carrying a large box of files and Friedman was waving several pieces of paper at Bell.

"Sir, you can't believe the things he was doing! Using his company card for personal expenses. Charging his long distance bills to us, too!"

"Outrageous!" Bell bellowed. "Let me see that!"

"It's evidence, sir," the man in the trench coat said in a gravelly voice.

The fly buzzed louder. Jay licked his lips. *Maybe if I dart out my hand,* he thought. *Maybe I could—*

"Nonsense. This is my corporation. This is my property." He scanned the phone bill. "What's this? A 900 number? The man's depraved!"

The fly was tantalizingly close. Jay's stomach rumbled.

"And what's this?" He grabbed a yellow credit card receipt from Friedman. "Curses? Hexes? What on earth is a toading?"

That got Jay's attention. "Oh, no," he whispered, realizing what Spivak had done. *Everything* Spivak had done. He shouted, "Get me a phone! I need a phone!"

He pushed Bell out of his way and dashed for the man's office. The fly buzzed above the outraged shouts of Bell and the others. Jay thought how good it would taste on his long, quick tongue.

"No!" he shouted as he raced across Bell's dense carpet and reached the enormous mahogany desk. The phone was perched near the corner like a big black dragonfly. He could almost hear it droning. A dragonfly would be so nice right now. . . .

Jay jumped forward. He leaped high and wide.

He grabbed the phone and began to dial.

"1-900-WITCHES," said the familiar, sexy voice. "May I help you?"

Jay said, "Ribbet!"

The witch cackled like a crone. "Oh, so sorry, whoever you are. You're too late! But it's nice to get the feedback!" Away from the phone she shouted, "Hey, Silvia, another successful toading!"

Jay let out a cry of anguish.

The fly buzzed into the room.

He dropped the phone, leaped, and caught the delicacy!

"Ribbet! Ribbet!" he shouted happily. Gulp! he swallowed it down.

Then he dropped to his haunches and hopped across the carpet and over the threshold.

Where a shoe loomed above him and . . .

Vend-a-Witch

ADAM-TROY CASTRO

Scott Engelman found the Vend-a-Witch among a bank of candy machines at the subway station.

It had been a soda machine yesterday, and in fact for as far back as he remembered. He'd been inordinately attached to the machine for years, in part because it stocked a brand of grape soda he'd loved since childhood and hadn't been able to find in any supermarket or convenience store since—but also because it had always given him what he'd paid for. This was a rarity, for Scott. Most other vending machines hated him; either they provided the wrong wares, or they held on to their treasures, humming insolently and with great pleasure as he jabbed the coin return in search of the honest transaction they were all so determined to deny him.

The loss of the one reliable vending machine in his life was a blow that Scott felt at the base of his spine.

He would have wept, but the Vend-a-Witch looked interesting, too. Its logo was a pictograph of a shapely witch in a pointed hat, backlit by the full moon as she rode a broom through the night sky . . . exactly like Elizabeth Montgomery in *Bewitched*, who was still one of the unmarried Scott's primary lust-objects. The push-buttons all bore the names of magic potions. There were four of them: *Miracle Hair Growth, Miracle Height, Miracle Strength,* and (his heart leapt at the words) *Miracle Love Potion.*

All fifty cents apiece.

Scott thought about it. It was the Miracle Love Potion that really intrigued him, of course. He'd never been lucky at love; women as a class had always despised him almost as much as vending machines did. If he could get a working love potion, and slip it to one of the secretaries at work . . .

. . . Still, it would be risky. He'd better be sure it worked first.

He inserted two quarters and pressed *Miracle Hair Growth.* The machine hummed. An empty paper cup labeled *Miracle Hair* slid down a chute and landed on the grille below. A nozzle emerged and filled the cup with a bubbling brown liquid that looked exactly like Coca-Cola. Scott drank, and immediately felt luxurious brown locks sprout from his previously denuded scalp, to nestle Tarzan-like at his shoulders.

He inserted another two quarters and pressed *Miracle Height*. The machine hummed. An empty paper cup labeled *Miracle Height* slid down a chute and landed on the grille below. A nozzle emerged and filled the cup with a bubbling tan liquid that looked exactly like chocolate Yoo-Hoo. Scott drank, and immediately felt his clothes strain and tear as his bones elongated, adding a much-needed ten inches to his previously shrimpy posture.

He inserted yet another two quarters and pressed *Miracle Strength*. The machine hummed. An empty paper cup labeled *Miracle Strength* slid down a chute and landed on the grille below. A nozzle emerged and filled the cup with a bubbling clear liquid that looked exactly like club soda. Scott drank, and felt his clothes strain and tear some more as his previously scrawny frame suddenly took on the physicality of a mightily thewed barbarian.

Grinning now, certain that he was about to cut a romantic swath through the entire female population of Manhattan, Scott inserted his last two quarters and this time pressed the button that said *Miracle Love Potion*.

Whereupon his lifelong bad luck with vending machines finally asserted itself.

As had happened a thousand times before, with a thousand different coffee and soft drink dispensers, the cup got jammed halfway down the chute. It didn't properly position itself under the nozzle, but instead hung above the grille at a wholly useless angle. When the nozzle emerged, the bubbling red liquid that looked exactly like Hawaiian Punch merely splattered over the cup and poured onto the grillework, forming a messy puddle that disappeared as soon as the drain beneath the grille could absorb it all.

Scott didn't have time to say, "Damn!" and start thinking about where he was going to find another couple of quarters.

Because, having tasted its own wares for the first time since being installed, the Vend-a-Witch suddenly decided that it was madly and uncontrollably in love with the godlike specimen of manhood standing before it. Damn the obvious differences between them! Damn its own mechanical limitations! Damn even what society thought! It had to have Scott, now!

And so half a ton of hot vending-machine lust sprung from its niche against the subway station wall to seize Scott in its flaming passionate embrace.

Not long after that, the Vend-a-Witch Corporation started stocking its machines with sealed cans. . . .

Shedding Light
on the Black Forest

Brent Monahan

Y ou've heard the tale; I know you have. But you heard it wrong. I can set the record straight; I was there when it happened.

They Germanized the alleged witch's name when they spread the story. Rosina Boccafine was of pure Sicilian stock—the old crone capital of the Western world. You know what I mean. The women turn ancient at fifty. Hair kinky and gray as iron wire. Thick, Mediterranean skin, gully-wrinkled after only five decades. Brown half-circles under eyes shining like polished coal. Most of their teeth missing. Errant hairs poking out from under their noses and chins. And of course, in that part of the world, *every* woman wears nothing but black once she becomes a widow. An image frightening enough in its totality. Yet Rosina managed to exceed the stereotype. She sported a large wart on her left nostril. She was also stooped to the point of hunchback from a lifetime of menial work. Finally, her voice sounded like a rusty-hinged barn door on a windy day. Such an easy target for the label of witch.

With the true gall of the pot calling the kettle black, they bruited it about that Signora Boccafine had murdered her husband of twenty-eight years, Signore Alfredo Boccafine. The simple truth was that what had first attracted Alfredo to Rosina was also what killed him. If she could be said to be a sorceress in any sense of the term, it was in the creation of food, both cooked and baked. Despite nearly thirty years of consuming his wife's miraculous bracciole, Alfredo once neglected to remove one of the toothpicks. Toothpick and unrolling beef lodged in his throat. Powdered cheese tumbled into his windpipes, and the spices swelled his vocal cords shut. *Addio*, Arturo.

Rosina had never had children of her own. Perhaps she had never wanted them. She was not the most patient or forbearing of women. But children she got aplenty after Arturo's death. She couldn't work her husband's farmland by herself, so she sold it. She should have used the money to open a bakery in some city. But she had heard tell that land was dirt cheap near Lindau, just above Switzerland. The tract she bought was, in fact, half a day's walk from Lindau, through the infamous Black Forest, along little more than a wolf path. One needed a compass to find one's way in or out. Which made it a virtual prison for those unfamiliar with the forest. Which made it a perfect location for a school for difficult children . . . another idea suggested to Rosina that she again, unfortunately, latched onto.

Lindau is only a day's ride on horseback to the borders of France, Austria, and Leichtenstein, as well as large parts of Switzerland. In no time at all, word spread that Widow Boccafine had opened a place she benignly called The Cottage, where embarrassments to well-heeled families could be stuck until age drained some of the vinegar out of them. That is how I, Jean-Claude Facheux, scion of the vintner family, ended up in the middle of the Schwarzwald. And that is also how Greta and Johann got there, too. Chance played no part.

When Greta and Johann Holzhacker arrived, she was twelve and he was eight. They told us, simply, that their mother had died and that their incarceration at The Cottage was a result of a wicked stepmother. Through my extensive research and the benefit of ten years' distance from the incident, I can tell you that their mother had not just died; she had been killed. The official report was that she had been murdered in her own kitchen by a vagrant, stabbed sixteen times in the back by a kitchen knife, not recovered. The vagrant (a sad fellow with a long history of insanity) had been hanged by the outraged neighbors before the law could question him. The father, Heinrich, had married just six months later. No one could blame him. He had a thriving lumber supply business to run. He needed a housekeeper and mother for his children. His second wife, Hanna, was only seventeen but had married Heinrich in spite of the gap between their ages and in spite of his children's reputations. She no doubt figured that they would both be out of the house soon enough, and if she gritted her teeth hard she'd be set for life.

But then more light was shed upon the murder. Being of true Teutonic stock, Hanna scrubbed the floors every day. Which is how she came upon the loose floorboard in Johann's room. And the blood-stained, missing kitchen knife beneath it. Looking at the exquisitely beautiful Greta and her innocent-eyed brother, Heinrich couldn't deal with the truth staring him in the face. In exchange for Hanna never mentioning her discovery again, he promised to pack Greta and Johann off to The Cottage.

The eight of us (ranging in age from seven to twelve) who had already been enrolled at The Cottage before Greta and Johann arrived were a bad lot. Typical antics had included filling shoes with horse manure, stealing money from parents' purses, setting fires, cheating at tests, throwing temper tantrums of monumental proportions, putting pins in infants' diapers, and tying junk to dogs' tails. The combined mayhem we attempted was enough to turn any woman into a figurative witch, and naturally we did not instantly change our natures just because we had come to The Cottage. Every day, Rosina's cackling voice sounded shrilly through the forest, and many a birch tree was stripped clean of branches for punishment. In retrospect, it's easy to see how Greta convinced us the woman was in league with the devil. But we were lambs compared to the Holzhacker children. Greta's long, blonde hair and lake-blue eyes made instant captives of the older boys, myself counted among them. But this was not good Xenough for Greta. The day she moved in, she shared with us two stories of the Holzhacker children's accomplishments, tales intended to show us that their new leadership had better remain unchallenged. Greta, it seemed, had guaranteed herself a lively twelfth birthday party by spiking the punch with mandrake root. Her guests had danced, sung, and chattered like ones possessed until they all collapsed from exhaustion. Johann's proudest moment was tumbling a priest from his donkey with a stone from his slingshot, the most dignified of many victims who had been knocked unconscious by one of the smooth, silvery stones he kept in his pockets for ammunition. The mention of smooth, silver stones should jostle your memory as an element of this affair. That is because the most accomplished of liars always sew in rags of real life to make the patchwork quilt of their fantastic tales look all the more true.

As I said, Rosina Boccafine was sorely vexed, night and day, by our antics. But she knew she had one advantage that could cow the worst of us: her culinary delights. Anyone caught misbehaving would be denied her delicious cookies and pastries. Those caught breaking the fundamental rules were denied the main course as well and given only bread and water. It usually worked with the original eight of us, because we were only mischievous and not evil; we concerned ourselves with the pure fun of a misdeed and not especially in making sure our tracks were covered. Not so with the Holzhackers. Their plan was twofold: to drive the woman insane with bedevilments, and to convince us she nightly rode that broom she worked so assiduously by day. Greta and Johann spent every spare hour collecting the most gruesome manner of insects to plant in Signora Boccafine's bedclothes. Her snuff was lightly peppered. They sawed another half-inch off her cane every few days. They rubbed a fine layer of lard across her spectacles, to make her believe her eyesight was rapidly failing. Always without being caught. Meantime, they had us quaking in our clogs by wondering aloud how a woman in the middle of a forest, never visited by hunters or butchers, could make beef goulash. Parents were not expecting any of us back, Greta declared. And even though we had witnessed the disappearance of none of our number, she added, it was only a matter of time.

But even the truly wicked slip up now and then. One day, Rosina's dog died in a ball of flame. Despite a frantic scrubbing in lye soap, Johann's hands still held the telltale odor of kerosene. The dog's pen, now empty, became Johann's permanent home. But he was still well fed. The same day as the dog was cremated, Rosina's spectacles disappeared. She was quite near-sighted and was reduced to feeling the fat on Johann's arm each day, to be sure that he was not wasting away on a hunger strike. That daily act was not lost on the young Miss Holzhacker, who pointed it out to all of us. On the fatal day prior to the incident, she told us all that she had awakened the night before and looked out the window, to see Signora Boccafine conferring with a goat who stood on its two hind legs. She had worn her usual black clothing and held her broom, but she also wore a pointed hat. She had gestured to the nearly full moon and then to the kennel where Johann Holzhacker slept. More than one bed was wet the next morning.

Each of us had particular chores around The Cottage, skills that would serve us in later life. Mine was milking the cows and taking them to and from pasture. The girls all had indoor chores. Greta's was helping with the baking. She had feigned a dull wit around Signora Boccafine since she arrived. Little did we know how well her ruse would serve her.

Clans throughout Europe are, to my way of thinking, all rather brutal. My people, for example, thought nothing of burning the Maid of Orleans alive at the stake. But the Germans have a special cruelty in their souls. It would never haveoccurred to a Facheux, using the ruse of stupidity, to shove an old woman into an oven and then latch the door. Her screams still echo in my head.

Greta (or Gretel, as she insisted she be called, to make herself seem more sweet) managed to lead us out of that deep woods. All the while we walked, she coached us in what to say. While her brother shot birds out of the trees with his smooth, silver stones, she warned us that, given our collective reputations, if we did not all tell the same exaggerated tale, the grown-ups of Lindau would suspect us of group murder. I frankly did not think that people in their thirties and forties would buy it . . . particularly the part about some of us having been turned into large gingerbread cookies. But this is, after all, a dark age in Europe and not the enlightened times of the ancient Greeks. Black cats die as soon as they are born, and the mice and rats run rampant in the streets.

Johann Holzhacker, or Hansel as his sister called him, died at the ripe old age of seventeen, in an inn brawl with college students. He may have traded his slingshot prematurely for a knife. It proved a good two feet shorter than the freshman's rapier.

Greta, I hear, has used her great wit and beauty to ensnare the heart of a king. A widower, it turns out. The only trouble is that the king loves his only daughter equally. In contrast to Greta, the girl's hair is as black as a window-frame, her lips as red as blood, and her skin as white as snow. I fear justly for the girl and believe it is only a matter of time before her life will be cut short. I pray that Greta the Witch should come to the horrible end she deserves. But such justice, it seems, is meted out only in fairy tales.

Suffer a Witch

MIKE BAKER

I'm a good witch, Moonshadow," Lucinda told the black cat that lay curled upon her ample lap, purring contentedly. Lucinda took a sip of herbal tea, nibbled on a slice of whole wheat toast topped with homemade elderberry jam, then scratched the cat between its ears. "Mommy's a good witch, isn't she?"

Moonshadow raised her head, stretched, yawned, then settled back down to sleep some more.

"That's a good kitty," Lucinda said aloud as she stroked her pet's silky fur. "Take a nice long nap. We've got a busy night ahead of us; you'll need all the rest you can get."

Glancing at the Greenpeace calendar hanging from the cabinet across from her, Lucinda smiled. Today was the day she'd been waiting for all year; at long last it was the most magical day of the year: October 31.

Once upon a time, back in the days when Lucinda had been Betty Michaelson, a not very attractive, slightly overweight, shy young woman who lived at home with her parents, she'd always thought of the last day of October as Halloween. That was back during her personal Dark Ages, back in the unenlightened time before she got in touch with the *Power from Within*, before she discovered the wonderful world of magic. Those days were long gone; now and forever this day was referred to only by its proper name—All Hallows' Eve—and it was always given the respect it was due.

Two events had changed Betty's life forever. The first was the death of her parents in a freak accident—the snoring Santa Christmas diorama they'd purchased on sale at the local Wal-Mart turned out to have faulty wiring; rather than create holiday cheer when plugged in, it exploded, killing them both instantly—shortly after she turned thirty. Betty's parents left her the house, plus a sizable amount of money. That, coupled with the insurance settlement, guaranteed that Betty would never have to work another day in her life. (Which, of course, she didn't.)

The second big event in Betty's life was the discovery of witchcraft or, more importantly, Starhawk, the mystical guru of postmodern witchcraft. Betty had read *Dreaming the Dark*, Starhawk's best-known work, so many times she could quote from it chapter and verse; not a day passed when she didn't open its pages. In fact, it was during one of her many rereadings of *Dreaming* that Betty decided to change her name to Lucinda, which she thought had a nice, magical ring to it.

Lucinda took to witchcraft like a duck to water. She made it her life, her reason for living. So fervent was her belief, she became more than just your typical suburban good witch; she became an activist witch as well. For far too long the sanctity and greatness of witchcraft had been mocked and reviled by a society poisoned by the bigoted slurs of organized religion and ignorant, ratings-obsessed daytime talk show hosts like Geraldo (who was notorious amongst the witch community for his annual "Halloween Lie-Fest"). It was time that people learned the truth, and Lucinda took it upon herself to spread the word whenever she had a chance.

One of Lucinda's ongoing, and most successful, projects was *Nice Witch Stories: The Magazine of Empowerment and Magical Exploration,* a quarterly fiction publication devoted to showing the world that witches were good people. *Nice Witch* was easy to read and user-friendly, designed to help people get in touch with, as Starhawk so eloquently put it, the *Power from Within* through life-affirming stories and poems about witches in all their magnificent, glowing, radiant humanity; witches embracing the mystical power woven through this wonderful world we live in.

Each issue of *Nice Witch* also contained recipes, diet tips (A Healthy Witch is a Good Witch), the latest news from witches the world over (Notes from the Cauldron), gossip (Witch Whispers), book, movies, television and record reviews, and mystical line-drawing illustrations.

When she wasn't working on *Nice Witch,* Lucinda spent her time writing to her local newspaper (which, she was sad to say, had a definite antiwitch bias; not once had they ever interviewed her, and they never ran the articles she sent them), and talking with her friends on the computer networks (Cyber-Witchcraft was the wave of the future, Lucinda believed; it was a simple, easy, cost-efficient way to get in touch with other witches, and Nature as well).

Lucinda had just finished her toast when there was a knock on her kitchen door. Gently lifting Moonshadow from her lap, she rose to her feet and answered it. It turned out to be Mabel Cooper, her neighbor and fellow coven member, right on time as usual. Lucinda ushered her friend inside, and together the two of them began preparations for that evening's sabbat. Mabel chopped vegetables for the munchies tray while Lucinda, with a little help from her blender, whipped together some of the sour cream, onion, and basil dip everybody had raved about at their last get-together.

Shortly after darkness fell, the doorbell rang. A frown creasing her brow, Lucinda looked up. *Who can that be?* she thought. *It's too early for the others to arrive yet.*

The doorbell rang again. "Trick or treat," a faint voice cried out from the other side of the door.

Sighing, Lucinda put down the cheese she'd been slicing into mystical shapes. This was one thing she *hadn't* expected this evening. Over the past few years, the number of costumed children who made the trek to her unlit, jack-o'-lantern-less door had grown steadily smaller and smaller as word that she didn't pass out candy had spread; last year she hadn't even been bothered at all.

If it weren't for the potential of reprisals—cleaning egg off of her house or picking toilet paper out of her trees wasn't her idea of a good time—Lucinda would have ignored her unwanted visitor completely. But she didn't want to risk it, so, silently cursing crass commercialism and youthful greed, she stormed out of the kitchen, Mabel hot on her heels. Grabbing a copy of the latest issue of *Nice Witch* off of her worktable as she passed, Lucinda reached for her front door, undid the chain, and opened it.

Standing on Lucinda's front porch was an adorable little blond-haired boy of about six dressed in a bright red devil costume. "Trick or treat," the boy said, extending pink hands that clutched a plastic pitchfork and a candy-filled plastic bag with a grinning jack-o'-lantern on it.

Peering around her friend, who was shaking her head disapprovingly at the sight before them, Mabel looked down at the little boy. "That's a scary costume," she said. "Who are you supposed to be?"

The boy flashed a gap-toothed grin. "I'm Lord Satan, Evil Ruler of Hell," he proudly exclaimed.

"Oh dear," Mabel gasped.

Saddened to the depths of her mystical soul to see such an innocent young thing fall victim to the manipulative forces that had warped this, the most sacred of all days, into a commercial holiday, Lucinda dropped a copy of *Nice Witch* into the little devil's candy bag.

"What's that?" the child asked, peering into the bag. "What'd you give me?"

"Read it," Lucinda told the boy. "You might learn something."

"Screw that, I want candy."

"Oh dear," Mabel gasped.

Looking up, the boy's gaze met Lucinda's. She caught a glimpse of a reddish glow in the child's eyes, then the child was gone. In its place stood a tall, thin, tanned, and handsome man clad in an Armani suit that had been specially tailored to leave room for the leathery wings sprouting from his upper back.

"Pleased to meet you," the man said, bowing his head and tipping its wings in greeting. "Hope you guess my name."

Mouths agape, both women stared.

The man smiled, revealing gleaming white teeth, each of which ended in a point. "Time's up, ladies."

Both women continued to stare.

"Oh well, I guess I'll have to tell you then. The name's Xeno, ladies, and don't forget it."

"Oh dear," Mabel gasped.

Still smiling, Xeno took a step toward the two women, both of whom slowly backed away. "You're probably wondering why I'm here," he said as he stepped into the house. "Why I've paid you this visit tonight."

Lucinda nodded her head.

"I'll tell you in just a minute," Xeno said as the front door swung shut by itself behind him. "But first, I have a question for you, my dear Lucinda. Do you believe in God?"

Lucinda hesitated a moment before replying. "Sort of."

Xeno gave a disdainful snort. "Sort of. How can you *sort* of believe in God. Either you believe he exists, or you don't. It's like being pregnant; either you are, or you aren't. There is no middle ground."

"Starhawk says that—"

"Frankly, I could care less what Starhawk says," Xeno snapped, cutting Lucinda off. "What's your problem, Lucy, can't you think for yourself? Are you so brain dead that you have to let some half-baked crackpot with a silly name do all your thinking for you?"

Lucinda bristled at the insult. No one, not even a well-dressed supernatural entity, talked to her like that. Taking a deep breath, she drew herself up to her full height. "Begone, spawn of Satan. I reject your domination." Drawing upon her inner power, the magical forces within which her reading of *Dreaming the Dark* had allowed her to tap, Lucinda focused it. Raising her hands, fingers splayed wide, she directed the *Power from Within* at the sneering demon. "Begone. I empower you to return to the hell from which you came."

Xeno smirked. "Empower this," he said, grabbing his crotch.

"Oh dear," Mabel gasped.

Xeno blew Mabel a kiss, then returned his attention to Lucinda.

"By the way, you're way off with regards to my heritage. I'll have you know I'm one of the fallen host, and I'm damn proud of it. I fell from grace with the Big Guy. I was there right by his side when he got booted out of heaven."

Lucinda peered down at her hands, a confused look on her face. She'd done everything *Dreaming* had told her to do, so why hadn't her magic worked?

"Want to know what you did wrong?" Xeno asked.

Lucinda raised her eyes, peered at the grinning demon. "What?"

"You didn't say the magic word."

"Huh?" In all her readings, Lucinda couldn't remember anything being said about a magic word. All words were supposed to be magic, if used properly.

"Blazimbo," Xeno told her. "If you want your magic to work, you've got to say Blazimbo."

Mabel snickered.

"You don't believe me?" Xeno asked. "Watch." Raising a perfectly manicured finger, he pointed it at Mabel. "Blazimbo."

What happened next was, without question, the most amazing thing Lucinda had ever seen. One instant her best friend was standing by her side, the next she was gone. Vanished. Disappeared.

Lucinda didn't know what to do; Starhawk had never discussed anything like this before. "Mabel?" she said, taking a step toward the space her friend had previously occupied. "Mabel, where are you?"

"Careful," Xeno said. "You wouldn't want to step on her now, would you?"

Lucinda looked down. Squirming about on the carpet inches from the toe of her left foot was a small, reddish-brown, lizardlike creature. It had a slimy, wet look to it, as if it had just crawled out of some muddy riverbed.

"Mabel?"

Grinning broadly, Xeno nodded his head. "You got it."

Lucinda glared at the demon. "You turned her into a . . . a . . ." she paused, struggling with her limited knowledge of amphibians, ". . . a slimy thing."

"She's a newt," he told Lucinda. "I turned her into a newt."

"But why? Why?"

Xeno shrugged his broad shoulders. "Seemed like a good idea at the time. Besides, your cat looked hungry."

Glancing down, Lucinda let out a startled gasp. Moonshadow was crouching over the newt, pinning it to the floor with a declawed paw. "No!" she cried. "Bad kitty!"

Moonshadow leapt back, a hurt look in her eyes. *I was just playing*, she seemed to be saying. *I wasn't going to hurt anything. Honest.*

Before her cat could get other ideas, Lucinda bent down and scooped up the newt. Raising it to eye level, she peered into one of its glistening black orbs. "Mabel? Are you all right?"

"She won't answer," Xeno told her. "Newts can't talk, you know."

"Change her back," Lucinda demanded.

"Or what?" Xeno asked, raising an eyebrow. "You'll hurt me real bad?"

Muttering, "Smart-ass," under her breath, Lucinda gently placed the newt in one of the pockets of her apron. When she looked up, she saw that Xeno was once again smiling at her.

"Why don't you just kill me and get it over with," she told the demon.

"Kill you," Xeno chuckled. "Whatever gave you the idea I was going to kill you?"

"But, but," Lucinda stammered. "But you're a demon."

"That I am."

"And demons kill people."

"Don't you think you're generalizing things a bit," Xeno calmly stated. "Just because I'm a demon doesn't necessarily mean I'm a bad person."

"According to Starhawk, demons are—"

"Don't start with that Starhawk shit again," Xeno snapped. "I warned you about that."

Lucinda glared at her tormenter.

"Now, it is true that I could kill you," Xeno told Lucinda. "But that'd be too dull, too predictable. No, I've got something a bit more . . . entertaining in mind."

Lucinda paled. Seemingly moving of their own volition, her eyes lowered to Xeno's crotch.

Noticing Lucinda's gaze, Xeno cringed. A wave of revulsion ran through him, making his wings rustle. "I don't think so," he told Lucinda. "You're not my type."

"Then what is it?" Lucinda asked. "What do you want?"

"It's simple, really," Xeno replied. "Are you familiar with the term 'suffer a witch'?"

Lucinda nodded her head.

"Certain personages in the Underworld, certain powerful personages, have suffered about as much of you as they can take, Lucinda. Now the Big Guy, he's all for freedom of choice—it's what we got booted out of heaven for, after all—but in your case, you've just gone too far. If you'd have been content to quietly follow your silly little religion, everything would have been fine. But *no,* you had to go and make a crusade out of it. You had to draw attention to yourself, with your magazine and your network postings and your 'Dear Mr. Editor, I'm a good witch who is disturbed about the bigoted antiwitch slurs your paper runs' letters and your nonrhyming mystical, magical poetry."

Spreading his wings, Xeno fixed Lucinda with his glowing red eyes. "What you've done, little Miss Good Witch, is make *all* witches look silly. Do you know how long it's taken to build up the belief of witchcraft as a heathen, evil practice? Centuries, Lucinda. Centuries of carefully planned public relations work."

Xeno bent over Lucinda. She could feel his breath upon her face. It was hot, and smelled slightly of sulfur. "That's a lot of hard work, and we're not about to let a bunch of flaky broads with low self-esteem, nada creativity, and loads of repressed sexuality mess it up. Am I making myself clear?"

Lucinda nodded her head.

"Good."

Outside, a car door slammed.

Stepping away from the cowering woman, Xeno glanced over his shoulder. "I'm about out of time, so I'll wrap this up. The reason I was sent here tonight was to right some wrongs, to restore the balance, *and* to make a much needed statement."

More cars arrived.

"Remember that cute little boy you answered the door for?"

Lucinda's attention shifted from the demon to her living room window. Something was going on outside; lights, and people, were moving around in her yard.

"He's hanging upside down from the maple tree in your backyard."

Eyes wide, Lucinda returned her attention to the demon.

"It's a terrible thing, really. Terrible. Now I'm not an expert on matters of this sort, but from the way the boy's throat was cut, and those symbols carved into his naked body, I'd say that it was a ritualistic killing."

Sounds from the front porch; the tromp of heavy feet on wood. Bright lights shown through the windows, dispelling the darkness.

"You know, it's funny how the local TV stations found out so quickly. It's almost as if someone tipped them off."

The doorbell rang.

Mouth agape, Lucinda stared at her front door. A tiny red-brown diamond-shaped head poked out of the pocket of her apron, checking out the commotion.

"Your time has finally come, Lucinda. Now the whole world will get a chance to hear about what a good witch you are."

Smiling broadly, Xeno waggled his fingers at Lucinda. "It's been fun, babe, but I gotta go. Ciao."

Xeno vanished.

The front door opened.

Slack-jawed and blank-eyed, Lucinda watched in helpless horror as the seekers of the truth, cameras rolling, microphones raised, descended upon her.

The Politically Incorrect Witch

Benjamin Adams

The first thing Goodie Jefferson noticed on awakening was the smell of fresh rain. *Damme,* she thought, *I fell asleep and got drenched. Bah*! She stirred in her bed of leaves, dragging her aching form up, inch by inch, by grabbing hold of the trunk of an imposing oak.

"That's damme odd," she muttered under her breath. She could have sworn that the trees in this part of the forest were naught but mere saplings—these were imposing giants, almost barren of foliage and ready for the winter. Still, it had been dark when she stopped to sleep; she must have been mistaken about their age.

Musty, decaying leaves clung to her dark, hand-woven traveling clothes. She brushed the leaves off irritably. *Wet, cold, 'n' filthy,* she

293

thought. *That's the last time I go a-midwifin' more 'n a day's walk from home.*

Counting time spent on the forest path yesterday, Goodie Jefferson figured she had no more than another six hours' travel; with any luck she'd be home by midafternoon, judging by the dim glow of the sun through the light gray overcast.

She looked around for the path, and began to worry.

"It was right 'ere!" she croaked, casting her eyes about wildly. "I knows it was! I followed the lights I set me own self, damme it all!"

The witch frantically replayed her memories.

Upon receiving word that Prudence Poroth was practically ready to give birth, Goodie Jefferson had set forth on the day-and-a-half trek along the forest path from Salem to Poroth Farm. Along the way, she'd scattered freshly made witch dust from the hemp canvas bag at her side, to guide her way with faint luminescence when she returned in darkness.

This was where the path had lain. She was *sure* of it. The light from her own witch dust had guided her.

"Oh, damme and double-damme!" she cried.

As if in response, a light, chiming sound—like children's laughter at play—issued from behind a nearby oak . . . and just as suddenly fell silent.

An annoyed expression crossed Goodie Jefferson's aged features. Oh, *now* she knew what was happening. Oh, yes.

Her own witch dust—carefully prepared from toadstools harvested at midnight under a new moon, newts' eyeballs, and dried radish mash —hadn't failed her at all.

"Show yerselves!" she barked suddenly. "Show yerselves, ye damme wee folk!"

The laughter pealed forth again, louder this time.

"Oh, ye divils," Goodie Jefferson screeched. "I'm not one ye want to anger!"

A sound suspiciously like a raspberry came from behind the oak.

"*Ooohhh!*" burst the witch, thoroughly exasperated. "Ye lure me here wi' yer damme faerie dust, and now ye taunt me like the children ye are. Well, I won't stand fer it!" She chose the direction opposite her unseen taunter and stomped away.

Behind Goodie Jefferson's retreating back, the tittering began

again, and continued for a long while; the self-satisfied giggles of someone who has pulled off the best practical joke of his or her immortal life.

After nightfall, Goodie Jefferson regretted her hasty departure.
These woods in which she found herself were odd somehow; diseased
and poisoned-looking, stunted oaks reached for the troubled sky with
gnarled and twisted limbs.

She forced herself to stop her strong, steady pace, and take stock
of her surroundings. As yet there was no sign of the path—no sign of
any path, for that matter. No light, either from her witch dust or from the
wee folk, showed to her eyes. Neither had she come to one of the many
small streams that should wind their way through this area.

The sky was still overcast, showing neither stars nor moon for
guidance.

"By damme," Goodie Jefferson murmured, "I'm lost, I am."

A wide, rounded rock protruding from the forest floor caught her
eye and she sat on it, catching her breath.

Oh, but this was a fine situation!

If only she'd been less prideful and dealt with the wee folk as they
liked. But Goodie Jefferson never bowed to anyone, neither man nor
faerie, and had always made do right enough. Why, on the trip to Poroth
Farm yesterday there had been that obnoxious goatherd denying her
permission to cross his land. As if any man could deny her that right.
Well, she'd taught him a lesson; the curse she'd laid on him would never
allow him to bare himself in front of any woman again without suffering
deep masculine humiliation.

But the faeries—the faeries had to be handled differently. She had
no doubt that even now the wee folk watched her from hiding, laughing
at her travails.

Well, let 'em, she thought. *I'll show the damme wee bastards I can
do all right my own self.*

The silence of the woods enfolded the witch as she reflected on her
circumstance, and she slowly became aware of how complete that silence held sway.

No birds twittered; no tiny paws stirred the leaves on the forest
floor.

As far as she could tell, the only living creature in these woods
was herself.

But slowly she became aware of something else in the darkness, another sound besides her own breathing and heartbeat. A faint *swoosh* in the distance ahead. It came and went without rhyme or reason; sometimes soft, sometimes loud and almost growling. Never before had the witch heard such a noise.

What matter of beast might that be? she wondered, not in the slightest interested in finding out.

Oh, but maybe that's what the wee folk wanted: her afraid and unwilling to confront this beast, whatever it was. Her blood boiled at the thought. Never would Goodie Jefferson be an object of faerie ridicule!

"Damme and double-damme!" she burst. Rising to her feet, she grunted as her creaky knees took her full weight again. *I'm gettin' too old to be wanderin' the countryside,* she reflected bitterly.

Aloud she snarled, "I may be old, but I ain't useless yet, damme ye!"

No answer came from the silent trees, and she moved on.

In another quarter-mile, the forest floor began sloping sharply downward. Gnarled roots protruded from the ground, showing evidence of recent subsidence. Up ahead came not the sound of rushing water that the witch might have expected under more normal circumstances, but instead what must be the source of the swooshing and growling noises she'd been hearing for the last fifteen minutes.

The sounds were strange, almost as if they were coming from a distance or around a bend, then becoming distant again, fading away. Occasionally there would come two or even more at once. Sometimes they even seemed to come from opposite directions, roaring past each other in constant anger.

Tentatively, Goodie Jefferson moved down the grade. The slant became more treacherous, and she began skidding downward.

"Ohhh, damme it to *hell*!" she shrieked.

A particularly pernicious old root stuck itself out of the slope directly in front of Goodie Jefferson's right foot. She wailed loudly as the root grabbed on and flung her out and down the incline.

"Aaaahhhhhhhhhh!"

Whump! The witch hit the ground roughly and began rolling down the slope, coated with damp earth and muddy leaves. After tumbling another twenty feet, she finally came to rest at the base of the incline.

Blearily, Goodie Jefferson staggered upright, brushing at herself. The ground here was flat and hard, gray like slate.

Suddenly she heard the growling swoosh once again, much louder than before.

She quickly looked up.

A pair of lights, brighter than the sun had appeared all day, were flying directly at her.

"Ye damme wee folk!" she bellowed. "Ye *bastards*! Ye've 'ad yer fun wi' me—now I'll show ye a thing or three!"

Digging frantically in her hemp canvas bag, Goodie Jefferson found the bag of witch dust at the bottom. *I'll turn 'em into toads. Or newts*, she thought. *Or ants, or maybe—maybe newt-ants!* That appealed to her, and she smiled wickedly as the lights flew toward her. "C'mon, ye faerie bastards!"

But suddenly, with a loud *sqwreek*, the lights stopped, and a brief moment later the growling sound also ceased.

"Hey, lady—are you all right?" came a very nonfaerielike female voice, accented strangely, but definitely human.

Goodie Jefferson blinked. She blinked again.

Witchcraft!

Where the lights had hovered a foot or so off the ground, now squatted the oddest-looking carriage she'd ever seen, like a metal box on black tires. A young woman's blonde head stuck out of an opening on one side of the box, regarding Goodie Jefferson with curious green eyes.

"Lady," the young woman repeated slowly, "I asked if you were all right."

"Ye needn't speak to me as if I'm stupid," Goodie Jefferson announced, giving her clothes one final tidying swipe. She fixed her gaze levelly on the young woman.

"Well," said the young woman, somewhat dubiously. "You looked like you were hurt or something."

"Don't concern yerselves wi' me," said the witch. Almost as an afterthought, she added, "Have ye run across any of them damme wee folk?"

"What wee folk?"

"Ye know, them damme faerie bastards!"

"Er—no. No, I haven't seen any, um . . . wee folk."

"Away wi' ye, then," Goodie Jefferson snarled and turned away.

"Wait! Ma'am!"

Reluctantly, the witch looked back.

Waving a beckoning hand, the young woman asked, "Um—do you want a ride?"

"Smells funny in 'ere t' me," said Goodie Jefferson. "Like tar or pitch or some such." Sitting in the back of the odd carriage—a Ford Pinto, by name—she peered out the window at the rapidly passing scenery. "Are ye sure 'tis safe to travel this fast?"

"I've been doing it for years," said Valerie, the young blonde. She seemed to guide the Ford Pinto with movements of her hand upon a wheel set in front of her. Goodie Jefferson peered forward with interest, watching every slight motion. Magic, to be sure.

"Ah," said the witch, "but I've 'eard tell that one may explode at speeds greater 'n thirty miles an hour; what d'ye say to that?"

Valerie glanced toward her with a sly grin. "If that were true, you would have been strawberry jam about five minutes ago. We're going fifty per *now*."

"Ah, I see," said Goodie Jefferson, who really didn't see at all, but didn't feel like pursuing the subject any further. She raised her eyes and stared forward at the road—lit by the same bright lights that she earlier had thought were the wee folk themselves—vanishing beneath the front end of this strange carriage.

Magic, to be sure. Indeed.

"So, what were you doing out in the woods at night?"

"Were on my way home from midwifin'," said Goodie Jefferson. "Up to Poroth Farm."

"Wow—really?" Valerie was impressed. "That's so *modern*, y'know."

"Been doin' it fer years," muttered the witch, echoing Valerie's earlier comment.

"*Years*? You're really ahead of the times. I respect that, I really do. I've been reading up on stuff like that, holistic healing, Wicca—all that kind of stuff."

Now Goodie Jefferson's interest was piqued. "Oh, yes?"

"Sure. Just take a look at some of those books in the backseat." Valerie hooked her thumb over her shoulder.

Looking in the indicated direction, Goodie Jefferson's eyes widened in shock. *These* books? These brightly colored, garish volumes? And the titles! *The Women's Encyclopedia of Myths and Secrets; What*

Witches Do; The Spiral Path; Wicca for the Solitary Witch; Sex and the Modern Witch.

"Ye—ye'd best be careful wi' books like these," the witch croaked through a suddenly dry throat. "Ye might find yerself swayin' at th' end o' a noose, or worse yet, burnt at th' stake." She shivered at the thought.

"What kind of talk is that?" Valerie asked, her voice turned icy cold. "Are you some kind of fundamentalist?"

"A what?" asked Goodie Jefferson blankly.

Valerie gave her another strange look. "You know, a Christian fundamentalist?"

"Whatever that is, ye can be sure I ain't."

"Well, what was with that weird talk about being burnt at the stake?"

"Why," burst Goodie Jefferson, "I'm a witch, same as yerself!"

And she began telling her story: of her encounter with the goat-herd, her return from Poroth Farm, and her encounter with the faeries.

Valerie laughed for a long time. "There's a heckuva lot more to being a witch than looking like one," she said.

"What're ye talkin' about?" demanded Goodie Jefferson. The toll of the day's events was finally wearing on her; she was feeling even more irritable than usual.

"You just don't have the proper attitude to be a witch," the young woman explained, a hint of smugness in her voice. "You come across as vindictive and nasty when you talk about these . . . these *faeries* of yours."

"What the divil does my attitude have to do wi' it? The wee bastards played a joke wi' me, 'n' I got a right to be angry about it!"

"A true witch doesn't state negatives or curse others. You have to harness your anger toward your—uh, your wee folk, and turn it to good."

Goodie Jefferson stared at her, mouth agape.

Valerie chanted in a singsong voice.

> *Eight words the Witches' Creed fulfil:*
> *If it harms none, do what you will!*

I'll do as I will anyway, thought Goodie Jefferson, but the young woman prattled on.

"You're just so full of negative energy. You have a lot of potential:

299

being a midwife is a good, positive act. But that curse you said you laid on that goatherd—"

"He deserved ev'ry bit o' it," muttered the old witch, her arms folded across her chest.

"But it's your responsibility to rise above such petty desires as revenge, and turn that energy toward something constructive."

"Says who, I'd like to ask?"

"It's your responsibility," Valerie droned on, "as a witch, to serve the will of the Goddess."

"The . . . Goddess," Goodie Jefferson repeated slowly. "What're you talkin' about?"

Valerie laughed then, the worst possible thing she could have done at that moment. If she'd taken the time to glance toward the passenger seat, she would have seen steam rising out of Goodie Jefferson's ears. "There, you see?" the younger woman continued blithely. "You can't possibly be a witch. You don't know *anything* of what it really means. You don't know the Law, you don't know about the Goddess, you don't know about White Magic."

Valerie began slowing the Ford Pinto, heading for the shoulder of the hard road.

"In fact—I think you're just a crazy old lady, who probably escaped from the mental ward in Salem, and I think I don't want you in my car anymore."

The Ford Pinto gently coasted to a stop while Goodie Jefferson fought very hard against the black thoughts filling her head.

"Go on now," Valerie said, pointing at the passenger door. "I'm sorry, but this is as far as I can take you. If you walk another couple of miles you'll come to town, and I'm sure someone can take care of you there."

"Ah, yes. Well, thank ye," the old witch said through clenched teeth.

"I hope you get help," the young woman said, her tone suddenly turned falsely solicitous.

Goodie Jefferson turned, one foot already on the ground outside. "I have somethin' fer yer troubles, missy," she said, fishing in her hemp canvas bag.

"Um . . . no, that's okay; I don't need anything," Valerie said, obviously preparing to flee in the strange carriage.

"Oh, I got it right here—"

A cloud of sparkling dust suddenly filled the interior of the Ford Pinto carriage. Valerie opened her mouth and yelled—

Well, no, she didn't yell, not exactly.

"*Croaaaaaak*," burped the rather large and ugly toad now sitting in the driver's seat.

The final remnants of the witch dust—carefully prepared from toadstools harvested at midnight under a new moon, newts' eyeballs, and dried radish mash—settled to the floor of the car.

"Ah, well. Serves ye right, ye damme nasty thing," grunted Goodie Jefferson. She reached back inside the car, picked up the Valerie-toad, and placed the startled amphibian inside her hemp canvas bag. One never knew when a toad might come in handy, after all.

The woods beckoned from the roadside. Her home was out there, somewhere; she'd find the faeries and make them take her back. The witch took one last look at the back seat of the Ford Pinto and looked longingly at the garish volumes.

The Woman's Encyclopedia of Myths and Secrets.

What kind of forbidden knowledge might she find there?

Goodie Jefferson smiled a rotten-toothed grin and turned away, toward the dark, inviting woods. *No, I'll have naught to do with such foolishness.*

The old ways were still the best.

Grue Love

DAVID ANNANDALE

So this is how Tanith and I met.

Mother Mayhem was an inveterate matchmaker. A discriminating one, mind you. She took her art seriously, and she had no patience for dilettantes who would go *Hey, George and Sandra have the same interests, the same incomes, and they live two blocks from each other.* Where's the challenge there? No, Mother Mayhem's speed was more along the lines of uniting a mermaid with an androgyne from Ganymede.

You probably think I made that example up, don't you?

Well, regardless, you get the idea. The course of true love may or may not run smooth, but as far as Mother Mayhem was concerned, the course *to* true love should be as im-bloody-probable as you could get.

I don't know if what happened was some sort of long-running master plan, or if Mayhem simply took advantage of a lucky set of circumstances. I had only. met her once before, in the late 1860s (about a century before Tanith was born, I might point out), when I helped her out with a particularly nasty and embarrassing curse on some stuffed shirt in the House of Lords. This was maybe twenty years before she moved to Canada. I have a soft spot in my heart for witches, so I tend to lend a hand when I can. Anyway, Mayhem was barely out of her teens at the time. It's massively unlikely that she kept me in mind until the 1990s and set up what happened. It's much more plausible that she took advantage of total coincidences. But I know Mayhem's track record, so I think it was a plot. Tanith agrees with me.

I didn't come on the scene until the race was almost run. Tanith filled me in on what happened up to that point. It goes something like this:

Tanith came home to Mother Mayhem from her first coven meeting. Mayhem no longer ran one (she was 145 years old after all, and her energies were beginning to flag) and so she had sent Tanith to one that had come "highly recommended" (by whom, no one seems to know).

"How did it go?" Mayhem asked. Her voice didn't just define "croak"—it legitimized the word's existence.

Tanith ran her fingers over the skulls on the sideboard. "I'm not sure." Her voice is a different story. Let me bend your ear about it sometime. But I'm warning you now, I'll be at it for a while.

"Why are you not sure?"

"It wasn't what I was expecting."

"It never is. You have to start slowly, you know. Give it some time."

Tanith shook her head. "No no, that isn't it. It's the whole atmosphere of the coven. It feels all twisted up and wrong."

"Wrong how?" Mayhem had been flipping absently through a spell book. Now she leaned back in her chair and put her arms on its rests. The light from the fire rippled over the canyons of her face, but couldn't push back the shadows hiding her eyes.

"Take the robe, for example." Tanith began to pace back and forth. She could feel a rant beginning. It had been building the whole evening, and now could finally get out. "They gave me a sewing pattern, *a sewing pattern*, to make it. And—"

"What's wrong with the one you've got?" Mayhem interrupted.

"It's black."

"That's bad?" The croak rasped in disbelief.

"Oh, it's *very* bad. Full of all sorts of unsavoury connotations, or so they tell me. No, what they want is green or orange or brown or yellow, or even white, if you can believe that. You know." Tanith raised her voice into bubbly, hippychick inanity. "The Colours of Nature." Singsong, head bobbing side to side as if she were delivering the punchline to a blond joke. "The Colours of Mother Earth. There's very little black in nature." Her voice dropped back to normal. "Guess they've never heard of night."

"This is wrong." Mother Mayhem did not sound pleased. She was sitting *very* still, which was usually a prelude to something *bad* happening to somebody. *Good*, Tanith thought, *I'm getting through.*

"It gets better," she went on. "No familiars. No spells except love and healing. No broomsticks, no—"

"No brooms!" Mayhem's outrage made the air in the room crackle in fright. The anger sounded so genuine that to this day Tanith still has some doubts about the whole thing being a setup. But then again, you didn't get to where Mayhem was without learning a thing or two about performance.

"No," said Tanith.

"Then how do they get to the Sabbath Place?"

"They don't. They hold the Sabbath in Germaine Holland's rec room. Or, if it's nice enough, in Assiniboine Park."

"And summonings?" Mother Mayhem's voice had faded to a whisper more incendiary than fire.

"You've got to be kidding."

"Group sex?"

"Oh, they used to have that. Gave it up last year, apparently. Something about being sensitive to private needs and needs for privacy or some such other nonsense. I think they realized it was fun and got uncomfortable."

"Sssssensssssitive," Mother Mayhem hissed. Outside, lightning struck a neighbour's oak. Said oak, having been so struck four times in the last week, finally said Screw This and gave up the ghost. It collapsed onto the neighbour's garage.

Tanith heard the crash and looked out the window. "The Wilsons are going to be ticked," she commented.

"Serves them right," Mother Mayhem replied. "They're always nosing around." She stood up. Shadows scurried to keep close to her robe. "This won't do. I will not have my ward in a coven so debased, so estranged from the old ways."

"They think they *are* following the Ancient Wisdom," Tanith said, amused. And sarcastic.

Mother Mayhem sniffed. "Do they now? Well, I am coming with you to the next Sabbath. And we shall see what we shall see."

The shadows around her robe giggled.

"Hello, Tanith!" Germaine's greeting had the wide-eyed warmth only certain people can achieve. People too stupid even to be naive. "How—oh!" She looked down at Tanith's robe. "You're in black," she said.

"That's right," said Tanith. She did her best to sound pleasant. "May we come in?"

"Yes. I'm sorry. Please do." Germaine seemed torn about which to be most upset about: Tanith's clothes or her own failings as a hostess. She moved aside. When Mother Mayhem stepped out of the night and into the hall, Germaine's hand went loose and let the door slam shut.

"This is my . . . foster mother," said Tanith. "She's come to observe."

"How do you do?" Germaine was trying her best, but sounding very uncertain. Then she took in Mayhem's robes and seemed (don't ask me why) to think she had found her footing. "And are you a Wiccan too?" Sprightly. Cheerful. Didn't have two brain cells to rub together. No neurons sparking here.

"I'm a witch," said Mother Mayhem, stomping the conversation flat.

Germaine's smile was beginning to look slightly desperate. "Well, everyone else is downstairs and ready," she chirped. Sprightly. Cheerful. Brittle as all get-out. "Shall we join them?"

"Hello, Tanith," Tod Holland called out as they descended. "Did you complete your worksheets?"

"Tanith's brought a guest, dear," Germaine broke in.

Tod's eyes lit up with the brilliance of sycophancy pure and holy when he saw Mother Mayhem. "Welcome, Wise Mother," he intoned.

"We are honoured to have you join us in the celebration of the Goddess."

"I'm going to be sick," Mayhem muttered under her breath.

"It only gets better," Tanith whispered back.

Mayhem's eyes darted around the basement. "Where do they hide the goat?" she asked.

"They don't."

"No goat?"

"No goat."

Mayhem grumbled something incomprehensible but definitely unholy.

Tod bustled over to them. "Will you be taking an active part in the Sharing of the Sabbath?" he asked Mayhem. "Or would you—"

"I'll sit," she said, puffer-fish friendly.

"Please." He was too busy fawning to notice that he'd just been insulted. He guided her to an armchair. It smelled of must and dust, as if it had been here to see the basement change from unfinished concrete and fibreglass insulation to the wood-panelled, carpeted exercise in suburban cliché it was now.

"Are you going to behave?" Tanith asked quietly.

"Of course not."

"Good." She went to take her place in the circle.

"Let us begin," said Germaine.

They joined hands. With Tanith the circle had twelve people. Mother Mayhem's presence in the room made thirteen. Down in hell, a faint flicker caught my eye.

"O Great Mother," Germaine intoned.

"Who cares like no other," Tod continued.

Oh brother, Tanith thought.

"Guide us to eternal light."

"That we might evermore do right."

The circle began to rotate counterclockwise. Tanith was surprised. There had been no widdershins last time. She glanced over at Mother Mayhem. Her fingers were tapping a convoluted pattern, and her lips were shaping words older than the city's bedrock. Tanith felt the ceremony move toward a strange fusion.

Meanwhile, that flicker had become a bright spiral. I spread my wings and flew up to take a closer look. I didn't know what to make of it. It seemed to be some sort of summoning spell, but I had never seen one like this. Usually, these things are tailored to a specific demon, with his or her name written all over it. Nothing like that here. And no binding component. What was this, some sort of free-form invitation, open to all?

"Come visit us!" Germaine shouted.

"Come visit us!" the circle echoed. Tanith joined in. She had seen Mother Mayhem's smile. This was going to be good.

"Oh come!" went the shout.

There was a moment of silence, and into it Mayhem dropped the name "Horogoth."

That's me. I saw my name appear in the spell. And there it was: an invitation with no binding. I had to check this out. I flew into the spiral—

—and bashed my head against the ceiling as I materialized in the Hollands' rec room. I pulled my horns out of the support beams and crouched down. I looked around. I didn't recognize the people who surrounded me, and it was clear that they didn't know me either. They were standing motionless, with looks on their stupid faces of such shock and surprise that they achieved a truly transcendental idiocy.

"Hello, Horogoth," said a voice I did know. I looked beyond the circle and spotted her.

"Hello, Mother Mayhem. Feel like telling me what's going on here?"

"Nothing much. Morons getting in over their heads. You know how it is. But I'd like you to meet my ward."

Someone stepped out from behind me.

"Tanith, this is Horogoth. Horogoth, Tanith."

"How do you do?" I managed, more than a bit flustered. Not because she was beautiful (which she was), but because of her eyes. There was a universe of wit and smiles in them that was knocking me straight into the next continuum.

"Fine, thank you," she said, and shook my hand. I saw that she was flustered too. Then we both did the I-realized-that-you-realized-that-I-realized thing, and we started to laugh.

Mother Mayhem was going from Wiccan to Wiccan, waving her hands in front of their eyes. None of them blinked. "I think their brain stems have snapped," she announced. "Well, I should be getting back home."

"Oh," said Tanith, "I'll—"

"No no, you two stay and get acquainted. I brought my broom in the car. I'll get home fine." She started up the basement stairs. "Oh, Tanith," she called over her shoulder, "did you know that Horogoth has never been to a Sabbath?"

"Really?" Tanith looked at me.

I shrugged. "Really."

"Why not?"

"Always seemed kind of pointless. And the group sex angle never did anything for me."

Tanith laughed. "You're not a prude, are you?"

"Oh no, not at all. Just a little . . ." I hesitated.

"Old-fashioned?"

"You might say that."

"Still," she said, "there's nothing that says you can't have a coven with a membership of one, is there?" She gently touched the tip of my wing. Thunderclaps went down my spine.

"No," I said, voice thick. "I don't think there is." I let my tail give her robe a little flick.

"Know any good Sabbath locations?" she asked.

"I can think of a couple."

"Well then." She locked her arm around mine and gave me one of those smiles her eyes had promised. "Let's check them out."

And so we did.

Dry Skin

CHARLES M. SAPLAK

Frank stood in the middle of the living room of his townhouse, absently lifted his shirttail to scratch at his rash, and tried to take inventory.

The funeral was three days past, but of course there were lingering traces of Deborah. Would there ever not be? They had lived together for about eight months, infinitely comfortable, with a few vague assumptions about marriage.

All of her clothes were now out, taken to Goodwill. The jewelry had been sorted through, and most of it was on the way back to Massachusetts with Deborah's dour sister Susan. Frank had saved a few things, mainly things he recognized as having bought for her—a silver cartouche, a pendant sculpted to look like a woodsprite, another sculpted to look like a mystic "dragonbone." She'd had a taste for the oddball, for some New Agey stuff.

And now she was gone.

The books were all separated out, and hers were boxed up to drop off at the library. It hadn't been an easy task, as she seemed to have made no attempt at classifying things into *his, hers,* or *ours.* Thus her copy of *The Book of the Dead* had been placed beside his current edition of *J. K. Lasser's*; her *Key to Theosophy* was between his copies of *What Color Is Your Parachute?* and *Directory of Directories.*

Even within individual volumes, she had managed to interweave the evidence of their individual lives. He'd flipped through all of her books to remove the paycheck stubs, used envelopes, photographs, and torn theater tickets with which she had marked her place as she jumped from book to book to dusty book. Her volumes were all crack-spined things culled from estate sales and odd bookstores. As he had picked memorabilia of their lives out of the pages, he looked at the illustrations —bizarre geometric diagrams, skeletons, exploded-view drawings of herbs and fungi—and wondered how a person of such grace and beauty could have such a fascination for the bizarre.

Frank raked at his scalp with his fingernails. He couldn't cry at losing her—it just wasn't in him. Nor could he rage or drink himself numb or mope. The only thing he really felt like doing was going on with his life. Occasionally he felt little twinges of guilt—*shouldn't I be taking this much harder? Isn't that what love means?* He suspected that he was keeping it all inside, buried so deeply and not marked, so that even he couldn't find it. That might account for his stress, and the itching. His doctor had recommended over-the-counter Numadryl, and had predicted that it would all clear up after the funeral. Frank half expected that if he could complete the process of tying up all the loose ends, separating things, it would disappear. He certainly hoped so. It was getting progressively uncomfortable, and when he'd looked at his back in the bathroom mirror after showering this morning, he thought he'd seen gray welts.

It was amazing how intricately their lives had become intertwined, how thoroughly she had managed to open him up and link herself to him. Their habits, their routines, their belongings, all mixed and melded.

But that was Deborah—she didn't recognize boundaries. In that way she reminded Frank of a persistent, outreaching system of tree roots. Even as he thought this, he gave a little shudder at the image, because of the other similarity between Deborah and tree roots.

Both were now underground.

The old cliché held a definite measure of truth: A piece of him was buried with her.

The mail dropped through the letter slot onto the foyer floor. Frank stopped scratching at his forearms to pick it up. The contents of the mail reminded him that the process of separating himself from the dead would indeed be a long one, perhaps never to be completed. Three of the five pieces were for Deborah.

One was junk, a preapproved credit card. The second was a request for donations to a local charity ("You'll be a Friend of the Animals for as long as you live").

The third appeared to be something personal, and in fact appeared to have been addressed in Deborah's hand. In the return address corner were these rubber-stamped words:

> Professor Abraham Perecardo
> Foreign Languages Department
> Gelflayne University

Frank opened it—had Deborah been alive he'd never have considered such an intrusion—to read the following handwritten message.

DEAR MS. DEBORAH NORVICK,

Thanks for the segment you sent me. I love a challenge, and this one sure took some tracking. It's not Czech, although your guess was close.

It's an archaic language called Old Church Slavonic, and translates thus:

> *Know (you) then that this spell will take the*
> *(twain), Be they husband and wife, father and*
> *son, daughter and mother, or sister and brother,*
> *and this rapture shall their minds and souls link*
> *as with gold chain so that what one knows the*

other knows, what one feels the other feels, where one goes the other goes.

P.S. Although the translation here is not exact, it captures the spirit of the thing (spells and incantations often depend on the spoken rhythm and context). The segment you sent me appears to be from some arcane alchemical or necromantic text. If you have more I'd love to see it.

BEST,

—DR. A. PERECARDO

Frank looked at the paper in his hand for a moment, but only for a moment. He decided that it made no sense, then crumpled it up and tossed it into a wastebasket.

Then, with an almost feverish sense of insistence, he scratched at the back of his neck. It wasn't until he felt something wet that he looked at his fingertips and saw, under the nails there, the pale blood and torn pieces of rapidly drying skin.

Gather Round and You Shall Hear

BILLIE SUE MOSIMAN

Too many people were dying.

Dessy felt Jake's hand brush over her naked left breast, but it was a mindless action. He was deeply entrenched in a paperback vampire novel and not really noticing her. He often did that, touched her as if to be sure she was there, and it made her feel beloved. If she came near him while he worked on the Volvo's old worn-out engine, he would forget the grease on his hands and reach for her hip, patting it a bit, the way you pat the head of a faithful dog. Or he might be watching a late-night horror movie and have his hand pressed between her thighs, warming her. At night in bed he couldn't sleep unless he had his arms cocooned around her body.

"Too many people are dying," she said now, unable to repress her thoughts.

"Hmmm. What people?"

She reached over and took the paperback from his hand. He didn't want to let go so she had to tug at it. He frowned, looking at her in consternation. "What people?"

She ticked them off on her fingers. "Last year I lost Uncle Ray. Remember the drowning accident, the riptide down at the beach?"

She waited until he nodded before going on.

"Then three months later it was my cousin Jamie. It was liver failure, but of course it was AIDS that killed him."

"I don't think I want to talk about this," Jake said, taking back the book from her. "It's morbid."

"Then my grandmother died," she said, pulling down the third finger and holding it to her palm. "I loved my grandmother so much."

"She was old. I liked her too, Dessy, but she was very old." He tried to find his lost place in the book, rifling through the pages until they made a whirring sound.

"Today I found out my cousin Lily has melanoma. Knots rose up all over her neck. She has maybe two months to live."

Now he looked up at her, the book forgotten. "Lily? The one with the five kids? Lives in Tennessee somewhere? Jesus."

"Not to mention your buddy, Connor. Got himself run down by a Metro bus. Now that's just crazy, Jake. Walking in front of a bus that way. He must have meant for it to happen."

"I *sure* don't want to talk about Connor." He brought the book close to his face, blocking her out. He and Connor had been friends for more than ten years.

"Don't you think that's too many people?" She couldn't let it go. She had never been able to let anything go until she'd resolved it to her satisfaction.

"When it's somebody you care about, it's always too many."

"Do you believe in witchcraft, Jake?"

"Hmmm."

"Black magic? Bad mojo or juju or stuff like that? I mean, you read about it all the time. What do you really think about the supernatural?"

"I wish you'd let me read this."

Dessy let him read. She couldn't tell him about the woman down the hallway, could she? Vera. Couldn't tell him she'd struck a bargain and a bad one.

That golden afternoon in her cramped apartment more than a year ago Vera had promised, "I can get you a man."

"I feel like such a ninny talking about this," Dessy had replied. "I know I'm not pretty. There are millions of pretty girls in this town and I'm not one of them. I'm overweight . . . okay, I'm fat. No one's ever been able to do anything with my hair. The cut's never right, the permanents fizzle. I buy good clothes, expensive clothes, and they hang on me like rags. . . ."

"I can still get you one," Vera said, standing by a scarf-draped table. "A man." She glided to a wall of shelves and took out one of the glass-stoppered bottles there. She sat at the table again and her face looked aged in brine in the soft gold sunlight spilling across from the windows.

"What's that?"

Vera smiled. It was like watching an icicle first crack and then hang precariously from an overhang. "It's what you drink to have a man love you."

Dessy licked her lips and thought this had been one of her more lame-brained ideas. Imagine going to a witch who advertised spells on a hand-painted sign in the door glass of the apartment vestibule's door. She didn't even believe in witches. She believed in *palm readers*. One had told her when she was sixteen that she would move away from that two-horse, dry, West Texas town into Houston. And she had. Predicted she would go on a trip to an exotic clime, and the first year she worked for the oil company, her boss, impressed with her capable and efficent skills, took her along as his secretary to Mexico City for a conference.

That must have been what caused her to timidly knock on the door of Room 311 and ask for a session. If a palm reader could tell the future, couldn't a witch *arrange* the future?

"How much does it cost?" she had asked Vera that day. "I don't have a lot of . . ."

"The fee is nominal. The monetary fee, that is." Vera smiled again and unease spread through Dessy like a chill from swallowing a chunk of ice.

"What do you mean?"

"Love is paid for in blood, dear Dessy."

"I still don't know what you mean. Maybe I should just go . . . I don't know why . . ."

Vera took hold of her hand across the table. The light was fading fast from the room. Shadows advanced from the corners, gathering like whispering old women at the funeral of a madman. Vera leaned forward and lowered her voice. "Not much blood. Just some, Dessy. A life on its way out anyway, one life here . . . and there. You'll hardly notice."

Dessy left then, her heart like a stone lodged hard beneath her ribs, a thing big enough and cold enough to kill her. "I can't," she had said, "that's unspeakable." She escaped Vera's grasp, hurrying from the dim, dusty room for the hallway and her own apartment.

A week later she was back. It was the loneliness that took her feet tracing the way to Vera's door, the desperation that raised her reluctant hand to knock at the door. "Remember me?" she asked, peering through the gloom at Vera's knife-edged face at the door crack. "The potion?"

"Ah yes, the man to love you," Vera said, stepping back and swinging wide the door to sweep her inside.

It had been explained to Dessy the deaths would come to those she knew, but it was coming anyway for everyone, and soon for these—the ones Vera must take to pay for the potion.

Dessy asked why; she asked it a dozen different ways, real pleading in her voice, but Vera was cryptic and kept her peace about why and how and who and when. She simply said, "He will love you and no other. He will always love you and forever."

Dessy signed the pact by nodding her head. That was all. She relented, feverish for a lover, for a friend and mate, for someone to look at her the way men looked at the women they loved. She nodded her head in acquiescence, took the stopper from the bottle, and drank down the sweetly vile potion from the blue bottle, gagging at the last, and then she had wiped her mouth with the back of her hand and asked, "Will I meet him soon?"

Vera smiled that smile that set Dessy to wishing she hadn't done any of this, took the few bills from Dessy's trembling fingers, and led her to the door. "It will be soon," she said. "No more than a few days."

And so it had been. Dessy met Jake at the company Halloween party. She was dressed as a ghost; she knew she hadn't any imagination, so why try to disguise herself as someone pretty? Besides, the flowing white shroud covered her heavy hips and full, ponderous breasts.

Jake stood in the corner, dressed as Count Dracula, watching as she entered the room. He wore a black suit, cape lined in red satin, and fake fangs that made him look boyish rather than sinister when he grinned.

He followed her to the buffet and offered to pour her wine (dyed black for the occasion) into the crystal goblets. He talked to her all night about vampires and sex and bats and sex and old movies and sex, and finally Dessy was so hot for him she thought she might fling off the shroud and grapple him to the floor right in front of the company president if he didn't stop talking.

Now they'd been together for more than a year and she had seen too many people die.

It had to be her fault. It ate at her like a slow fire, burning and smoking low in her midsection so that she couldn't enjoy being loved. Jake's attentions only reminded her people were paying with their lives. Every time he touched her, she cringed, thinking of another funeral, another casket, a grave yawning. Would it never end? Would the debt never be repaid?

She might have been able to live with the guilt—*might have*—for she loved Jake and their life together. She couldn't contemplate a time in her life without him. She might have found a way to accept the deaths if it hadn't been for the headaches.

"I can't read anymore, it hurts so bad!" Jake threw the latest vampire fiction across the room from the bed and grabbed the sides of his head with both hands. He shook himself as if to shuck off the pain, and then he groaned.

Dessy went for a cold bath cloth to bathe his neck and forehead. She brought back aspirin and a glass of water. Nothing seemed to help.

"You'd better go to a doctor," she said, worry creasing her face.

Brain tumor, they said. Three of them, specialists, standing around his bed in the hospital where Jake lay nearly comatose from a morphine drip. Definitely a brain tumor, that's what the scans showed. It was large. It was deadly.

Jake was going to be taken away from her.

She must set it all straight again if she could. That first fear that had turned her heart to stone now melted to volcanic lava that scored her and left her racked with tremors, her cheeks wet with tears. She rushed home to the apartment house, ran up two flights of stairs to the third floor, to Room 311.

She knocked, banging on the door with both fists, screaming with the terror and dread of losing all that she had ever loved, all that she had ever had.

The battering went unanswered. Dessy called and no sound came from within 311.

Down the stairs again, racing, leaping down them three at a time, staggering, she hit the first floor and banged again on the super's door. "Let me in! I have to talk to Vera. Let me in now!"

The door opened on a chain and Mr. Caramini looked out at her, concerned and not a little frightened. "What's all this about?"

"Where's Vera? Three eleven!"

"Dessy Mitchell? What's wrong with you? You look a mess, crying that way. There ain't no one in three eleven, you know that."

Dessy's voice went up an octave. "Vera, the woman in three eleven who put the sign in the door. . . ." She turned to point and only then did she see there was no sign. But it had been there just the day before, she was certain of that. She swallowed and put a cap on the panic that was trying to shatter her mind. "Vera." She said it just as plainly and unemotionally as she could so he would understand. "She had apartment three eleven, third floor, down the hall from my apartment. She kept a sign in the window. Right there." Now she did point. "It was there for months."

Mr. Caramini closed the door, undid the chain, and stood facing her. "Honey, you're mistaken. Three eleven's empty. Been empty for a couple years. You never heard from the other tenants about the murder in there?"

Dessy felt her knees go weak. She sagged against the door frame, her breath whistling out of her like steam from a kettle.

"That was before you moved in. I'd 've thought someone would have gossiped about it to you by now, though I do see you and your young man tend to stay to yourselves a lot. Was a terrible thing, messy. I had a time, I can tell you, getting folks to take the other apartments for a while. Bad karma, you know."

"What happened?" she asked. Not that she cared. It didn't matter, did it, what happened; what mattered was that she had struck a deal with a mirage, a phantom, and there was blood to pay.

"It was a middle-aged couple, devoted you would have thought them, like lovebirds. Always holding hands, or he'd have his arm around her shoulder, always kissing here in the lobby when they thought no one was looking. Well, sort of like you and Jake."

Dessy closed her eyes and saw the hospital room with the doctors ringed around the bed like white vultures, hanging over their patient they could not save. They sighed and exchanged guilty glances and told her how it might turn out all right, you never could tell with these things, it could stop growing, there were miracles every day, they'd seen them. Lies. Lies to keep her from cursing them, from falling apart and making a scene.

Mr. Caramini's voice was like a glass chime, tinkling in a soft breeze. She tried to listen to him, to make out the words.

The woman, Veronica Oren, found out her husband had cheated on her, he had betrayed her, the love wasn't as strong as she thought. Driven to a jealous rage, she'd waited behind the door of 311 for him to come home one night. She stabbed him so many times there was blood on all the walls and even in the hallway, pools of it, rivers and streams of it that leaked down the stairs, dripping one after the other, down and down.

Dessy left before he had finished the tale, moving up the stairway in a trance, mumbling. She knew how it ended. Vera/Veronica had been put to death by the state of Texas for her crime of passion. Paid for her love with blood.

On the third-floor landing Dessy paused, went to the closed and locked door that had opened for her a year ago. She stood with her head pressed against the cold unyielding wood. She whispered pleas, promised her entire family, her firstborn, promised anything to save him, to save Jake.

From inside only the shadows whispered back, gathering from the empty corners that were darker than dried blood, darker than love scorned and lost.

Dessy thought she heard them.

You will be alone again, they chorused. *You gave away too much,* they hissed.

Too many people have died.

Fish Witch

Lois H. Gresh

Caretta dove into the ooze of the trench floor. A slick flash through murk, and the eel buried its jaws into the flank of a fangtooth fish. Tremors rippled down Caretta's tail. The eel flitted into the warm sea waves, leaving the fangtooth a rag of bone and skin.

For the moment, Caretta was safe.

High above, strung across the upper edge of the subducting slab, algal blooms flickered red. Caretta floated upward, mouth twitching, teeth-needles clicking. The water vibrations, the sting of the tiny male corpse embedded over her belly lights: everything pulled her up the rock ridge toward the algae.

At the top, she chewed the corpse from her side, then set off for the beach to lay her eggs. Her flippers clung to the sharkbone, which zipped her over the peak of a volcanic sludge mountain and down its craggy slope.

Eventually, the sharkbone swept her onto the beach where she had hatched long ago. Back then, the miasmic brew had effervesced with kindly spirits and tranquil visions. But now the brew was black ooze, death, and in it she saw the future of her species: the killings, the tortures, and the waste. She forced herself through it, then past the digging machines and the dead fish; up, up to the birthing place.

She remembered the crack of her shell and her first gasp of air, the warmth of a beating sun, the stars twinkling like phytoplankton in oil; the slap of the cool clear sea when she had slipped into its shield . . . so long ago.

In a sweltering ache, she gave herself back to the beach; and she begot Cornechia, who begot Fortuna, who begot Mydasta . . . and then Softflanks begot Tearl, who would become the most evil caretta of all.

Orphans splashed in the glass-enclosed Bath. On their shoulders, sun-flecked water glistened like fairy dust.

317

Sare dangled from an exercise rope, her nostrils filling with acid. She sniffed, just to be sure; and with a pang of terror, realized that the outside was seeping in again.

Carol, the oldest orphan and next in command after Sare, gripped her side and grimaced. Blue-lipped children shivered and cried. Sare knew how alone they felt, for she, too, had been stranded at the Los Limbos orphanage, not knowing her parents or even whether she had any.

She heaved herself from the water, sloshed up the stairs to the control room. Otto, the chief engineer, was twiddling dials beneath the hydrophonic tubes. A bush of black curly hair hid his face.

Sare's white braid slithered down her chest and clung like a wet snail. Her side was itching something fierce. "Come on, Otto, *do* something. *Please*, before it's too late."

Otto stared at the transmission screen, which showed a small school of turtles scuttling down the side of Trank Volcano one thousand miles offshore. "Look at those frequencies, Sare. They're higher than anything I've ever recorded."

"Otto, listen to me. You have to seal the tunnels. You have to do it *now*."

Otto scowled and turned from his turtles to the glass wall. Brown mist floated over the five Bath pools, where exercise ropes hung idly over two million gallons of water. Rather than children's laughter, Sare heard seawater roaring through the tunnels within the concrete walls and waves slamming against the Los Limbos orphanage.

Otto's teeth were white pearls in oyster-pink gums. "I swear, you bleached-out albinos are all the same: stinkin' sterile and hooked on everybody else's kids. Just sit tight. I'll have Moe go down and fix the machines. Okay?"

Sare itched to slap him, but instead wrapped her fists around her elbows and squeezed. Otto was Boss.

Something blipped on the screen. Out where the sea was two thousand feet deep, turtles were pulsing messages. The frequency *was* amazing: blips between eight and ten thousand cycles per second, more than any sea creature Sare knew about—and now the frequency plummeted . . . down, down to twenty-five cycles.

A whiff of fetid air . . . and the cramps hit her, and Sare fell against Otto's shoulders, clawed at his thin shirt, recoiled as her fingers scraped his hairy skin.

He ignored her. He twisted a knob and scanned the ocean with ultrasonic sound: short high blasts at frequencies of twelve thousand cycles, then fifteen thousand. The blips scattered, thrashed, stormed together. "Sare, something's coming to the Bath, something intelligent, something that's very determined."

Sare tried to focus on the blips, but the filthy air swam up her nostrils into her head, and everything swirled; and all she saw on the screen were her own pink eyes, reflecting off the glass like two bloody tears.

Tearl dangled a luminous lure from her forehead fin. Her spell leaked from the lure into the water. A sticky web of mucus contracted across her belly. Her side ached: the side with the sperm sac.

A male caretta croaked. She felt the fibrillation of water as he rubbed his muscle across his gas-filled swim bladder.

She intensified the voltage of her spell blips.

His transparent swim bladder bobbed before her eyestalks. His little fins undulated. His mouth suckered her side; and her sperm sac swelled and its fleshy folds embraced him. Her mucous web tightened around his tiny body and smothered him. He gasped and his mouth stung her a final, feeble time.

For a moment, Tearl was sorry that he had died, but then she dipped her head into orange phosphorescent ooze and sniffed for shrimp and breadworm.

Something jabbed her.

She turned and in the guts of the trench saw Hardback's forehead fin twinkling an iridescent blue; the fin loomed over Tearl's eyestalks, jabbed again.

Hovering near Hardback were green-pearled belly lights: Tearl's closest friend, Goblips.

Hardback's vibrations were clear: *Before we leave for the birthing place, we're going to eat Jellywriggler. With or without you, Tearl. If you want a safe journey, you'd better join the coven.*

Tearl's flippers stirred the water: *Jellywrigglers live in colonies. They build things. They're as smart as carettas, maybe smarter.*

The lure on Hardback's forehead fin spurt electricity. *A fish is a fish, Tearl; doesn't matter that one is bigger or better, that one thinks a wee bit more than another.*

Tearl said, *I won't kill intelligent fish.*

Hardback circled her, a shiny whip. *Stupid Tearl, when will you learn? We have no time for petty morality. Jellywrigglers are dumb. They live with males.*

Carettas could be so cruel and shortsighted. They spent too much time luring males and murdering innocent fish. On good days, they went for sharkbone joyrides and pillaged local fish colonies.

Goblips said, *Come on, Hardback, leave Tearl alone. Why pester her? She looks sick to me, like maybe she just got the sting.*

Ah, dear Goblips; she was the only one who understood anything.

Hardback's sac sagged from the weight of eggs. *You two can stay here and starve for all I care. I've got eggs to lay. And to make it to the beach, I have to fill my belly.* She streaked off in a brittle blue flare and joined the coven by the rock ridge.

Goblips chewed the male corpse from her flesh and spit it into the orange ooze of the trench floor. *I don't like this birthing business any more than you do, Tearl—why we have to put up with male parasites is beyond me—but face it, girl, we have no choice.*

What choice did carettas ever have? The males always died, leaving carettas to carry on all of life's work. And carettas survived only through spellbinding blips and luresaps, through trickery and treachery of the worst kind.

Tearl was tired of playing witch to the fish, tired of smelling their fear and hearing their death screams in her dreams. She stole a look into her crystal-shelled back. She hoped to see something good, but all she saw was the caretta's future: blood everywhere and mass death, and the carettas rejoicing, applauding each other for the great suffering they caused.

Tearl did not want this future.

Goblips called: *Come on, Tearl. If you don't help, the others will get mad and rip you to shreds.*

Tearl hopped on her sharkbone and pushed off the bottom ooze. She jetted to the ridge where the carettas waited, blipping current and spitting Jellywriggler luresap.

Something flipped into the circle of carettas. A Jellywriggler: all tentacles and soft meat, large jelly-filled head, eyes more succulent than seaweed.

Tearl tensed; nothing tasted better than Jellywriggler, nothing. It took all her strength not to leap and kill and devour the fish, leaving nothing for the others.

The Jellywriggler squealed a melody of pressure blips and strained the water for luresap.

Hardback dove. Then Goblips. The water spit blue and green and brown . . . and blood.

Tearl dove, too. She could almost taste the sweet meat on her lips.

Hardback's mighty flippers held the Jellywriggler down while Goblips zapped the fish with voltage.

The Jellywriggler shrieked: fear, pain . . . *anguish.*

And a smothering sickness descended over Tearl. She hovered by the rock ridge, her stomach hollow and cramped.

Somewhere far behind, a Jellywriggler's teeth ground against rock, and Tearl knew in the empty pit of her belly that it wailed for its lost mate.

Carol staggered into the room, slid on the wet floor, gripped the cot. "It hurts so bad, Sare. What's the matter with me? What's happening?"

Sare stroked the girl's white hair, then tied it back into a braid. Carol's blood beat against her eyes: red, then pink, then red again. A true albino.

Sare said, "The cramps will pass. The outside air does it to all orphan girls."

She covered Carol with blankets, then climbed the stairs to the control room, where Otto was staring at blips on the screen. "Look, Sare, the turtles are almost here. They're communicating with us. Listen!"

He jabbed some buttons. An eerie whine spiked the room.

"For God's sake, Otto, turn it off!"

But he just laughed; and his teeth glistened; no longer tiny pearls, they dangled now like barbs.

She must be seeing things, losing her mind. She turned . . . *must get out of here . . . must go . . .*

But she was under some kind of spell, a spell triggered by the turtle blips, and her feet wouldn't budge. Blipping fuzz bounced from the walls and reverberated in red spasms across her eyelids.

And the blips hit Otto, too, and possessed him; he leapt from his chair and whirled around the room, dancing like a lunatic to the crazed blip beats, jumping with the peaks, crouching with the whines.

He was mad, crazy mad, more nuts than Bob or Jet or Phillipe had been before they died. Otto, a sick bedraggled creature of the sea: withered body spindly as dead-limbed coral; hair tendrils all bunched and drooping moplike over his face; tufts of shoulder hair glistening with oil.

He looked very weak . . .

Sare could throw him to the floor. She could finish him off. She could force him to . . .

. . . to . . . do what?

Hardback's vibrations were strong: *Something weak and stupid: Jellywrigglers! Girls, get ready to attack.*

Goblips swam alongside Tearl and said, *You'd better attack this time.*

But the coven isn't hungry. There's no need to kill these fish.

There's always a need to kill, dear. What else is there to live for? Goblips flashed her green-pearled belly lights. The lure on her forehead fin fired luresap into the phosporescence swirling around the frosted coral. A parrotfish flitted past and dove behind a prickled urchin ball. Goblips scooted after Hardback.

An iridescent blue flash told Tearl that Hardback wanted her help. Reluctantly, Tearl swam after Goblips and pretended to join the coven.

Hardback flipped, and all the carettas lunged after her, except Tearl, who pulled back at the last moment.

The water was a murk of sand and muck and blood, and Tearl's eyes stung; and by the time she could see again, piles of carettas were heaving their death sighs.

She turned and tried desperately to find the green-pearled lights that would tell her that Goblips was okay.

She remembered the future she had seen in her crystal-shelled back. There would be more carnage and more pain. The fish colonies were doomed, for she had seen happy carettas dancing in a sea of death.

Hardback was dead. Goblips was wounded, one flipper punctured and bleeding, belly scourged by claws.

Everywhere were Jellywriggler carcasses: draped across the coral limbs, tentacles and succulent meat strings waving in the current, oozing jelly heads beckoning.

Goblips gulped meat and jelly. Her mangled flipper hung from her shoulder. Her belly streamed blood.

Something loomed nearby, something large: a Jellywriggler with sad, drooping eyes. The Jellywriggler vibrated; it was trying to tell her something, but Tearl didn't understand.

What is it? What do you want? she asked.

The fish tried to push her back toward the volcano and the home trench.

Tearl didn't want to hurt the Jellywriggler. She slapped it away. She was so tired of being an evil caretta. She crushed some argonaut shells, sucked out the eyes and slurped down the tentacles. It made her feel a little better, for argonauts were *food*: they didn't think, they didn't dream, they didn't laugh or cry.

But that night, Goblips died, and a dark emptiness dug its way into Tearl's heart. If not for the Jellywrigglers, Goblips would be alive. Goblips, her best friend.

Tearl cast her luresap into the water, flung her spell as far as she could. Tearl would kill anything that got in her way, for it no longer mattered.

Otto's hair fell out in clumps. He reached for the dials, his arms craggy and mottled like starfish limbs. His fishy odor: such a perfume he secreted into the brown murk . . .

. . . so sexy, Sare wanted to scream.

He said, "Only two turtles left, both in the coral reefs outside the orphanage."

Sare untwined her snail-white hair. Oil streamed from her pores, plastered a hair halo around her face.

Otto turned from his screen. His eyes had the sheen of polished shell. His teeth barbs chattered. He was so weak, she could barely control herself. She secreted more lure, and the mucus dripped and brightened the white of her hair.

He moved toward her—"I want you but I don't know why," he said—and she laughed—a wild shriek of a laugh—and grabbed his head and crammed it against her side where the goose bumps pricked. His eyes waxed. His barbs stung: once, twice, over and over, until finally she slammed his head into her sperm sac and smothered him.

She staggered back, tingling, dizzy with joy. Her side no longer itched.

Brown air billowed through ducts and tunnels and vents. In the Bath, male orphans wilted and females glowed.

Otto should have listened to her. He should have fixed the filters.

The natal beach was minutes away. Tearl was the only caretta left. If she didn't lay eggs, there would be no next generation.

The Jellywriggler's fat body danced in the current, flitting past sludge lumps and oil-coated birds. Tearl smelled its fear. She tasted its terror.

So excited now; she had no choice. Her flippers grasped the sharkbone. She surfed circles around the Jellywriggler, slowly, then faster. She tightened her web, spinning now in fast wild loops.

The Jellywriggler squirmed, eyes darting for escape routes; but Tearl was swimming too quickly, and there was no way she would allow the fish to live. She was *caretta*: greedy, wicked, and deadly. She would cast spells. She would lure males. She would kill anything that caught her fancy.

She socked the Jellywriggler to the ocean floor. She zapped it with a voltage so high that the fish flared and collapsed, and then she plunged her lips into the succulent morsel and sucked. But the excitement was gone—it was only the killing that she liked—and so she left the bloody body there to rot.

She forced herself through the black ooze, up, up to the birthing place. A touch of gummy sand, and her flippers ached. She remembered the crack of her shell, her first gasp of air. In a sweltering ache, she gave herself to the current, and it pulled her toward shore.

But the sea did not lap upon the beach. Instead, it swelled and it slammed her against something hard; and the blood flowed from her flippers and her belly and her head; and she struggled for sand—

but found none!

She groped along the hard wall until at last she found an opening, and then she crawled into the tunnel and let the water slosh her along the slimy sides to a broken net within.

This thing—whatever could it be?—was where her natal beach had been. This thing was filled with water.

And who were these strange creatures with white tentacles and glowing pink eyes?

Everywhere were dead males, all frail and suffocated. Splashing around them were females: strong with sacs bulging from their sides. Laughing. Croaking. Eating the male flesh.

Tearl tasted joy, and it was sweeter than the Jellywriggler's death cries gurgling in her ears. The males smelled good.

She deposited her eggs in the tunnel, and then she swam across the pool to meet the other carettas.

The Hammer of Witches

MARK KREIGHBAUM

Naked and exhausted, Madeleine stumbled along a riverbank through a nighttime storm. The slender young witch's bare feet slipped in the damp arrowhead and pickerelweed of a slough. She struggled through the tangle of vines and plants beside the stream. Wind-driven rain stung her naked body like wasps. Her lungs ached and her sides felt as if they were being pierced with needles. Her enemies were close behind—she could hear the crackle of their walkie-talkies and the baying of their damned dogs—but the river spirits she'd begged for help would delay them, she hoped, until she came up with some kind of plan. With any luck, the neo-Inquisitors might even lose a hound or two. Madeleine shook her head. Luck was in short supply for her these days.

She paused to lean against the trunk of a large goat willow. With a yelp of pain, she jerked back at the touch of the bark on the raw wounds on her back that she had managed to forget for a moment. In a sense, the half-dozen whipcuts that burned down her back had saved her life. The neo-Inquisitors, drunk with the delight of capturing a real witch, had not waited for their master, the Hammer of Witches—so named in dubious honor of the old *Malleus Maleficarum*, the fifteenth-century handbook used to hunt and test suspected witches—but instead made the mistake of flogging her before injecting her with synthetic witchbane. She'd used the delay to weave a hasty illusion that allowed her to escape into the woods behind the motel. She might have eluded the fools completely, but their leader, who had been establishing his credentials with the motel operator, joined his pack and brought a seasoned eye to the hunt.

Madeleine had glimpsed the Hammer only once and that was enough. Balding, a little under five feet tall, he wore tailored white robes embroidered with the crimson sigils of his office. A bandolier of witchbane in silver vials crossed his narrow chest. Though physically unremarkable, she could sense the ferocity of his hatred preceding him like a torch. But he was no fool. Once on the scent, none of her tricks and small glamours deflected him for long.

Madeleine squatted and settled against the tree, careful this time to spare her back. Surprisingly, the willow possessed a flicker of the Worldfire. She sensed that it had nurtured this ember of power for centuries. The tree offered her this meager strength, like a faithful but old and crippled dog nuzzling its master. She stroked the trunk fondly and allowed herself a rueful grin. Such a tiny touch of magic would allow the casting of a momentary illusion, at best, even with the song of midnight approaching, when a witch's power is at its greatest and the wheel of change easily spun.

"No, *Saile*, I won't take your small pride. I need a true flame of the Worldfire now. But you're brave as the rowan, old one, and you have my thanks."

The willow's tender life-warmth eased the chill of terror that gripped her. Madeleine sighed and closed her eyes. The witchfinders had been chasing her for weeks. She'd used her power to save a child from being struck by a car and so revealed herself. In the last three days, she'd managed no more than an hour's uninterrupted rest, and that filled with nightmares. She didn't dare return to her coven's secret cromlech, the henge where they pooled their power, because it would endanger all her brothers and sisters. Oh, how she missed her coven, the splendor of midnight rituals, the joy of exploring the natural world in a dozen different forms. Changing bodies with her fellow witches was as simple as desire and a kiss. They must not be endangered! Better that she draw the hunt far away and spend her last reserves of power distracting the evil witchfinders from rooting out her coven. But the chase was nearly done. In the end, she would speak the Dolorous Word and commit suicide rather than submit to torture and the betrayal of her coven. She was so tired. A weariness as vast as a starless night descended.

Thunderclaps, like God snapping the bones of giants, jerked her out of a doze. For a moment, she didn't know where she was, or why she was naked and shivering. But under the wail of the wind, the cry of the hounds reminded her. They were so close! Fool, for falling asleep. They would be here in moments. Madeleine looked up at the clouded sky and blinked as sheets of rain swept over her.

"Sweet Lord bear witness, I have never used the Craft for ill." Her voice shook.

Her innocence meant nothing to the Hammer and his accomplices. The world had fallen into a dark age, where the crimes of a few evil witches who perverted the Worldfire led once again to the indiscriminate persecution, torture, and murder of innocents. This time, it wasn't only papal bulls sealing their fate, but statutes and national security directives. Did it matter to the Hammers of the New Inquisition that good witches had hunted down and punished the creature who assassinated the President? No. They had license to hunt and kill and torture, and that would always attract a certain kind of man. And woman. The Inquisition had become an equal opportunity horror.

Just then, the Hammer and his pack of witchfinders burst out of a thornbrake and confronted her. The Hammer's fine white silk robe was muddy and torn, and the tufts of his balding hair stuck out in all directions. All of his hunters carried powerful lanterns, and the dance of their lights was like a whirl of fireflies in the sheeting rain. Their short, homely leader grinned and Madeleine saw the way his bulging eyes moved over her naked body. *You won't have that satisfaction of me*, she thought, and readied the Dolorous Word in her mind.

The Hammer stopped his pack a good distance away. The witchfinders shouted insults and jeers, though she noticed they kept their distance. They'd learned a bit of respect for her wit during the weeks of the chase. The Hammer passed his lantern to someone and moved forward alone. In one hand, glittering with rings, he held an air injector loaded with a vial of witchbane, in the other, a glowing cross. He inched closer to her. The cross was really a sensitive detector of human electromagnetic emissions and it glowed when brought within a few feet of a person whose aura revealed the potential for the use of witchcraft. Right now, the cross glowed a weak blue.

"Almost spent, eh, darlin'?" He spoke in what sounded to her like a fake southern accent. The leer scrawled on his homely features made Madeleine's stomach twist with revulsion.

She rose up to stand before him. She'd die on her feet, at least. The Dolorous Word was ready. She should speak it now, but she couldn't find the courage. Why did they have to hunt witches? She had never harmed anyone. Again, she saw how his piggy little eyes roved over her body and it made her sick. She wanted to charge him, scratch out his eyes. But that would be foolish. The Hammer was a trained witch hunter. He would be ready for such an attack. The Hammer's witchfinders, a scraggly pack of three men and a teenage boy, hung back several dozen yards under the shelter of a copse of willows to keep out of the driving rain. Obviously, they had full confidence in their master. And why not? She *was* spent.

The Hammer came within a couple feet and studied her cautiously. Clearly, despite his taunt, he feared she might have one last gasp of power. Madeleine opened her senses to the night and realized that it was nearly midnight, the zenith of a witch's power. He was right to be careful. Had she access to a cromlech, or even a ley, he would be hard pressed to save himself. He studied the digital display on the cross as it measured her resources, until he was satisfied that she was no danger. He put away the cross and drew out a garotte. He crept a step or two closer.

"Ah can make the end quick for y'all," he murmured, violating her with his hungry gaze. He showed her the garotte and went on in his affected drawl. "A nice stranglin', instead of a long night of burnin'."

Madeleine couldn't help herself; she let out a moan of terror. The Hammer grinned. She swallowed and closed her eyes briefly. The willow behind her responded to her flare of extreme terror by pouring the small well of power it had stored for over three hundred years directly into the young witch. Madeleine felt the jolt of the Worldfire as it burned along her veins. Midnight echoed in the darkness, the hour tolling in her blood like a silent bell—the hour of the wheel of change.

The Hammer raised his eyebrows and smirked. He held the witchbane injector ready. But he had put away his cross, so there was no way for him to know that she had just received a touch of power that could be made into a brief illusion and, she abruptly realized, one other simple spell. His pack was still a good distance away, unable to see all that occurred. Suddenly, Madeleine had a plan. Letting her voice shake, which was no effort since she was frightened to death, she spoke:

"You p-p-romise not to make me . . . suffer?"

"Certainly, darlin'," he said. "Let's just give y'all a little old 'bane heah and have us a nice time."

Madeleine nodded and extended her scratched and bloody left arm. At the same time, she cast a small glamour. The Hammer used the injector on the arm before him and relaxed visibly after. He swaggered close to her and slipped the garotte around her neck, but he didn't tighten it. Instead, his blunt little hands wandered over her body. She noticed that he was a good three inches shorter than she.

"Would you . . . would you kiss me?" asked Madeleine.

"Why not?"

He stood up on his toes and placed his mouth greedily on hers. Madeleine gave herself over to the kiss and spoke the word of transfer that she had used so many times with the members of her coven to switch bodies when the midnight wheel of change was spun.

The Hammer realized instantly what she was doing, but it was too late. In her new body, Madeleine jerked the garotte tight so that no word could escape the Hammer's new lips. Still, he managed to form a silent word of question as he died.

"One last illusion," she whispered to the man dying in a young witch's body. "The illusion of my arm that you thought you injected." He jerked with a strangled cough of laughter.

After some minutes, he was gone. Madeleine looked down at the corpse without any true feeling of triumph, nor much either of remorse. He had given her no choice. She reached out to touch the bark of the willow, though.

My thanks, Saile. You will be remembered, she thought. But there was no answering warmth. She was no longer a witch. She was deaf now to the natural world. Almost, she would have preferred death.

She turned to face the pack of witchfinders. They were laughing and shouting with unholy glee at the murder of the young witch. Fooling them into believing the Hammer was still alive would not be easy. She was now a powerless mortal, forever cut off from the Worldfire. But if she succeeded in her masquerade, then she would have a new life to spend protecting her brothers and sisters from the hunt. And she had a new trick to teach them that might save many more witches from the evil of the neo-Inquisition.

The Hammer of Witches might finally become a tool for justice, after all. Madeleine glanced back one last time at the willow. Her eyes stung with tears. *Goodbye, my friend,* she thought. And did she only imagine a last wisp of Worldfire brush across her cheek like the memory of the sun? She must have imagined it. Even so, the new Hammer of Witches smiled.

Witch Hunter

Douglas Hewitt

Brenna Pratt heard a heavy thump on the porch. The Georgia farmhouse was old and sometimes the wind shifted its timbers, but the thump unsettled her. She dropped her fork of spaghetti and stood. Someone moaned. Listening intently, she walked to the front door and looked out the window into the soft light of dusk.

"No!" she cried, throwing open the door.

"Brenna," her mother gasped, arms folded over her stomach as she lay in a fetal posture. "Tired. Not much time. Listen to me."

Brenna knelt and placed a hand on her mother's shoulder, careful not to jar the body, and noticed blood seeping through her mother's fingers. "I'll call Dr. Litton."

"No time. He'll come for you next."

"Who?"

Her mother's voice weakened. "Murdock. A witch hunter."

"Witch hunter?" Brenna thought that perhaps someone running for mayor of Durham was starting a headline-making religious crusade.

"Run," her mother said, eyes bulging. "Run and don't look back."

Brenna touched her mother's arm. Ice cold. "I'll get a blanket and call nine-one-one."

"Too late. Run . . ." Her arms dropped. Through a wide rip in her green sweater, a red tide spilled.

Brenna fell back. Her mother had been gutted. This *witch hunter* had cut her open like an animal, killed her. Brenna felt the connection go dead, like a severed telephone line.

She pushed herself up and hugged her mother, rocked the limp body. *How can this happen! Cruel, wicked world . . .*

The days of witch hunting were over, or so witches believed. They ended because witches enjoyed solitude—Brenna more than most. Living near nonwitches tended to dilute their powers. Who wanted that! Besides, people believed witches did not exist. And why not? They rarely encountered them. And everyone in the modern world felt scientifically superior to the superstitious believers of the past. Hah, what a joke! Did the common man have any common sense? No, buffoon!

But Brenna sensed a flaw in her logic. If she desired solitude, why now, when she had never felt so alone, did her soul retch with despair?

Confusion swamped her thoughts. What did life mean? Alive one moment, dead the next. A spark extinguished. Time was chaos.

Murdock . . .

The name struck an evil resonance from a childhood tale dimly remembered. Did Murdock really think witches were evil? The ironic bitterness. Cram it down your throat! Being a witch had nothing to do with the manifestation of one's afterlife. Witches protected themselves, but was that a crime? Of course, they advanced their causes, from zoning ordinances to land deals, but that was all. Books claimed witchcraft was an outgrowth of the Dark Ages, filling the void left by Christianity's retreat to monasteries. Perhaps Murdock's appearance signified humanity's relapse into darker times.

No! The sisters of witchcraft must unite.

She leaned back, wiped her eyes, and breathed slowly, calming herself. There was another life to consider, the child in her womb. If Murdock were coming, she had to think clearly and act fast. The great adaptable human mind—shrugging off the death of a mother! Callous? No. Brenna was a caring, nurturing mother-to-be. And witches, often thin and running high metabolisms, did not get pregnant often.

Her daughter—a spell had revealed the child's gender—must have an opportunity to exist, to experience the joy (and yes, the bitterness) of life. Men like Murdock failed to understand this. They had not a clue how to nurture life. Destroyers! Failures! Men had their strengths, of course, and were perfectly capable of love, but they could never yield nourishment to a suckling infant.

Alone.

She reached down, took the leather pouch from her mother's hand, and rose, intending to go inside and collect her amulets and powders.

Lydia. I'll name the child Lydia.

A voice stopped her, a hoary voice of power and death—"Brenna, is it? Touching display, but pathetic. Ready to join your mother?"

Standing in the front yard, he appeared large and well shadowed under the nearly full moon. He wore an orange-brown camouflage outfit, clean and creased, and held a polished compound bow. A quiver of arrows was strapped over his shoulder. A combat knife hung in a sheath clipped to his belt.

"My mother was old and weak," Brenna said. "You won't find me so accommodating."

"You think she was my first?"

"I have no idea." Brenna doubted she could outrun Murdock, and locked doors probably meant little to him. Only witchcraft and her wits remained.

"I've killed hundreds."

"Always the same way? At close range with your knife?"

He pulled out an arrow and notched it. "No."

She edged toward the door. "You arrogant cocksure bastard! Maybe I'm not a witch. How many innocent people have you murdered?"

His smile lacked mirth. He walked toward her and touched his nose. "I got a keen sense about me. I smell your sluttiness. Thick, it is— thick and slutty. You're the one that drew me to this town. I can smell other witches now that I'm here, but you! Pregnant! Your stench slows wind."

"You cannot kill all of us."

The smile vanished. "We shall see. Prepare to die. Fear no more the heat of the sun, nor the rage of winter."

She ran inside and slammed the door. Something *thwacked* it. She looked. The arrow's four-blade tip had splintered halfway through. Her eyes widened. The sight transfixed her. Footsteps pounded the porch's planks. She locked the door. It bulged inward. She backed away. Another impact. She ran toward the back door, through the kitchen, grabbing her keys from the counter. As she turned the back door's handle, a crash of wood announced the front door's demise. "Honey, I'm home," Murdock bellowed.

Stumbling down steps, she realized he would catch her before she could reach her truck.

She stopped, reached into her mother's pouch, and took a vacuum-sealed plastic packet of powder, color-coded green. Rare roots and chicken bones ground to dust. She ripped the plastic and tossed the contents into the air. She danced furiously, circling, pumping elbows and knees. Green mist billowed from the falling powder toward Murdock.

Weakened more than she would have thought possible by a single spell, she ran with awkward strides to the driveway. The confusion spell was powerful, but would only work for a few minutes.

She climbed into her Dodge Ram truck, started the engine, and sped down Deep Creek Road toward Durham. She spotted Murdock's car, a Taurus, but decided against stopping to sabotage it. No time. But where should she go? Perhaps she should leave Georgia. No, he could track her anywhere—*sniff her out.*

She had to kill him. But she felt weak. Drained. Maybe stress had caused the spell to draw more power out of her than normal.

Still, her mind screamed, *Kill him! Be vicious. Dammit, it's self-defense.*

Maybe she and her friends in Durham could overpower him with a group spell. Lay him out cold. Then she would slit his throat—or bind him and let him wake and torture him first.

A shadowy movement off the side of the road caught her attention. A spruce tree. Falling. It would block the road. She stamped the accelerator. Thought she would make it. No! *Whumph!* The truck rattled and clattered and pitched violently before stopping. She got out. The back of the truck bed had been crumpled, shearing the rear tires. A trap? She supposed Murdock could have used a remote-controlled explosive, or a timed fuse.

Headlights appeared. She scrambled to her right, up an embankment, and hid behind an oak tree, realizing the Chattahoochee National Forest could conceal her for years. Perhaps she should retreat into its depths, protect others by drawing Murdock away.

The Taurus stopped. Murdock emerged like a hungry bear from its winter hole. "You can't hide from me. Your stench carries well." He circled in the Taurus headlights, his head angled up, and stopped as he faced the oak. "Won't be long now. Give up and I promise your death will be painless."

She dug into her mother's pouch and found a tiny porcelain jar of masking cream. *No, save that for later.* Later? There might not be a *later.*

Trusting her instincts, she chose a yellow-coded packet. She broke it, threw the powder over her shoulder, and whistled sharply three times. The spell weakened her; she dropped to her knees.

"Time's up," Murdock called.

She peered around the tree. Murdock marched toward her, his gait confident and strong, showing no lingering effect from her first spell.

As she struggled to her feet, as arrow struck the oak. She lurched ahead and walked hunched into the forest. An arrow nipped her ear. Blood trickled down her neck.

A pack of shadows pattered out of the woods toward Murdock. Foxes. The second spell had worked.

Murdock's cry turned quickly from surprise to pain. Foxes yelped excitement. One yelp was cut short, strangled.

Leaving Murdock to deal with them, she found a spiritual reserve of strength, a resolve based on the belief that she carried the future of witchcraft on her shoulders. She scrambled up the slope to a ridge, then followed it south, her stride gaining a measure of consistency. With no underbrush to impede her, walking was not difficult, but it seemed branches scratched her face and arms continuously, as though trees were trying to peel her skin.

The ridge would take her into Durham, three or four miles away. She had to warn the others about Murdock.

She fell several times, sprawling onto rotted leaves. But her reservoir of strength powered her up each time. After walking two miles, she spotted a floodlight to her right, perhaps a quarter-mile away, illuminating a barn needing repair. The Clement farm. The Clements were good people, and their son, Blake, was her fiancé, but they had no special power. They had a phone, though, and Blake's Camaro could speed her out of Georgia in no time at all.

She walked toward the farmhouse, optimism spelling. Maybe she would make it. Maybe Murdock was not as powerful as she had imagined.

Thwack!

She stared at the arrow, its tip deep in the trunk of a pine. The shaft's alignment indicated the shot had come from behind. But how far back?

Deciding she was too weak for a spell, she jogged clumsily toward the Clement house. Arrows whipped past. They sliced surface layers of skin on her legs and arms. She grew numb and realized Murdock might catch her before she reached the house. She worked her hand into the pouch, grabbed three powder packs, ripped them open with her teeth, and flung them, muttering a few words of power. Full incantations seemed impossibly difficult—like calculus—which she attributed to loss of blood.

Murdock's laugh echoed. His voice sounded amplified, strong, virulent. The spell had failed.

She stumbled onto the Clement yard. The elder Clements would be at the council meeting, but the Camaro was in the driveway. At the porch, she glanced back. Murdock emerged from the treeline. He appeared taller by six inches than when she first saw him. His shoulders looked wider. His biceps had thickened, ripping through his shirt. Smiling wickedly, he dropped the bow and grabbed his knife.

She tripped on the porch steps, scrabbled inside, closed the door.

"You should always knock first," Murdock yelled.

How could he be so strong after three spells! The truth hit her. She had assumed Murdock was a witch hunter because he wanted to rid the world of witchcraft. But that wasn't it. He was a creature feeding from the power of witches. A monster. He had baited her all evening, tricking her into using spells, and he grew stronger each time. He must have also fed from her mother, who had complained of being tired.

"Brenna!" Blake cried from the doorway into the living room. A moment later, he was at her side. "What happened? Christ, you're bleeding all over. I'll call Dr. Litton."

"No time."

"But—"

"Someone's out there." She stood and staggered to the living room. "He wants to kill me."

"I'll get my shotgun."

She nodded.

Taking the porcelain jar from her mother's pouch, she twisted the lid off and wiped salve over her face and arms.

Blake returned, loading shells into the shotgun. "Ready."

She handed him the pouch. "Put this in your pocket."

He stuffed it into his jeans pocket and eyed the back door. "How close was he?"

"At the edge of the backyard."

He stepped into the kitchen. She followed him and scanned the counter, spotting a paring knife. She grabbed it. "Look out the window," she said. "He only has a knife."

He shifted to the window and nudged the shade.

Brenna stepped to the door, saw it was still unlocked, and edged back into the darkened pantry.

"I don't see anyone," Blake said cautiously.

The door whipped open. "Time to die," Murdock said.

Blake aimed the shotgun, but before he could fire, Murdock sprang forward, jerked the gun away, and lunged with his combat knife.

Sliding forward, she saw a slight hesitation in Murdock's thrust.

Perhaps he had realized at the last moment that his target wasn't Brenna. But the pouch reeked of witchcraft. Murdock had attacked what his senses told him was his objective.

The knife penetrated Blake's throat, severed his spine.

She swung the paring knife, throwing her weight into it, and the blade slid in cleanly, flat, between ribs, into his heart. His body convulsed. Blood splattered onto her hand. He whimpered, fell, and lay motionless. Dead, she was sure, because she felt suddenly infused with power, as though his death had released all he had acquired. Her wounds healed in seconds.

She drove Blake's Camaro to her home, avoiding Deep Creek Road, certain everything would work out all right. She felt comfortable being alone, and with Blake and her mother dead, she would experience more solitude now. Odd, a peace of mind brought on by violence. Blake would not have been a good husband anyway. Too much of a family man. He'd be home too much.

Stepping out of the Camaro, she rubbed her stomach. "I know you, Lydia," she whispered. "Like mother, like daughter. I'll not be around much after you come of age."

But that was okay, too. Brenna would be too busy expanding witchcraft's influence, protecting her kind from the likes of Murdock.

Sorrow Laughed

Tom Piccirilli

At Julia Tether's art opening, a shirtless waiter fluttered over, handed me a glass of champagne, struck a pose with his red nails extended, and shrieked, "Oh, so you're the one! The party's almost over, it's about time you arrived! Everyone's been dying to meet the dashing muse."

I sipped and said, "What in the hell are you talking about?"

He wriggled a finger at me, black suspenders cutting twin paths through his hairy chest, the pink bow tie slightly askew. "No need to be modest! You're nearly half the show, and the works are selling . . . no, no, they're *melting* off the walls. Mrs. Delaney bought the twelve-foot not a minute after she walked through the door, and the woman's been simply *panting* over it all night. Believe me, take her and make yourself happy; she's wealthy beyond dream."

I'd met Julia Tether briefly several weeks ago at the Museum of Modern Art, as she sat crying in line behind me at the water cooler. It didn't take long for the hyperkinetic artist to dissolve into discourse, telling me her trials and travails on the New York art scene, quoting from the scathing reviews she'd received, and urging me back to her apartment where I could peruse her latest works. I'd done so, finding them quite good, but ultimately a bit unfulfilling—though certainly she proved to be better than the reviews led one to believe. After some take-out Italian, a bottle of wine, and an invitation to both her bed and tonight's gala opening, I'd turned down the one and thought it only right to stop into the second for a moment, to pay due to Julia at what I suspected would be a disappointing night for her.

The waiter gripped my face the way a loving aunt pulls the cheeks of a child, and I somehow found it within myself not to break his jaw. "Oh, go on, Julia's in the corner talking shop with the critics. To think they lambasted her six months ago, and now the toadies are nearly down on humble knee ready to propose." He let go and resumed fluttering among the crowd.

My second self rose, scrambled up my back, and nuzzled my neck. *Did you see that? The guy had pierced nipples. What is it with some people? The inquisitors used to do that checking for devil's marks.*

People dressed in Greenwich Village regalia accosted me as I walked by, shaking my hand, touching; transvestites with serpent tattoos, women in blue pumps and black capes, the elite real estate moguls in three-piece suits, and fashion models I recognized from designer-jean commercials. The *Penthouse* Pet of the Year took my hand and gave it a hearty shake. Several times I was called a muse, kissed by strangers, drinks thrust upon me, and my business card requested. I still didn't know what anyone was talking about.

And I always thought we were kind of weird, Self said. My familiar crawled down my leg and crept forward through the gallery, agilely avoiding feet. *Aw, hey wait a minute.*

What?

Look at the walls.

They could hardly be made out in the throng, everybody loud, the smell of sweat and marijuana prevalent; oddly positioned track lighting threw strange shadows across Julia's dark paintings, all blacks and grays

337

with thick swirls of underscoring white and tinges of red. I recognized two as works I'd seen in her loft, but the others—here was the muse—the others were of me and not me, myself and Self.

"Oh, cripes," I muttered.

I noted seventeen paintings of me before I gave up counting. She had captured an essence that gave me chills to look at, knowing she possessed a sight I had not recognized while drinking our wine. She'd not only seen and unearthed a secret, but had then presented it for public viewing. Centuries ago that would have been more than enough to condemn a man—a finger pointed, a hysterical child's accusations. Self cooed and jabbered, reminding me of the witch trials in Bury, St. Edmonds, England, where sixty-eight had gone to the gallows.

I was on the wall: My face smeared in broad dimensions, close-ups, elongated, twisted, and drawn to a near photographic perfection, she'd used me at every angle. In each painting, peering from behind my head, from up out of my chest, kissing my neck and licking my ear, hopped a shaded figure that wasn't quite a face or a form, an unperson not me but not so different.

Julia Tether caught a glimpse of a bane she wasn't doomed to carry but had somehow become her burden: bordering my portrait were ancient sigils and the hexagram Seal of Solomon, hex signs and pentacles, fertility symbols she could only know if she'd read the grimoires of Abin-sur, swastikas, solar wheels, the horned women and Sumerian mother goddess, and a ten-foot image of Baphomet, the Judas goat-devil of Aleister Crowley, with its arms around me in familial embrace.

I whispered, "Holy God," and laughter resounded in my mind.

She didn't do too well getting my good side, Self said.

I floundered through the crowd searching for Julia, and though the gallery wasn't exceptionally large, it had been split into alleys and hallways designed to spotlight each of her works. Finally I grabbed a different waiter and he pointed me to the far corner, where the murals and mobile bar had cordoned off a section of the mazelike place.

Julia Tether stood encircled as if bound for the stake. She looked as if she hadn't slept since the day she'd met me—eyes flitting and shadowed, makeup failing to camouflage the baggy pouches and heavy stress lines around her mouth. Her bountiful auburn hair was pulled back in a heaped pony tail. She tittered hideously as the *Penthouse* Pet finished telling her a joke.

I took her elbow. Julia turned, smiled at me, and said, "Well, if it isn't the poor damned soul," and collapsed into my arms.

Apparently this was considered chic in the art world; as I carried her back into a lounge area, I heard a smattering of applause for Julia's dramatic display. I opened the door, laid her on the divan, and pressed my hand to her forehead. After a moment she groaned, mouthed a string of words in a millennia-dead language, then sighed and settled back.

Has she been hexed? I asked.

No.

Spells of any kind?

No, it's the effect of her own emotional imbalance. She's sensitive, and obviously caught a glimpse.

Of what?

Me. Or maybe something coming for her. Or for you.

I waited an hour while Julia slept peacefully, the furrow between her eyebrows easing as the glimpse drained free like poison into a poultice. A knock at the door drove Self to the knob, where he bared his teeth. A lady's giggling voice, slippery with double entendre. "Oh, Julia, dear, we're all going on home now. You can lock up when you're finished with your latest artistic effort. Don't strain anything now, you've interviews all tomorrow afternoon, and please, remember not to get any of that awful lead-base in places it might prove most frightful to remove." I expected her to end with a "Ta-ta" but thankfully, she left without another word.

Julia opened her eyes and murmured, "Please, I'm thirsty," swallowed thickly and said, "And I love you." I found a bottle of seltzer on a table near the window, but by the time I poured a glass she'd fallen asleep again.

Do you have this effect on all women? Self asked.

It took only a few minutes of poring over the paintings to find what I was looking for: Hidden in the subtle symbols of Mrs. Delaney's twelve-foot work, Self and I were looking off at something in the distance, both of us squinting. There, in the faint glint of our eyes, was a nearly imperceptible face I'd been warned against in prophecies when I was a child, and again spoken in whispers by Native American ghosts on the spectral highways I'd hitched in my youth: it was called Sorrowsire.

"What in the hell . . . ?" I said and was blown through the air by a killing hex striking deep in the middle of my back. The stink of my own burned flesh surrounded me. I screamed and landed fifteen feet away on my face, tumbling and rolling, toppling easels and art. An explosion of black static blazed in the center of the room, my shirt in flames. Self patted me down and spat out the fire.

The waiter with the pierced nipples and suspenders stood over by the painting, grinning insanely, completely taken over. Trails of cocaine lined his upper lip; he must've been in the bathroom the whole time. Cackling didn't describe the sound he made, or the viciousness it contained. He wriggled his fingers at me again, and langorously transformed inch by inch like a redesigned portrait.

Skin unwound and altered like hot wax, reforming, thin and ropey and fat and taffy-pulled, as if a great hand were squeezing: the body went first, clothes shriveling and shifting, the smell of freshly harvested wheat and arcana wafting through the air, mold and wet cloth. His eyes vanished into slits, nose receding to a charred lump, until only the red lips remained drawn across a scarecrow's potato-sack face. Sorrowsire took this form during its days in Salem, walking among the crops of New Englanders, spreading madness among their children. Its lips scurried across the sack in mockery of a mouth, raggish, tatterdemalion garments clinging to a warped skeletal structure, bones always moving. "Necromancer, there's a circle in hell set aside all for you."

I coughed and gagged on blood, finally managed to say, "You have a grudge for some reason?"

"Not in particular. Let's just say I don't like the company you keep."

What's happening here? I asked.

We met a long time ago, Self told me. *On a level I never mentioned. It commanded a legion in Beli ya'al's army to take over the world against Satan.*

Let me guess. You deserted.

Something like that.

"Time to pay what's due," the scarecrow said, its stuffed hands alive with hellflame. Malignancy has a weight, and I could feel it pressing down from the demon, the air clammy and oozing. I unleashed a protective spell and dove for cover at the same instant Sorrow foisted a banishing curse, glowing sigils whirling through the room, a hot wind blowing burning hay and smoke into my face. The room was on fire, the paintings curling at the edges, Self and I sizzling and bubbling. Sorrow pushed back harder—broad smile arching ear to ear as it cackled—

throwing up incantations I could barely understand. No wonder Salem never had a chance. I parried the spells one by one, out of breath and weakening beneath the fierceness of its majiks.

Self raced up the scarecrow's back and repeatedly bit and ripped, tearing out clots of hay and flesh and fetid mucus. Sorrow barely seemed to notice.

Then Julia walked in, and screamed. She looked at me, my hands glowing blue with an Assyrian spell, the room burning. I dove and made an attempt to tackle her, catching her around the legs and hauling her down. Sorrow threw a hex at our heads, and the nearest wall gave way. Julia clung to me and said, "What!" She raised her face, eyes blacker than before, all that vitality from the day at the water cooler completely eradicated.

Self scrambled and cartwheeled and leaped, his claws caked with ichor.

Tear it up, I ordered.

Can't, it's too strong, Self said. *This clown's the Rambo of nine circles. Help me.*

How?

He repeated, urgently whining now, *Help me!*

The door to the gallery had shattered during the fight, and through the smoke I could see a crowd milling in the street. I shoved Julia forward and whispered, "Now," stood and grabbed the scarecrow by the neck, hoping to keep it off balance long enough for her to get out. I brought it back to the physical, jabbing the thing in its grotesque face, kicking at a groin I knew wasn't there, chopping and elbowing. Sorrow laughed.

It smacked me with a backhand that lifted me off my feet and put me through a coffee table. I felt my legs snap easier than I thought possible, my own shriek deafening me. Rolling in excruciating pain, gritting my teeth, I looked up just in time to see Julia, with her hands over her heart, fall to her knees, trying to hold in the blood pumping from her chest. A spear of one of the broken frames protruded from between her breasts.

Sorrow grinned. Self ran over and danced in falling streams, unable to let it go to waste, the shower revitalizing him. He glowed and giggled, drinking, finding the help he needed. Rushing back, he did a jig now on the scarecrow's shoes, reaching up and disemboweling what had no bowels. He sprang forward and tore into Sorrowsire again, their auras colliding, the heat and brilliant light setting a different kind of fire beneath them. Sorrow's cackling ended, and took on a different tone, the maliciousness now spiced with something akin to fear, or ecstasy. Sacrifices were power. The black static rewound, flashing faster and faster toward its center, a portal opening and shutting like a gaping set of fangs, and the scarecrow—now reverting to the screeching, weeping waiter—fell through.

I crawled to Julia, my knees spiked with agony. I took her face in my hands. She raised her fingers to my cheek, and coughing, spitting blood, it took her forever to say, "I'm sorry. I think we might have liked each other." I believed her, and tried to kiss her, too late. Her head drooped back, until she rested like a sleeping lover across my lap.

Self clambered onto my knee, his magic mending me as I held back screams, ligaments and muscles rejoining bone. *We have to go*, he said.

I held her in my arms, a new painting spreading beneath us. *Did Sorrow do this or did you?* He kept working, healing me with his gentle, loving touch. I groaned in relief. *Did you kill her?*

My second self responded, innocently enough, *Who me?*

A Spell of Research

BRAD STRICKLAND

I want witches," insisted their visitor. "Not dabblers or gaudy-strut pretenders, not mummers or mountebanks, but your true witch, your hag astride a hailstorm, your night-flitting acolyte of the Evil One. Do you—do you understand me?"

Sibyl, pouring tea, looked at her two neatly dressed spinster sisters. Gertrude was rolling her eyes independently in their sockets to indicate her opinion of this fellow's sanity, Ermengold staring at the gentleman with the fixed gaze and dreamy smile of someone easily five and a half sheets to the wind. "Yes, dearie," murmured Sibyl. "Here, have a nice cuppa."

Their guest, an egg-headed balding fellow of middle age, took the cup and saucer suspiciously. "Some infernal brew?" he asked.

Before he could launch into another dithyramb, Sibyl soothed, "Just tea, dearie, that's all. Oolong."

"It's an anachronism," Gertrude said. "We do that."

"Have a nice cup of anachronism," added Ermengold, with a half-stifled hiccup.

"Now, then," Sibyl chirped brightly when they had all been served. "To business. Master—Will, was it?"

"Aye, madam, an humble—"

"Yes, to be sure. Well, I must say it's very flattering to have someone come all the way down from London and all to our little cottage—"

"Your hovel."

Gertrude began to swell like a toad. "I *beg* your pardon!"

Master Will practically threw his cup to the table. "No, no, I expected—that is, this is a very nice cottage, it's only that witches are supposed to live in—"

An unsteady Ermengold leaned forward and began to dab at their visitor's thigh with a napkin. "It won't stain if you put a little cold water on," she said. With a dreamy smile, she went on dabbing for rather a long time.

"Yes, that's quite enough dear," said Sibyl. "Now, Gertrude, behave yourself. Master Will, the very first thing you need to understand about witches is that we tend to resent stereotyping."

"Stereo— Madam, you have me at a loss."

" 'S not invented yet," mumbled Ermengold. "What a nice codpiece you have."

Master Will crossed his legs. "Er, thank you, methinks the discoloration has blanched."

Ermengold gave him a wobbly smile. "Oh, d'you know Blanche?" She yawned, muttered, " 'Scuse me," and immediately fell back in her chair, sound asleep.

"She's been sampling last year's wine," Sibyl explained. "Poor dear, no head at all for alcohol."

"You could also omit the terminal prepositional phrase," growled Gertrude.

"Ah—yes," stammered Master Will. "Where were we?"

"Witches hate to be thought of as, well, evil old crones. We aren't really." Sibyl sipped her tea. "We serve as midwives and healers, mainly."

"But wicked curses, mouthed aloud on a wind-whipped blasted heath—"

"Wind-whipped hogwash," said Gertrude with a snort. "Look, you, we live in a kingdom that has, what, maybe two hundred physicians? And how many thousands of people does that leave without proper health care, hmm? And the physicians themselves, Lord, what a bunch of quacks! Studyin' Galen and Hippopotamus and I don't know what else when they might be discoverin' the elementary principles of sanitation—"

"But you must have curses," moaned Master Will.

Sibyl frowned a you-behave-yourself glance toward Gertrude. "Oh, of course we do. Some people just feel better if they think their enemies are under a curse. That doesn't mean they work, dearie."

"Your words leave me mazed, madam."

"And that's not so hard to do, either," growled Gertrude. "Look, it's simple. Bloke comes to you wantin' revenge against some other bloke, all right? So you listen to him and decide he's got a real complaint, nothin' that any court in the land would do anything about, but he's right and his enemy is wrong. So you go through a lot of nonsense with a cauldron and smoke and mirrors and you tell the first bloke that the second one now has a curse on him, and all he has to do is wait. Sooner or later it works, all right?"

"You bring evil to the malefactor?"

"Evil, weevil!" snapped Gertrude. "Life's not fair, sonny. Everyone has a share in the miseries of this world. Soon or late, the second bloke's goin' to be wretched and reelin', and then the first bloke feels better. On account of he *thinks* he had a hand in evenin' things out, understand?"

"But the cauldron—"

"We usually boil our dainties while the client's lookin' on."

"*Ger*trude!" said Sibyl, shocked.

"Well, we do." Gertrude sniffed. " 'Course, the client thinks it's some ungodly brew, but it's just undies. What of it? Undies need boilin' now and again, same as anything else."

"Be that as it may," Sibyl said in a lofty and cold voice, "curses are not our specialty. Oh, I suppose if we put our minds to it, we could come up with some dire magic, but no one ever truly needs that, dearie. And what we generally do is to make healing compresses, soothing draughts, and healthful tonics. All natural ingredients."

Master Will looked puzzled. "But 'tis well known that in a witch's brew go such elements as limb of frog, hair of dwarf, eye of newt—"

Ermengold woke up, smiled, murmured, "Oh, d'you know Newt?" and went back to sleep.

"I'm afraid bread mold is about as disgusting as we get," apologized Sibyl.

Their visitor sighed. "Alas, my mission is in vain."

Gertrude leaned across the table. "What do you want to know about witches for, anyway? Not one of those Puritan witch-finders, are you?"

"No, no," said Master Will, rising from his chair in some haste. "I am a player, ladies, and a humble writer of plays. I am working on a tragedy at present, and I thought some witches—only such, well, such *nice* ladies as you are would never do."

He looked so downcast that Sibyl said helpfully, "You could just make them up, you know, dearie."

"Yes," agreed Master Will. "Yes, I suppose I could." He sighed. "Well, I must be away if I'm to return to London tonight. Tell me, have you a pen, ink, and paper about?"

Of course they had the paper and ink, and Abigail, the yard goose, contributed a quill. Master Will hastily scribbled something. "Here." He handed the freshly written paper to Sibyl. "Present this at the door, and you and your sisters will be admitted free of charge. I thank you." He clapped his hat on his head, swirled his short cape—he was good at swirling, Sibyl thought—and made his exit.

Gertrude scowled at the scrawled paper. "Hmpf. Calls himself a writer. I've never seen such sloppy penmanship."

As it happened, the sisters were not able to avail themselves of the free offer for some months. Then, after a particularly busy season of childbirths ("What was in the *water* nine months ago?" wondered Ermengold) and an epidemic of thrush among the resulting infants, the exhausted trio decided that a bit of a holiday might be in order. They traveled to London in some style, riding in a reasonably new wagon with a reasonably young mule drawing it, and found the theater near the Thames.

Only after the play had begun did the three sisters realize they were witnessing the fruit of their visitor's research.

A hunched-over man, clad in nasty-looking rags, stirred an obviously empty cauldron while another chanted, "When shall we three meet again, in thunder, lightning, or in rain?" A third actor joined the group, just as hairy, ragged, and repulsive.

"I never," whispered Ermengold, who when sober was rather prudish.

"They're ugly," Sibyl said in despair.

"They're *men*," Gertrude said in real anger.

They did not stay for the end. In leaving, they paused in a huddle at the corner, conferred for a few moments, and then, with grim visages, turned to face the theater. A real curse doesn't take a cauldron and disgusting ingredients. It just requires a witch's anger, brought to at least a steady simmer.

And they were *boiling*.

At a table in the tiring room of the Globe Playhouse, Will Shakespeare sat with his head in his hands. "Burbage?"

"Broken leg," the prompter said sorrowfully. "Out for the rest of the season."

"Kemp?"

"Says he doesn't feel funny. Won't go on this afternoon."

"Method actors," groaned Will.

"And our leading lady may have a case of the pox—"

"He's only twelve!" roared Will.

The prompter shrugged. "You know, it seems to me this has been going on ever since we started with *Macbeth*."

With absolutely no warning, a helmet carelessly placed on a high shelf rolled off. It made a gonglike sound as it bounced off the head of the prompter, who toppled forward with a displeased expression on his unconscious face.

Will looked at him for a long minute. Then, with a sigh, he rose and went to the stage. A somewhat diminished and maimed group of actors waited for him, silent and apprehensive.

"Your attention," Will said. "Since we have sustained so many, ah, casualties, we shall forgo this afternoon's production of *Mac*—" He paused, and even though no helmets hung above the stage, a shiver ran up his spine. "Of—of the Scottish tragedy," he finished lamely. "Let's give them Kit Marlowe's *Doctor Faustus* instead."

"It's not ours, Will," objected someone.

"We know it, though," Will snapped. "It won't hurt this one time."

"All right with me," said the morose clown Kemp. "One play or another, what's the difference? I don't give a curse myself."

Will frowned at these last words, started to speak, and thought better of it. Which was really a pity, because if the goal of the theater is to bring truth and beauty into our lives, then at that moment he was right on the edge of being halfway home.

How the Cookie Crumbles

MOLLIE L. BURLESON

Timmy stepped carefully over the dead branches. Wouldn't do to get hurt this early in the game, not when he had such a long way to go. Mother . . . funny how she always found out. Every bad thing he'd done—she always knew. Even about hanging Chessie from the branch. Damned old cat had hollered good and long. Maybe it was true about a cat having nine lives. Sure took *him* long enough to die.

The piney woods closed in around him as he made his way along the faint path. *Well*, he thought, *I'm through this time. I'm never going back to that house, or HER! Who needs her and her scolding? Always complaining, always picking. And she talks about ME! If I wasn't sure she was my real mother, I'd think she was my STEPmother. She's pretty handy with that strap. It's good for me, she says. Hah. Says I'm evil, real evil, like Dad; says she'll beat the devil out of me if it kills her. Well, she's taken her last swipe at me. I'm gone.*

He cautioned his way over some stones in the creek. Pausing on the other side he sat on a large, flat rock and surveyed his surroundings. The woods were dark and silent and deep. The tiny creek burbled strange and curious sounds as it made its way down the hill. Timmy took off his backpack and opened it, burrowing to the sandwiches he had packed. *There's plenty of food here. Should last about a week. By then I'll be far enough away from her.*

He'd thought a lot about leaving home the last few weeks, and now after the cat incident and the resultant strapping, he'd decided to do it. To pack up and leave. For good. He was big for his age, looked fifteen at least. No one would guess he was only twelve. He'd planned it out very carefully, had stolen what money his mother had, made sandwiches and packed food and essentials, and had crept out early this morning, just at dawn when the chickadees started their cheerful "dee-dee-dee"-ings. Nasty little birds. They made excellent targets for his pellet gun.

Timmy didn't feel he was bad doing these things. They were just part of him, something he *had* to do. And did. He considered himself a pretty cool kid, cherubic-looking, rosy-cheeked, and fair. It was this innocent look that had saved him many times in the past. But not with Mom; she knew better. Maybe if he had stayed longer with her he might have . . . No, it was best not to think of what he might have done.

Finishing his lunch, he tossed the wrappings into the creek and, kneeling, leaned over and cupped some crystal water to his lips. Not bad. *I have food and water and my sleeping bag. Plus about twenty bucks to tide me over till I can get a job. Or steal something.*

Looking at the sky and the lack of shadows, he estimated that it was nearly one o'clock in the afternoon. Better be getting on. He strapped on his pack and set off toward what he thought was the west. "Go west, young man," he had heard in some class or other. School. Actually, he was good in school, especially in English. He had read books voraciously ever since he first stumbled over the words in the Golden Books series, and loved, most of all—though he would *never*, even on threat of losing his life, admit it—fairy tales. Their sense of adventure, of magical beings, of another, better kind of life, appealed to him, and he lived most of the time in a world created from their reading.

Lost in thought, he stumbled over a fallen log that had been hidden under a pile of skeleton-fingered oak leaves, and fell headfirst into a brier thicket, knocking his head against a stone. Dazed and disoriented, he picked himself up and sat shakily upon a rock. *God, I've got to quit daydreaming or I'll wind up dead here in the woods and no one will ever find me.* He felt his forehead and encountered only a small bump, no blood, and shrugged his shoulders and stood up. *That'll teach me, I guess.* He trudged on through the underbrush trying to stay close to the stream, which for the most part was petering out. *When the sun starts to set*, he told himself, *I'll be sure which way I'm heading and I'll be okay.*

Hands deep into his pockets, spirits dampened, he struggled onward. *Maybe leaving home wasn't such a good idea. Soon it'll be night and . . . aw, come on, stupid, you're not afraid, are you? So what, if fat Billy Perkins went into the woods last year and never came out. Who cares? He was such a goody-goody.* Squashing a cricket, Timmy spit a huge hawker and moved on.

The hours passed. He moved across crystal mountains on white steeds, battled dragons, and turned slimy frogs back into rosy-cheeked maidens. He escaped from ogres and kissed black-braided milkmaids. He stalked primeval forests. He smelled something—what was it he smelled? Awaking from his reverie, he sniffed the air. Was it his imagination or did he smell something baking? Baking? Oh, sure, someone was baking way out here in the woods. Yeah. He must really be hungry, smelling things like that.

The sun had begun westering in the sky, casting sinewy shadows upon the pine-needled forest floor. At least he was heading the right way. He noticed a slight movement in the brush on his left and froze in his tracks. A small flaky-skinned lizard scuttled out onto a rock, trying to catch a few slanting rays of sunlight. It closed its eyes, basking in the glow. As quick as the lizard's own tongue, Timmy's hands snaked out and caught the lizard by its fleshy middle. "Well, what do we have here?" He held the animal close to his face and peered into its eyes. "Mr. Lizard. How do you *do?*" The creature, terrified of the boy, let go a stream of hot liquid. "Pee on me, will you, you rotten little bugger!" Holding the lizard by its tail he whacked it against the trunk of a tree, and tossing what was left of the animal back into the brush, he rubbed his blood-spattered hands on his jeans and walked on, the lizard completely gone from his memory.

The shadows were longer now and the sun was beginning to hide behind the distant mountains. Trees overhead leaned conspiratorily together, forming a cloistered archway. The lightgrew steadily dimmer.

He was weary and his feet hurt. Stopping beside a log that had fallen upon the trail, he sat down, unlacing his sneakers and massaging his toes. *God, I'm dead. Beat. Hungry, too.* He opened his pack and pulled out a roll and a hunk of cheese. Popping open a can of root beer, he munched and sipped and thought: *Guess I'd better be stopping for the night before I lose the trail.* A tendril of odor assailed his nostrils. *Is that the root beer?* He sniffed at the can. *No.* He breathed in deeply. *Ummm.* Something delicious. There *was* something baking nearby. Tossing the can into the brush and rubbing the cheese crumbs off his pants, he retied his shoes and threw on his backpack. Following the scent—definite and pungent now—he came to the edge of a clearing.

In the gathering darkness he could just make out a small cottage.

It looked cozy with the warm yellow light shining from the windows and smoke curling lazily up from the chimney's throat. The smell was even stronger now. He hurried across the meadow. In the last faint glow left in the sky he peered closely at the cottage. If he didn't know better he would swear that it was made of gingerbread. Hold on, Timmy, you've been out in the woods too long. *Gingerbread*. Wait a minute! He remembered his mother talking once about real gingerbread houses in town—what did she call them? Carpenter Gothic, that was it. And it does look like gingerbread. Kind of. But that smell, now . . .

He walked up to the door and tried the knob. It was unlocked. He pushed open the door and was immediately overwhelmed by the wonderful fragrance of warm and steaming gingerbread. He could sure eat some of that! He was starved.

"Anyone home?" He peered into the room, which was lit by kerosene lamps. A huge blaze roared in a stone fireplace and an old black tom was perched upon an ancient rocker. The furniture in the room was plain but looked comfortable. Over in the corner stood a huge black old-fashioned stove with shiny metal handles. It must have been very hot, for it glowed red.

On a long well-scrubbed wooden table lay masses of gingerbread men. Some were small and others large. There were some frosted with shiny white icing and some with raisins for eyes. He ran over and grabbed two cookies, stuffing them into his mouth.

"Stop!"

He froze.

"How dare you sneak into my house and eat my gingerbread!"

He turned around to find a little old lady, face gnarled and wrinkled like one of those apple-face dolls he'd seen at county fairs. She wore a dark calico dress that hung down to her ankles, and black high-topped shoes that peeped from underneath the hem. Her hair was gray and tied up in a bun, and loose tendrils of it hung wispily about her face. She regarded him with beady, birdlike eyes.

Unruffled, Timmy said, "I didn't sneak. The door was open and I just walked in."

"Just walked in," parroted the old crone. She leaned closer and peered myopically at him. Reaching out, she pinched his arm between her long bony fingers.

"You're nice and fat." Her voice became liquid and specks of saliva formed at the corners of her mouth.

"I suppose next you'll be telling me that you're going to throw me into that oven and turn *me* into gingerbread," he laughed.

"Smart little boy, aren't you? Maybe you're just *too* smart."

"Yeah. I'm smart. I've read all the fairy tales and I know who *you* are. You're a witch!"

"Of course I'm a witch, and I will indeed bake you into a ginger-bread boy. I've baked lots of them; you'll be no different."

He tossed his head scornfully and grabbed for another cookie. "Just try it, lady. You don't know who you're fooling around with."

He had the cookie in his mouth and chewed up and swallowed before she could speak.

"*That* was Gary Wilson. He was the nicest boy I've ever baked."

"Wait a minute. If you're *that* witch, then why aren't you dead? I remember reading that you were thrown into your own oven by—"

"Oh, those two brats! Little good it did them. I'm a witch, you know. Witches like fire."

"I thought witches were burned at the stake."

"Oh yes, they were, once. But they always come back. Like a bad onion or a rotten cabbage." She chuckled a high-pitched cackle at her own humor. "The witches of fable live forever."

Timmy perched on the tall stool that stood beside the table. "So you came back."

"Yes. And now it's your turn. But before I toss you into my oven, I must know your name."

"Why should I tell you anything, witch?"

"Because you won't be able *not* to," the crone croaked as she clamped bony fingers over his arm and held him in a viselike grip. "Your *name*, boy!"

Timmy struggled to control his tongue, but some force compelled him to speak. "Uh . . . I'm . . . Timmy Block."

"Timmy Block." The old dame savored the name on her cracked lips. "Timmy Block? From Centerville?" Her black caterpillar eyebrows inched up. "Not the Timmy Block who tortures ants and squashes bugs and hung his mother's cat from the backyard tree, and plays funny little games with lizards? You're *that* Timmy?"

The boy, eyes cast downward, nodded assent.

Releasing her hold on him, the withered woman stepped back and gazed intensely at the boy. "Timmy Block . . ." Her thin shriveled lips snaked upward into a crooked smile. Her eyes glittered like beads of jet.

She nodded and grunted something under her breath and scuttered crab-like to her rocker and sat down. She began to rock, back and forth, back and forth, while her cat stretched and yawned upon the hearth.

Timmy watched her in amazement, and then an understanding slowly dawned. He grinned.

"Have a cookie, Timmy, and throw another log on the fire. It's going to be cold tonight."

The boy heaved an apple log onto the dwindling fire. Walking over to the table, he surveyed the cookies lying there, searching for just the right one.

He found it, an especially fat and chunky one just like Billy Perkins. He smiled. And bit its head off.

Coming Out of the Broom Closet

LAWRENCE SCHIMEL

I can't stand all these secrets," Robert had told him. "I feel you don't trust me. Hell, I feel I can't trust you. How do I know you're not having an affair behind my back? It certainly seems likely."

"It's not that," Eric promised.

Robert left him anyway.

"But how can I know? I can't live with these secrets anymore."

Now, everything reminded Eric of Robert. He was driving himself crazy with loneliness as he moped about the apartment they had shared these past seven months. Eric would suddenly notice something out of place, a gap in the bookshelf, his own battered old boombox where once Robert's fancy stereo had been, and the realization that Robert was gone would come crashing in on him once again. The fact that no one complained when he squeezed the toothpaste tube from the middle, complained and half-patiently, half-exasperatedly rolled the tube anew from the bottom each night. What had become Eric's favorite clothes were no longer in his closet, because they had never been his. It was all driving Eric absolutely berserk and there was only one solution he could think of that gave any hope for a second go at things. It was probably too late already to save their relationship, but Eric was determined to go through with it, as his only hope.

The time had come for him to come out—as a witch.

"You'd have thought it would be easier the second time," Eric confided to his reflection one morning, a week after he had begun to tell his friends, as he waited for the shower to warm up. "Coming out."

Gregg, who'd been Eric's best friend since sophomore year in college, had spewed strawberry milkshake from his nose when Eric told him. He apologized profusely, of course, when he saw that Eric was serious, but as he mopped up the spilled shake it only sent him into further paroxysms of laughter.

Eric sighed and stepped into the shower, lathering himself with soap. His friend Marilyn's reaction echoed in his mind: "I mean, everyone already knows you're a fairy, but aren't you taking this joke a little too far? But while we're on the subject, how much would you charge for a jar of Love Potion Number Nine? I wouldn't need all that much, just enough to get Jon Bon Jovi to fall madly in love with me. . . ."

It was no joke. Eric couldn't see why no one understood that. In his anxiety, worrying over his friends' reactions to his news, Eric nicked himself with the razor as he shaved his leg. Staring at the blood, he was reminded of how it had gone when he'd told his parents.

His parents had been alarmed when he'd called them up and said he had something to say to them, to the both of them. But they didn't treat him seriously once they knew. "At least it's not AIDS," was all his mother could say, repeating it over and over again, although whether to herself or to her husband or to Eric he was never sure.

Eric splashed water over the cut and finished shaving. Everyone had laughed at him. Eric wanted to cry. He tried to pretend it was just the shampoo in his eyes.

And to top it all off, Robert had already moved in with a short, Mexican bodybuilder he'd met at the Tunnel of Love. So much for salvaging that relationship, Eric thought wryly as he toweled himself off. Robert and he were supposed to still be friends, but Robert didn't have the time to be supportive of Eric's second "coming out," what with his new beau and all.

And I sure need all the support I can get, Eric told his reflection as he finished shaving the stubble from his chin. He powdered himself and pulled on nylons and a padded bra, followed by a black dress. Eric wished for the hundredth time that he and Robert were still together; it would make this all so much easier on him. He wondered if there weren't some love potion he could make, to get Robert back, but all the love potions he knew how to make were het. Perhaps a bit of experimentation . . . Switch the ingredients of . . . But Eric was afraid to do anything that might hurt Robert. He was still very much in love with him, for all that Robert had left him for another man. Or left him and found another man. Same difference. Robert had gotten over him already. Maybe Eric would turn the bodybuilder into a toad. . . .

"You're stalling," Eric said aloud. He regarded himself in the mirror, wondering whether to bother, and deciding he'd better. He opened his medicine cabinet and began pulling down makeup: rouge, mascara, lipstick, eyeshadow.

Much as he dreaded the thought of it, if he was going to do this right, just as he had to come out to his friends and family and tell them he was a witch, he had likewise to come out to his coven, and tell them he was a man. Eric only hoped he survived the experience.

Bat's Blood for Flavor

ADAM NISWANDER

The tiny black-clad old woman showed up at the Your Way Grocery Center one Wednesday in mid-August just past noon. Dwarfed by her shopping cart, she moved quietly up and down the aisles, peering out of small, black, birdlike eyes over her comically elongated nose—a nose tipped by a huge red and purple wart. Thereafter, she appeared every Wednesday at the same time, regular as clockwork.

She paid cash at the register, so no one had occasion to ask for ID or even her name. Her unfortunate disfigurement made the cashiers uncomfortable, so they never looked directly at her as she checked out, except furtive glances when she fumbled in her purse. Each time she shopped, they heard her say the same thing. "I wish this store was more sensitive to the needs of its special clientele."

When the old woman left, the employees watched, shaking their heads in disgust that such an unpleasant-looking person wandered freely out in public.

Robbie Ripple, the bagboy with the most experience—he had worked for Your Way for over six months—watched the old lady as she pushed her cart around the corner and down the alley to the loading dock. The boy jokingly commented to one of his co-workers, "That must be where the old witch parked her broom."

Gordon Donner—at twenty-eight, the youngest full-time manager in the chain's history—had just transferred in from the big city. Something of a martinet, he ruled his store with all the delicate subtlety of Benito Mussolini. Gordon heard Robbie's comment and grabbed him by the shoulder. Pushing the boy outside, he spoke in a loud voice. "That will be enough of that, Robert! You are not ever to refer to our customers in derogatory terms. What's gotten into you? The lady may be ugly as sin, but that doesn't make her a witch."

The boy lowered his head in shame, a deep red suffusing his face and neck. "I'm sorry, Mr. Donner. I was just jokin' around."

Gordon glared at the boy a moment longer before he said, "See that it doesn't happen again. Now go back in there and get to work."

The boy fled.

Gordon looked toward the alley, and saw the old woman standing there, watching him. He cleared his throat and returned inside. *Christ! I hope she didn't hear me,* he thought.

A week later, Donner stood by the seafood showcase in the rear of the store, directing arrangement of the clams, oyster, shrimp, and crab, when he felt a tap on his shoulder. Turning, he discovered the old lady.

"Are you the manager, young man?" she asked.

Gordon found himself compelled to stare at her nose. The wart stood out like a flashing psychedelic sign, raspberry red and neon purple. He could not wrench his gaze away. Mortified by his own behavior, he stammered, "Uh . . . uh . . . er . . . uh . . . yes, ma'am."

She seemed amused. "Could you special order some toad's feet for me, young man?"

Fascinated with her nose, he barely heard her words, then realized what she had asked. "Uh . . . what?"

She shook her head. "So rude," she muttered to herself. "I asked, young man, if you could special order toad's feet!"

Donner couldn't even organize his thinking enough to formulate a reply. He blinked at her, nervously, as her nose seemed to flash before his eyes.

"Were it not for the fact that this store carries ingredients necessary to my work, I would cease shopping here altogether," she snapped, then turned and stalked down one of the aisles. *Jesus!* thought Gordon. *She's crazy as well as ugly!*

Curiosity compelled him to follow her. He saw her enter the Gourmet Foods aisle and pause before a waist-high shelf. She selected several items, dropped them into her cart, then glared at him before heading up front to the registers.

Gordon waited until she was out of sight, then went to the shelf. Stacked neatly were small containers—boxes, jars, and cans. He bent to look at the labels. "What the hell!?!" he exclaimed.

The small box read DRIED BAT'S BLOOD.

The tiny jars contained a viscous yellow liquid with clouded orbs floating in them. The label read EYE OF NEWT.

The cans were red and white, like Campbell's soup, but they were not the old favorites. The brand was Toil & Trouble, and the flavors left him stupefied. He read aloud, "Frog's Tongue, Cream of Rat, Spider's Web, Roast Floaters . . . what the fuck?"

Donner looked up, expecting to see his employees grouped around, stifling their laughter. This had to be a joke!

He was the sole occupant of the aisle.

Angrily, he stalked up to the register, grabbed the PA mike, paging his head stockboy, Marvin Crump.

When Marvin arrived, he looked concerned. "Are you all right, Mr. Donner?"

"What do you mean by that?" demanded Gordon.

The young man spoke in a low tone. "You . . . uh . . . shrieked over the intercom, sir."

The manager was taken aback. "I what?"

"You shrieked, sir," replied the boy. "I thought you were dying."

Gordon looked around and saw that a small crowd of shoppers and almost half his staff were staring in his direction, heads together and whispering among themselves.

Self-consciously, he stood straighter and smoothed his clothing. He took Marvin by the shoulder and led him toward the Gourmet Foods section.

"I want to know the meaning of this, young man," he said in a fierce whisper. "What the hell is that stuff doing on my shelves?"

Marvin followed his sweeping gesture and peered at the area indicated. He looked back at his boss, puzzlement clearly distorting his features. "What stuff is that, sir?"

Gordon sputtered. "What stuff? *This* stuff!" He reached forward to grab the box of dried bat's blood and stopped. The macabre items were no longer there.

He looked right and left, trying to figure out where the shelf had gone.

The usual store stock sat on display.

Gordon grew faint.

"Do you feel okay, Mr. Donner? asked Marvin solicitously.

"Huh . . . what?" The manager had gone pale. "Uh . . . no, Marvin, I don't think I do. I'm going back to my office and lie down for a while. Call me if you need anything." With that, he wandered off down the aisle and turned left toward the Employees Only door.

Crump watched him out of sight, then shook his head silently.

During the next few days, everyone noticed the change in Mr. Donner. He no longer acted like a dictator. He seemed to have lost his confidence, speaking in a mumble, wandering the aisles as if looking for something.

The following Wednesday, Gordon watched through the wire-mesh security window of the Employees Only door until he saw the old woman enter the store. When she turned her back, he slipped out and followed her.

This time, when she turned up the Gourmet Foods aisle, he crept up behind her.

She spoke without so much as glancing in his direction. "The Bat's Blood really enhances flavor. Did you know that?"

"What are you saying?" he demanded, shouldering her aside and grabbing the box from her hand. DRIED BAT'S BLOOD.

It hadn't changed. Feelings of triumph raced through him.

He held it firmly and shouted at the top of his lungs. "M A R V I N!"

The stockboy came racing around the corner as if propelled by a sling. "Yes, Mr. Donner?"

Gordon smiled triumphantly and held the box aloft. "This is what I want to know about, young man. Just what are we doing with this junk in stock?"

The boy came up to him and Gordon thrust the box forcefully into his hands. Marvin looked at it, then back up at his boss, fear in his eyes. "What's wrong with imported liver pâté, sir?"

"What?" Donner snatched it back and stared at it in disbelief. "But it was Bat's Blood! This lady here saw it, didn't you . . . uh . . ."

The boy and he were alone.

"Where did she go?" the manager demanded.

"Who?" asked Marvin.

Donner glowered at the boy with such rage that Marvin actually cringed away. "THE WITCH! THE WART-NOSED WITCH, YOU IM-BECILE!"

The stockboy continued to back up. "I don't know who you're talking about, Mr. Donner." Then he turned and rushed out of sight.

"SHIT!" Gordon bellowed. He turned to the shelf. It contained the usual innocuous items. He rushed up the aisle, yelling, "STOP HER! DON'T LET HER OUT OF THE STORE!"

The customers and staff ran in panic as he waded into the crowd, shoving people aside, shouting, "WHERE IS SHE? DON'T LET HER ESCAPE!"

Robbie, Marvin, and several of the other boys had to tackle him. Pinning his arms to his side, they frog-marched him back to his office.

Gordon Donner lost his job and was admitted to the psychiatric hospital for observation. He kept muttering about witches buying bat's blood in his grocery store. The owners of the Your Way Grocery Center replaced him quickly with a local man.

The following Wednesday, the wart-nosed woman returned to do her shopping at the usual time. The new manager saw her in the Gourmet Foods section and approached her.

"Hi, Wanda. How's tricks?"

"What? Oh, fine, Asmodeus. How's the new job?"

"Great! Just great!" His face crinkled into a smile. "I never thought it'd happen, though. The mortals just don't like our kind intruding in their daily lives."

"Nonsense," replied the woman, black eyes twinkling. "They just need a little more bat's blood in their diet. It enhances the flavor re-markably, did you know?"

The new manager nodded. "Yes, I'm a longtime aficionado myself," he said, "and I have a lot of other swell ideas for changes around here."

"Porcupine Pasta?" asked Wanda.

"Oh, yes, of course," replied the man. "Plus stuffed ferret skulls, green snail jellies, pickled dog cookies, and, as we get closer to Hallow-een, maybe even poisoned apples."

"How wonderful," Wanda said laughing. She took his arm and they strolled down the aisle, chattering gaily. "I have a really good recipe for monkey-brain pie. . . ."

The Metropolitan Menace

GORDON LINZNER

Dim lights made the basement seem even more cavernous. A man in a three-piece suit removed a small sarcophagus lid. His two companions studied the contents, or rather, their lack.

"I ask you, Miss Slade, who'd steal a cat mummy?" he said.

The silver-haired woman fingered a five-sided charm on her neck-lace. "When did you say you found it missing, Mr. Peterson?"

"Two weeks ago."

"When was it last seen?"

"We had an inventory in May. We only found out this soon because one of our directors was concerned by the Egyptian government's re-quest that such remains be interred. Of course, I believe they were referring to human remains. . . ."

"She's not listening," said the burly man at Slade's side.

The shorter man frowned. "I see. Mr. MacElroy?"

"Kirby will do. She's considering things beyond your ken; mine, too, usually."

"Looks to me like she's just playing with her jewelry."

"That's when things get interesting. Tell me, Peterson, with all these relics down here, why does the Metropolitan Museum have such a dinky, almost forgettable Egyptian room?"

"Public interest in ancient Egypt dropped off sharply after the Tut exhibit. As assistant curator I try to get as much of this as possible into the public eye; some things don't generate enough interest. No one wants to look at a mummified cat."

"Someone did."

"How long does a job like this usually take, Kirby?"

"Two months," said Evelyn Slade, looking up.

Peterson blanched. "So long?"

Slade shook her head. "Your mummy. It's been gone two months and a week. And something else. This museum intrudes on Central Park. You must have vermin problems, Peterson."

"The rooms are sealed."

"You're evading the question. Do you get mice? Rats?"

"Once in a while. The situation's under control."

"How? Feline defenses?"

"Fe—? Oh. Yes, we have a cat."

"A female. And this mummy belonged to a tom."

"I'm not sure."

"I'm telling, not asking. Kirby, how's your tracking?"

MacElroy scowled. "A wee rusty."

"Can you find that cat? The female?"

The big man shrugged.

"Do it. Peterson, come with me. We're going to follow the path of your missing relic."

"Is that possible? I mean, two months . . ."

"I just said so. I'll be surprised if we don't meet Kirby at the end of our trail."

Slade led the way, pausing now and then to concentrate before choosing a new direction. A bewildered Peterson snapped up what scraps of information she offered between trances.

"Everything leaves traces," she told him. "Your own body constantly sheds skin, replacing itself every seven years. Actions and emotions can resonate for years, even decades. Too slight, usually, for most people to detect, though sufficiently powerful ones can be sensed. People call them ghosts."

"You're following what, then? Scraps of mummy wrappings?"

Slade grimaced. "Any decent forensic detective could do that.

There's more here. This look familiar?" She swung open an empty packing case, revealing a grayish-yellow lump.

"Our mummy?"

"The shell, anyway. Listen."

Peterson strained his ears. "I don't . . ."

"Shh."

He heard it now: a faint thrum, like a small generator running
down.

"This way," Slade said.

They traced the sound to an emaciated orange tabby lying on a
tarp behind a pedestal. Four tiny, very still kittens, with orange and
black markings, nestled against her belly.

"Melon," Peterson identified.

The cat looked up at him. Then her eyes glazed over. A sharp cat
urine odor filled the air.

"Must've been a complicated birth," Peterson said. "An hour earlier, we might have saved her. Or her kittens."

"Yes," said Slade, "but not from the rigors of birth. How old was
Melon?"

"Four, five years."

"She looks twenty, too old to bear a litter. Keep looking."

"For what?"

"The other kitten. Damn, Kirby should be here by now!"

"Any chance of an explanation, while we're waiting?"

"I hate explaining to clients," Slade complained. "They always
interrupt to tell me how impossible or insane it is. And there usually
isn't time."

"I'll be quiet."

Slade sighed. "Your mummy housed, for lack of a better term, a
soul, probably a wizard's. No, you promised! A kind of immortality can
be attained through mummification, which preserves body traces. This
wizard infused his essence into a cat to be buried with his pharoah and
eventually revive himself."

"All this you learned with your pentagram?"

"And experience. Focus means nothing if you can't read what you
pick up. You're taking this in very well. I'm impressed."

"I'm stunned. Why come back now?"

"Perhaps this was his first time near a female cat in heat."

"He impregnated Melon?"

"And, having thus transferred his 'soul,' abandoned the mummy. He was too weak to control her; he needed a new, unformed mind. He had to wait until she whelped."

A thunk came from the next aisle.

"Your associate?" asked Peterson.

Slade fingered her pendant. "Something's wrong."

They peered into the aisle. MacElroy's muscular frame leaned on a shelf, shoulders slumped, knees bent, eyes fixed on a coal-black kitten that could have fit in the palm of his hand.

"That looks almost old enough to wean," whispered Peterson.

"He could have been full grown. Luckily for us, siphoning life forces can be a wasteful process."

"What's happening to Kirby?"

"The same thing that happened to Melon and the rest of the litter. He's consolidating power by draining others."

"He?"

"Or she. The mummy was male, but . . ."

MacElroy's knees struck the cement floor.

"No more time." Slade stepped into the aisle.

The kitten's ears twitched. It turned to glare at Slade, who was focusing on it through her charm. The eyes glowed red, stronger than a normal cat's, fueled by some internal fire. MacElroy shook his head, then sank to the floor.

An electric current ran through the pentagram. Slade almost dropped it.

"Peterson," she gasped.

"Yes?" he said from hiding.

"Need ankh."

"I didn't quite get that."

"Egyptian cross. My focus isn't . . ." She stopped talking, concentrated on warding off the cat's mental attack.

"Sure," said Peterson. "There're dozens around here. Somewhere." His footsteps faded.

Long minutes passed. Slade and the kitten were locked in a standoff. Though hours old, the latter possessed energy from its mother and littermates, and who knew how much from MacElroy. It also seemed to sense Slade was bigger game.

The pentagram grew hot. Slade shifted it from hand to hand. The kitten used the charm against her, drawing on the power she tried to invoke on her own behalf. If she put it down, though, she'd have no protection; if she ran, MacElroy was doomed.

What was keeping Peterson?

Slade braced herself against a pillar. Those red eyes pulled at her. She locked her knees, resisted the urge to kneel, sit, surrender. Sweat soaked her peasant blouse, chilling her.

Suddenly, the eyes were gone.

"You okay, Evie?"

Slade blinked. In the shadows sat Kirby MacElroy, holding a fiercely leaping cloth bag at arm's length.

"That's what I like about you, Kirby. You know the value of brute force."

"I just scooped the critter up."

"That won't hold him long."

MacElroy twirled the bag. "The floor looks nice and hard."

"I'd rather you not do that, Kirby. That kitten's as much a victim as its kin. The being possessing it isn't wholly fixed, or it wouldn't be stealing lives to build up its strength."

A gash appeared in the bag's side.

"If you have a plan, Evie, you'd better start it fast."

"If Peterson gets back here with that ankh . . ."

Kirby scowled, felt in a pocket with his free hand, and tossed Slade a pendant. "I got this at the gift shop."

"Why didn't you tell me?"

"You didn't ask. It's only a replica."

"As long as it's culture-specific."

A paw widened the gash. Two red eyes glared at Slade.

"Here, kitty," she said, placing the ankh atop her pentagram and bringing her concentration to bear once more.

A yowl echoed in the cavernous basement.

"Miss Slade!" Peterson raced up. "Are you all right?"

"Naturally." Slade pulled at her damp blouse. Steam rose where the pentagram touched moist flesh.

He held out a small iron ankh. "It seemed to take forever to find this."

"You should have tried the gift shop," said MacElroy, stroking the purring kitten in his hand.

"Is he, it, I mean . . . ?"

"Perfectly harmless, now. For a cat. It'll be a couple of months before he replaces Melon as a mouser."

"I doubt anyone on staff has the patience to nurse an orphaned kitten. Especially one that's been possessed."

Slade shrugged. "Then I'll take him."

MacElroy frowned. "Evie, you hate pets."

"I dislike the concept, but I did save his furry butt. You know, Kirby, some clients are disappointed when they don't see a boiling cauldron on my desk, a black cat on the mantle, a flying broomstick by the window."

Peterson blushed.

Slade grinned. "What can it hurt to meet one of those expectations?"

In the Cards

MARTIN R. SODERSTROM

The Metro Toronto Convention Center was immense; hundreds of square feet that spent most of its time as dark, unoccupied open space. Then there were the other times: colorful and busy booths ate up what had been empty air accompanied by hucksters with as many styles of sales showmanship as horror movies had sequels. Most of the time the cap-toothed smiles rested atop dark blue suits, lost in a cloud of GQ-style cologne. Most of the time. Every now and then the different would take residence, trying desperately (though usually in vain) to show how sensible it was. This was one of those days.

The Psychic Fair had come to Toronto.

"How much longer, Jack?" A tinny female voice hissed out of the earphone plugged into Detective Jack Spartan's ear. "My hands are getting chapped from having my palm read so many times. By the way, if you see any tall dark strangers, tell them I'm over in the crystal ball exhibit."

Jack smiled as he self-consciously touched his ear and looked for a private place to respond to his partner's wit. He rounded a corner and found a small collection of empty chairs arranged before a television and

VCR on a rolling cart. The sign outside the entrance said the next show was at 3:15, more than half an hour away. Jack furtively glanced around and then slipped over the velvet ropes. He made his way into the mock theatre until he was positioned behind the cart, out of sight from passersby. He reached inside his jean jacket and withdrew a small microphone that was attached by a thin wire to a transceiver pack in his pocket.

"Funny, Connelly. Just keep looking for the cards," Jack said into the mike. His tone wasn't cross, but he knew he didn't sound like himself. And he knew if anyone would pick up on it, it would be Janna Connelly, his partner.

"You okay, Jack? I was just joking. I've swept the west end of the hall and no one's using any kind of Tarot cards over here. It was a good hunch but I think it's a bust."

"Yeah, I'm okay. Sorry. Case is getting to me. I think you're right about the hunch, though. I haven't seen any—" Jack lost his train of thought as he spotted a sign just outside of the small theatre:

WITCHCRAFT ON LEVEL 2

"Jack? Say again, Jack, I lost you."

"I'll be a son of a bitch," Jack said as he fingered the rabbit's foot keychain he'd picked up on one of the display tables.

"What?"

"Meet me out by the escalators, Janna."

"What for? What's up, Jack?"

"That Karma Corn you bought me for lunch is kicking in."

"Huh?"

"Just hurry up," Jack said before he slipped the microphone back into his jacket and headed out for the escalators.

It didn't look *Halloweenish* at all, which is what Jack had expected. Passing through the double doors into a considerably smaller area than on the first level, Jack nodded to the right and Janna headed off to look around one side of the hall while Jack went to the left. There were no salesmen or hucksters here, most of the booths and displays manned by a single person. Most of them were women, but there were a few men around. Some of the booths were packed with shelves of old brown and red books for sale; others were simply tables covered with a scattering of small colored vials and bottles, tiny handwritten price tags affixed to each of the containers. Jack logged all of this to his memory, but gave it little attention. What did catch his eye were the tables covered with cards. There were several such tables, most of which were manned by card dealers without subjects, just slapping cards down and mumbling to themselves before picking up the colorful display and shuffling out a new hand. It looked like some kind of solitaire tournament.

Jack knew he wasn't all that far off. His research over the past few months had revealed that the fifty-two-card deck that was used for bridge or gin rummy every Saturday night had evolved out of the Tarot deck. The presence of the cards excited Jack, but none of the decks he passed matched the cards he was looking for—the special earthy-colored tickets that followed the murders.

There had been five to date. Five brutal slayings with no rhyme or reason. The only clue he had was a small stack of five Tarot cards back in the evidence locker. But little of this case made much sense. Like why did the cards show up twenty-four hours after the murders? And how did the murderer get past the police to leave them? It was frustrating. Jack and Janna had been to just about every occult bookstore in the city. All of them had bizarre inventories, most including a few different styles of Tarot cards, but none that matched the ones from the crime scenes. The Psychic Fair was a shot in the dark. Jack was losing hope fast, knowing that the pattern of murders meant that another victim would be slain in the next eighteen hours if he didn't—

"Jack!" Janna's voice was clenched and excited. Jack touched his ear and turned to look at the expanse between him and Janna. The room was small enough that he could see all the way across it. Janna was in the corner by a steel barrel that served as a garbage can, with her back to the room. "I *found* them!"

Jack felt a charge shoot through his veins. Janna turned and held up three fingers and then pointed down one aisle. Jack tracked his eyes down the aisle until he was looking at the third booth in. An elderly woman seemingly buried in scarves and cloaks sat at a small covered card table. She too was playing what looked like solitaire. And even from this distance Jack recognized the cards. Forcing himself not to run, he quickly moved towards the aisle. But just as he reached the door, a crowd of about fifteen teenagers flowed through the entrance, blocking his way. He tried to push his way through, but the laughing teens just pushed back. He pulled the microphone from his jacket and was about to speak into it when one of the teens smacked into his arm. The force yanked the microphone's cord right out of the transceiver pack. With little other choice, Jack turned and headed the other way.

He swept down the far aisle and then pushed past a few milling couples in the rear aisle, receiving profanity and a few shoves for his efforts. Finally he turned into the far end of his target aisle. The old woman was sweeping her belongings into a huge cloth bag. When she was finished she looked up right at Jack. *Damn!* He started to run at the same time she did. But she was closer to the door. If she made it out of the room first and down one of the escalators, they'd lose her for sure. Jack was about to shout when Janna stepped out from behind a partition and grabbed the woman. They struggled for only a moment before the woman gave in to Janna's superior strength. Janna looked up and smiled at Jack as he briskly walked over to them.

They had her. The killings would stop.

After filling out the requisite piles of paperwork, Jack rushed downstairs and into the interrogation viewing room. Inside the darkened room was a table and several chairs. The only things on the table were a couple of well-used ashtrays, some notepads, and a cup of pencils. The room's walls had several closed curtains at various points. Jack sat in one of the chairs and pulled the drawstring to open one of the curtains. Behind it was what looked like a simple window opening into a brightly lit room with a table and some chairs in it. The old woman was seated at the table, smoking quietly and staring right at Jack. He knew she couldn't see him through the two-way mirror, but it still gave him the creeps.

Damn, Jack thought when he realized the paperwork had taken so long that he'd missed Janna doing the initial interrogation of the woman. He was about to get up and leave when the door opened and Janna came in. She closed the door behind her and sat down. For a few moments they just looked at the old woman through the glass and didn't say anything. Something was gnawing at Jack, but when he almost had it nailed down, Janna spoke.

"You first," she said.

Jack tore his gaze away from the window and opened the file he'd brought down with him. Scanning his notes, Jack told Janna everything he'd managed to find out based on the woman's identification. It was sketchy, at best. Her name was Maria Kuprek, sixty-three years old, and she lived in a house in Etobicoke. No priors, no outstanding debts—nothing. She was the kind of person who could fall off the face of the earth and no one would really notice.

"She's a witch," Janna said as Jack closed the file. "Or, at least, she thinks she is."

Surprisingly enough, Jack had no trouble accepting this, considering where they'd arrested her. But it wasn't just that. In the months that they'd spent going from occult store to occult store, Jack had become anesthetized to Toronto's underworld. It was a section of society that he hadn't even known existed, a community that flowed and thrived beneath everything else that appeared on the surface.

"I want to talk to her," Jack said as he stood up. Janna had relayed little information, saying she was uncooperative.

"What? I told you, Jack, there's no point. She only answers every third question and even then she seems to be in a world all her own. I think we need the psych team on this. She's whacked."

"Hmm. I still want to talk to her. Go get the cards we confiscated from her. I'll meet you in there," Jack said. He pushed past Janna to let her know he didn't want to discuss it.

"All right, all right. I don't know what you hope to accomplish, but you're the boss. I'll try and grab a uniform to come in while I'm at it."

"I hardly think that's necessary," Jack said sarcastically. SOP was to have a uniform present while questioning a suspect for the protection of the investigating officers. But this woman was no threat. At the speed she walked it had taken them twenty minutes to get to their car from the convention centre.

Jack left Janna and walked down the hall towards the door to the interrogation room while Janna headed out to the evidence lockers. It was then that Jack finally grasped what was bothering him—it was Maria's frailty. Two of the murder victims were men. Large men. But Jack wondered if she'd have even been able to overpower the women. He recalled the arrest and how Janna had easily overpowered Maria while she was trying to get away. As he opened the door to the interrogation room, Jack knew this woman was no murderer. She was connected to the murders in some way, but if she was a murderer, he was a ballet dancer.

Jack had been trying unsuccessfully to talk with Maria for fifteen minutes when Janna entered the room. She closed the door behind her, put the stack of cards down in front of Jack, and then sat in a chair by the door. Before Jack had a chance to pick the cards up the woman reached out and snagged them. It was odd. The cards seemed to melt into her hand like an ammo clip slipping easily into the grip of a gun—hidden and deadly. Jack reached into his pocket and withdrew the five cards he had in a plastic baggy: the ones he'd recovered from the murder scenes. Maria reached for them but Jack quickly pulled them out of her reach, still holding them in the air. Maria's gaze was frozen on them.

"We need your help, Mrs. Kuprek," Jack said in a quiet, soothing tone. "We know you're no murderer, but I think you know who is." Jack ignored Janna's sudden reaction to the statement. "What do these cards mean? Why have you been leaving them at the murder scenes? What are you trying to tell us?"

Maria slowly lifted her hand until it hung in the air before Jack, palm up. She was asking for the cards. The items had been scoured by the lab already so Jack didn't see the harm, especially if it got Maria to cooperate. He gave them to her. Maria slowly but methodically opened the bag and withdrew the cards, immediately placing them strategically on the table before her. She placed them so that they formed a cross: three cards in a vertical line with the other two cards placed on either side of the centre card. Jack looked down and saw that she had placed them for him, the faces staring right side up to him.

In the past few months, Jack had come to understand the Tarot and its various uses. This cross was a way of saying something. The centre card depicted the situation being conveyed. He looked down and saw that the centre card was *The Hanged Man.* Jack searched his memory and recalled that this card in that position meant an obstacle. Jack pondered this as he looked at the card above this one, which depicted a commentary on the situation: *The Empress.* This meant that the situation, the obstacle, concerned a woman. Next was the card below the centre card, which would tell the meaning of the situation: *The Moon.* Jack struggled with his memory and finally realized that the three cards meant a woman had caused an obstacle and was, in some way, a fraud.

"The murderer's a woman? Is that what you're saying?" Jack asked Maria, but she just quietly pointed down at the table. Jack realized she wasn't going to tell him straight out. He'd have to figure it out on his own. He looked back down at the table.

"This is crazy," Janna said. "You can't really be—" Jack shushed her and continued his reading.

The card to the left of the centre indicated a "for" force: *Justice.* That one was obvious. He then looked at the card to the right of the centre, which should indicate the force against: *The Devil*. The force against had some kind of power in the situation, Jack realized. Finally, Maria placed a sixth card up and to the right of the cross. This was the result card. It would tell what the result of all the other cards would be: *Strength*.

"A physical resistance?" Jack asked, looking up at Maria. She slowly closed her eyes and nodded. "Okay," Jack said, collecting his thoughts, surprisingly excited about the card-reading activity. "So a powerful woman is the murderer. And somehow she's causing an obstacle in the investigation . . . maybe through the use of her power. And the result once she's identified will be a physical struggle." Maria nodded.

Janna stood up. "This is nuts. Let's just put her in a cell and book her, Jack. Why are you bothering with this nonsense? Don't you see—" Jack ignored her.

"A woman with power. A politician? Or is it power in the business world? A powerful businesswoman?" Jack mused.

"Jack!" Janna shouted this time.

Jack looked up at Janna, at her exasperated and worried face. Then a realization came over him that sent a shiver up and down his spine. He slowly turned his head back to Maria, his eyes taking longer to leave Janna than his head.

"A policewoman?" Maria slowly nodded.

Jack looked back at Janna and just stared. Janna seemed to be trying to force a smile.

"Janna?"

Janna looked like she was about to say something, but then the phony smile drained from her face and Jack felt his heart leap as she fumbled at the clasp on her holster. Jack leapt out of his chair and was on her before she could get the weapon out. She was strong, solidifying Jack's conclusion even more, but Jack was stronger. After a brief struggle, Jack had her gun and held her against the wall with his shoulder as he cuffed her. Once she was under control, Jack looked back at Maria.

She'd scooped up the cards from the table. She shuffled the earthy deck and then began dealing new cards out on the table. Jack looked away. He'd seen enough in those cards.

Plague

Ernest Leong

Governor Yang quietly stroked his long whiskers as he sat in the Court of Justice, studying the three prisoners before him. All were on their knees, their foreheads touching the cold marble floor. Khan, Yang's Captain of the Guard, stood behind them, his hand on his sword. He tried to hide his concern for the Governor, whose face was mottled with red splotches—a sign of the advanced stage of the plague that wracked his body, and had already killed half the city's population.

"One of you," Yang spoke in smooth Cantonese, "is a warlock or witch who has brought plague to our city. You are also a very good liar, but you will be exposed in due time."

Yang coughed hard, and spat blood into a nearby spittoon. He straightened, smoothed the folds of his Imperial blue robe, and nodded at the turbaned man. Khan immediately grabbed the man's head, yanked it up. The Governor blinked away sweat dripping over his eyelashes as he studied the hard, cruel features of the Arab's face.

"Arab," Yang began, "we have watched with great admiration while your Khalif and his Islamic hordes sweep east, ever closer to the gates of our glorious Empire. For the moment, our Emperor has chosen not to mobilize against you."

"Your Emperor is very wise," the Arab sneered.

"Silence, dog!" Khan snapped, striking him across the face with the back of his hand. "You will not speak of our Emperor that way."

"Then kill me!" he retorted. "At least I die knowing I have helped our glorious cause. That's more than can be said for you, Governor."

Khan raised his hand again, but Yang shook his head.

"Chinese and Arab have profited in the past from trading, but perhaps your leader desires more?"

The Arab raised his head, glaring at Yang.

"The Khalif needs no cheap sorcerer's tricks to get what he wants."

Yang smiled grimly, as he nodded at the next prisoner. Khan kicked the second one straight. It was Mrs. Po, an old hag bent with age, and whose face had wrinkles too numerous to count.

"And you, Mrs. Po," the Governor said, as he opened a scroll he had taken from his sleeve. "It has been well documented by the district magistrate how you have sworn revenge against our divine Emperor. And since you are a master of black magic, who is better equipped to bring plague and pestilence?"

"It was not I, Lord," she answered, in a soft, frightened tone. "My vendetta is against the Emperor only, whose verdict took my only son from me in the foulest way."

Yang said nothing for a moment, as he lit two incense sticks lying on the heavy wooden table.

"Your son was found guilty of raping and murdering three young girls. He confessed his guilt immediately, without torture. The sentence that he be drawn and quartered was just, and no fouler than the acts he himself committed."

A long wail escaped from the woman's lips, that made even Khan's hair stand on end. She kowtowed, knocking her head on the floor with each bow.

"I swear on the soul of my long-suffering son, it was not I, Lord!"

"Enough!" the Governor snapped, in a rare display of temper. "Show me the last prisoner!"

Khan poked the last man with the butt of his sword. A soft, corpulent man in rich silk robes looked up, terror-stricken, at Yang. His breath was short, raspy.

"Merchant Wu, though it has never been proven, it is strongly suspected that you have profited in the past by trading with foreign barbarians from the West, though this is strictly forbidden, and punishable by death. Could it be that, for a price, you now deal in death for an as-yet-unknown enemy?"

"No, Lord, no!" Wu cried out, his fat stomach shaking like jelly. "The Emperor has always been kind and generous! I would never be disloyal! Never!"

Yang studied each prisoner carefully, as he fought to keep his teeth from chattering. He pulled his robe closer around him.

"We shall see," he finally muttered.

Yang reached under the folds of his robe, took out a blue pouch. His breathing was hoarse, but still controlled.

"The problem here is not who hates the Emperor most, but who is best equipped to conceal his or her true self. For it is clear no mortal creature could inflict this much death this quickly."

While Yang opened his pouch, Khan quietly drew his sword, watching the Governor for the signal to strike. The Governor produced a trigram (an eight-sided mirror) from the pouch. It gleamed brightly in the light, making the prisoners, and even Khan, wince and turn away.

"A trigram reveals nothing!" the old woman cried out.

"By itself, no," Yang replied, "but with the smoke from these incense sticks, the outline of the immortal will be shown in this mirror."

The prisoners kneeled, breathless, oblivious to the pain in their joints, as they watched the fragrant smoke twitch and crawl in the air current toward them. The Governor also seemed to forget his own illness, as he intently studied the trigram. Finally, he smiled, looked slowly up, and pointed.

"You."

Khan's blade slashed cleanly through the Arab's neck, killing him instantly, as the turbaned head rolled to the balcony. The others stared in a mixture of horror and relief.

Wu's lips convulsed as he fought to get the words out.

"Wh—what about me?"

Yang turned to his faithful captain.

"See him safely out of the palace. And have a messenger ride to the Capital with this proclamation." Yang held out a scroll. "The danger is gone."

"Yes, lord! I shall go myself!" Khan bowed, as he herded Wu out, shutting the great hall doors behind him.

When he was sure he was alone, the Governor descended from the dais, stood over the corpse. The sweat, chills, even the red splotches magically disappeared as he stared, mesmerized at the blood streaming from the dead Arab. An animal growl escaped his lips. He fell to the ground, and began to lick the blood. As the smoke from the incense sticks flowed over him, his body slowly transformed. It became longer, with a scaly red tail. Wings sprouted from the creature's back, and its dark brown eyes were now a bright jade-green.

"Now now, little one," came the voice of Mrs. Po from the shadows, "we must try and control ourselves."

The old witch cackled as she emerged from behind a pillar. She hobbled over to the creature, and scratched behind its ear.

"You did very well," she whispered. "The Captain himself will deliver the message, and with it, sow the seeds of a new plague in the Capital. No one kills a Po with impunity!"

The creature growled softly and rubbed its lizard head against its master's lap.

Under Control

DANIELLE D'ATTILIO

Nothing worse than a bored witch, I always say. I know; I live with one. Don't believe there's real witches that cast spells? Well, I got one sitting in the middle of the kitchen floor right now, doing something no normal wife should be doing, and one dead neighbor lying out in his backyard. I can see him from here—most of him anyways. Not his feet, though, 'cause they're hidden behind the porch. Been there most of a week now. I can see a small cloud of flies hovering over his body. But the crows won't peck at him. No siree. They swoop in and get a sense of what done him in and swoop right off, they do. My wife did it to him. Cast a spell that killed him, she did. No particular reason. Bob Waterman ain't done nothing to her. She just done it for fun. Like I said: Ain't nothing worse than a bored witch.

I seen her looking funny at Gretta McCutchen down at Symm's store the other day and knew something was gonna be up. She was eyeing Gretta and her big belly—she's about to drop her second child, she is. Big as a house. I got a feeling that what Marg's dishing up in the kitchen right now is for Gretta, and it ain't no apple pie. Been out in the woods collecting all kindsa plants 'n' roots 'n' stuff this mornin'. I don't know much about it—it ain't *my* sorta thing. But what's simmering in that pot smells mighty peculiar.

Gretta, she don't know about my wife. Not many folks do—and those who do dare not speak of her. Sheriff Potts knows, but he steers clear of our place. Can't say as I blame him. Marguerite—that's my wife —done in his depity last year. Potts come out to our place to question her about it, then starts accusing her of this 'n' that. But Marg wasn't nervous in the least. She just pointed her finger at Sheriff Potts, and

374

suddenly he gets a pain in his groin and drops to his knees. They held each other's eyes for a few moments—I was standing right there—and something passed between them. Him holding his balls and her squinting her eyes 'n' snickerin like she does. After he fled the yard, Marg just laughed and laughed. She ain't crazy though, she's just plain mean. Enjoys it, she does.

The undertaker's hack just left Bob Waterman's place. Suz—that's his wife—finally got back from Greensboro, where she'd been tending her sick mama. We didn't see her get back, but she must've been the one who called. I know that Judd Trader passed by Bob's place a few days ago, but kept on going. Same with Stu Farley. No way they could've missed Bob lying out there as dead as cordwood. They know about Marg, and have the good sense to keep their traps shut. Anyway, Ned Blackman rolled up in his beat-up black hearse that's been around since the Korean War, rolled up and took one look at Bob and shook his head. Then he looks right across the lane at our porch, where Marg and I were sitting. Marg went to raise her finger, but I put my hand on it and she put it back on her lap. Reluctant-like, I might add. I felt it twitching under my hand. Sometimes I think that that thing has a mind of its own. I know better, though. Marg does like to have her fun and gets a bit antsy when she's denied it.

"Not now," I says to her. "It'd be too much of a coincidence doin' Ned right there along with Bob. Sheriff Potts'd be sniffing around here again, and I don't think he'd come alone."

"Let 'em all come," she says, but kept her finger still. We rocked and watched till Ned pulled away. Marg just leaned back in her cane rocker and let the sun shine on her face. Beautiful, she is. Long hair the color of cornsilk. Bottle-green eyes and red, full lips. Her body's got all the right curves. Looks real fine in those blue jeans she always wears. Creamy soft skin, too. Draws appreciative glances.

She's one hundred 'n' seventy-four years old.

We never stay in one place for any stretch of time.

After a while she up 'n' said that she was off to visit with Gretta McCutchen. Don't know what she's got in store for her, but she strapped a bundle to the satchel of her bike and peddled off down the road, the bike kicking up a bit of dust in her wake. I just kept rocking.

* * *

Gretta McCutchen had her baby the night before last—I heard the news down at Symm's yesterday. Something went wrong. REALLY wrong. Everybody was talking in hushed tones 'n' all, but I heard that it was born with a full set of teeth. Sharp ones at that. Gretta didn't know till she took it to her breast . . . and the baby bit her nipple clean off. Wonder what was in the pie that Marg gave to her!

Folks are starting to talk, now. I was in the fabric store today, behind some big rolls of denim. Heard a few of the women mentioning Marg and Gretta in the same breath. Don't know how they put the two together. Their mouths snapped shut when I came out from behind. Doris Horton went white as a sheet when she saw me and fumbled while cutting me a swatch of that denim fabric. Just about clipped her finger off. Guess it's about time to be movin' on. I swear that the next place we get to will be the last. Real tired of moving, I am. But we won't be going anywhere just yet, not until the corn's come on good enough.

Suzy Waterman ain't come outta her house since they hauled Bob away, but we seen her face in the window, staring across at us. I put my own face close to our window and stuck my tongue out at her. I didn't hear it, but I think she screamed.

Marg is out collecting more roots. Nothing else to do, she said, but I saw that twinkle in her eye before she left and knew she was scheming again. I got a hunch that she's got a surprise in store for Suz. Think I'll have a talk with her when she comes back; too many tongues wagging about us right now. I could follow her out into the woods, but I got my own project that I'm working on.

I look as old as I am—sixty-two. Never cared to take those potions that keep Marg so young. Never quite trusted her not to put something in it . . . although in my heart I know that she'd never dare do that. Not to me. And you're probably wondering why I ain't scared to just up and leave her. She *is* a mean one—meaner 'n her mama was. But she ain't mean to me.

Too late to do anything about Suzy Waterman. Marg came in just now, smiling fit to split and muttering something about nosy neighbor's noses. There's a small lump in the pocket of her jeans. Guess we'll have to get going sooner than I'd hoped.

Time to go out and check the corn.

*   *   *

Marg noticed a few wrinkles on her face. She's whipping up a batch of that fountain of youth again. I suggested that maybe cutting her hair would give her a little lift, that it's getting a little scraggly lookin', which ain't exactly the truth. She let me trim it while the concoction bubbled on the stove. Hope no one goes over to visit Suzy Waterman just yet.

I do love her, but she's gettin' outta control just like she did in Anniston, Alabama, back in '52. They blazed the house and chased us through the woods until we got far enough ahead for Marg to stop and do something about it. Didn't mind all those men dying, but it sure was a waste of good hunting dogs. It's gonna happen again, I just know it. But Marg, she don't care. "Let 'em come," is what she said. Sounds like she's kinda lookin' forward to it. Not me. I put my foot down and she raised her finger at me, but then thought better of it . . . as she damn well should.

Time to skedaddle. No one's shown up at the Watermans', but someone will be looking in on her soon. I'm packin' up and gettin' out. This'll be the last time.

The corn came on enough to collect some silk, and I'm done sewing them tiny blue-jeans, done with my project. Thank goodness Marg let me cut her hair. Even snuck a few jars of that fountain of youth potion when she wasn't looking; they'll be hunting for a man in his sixties. Besides, I'm getting tired of being old. No sense in being old when you don't have to be. Gonna start a new life. Gonna work a little magic of my own.

You see, I've made a little Marguerite doll.

I'm tired of moving around.

Dressed to Live

C. BRUCE HUNTER

Nicola followed the slave girl's directions to the letter. Through the cane field to the edge of the jungle. Then down the old road. Past the ruins of the Spanish mission. And finally along an overgrown path that led to the witch's house.

She held her lantern low to keep from showing a light. In twelve years of living in the islands, she had learned most of their dangers, and she was determined not to let anything stop her now. This might be her last chance to escape, and she was damned if she'd let it slip away from her.

She soon lost all track of time, but that didn't matter. From the moment she entered the jungle, she had been guided by a small yellow light winking at her through the foliage. She knew it was an illusion. The growth was too thick for any light to penetrate it. But she had long ago stopped trying to make the happenings of this place conform to her own logic.

At first, she had taken the slave girl's story on faith. Now she could see the proof of it. The light came from the witch's house, and that was all that mattered. She would follow it to hell if she had to.

As she fought her way along the path, branches and vines seemed to reach out for her. But she would not be driven back. She pushed them aside, gathered her cape more closely around her, and followed the light.

It seemed brighter now, more constant. She pushed through one last veil of vines and found herself in a small clearing. In its center stood the witch's house.

It was more shack than house, a simple frame clad with unpainted boards that had weathered to a dark gray, and roofed with a yellowing thatch of palm leaves. The place looked common enough. All that marked it from the usual slaves' quarters were the charms on the porch. They hung from large nails—feathers and skins and bags of things Nicola didn't want to know about. And all arranged in patterns only the islands' natives would recognize.

She approached cautiously. The slave girl had told her it was the only house in the jungle, but she would take no chances tonight. She held the lantern up to look for markings on the door.

Just then it opened and Nicola came face-to-face with the witch.

She almost dropped the lantern, the old woman had startled her so. The twisted body and withered face were a vision from hell. Framed by flickering candlelight from behind, the witch looked very ancient and more than a little evil.

It took Nicola several seconds to regain her composure. She swallowed hard and forced herself to speak.

"One of the girls told me . . ." she said, pulling a wadded scarf from her pocket and half holding it out to the witch. "I need your help. I just can't go on. . . ." Her words choked into sobs.

"It don't matter, child," the old woman smiled. She took the scarf from Nicola's hand and retreated into the house.

Nicola started to follow, but something stopped her. She stepped hesitantly forward and stood just inside the door while the witch limped to a small table lit by a circle of black candles.

The old woman strained to lower herself into the room's only chair, then placed the scarf on the table and carefully unfolded it. She laughed when she saw the fist-sized clump of freshly cut hair.

"I suppose that's more than you need," Nicola said, nervously rubbing one hand against her cape.

The old woman's laugh faded to an enigmatic smile. She reached deep into her apron pocket and pulled out something wrapped in a black cloth. She placed it on the table and unfolded the cloth to reveal a very small, crudely carved wooden doll.

"It jus' takes a little," she muttered as she teased a few strands of hair from the clump. Squinting through smudged glasses, she fastened the lock of hair to the doll's head with a dab of glue from a small pot on the table.

"This binds his soul to the doll," she explained. "It be how the spell work."

"Somehow I thought it would be more involved . . . more complicated." Nicola twisted her hands nervously around the handle of the lantern she still held in front of her.

The old woman looked up from her work and offered another smile. "The doll's power is simpler than mos' peoples think. It be nothin' more than conjurin' up the right power to do your biddin'. You jus' needs to know how to do it." Reaching into her pocket, she pulled out a piece of red twine and showed it to Nicola. "Pay attention, child. You tighten this around the doll's neck. That does the trick."

She pressed the hair against the doll's head with finger and thumb and held it in place until the glue was dry enough to keep it from falling away. Then she gently laid the wooden figure and the twine on the black cloth and slid them to the middle of the circle of candles.

"Remember," she cautioned, "you mus' tell him about the doll. Else it won't do its work." With those words she leaned back in her chair and busied herself brushing away scraps of hair that had fallen into her lap.

Nicola fidgeted with the lantern for some time, not knowing what she was supposed to do. Then she remembered that she had to pay the witch. Digging into the pocket of her tattered cape—the pocket that didn't have a hole in its bottom—she retrieved a handful of crumpled banknotes and offered them to the witch.

The old woman didn't take the money. Instead, she tapped the table with one bony finger. Nicola dropped the money on the table, just outside the circle of candles, then took a half step back.

The witch picked up the doll and blew on it to see if the hair would hold. When it did, she smiled broadly, wrapped the doll in its cloth, and handed it to Nicola, who took it in a trembling hand and nervously slipped it into her pocket.

"How long will it take?" she asked.

"Not long," the witch said. "The magic works quick. An' don't worry, child. He won't suffer none."

Nicola barely heard the words. She had already turned up the wick of her lantern. Then she buttoned the collar of her cape in spite of the night's humid heat. Awkwardly making her way to the door, she slipped out of the cottage and rushed into the night. This was a horrid business, and she wanted to finish it quickly.

The sound of hacking coughs from the bedroom sent a shudder up Nicola's spine and through her shoulders. She had never gotten used to that sound, and tonight it seemed to dig into her soul.

She had stalled as long as she could. She had taken time to blow out the lantern, to place it securely on the shelf, to take her cape off and throw it across a kitchen chair. But her husband was still in the bedroom, and sooner or later she would have to face him.

Everyone has a breaking point, she told herself. It wasn't fair. She had been a good wife; most would have given up long ago. Still, she could barely face the task that lay before her.

Taking several deep breaths to steady her nerves, Nicola stepped up to the door and pushed it with the tips of her fingers. It creaked open, slowly, while a sickly sweet odor reached out for her. It clung to her skin as she entered the room.

As the door opened farther, a shaft of light from the kitchen knifed its way to the bed. There it illuminated the withered body lying on blood-stained sheets.

"Is that you, Nicola?" he rasped.

Nicola struck a match and lit the candle on the table, but it did no good. Geoffrey's eyes had weakened with the rest of his body until he could make out only the barest shapes of things. He lay on the bed looking at her, or at least in her direction; she was sure he could no longer see even the short distance across the room.

"Yes, Geoffrey, it's me," she whispered. Her words were scarcely more audible than the pathetic wheeze that answered them.

When he held out his hand to her, she inched farther away. "I'm sorry, Geoffrey," she said, speaking more loudly, because it was important for him to hear what she had to say. "I can't go on like this."

His lips moved slightly, but no sound escaped them.

"I've got my own life to live," she said as tears formed in the corners of her eyes. "I just can't go on. There's no money left, and all I can earn goes to the doctor. . . ."

Her words trailed off. There was no point in saying all this. If Geoffrey could still understand anything, he knew how much of a burden he had become. It would be kinder to do it quickly. Besides, she couldn't imagine that he really wanted to go on living. It wasn't fair to either of them.

"I've bought a doll from the witch." Nicola forced the words out rapidly. "She promised me that it would be painless. Then we'll both be free."

Geoffrey's eyes widened, but he didn't seem to understand what he was hearing.

"A *voodoo* doll," Nicola whimpered. "She showed me how to tighten a string around its neck. I can't bring myself to do it any other way. She *promised* you wouldn't feel pain."

Geoffrey tried feebly to push himself up. His eyes were wild and his body trembled.

"You know I don't want this," she pleaded, "but I just can't go on any longer. It's more than I can bear."

She knew he understood now; she knew his soundless words were a curse for what she was about to do. But there was no other choice. She turned on her heel and ran back into the kitchen.

Geoffrey's exertion changed to another bout of hacking and wheezing. The sound dug into Nicola's head until she thought she would scream. She covered her ears and took a deep breath. It would be only a few more minutes, she told herself. And it was really the kindest way for both of them.

Grabbing her cape from the chair, she reached into the pocket. *Only a few more minutes.* She pushed her hand deeper into the pocket. The doll wasn't there. It must be in the other pocket. She turned the cape around and fumbled with the folds of threadbare cloth. But even before she put her hand in the pocket, she could tell by its empty feel that the doll wasn't there either.

She tried to recall which pocket she had put it in. When she remembered she slumped into the chair and shook her head violently. It had been the one with the unmended hole in its bottom.

Nicola burst into tears. They came uncontrollably, and only when they had washed away most of her tension did her head clear enough for her to see that all was not lost.

It was only a few miles from the witch's cottage to hers. The doll had to be on the road somewhere between the two.

She jumped up from the chair and took the lantern from the shelf. After breaking three matches in her hurry, she got one to strike, lit the wick, and rushed out into the early morning darkness to search for the doll.

The sun was high above the horizon when she finally gave up hope. Hours of retracing her path back and forth along the road had been fruitless. The doll was not to be found.

Later, when she could think clearly again, she might try again. But for now she was too exhausted to try anymore. Her body ached for sleep, she could barely open her eyes, and her legs were so sore she could barely move them.

The empty lantern dragged on the ground as she trudged the last few yards to the cottage. Maybe Geoffrey would be asleep. At least then she wouldn't have to confront him. She needed time to work things out, and her emotions were too drained to deal with it now.

The front door was partly open. She went in, pushing it aside with her shoulder, and let the lantern slip from her hand.

She inched toward the cot that stood against the far wall, her feet sliding heavily across the gritty floorboards. She was almost there when Geoffrey emerged from the bedroom.

She stopped and stared; her tired mind saw him as an apparition floating across the room, but she was too exhausted to react. Geoffrey was washed and dressed for the first time in more than a year. He was shaky, leaning heavily on his cane. But he was standing. And even his thick, gray-black scraggle couldn't conceal the trace of color that had come back to his face.

Nicola found herself on the cot, although she didn't remember sitting down. Too tired to fight through the haze that muddled her thoughts, all she could do was watch her husband hobble about the room.

"You should have waited," he said as he took a piece of paper from the kitchen table and waved it at her. "I know what you said last night . . . or was it the night before?" He thought for a moment, then dismissed the question with a wave of his hand.

Nicola had forgotten her need for sleep. She sat on the cot and listened passively to the voice she had loved long ago, before it had faded to a sickly whisper.

"I was stronger this morning," Geoffrey was saying, "strong enough to get out of bed. And less than an hour ago a solicitor came with this letter.

"It's an *inheritance*," he leaned forward to punctuate that last word, "from an uncle I'd almost forgotten. He went to sea before I was born, and now he's left me his fortune."

Geoffrey continued, but Nicola didn't hear the words. Her mind focused on the paper in his hand and slowly—very slowly—she came to understand what it meant.

"Then we don't have to live like this any more," she said, in a little girl's voice.

"We?" It was only one word but it said more than enough. "Do you think I could live with a woman who was going to kill her sick, helpless husband? You really should have waited. If you'd hidden your true colors for another day, I'd never have known."

Geoffrey stopped talking when he heard a carriage approaching. Its wheels squeaked to a halt just outside and he looked through the window to see who it was.

"That's the solicitor come back with a carriage for me." He took his wrinkled, soiled cape from a nail on the wall and started to drape it over his shoulders. Then, as an afterthought, he looked at it and threw it on the floor.

"I can afford a better one now," he mused as he disappeared through the cottage door.

"What about me?" Nicola asked, her voice still that of a little girl.

"You can stay here if you like," he called from outside, "if you can keep up the taxes. It doesn't matter to me."

A few seconds later, with a rattle of baggage and hardware, the carriage jerked into motion and rolled away.

Geoffrey laughed as he felt the wind in his face, and when the carriage passed the baker's cottage down the road, he waved at the baker's wife, who was bringing a tray of loaves from the oven. She returned the favor with a smiling nod as she carried the tray into the house.

"And what's that?" she asked as she squeezed past her daughter, who was playing in the doorway.

The little girl looked up from the nest of toys she had arranged on the floor and smiled, "It's a new doll."

"Where did it come from?"

"I found him in the ditch this morning. He was all dirty, but I cleaned him up." The girl strained with a pair of scissors to cut a piece of black cloth to the pattern she had drawn on it. "And I'm making him a fine coat so he can be a gentleman and live happily ever after."

384

Common Grounds

P. D. Cacek

eena felt her fingers tighten around the stone pestle as she watched the trailing wisps of golden hair disappear around the "Illuminari" aisle.

It was her.

Had to be her.

The Bitch.

From hell.

Dropping the pestle into the dried mudwort she was supposed to be grinding, Geena dusted her hands off on the black New Age/Ancient Ways shop apron and sidestepped around the narrow preparation table and walked toward the back of the store.

Stopping only long enough at the candle aisle to straighten the TWO FOR ONE SALE sign.

To make sure the golden woman in flowing white gauze was the Bitch in question.

She was.

Ken's new girlfriend.

Geena had seen her waiting across the street—long tanned legs crossed at the ankles, breasts *almost* covered by the scoop neck running shirt—leaning against the front bumper of Ken's Z-car (*impatient*) while he tucked the last of his stuff into the duffel bag they'd found (*together*) at a flea market and tried (*again*) to explain that it wasn't Geena's fault and that he still hoped they could be friends and that he was sure she'd find someone else.

Thanks for the five years.

See ya, kid.

Geena's stomach had twisted into a knot by the time she'd gotten to the back wall and found herself staring blankly at the shelves of I'M THE INCARNATION OF YOUR WORST NIGHTMARE, W.P.N—WICCA POWER NOW, DON'T GET FAMILIAR WITH MY CAT, and I'M A WITCH, WHAT'S YOUR EXCUSE? T-shirts.

"Oh, excuse me, miss," a voice said, "do you have this in extra large?"

Geena blinked and turned her head, found the source of the question—a beach ball of a woman in African-print caftan and matching turban holding up a I ♥ THE GREAT HORNED ONE tee.

"B-bottom row," Geena said automatically. "Right next to the Salem Sucks headbands."

The woman smiled her thanks and Geena turned. Right into her ex-lover's new love. Bright green eyes sparkled above the pert little nose and gleaming white smile.

"I was wondering if you could help me?"

Geena swallowed hard and wiped her hands against the front of her apron again even though they were as dry as bone. The Bitch's hands, long tanned fingers ending in pussy-pink nails, were wrapped around two candles (*cheap cow was taking advantage of the two-fer sale*). Both black.

Figures.

Ken always did like living dangerously.

Except with her.

Geena cleared her throat of the lump that had somehow formed there and forced herself to smile. *Faking it,* as Ken used to say. Their last three months together.

"Of course," she said. "What can I do for you?"

The Bitch took a deep breath—just large enough to let everyone in the general vicinity know that her firm and gravity-defying breasts were real. And not Memorex.

Geena folded her arms over her own twin B-cup wonders and fought the urge to see if the spun gold tresses cascading around the heart-shaped face were just as real.

"I'm planning an intimate little dinner tonight and I need . . ." The Bitch giggled lightly. *And Ken thought THAT was real?* "Oh, this is so silly."

"No, please," Geena said, letting her arms drop from the stranglehold. "You'd be surprised at some of the questions I'm asked."

Both the giggle and smile disappeared as the Bitch glanced toward the fat woman still browsing through the Satan-Slogan™ shirts.

"I'm sure," the Bitch mumbled, then—smile and sparkle back in place—flipped a thick curl back over her shoulder and said, "I'm planning an intimate dinner, tonight . . . just my boyfriend, and I thought

. . . oh God, this really is ridiculous . . . but a friend of mine said she once got a . . . potion or something that really turned her man on and . . ."

She giggled again. Tossed her head. Inhaled.

Geena tried not to get physically ill.

"Was it a premixed potion?" Geena asked instead, motioning the Bitch toward her workstation. "Or was it a special blend?"

The bright green eyes blinked—once, twice—as dazzling white teeth raked the full bottom lip (*painted to match the nails, naturally*).

"I'm. Not. Sure," the Bitch said.

"No problem," Geena said, turning and punching up *Potions/Love* on the workstation's computer terminal. "What's your friend's name?"

"Um . . . Elizabeth Jarvis . . . and I think she was in about a month ago." More giggles followed by a lengthy sigh. "And if she wasn't lying about Stan's reaction . . . Yes, I *definitely* want some of that."

Geena ignored the last statement and concentrated only on the name, finding it in the middle of the sixth page. Jarvis, Elizabeth—Love Potion #134-B/liquid prepac/aisle 14/section 3/serial number . . .

Standard stuff that came from a distillery up in Maine. Sort of a generic, non-habit-forming Spanish Fly. The same kind of thing you could get from a bottle of Tequila at a quarter of the price.

Geena scrolled down another three pages before turning around. Frowning. Shaking her head.

"Ummm," she exhaled slowly, "I'm afraid your friend's potion was one of our special orders. It requires all fresh ingredients and I'm terribly backlogged today—"

"Oh, dear," the Bitch moaned, pouting, heartbroken, bright green eyes inching their way up Geena's face, "and I so *wanted* it tonight. Just for fun . . . you know."

Geena knew, but let the power play go on another few seconds before collapsing under the weight of the beautiful blonde stare.

"Well-l-l-l-l," she sighed. "Okay. *When* do you plan on serving . . . dinner?"

"Around ten," the Bitch said. "I've always preferred dining in the true Continental style. Much more civilized, don't you think?"

Depends whether I feel like a McFish sandwich or Chicken McNuggets that late at night, Geena thought as she flipped through the Rolodex of botanicals next to her mortar, pausing occasionally to either nod, "um-huh," or scribble down the name of an herb.

"Okay . . . and I'm only doing this because your friend's such a good customer. . . ."

Geena stood on tiptoe and glanced quickly toward the single cash register at the front of the store. Mr. Collins, her boss, was handing the fat, beturbaned woman a red-on-black New Age/Ancient Ways paper bag and mouthing his thanks and please come agains.

"Okay," Geena said again, lowering her voice, "I'm not supposed to do this, but . . ." Another quick glance—for effect. "The store closes at eight; if you can be back at nine I'll . . . I'll make sure you get what you need."

A look of divine presumption washed over the Bitch's face.

"Why *thank* you. How *nice* of you. Nine will be perfect, but . . ." Blink. Wink. Giggle. "Of course, I really don't *believe* in any of this. I just think it would be fun to, you know, see if it works."

Geena blinked, winked, and giggled back. "I know what you mean. I just work here."

Twitter, twitter.

"Oh, now about these candles . . ." the Bitch asked, "do you think black or shall I go with the red?"

Geena folded her hands over the list of herbs, in case Ken's new lover could read upside down and translate the combination back into the ingredients for spaghetti sauce, and smiled.

"Oh, I think the black," she said. "Can't ever go wrong with good old basic *black*."

The Bitch was twenty minutes early.

But Geena was ready for her.

"Oooo," the Bitch said as Geena closed and relocked the door behind her, "I just *love* that outfit. . . . What do you call it? A dashiki?"

Geena grunted something she hoped would pass for an answer and led the way to the tiny classroom/lecture hall in the converted store room. Incense of white sage and powdered vervain washed over them as Geena opened the door and motioned the Bitch inside.

Alternating white/black/red candles glimmered at the points and junctures of the pentagram Geena had chalked onto the bare wooden floor. A bronze knife, its handle wrapped in 100 percent, artificial human skin, lay in a circle of powdered bone and alexandrite between the outstretched legs of the star.

"Impressive," the Bitch said, taking the only chair at the star's head. "This *is* part of the total cost, isn't it? Lizzy didn't say anything about a floor show."

"Lizzy was sworn to secrecy," Geena said, stepping into the circle with the knife. "But don't worry, this part's free."

"Oh." Long, jean-clad legs crossed one over the other and breasts swelled beneath a top so sheer Geena could see every detail of the (*ridiculously*) frilly bra and dark nipples. The Bitch dropped the red leather clutch purse into her lap and patted a stray golden curl back into place. "All right then, go ahead."

Smiling, Geena pulled the incense deep into her lungs and released the silver shoulder catch on the ritual tunic, heard the Bitch's startled gasp as it fell to reveal her naked body.

"What the *hell*—?"

Famous last words.

Geena picked up the knife with her left hand as she leaned forward and sprinkled the powdered amethyst and moonstone she'd concealed in her right over the flame of the nearest black candle.

"As you are," she said to the wide-eyed Bitch, "so am I. As I was, so may you be."

The knife felt icy as it pierced the flesh between Geena's breasts. But the scream, although it started in her voice, ended in the Bitch's.

The transformation took less time than the spell book said it would. Less than the blink of an eye, instead of the minute and a half the book listed. Not that Geena was terribly surprised. Spell books just weren't what they used to be.

Opening the clutch purse, Geena stood up and looked down at the crumpled body sprawled across one leg of the pentagram. And grimaced. God, she really should have gotten out in the sun more.

But there was no time to think about that now.

Flexing the still unfamiliar muscles, Geena snapped open the matching leather wallet and nodded at the fashionable address listed on the driver's license (*even the picture looked good*). Snapping the wallet shut, Geena checked the time on the (*real*) gold watch that encircled her perfectly tanned wrist and plucked the corners of the slightly wider, definitely more sensual mouth.

It was just nine.

Which meant she'd have just enough time to get "home" and make dinner.

Before Ken showed up.

They decided to skip dinner.

And get right to dessert.

Geena couldn't remember Ken ever making love like that in the five years they'd been together. Maybe he really did prefer big boobs and blonde hair. (Geena'd been a little disappointed to discover that the Bitch really *had* been natural.)

Or maybe he'd just been overwhelmed by the fact that he'd opened the door to her call and found her bare-assed and spread-legged on top of the dining room table.

Whatever the reason, Geena wasn't going to think about it too hard. The fact was that they were together again and—even though he'd called her by the Bitch's name all through their three bouts of sexual one-on-one—that's all that mattered.

For the moment.

Geena cocked her head, listening to the steady buzz of Ken's exhausted snoring coming from the bedroom, before returning to gaze at her new reflection in the bathroom mirror. *Too much hair,* she decided, lifting the heavy locks off the back of her neck. But maybe she'd leave it like that. For a while, anyway.

Smiling, she lowered her arms and licked her lips. Tasted Ken on them and sighed.

She'd have to remember to roll the portable television into the bedroom so she could turn it on first thing in the morning.

Geena watched her sparkling white teeth chew absently on her newly poutable bottom lip as she tried to work out the timetable.

Let's see. . . .

Mr. Collins usually opened the store around six-thirty (to catch the early morning witch crowd) . . . so that meant the media vultures would have plenty of time to circle in and report on the latest piece of urban unpleasantness by the seven o'clock news.

Yeah. Plenty of time.

For them to report on the apparent Satanic ritual murder of one Geena Beaumead.

And for Ken to react to the apparent Satanic ritual murder of his one-time true love.

A reaction that BETTER take place, Geena thought, and blew herself a kiss, *if he knew what was good for him.*

She's My Witch

NORMAN PARTRIDGE

We parked in the old cemetery that night, the Ford coupe I'd boosted up in Fresno wedged so tight between a couple of crumbling mausoleums that we could barely open one door. It seemed we'd spent the entire summer that way—sitting in one stolen car or another, talking or making out while we listened to the latest rhythm 'n' blues tunes on KTCB. Shari liked the old cemetery because it was real quiet. No one else ever came there, even in the daytime. As for me, I'd gotten used to the place. I wasn't crazy about it, but I was crazy about Shari.

That summer it was like no one else existed. The rest of the world couldn't touch us.

"Tonight's no different," I said. "Whatever's gonna happen later . . . well, it's just gonna happen, however it does."

Shari's hand slipped out of mine, just seemed to melt away. Her gaze was welded to the dash, like if she squinted real hard she'd actually be able to *see* LaVern Baker through the radio.

She wouldn't look at me at all, and I don't think she really heard the music, either. "I don't know," was all she said. And then she shook her head, her dark hair washing over her face like a silent wave.

I couldn't see her face at all, and I couldn't stand to be apart from her that way. Sitting there in a stolen car with my girl, her hair as black as night, her dress just as black . . . and having her whisper those three words in the darkness, like she didn't have any faith in me—in *us* —at all.

Those three words parting the only lips I wanted to kiss. And Shari not even looking at me when she said them, afraid that I'd see her doubts hiding in her eyes.

My girl, sitting there in a boosted Ford parked in her favorite place in the world, trembling, like she'd rather be somewhere else. *Anywhere* else. And who could blame her? Christ, with the things she'd discovered that summer, she could have had anyone. Sticking with me was just crazy, just—

Unsure, I reached out, my hand barely brushing her bare shoulder, traveling that delicate ridge of collarbone, exploring her slender and perfect neck. My fingers drifted through her hair, my movements surer now—I gotta admit it did something to me, just like always. I found her chin and gently turned her head in my direction, brushing that midnight hair over one shoulder.

There were those beautiful eyes of hers, alive with mysteries she could never share. Those full lips, containing all those secrets that she would never speak. Like I said, it did something to me. Just like always. I moved in to kiss her, and she didn't move away. It didn't start out like much of a kiss, but it shook me up the way I hoped it would.

When it was over, I really had the itch. I wanted her more than ever.

One look, and I knew that she felt the same way. A tear ran down one smooth marble cheek. I wiped it away, and it smeared on my callused fingers, and I found myself wishing that I could crush it in my fist.

She said, "I just want everything to stay the way it is."

"Don't worry, little darlin'," I said, trying to sound more confident than I was. "Tonight it's you and me. Just like it's been all summer, ever since you and me became an *us*. Those jerks are in for a big surprise." I slipped one hand around the back of her neck, but not in a rough way, and with the other I twisted the rearview in her direction. "Just look at you, Shari. You're not the same girl you were when school let out."

Shari stared at her reflection. She didn't blink once, and a shiver rocketed over my spine like someone was stepping on my grave.

"No," she said finally. "I'm not the same person. This place . . . and you . . . you've given me so much, Johnny."

She pushed the mirror away, looking at the cemetery through the mosaic of kamikaze bugs plastered to the old Ford's windshield. Low fog bathed the ring of tombstones where she'd danced a couple of nights back with nothing covering that beautiful marble skin of hers but the blood of a black cat. I wanted to tell her that everything was going to be okay, but I could see that she was spooked, just as spooked as the first time she visited the cemetery. That was back when she was just a scared kid in hand-me-downs who'd been broken by other kids because she couldn't bear to look anyone in the eye, before the black dress and the red lipstick, before I took to parking boosted cars in the long shadows between two jagged mausoleums, before all the secret kisses and all the things that went with them.

So much had passed between us that summer. We'd made a world of our own, and no one else knew anything about it. But with school ready to start up, our world was going to change. We'd have to face those other people again. I thought I had it all figured out. But with Shari so rattled and uncertain, I couldn't help but worry.

Her voice trembled. "Sometimes . . . this summer . . ." she began. "It just doesn't seem real. I keep thinking I'll wake up, and it will have all been a dream. I keep thinking that maybe I'm imagining you. . . . I always had a crush on you, y'know? And I keep thinking that I'll wake up, and I'll be back in school with all those people, and you'll be here. . . ."

I nodded. She took my hand then, her fingernails digging into my palm like little knives. I couldn't help but shiver; she couldn't seem to let go. Her face had disappeared in the darkness—there was just a little razor cut of a moon in the sky, and the night was coming on hard, clouds blanketing the stars.

"I keep staring at that moon," she said. "I keep thinking that it looks like a sickle."

She couldn't stop shaking. "I'm afraid the moon's going to slice down out of the sky, Johnny," she said, her fingers locked in mine. "I'm afraid it's going to cut us to pieces."

The carhop's roller skates made an icy little rumbling sound as she drifted across the parking lot, away from the stolen Ford.

When she was out of sight, I lifted the Coke off the little metal tray and handed it to Shari. Then I reached under the seat and found the cardboard box. Inside was a Revell model kit that I'd bought in Fresno the same night I boosted the Ford. I slipped the lid off of the box, revealing a miniature '48 Chevy.

"Wow." Shari smiled. "It looks just like it."

"Yeah, I'm a real artist." I wasn't bragging. I'd done a good job. Customized it just right. Two-tone paint job—turquoise and black. Every detail reproduced, right down to the miniature tornado swirling on the hood.

I handed the model to Shari, then rummaged through the unused parts in the bottom of the box until I found the decal sheet. I traded her the sheet for the Coke. She ran her fingers over the decals, whispering a few words.

I knew better than to listen. Instead I stared between a couple of dead moths splattered on the windshield, studying a turquoise-and-black '48 Chevy parked over by the bowling alley.

Shari dipped the decal sheet into the Coke. She let it sit for a minute, until the decals started to drift away from the backing.

There were two license plate decals. She attached one of them to a blank plastic plate glued to the trunk of the model.

The other floated on the surface of a Coca-Cola ice-flow. Shari stared down at it as she took the glass from my hand, then glanced over at the Chevy parked by the bowling alley.

"You promise not to blink, right?" she asked. "I mean, you're not going to get distracted by a carhop who's a dead ringer for Anita Ekberg or anything, are you?"

When the girl you love asks you something like that, you've got to laugh. "Baby, I'm just like the Flamingos," I said, and then I sang the rest of it—"*I only have eyes for you.*"

Shari hustled on over there. My ears were treated to the sweet little staccato rhythm of her high heels on blacktop, but my eyes got the better part of the deal when she bent low behind the '48, her tight dress riding up over firm thighs.

The fingers of one hand dipped into the Coke. Then she reached out, kind of tenderly, the way she sometimes did when she ran a finger over my lips. But her finger only traveled the length of the Chevy's license plate, leaving behind a decal from a Revell model kit.

And then the two of them showed up, right on cue. Slammed out of the bowling alley like they owned the world, swaggered across the parking lot.

Shari barely had a chance to straighten up. They both saw her at the same time, saw that black dress hiked up to the limit, that red lipstick, saw everything through a testosterone haze.

Nick Bradley was the smarter of the two. He got his mouth open first, saying, "You like the ride, huh, honey? You maybe wanna go for a ride?"

"Course she wants to go for a ride." Marty Hyde's brain had finally kicked into gear. "But it's *my* ride, and I got the keys and the master switch." Marty jingled his car keys as punctuation, shoving Nick with one shoulder, Nick stumbling in spite of himself. "We don't have to make it a party," Marty added. "Unless you want it that way, angel."

Shari looked both of them dead in the eye. She refused to blink, and they . . . well, I'm sure the idiots wanted to blink, but they just *couldn't*.

Nick caught Shari's thought-wave first. He laughed, shaking his head. "Naw," he said. *"Naw!* It can't be!"

Marty caught up. "Sharon? Sharon Heep? Is that really you?"

Shari's eyes were daggers now. The corners of her mouth were playing with a smile, but just playing. And then she batted her eyebrows —a wicked twitch. Stirred the straw in the Coke and took a dainty sip. . . .

"It is her!" Nick slapped Marty on the back. "It *is* the Heepster! Jesus, Marty, it looks like old Sharon's been to charm school this summer!"

"Slut school, more like it," Marty replied, ever the quick wit. "Hey, c'mon, Sharon. Let's go for a ride, just the three of us. Let's see what you've learned this summer."

I said, "You guys got room for one more?"

Nick and Marty whirled. They hadn't heard me coming.

Once again, Nick caught on first. "Johnny!" He gasped, a look of horror crossing his face. "No . . . it can't be—"

Marty cut in with the clincher: "Christ, Johnny . . . you're dead!"

I nodded, flicking open the switchblade that Nick had buried in my guts back in June.

They froze—eyeballing the knife, their faces pasty white—so I decided to help them out. "Let me steer you fellas in the right direction," I offered. "This is the part where you're supposed to run for your lives."

"Don't confuse them, Johnny," Shari said. "Don't be so literal."

"Sorry, fellas." I snapped the blade closed. "I mean, you don't have to *run* run—you can take the car."

Nick and Marty just stood there, staring at us as we returned to the Ford.

"Man, can you believe that they're so stupid?" I said.

Shari took my hand. "Believe it, daddy-o."

Behind us, the Chevy's engine finally rumbled alive.

Four new tires burned rubber.

Nick and Marty were gone.

Pretty soon, they'd be the *gonest.*

"What was that junk you put in the Coke?" the carhop wanted to know.

Shari laughed. I didn't do a very good job of keeping a straight face, myself. But I did manage to set the model car on the serving tray.

"Decals," Shari explained between giggles.

"Yeah," I said. "We're a couple of hobbyists. We get together and build model cars. I guess we got a little sloppy tonight."

"It could have been worse." Shari's voice was suddenly real serious. "I mean, we could have gotten glue all over the french fries, or paint in the cheeseburgers, or something."

The carhop didn't seem to catch on. She frowned as she set a fresh Coke next to the model car. "Well, just don't do it again. Those darn what-cha-ma-call-ems are stuck to the glass. I bet it's going to take a razor blade to get 'em off. I mean, only a *gomer* would want to drink *Coke* out of a glass that says *Chevy.*"

"Sorry," Shari said, and deep down I'll bet she really was sorry for putting the carhop to all that trouble.

The carhop skated away. We dug into our cheeseburgers, which hadn't even had a chance to get cold. Shari said, "I didn't think I'd ever want to eat again."

"You were really nervous, huh?"

"Are you kidding?" She swallowed another bite. "And it isn't like we're out of the woods yet."

"Sure it is."

She sighed. "C'mon, Johnny. We still have to go back to school. We still have to face everyone else."

"So what?"

"I mean, all the stories and everything . . ."

I shook my head. "It's like I said: this one little step, and it's all over. Nick and Marty were the biggest, toughest monkeys in that damn zoo. With them gone, it'll be easy."

"But what about you? Nick and Marty talked, y'know. I mean, I never would have found your grave if I hadn't listened to all the stories that were going around. And there'll be lots of questions when you show up again. Think about it, Johnny. You're going to have to explain things. Your parents are going to want to know what happened—"

"Those rummies?" My lips twisted into a smirk. "They'll be sorry to see me walk through the door. My old man will worry that I'll cut into the beer budget or something. Maybe I'll just stay in the boneyard. It's gotten so I kind of like it there."

"But everyone else—"

"Screw everyone else. Screw their questions. Who's gonna have the guts to ask 'em, anyhow? Who's gonna come up to a guy who's supposed to be dead and buried in an unmarked grave in the old cemetery . . . especially when the studs who supposedly gutted him and put him six feet under turn up dead? Who's gonna say a thing to that guy when he comes waltzing into school with a girl on his arm?"

Shari nodded. "Not just any girl. A *freak* who believed in ghosts and witches and things that go bump in the night. A *freak* who everyone laughed at." She took my hand. "Until she found someone who taught her to believe in herself."

"Yeah," I said, "but you had to dig me up to do it."

"Sometimes you have to be real desperate before you can really believe." She kissed me, a sweet schoolgirl peck on the cheek. "And, anyway," she added slyly, "some things are worth a little digging, y'know?"

We finished the cheeseburgers and drove back to the old cemetery, parking the stolen Ford between the same two broken-down mausoleums. Like I said, there was barely enough room to get one door open, so we both slipped out the driver's side. I left the radio on, because Dinah Washington was singing "My Man's an Undertaker." Somehow, it seemed appropriate.

There was a marble slab a few feet off. Spider-webbed with cracks, but pretty much level. I set the Chevy model on top of it.

"I wonder where they are," Shari said.

"Let's find out." I knelt down, put my ear to the plastic hardtop. "Wow, I can hear the idiots yelling at each other. But I can't figure out what surprised them more—that I'd come back from the dead, or that you'd turned into such a dead solid knock-out."

"Real funny, Johnny."

"Yeah." I sat on the slab. "Sorry. But I gotta tell you, Shari—your legs really made an impression on them."

"Why, Johnny Benteen, you're such a card." She laughed. "I never would have guessed that a dead guy could possess such a keen sense of humor."

"Ouch. Score one for the sexpot sorceress."

"This is so weird."

"The weirdest."

"Let's get it over with."

"You want to do it?"

She turned away. "I don't even want to *watch.*"

I slipped Nick's switchblade from my pocket. Flicked it open. Pressed the sharp metal point against the miniature tornado that swirled on the model's flimsy plastic hood.

"Look away, little darlin'," I said. "Look up at that pretty sickle of a moon."

The Angel

CHRISTIE GOLDEN

Kat had loved the Angel for as long as she could remember. He had always been there: the gentle, unseen force that moved her crib's hanging mobile when the air was still; the friend who would always listen when Mommy and Daddy were too busy; the solace when she cried herself to sleep during the turbulent teenage years.

In her childhood, he was her "imaginary friend"; as she grew older, she saw the wisdom in not speaking of him. But he was always there. She could feel his love and laughter in the summer breezes; his gentleness eased her through the winter's chill. And when friends proved false, he came to her in dreams, and she knew she yet had one Friend who loved her. She simply could not imagine life without him.

Her only friends at school had been the other societal rejects: the geek with inch-thick glasses, the fat girl who laughed harder at her weight than anyone else did in order to be accepted. Kat was one of the army of the unwanted, and it didn't much bother her. Not when she had the Angel.

She paused in her conversation, suddenly not wanting to go on. The rest of the coven was hanging on her words, wide-eyed, eager.

"It's okay, Kat," Marjorie said, placing a gentle hand on her friend's bony shoulders. Kat smiled.

The coven had been little short of a miracle for Kat. She would have been called "fey" in centuries past. Tiny and slender, pale and dark-haired, she was excruciatingly shy. When Kat had learned that the vice president of the college science fiction society was a Witch, Kat had been intrigued and had stammered a few questions. One thing led to another, and finally to the coven, Marjorie, and the incredible confession Kat was now making.

She blushed. "I know it sounds silly," she murmured, "and I'd understand if you don't believe me."

Alex, the High Priest, shook his head. "Oh, Kat, of course we do. Everybody here knows that there's more out there than we can see."

"Or hear," Dan put in, with his infectious grin. Dan often "tranced," speaking with the voice of the God. Everybody chuckled. Seriously as they took their religion, there was always a place for good-natured humor. Kat found herself wondering, as she often did, why witchcraft had gotten such a bad rap. It was a gentle, loving religion, based on respect for life and the earth, a thing quite separate from Satanism. It was a shame more people didn't understand it better.

Marjorie squeezed her shoulder. "Go on. We want to hear about the Angel."

And so Kat continued.

She had never actually seen him with her eyes, she explained, only her heart. She knew what he was saying, without words; theirs was a communication that defied logic, but was undeniably real. The Angel came to her most clearly in dreams, incredibly beautiful, unspeakably alien, eternally loving. And how could she help but love him back?

Kat was speaking about Russ before she knew it, telling the intimate details of her only lover to this group of relative strangers quickly, before she had time to regret it. Russ had loved her, but he couldn't understand her. And he had thought her insane when she told him about—

"It's okay, Kat," Marjorie soothed, holding the girl as her thin frame shook with sobs. "Not everyone understands. Not yet. But we do. We love your Angel, because he loves you."

Murmurs of assent flowed through the coven. Gentle, caring hands were reaching to comfort her. As Kat held onto Marjorie and wept, she kept secret the one fact she knew: Russ could never have satisfied her, hard as he had tried. He was not an Angel; and Kat had loved the Angel for as long as she could remember.

Kat thumbed her Shakespeare and nibbled absently on her third Krispy Kreme doughnut. "You eat all that crap and you never gain an ounce. Wish I knew how you do it," Marjorie muttered as she sipped her black coffee, wincing.

Kat laughed. "I do, too. I'd market it and make a million." She washed the doughnut down with a swig of A&W. Marjorie was still looking at her.

"Kat . . ."

"Hmmm?" Gods, Hamlet had his problems, didn't he?

"About the Angel . . ."

Kat stiffened. They had never discussed the Angel outside of their coven meetings. "I'd rather not. . . ."

Marjorie flopped down on the bed beside her, her French final forgotten. "Do you think there's a way we could see him?"

Kat's stomach knotted, and she concentrated on her Shakespeare. *The ghost of Hamlet's father represents—*

"I mean, maybe Dan could go into trance and channel him through."

"He doesn't talk."

Marjorie paused. "Oh." Kat went back to her book, hoping that would be the end of that. She didn't want to share her Angel with—

The book tumbled from her hands.

He was there, his warm presence in her mind like a sudden fire, and she was weak and yet strong, as always when he visited. She realized with a thrill of joy and surprise that he wanted to share in her world, her plane of existence. That world was full of *colors*, he was "saying"; full of so many diverse and beautiful things. And she, Kat, was the most beautiful of all. . . .

Marjorie's image was swimming as Kat looked at her. Why did Marjorie care so much?

Because Marjorie's never had what I have. She wants a little magic, too.

"No," Kat managed, her voice raspy, "not a trance. I'm going to bring him through. You'll love him, too, Marj, and I want to share him with you."

There are more things in heaven and earth, Horatio, than are dreamt of in your philosophy.

Marjorie's eyes were bright with wonder and joy.

At the next coven meeting, Alex doused their pleasure. "No," he said flatly. "I refuse to bring such a being into our plane."

Kat closed her eyes. *That's that,* she thought to herself.

"Oh, come on, Alex," she heard Marjorie arguing. "So far it's all been words and good feelings, nothing more."

Dan frowned, his baby face going somber. "You're wrong, Marj," he said softly. "I've brought something through. I've brought the God through."

Marjorie colored, her round cheeks flushing. "I didn't mean it that way. But . . . this is something real. We can see it, touch it, learn from it. Kat's got a friend from Fairyland, people, and we've got a chance to meet him!"

Alex's bearded face was thunder. "We don't know what this place will do to him. We don't know if we can send him back."

"He wants to come," Kat said softly. "He trusts us, and he wants to come. He wants to be mortal, to take the risks."

"If you don't want to bring him through at the next meeting, Kat and I'll do it by ourselves," Marjorie threatened suddenly. Kat glanced at her roommate, surprised. They had made no such bargain. Why was Marjorie lying to her covenmates?

A nameless fear fluttered through Kat, a foreboding of danger. She had opened her mouth to agree with Alex when the High Priest spoke. "Very well," he said, defeat in his tone. "Next Wednesday."

The air thrummed with power.

The incense wafted up to the ceiling, the candles glowed, all was in readiness. The altar was laid out carefully: There was the ritual knife of iron for the God, the cup of water for the Goddess. A seashell marked the element of Water and the direction of West; a feather stood for Air and the East; Earth was a dish of rich loam, placed in the North; and a red candle burned with the element of Fire and the South.

Kat tried to keep her breathing regular. *Tonight . . . she was going to be able to see him tonight. . . .*

She didn't even hear what Alex was intoning. He looked quite awe-inspiring in his formal robes; tall and bearded, he was a High Priest to be reckoned with. He finished whatever it was he was saying, and with the knife, cut a "doorway" in the air. He turned to Kat, and with a troubled expression, nodded that she might begin.

Kat stood on wobbly legs, silently calling the Angel. What if he didn't come? Alex would be pleased. He still thought the divine creature would be in danger in this world. If the Angel didn't manifest, would he—

But then he was there, warm, sweet as a breath of spring in midwinter. He was coming. He wanted to be with her.

Kat's whole body was shaking violently. She raised her hands and slowly put them into the "doorway."

And gasped as a sudden warmth brushed her fingers. Almost, she jerked away.

Let me come. Let me be with you.

Wasn't this was she wanted? Wasn't this what she had dreamed about all her life? She couldn't refuse him now.

She opened her hand.

His grip this time was sure and strong, but gentle. She felt invisible, slender fingers twine about hers, and her heart jerked as it beat. She gave a little tug, and began to pull him through. She was only dimly aware of the rest of the coven crying out in astonishment and excitement.

Light blazed about her, and as her eyes adjusted, she saw the strong, perfectly formed hand that held hers so trustfully. It became an arm, golden and sleek, and bit by bit, the Angel slid into her world. He was all sunshine and summer, light and laughter and golden as morning, his skin slick with moisture as a newborn's. A face emerged from the light, more beautiful than even she had dared dream. His curls were dark gold, wet against his head.

He was halfway through now, halfway through this birth into a human form. She had both of his hands in hers now, and was pulling with all her might. Wings the color of wheat were damply plastered to his sleek back, flapping wetly as he struggled. With a rush, the Angel collapsed onto Kat, his beautiful body, slender as a youth's, twitching as it sought air.

I am here for you. Long have I loved you, never could I be with you, but I am here, I am here!

His amber eyes shone, his joy shot through her, and she gloried in the beauty and wonderment of it all: what did the world know of her joy, of her reality, when this glorious creature had come to her out of love?

So keen was her ecstasy that it was several seconds before she noticed that the radiant eyes were dimming, their expression changing from rapture to puzzlement as the honey-colored fluid that passed for divine blood oozed across his back and trickled down his shoulders. Marjorie had stabbed him with the altar knife, the iron knife, the one thing that could kill one of the Fair Folk, and it protruded from the spot directly between his golden wings.

As a horrified Alex and Dan wrested her away from the Angel, Marjorie was laughing insanely, unable to bear the sublime joy, filled with wonder that she could not tolerate. And Kat wondered in a detached part of her brain why someone didn't stop that horrible sound that went on and on and *on* until she realized that it was her own screams echoing endlessly endlessly endlessly. . . .

The Good Witch of the North Wing

STEVE ANTCZAK

Y ou know," I say as we drive along the twisted country road, "if it hadn't been for her, I wouldn't be the man I am today." Maxine looks out the passenger window. Dogwoods are bare. Fall is almost over, winter is fast approaching. Jacket weather, but not glove weather yet.

"Who are you today, Max?" she asks smugly. I look at her, but that can't be what she said. She's never in such cruel humor, and where would *she* get off asking a question like *that*?

"What'd you say?" There's an edge in my voice. I know by the way it gets her attention.

"I said you must be pretty excited about today, Max. Did you misunderstand me?"

"No," I lie. She knows I lie. Used to be I *never* misunderstood her.

403

That was *before*. It's much easier to know what a person says when that person is as much a part of you as Maxine was a part of me.

"You did."

"Okay, I did. Sorry. Nervous, that's all."

"I know. Are you?"

"What?"

"Excited?"

"Yeah, sure."

Excited at first. Now I'm wondering. Is this a good idea, visiting Glenda after so long? Will she remember me?

Us. I sometimes forget Maxine was there. Sort of. No, she *was* there in mind and body, they just weren't connected at the time.

I should explain.

It was three years ago. So much has happened since . . . it seems a *lot* longer. In that time we had little Maximillian II, and now he's almost six. We keep this a secret. Not because we're ashamed of him, no, we're proud as parents can be, that's the truth. We spoil him, but why not? He's six when he should be three; is this *his* fault?

That's not why we're going to see Glenda, though.

I admit I feel guilty. This *is* the first time I'll be seeing her since I left, and I'm visiting because I *want* something from her. If Glenda hasn't changed, she won't mind. She never felt better than when she felt *needed*.

"Can we stop soon?" Maxie asks from the backseat. He'd been asleep; now he's awake.

"Max wants to stop," I tell Maxine.

"I *heard*," Maxine says in that annoyed voice she uses on me when something offends her. I know why she's offended this time. She doesn't like me repeating what Maxie says, because she doesn't always hear him. She does it to me, but it doesn't bother me. *I* know I can't hear *every* word that comes out of his mouth.

The next rest stop is another fifteen minutes, so we get there before Maxie gets irritable. He's not perfect. He whines when he has a reason to whine, even if it's not much of a reason, like most kids. Maxie goes to the men's room while Maxine gets overpriced sodas to take with us, so we'll have to make another pit stop in an hour. I'm just as guilty as the next guy, because if there's a Coke there for me, I drink it.

When we get back on the road the scenery begins to look familiar. My mood darkens. My memories of this area aren't particularly pleasant. Maxie senses this and becomes a perfect angel the rest of the ride. Maxine's mood mirrors mine, and may be darker.

Her body remembers, but her mind doesn't, which is good. Two orderlies transporting her from a homeless shelter in Savannah decided to stop for recreation. They pulled off the side of the road, under cover of the trees, and used her body for pleasure. It was a nightmare Maxine sometimes had, so I told her the truth, but pointed out it had not been *her* at the time. The nightmare was very infrequent now. The orderlies had been discovered and dismissed, not charged. They were free men now, living full lives, hopefully unable to sleep at night as well as they might have.

"There it is." Maxine points ahead to a clump of dogwoods . . . perfect cover when covered with greenery. She stares at that spot as we pass, turning in her seat to watch as it recedes into the distance. Then she turns back around and sits stoically in silence.

I say nothing. Words wouldn't help right now.

Then there's the sign: BETHLEHEM HOUSE. We residents called it Bedlam, when it was under state jurisdiction. Now it was part of the Peachford Foundation, people buying institutions all over. I hoped they treated Glenda as well as the state did, once they found out *who* she is.

A witch. Not just any witch, but the witch L. Frank Baum had known before writing *The Wizard of Oz* and the other *Oz* books. She was crazy then, but at that time it was considered par for the course for witches. Ever see a real shaman or seer? Nutty as a Snickers bar, loopy as a hippie hallucinating on LSD . . . They see things we can't see, do things we never dream of doing. That kind of, and I hate to use this word because it's not what I mean, but that kind of *power* will crack *anyone*.

"Max!" Maxine yells. I almost miss the turn for Bethlehem House. Up the long, black drive to the gatehouse.

"Max Silverberg," I say. The gatekeeper checks his list.

"Hey," he says, then grins. "I remember you. I'm Henry the Gatekeeper, remember?"

I remember. He's been gatekeeper for longer than I've been alive. Rumor was that he'd been a "resident" when the place was still under private ownership, and got the job because he followed all orders without question. Would've made a great Nazi.

"How are you?" I ask, wishing he'd just wave us on through, but I act friendly now that I'm here. I feel like I'm in the spotlight. Everyone who knew me *before* will be watching. *Is he still holding together? Should we get his old room ready?*

"You know how it is, Max." He looks past me at Maxine. "Isn't that . . . ?"

She waves. "Hi."

Henry grins, that insider's grin to let me know *he* knows what's what—not insidious, just another form of elitism. I wink, to make him feel all warm and special inside. One thing I've noticed about people who know about me, who knew me *when,* they think I'm either a savant with the wisdom of Solomon, or a blathering idiot who doesn't know the difference between night and day.

Henry waves us through.

"It's changed," Maxine says with a touch of awe in her voice. In three years the place has grown. The main building has sprouted two arms extending out at an angle, ready to embrace us as we drive up. The lawn is nicer, with trees, shrubs, ponds, paths, gazebos, and benches. Some of the more responsible residents are out, alone and in pairs. I recognize no one. The drive curves around to the front entrance.

"I don't like this place, Daddy," Maxie says. "Can we go home? I don't *want* my present!"

I glance at Maxine to see if she heard. . . . She turns around to answer for me, "Now, honey, you were excited when we told you what we had planned. . . . You *said* you wanted to meet Glenda the Good Witch, right?"

Maxie's seen *The Wizard of Oz* a dozen times since we got the video. We told him that Glenda in the movie isn't the same as ours. He understands about actors and movies.

He reluctantly climbs over the front seat to get out with me. We never let him go out the back. . . . It would look pretty weird to someone when they didn't see anyone get out.

"I am a little nervous," I confess to Maxine.

She nods. "Me too."

The lobby isn't different. The man there to greet us with a big smile hasn't changed either.

"Max! Maxine!"

"Mr. Hale," I say, "Good to see you looking fit."

"Oh!"

"It's true." Maxine gives him an exaggerated once-over. "Mmmm. How do you do it?"

406

Hale inflates with our stroking. Old habits die hard. We're lying through our teeth, of course. I'm surprised to see him walking under his own power. The director of Bethlehem House is overweight, smokes, and spends his days sitting around reading case studies of the residents and psychiatric journals. To give him credit, he was a staunch anti-Freudian when it was virtually impossible to be taken seriously in his field without making even vague reference to Freud. His stance had a lot to do with why the place went through lean years, because he couldn't get funding.

"Please." He shakes my hand with a loose grip, gives Maxine a wet kiss on the lips. "Call me Lawrence." To let us know he accepts us as sane equals now.

"Okay, Lawrence," I say. Then, "How's Glenda?"

He fends off the question with a wave of his chubby hand. "Glenda will always be Glenda."

"Where is she?" Maxine presses the issue. She wants to spend as little time with Hale as possible. He was the one who'd dismissed those orderlies, but he also saw that they got off without criminal prosecution. Rumor had it they'd been supplying him with companionship from the wards. Maxine has told me the thought of Hale makes her feel unclean. She doesn't know if he used her body or not. I give people the benefit of the doubt, but in this case I tend to assume the worst. "I'd like to see her," Maxine says. "It's been so long."

Hale checks his watch. "She should be eating lunch now. Let's join her!"

"What about the boy?" I don't want to wait *too* long to get to the purpose of this visit.

"Right," Hale says, as if he'd forgotten. "He'll be brought down." He waddles over to a phone without buttons, picks it up, talks, hangs up, smiles at us, and says, "Okay! Let's see Glenda."

We follow him, down a hall, past a checkpoint where we're given guest badges, past where I remembered the cafeteria used to be. It's not there.

"Where are we going?" I ask, trying not to sound scared. As soon as you start to question things everyone else takes for granted, when you've already been committed once, watch out.

Hale glances back. "The North Wing," he says. "A new addition. We moved Glenda there a year ago."

"The North Wing."

"Yes." A smug chortle. "Too bad *she* doesn't understand the reference. She'd appreciate it."

It's easy to tell when we go from the old to the new. The halls get wider, whiter, with sprinklers poking down from the ceiling. Better lighting. The effect is antiseptic, less inviting than the hardwood floors and brass-mounted candelabra of the old part, but maybe this *is* better, I don't know.

"Despite Spartan appearances," Hale says, "this wing is quite cozy. Bigger rooms, all with color TVs."

I don't say what I'm thinking. Large rooms, bright lights, and too much TV are partly why some of the people are here in the first place.

The cafeteria is a haloed affair of white tile and polished chrome. Round Formica tables scattered throughout, an improvement over the long rows of tables in the old cafeteria, like the ones used in prisons. I wonder if the food is any better, despite the gleaming mien.

Glenda sits alone, spooning apple sauce, heaping mounds of it, into her mouth. If you've seen the movie, you'd pass this woman right by and not even begin to imagine that she was *the* Glenda, the Good Witch of the North.

"*That's* her?" Little Max asks in utter disbelief.

"That's her," I say. Hale glances at me, a question in his eyes, but I smile at Maxine as if that's who I'm talking to. She smiles back; I don't think she heard Maxie.

Glenda looks like a Norman Rockwell granny on acid. Silver hair that started the day in a tight bun sticks out in loose strands all over her head, as if she stuck her thumb in a wall socket. She's wearing gigantic earrings, dangling silver baubles like Christmas tree ornaments. Pinned to the top of her hair is a black lace hat, deceptively tilting to one side, threatening to fall off. Her eyes are wide and blue as the ocean, and as deep and wild.

Hale approaches the table timidly, which reminds me that as much as he enjoys the prestige of having her here, she scares him.

"Glenda, you have visitors."

She looks up from her apple sauce, lumpy globs of it drop into the bowl from her mouth. Her eyes stay devoid of emotion.

"Mannequin," she says in a dismissive tone. "Stuffed shirt." She looks past me and Maxine, and suddenly those eyes alight with blue fire.

"There!" She points between Maxine and me. "Between the air! I see green eyes, I see blond hair!"

Maxine whispers into her hands, cupped over her mouth, "She sees him!"

"Glenda," I say, "it's Max. Remember?"

She looks at me, smiles, but the fire dims in her eyes. "Mirror Man?" A frown. She looks at Maxine, at me, back at Maxine, at me again. "Mirror Man, Mirror Woman . . . Mirror *Child!*" Now the flames leap from her eyes. It's difficult to tell if it's really happening or a trick of the imagination. No matter, she knows what's going on. I can tell she remembers, and she knows why we're here.

Then Hale says, "The child."

I look where he's pointing. An orderly wheels the boy in, then goes.

Brown hair, emerald green eyes, and he looks almost as I've been imagining Maxie would look to . . . others. To us he'll continue to look the way he always has. Like love.

"Sure the kid's gone?" I ask Hale. We'd discussed it over the phone during the weeks leading up to this visit, but I'm still uneasy about it. "Vacant?"

"Look at those eyes," Hale tells me. "There's *no one* there."

"Nobody home," Glenda says. "Ding dong! Nobody hooooommme!"

I look at Maxine; she nods.

"Glenda," I say. "Glenda, please listen."

She looks at me, doesn't say anything, but her face is alive with a mischievous aura, grinning like a Cheshire cat. I fully expect the rest of her to vanish. Wouldn't be the first time. I got used to that trick when I lived here.

"The little boy with the blond hair and green eyes wants to be real. Can you make him real?"

She looks at Maxie. Hale looks at approximately the same spot, but sees only the gleam of a newly waxed floor.

"Real little boys get hurt, you know," Glenda says. "They scrape their knees and bleed. Real little boys get yelled at for tracking mud across the carpet. Real little boys cry."

"I still wanna be real," Maxie replies.

"Wouldn't you rather have a finely carved wooden body like Pinocchio?" Glenda asks. "Never grow old, be young forever and ever like Peter Pan?"

Glenda is pulling out all the stops. All pretty little beads to dangle before a six-year-old boy, but I know that's all they are, too. Beads. Trinkets.

Maxie believes Glenda can do those things. Maybe she can. I know what she did for me, over three years ago. What she did for Maxine.

For some reason I think of the movie *Who's Afraid of Virginia Woolf?* Not my favorite movie. I just don't understand how two people can be so cruel to each other. Perhaps if Glenda weren't around to make our dreams real, or to give hope that they *could* be real someday, Maxine and I wouldn't be so far from that. Exchange one kind of madness for another. I like to think we're just not that kind of people, but I see similarities.

We had to dream Little Max up, because Maxine and I can't have children nature's way, and won't adopt. We wanted a child that was *ours*.

"I wanna be *real*," Maxie says. "Make me *real, pleeeeeaassse!*"

I'm proud to hear him say "the magic word" . . . and Glenda nods, closes her eyes. A beatific smile spreads across her face as she turns it up toward the sky, way up high, and there are three taps as she clicks the heels of her shoes together. I feel wind on my face, warm, and I feel my heart swelling with love that we had known only a shadow of before—

"Max! Look!" Maxine yells. I open my eyes, which I don't recall closing.

The kid stirs. His little brown-haired head twitches from side to side; he groans, and suddenly his eyes open. He looks at Maxine.

"Mommy?"

Maxine cries out, rushes to the wheelchair, and lifts him out into a hug. "Yes, Mommy's here!"

She turns around so her back is to me. Maxie looks at me now, and I give him my best Dad smile, like I imagine my father would have given me had he ever decided to smile.

"Way to go, son," I say. His reply is to smile back, the happiest kid on earth because he's just won the approval of his father, not realizing he's had it all along.

"Bubble bubble, toil and trouble," says Glenda, gleefully playing with her apple sauce again, having forgotten us. *Gurgle and burp.* She thwacks her spoon into the apple sauce. It splashes up all over her face. She sits there, stunned for a moment, then exclaims, "Jimminy Cricket!"

Fiddlesticks

T. Diane Slatton

The dwarf Sir Cranston Pitts hated the witch. The passion with which he despised her burned as brightly as the love he'd wasted on the Queen's lady-in-waiting. But it was the witch he thundered toward in secret night, bringing her a gift he stole from the palace.

He twirled a bullwhip above his oversized head and flicked it "Crack!" at the lead horse's ear. When the steeds bolted near panic, he threw aside both whip and reins to grip the plank seat so he would not tumble backward into the wagon's haybed.

He shuddered when the witch's hovel came into view. Moonglow illuminated smoke blooming purple-black from her chimney. A gnarled elm stood sentry in the blighted front yard, its branches decorated with blood-stained leather boots and satin shoes that had no doubt belonged to the unfortunate travelers who'd passed this way before.

A stench like rotting flesh called tears to his eyes, but his mission made no time for sickness. Snatching up the reins, Sir Cranston Pitts stood atop the seat and tugged until snorting, straining horses stamped to a halt.

"Baljataur!" he called.

Bile leapt to his throat when lamplight appeared at the hovel's only window and a tattered green curtain moved aside to reveal the witch's tattered green face. He forced a smile, flourished a stubby arm toward the prize hidden within his wagon's haybed. The loathsome face disappeared and, almost instantly, the front door creaked open.

An enormous fan-backed lizard slithered escape from the hovel, then the delicate clip-clop of the witch's footless stumps crossed the porch.

"Madame Baljataur," he said with a bow too low for sincerity. "I come to beg truce, old friend. Remember now that it was my King who banished you from service as Royal Sorceress. It was *he* who ordered the monks to cut off your feet and cast you out into the woods. Do not

411

continue to blame me for your fate. Recall that I was only your lowly assist—"

"Only my low-low assistant. Ha! You, who fled to warn the King that I suckled his son at my inferior breast."

Sir Cranston Pitts raised from his bow, swallowed disgust, wrung his hands to appear contrite. "I see it after all these years, Baljataur. You meant the Prince no harm. It was love for the Royal Infant, not jealousy toward the Queen, that caused your desire to mother him. But as you must realize, madam, I was not merely your assistant. I was bound by duty to be the baby's protector."

Seeing the witch's mouth turn up in a hateful smile, he pointed a tiny finger of accusation at her. "*You* lived within the palace, woman! You knew how my eyes must have seen it—a peasant witch hiding in the wine cellar taking intimate liberties with the heir to the throne! I *had* to report the appearance of evil."

"FIDDLESTICKS!" Baljataur screeched past mold-specked teeth. She cackled laughter, her withered bosom heaving beneath a dust-caked gown. "Where hides the dwarf's happy bell's-cap? Where is your punchinello scepter to mock your King's rule, idiot jester?"

Sir Cranston Pitts's hands curled into fists, a movement instantly regretted when a blow was delivered to his chest by—what? Before he could regain his senses the same force lifted him, hurled him crashing to splinter wood on the porch.

"Mercy!" he wailed when the witch rested the tip of a footless stump atop his chest.

"Good eve, Fiddlesticks. Do you offer me *your* position in Royal Court to replace my honor gone-gone?" She removed the stump from his chest, seized his silk-and-lace collar, snatched him up, mindless of his feet wildly kicking at air. "Does the jester bring me back all my fine shoes—and the feet to put inside them? Or do you offer me your own!"

"Not jester!" Sir Cranston Pitts angrily said. "No more lowly hag's assistant and no more am I called Fiddle—" His scream cut through the dead night as the witch flung him high and away. His child-sized boots sucked themselves from his feet and flew to dangle from the elm's branches even as he crashed face-first into the wagon's haybed.

A chill wind howled through the forest. The dwarf rolled onto his back, panicked at the sight of destruction's handmaiden leaving the porch to claim him.

"A gift!" he cried. "*More* than a gift I offer you for my life. It is the greatest treasure. . . . Revenge."

The witch gasped, her yellow eyes sparkled near gold-dust.

Sir Cranston Pitts moved his trembling hands swiftly to brush hay from rich velvet boots half-exposed. "It is—"

"I *know* what it is, Sir Fool. You bring David, Prince Gaspari! You give-give a prize not yours." Baljataur slid her stumps through high spokes in the rear wagon wheel and hoisted herself up to uncover the rest of the sleeping Prince. She kissed his full, ruby mouth and smiled, which made her look all the more hideous. "What spell do you cast?"

The dwarf shook his large head. "No spell. Only sleeping powder in his wine. The rest is for you to do, old friend. The palace monks have seen to it that our walls are protected from you all these many years. But here in your house the Prince will be rendered worse than vulnerable. Strike now! I challenge you. Take your worst revenge upon the King through his son."

The witch turned to regard him. Though her expression was still, Sir Cranston Pitts felt accusation. "You doubt the purity of my intentions," he said, sounding wounded.

Baljataur slung the Prince's limp bulk onto her shoulder with little more exertion than made her grunt. The disturbance of her garments brought moths flitting out as she moved like a nightmare ballerina en pointe on her stumps up to the porch, inside the hovel.

With imagination unleashed, the dwarf considered the morning to come. He would, of course, fake grave concern when the King and Queen wondered aloud why their charming son did not awaken them with his lute music. Moments after, the lad's private manservant would shriek riotous alarm at not finding the young satyr tenderizing his hide in the palace baths.

Best of all—oh!—wouldn't the Queen's fragile lady-in-waiting need a gentleman's touch to console her? A small, desperate gentleman perhaps . . .

He rubbed miniature hands together, bent to take up the reins, froze. *He needed his boots.* They were his only pair. The monks could be faulted for the Prince's disappearance, but if both the boy *and* Sir Cranston Pitts's footwear turned up missing on the same morning—!

Gulping terror, he considered the impossibly high branch his boots had been banished to, then he climbed down from the wagon and up onto the porch.

He stood in the doorway looking around from jar-laden shelves to moth-shadowed lamplight to nests of cobwebs like cyclones high and low in every corner.

The witch's thick, white hair hung loose, nearly alive in its writhing movements around her shoulders. Her black sleeves were pushed up; her fingers danced through smoke curling angry red from an iron cauldron. There was no flame under the big, bubbling pot, which was testament to the power she still possessed.

His eyes lifted to David, Prince Gaspari, who now hung from the peaked ceiling by chains clamped to his wrists. The lad still slept with an angelic smile playing around his lips as if he were lost in pleasure.

"He is grown-grown," the witch sighed.

Sir Cranston Pitts could not hold back a sneer. "Too big, I say! Do what you will, old friend. But please. I require my boots."

The cauldron moved scraping across the wood floor with the witch walking on leg-stumps behind, not touching it. When the thing stopped in the center of the room, the sleeping Prince's feet dangled only inches above its bubbling contents.

"See his boots?" the dwarf pointed. "I swear he has taken upon himself your own love of grand footwear. He owns many boots. Many shoes. I can deliver them all to you in a week's time. . . . Please, madam. I possess only a single pair!"

"Here." The witch jerked her head toward a stepladder on wheels. "There." She gestured toward dusty jars on rotting, wood shelves. "Here and there!" when he did not move.

Sir Cranston Pitts understood her command. He rejected it. How dare she order him—an Honorary Knight of Royal Court—to assist her as if he were still *Fiddlesticks*, the lowly jester. He would have stood his ground all night if not for the sound of fast footsteps padding up the stairs outside.

He scurried across the room, up the ladder just as the witch's fan-backed lizard ran inside. The front door slammed and the dwarf saw his trap.

"Baljataur," he begged. "I mustn't. I *cannot* play a part in the Prince's destruction."

The witch squinted yellow eyes at him, grunted a sound either amused or disgusted. "You will help," she said slyly, "if you will have your footstuffs back." Taking up a large paddle, she began stirring the thick, crimson liquid in the cauldron. "Metal shards with shavings of ice."

Sir Cranston Pitts sighed, drew upon years-lost memories as he took fast inventory of the spellcaster's jars. He remembered that the witch never labeled anything, for she was every bit as illiterate as she was ugly.

The ladder shot splinters up through his socks into the tender soles of his feet as if it heard his insult. Tears sprang to the dwarf's eyes, clouding his vision even as a jar full of mirrored sparks almost jumped into his hand. He came down the ladder and limped to where Baljataur stood. She took only a pinch, but he fled and was back up the ladder by the time tongues of flame danced atop the bubbling mixture.

"A gargoyle's loyalty."

Gargoyles have no loyalty. He stalled, plucking splinters from his feet, thinking about this ingredient the witch requested. At last he brought down what appeared to be a jar of glowing worms. "Make the Prince small?" he said hopefully. "Smaller even than me. *A slug!*"

The witch scooped out a handful of the jar's contents, which she cast into the pot.

Sir Cranston Pitts fled again to the ladder. Climbing to the highest rung, he watched smoke that turned poisonous orange as it rose and slithered serpentlike around the Prince's ankles.

"Wake!" the dwarf spat through clenched teeth. New waves of hatred washed over him at the sight of David's black mane of curls framing the face more seductive in sleep. The boy's graceful hands twitched, drawing attention to their size. Too big. All about him—his shoulders, his arms, his thighs—everything was far too big.

"Kill him," Sir Cranston Pitts begged.

The witch seized her scaly pet from the floor and bit hard into the soft, white flesh of its underside. She wiped its blood from her ancient mouth, then snatched the still-beating heart from the lizard's dying body. After dropping the organ into the cauldron, she hurled the limp carcass at her assistant's feet.

The dwarf yelped and bit back angry curses as the reptile fell to its final rest on a bottom shelf.

Baljataur lowered her head, muttering an incantation that wound the orange smoke-snake around the Prince's body until it engulfed him from ankle to chest. "Baby's trusting laughter," she ordered.

Sir Cranston Pitts did not move. This last ingredient was a *gift*.

The same gift, in fact, that the hag claimed she had been bestowing upon the Prince when she was caught suckling him.

"Baby's trusting laughter!"

He swiftly brought down the familiar jar that seemed filled with nothing but air. The witch held this treasure to her withered bosom, her expression of twisted rapture the very same as seventeen years before when she held the King's only heir.

"Yes!" the dwarf cried when the jar was opened and a purple mist was sucked into it from David's nose. Of course. She was merely *taking back* her gift; for when she dealt the boy his doom he would have no more need for trust or laughter.

A shadow of guilt arose when Sir Cranston Pitts remembered how the joyous Prince, only hours before, had raised a glass "To love!" before swallowing the drugged wine. The dwarf had then leapt onto the lad's bed to stand tall and powerful above the sleeping form. For a long time he stared down at the comely mouth and big body, nursing fantasies of a sword unsheathed to spill royal blood on silken sheets.

"Ladder!" the witch barked.

He wheeled the stepladder close and climbed up to see what she stared at down in the cauldron. Baljataur waved her arms, causing smoke to move aside and flames to drown.

"See all-all," she whispered. "Clearness of truth. Purity of truth."

Gripping the sides of the ladder, he leaned forward until his own reflection shone in the calm, red liquid. It was not mere reflection, for there was David, Prince Gaspari—not hanging unconscious by his wrists above the iron pot, but sitting serenely in the palace gardens playing his lute.

Sir Cranston Pitts beheld the moving images. He heard the tune the boy played, heard his own footfalls as he danced close to where David sat. *Why did the Prince never laugh at me?* the dwarf thought, watching his ridiculous self: stubby arms flailing, stubby legs waddling, oversized head bobbing as if the neck could not sustain its weight.

"Stop dancing!" he shouted into the cauldron.

As if it heard, his image stopped and sat cross-legged in front of the Prince. David laid his lute on the grass and shielded his eyes to look at the noonday sun.

"Greetings come to me," the lad said, "from King Gustav of Prussia. It seems my marriage to his daughter has been arranged. Did you know of this, Sir Cranston?"

The dwarf shrugged at first, then nodded when the Prince's searingly honest gaze fell upon him.

"I remember that day! Last week!" cried the dwarf perched on the witch's ladder. The images in the cauldron took no notice of this interruption.

There, the Prince tore up a handful of grass and hurled it into the wind. "How very thoughtful of everyone to fix my life for me. What is the King of Prussia's daughter's *name*?"

"Details," the dwarf snorted. "The importance lies in the size of her dowry. . . . And she still has all her teeth."

The Prince groaned.

"It is all to the good, Your Highness—to end your foolish talk of venturing out into the world. Did you not realize that saying you long to hunt the wild boar like a common woodsman would drive your mother half mad with worry? The queen thinks a wife will keep you safe here."

"Safe from *what*—the awful, footless witch? I daresay, old fellow, that if Madame Baljataur held any ambitions of seeing me dead all these years, she would have overrun my father's parasitic monks on one of many occasions when they are too drunk to protect me."

Sir Cranston Pitts' reflection crossed himself, as he always did when the Prince spoke ill of the palace Holy Men. "Your duty is to marry," he said firmly. "You must ensure our King an heir, and ensure our peaceful relationship with Prussia."

"I am already married."

"To a leg of lamb!" the dwarf laughed, pinching one of the boy's beefy arms.

"No, *truly*. In the palace chapel we pledged love to one another with God our only witness." The Prince's eyes fell; he blushed furiously. "We pledged love again that night in my bed."

On the ladder in the witch's hovel, Sir Cranston Pitts felt the same dread knotting his belly as it had on that sun-drenched day his murderous plot against the boy began.

It was David's own fault, he reasoned. There were a hundred women living in service to the King's household. At least sixty of those were unmarried, and of that sixty approximately forty were virgins. The Prince could ruin them all if he wanted to. Sir Cranston Pitts only wanted one virgin for himself: the Queen's lady-in-waiting.

"She is Lady Clymestra," the Prince in the cauldron-garden confessed. "Perhaps you know of her—my mother's lady-in-waiting?"

The dwarf watched all color drain from his reflection's face as it stared, blinking dumbly at the Prince.

"I know what you will say, Sir Cranston—that she is a mere servant, a peasant, *unworthy*. You will warn me to hold my tongue lest the monks hear of my sin. Well, I don't care. I must tell it, for there can be no sterile arranged marriage for me. The scent of the hunt is now alive in my nostrils. No cause for worry; I need never leave this house, for Lady Clymestra *is* my freedom. I have tasted the forest and the world beyond in her intimate chambers. I come on my knees, rapt and prayerful at the church of her perfumed thighs. I am reborn—"

"VILE!" Sir Cranston Pitts hopped up and down on the witch's ladder. "EVIL!" He swung tiny fists at the Prince's velvet-clad feet hanging only inches above the cauldron. He almost lost balance, but death would not matter if he could take the lascivious young bull to hell with him.

Baljataur stepped back, cackling laughter when the dwarf landed a blow and the Prince's eyes flew wide. Sir Cranston Pitts stopped punching and screamed, "Beast!" up at the boy's startled face.

David, Prince Gaspari's eyes darted from the dwarf to the witch to his own dire situation back to the dwarf. "Sir Cranston," he said haltingly. "Not one man in my father's house would I call 'Uncle.' None save *you*. Do you wish to steal next spring from me? Will I perish without a look at my child to be born then?"

Sir Cranston Pitts clamped hands over his ears and roared, "Do your worst! Kill him now!"

"Then damn you!" the Prince shouted back. "Damn your long life and everything you touch!"

The witch's laugh screeched beyond all sanity. She punched her own breastbone with both fists, then thrust hands outspread as if she would embrace the cauldron.

Snap! went the ceiling chain. Sir Cranston Pitts shouted surprise, leapt down from the ladder when the Prince fell with a great splash into the scalding fluid. Baljataur used her stirring paddle to hold the big lad under until, at last, he ceased his struggle.

The dwarf waited for joy to overtake him. Or relief. Or vindication at the very least. The feeling that finally swept him was nausea. He vomited on the wood floor, staggered dizzily backward, jumped at the noise when the witch threw her paddle clattering into a spider-webbed corner.

"All-all is mine!" she cackled.

Fluid in the cauldron belched, spewed its red-drenched contents ceilingward. With a new explosive laugh, David, Prince Gaspari spun like a dervish where he had been before above the iron pot. But now he hung suspended by *nothing*. The witch below him ran once around the cauldron, then she crumpled into a steaming heap on the floor.

Dead.

Sir Cranston Pitts screamed abject terror and bolted out into the night. He scrambled up onto his wagon, snapped the reins, whipped the horses to speed him through suddenly menacing woods.

"Open!" he shouted at the palace gates even before he'd crossed the last drawbridge. Once more on royal soil, he slowed the exhausted steeds and slipped them back into the stables, but no sense of safety accompanied him to his bedchamber.

Heartsick now, and fearful, he opened his shutters to await whatever damnation would surely befall him. He must have fallen asleep on his small window seat because it was there he found himself when his mind leapt to startled wakefulness at the distant sound of a lute.

He slid to the floor with full knowledge that the night before had been no mere drunkard's dream. His socks were encrusted with filth and his only pair of boots was gone. He walked to his door and out; he trod long passageways of gleaming black floors and white marble pillars; he followed the strangely mournful tune that drew him to the baths.

The music stopped, causing the dwarf to wring his hands with apprehension. He tiptoed around nude statues and copper candle-bowls to where mist swirled up from the large, shallow pool cut out in the floor.

"Damned hot," said David, Prince Gaspari. "I feel as though I am being cooked."

A tremor rippled through the dwarf at these accusing words, and the new edge of viciousness in the Prince's voice. Sir Cranston Pitts glanced fearfully at discarded, crimson-slick clothing nearby.

"Fetch Lady Clymestra for me." The Prince threw his elbows backward onto the pool's ledge, raised his hips, lowered them again in a shockingly wanton gesture. "Tell her to bring cool water. And boots— several pairs of my finest."

The dwarf crept closer, though his flesh crawled with every step.

"Inform my father that I refuse to marry the King of Prussia's daughter. I welcome any resulting declarations of war, for why have only a dowry when there is an entire *country* for the taking!

"Oh, and after you put on your happy bell's-cap to make me laugh, Sir Fool, do throw open the wine cellars to the palace monks. We must keep them occupied at all times, yes?"

Sir Cranston Pitts froze, watching the loving attention with which the Prince washed his big feet. Moisture slid from underneath the dwarf's arms, stinking fear and guilt that filled him with fresh thoughts of murder.

"You cannot move?" the boy said coldly. "Allow me to help."

A ball of fire rose from the bath, shot past the dwarf's ear, blasted a small, chiseled male nude near the doorway to bits. Sir Cranston Pitts jumped nearly a foot into the air, then fell trembling to his knees when an enormous fan-backed reptile slithered into the room, into the bath with David.

"For-*giiiive!*" the dwarf sobbed.

The Prince's eyes—like metal shards and shavings of ice—sliced through the mist. "I forgive, Jester Fiddlesticks. Forgive all-all and pledge you a gargoyle's loyalty from my heart . . . the heart of a lizard reborn."

Empty Jar, Empty Chest

STEPHANIE D. SHAVER

She was like a goddess in beauty, and just as unattainable.

Regan was a slight girl, narrow-hipped and dark-eyed, virgin as fresh snow, and quite unattainable to a lowly sometime-hunter, sometime-poacher who wore ratty furs and hide. Terent had tried very hard to win her—flowers, gifts, all the pretty things a girl could want. And she had turned them down, every one.

"I've tried everything," he complained one day (as he was oft known to do) while he was purchasing a bag of waybread from the baker's son, Deits. "I know she would love me if she could only see what I am, how much I could give her! I mean—who *wouldn't* love me?" He snorted, chewing on his beard in frustration. "But I'm nearly at the end of my rope! What next?"

"How about magic?" Deits asked casually.

Terent raised an eyebrow. "Magic?"

"Oh, aye. Don't you know of the witch?"

"The one in the wood?"

Deits nodded.

"What of her?" the hunter asked curiously.

"She may be able to help . . . if you truly love Regan."

"Of course I do!" he said, adding mentally, . . . *her lips, her hips, her eyes, her thighs . . . well, what I've SEEN of her thighs. . . .*

The baker's son nodded, then, pausing, said, "She helped me find my love."

"That's nice," Terent said brusquely. "Can you tell me where she lives?"

Deits nodded, and, after taking Terent's money for the waybread, took him outside, pointing northward and rattling off some directions.

"You will need money. She will ask payment."

Terent nodded. "Of course," he said, and rubbed the hilt of his blade. Sage . . . wasn't the juice of sage, and some other plants, said to repel witches . . . ? In his mind, he scanned the herbs he had seen growing through the very wood he hunted, and smiled.

"Of course," he repeated, and, without thanking Deits, went on his way.

Terent heard a voice muttering, just before he raised his fist to pound on the door, "Empty jarses means empty cauldron. Ah, Raven, what now?"

Knock, knock, knock.

"Who ist?" The patter of feet against a wooden floor. "Who tapses on my door?" The door rattled, as if someone were shaking the handle. "Who ist? Answer!"

"Terent Hound!" he yelled back. "Come for the witch!"

There was a sqwuak, and a "Come for the witchses, has he? Will turn him into a toad, thist witchses shall!"

"No! No—I mean, I came to speak to you—"

The door swung open to reveal an ill-lit cave of a room and a stringy, dingy, hunched figure in drab gray. She pushed a strand of hair out of her eye, and looked him up and down.

"What does Terentses want with Malana?"

Terent swallowed, his mind turning in a thunderous circle. Malana? Did witches have names? He thought they yielded them to the god Raven in exchange for their power. No matter. It was not a name he needed.

"Witch? Are you the witch?"

"Aye!" Malana said, and cackled. "Yes! Witchses! Come in, child-soul. You lets too much cold in."

He shuffled in, and the door slammed shut, the bar falling home with a clack. He swallowed, then reminded himself of the knife at his hip. No witch would harm him tonight.

"So, what does Houndses want?" the witch asked, shuffling over to a large black cauldron and taking a delicate sniff of its contents.

"A charm, ma'am. Just a charm."

"Oh? *Just* a charmses? No such thing." She reached up to a shelf, and took down a jar. She shook the contents, listening, then, smiling, opened it and dumped the contents in. "No such thing, *just*acharmses," she repeated, and smiled at him.

"A . . . love charm."

She raised a brow at him, and, reaching over, grabbed a broom from beside the fireplace. She bared her teeth. "Ah! Child-soul wantses a woman to fall in love, eh?"

He nodded.

"Then charmses ist not what he wants! *Potion* ist what he wantses!"

He had to stop himself from caressing the handle of his blade.

"Potion, charm, whatever. I just want her to fall in love with me."

"Ahhhhh . . . do you?" The witch's eyes flickered. "One-sided true love? Or true *lustses?*" She flicked a half-smile. "Malana won't do ist."

"You must!"

The witch—who had turned toward her cauldron and begun stirring it with the handle-end of her broom—turned back around and raised a brow. "Mustses? Strong words, little hound. No, Malana *mustn't.*"

She turned back to her cauldron. Terent swallowed, then stepped forward, and, in the smooth motions of the hunter, the hound, drew his knife and placed it at her throat. She froze, straightening a little from her hunch as he grabbed her hair and hissed:

"Yes, you mustses."

* * *

422

The potion was red when it was poured into the bottle. It took all of an hour to make. Terent kept the knife out as she prepared the potion, and the witch actually seemed to whimper whenever she looked at it, making warding signs and keeping a good distance from him.

"Ist done," she whisper-hissed, capping the bottle. "Now putses knife away!"

"No," he said. "Not until you give it to me."

"Takeses ist!" she yelled, pointing to where it sat. "But takeses knife *away!*"

He smiled, going over to where the bottle rested on a table, and, lifting it—it was slightly warm to the touch—shoved it in his pocket. He bowed slightly, ironically, and then went for the door.

"Remember!" he heard her shout as he made his way out the door of her cottage and toward the open wild of the woods. "One drinkses, then the other. Both mustses declare love, and mustses be by the river, and mustses be *tonight! Remember!*"

He scarcely heard her as he went toward the village he, and his Regan, lived in.

She was brushing her hair out by the moon—purported by the women to keep hair lustrous, purported by the priests to teach them women's evil—when he came calling. Her father's home sat on the outskirts of the "village" (only called so because it paid the King's tax), and her window faced toward the wood.

"Regan!" he whispered as he stepped out of the shadows and into the radiance of the moon and her beauty. "Regan!"

She searched the area with her eyes for a moment before nailing him with her gaze. She sighed heavily when she saw it was him. "What *now*, Terent? What do you want?"

"I—have something for you," he said. "A . . . gift."

Regan looked at him with open, cold curiosity. "Really? Let me see."

He held up the bottle, and thought for a moment. "It is a potion . . . of beauty."

She blinked. "Oh!" She breathed deeply. "Give it to me!"

"No," he said, stepping back a pace. "I must . . . you must come here, first."

She raised an eyebrow. "Oh, please," she said. "You think I'm actually going to fall for that? How do I know you're not just trying to lure me outside to rape me?"

"How do you know I really *don't* have a beauty potion?" He stepped back another pace.

"Terent!"

"Come, Regan. I promise not to hurt you. Come with me. . . ."

She frowned, and he saw her considering. Silently, he held his breath. This had to work; he couldn't simply drag her off to the river. This had to work . . . it just had to. . . .

"P—romise?" she said at last.

"On my knife," he said quickly, quietly.

"All right. Let me get my cloak."

He smiled with relief in the shadows.

"Terent, where are we going?"

He kept his hand around her wrist, wondering at the softness of her skin, lily-petal smooth against his rough fingers.

"We must drink the potion by the river."

" 'We'?"

He smiled. "There is enough for both of us."

"Terent!"

"Shhhh. . . ." He stopped. "Hear that?"

She sighed. "Sounds like the river."

"It *is* the river." He tugged her along. "C'mon."

The river was glittering like liquid diamond over granite shores in the night's wan light, and he sat down next to it with a triumphant flop. He had her here. Now, just one more thing.

"Say you love me."

"*What?*" she said, sitting down and staring at him like he had gone mad.

"It's part of the potion," he said. "Say you love me; you must say that to make it work."

She sighed, rolled her eyes, and said, "Terent, I love you."

He smiled and removed the bottle from a pouch at his side. He uncorked it with an air of ceremony, took a sip (it tasted foul), and said, "I love you, Regan."

"Gimme!"

He handed it to her, watching her drink it with a hungry greed, and then waited.

She stood. "Okay, when does it work? You're still ugly."

"Am I?" He felt a sudden, pleasant rush of heat, and his stomach flopped. He wondered if she felt the same.

She made an annoyed, huffy noise and pushed herself back to her feet. "Yes, you are. . . ." Her voice dropped away, and she stared at him silently, her eyes going glassy. She shook her head drunkenly, and then said, "Oh, Terent." She licked her lips, breathing heavily. "Oh, Terent—"

And dropped like a lead weight.

He blinked and reached over to gather her in his arms. Her love for him must have made her swoon, yes, that was it, and his kiss—his kiss would wake her. Of course . . .

He bent his head to kiss her, to wake her—

It was then that the witch's poison fully hit his less delicate veins, and he crumpled silently over her body.

She pointed toward the blade on the hound's hip. "Deits, take that Raven-cursed knife away. Forsworn it is and therefore now no more than a dagger to me, but still . . ."

The witch's consort smiled at her. "Speak no more, m'lady." Stooping, he picked up the knife and tossed it into the river. It vanished, the ripples it created blending with the others made by the moving water. "Did he try to kill you with it?"

"Oh, no. Just threatened me. I'm sure he fancied it a secret weapon." She shook her head. "Secret—gah. As if I wouldn't feel its presence the moment it entered *my* home." She snorted, and rolled the bodies over. "Good thing the girl's cloak is long. We can drag them back to my home with them on it."

Deits smiled at her, and stroked her hair, now long and blonde, her lips a deep red. Not beautiful, but striking. Ah, yes. Very striking, his witch.

"Will they be noticed?" she asked.

"Eh? Oh, no. I was very careful, m'lady Malana. They're more likely to believe that Terent stole her away. And Regan wasn't well liked."

The witch smiled. "Good, and good."

"What now?" Deits asked softly as he hauled Terent's body onto the cloak. "The hearts of two untrue lovers—that's what you said you needed, right?"

She smiled grimly, displaying her sharp little teeth, her voice slipping into a rattling hiss, "Aye, Deitses—empty chestses means full cauldron! Ah, Raven, what do I need next?"

Brownouts

BILLIE SUE MOSIMAN

It wasn't working. Nothing she tried lately would work. All her spells failed her, and with them her confidence plummeted to its lowest depths.

"Can't you do something? We're going to lose the ranch if you don't help."

Guida sighed deeply as she glanced from her needlework to her husband. "Then we'll have to lose it."

She stuck the needle through the coarse cloth and pulled the scarlet thread through to the other side. It was a sampler detailed with the names of the goddesses. Soon she might not have a place to hang it.

"Where will we go? What will I do? I can't feed four kids on some clerk job in town."

Brady took that moment to run into the room yelling, "Martha wet her pants, Mama! I *told* her she was gonna get a whipping if she didn't go to the bathroom and she wet herself anyway."

"Tell Martha to come in and I'll change her."

"I hope you whip her, Mama," Brady said over his shoulder as he raced out again.

Jim put his fingers through his hair. "I don't know how you stay so calm. These kids drive me crazy and here we are going down the tubes, not enough in the bank to buy feed for the cattle, and you sit sewing."

She put aside the hoop of cloth. Martha was at the door, peeking from the doorframe with an ashamed look on her face. "Come on in; it's all right, Martha. Mama'll fix you right up."

"Will you try again?" Jim asked.

"I'll try."

"Do you promise?"

"I promise."

She went into the stable once she had finished cleaning up Martha and putting all the children to bed for noonday naps. The cattle didn't come in here much until the weather chilled and they wanted shelter from winter storms.

In the loft where Jim kept bales of hay, Guida had made a quiet place for herself. Behind a stack of bales she had thrown a quilt on the rough haystrewn boards. She kept a candle, matches, and her book of spells on the sill of a grimy window set into the wall nearby.

There was no privacy in the house, crowded as it was with all the children, and the stable loft was the only place she could find to concentrate on creating magic.

Magic. The most beautiful word in the language, any language. If only she could recover her power to perform it. When she met Jim, when they were young and energetic members of the local coven, she had been one of the most potent witches in all of West Texas. With that power she helped Jim find the right land and build a working ranch with horses and a respectable cattle herd. Then the children began to come and her power waned with each succeeding pregnancy. Alarmed, she went to the priestess and asked what was happening to her.

It was simple, really. The more children she produced, the more earthbound she was, the more strands she had binding her to the mother soil. The more earthbound, the farther away from her Protector she moved.

"Why do you think so few of us have babies?" the priestess asked. "We aren't like normal women. We squander our gifts if we try to live out an average woman's life of motherhood. Sex renews your energy. Birthing and caring for children drain you."

Guida tried not to get pregnant after Jersey, her second son.

Mistakes happen. That's what the doctor said, checking her intrauterine device. "Maybe we should try another method."

The birth control pill failed and she found herself pregnant with her fourth child, Martha.

And now she was pregnant with a fifth baby. Her powers were almost gone as it was. Once the child she carried was born, she expected she would be stripped of all powers forever.

She lit the candle and set it back on the sill away from the hay bales. She opened the book of spells and studied it for some time. She had used most of them at one time or another: the spell to heal (Brady came down with measles and almost went blind), the spell to keep a man at home (Jim had wandered from her bed during her fourth pregnancy, taking up with a barroom girl in town), the spell of fertility (this one was used on the plowed lands where Jim grew his own corn for the cattle).

There appeared to be no spell for insolvency. There was one to bring money, but she had been casting it for six months and it was not working.

Her gaze paused on a page and she read the spell there slowly, carefully. *Spell of Deceit.*

Guida sat back, letting the book lie open in her lap. Maybe this one would work. The county tax assessor was coming in the morning with a writ stating they were taking over the ranch for back taxes owed. Could she deceive him into believing they had been paid? By the time the spell wore off, she and Jim could make enough to really pay them and the assessor would never know the difference.

She turned back to the book and studied the spell until she had it memorized. Then she put it aside on the sill, bowed her head, and began to pray for intercedence. For the power of deceptiveness.

Something must save them. Or else where and how would her children be able to live?

Jim stood alongside Guida, reading the formal papers from the tax assessor. Before through the first paragraph the black typed letters on the page began to wiggle and move, dancing like electrons around a nucleus.

Guida smiled mysteriously and heard the official say, "What a lovely smile you have, Mrs. Frederickson. I'm so glad I brought this out for you and your husband to see today. I know it takes a load of worry off you both to know everything has been filed and the ranch is all paid up."

Guida handed back the changed document and said, "Thanks so much. It was good of you to come all this way to let us know."

As he drove away Guida said to her husband, "Well, that's the first spell that's worked for me in months."

"What spell?" he asked. "Sometimes I think you speak in riddles just to make me look stupid, Guida."

That was the first inkling Guida had that something had gone wrong.

The next instance happened less than an hour later when Brady came to her with another complaint about his little sister. "Martha won't play house right. She keeps making me sweep the floor. Will you make her behave, Mama?"

"Tell Martha to come here and I'll speak to her."

Brady stood there, puzzled.

"Well? What are you waiting for?" Guida asked.

"I don't know, Mama. Didn't you call me?"

"I thought you wanted me to talk to your sister about the rules of playing house."

"Martha's fine. I love Martha. She knows how to play. Can I go now? She's waiting for me to sweep the floors."

After she'd dismissed him, she wondered what in the world was happening. Had she deceived Brady into believing his sister was a paragon of virtue? And Jim. Had the spell in some way spread out from the papers to his mind, deceiving him into thinking there had been no spell cast to save them from paying the taxes?

She had never seen a spell travel so rapidly from one event to another. It could turn against her and finally wreck everything if she didn't control it.

She hurried to the barn, climbed to the loft, and took up the book. She reread the spell, her lips moving as she went over the words. Had she left out one, mispronounced a word, added in something she shouldn't have?

That night in bed Jim turned to her and whispered, "I never thought I'd be married to a movie star."

Shocked, Guida said, "What?"

"Honey, my world is perfect because of you. There's a thousand men in Hollywood who would have wanted you, but I was the lucky one. I just wanted to tell you how much I love you."

He thought she was someone else! Now the spell was mutating so that the people it controlled grew to deceive themselves without her having anything to do with it. Had Jim always fantasized being married to some movie queen? And now believed he was?

In the morning she'd have to find the priestess and ask for help. This was a disaster.

"Weren't you in class the day I told the apprentices not to use that spell without supervision from higher ups?"

"I must have been absent. I don't remember anything of the sort."

"Well, you've caused yourself a great headache, Guida. You're going to have to reverse this spell. If you let it go on, eventually no one will know who you are. Everyone you meet will deceive himself into thinking you're someone else, someone they've admired or had a craving to know."

"This is terrible! My husband thinks I'm a movie star. This morning my children thought I was Miss Roshack, their favorite teacher at school."

"Hurry back home and call for a reversal before it gets any worse."

Guida stood from the sofa and moved quickly to the door. She turned back to ask how long would she need to pray and the priestess astonished her by rising, coming to give her a hug before she stepped back to say, "I'm so glad you visited, Rita. I thought you'd never come on a trip all the way from Spain to see me."

"Rita?" Now her mentor thought she was a long-lost sister.

She must hurry home to the loft. She had no time to lose.

The day wore on toward night and the light dimmed in the stable, casting shadows like black bars across the empty spaces.

Guida dropped the spell book from her hands and turned to move smoothly, gracefully to the ladder leading down to the stable floor.

On the way to the house she touched her hair and thought, *I should have my hair seen after. It must be a fright.* She looked down at her faded dress and thought, *I need new vestments. This ragged apparel will not do.*

As she opened the front door, her children greeted her with cries of delight. They called her Miss Roshack, but that was all right, the dears. They could call her anything they liked as long as they were well-behaved. They couldn't very well address her as Diana, Goddess of Moon, Forest, Animals, and Childbirth, could they?

Orpheus came from the kitchen, an apron tied around his waist. Even in a rancher's dusty clothes, old boots, and the apron, he made her heart accelerate. She had always known he would make a good mate. If he would follow Eurydice into the bowels of hell, he would be true to his Diana. "Hi, sweetie," he said. "I thought I'd make dinner tonight."

She nodded at him and smiled regally. "I'll entertain the children," she said, sweeping her skirts aside as she sat down in the throne.

"Come now and sit at my feet," she ordered, reaching out to touch each child on the shoulder.

She rested her hands on her growing stomach then and began to tell the tale of olden times when there were theaters and coliseums and chariots full of adoring worshipers who came to give the gods and goddesses their due.

She concluded, "Though the time has passed from that golden age to this new one, we are back once again to create the world anew."

The children all beamed in enchantment.

Diana thought that tomorrow she would cast a new spell, adding more cattle to the ranch, building a forest glen where the children could play in running brooks, and maybe she would have the moon shine all throughout the day to signal a fresh beginning in the land.

Small Workers

Lois Tilton

It was a *big* ant, a big shiny black ant with big black pincers. Nettie jerked her fingers back to save them, and the ant gave her a dirty look before it disappeared back under the foundation. *"Eeeuuuuw!"*

"What the hell are you looking at? Shit." Carl elbowed her aside as he knelt down to see for himself. "Carpenter ants!"

He pulled off a damp, crumbling splinter of wood from the siding and revealed a half-dozen of the ant's relatives, who scuttled to safety in the tunnels honeycombing the wood. "Eeeuuuuw!" said Nettie, and again when Carl picked up one ant and savagely pinched off its head from its body.

"Shut up, will you?"

The ant's legs were still kicking, the pincers on its severed head still slowly opening and closing, as if it wanted with its last gasp of life to dig its mandibles into Carl's flesh. But it couldn't reach him as he stamped away into the garage, returning a few minutes later holding a black aerosol can with an elaborate nozzle. "Get out of the way," he said to Nettie, pushing her back as he shook the can so its contents fizzed slightly.

He depressed the nozzle, and a high-pressure jet rushed out with a hiss of propellant gas, spattering against the foundation of the house.

431

Nettie stepped further backward as she smelled the sharp, acrid chemical odor. "Isn't that dangerous, breathing those fumes?" she called to Carl.

But he ignored her, proceeding at a half-crouch along the length of the foundation, spraying the ant poison. Nettie glanced up to see their old neighbor, Mrs. Hagopian, frowning in worried disapproval at the edge of her immaculately groomed lawn. Mrs. Hagopian didn't like pesticides or other chemicals. Nettie sometimes wondered how she kept her lawn so perfect without using anything on it, but the demarcation between the plush greensward of Mrs. Hagopian's grass and the scraggly weeds growing in their own yard was painfully obvious.

Then Carl came back around the corner of the house, cursing and shaking the can of insecticide. When it sputtered emptily no matter how hard he shook it, he flung it into the bushes. "Damn thing's empty," he snarled, heading back to the garage. Nettie bit her lip, but Mrs. Hagopian was gone.

Nettie retreated into the house. When Carl came in about a half hour later, he reeked of pesticides. "Eeeuuuuw," Nettie said from the stove, but he gave her a look and went to the refrigerator for a beer.

"Did you kill all the ants?" she asked.

"How the hell do I know if I killed them all? I sure sprayed the hell out of them, that's for sure. Hey, there isn't any beer!"

"Yes, there is. I bought a case yesterday at the store."

"Well, then, where the hell is it?"

She went to the refrigerator, pulled out a can.

"What are you hiding it back there for? Sheesh!" He popped the top and slurped quickly at the foam boiling out of the can, cursed because the beer wasn't cold enough.

"That's why I put it in back, where it's the coldest," Nettie explained. "That's as cold as the refrigerator gets."

"Piece of junk," Carl said. "This whole place is a dump. Rotten wood—looks like a goddam Swiss cheese. Full of ants . . ."

"They're so *big!* Don't you think, maybe we should call an exterminator or somebody?"

"Yeah, like I can afford to pay some exterminator." He drained the can. "Get me another one. And when's that slop going to be ready? I'm hungry."

* * *

432

The next morning, after Carl had gone to work, Nettie went out and crept nervously up to the place where she'd seen the ants. Their twisted, inch-long bodies littered the cracked ground next to the foundation, curled into tortured fetal positions. Nettie drew back. A shiny black head with vicious-looking pincers was emerging slowly from a crack in one of the cinder blocks.

"Oh-oh." Carl wasn't going to like it when he saw the ants were still in the house. He was going to be real mad. Nettie bit her lip nervously. When Carl got mad—

"Not good. Not good." Nettie jerked her head up. There, standing behind her, was Mrs. Hagopian, all dressed in frowsy black down to her ankles with a knitted black scarf tied under her chin. She was shaking her head. "Not good, to spray, to kill small workers."

"But . . . Mrs. Hagopian . . . they're *carpenter* ants. They're like, eating the wood! And we can't afford an exterminator, Carl said so."

"Your man, he spray poison. Your husband. He good man?"

"Carl? Well, I guess. Well, sometimes he gets a little mean. . . ."

The old woman reached out a hand to pat Nettie on the shoulder. It was covered with brown blotches, and the joints were so swollen and twisted Nettie wondered how she could manage to open and close the fingers. "You a good girl. I help. You want small workers to go?"

Nettie blinked. "Yes, please."

"Then go inside to kitchen. Get flour, get sugar, get salt. Bring here."

Curious, Nettie ran to do as she was told. The old woman took a pinch each of flour, sugar, and salt between her finger and her horny thumb and rolled them together, muttering words in some strange language Nettie didn't understand. Then she sprinkled the white mixture in front of the crack in the foundation where Nettie had first seen the ants. A six-legged black body emerged, then three others, and suddenly there were a hundred ants pouring out of the foundation, and hundreds following them.

Nettie screamed, running backward, brushing at her legs as if the swarm of ants were crawling up them. But Mrs. Hagopian stayed where she was, bent over, crooning foreign words to the insects. And like a stream of oil, the black ants flowed out of the cinder blocks, past the old woman, and on into the lush thick grass of her lawn.

She looked up at Nettie, gave a cheerful nod. "Not be afraid. Small workers not hurt you. Come. See."

Nettie really didn't want to, but there was Mrs. Hagopian, standing there, beckoning to her. Cautiously, she approached, looking down at her feet in case ants jumped up on her. But they were all disappearing into Mrs. Hagopian's lawn.

"Come, see," the old woman said again, and bent down, parted the grass. Nettie nervously stood behind her and looked. There were the ants, the carpenter ants from her house and other ants: big ones, little one, black ones, red ones. Thousands of ants, all swarming in the grass. As she watched, Nettie saw them grooming the lawn, clipping the grass blades, carrying off weed seeds, loosening the soil around the roots.

"Small workers," Mrs. Hagopian said smugly.

And indeed, wherever Nettie looked, there were ants at their tasks, cleaning off the sidewalk that led up to the house, carrying off leaves and other debris, down to individual grains of dirt in the jaws of the smallest red ants.

"How do you get them to *do* that?"

"Secret from old country. Young woman marry husband, work hard. Hands . . ." She held them up. "No more can work. Old woman have small workers to help. From my mother I learn. From her mother. Old secret."

Nettie watched the ants for a few more minutes. Actually, when you *looked* at them, it was kind of neat, really. "Do you think you could teach me?"

The old woman took her hands between her own. The palms felt like warm, rough leather. "You are young woman. Strong, strong hands. But I have no daughter. You good girl. I teach you."

And so Mrs. Hagopian taught Nettie how to mix the flour, sugar, and salt, the words to use to call the ants, to control them. It was weird, at first, and Nettie still didn't like the really big black ants. But after a while, it was kind of neat to see them picking up the crumbs from her kitchen floor and taking them to the garbage, two lines of them, coming and going. The more she learned, the more it didn't seem weird at all. And the house was cleaner than it had ever been.

Even Carl noticed, though of course she never called the ants to work when he was around. It was too bad, though, that she couldn't set the ants to working at night, which Mrs. Hagopian said was the best time.

But then Carl got laid off, and suddenly things changed for the worse. With him lying around the house all day, the place got to be a mess, and Nettie couldn't call the ants to help clean it up. He got meaner, too, being out of work, and he started to drink a lot more.

One night, when crying herself to sleep didn't work, Nettie crept out of bed to the kitchen, mixed the flour, sugar, and salt, and whispered the words to call the ants. In the morning, the floors were clean and the burned-on food was gone from off the stove. Encouraged, she called the ants again the next night, and the next, and things started to get better again.

But then Carl, who was drinking a lot of beer before he came to bed, got up in the middle of the night to go to the bathroom, and afterward he decided to go get a sandwich in the kitchen. Nettie was suddenly yanked out of sleep by the sound of curses.

She ran in a panic down to the kitchen, and there was Carl, swearing and stomping on the ants. "Shit! Look at this! Look at all these! Damn, there must be a million of 'em! Don't we have any ant poison?"

"I . . . don't know."

Something in her tone made him turn around. "What's the matter with you, anyway? Look at all these damn ants! What've you been doing? I bust my butt every day, working, and what do you do? This dump is filthy! Ants, all over the place!" He jerked open the cabinet door under the sink, started tossing stuff out, looking for ant poison. At last he came out with a can.

Nettie didn't know what to do, what to say. "No, I . . . oh, don't!"

A familiar look came over his face. "Don't you tell me what to do, bitch! You don't take care of this, I'll have to. Now, get out of my way." With a slap to the side of her head, he knocked her aside, then started to shake the can. But it was empty. He cursed, threw it at her. "There's never anything in this house when I need it! Why can't we have a can of ant spray that isn't empty? What do you do with the money I give you, anyway?" He pulled her to him, hit her again. "Answer me, dammit! I'm talking to you!"

Two days later, when Carl had driven to the store for more beer, Nettie crept out of the house. Mrs. Hagopian was out pruning her roses. The carpenter ants, with their huge jaws, took only a minute to gnaw through the stems.

435

The old woman glanced up at Nettie's bruised, swollen face, nodded knowingly. "Ah, your man, he beat you."

Nettie put up a hand to hide the black eye. "He got up at night and saw all the ants in the kitchen," she said apologetically.

"Hagopian, he use leather strap, razor strap."

"Your husband?"

"First husband, Hagopian. Long time ago."

Nettie was curious. How *old* was Mrs. Hagopian, anyway? "You had more husbands?"

"Eight. Eight husbands. Some get drunk, some not. Man always like to beat wife. But young woman think, need husband." She shook her head.

"You had *eight* husbands?"

Mrs. Hagopian shrugged. "In old country. Things different, there. Eight husbands, yes. But small workers better."

At the moment, with her face throbbing, Nettie couldn't help but agree.

Mrs. Hagopian leaned closer. "You want know more secret? Old country secret?"

Nettie thought a moment, then nodded.

It was late before Carl got home that night, but still he demanded dinner the first thing he came into the house.

Wordlessly, Nettie set a plate in front of him.

"What's this slop?"

"Dumplings. It's a recipe I got from Mrs. Hagopian. Just a little flour, sugar, and salt. She told me she used to make it for her husband, back in the old country."

A Wild Imagination

LISA LEPOVETSKY

I'll be the wild mustang, and you be the cowboy. You have to capture me and tame me for the rodeo."

Debra shook her brown curly mane, and trotted off across

the backyard before Jerry could answer. She heard his high-tops pounding on the wet grass behind her, but she wasn't worried. She could always outrun him. She could outrun all the boys in the neighborhood. Rainwater dripped from the willows onto her back as morning fog dampened her T-shirt. A late-night thunderstorm had mined the lawns with puddles and mudholes.

Mama would have a fit if she caught Debra out here without a jacket, but Mama had left for her "group," as she called it, early in the morning. She wouldn't be home until nearly noon. Mama's "group" was a bunch of women who dressed in white robes and danced around in a circle, singing songs in strange languages. Debra wanted more than anything to be part of that circle, to dance with the women in the morning light. She wasn't allowed to join in yet, but she'd watched from between the banisters when Mama didn't notice. She'd even memorized some of the strange words she heard them chant.

Dad didn't approve of the "group," but he didn't say much. Debra suspected he didn't really know what they did in their circles. Maybe he didn't want to know. He just grumbled to himself and got that tight, dark look on his face whenever Mama mentioned the other members. He always seemed edgier on the days she met with them. Usually Debra was especially careful to behave herself those days, to avoid the lick of his belt or the wooden spoon.

But not today. Today, she wanted to think only of herself and the moment, to run faster than Jerry, faster than any boy, to fill her lungs with the morning dew. Debra inhaled her freedom, laced with the scent of roses from the garden. Mama's herbs were scattered throughout the flowers, and their musky, spicy odors seemed to give her extra energy. She bent forward, feeling her muscles tighten as she sped off, leaving Jerry far behind.

As she ran through the yards and empty lots connecting their small-town neighborhood, Debra turned her vision inward the way Mama had shown her, and felt the familiar metamorphosis begin. She whispered the words she'd heard her mother sing with the group. Her ten-year-old legs thinned and lengthened, and as she leaned even further forward, her arms repeated the process. Fingers and toes clenched tightly, hardening like solid fingernail fists into unshod hooves that kicked up the soggy turf passing wildly beneath her. Her neck stretched and arched, and she tossed her narrow head in the sheer joy of being a horse.

"Hey Debra, wait up," Jerry panted somewhere in the whiteness behind her. "I can't see you anymore. Where you going, anyway?"

As she galloped toward the dirt rectangle the Ericksons used as a makeshift tennis court, Debra whinnied with delight. He could follow that sound if he wanted to find her. She didn't answer his question, directed at the person she used to be. The child Debra didn't exist now, only the wild mustang and the prairie. She could almost see the tumbleweeds and cacti outlined by the fog.

Pretending not to hear Jerry's calls, she plunged headlong into the tennis court, waves of thick ocher mud sliding aside to make room for her. She felt the delicious suction of the flooded dirt surface against her galloping hooves, and the wet mud splashing against her loins. She neighed again into the mist.

Jerry's voice beat heavily into the dense air with each step he ran. "Debra, cut it . . . out. I don't . . . want to play this . . . stupid game anymore. I'll get you . . . back for this."

The wild mustang wasn't even tired yet, but the muck had slowed her down slightly, and Jerry was closing in, running around the grassy edge of the tennis court. She heard his voice level with the pounding of her heart and hooves as she gained solid ground again on the other side. She felt a thrill of fear at the denim smell of him and wanted to run, but the chainlink fence rose before her. She whirled to face him.

"Hey, Deb," he panted, leaning to one side, his hand holding his waist as though he'd fly apart if he let go. "Your dad's gonna . . . be real mad. He's always yelling at you . . . to keep outta old man Erickson's court. You're gonna get it . . . when he finds out."

The filly that had been Debra tried not to listen, prancing irritably on the small border of wet grass, but she felt her neck muscles begin to shorten, and her hooves softened painfully into flesh and bone. Frustrated tears joined the wetness of the fog on her face, and she was glad he couldn't see her very well through the pale mists. She tossed her head once more in defiance, and tried to whinny. Her voice sounded small and thin to her shrinking ears.

Jerry stepped closer, and pointed at her feet. "Where're your new sneaks?"

The little girl Debra looked down. Both shoes were gone, and her socks were thick with mud. Glancing out, she couldn't see any sign that she'd ever stepped into the thick mud of the tennis court. She knew what her father would say if she returned home shoeless, especially today. He'd probably paddle her, and even Mama's pleading wouldn't help.

"Your dad's really gonna beat you when he finds out." Jerry might have been reading her mind. She didn't even have to look at his face to see the satisfied smile. It coated each word he said.

Debra sighed and stepped back into the court. The mud felt slimy now, and rose well above her ankles. She shivered, wishing she'd worn her jacket after all. She moved her hands through the cold orange goop till they were numb.

"I'll find them," she said, her voice surer than she felt. "I'll rinse them off and dry them out. He'll never know. Come on and help me find them, Jerry."

"No way, José." He watched her from his grassy perch for a minute. Then he spoke slowly, quietly. "Dads have a way of finding things out, you know. It's almost like they're psychic or something."

Debra stopped searching and straightened up, her hands so coated with mud they looked twice their normal size. She eased her feet through the muck until she stood before him.

"How would Dad find out, Jer? Who's gonna tell him?"

His eyes glanced down. "I don't know," he mumbled. "You just should be prepared, that's all."

Debra pictured her father reaching for the wooden spoon, the one Mama used to make birthday cakes for Debra. The one that left red welts on tender flesh for days. When she pictured Dad's face, he looked like Jerry. Jerry would be Dad someday. Debra shuddered.

She glanced again at her hands and feet, so heavy with mud they seemed more like paws—big, hairy lion's paws. She closed her eyes and muttered the familiar chant, feeling all her muscles thicken, strengthen, and the hairs on her neck bristle. Her breath burned in her nostrils and she licked her lips as she hunkered toward Jerry.

"Let's play big game hunter," she growled, and leapt on him.

Jerry had no chance to answer as she caught his throat between iron jaws and tore. Warm blood splashed her T-shirt, washing some of the mud away. Her sharp claws dug joyfully into the earth as the jungle sun broke through the mist and shone on her rippling fur.

Her roar rang like laughter in her ears, like the joyful song of white-robed women dancing free in the daytime.

Quiet, Please

RICHARD PARKS

I told you I'd get it. Miss Ganny's replacement is deaf as a post." Dan Little held up the sign, the lettering easily readable in the bright moonlight. The night was warm; we were both shirtless. Dan's normally pink face was flushed even redder with excitement. I wasn't excited at all, though I tried to pretend for Dan's sake. Standing on the edge of Canemill Unity Cemetery at two to midnight didn't seem like cause for excitement. Mostly I was just scared.

"You really think this is a good idea?"

Dan smiled. "You ain't turning chickenshit on me now, are you?"

I tried reason. There wasn't much else left at this point. "What if someone sees us, Dan? Chief Williams himself got on the Channel 6 news and said they got a 'Satanic cult' on the loose after that desecration last month. They catch us and the *last* thing they'll do is lock us up!"

"That's election talk. Besides, what do you think they'll do?" Dan asked, grinning. "Strap a Bible to our ass and set it afire? You worry too much, John Lee Hook."

My whole name. Dan might have been fifteen but he was at least twenty years' worth of stubborn. No point arguing now; the best I could hope for was to get it done and get out. I didn't have many friends, but sometimes hanging on to one seemed more trouble than it was worth.

"All right. But how we going to do it?"

He handed me the sign and then reached into the knapsack he had slung over one skinny white shoulder. He produced a sliver of metal that glinted in the moonlight. "Masonry nails. There was some left in Daddy's shop."

I'd almost forgotten Dan's father. I gathered they didn't get along too well, but Dan hardly mentioned him at all until three months ago in the library, when he looked up from his hot-rod magazine and said, "The bastard died yesterday."

I'd asked who that was, of course, and he told me. Then he called

440

him another name, and then Miss Ganny wheezed at us to be quiet, as she always did, and that was that until now.

"I forgot to ask—is your mom doing okay?"

He laughed and put the nails away. "She has a new boyfriend already. His name's Mike. He's a mean bastard too. Mom likes mean bastards." He seemed to consider. "She must, anyway. Daddy used to slap her around and now Mike does." He shrugged. "Like she just couldn't wait or something."

I shrugged. "Mom says some people can't help the way they are . . . you know, like it gets to be a habit. Maybe they do what they do over and over 'cause they don't know nothing else. Or maybe they're born that way."

"Maybe you think too much, John Lee."

If there was a right thing to say following that I didn't know what it was. We both kept silent as we walked along outside the chainlink fence around the cemetery. Dan ducked between two tall azalea bushes and slipped through a neatly cut hole in the fence.

"How'd you know about this?" I asked, crouching low to follow.

Dan turned to face me. "I made it," he said proudly. "Took me almost a week with a keyhole saw, coming out here every night. Just finished it last month."

But they'd buried Martha Ganny not a week ago. "How long you been planning this?"

He shrugged. "You mean ol' Ganny? Hell, I thought the old witch would never die. This was for something else."

In the strong moonlight the headstones themselves looked like pale bones sticking up out of the earth from a shallow grave. We moved as carefully as we could through the stones, though that was mostly to keep from stubbing toes—the low stones didn't catch light so well. We were quiet but not overly so—Dan had already arranged for Lou Simms, the caretaker, to find a "present" of a bottle of Jack Daniels that Dan had swiped from somewhere. The old guy lived alone and it wasn't likely he'd hear anything till late morning.

Dan passed one more grave without even breaking stride, but I pulled up quick. "Lord . . ."

The earth had recently been disturbed, but that's not what got my attention. It was the headstone. It had been broken apart by repeated blows and none too well put back together, but the name was still—barely—legible.

" 'Matthew Little.' That was your father, Dan."

"I know my daddy's name, John Lee. Don't you?" he asked. His smile was nasty.

"You know damn well I don't," I said, "so stop being such a sorry-ass. It's just that they didn't give any names on the news. I didn't know your father's grave was the one wrecked, though I guess you did. I'm sorry."

"I'm not," Dan said. "I did it." He turned his back on me and kept walking. After a moment I followed. I don't know why. I was trying to be a friend, I guess. Just not very good at it.

"Well?" he asked after we'd gone a few yards. "Aren't you going to ask me why? I think you want to."

"Didn't know things were *that* bad between you. That must have been rough."

"You were lucky not to have a father," he said after a bit. "At least not one like mine."

"But what was the point of breaking his headstone?"

"Same point as being here now. Funny thing. After they're dead, a person's outlook on life seems to change." He grinned. "When Daddy was breathing he'd beat the hell out of me if I so much as *touched* anything that belonged to him. Cigarettes, beer, girlie magazines . . ." He grinned. "Or his tools. Then I used his own sledgehammer to break his own headstone, and he didn't say a damn thing. Not one word. I dug halfway to the coffin before I ran out of time. Nothing. He just didn't give a rat's ass anymore, but it sure felt good to me. This is going to feel good too."

"She only yelled at us now and then. It was her job."

"We ain't gonna break nothing, John Lee. It's just a joke."

Right. Joke. Ha ha. I'd heard it was bad to speak ill of the dead, but nobody said nothing about kidding them. And it *was* kinda funny. I could just picture the look on the face of anyone who knew Miss Ganny, to come here and see what we'd done—

"You got the flashlight?"

Almost forgot. We hadn't done it yet. Dan's question brought me back to where we were. We stood now in front of a gravesite topped with a stone box shaped like one of those little Roman temples in our history books. Only it wasn't marble, that's all. The surface had the gray sheen of concrete. There was money in Ganny's family but apparently not that awful much.

I held up the flashlight. "Here."

"Shine it on the side, doofus. You want me to smash my finger?"

I shone the light on the side of the little mausoleum while Dan fumbled around in the pack for the masonry nails and his Daddy's hammer. "Great. Give me the sign."

I'd almost forgotten that, too. I handed it over, glancing around to see if anyone was about, but as far as I could tell there was just me, Dan, and a wide field of stones. "Let's get this over with."

"Hold onto it a sec, John Lee. And hold that light steady while you're at it."

Dan pushed the sign against the concrete and held it in place with his palm while he fumbled the first nail into position with thumb and forefinger. The first blow rang dull and hollow. The lettering on the sign was clear and bright in the flashlight beam.

QUIET, PLEASE.

It was just a sign, swiped from the side of the counter from which Martha Ganny had worked for more than forty years. Her whole life among books and quiet. I think she liked the quiet as much as the books. She had seemed to resent even the small hacking coughs she couldn't help but make since I'd known her. And she sure wouldn't stand for noise from anyone else. I still remember the day Mud Johnson wouldn't shut up. He called her a witch. She said if that were the case she saw no reason why she shouldn't turn him into a frog and cook his legs for supper if he wouldn't keep quiet. She said she'd do it. He believed her.

I think we all did.

Not that I blamed her for that. I liked the quiet, too. It was one reason I came to the library after school. To read, and be safe for a while. Dan came for mostly the same reasons, I think, and maybe that's why we tried to be friends. I think safety mattered more than quiet, now that I knew more about him. And he always wanted to talk. Maybe not about his father or family or anything that was really bothering him. Just to talk. That was our whole problem with Miss Ganny.

"John Lee . . ."

"What's wrong?"

Dan had stopped, almost in mid-swing. He stared at his hand where it touched the sign and the stone. "This feels strange."

"Strange how? What are you talking about?"

He didn't act like he was too sure himself. "It's almost like . . . like I'm leaving. Like I'm not here."

"You look 'here' to me. We both are. Hurry up!"

He shook his head. "I can barely see you. Why are you standing so far away?"

I took a step closer. "There. That better?"

"John Lee?" It sounded like a lost voice, crying in the wilderness. "Where are you? Get me out of here!"

I reached out and grabbed his shoulder. "I'm right—"

"—here."

"Quiet, please."

We were at the table by the magazine racks. Dan had his hot-rod magazine, I had my science fiction paperback. Miss Ganny came out from behind the counter, the wrath of God in her eyes. Part of me still knew that I stood in the moonlight, my hand on Dan's shoulder, but that didn't help a bit.

"I honestly don't know why you come here," she said, her voice wheezing from the emphysema that killed her. "This is a library, not a place to carry on like banshees. Don't you boys know that?"

"There's nowhere else to go." I don't know if I actually said anything, but the memory was still there. It's what I always said, whenever the argument arose. It had happened too many times before. Maybe one too many times.

"Quiet, please," she repeated.

Maybe some people can't help the way they are. And maybe they just couldn't stop. Like Miss Ganny, dead now and still thinking she was in her precious library and making us be there too. Miss Ganny couldn't stop. And Dan couldn't stop. Not even then.

"Go to hell, you old witch," he said.

Miss Ganny looked at him. If she'd looked at me that way, I'd have died on the floor of whatever this place was, real or memory, but Dan didn't even blink. I don't think smashing his father's grave had felt so good to him at all, because if there had been more anger in him than he showed in his eyes right then, I don't think his body could have held it. It was as if everything that had ever hurt him in his life were rolled into one package and given the name Martha Ganny.

"Go to hell!" he said again, and then again as if the sound of it was music to him. "Go straight to hell!"

Whatever was left of human in Martha Ganny was gone now. Maybe Mud Johnson had been right about her. Or maybe Dan sent it away. Either way, now it just wasn't there.

"Young man, hold your tongue or I'll hold it for you."

"Go to h—"

I didn't even notice all the people and cars lined up waiting at the hole in the fence when I finally managed to scramble through and more or less fall down in front of them. I remembered Chief Williams's round red face from the TV. People with cameras stood behind him and suddenly there were a lot of flashing lights.

Chief Williams looked entirely too pleased with himself.

"Turns out Mr. Simms remembered someone had given him a good bottle of whiskey before the first time this happened," he said. "Turns out he had enough unpickled brain left to call us. You're under arrest, son."

They didn't do any more to me than they were supposed to do. I felt like Chief Williams would have liked to if the cameras weren't around but it was an election year and the cameras were what really mattered. After I was handcuffed for the reporters he personally marched me back into the cemetery, and just before he made them shut off the cameras we found Dan right where I'd left him. All except his tongue, of course.

They keep asking me about that.

I tell them over and over where it is and they look at me funny and ask again. I don't know why, but I am trying to be patient—some people just can't help the way they are.

A Hundred Wicked Little Witches

STEVE RASNIC TEM

That's enough, that's enough now," Jack whispered to the witch of wallpaper, whose face stared at him from every inch of the wall, her eyes bright and piercing as needles, her mouth a thin line of disapproval. But like all the others, she would not stop.

They would not stop: the witch of belly, the witch of walk, the witch of tongue. They had no sense of caution, of precaution, of decorum. They had no sense of the limits of a man's toleration, the limits to which a man might go. They had no, made no, sense. Jack tried to forget them, tried to manage without them. But they had the power, and only they could make the decision to let him go. The witch of charms might encounter him on the street, and she might force him to follow her blocks out of his way, simply on a whim. The witch of a glance might distract him at work, denying him promotions and the respect of his peers. The witch of lingerie might keep him awake all night, his mind so filled by the unobtainable that there was no room for sleep.

And if he objected, if he balked, if he shouted that he'd had enough, his fellow passengers on the bus, or the pedestrians sharing his sidewalk, would turn, would look uneasy, and gazing past them he would inevitably encounter the icy stares of fourteen highly annoyed witches. He knew this for sure. He'd counted. Each and every time, he'd counted.

Women were like that, as his father had told him. All of them witches, as his father had told him. Each with her own special power. Each with love to give and love to withhold. Each with the talent to destroy him in a hundred little ways. The witch of impatience and the witch of boredom. The witch of adultery and the witch of dissatisfaction. The witches of intolerance, aggravation, and greed.

Jack's own mother had been a witch of neglect. After she had him she didn't want anything else the rest of her life, including—most especially—him. She became a sad waitress during the day and a witness to street accidents at night. The only times he could remember her actually speaking to him before his father finally came back one day to take him

446

away was when she told him how to handle strangers: "Go away with them. Do what they want to do. They always tell better stories than the ones you hear at home."

When Jack was a small child the witches were appropriately small and enigmatically sinister. The witch of holes might lead him into the smallest place, even though he was much too large to fit. The witch of food gave him stomachaches even with his favorite meals. The witch of whispers told him secrets he'd be better off not knowing. They were full of tricks, misrepresentations, and disappointments, these witches. They taught Jack what he might expect the rest of his life. The witch of shadows filled the darkness with an impossible number of presences, breathing unseen and speaking in code. The witch of kisses filled him with an intangible longing. The witch of silences refused to answer any of his essential questions.

"Answer me! Talk to me! Say anything!" Jack shouted into the darkness, but the witch of solitude was not to be seduced.

During his teen years Jack dated every witch on the menu, and some other witches none of his friends could imagine. He followed the witch of legs one day until she lost him in a field of dining rooms. He kissed the witch of mouths so long and fervently that she stole his voice and used it to make crank phone calls. He fell asleep with the witch of smells and woke up with the witch of what's left.

Jack had grown cynical by the time he went off to college. With each new woman he met, his first thought was *Which witch is this?* Occasionally he might encounter the witch of hope or the witch of promises, but invariably he'd be left with the witch of nothing special.

Then came the day he met Marsha. She made no particular impression on him initially, which was unusual in itself. No handy labels presented themselves. She was a lawyer in a small firm downtown. They met at a party thrown by mutual friends. Apparently there'd been some matchmaking going on, but he hadn't known this at the time. Marsha was small and quick, with piercing black eyes that flashed as she talked. "You're full of it, Jack," was perhaps the second or third thing she ever said to him.

Her insulting him that way was almost a relief. Marsha was surely the witch of attitude, and having made that determination he could at last feel comfortable with her. He knew what to expect from her.

But as he realized later, her comment wasn't far off the mark. He'd been expounding, after too much drink, on his theory of witches. He'd felt secure that the people listening to him believed him to be merely fabricating a witty, extended conceit, with no idea that he really believed it. Marsha, however, saw through him almost immediately. "I know you can't see it right now, but you're full of it, Jack."

"Full of it? Full of witches, you mean."

Marsha sighed, turned away, then immediately turned back to him. "Will you come over for dinner tomorrow night?" And she smiled. A witch of surprises? But when he looked into her face at that moment, he would swear she was the witch of eyes.

All the next day Jack was plagued by the witches of shyness, embarrassment, and nerves. Every time he looked in the mirror they were there, telling him how bad he looked, how unimpressive he was. The witch of disinterest fell asleep while enumerating his faults, melting into a silver pool when he turned the hair dryer on her. The witches of jibber, jabber, and yakkety-yak screamed when he slammed his bathroom door on their criticisms.

Jack kept going to the mirror to check himself, intent on making the best impression on her that evening. Unfortunately the witch of bad hair had flown through the window that afternoon: it looked as if he'd caught his head in a mixing bowl. To add to that, the witch of middle age was growing a crop of white hairs inside his ears, and the witch of septic tanks had performed unspeakable magic on his breath. "Bug off!" he shouted to the ceiling, and the witches of cobwebs, dust, and lost memory scattered to points unknown.

"Damn, I look terrible," he said to the mirror, and the witch of gaunt reflection winked back. He shattered the glass with his fist, and bits of seven forgotten little witches tumbled to the tile floor, their eyes dull and inattentive.

The drive to Marsha's apartment was short but nerve-wracking. He missed the turnoff and ran over the witch of roadkill, drove around lost through a suburban tangle of ranch-style homes and the lairs of condominium witches for almost an hour. All the pedestrians he saw were women, or reasonable facsimiles, and all these women—he knew—were witches. So he refused to stop and ask any of them for directions. A few approached his car at an intersection—among them a witch of no visible means and a witch of immense proportions—but he stepped on the gas and rode away before they could grab the door handle.

In front of a church he counted four small witches-in-training in their school uniforms filing past with their leader, staring menacingly at his car, daring him to run over just one. In fact, the idea would never have occurred to him: It was the small witches who filled him with the most painful mixture of pity and fear.

Marsha's house was a split-level with a high hedge all around, no doubt to keep whatever particular rites she practiced a secret from male neighbors or arriving suitors.

"I'd pretty much decided you'd chickened out," she said to him when she opened the door. "What's the matter—the traffic witch cause you some trouble?"

He stepped back as if slapped. She *knew* of the witches! Of course, *all* the women knew—it was their birthright. But he had never had one admit this so readily before.

Marsha made him uneasy, and yet he was drawn to her irresistibly; she had become his witch of greatest appeal. Just as in the past he had fallen in love with no help for it for the witch of thighs and the witch of perfume, the witch of high breasts, and the witch of the perfect nose, or for Marsha's previous, most threatening rival, the witch of sweet reassurances.

"You look like a man who's been dating all the wrong women," she said with a laugh and a wink. He couldn't understand what she was talking about.

"I've never been too good with women," Jack admitted, thinking back to the witch of broken dates and the witch of screaming tantrums. "I've never known quite what to say. I never know what they want."

"I suspect it has more to do with what *you* want, Jack," Marsha said, this witch of smiles.

She reached over and took him by the hand. She pulled him to the couch and with her higher power forced him to sit down. She stroked his hand and whispered reassurances. She told him, "Let go," and "There's nothing to be afraid of." It was all too much. She was obviously some sort of witch of deception. He ran away—escaped—from her apartment and back to his own home. He ignored the witch of poverty panhandling in the street. He rudely brushed off the witch of opportunity who accosted him in the elevator.

"They don't understand, not any of them," he said to his empty four walls. And four witches of loneliness nodded. "I do my best, but I really don't know how to please them." Five witches of frustrated desire raked their claws across his clothes, exposing his cool flesh. "I'm so

449

scared of them I don't know what to do!" And three enormous witches of suicide began to open him with hammers and razors and knives.

"Open him! Open him! Open him!" they cried in unison, as his skin split and ribs parted. Then they reached inside him with their thin, wrinkled hands, to retrieve their sisters, the hundreds of witches who had always lived inside him, craving his attention.

Silhouette

MARK McLAUGHLIN

I need about five hundred copies." Knutson squinted at the pale, dark-haired clerk's name tag. Bright blue italics enthused WELKOME TO KOPY-KWIK! over black vinyl lettering: SILHOUETTE. "Is that your first or last name?" he said, nodding toward the tag.

The young woman blinked her night-black eyes. "It's what I'm called." She pointed to a wall display of paper colors. "Which would you like: white, yellow, blue, lime, or hot pink?"

"*Definitely* hot pink." A lazy smile stretched across Knutson's face as he leaned forward on the counter. He was a lean, thirtyish man in a black tank top and sweatpants. "Does anyone ever call you Silly?"

"I could ask you the same." Silhouette *tsk*ed, lifted his right hand from the counter, and worked a crumpled flier out of his grasp. "Look what you've done."

"That's okay. I'm just gonna stick the copies under windshield wipers. They don't have to be perfect." He shrugged, and his long blond hair tickled the flaming skull tattooed on his shoulder.

"The machine needs toner, so it'll be a while." She nodded toward a chair by the door. "You can wait over there."

Knutson remained standing. The pale woman took a plastic container from a sky-blue shelf and carried it to the sky-blue photocopier at the far end of the shop. Sky-blue was also the color of the wallpaper, counter, cash register, and the clerk's long frock. Origami birds and bats and insects hung by threads from thumbtacks in the sky-blue ceiling.

Silhouette turned toward him. Studied him. "Weren't you in here last week?"

Knutson yawned. "I can't remember."

"I'm sure you were. . . . You copied a recipe torn out of the newspaper."

"Must have been someone else. I can't cook." He looked toward the small front window. The parking lot was empty. "You must get lonely, working all by yourself. They should get you a helper."

She shot him an irritated glance. "For your information, I *am* 'They.' This is my place. I've got my own way of doing things."

"Oh. Sure." He watched as she finished loading the toner. She wiped the machine with a handful of white cloth. . . . Silk? Knutson squinted: was she really using silk to clean a copying machine? Her hand flipped back and forth as she wiped. On the side of the machine, black vinyl letters read: KOPIES SO KWIK, YOU'LL THINK IT'S MAGIK!

Silhouette slid a ream of hot pink into the paper tray. She opened the lid a crack and slid the flier into the machine. She punched buttons and bright green light seeped from under the lid. Paper whisked out of the front of the copier, collecting into a neat, rectangular pink column.

The clerk tapped her foot for a moment. She watched the growing stack of copies. Then her eyes opened wide as she grabbed one from the pile. "Your flier. It's for—"

"Sudzy's Car Wash." Knutson backed toward the door. "So?"

A hard look crept into the clerk's eyes. "They closed down two weeks ago."

Knutson turned the handle on the door's lock.

"You just leave me alone." Silhouette whispered. "I expect people to leave me alone."

"Come on, honey. The customer is always right." Knutson's lazy smile grew into a sideways leer. He ran up to the counter: the small gate sealing off the work area wouldn't open when he hit it, so he simply jumped over. He wondered for a moment how much money was in the cash register. On the side of the register, black vinyl proclaimed WE DO THINGS RITE!

"This is my place—my *business*—and what I say goes." Silhouette laid her hand on the corner of the copier. With only a small push, she spun the heavy machine around.

A flurry of pink cascaded toward Knutson. He batted the paper tempest away as he moved toward the clerk. Soon his fingers were covered with stinging paper cuts.

"Your kind doesn't know when to stop!" Silhouette's voice took on

451

a high, shrill tone. "I try to run a nice little business. And where does it get me?"

Knutson was now only three feet away from her. She moved her hands toward the ceiling in a series of frantic gestures; her dark eyes grew wider, wider. He reached toward her—to crush her to his chest, to drag her to the floor—

He heard a barrage of sharp snaps. He looked around and was immediately sliced across the nose with a paper wing. Crisp white bats and locusts circled around his head, slicing and poking him, whipping him with their broken strings. Elegant white swans tried to peck out his eyes.

He curled up on the floor, his hands over his face. For several minutes, the paper creatures continued their assault. Something sharp entered his right ear; hot pain blazed through that side of his head, and he screamed. Suddenly, the whirring and whizzing of flying paper stopped. For a moment, there was silence. . . .

Then a shrill, anguished cry filled the room. *We just wanted to fit in.*

Knutson's breath caught in his throat.

We?

He turned his head and peeked out between his fingers. He was just in time to watch the clerk point down at him. The copying machine opened its toothy lid and bellowed ravenously.

Master Tape

RICK HAUTALA

Abigail was feeling nervous, and she was very tired.

For the last three nights, she'd been awake for most of the night . . . ever since she received that "official" letter from Louie Phillips.

Louie the Scumbag, she always thought whenever she thought about him . . . as if *Scumbag* were his God-given last name.

Talking to Louie over the phone was always bad enough, but today Abigail had to go up to the office and *deal* with him, face-to-face.

That was never easy.

The instant she entered the offices of Caribou Ranch Records—a plush, well-appointed corner office that looked down on Congress Street from the sixth floor of the Canal Building—her first thought was that it was much too cold.

Cold as a witch's tit!

She had to bite down on her lower lip to stifle a ripple of nervous laughter.

Shivering, she sat down but had to look away from him when he leaned toward her across his desk and smiled at her.

She couldn't *stand* to see him smile like that.

She had always thought his teeth looked much too large for his face.

All the better to bite you with, my dear, she thought bitterly, thinking that it was the *perfect* look for a slime-ball record producer like Louie.

Lacing her fingers together in her lap, Abigail glanced out one of the office windows, where thick wedges of ice, stained brown by the city air, clung like ruined spider webs to the corners of the glass. Off in the distance, she could hear the warbling wail of a police car or ambulance.

Yeah, and they'd be calling for an ambulance for YOU soon, Mister Scumbag, if I had MY way!

It took a great deal of determination and effort, but she turned and looked back at Louie.

"So . . . you *do* have the tape with you, I assume," Louie said.

His voice slid up the scale, dragging out the last word as if it were something that tasted irresistibly delicious. He ended with a not-so-subtle *I've got you by the short-'n'-curlies, honey, and you know it!* grin.

Once again—as she always did whenever she had to deal with Louie face-to-face—Abigail thought about how big his teeth looked. They looked like tiny dinner plates . . . or little white shovels that could just chomp and *chomp* and *CHOMP.*

Just like what you're doing to my career, she thought, and the bitterness of the thought was a palpable taste on the back of her tongue.

As much as it hurt to do so, she sighed and nodded. Reaching one hand down, she patted the large gray tape case she was clutching on her lap.

"You know," she said, her voice almost breaking before she

sucked in a quick sip of air. "You . . . you don't have any right to . . . to *do* this . . . to *force* me to turn it over to you."

As often as she had rehearsed that particular line on her way over to Louie's office, it came out halting and unconvincing, even to her own ears. A *scumbag* like Louie, who was used to screwing people to the wall on a daily basis, surely wasn't going to be intimidated by the likes of her.

"Oh, is that so?" Louie said, leering all the more at her.

His wide, flat teeth gleamed like shiny porcelain in the diffused light of his office.

"Well, then, I suggest you take another look at your record contract, sweetheart. I paid for the studio time, and that tape belongs to *me!*"

Abigail cringed away from the vulpine look in his eyes. She wanted to—but didn't dare to—tell him that, while the master tape might be his, every damned song on it was *hers!*

Louie smiled, his lips parting even wider to expose both top and bottom rows of his teeth all the way to the gum line.

"And you signed that contract, baby. Nobody made you sign it. You *wanted* it, so you damned well better learn to *live* with it."

Squinting slightly, Louie sniffed laughter through his nose. A foamy bubble of saliva formed in the corner of his mouth, but he wiped it away without a thought.

"Otherwise," Louie went on, still smirking at her, "I'd just have to have *my* shark call *your* shark, and we can thrash the whole thing out in court, if *that's* what you want."

Squeezing and wringing her hands together, Abigail looked down at her lap and slowly shook her head.

"*No?*" Louie said with a hearty laugh. "Did you shake your head *no?* Well, I didn't think you'd want to go that way because—frankly— you and I both know you don't have the . . . shall we say, the 'necessary resources' to go that route with me, do you?"

Lacing his hands behind his head and looking satisfied, Louie leaned back in his plush leather chair, making it creak like a string of exploding firecrackers. His smile widened all the more, and Abigail couldn't help but wonder if his mouth could possibly stretch any wider.

Maybe it will spread all the way around to the back of his neck, and his head will pop off! she thought; but instead of seeing the humor in that thought, it filled her with a grim sense of satisfaction or expectation.

454

"So-o-o-o," Louie said after a lengthening moment, letting the word drag out slowly again. "Are you going to give it to me now?"

Abigail grasped the cloth handle of the tape case tightly and cleared her throat.

Catching her hesitation, Louie arched one eyebrow, leaned forward, and said, "Yes, my dear . . . ? You have something more to say . . . ?"

Abigail could see how much he was enjoying this, and she hated him all the more for it. Biting her lower lip, she nodded her head curtly.

"Yeah . . . well . . . I should . . . should probably tell you that I . . . I worked on it—on the album a . . . a little more."

"You *what?*

Bright purple lines of broken blood vessels spread like a ladder of lightning across Louie's face.

"Well, I hope you don't think *I'm* paying for any more studio time! I'm telling you right now, sweetheart, if you screwed with this—"

"Oh, no . . . no. It's still the same record," Abigail said, fighting hard to keep her voice steady. "Every song's exactly the way it was. I just . . . just redid a bit of the vocals, is all. I . . . I wasn't satisfied with them."

"*You* weren't *satisfied!*" Louie bellowed.

The color rose higher in his face, and all Abigail could do was hope that he'd bust a blood vessel.

"Well *I* was satisfied with it the way it was!" he shouted. "And as far as I'm concerned, that's all that counts!"

Clenching his fists, he suddenly leaned toward her across the expanse of his desk. Raising one hand, he shook a forefinger at her.

"And I swear to Christ, if you screwed with that material, I—I'll sue your lily-white ass from here to Fiji!"

"They . . . they're *my* songs," Abigail said, surprised that she could speak at all. Her hands were slick with sweat as she patted the sides of the cloth tape case.

"That very well may be," Louie said with a snarl, "but it's *my* record, and it's going to be put out on *my* label, so only *I* have final approval! If you don't believe me, just read clause eight in your contract."

"I didn't mess with it. Honest," Abigail said, trembling inside. "Go ahead. Listen to it."

With a quick nod of her head, she indicated the tape deck and speakers on the mahogany shelf between the windows behind Louie.

"See for yourself. I just overdubbed the vocals to . . . to punch them up . . . give them a bit more depth."

She held the tape case out to him, and Louie snatched it from her so fast her finger got caught on one of the metal clasps and broke a nail. Wincing, she looked down at her finger and smiled thinly when she saw the ruby-colored bead of blood, welling up from her cuticle.

Louie didn't seem to notice or care. He was too busy opening the case and taking out the master-ready tape. His face was still flushed with anger, and his hands were shaking uncontrollably as he threaded the leader tape through the machine's tape head.

With barely a glance over his shoulder at her, he said, "I promise you, babycakes, if you've altered this tape in *any* way, I'm gonna sue your skinny little ass!"

Abigail's breath was caught like a fishhook in her chest. Unable to speak, she simply nodded at him and stared at the tape deck.

Still growling under his breath, Louie jammed down the *play* button, and the tape began to roll.

After several seconds, an opening guitar riff filled the office, drowning out everything—even the high, rapid flutter of her heartbeat in her ears. A faint smile touched the corners of her mouth, but she said nothing as she tried to settle back in her chair and listen.

After the opening bar, the drums and bass kicked in; then, after another few seconds, her voice swelled up until it reached full volume in a sustained wail that sent a shiver racing up her back.

Frowning, Louie glanced over at her again and scowled. His jaw was set with grim determination, and his upper teeth were exposed, making him look like the jackal he was. Abigail's recorded voice began to sing "After the Rush."

"Hmm . . . sounds okay to me," Louie said after a few seconds of listening.

Abigail could barely hear him above the sound of her music, but then, as her voice spiraled into the chorus, another voice, so faint it almost wasn't there, came through the speakers.

Louie's expression dropped, and his face went pale.

"What the hell—?" he asked. "That wasn't there before. Who the fuck is that singing?"

He stripped his lips back, and his wide teeth flashed like fangs as he glared at her.

Abigail forced a smile as she focused on the second voice. It was almost—but not quite—buried beneath the mix. Like a tantalizing wave of the hand seen dimly through a thick mist, the second voice wavered up and down with an odd echo effect as it gathered strength.

"That's the second vocal track," she said, struggling hard to remain calm and not start laughing out loud.

"But that . . . that's not even *you!*"

Louie looked like his head was about to explode.

"That's a . . . a goddamned *man* singing! And it sounds like you're playing his vocal track backwards! What the fuck are you trying to pull here?"

Abigail tried to ignore him as she nodded her head in time with the music. The two voices were mixed so high they quickly dominated the sound of the instruments. Like dancers . . . like lovers, the voices twined in and around each other, weaving up and down.

Abigail closed her eyes and, for a moment, imagined that the voices were two fast-growing strands of eglantine that were so entangled they were becoming indistinguishable. When she opened her eyes again, she couldn't tear her gaze away from Louie's expression of pure, blind anger.

"But this isn't . . . No! This is *not* acceptable!" he shouted, shaking his clenched fists above his head. "This is absolutely *not* acceptable!"

Before he could continue, he paused and, wincing slightly, raised one hand to his mouth. A look of perplexity, then of utter shock filled his eyes when he took his hand away and saw the pink smear of blood on his thumb and forefinger. His frown deepened as he skinned his lips back and grasped one of his front teeth and started to wiggle it back and forth.

"Jesus," he whispered, shaking his head.

Abigail couldn't hear him above the steady wash of music, but she had a pretty good idea what he had said. Her own smile widened all the more as the man's voice she had recorded backward continued to weave in and out with her own voice.

"So who the hell *is* this singing with you?" Louie asked with a snarl, his eyebrows lowering like storm clouds.

Abigail wanted to laugh out loud when she saw the thin trickle of blood that was running like a scarlet ribbon from one corner of his mouth. At first Louie seemed not to notice it, but then unconsciously he wiped his chin with the back of his hand and froze when he glanced down and saw the dark red slash of blood across his wrist.

"What the—?"

Reaching up with both hands, he felt around inside his mouth. Then he grabbed his front tooth again and started to wiggle it back and forth, hard. Sweat glistened like dew on his forehead.

Abigail almost squealed with joy when she saw his front tooth shift back and forth like an ancient, teetering tombstone. Then, with a sudden *snap* that seemed almost as loud as a gunshot, Louie's hand pulled away. His eyes widened with genuine shock—maybe even terror—as he stared at the bloody stump of tooth he was holding between his thumb and forefinger.

At first he seemed too stunned to notice the pain; but after a moment—as Abigail's voice and that other voice continued to wail away in the background—his eyes clouded over. He cleared his throat with a deep, watery rattle, then leaned forward and spit a clotted glob of blood into the cup of his hand.

Abigail held her breath.

It was *working!*

Before he could find a tissue or something to wipe his hand on, the trickle of blood coming from Louie's mouth suddenly gushed, running so fast it dripped in a steady stream from his chin onto his chest and lap. His eyes were now frantic with fear as he started to rise from his chair, then sat down heavily and stared vacantly at Abigail.

When he opened his mouth again and tried to speak, several more teeth shot out and hit the top of his desk, rattling on the wood like little lead pellets.

Abigail didn't say a word as she rose slowly from her chair. All the while her eyes were locked onto Louie, who was now slumped forward and reaching out to her with one trembling hand. The other hand clasped the padded arm of his chair, but it couldn't support him. Moaning softly, he slid slowly to the floor, looking like he was melting.

Moving with a quick, dancelike skip, Abigail came around the side of the desk and looked down at him. His white button-down dress shirt and tie were now saturated with a spreading bib of blood. His shirt clung to his heaving chest as he looked up at her and panted heavily, like a dog in August.

And that's just what you are, Louie, she thought but still didn't quite dare say to him. *Nothing but a cheating scumbag dog!*

Louie's eyes were pleading with her for help. With a thick, bubbly groan, he rolled his head to one side and hit it against the leg of his chair. He winced when he tried once again to speak, and more teeth fell from his gaping mouth onto the floor. Abigail almost couldn't see them inside the thick wash of blood that was flowing from his mouth.

Her smile widened even more when she glanced over at the still-running tape deck. The music and voices—especially the male voice that had been recorded backward—were subtly but steadily gaining strength, shifting into a low, sonorous chant that soon overwhelmed the steady musical backbeat. The words were unintelligible, but they throbbed with an undeniable power. Abigail felt a twinge of pain in her own jaw and knew that she had to get out of the office soon.

She looked down at Louie, satisfied that he didn't have enough strength to get up from the floor and turn off the tape machine.

That was good.

The song would keep running while she got away and he bled to death.

It really *was* working!

She turned to leave, but then, kneeling down and leaning close to Louie's ear so that, even through his panic and pain, he could hear her, said, "Oh, you wanted to know who that is singing with me. . . ."

Louie's eyes were glazed with pain. His face was as white as his shirt, and his body was starting to twitch as though an electrical current were playing through him. He looked so far gone that he wasn't even on the planet anymore, but Abigail almost didn't care if he could hear and understand her or not.

It didn't matter.

It was the effect . . . the *power* of what she had recorded that counted.

"Remember you wrote that letter, threatening to sue me if I didn't deliver a master-ready tape of my new album?"

She had been smiling so widely and for so long that her cheeks were beginning to hurt. She had to massage her jaw before she could continue.

"Well . . . that's who's singing with me."

The male voice now dominated the music, chanting in low, som-

ber, almost inhuman tones that reached down into her heart . . . into
her soul. . . .

"That's my Master's voice."

The Edge

ADAM MEYER

Usually an owner only asks you for a meeting when the team is
playing poorly and he doesn't know who else to blame. But the
Bobcats were in first place by four games, and here it was
mid-August. In the year-plus I had been managing the team, Briscoe
had never been a meddling owner and I didn't expect him to become one
now. So again, why the meeting?

Briscoe's office was the size of the apartment I lived in when I
played in the minors, only a hundred times more elegant. It had plush
carpet and gray walls and an oak desk with brass trim, elevated on a rise
near the window. Behind Briscoe was a panorama of the city, tiny yellow
lights sparkling in the purple haze. I sat in a leather armchair across
from him, trading personal small talk and baseball banter. Finally, he
leaned forward with a sense of purpose.

"I'm very satisfied with how the team has performed," he said,
which is not usually how these meetings begin.

"Good." It was all I could think of just then. "I feel very good
about our chances to go to the Series."

"So do I." He plucked a candy cane from a glass jar on his desk
and offered one to me. I declined. Tearing off the cellophane, he studied
me. *Does he know something?* I wondered, but that seemed unlikely.

"Is there some problem I'm not aware of?" I asked.

"Absolutely none. I couldn't be happier." He licked at the candy
cane. "Which leaves you wondering why I brought you here. That's
okay, I'm wondering myself."

The sky darkened from purple to blue, and the moon appeared
behind a row of steel-and-glass fingers. A helicopter swooped toward the
river. Cars crawled along the tiny black ribbons that were the road. I saw
Briscoe's reflection in the mirror, and part of my own.

"You worked with Lou Nicholson, didn't you?" he said, as if he didn't know.

"He was my mentor."

"One of the greatest managers of his time."

"*The* greatest," I corrected. "As a player he won four World Series with the Yankees, and as a manager he won six. Four with the Giants, including their last before they left New York, and two with the Boston Braves."

"That's quite a résumé. Yours isn't so bad either."

"I suppose that's why you hired me."

"It is indeed."

A career-winning percentage of over .600, four World Series appearances, and three rings to show for it, plus a reputation as someone who didn't believe in losing. I'd had my pick of teams when my contract with Chicago expired, and I'd chosen Briscoe's. Now I was wondering if I would regret it.

"Let's look at some of the things that have happened since you joined the team," Briscoe said. "If that's all right with you?"

I shrugged. "Fine."

"April of last year. Moddy Rodriguez, who was an all-star on your championship team in Chicago but has been plagued by back troubles, suddenly finds himself healed. He goes on to have a career year. Thirty homers, a hundred RBI, fifth in MVP voting. He signed with L.A. for this season and he's hardly batting his weight."

"Moddy worked very hard last year. Perhaps his habits have changed."

"It seems to me you brought out the best in him."

"I hate to take the credit for what he accomplished."

"But you can't deny that other players who some considered washed up have flourished on your teams."

I shrugged. "I take pride in helping players to fulfill their potential."

Briscoe slurped on his candy cane. "Now what about Heath Summers. He's been a career .500 pitcher. But this year he's throwing like Cy Young and Nolan Ryan combined."

"These things happen. I can't explain everything. I know the pitching coach has done a lot of work modifying his mechanics—"

"His mechanics look the same to me," Briscoe said.

He knows, I thought.

461

"The changes are subtle," I said.

"Yes." Briscoe took the candy cane out of his mouth and used it to punctuate his speech. "On the other hand, look at a player like Norv Dollinger."

"There's a guy who hasn't prospered, unfortunately. Of course he's been hurt most of the year."

"Yes," Briscoe said, as if tasting the word and finding it bitter. He rolled his chair to the window, touched a finger to the glass. His face was hidden by the huge armchair but I could see his reflection; he seemed to be frowning. "Dollinger was quite a bit of trouble early in the year, though. Complained about his playing time. Tried to stir up sentiment against you with the rest of the team, or so I hear."

"I don't know if there's anything to that. Dollinger was a little frustrated is all."

"I've also heard he was the 'anonymous source' that kept badmouthing you to the *Post.*"

"I've heard the same, but again, I don't put much stock in rumor. I prefer fact."

"That makes two of us." Briscoe snapped off the end of his candy cane in his teeth. "And the fact is Norv Dollinger has been on the DL for two months now. The doctors can't seem to figure out what's wrong with his leg. That's a fact."

"I'm sure they'll take care of it."

"Yes, I'm sure, too. But let's not dwell on the negative. We're tearing up the division. Toronto's the only team within striking distance, and they're coming to town for three games next week. We could deliver a knockout punch."

"I hope so," I said.

"And then look at Bobby Anderson. He's on pace to hit over fifty home runs, knock in a hundred forty, and bat well over three hundred. That's quite remarkable."

"Yes," I said, suddenly unsure of where this was headed.

"He'll be a free agent next season. With those numbers, it'll cost a small fortune to sign him. I'm not going to pretend that this team doesn't earn a lot of money. It certainly does. But what Anderson's going to ask —quite frankly, it's extortion."

I shrugged. "These days, that's what it costs to keep a superstar."

"I know. But what would happen, do you think, if Anderson fell short of those projected numbers?"

462

"Not much chance of that unless you sawed off both his arms."

Briscoe laughed, but it was as artificial as the turf in Madison Stadium.

"He'd be worth a lot less money if his numbers weren't quite so high."

"That's true," I said, and suddenly I understood what he wanted. "But what about the World Series? Our chances of winning the division alone would go way down if Anderson was hurt."

"I suppose, but the only competition is from Toronto, right?"

I nodded.

"If they suffered a mishap or two themselves, that might hold them back, don't you think? At least long enough for Bobby Anderson to recover from his . . . injury."

"Baseball is a strange game," I said. "You never know what might happen. Bobby could get hurt for a little while, but be in tiptop shape for the playoffs. Toronto could suffer a few setbacks of their own and fall out of the race. Yeah, I could see that happening."

"I should tell you why I brought you here then," Briscoe said, smiling now. "I was thinking of restructuring your contract. You've done such good work, I thought a small raise might be in order. Say two hundred thousand?"

"Normally I would agree, but this is a lot of work. Better make it three."

Briscoe opened his mouth. A baseball owner by vocation but a lawyer by profession, his natural instinct was to argue. He suppressed it, however, and stuck out his hand. I shook it.

"Let's go, Bobcats," he said, dropping his candy cane in the trash.

I smiled. "Rah-rah."

Back at my townhouse I searched through my current set of baseball cards and set aside several, including Bobby Anderson, the Bobcats' center fielder, and Red Rawling, Toronto's perennial all-star first baseman. Baseball cards weren't my only hobby. I also collected hair specimens and clothing scraps from the locker room, and saved these in small Ziploc bags labeled with the name of the appropriate player. I had six boxes full in the hall closet.

In the kitchen I fashioned a powder from various ingredients, including oregano, lemon juice, rubbing alcohol, cremated flesh, and some rare herbs grown only in certain Haitian locales. I brushed some powder onto each of the cards I had set aside, along with the stray hairs and bits of clothing. Nothing to do then but wait.

I turned on the TV to pass the time. There was a ball game on. Cleveland and New York. The Indians were ahead by three runs, but the Yankees had a feisty team. I had to be at the ballpark early the next morning for batting practice, but I couldn't sleep. I watched the game and swallowed a few beers and looked at the cards lined up neatly on the table, daydreaming of the next World Series. First I picked up Bobby Anderson's and snipped it neatly in half with the scissors, cutting right through his chest. It was a terrible thing to do, really. A few years down the road, Anderson's card would probably be quite valuable.

Do No Harm

PAMELA D. HODGSON

itches don't raise no dead spirits." The kid stuck out his lip at me in a look that was half sneer, half pout. The train rounded a curve, forcing him to lean against the cold steel wall of the vestibule to keep his posture and his attitude.

"Witch of Endor did. It's in the Good Book." Softly rolling green pastures drifted by the round-cornered square window behind him. Fertile. I wished I could get off for a bit and walk, feel the wet squelch between my toes. Been a good hundred years since I did that. Pick some wild herbs. Build a fire. Not have to talk to anyone. Not have to go back to the ER, ever.

"No witches in the Bible." He patted the pockets of enormously baggy jeans, dug out a single lonely, battered cigarette, and struggled against the train's undulating motion to light it. Pungent sulfur smell leaped up when he lit the first match. Made me hungry. The match fluttered and flickered out as it touched the cigarette. He tried another.

"Witch of Endor. Raised Samuel. Told Saul he would die because he turned away from the Lord. Go ask the reverend. Ask your mama." If either had set eyes on him recently, I'd be damn surprised.

He failed to get the cigarette lit, flung it down and ground it to bits under the heel of an expensive high-top sneaker. His hair hung over his face in a flap of chestnut-colored bangs so I couldn't see whether he was crying. *Nothing of his mother's white blondeness in him,* I thought. *Not much of his mother at all.*

He'd said he didn't believe I could raise his dead father's spirit, but he had come this far, left the city and got on the train with me to go where his father had died, so he must have believed something. Anyway, I'd known him since he was a tiny thing trailing along behind his big sister Callie in her Girl Scouts uniform, eating Golden Trefoils on my kitchen floor while Callie sat at the table, legs crossed at the ankle, hands folded. I watched the little boy out of the corner of my eye. Something powerful in that boy. Something scary.

That's almost nine years ago. Funny how when you're a witch the people who most need you find you on their own, without knowing to look. Callie had finished high school at sixteen, went off to the state U, and not so much as written home. She wrote me though. Said her brother was threatening her boozed-up mother, taking money from her purse, and she was tired of being the peacemaker. She wasn't coming home for break. I thought it might do them both a world of good to have her back for a few days, but I wasn't going to push the girl. She'd been sitting in my kitchen chair after school telling me her business and crying on my shoulder for too many years. I could have brewed up a little something, cast a spell, made her come home anyway. But I stopped doing that long ago; got me in too much trouble. Stick to healing spells, such as I can manage, modern technology having mostly outpaced my craft. Mostly I'm just that old nurse's aide down at the hospital who seems to have a way with folks.

But Callie . . . well, I never had a daughter of my own. I didn't tell her about the neighborhood pets turning up in the trash cans behind the gas station, with paws torn off, skin peeled back, left for dead, and Tommy with blood and fur on his jeans. She should have some peace.

For Callie, I'd fed Tommy when she couldn't or his mother didn't, and I bought him a pair of shiny black leather loafers to wear to his eighth-grade graduation. And I tried to watch out for the animals. But when he went missing for three days, then turned up on the corner by the bus shelter with a gun-shaped bulge under his smelly T-shirt, I wanted to back off. I could sense him, had dreams of him standing at a crossroads. You could say he haunted me. I wanted to stay away from him, not so much for the roughness, but more like I felt a ripple in the world when I was near him too long. Shook me up bad.

Callie would want me to do something. She wouldn't say it, but it's what she'd want.

Don't know why I did it, or even when I decided what I was going to do. I just did it. I offered Tommy a change of scenery; raising his father's spirit he didn't much care about, so he said, but I could see otherwise. Could see it in the sparkle and tremble in his eyes. Which is why I figured that under the long lock of hair he was probably teary on the train, and why I just let him be and rocked my way back to our coach seats.

I'd never raised any spirits of the dead before. But I knew I could do it, just the way you know you could walk all the way home from work if the bus never came and you had no other way. You don't do it, because you don't have to, but you know you can. It's obvious.

It had taken some trouble to find out exactly where Tommy's father had died, given that neither little blonde Callie nor the boy had been told much about it, and whenever I asked their mother, she burst into a tirade or tears. Finally I'd found out by asking around the block; sure enough, old Mrs. Medina, whose apartment always smelled like fresh mint, she remembered when it happened. "Dey say he left and killed himself, is what dey say," she told me, the fresh scent—crisper and greener than the toothpaste smell that most people think of as mint— wafted around her like a cloud. If you shifted your weight closer or farther, you could tell exactly where the mint aura ended. "But I remember it, yeah. He went off to Chicago for getting a job, he did. And dey found him dead at Hammond, in Indiana, it is, in de alley by de train. Got off before his stop, don't know why. Either he hit his head when he fell down drunk, or somebody hit it for him. He was like dat boy, was his father. Something strange about dat boy."

The ground flowing past the train wasn't yet Indiana flat, all one shade of green—we were still a couple hours east of Hammond. I leaned against the window and collected myself for a rest, because you need energy for an undertaking like this. Tommy ambled back to the seat and plopped down next to me. I could hear the scratchy blur of music bleeding from his Walkman's headphones over the rumble and hum of the train. I let my head fall against the window. The cool glass—or maybe it was him being so close—chilled me a little, and I drew my knees up. Tommy leaned his seat back and rested his heels on top of the seat in front of him. Don't think he slept. I did.

"Hammond. Hammond, Indiana, in about five minutes," one of the train crew hollered, snatching down the paper markers above our seats that showed our destination. I shook myself awake and looked around for Tommy.

"Your boy's in the vestibule there," the woman across the aisle said, and smiled. I shoved my sweater and a magazine into my bag and slung it over my shoulder. I hoisted Tommy's khaki backpack over my other arm and bumped my way to the doorway.

The boy was leaning where he'd been before, arms folded tight and lips clenched. Smells of factory grit and burning oil leaked through the seams of the doors. I held out his backpack. After a moment, he unfolded his arms and took it without looking at me. Modest frame houses —smaller than home in Cleveland, but better kept—skated by the window behind him. His hair flopped down over his eyes again.

The rhythm of the train got more ragged as it slowed down, so that my feet were rocking over the textured bumps of the floor. I shifted over to let the train man pass, which put me close to Tommy. I felt a burst of heat off the boy and stepped back soon as I could. Train man flipped up the floor to reveal steps and opened the door as the train grumbled to a stop. A black woman and her three tired-faced, blanket-hugging daughters piled off with us. A big man in work clothes met them on the platform, wrapped all three girls in the loop of his arms. Nobody met us.

Which alley was the question; I hoped I would be able to tell. We got down off the platform, out in the street, and I paused to feel around for a tentacle of direction, a whisper of something in the autumn air. Tommy swatted his hair out of his eyes and his voice was husky. "This way," he said. Now the boy had no way of knowing, unless he could sense it too, had a natural gift. Which would explain why he made my teeth ache.

He walked hunkered down, his backpack in front of him and his body rounded over it, not looking back. I followed the tail of his loose blood-colored T-shirt that flapped in rhythm with his walk. He went up a block, cut through a deserted parking lot—it being Sunday, the commuters were gone, as they must have been when his daddy died—and around another corner into an alley behind a warehouse. A big refrigerator hummed, filling up the alley with its whine. Off a ways, a car backfired. Tommy stopped.

Smelled like motor oil and piss. The other smell was sick-sweet, rotting corpse and flowers, drifting by in a stream exactly at nose level.

467

Looked like the spirit wasn't going to make it hard for me at all. Spirits are like people, I guess: the ones that need a witch tend to find one.

I let my bag slip off my shoulder and reached for Tommy's hand. It was clammy and limp, like holding a fist full of raw squid. But his back was straight and stiff as a school principal's, and he squinched his eyes shut. I closed mine too, pictured Callie in my mind when the thought of giving up and getting away from that boy started to wangle its way into the front of my mind. I took a deep breath and mouthed the words of power. Tommy's fingers quivered against my palm.

We opened our eyes at the same time. A different set of buildings lined the alley—older, used to be stately but fading into rundown. Except the warehouse, that was the same, but it was brand new, with fresh, sharp-edged golden bricks and clean white mortar. High-pitched whine of some kind of engine coming from inside. Tommy's father—no mistaking him, the boy favored him powerfully, with that chestnut hair and broad cheeks—leaned against the wall, breathing hard, his cheeks and eyes red and his pale lower lip working as if trying to speak. He looked real as you and me. But he was carrying his own ghost of a memory.

The shadow shape of a man with a tire iron stood a good two yards away. Tommy's father could have run, probably, and made it, but he reeked of beer and vomit—he wasn't going anywhere. He glanced over toward me, imploring, but I shook my head. I can't change what's past.

The ghost-man with the tire iron advanced, talking low. "Who do you think you are, sleeping with my wife and then calling her a whore?" he growled. "You, man—a guy who made his own wife raise a child you fathered on some other woman." Tommy started. "And tell her you're coming out here for a job, so you can maybe make another bastard. Thought I would be outta town when you got here, huh?" He took another step.

"I love my son" is what Tommy's father whispered.

Tears streamed down the boy's face, striping it. He drew in air, trying to suck back the sobs. The shadow-man's ghost tire iron arced down and cracked Tommy's father on the side of the head. We could hear the bone crunch and smell the boozy blood as he fell. Tommy screamed. I expect the funeral was closed casket.

I wrapped the boy up in my arms, stiff and shaking. When the shadow-man was gone, and just the solid spirit of his daddy, upright now, but with the fatal dent in his head, stood waiting, hands open to us,

I turned the boy's head to see. "It's okay, sweetie," I cooed, until he opened his eyes.

"Daddy . . ." he croaked. He took a long deep breath and pulled away from me. His eyes narrowed a bit. "Dad, I'll make it right." The man looked at me, back at the boy, and shook his head.

Tommy wrapped his arms tight around himself and closed his eyes. His father slipped out of existence, and the whole alley faded back into its present state. The urine smell was sharper than before and the heat coming off the boy all but singed my hair.

The gravel around us shimmered and quivered. I shook my head to clear it. I hadn't let the spirit go; Tommy must have done. Or maybe the footsteps I heard smacking the pavement of the gangway next to the factory had scared the ghost off. I could smell the man before I saw him —tang of a fat man's sweat. He rounded the building and sauntered into the alley. Although he was pounds heavier and twelve years' hard lines were etched into his face, I recognized him as the shadow-man. But real this time, for sure. I dug my fingernails into Tommy's shoulders. The boy's eyes flicked open.

"You killed my father," he hissed at the man, pulling himself free of me. "You murdered him."

The man's eyes narrowed nearsightedly, then the light of recognition clicked on and quick, he made his face blank. "Don't know what you mean, young man. Ma'am, is there something I can help you with?"

Tommy hiked up his long T-shirt to paw in the pockets of his baggy pants, his eyes never leaving the man.

Before I could think what to do or say, Tommy drew out his hand, and it was full of metal. It was a little tiny gun, not one you would even think to worry much about if you didn't know from yanking bullets out of bodies five days a week that it could punch a long deep hole in a person without hardly trying. Tommy raised it and pointed it at the fat man. I felt like I'd walked into a TV movie. "Tommy, child, put that thing away! Where'd you get that?" I said. I felt like I should do more, but I'd been staying out of harm's way for so long that I froze up trying to figure what.

The boy didn't waiver. I saw the muscles in his hand shift and tighten, his finger clenching the trigger just a little tighter. I closed my eyes and set out to cast a spell that would keep him from firing the gun. I trembled with the strain of trying to clear my mind and do the work so quickly, so urgently. Not to mention my skin-crawling feelings about the boy. My eyes kept fluttering open to see what was going on.

The boy shrieked, high and small. The fat man slammed his open hand into the side of the boy's head, and used his body to pin the gun arm against the warehouse wall. Tommy wailed and kicked. I found enough breath to scream. That was all.

The gun clattered to the ground and so did Tommy, pawing for it. The fat man went to kick him, but Tommy snatched his big beefy calf out of the air and pulled him down. But the big man landed nearer the gun and came up with it.

I saw Tommy fall before I heard the pop. Don't know if that's because light travels faster than sound, or because it took that long for the sound to register for what it was. Blood made a dark spot on the stomach of his T-shirt, and his face turned paler than his mother's.

The fat man was gone when I turned around, but he must have had some shred of decency left in him, because an ambulance roared into the alley in the time it took me to mop the sweat off Tommy's face and jam a handful of T-shirt like a plug into the wound. I know lots of healing spells, but none of them powerful enough for gunshot. Modern technology having outpaced witchcraft, as I said.

People who need a witch find one. Saul found the Witch of Endor, but it didn't change his dying. I found Tommy, but a boy mixed up with guns is going to get shot one day. You turn away from your path and it happens. Now I have to go tell Callie.

Magician's Assistant

ADAM MEYER

h ot, stifling darkness. Thirteen candles positioned at intervals around the room cut orange holes in the gloom. A mixture of fear and anticipation hung thickly in the air, like smoke.

"Michael?" Madame Suzie asked. "Can you hear me, Michael?"

Everyone held hands so that, in Madame Suzie's words, "the spiritual energies might flow from one body to another." Annie Collins was seated with the medium to her left and a lawyer named George Jackson to her right; he claimed to be a huge fan of Annie's late husband, Harry.

"Can you hear me, Michael? If you can, say something."

A dramatic pause.

"Yeah, I hear you."

Madame Suzie's voice was high-pitched and contained the slightest traces of a southern drawl. The voice of Michael, the spirit whom she pretended to contact, was soft, deep, and had a distinct Brooklyn accent. Both voices issued from the medium's lips.

"Michael, how are you?"

"I'm dead, how the fuck do you think I am?"

"Please, Michael, I've warned you about that language."

"Pardon me."

Like so many other mediums, Madame Suzie had practiced long and hard to perfect the deep, male voice belonging to the imaginary spirit Michael. Smiling, Annie listened to Madame Suzie banter with herself.

"Michael, I need your help." Madame Suzie waited, then added, "Will you help me?"

"Why should I? Why the fuck should I?"

"I have guests, Michael. That's hardly proper language."

"Listen, I'm doing you a favor; I can fucking talk however the fuck I like."

"Does that mean you'll help me, then?"

"I just said I would, didn't I?"

"Yes, you did. Michael, have you ever heard of a magician named Harry Collins?"

"Shit no. He must've been after my time."

"In any case, I have his widow, Annie, here with me, and she'd like very much to talk with him. Do you think you could find him for me?"

"Give me a few minutes, all right?"

Annie listened to the sound of her own pulse. The lawyer, Jackson, tightened his grip on her right hand. She clenched her teeth.

"As long as you need," Madame Suzie said.

Waiting in the darkness, Annie found herself remembering the past. She recalled fondly when she had first met Harry Collins, over twenty years ago. She was his assistant at first, then became his lover, and soon his wife. Eventually, through a combination of charisma, talent, persistence, and luck, Harry moved from grimy nightclubs to fancy theaters, where he soon played to full capacity crowds night after night.

By then he was no longer the same Harry, he was a millionaire and a star. Annie still loved him, as she always had and would, but part of her longed for the days when they'd performed side by side in crappy clubs for five bucks a night and the audience's applause.

A sound startled Annie from her thoughts. It was a whistling, like the sound of an old man's shallow breath.

"Harry? Is that you?" Madame Suzie asked.

"Yes," said a soft voice. Not from the medium's mouth, but from some far corner of the room. A speaker, Annie presumed.

The medium turned to her. "Say something to him, dear."

Annie, faking all the emotion she could, called out, "Harry? Darling?"

"Annie." The last syllable was drawn out for several seconds. "My Annie."

"Oh, Harry, I can't believe it's really you!"

In the center of the table, a pale smoky figure appeared. The face was barely discernible. It might have been Harry, Annie thought. Then again, it might have been just about anyone.

Numerous gasps, cries of shock. Not for the first time, she was amazed how all it took was a few gimmicks to make people believe the impossible. But then, that's how Harry had made his living.

"Would you like to ask the spirit a question to prove that he's really your husband?" Madame Suzie asked.

"Yes, I would." Annie felt her heart hammer inside her chest. "Who's the greatest magician that ever lived?" That was Harry's cue; Annie freed her hands from those who held them on either side and stood.

A voice cried out, "I am," and she had a glimpse of a tall figure wearing a satin cape just as the candles were suddenly extinguished.

Annie lunged for the door. Once she was in the hall outside the room, she sighed in relief. Soon others would try to escape the same way, but would find the door mysteriously locked.

Annie found her way to the living room. Sat on the sofa, covered her ears with her hands, closed her eyes. Yet she could still hear the pounding on the door and walls, the screams and howls and cries of agony, the oppressive silence that settled in once the massacre was over.

Her eyes flicked open. She stared out the window at the ink-black night. Pale moonlight painted the carpet a shadowy gray. A hand touched her face.

There was an instant of sharp terror, then flooding relief.

"You scared me," Annie said.

"I know."

She looked at his face and thought he might have been smiling.

"Brilliant performance," Harry said.

"What did you expect?"

"Nothing less."

Harry's lips found Annie's, his cold tongue slithering between her teeth like a slug.

"I love you, Annie."

"I love you, too," she said.

It was the truth. But there were nights, like tonight, his dead-cold skin pressing against hers, that she wished she had never helped bring him back from the dead.

Bad Things Happen on Halloween

LUCY TAYLOR

I'd rather be home where it's safe tonight," Lillian said. "Too many bad things happen on Halloween."

We were sitting at the L.A. Diner on 28th Street, eating cheeseburgers and malteds like a couple of teenagers.

"I thought we were going to Pearl Street for the Mall Crawl," I said.

"I'd feel better at home. Halloween is too dangerous."

"You mean drunk drivers? Rowdy kids?"

"Witchcraft," said Lillian, with such seriousness that I almost laughed. "Halloween is the big holiday for witches and Satan worshippers. I heard on a talk show that one in ten people in Boulder is involved in the black arts."

I tried not to show how hilarious I found the seriousness with which she uttered this statement.

"Yeah, right, and three out of ten have been abducted by aliens, held captive in UFOs, and made pregnant by Elvis. That stuff's just talk show hype to get ratings. Nobody takes it seriously."

For all the impression I made on Lillian, I might as well have been speaking Swahili. She glanced behind her at the door, where Raggedy Ann and Andy were making their entrance just in front of the Tin Man. "The witches hold ceremonies in secluded places and sacrifice innocent people. They torture them to death as an offering to Satan."

"If Boulder is a hotbed of murderous witches," I said, ever the rational male, "then why aren't the police investigating it? Hey, why not the FBI? Why don't we read about any of this in the *Daily Camera?*"

"Because it exists right up to the highest levels of government and law enforcement."

"Another conspiracy theory," I sighed, taking the check from the roller-skating waitress. "Next thing you'll be telling me JFK was a warlock who got shot by the head of a rival coven."

Lillian glowered at me. "Don't joke about this, Matt. I'm serious. I want to go home. And I don't want to be alone either."

Now that put a different hue on things. I'd been hoping to go home with Lillian ever since I met her on the Pearl Street Mall a few days earlier, where I was playing my guitar for change outside Pasta Jay's. Lillian had struck up a conversation and invited me to have coffee with her at the Boulder Bookstore Cafe. I'm not used to good-looking women being so friendly right off the bat, but I figured she liked my music and my East Texas drawl.

Lillian got into her Mazda and I followed her in the battered old Ford that had brought me to Boulder from Denton, Texas, after I lost my job there two weeks ago.

She lived a few miles north of town in the mountains, past some horse farms and up a winding dirt road, in a three-story frame house encircled with pines.

"Thanks for coming home with me," she said, unlocking the front door.

Hey, at that point, I would've told you Halloween was my favorite holiday.

We went inside, Lillian preceding me. "There's a lamp across the room, Matt. Would you turn it on please?"

I made my way across the dark room. There wasn't much furniture and what there was had been pushed back against the walls where it cast large, looming shadows. I could see why Lillian got the creeps living alone here.

Especially since some of those shadows were changing shape, unfolding like lawn chairs, elongating.

I grabbed for the light.

There must've been twenty people standing in a circle around me. All wearing long robes, all carrying daggers. The walls were covered with Satanic symbols.

They lifted their daggers in unison, started some weird kind of chant that sure as hell wasn't Gregorian. Every now and then I recognized Lillian's name in the words and I realized they must be honoring her.

Lillian came toward me. Took my face in her hands and brushed her lips against mine. *"Now* do you believe in witchcraft, Matt?"

"Bad things do happen on Halloween," she said, smiling, just before the daggers came down.

Midnight Oil

L. S. SILVERTHORNE

er spirit lamp burned in the grass beside the jack-o'-lantern. Pumpkin-orange flames danced in the cold winter's night as she waited on the edge of the circle. They would come tonight as they did every eve of Beltane. Flames licking their smoky heels. Bass voices moaning above the clacking of dead leaves. Smoke charring the air. Dust rising. This time, their midnight gathering would end differently. The Witches of Beltane would come to reclaim those burned centuries before, luring out a victim to trade. Circles in the grass marked their point of combat. Their victim was her next-door neighbor. They had filled his head with lies and now she waited, turning the spirit lamp down low. Finally, she knew their weakness.

At 11:45 P.M., Jake Quillen awoke to screaming on his front lawn. Groggy, he crawled out of bed, throwing on his robe as he staggered down the stairs. A young teenager huddled on his stoop, stringy blonde hair draped across powdery, tear-stained cheeks. Blood streaked her pink flannel nightshirt, drying like watercolors on her palms. She clutched his arm, grinding the terry cloth against his skin until it burned.

"You've got to stop her," the teenager shouted.

Jake frowned. "Kerri, is this some sort of Halloween prank? Halloween isn't until tomorrow night and this kind of thing isn't funny."

"It's no prank, Jake," she shrieked. "She—she killed my dog."

His mouth gaped. "Who killed your dog?"

"Your neighbor, the witch, that's who! Look!" Kerri pointed at the dark green circle glistening on his front lawn. A tiny gray form slumped in its center.

"Reneta Ames killed your dog?"

Kerri nodded emphatically.

Several times this week, Jake had seen the woman burning an oil lamp on her patio, electric lights blazing behind her in the kitchen. Kerri and her friends had told everyone that the Ames woman stole neighborhood pets, prayed to the moon, and cast black magic in her backyard. Now, no one would go near her house. He didn't know what to believe.

"I'll call the police."

Kerri's grip tightened. "No, please," she urged, yanking him toward the yard. "Bury my dog first."

He gazed into the sad green eyes and nodded. First, a decent burial for Fifi and then a call to the police. Barefoot, he padded across the yard, Kerri a few paces behind him. When he reached the circle, Reneta Ames stepped out of the brush. Her sable hair was tied back from her face. She stood nearly as tall as Jake.

"Don't take another step," Reneta ordered, pointing at the circle's edge.

Jake halted in mid-stride. "What kind of monster are you?" he shouted. "Killing a kid's dog."

Her mahogany eyes widened and she turned her gaze to Kerri. "Tell him who killed the dog."

Kerri nudged Jake forward, hiding behind him. "Don't listen to her, Jake. My dog deserves a proper burial."

"Get her yourself, Kerri," said Reneta with a wry smile. "What's stopping you?"

"Jake," Kerri pleaded, her voice turning frail. "I'm frightened. Please make her leave. She's a witch, I tell you."

476

Ignoring Reneta, Jake stepped over the circle's edge and moved toward the dead animal. He bent toward the cold, stiff poodle's body and slid his fingers beneath it, but the body turned to ash in his hands. Something moved within the green circle. He turned. Shadowy figures rose from the earth. The air smelled of damp hay and dirt. Two thick, splintered poles punctured the earth, rising up into the cold night sky. Bundles of dry twigs lay around the bases of the wooden poles. Darkly clothed figures streaked across the lawn and paused beside Kerri, skin whitewashed, eyes pinpoints of cruelty.

"The Beltane sisters," said Reneta with a sneer, "and right on time."

From the brush, she rolled out the flickering jack-o'-lantern, sending Kerri and her sisters into hurried steps backward. The gray figures mixed with the darkness like ashes on slate. Voices deep and desperate reverberated around Jake in raspy whispers.

Jake tried to escape the circle, but the twigs coiled around his legs, forcing him against the stake.

"It seems we're having a bonfire in your honor, Jake," Kerri said with a steely laugh.

Hands like wisps of darkness held Jake against the stake.

"Kerri . . . why?"

"Every eve of Beltane, the earth yields up the ashes of my sisters burned at the stake. Only a trade of human spirit will free them from their circles."

"She's been collecting them all over the country," said Reneta, backing away.

Kerri reached into the sky and plucked a spark from it. She rolled it around in her palm and then threw the spark at the twigs. Jake screamed as oily black smoke rose up in a wide shaft followed by a ring of crimson flames. Heat roiled against Jake's face, chafing cheeks, scorching robe.

Spirits moaned until a shrill, piercing scream rippled through the stillness. The terrified spirit of a bound woman plunged up from the earth and hovered beside Jake, her hair and body set aflame. He smashed his eyes closed as the burning spirit wailed in agony.

Reneta slipped back to the brush and slid out the spirit lamp, the oil base nearly empty. Another grating scream ripped through the silence, startling Jake. He opened his eyes and kicked at the flames. Skin blistered. The spirits wept. Others leaped up from the dirt, flames wild and pitching. Reneta turned the wick up until the spirit lamp's umber flames danced in the night air.

"What are you doing?" Kerri shrieked and stepped back. "Take it away, do you hear! Take it away!"

Reneta waved the lamp at the Beltane Witches. Kerri drew her arm over her face, stumbling back from the circle.

"Don't fear it, ladies. Look closer."

When Reneta was an arm's distance from Kerri, she swept off the globe. Instantly, Kerri was mesmerized by the flame. With wide, crimson eyes, she watched it flicker and sway in the darkness. Her solid form began to fade. Skin turned translucent. Finally, her body dissipated into a wisp of smoke drawn into the lamp's flame. The clear oil turned red, the level rising a half-inch. One by one, the other witches turned to smoke, followed by the burning spirits. Ribbons of smoke slithered into the lamp until the oil's base brimmed with crimson oil. The fire at Jake's feet quickly fizzled and sank into the earth. With a groan, the stake receded back into the earth, leaving Jake standing alone in the center of the yard. Somewhere in the distance, a dog barked. He could only stare at her, dumbfounded.

Reneta held out the lamp to him. "It's a spirit lamp. Dark Witches like the Beltane Sisters fear fire but are drawn to it like moths. Fire forges good from evil. What isn't good burns away. That's why a white witch cannot burn." She held a finger in the flame, making Jake wince, but her skin did not even redden.

"Kerri sure played me for a fool," Jake said with a sigh. "I thought you were victimizing her."

Reneta shook her head. "She knew you would never suspect a child—especially with me there to blame." She motioned him across the yard toward her house. "Care to burn a little midnight oil?"

Jake smiled. "Love to."

They talked about All Hallows' Eve and the Salem witch trials. Reneta told him all about the Witches of Beltane, their annual gatherings and their fear of fire. When morning came, the oil lamp was empty. Reneta gave Jake the jack-o'-lantern with its thick white candle inside to ward off the Witches of Beltane. There were many more than those who appeared on his lawn. Gratefully, Jake accepted it.

Every Halloween, a smiling jack-o'-lantern burns on Jake's porch to keep the Witches of Beltane away from his door.

Invitation

Katherine Ramsland

I usually hated Halloween hype because it meant getting sent on assignments to do ridiculous stories about vampires and witches. It was all so contrived and we alays found people willing to do something dangerous or idiotic to get mentioned in the local paper. Plus, these people were weird! I mean, who would file down their own teeth into pointed edges or claim to travel sans body except someone totally off the wall? Although I was merely the photographer on these outings, I always had to stand around and listen to their bogus descriptions of supernatural powers. But this assignment was different. This one turned out to be dangerous.

First of all, this "witch" was a man. I know, I know, I'm supposed to use the word *warlock* or *wizard*, but he didn't. I think it was because he identified with a force that defied gender splits. And the other odd thing about him was that he wasn't seeking publicity, not this guy. The reporter I worked with—Kimm—had heard about him from a friend and had decided to follow up the lead to try to get a unique story.

"He's reclusive," she told me on the way. "I had a hard time talking him into seeing me. So don't show him the camera or anything like that until I say. And maybe we won't get any pictures, but I want you along just in case. I didn't tell him I'm a journalist. I just said I needed his help."

Fine, I thought. *I'll get paid.* I needed an assignment like this anyway to get my mind off my neighbor—a former friend and confidant —who was suing me for some imagined transgression. The suit not only pained me and caused enormous amounts of stress, it was costing me. Plenty. I often wished I had some of these powers other people claimed to possess. Like the woman last Halloween who had told us that every time she had an altercation with a man, the man died. I hadn't believed her, but I'd liked the thought. Such power seemed very appealing just now. I wanted my neighbor to die and I'd fantasized about sending him into her path, certain that his abrasive personality would ensure his demise.

I checked my camera, saw that I had only used eight frames, and thought ahead, anticipating what our subject might tell us. Maybe I could ask some advice. Like how I could kill my neighbor with the blink of an eye. Something like that.

Let me just say, this witch, or whatever he was, was a shock right from the start. I never even heard Kimm introduce me. I just stared at the guy. He had presence, I'll give him that, but more startling were the dark blue eyes. They were almost too intense but framed by laugh lines that exposed a thorough enjoyment of life—or of me. I'm still not certain which.

I think his hair was dark and longish, but I don't recall. That's pretty unsettling, considering I'm a photographer and I pride myself on being observant, but I was riveted by the eyes. I think I embarrassed Kimm because she said to me afterward that I should have been more professional. I don't know what I did exactly, but I know that something *happened.* To me.

The funny thing was, the guy didn't have much to say. I wasn't sure why he'd even agreed to let us crash in on his evening. Kimm kept pressing him with questions about his practice as a witch and he offered only vague responses. But he kept watching me with those eyes. I felt that *I* was the one who had been invited, not Kimm. Like the witch was waiting for something from me. At one point in the evening, he quickly reached over and touched me. I pulled away but not before I felt the heat from his fingertips on the back of my hand.

I wish I could tell you more of the details of that meeting. But if I could I probably wouldn't be describing this to you. I just know that when I left his house, I was different. And he knew why.

My first indication that something had changed was when I indulged in my usual daydream of making the senior photographer leave the paper so I could have his office. And within a few days, a family tragedy required him to resign and move to another city. I was a little disturbed, but thought it merely a coincidence. Still, I got the office.

At one time or another, we all want our wishes fulfilled, despite the hackneyed injunction to "be careful what you wish for." We just want satisfaction. But not satisfaction with a price, so when such "coincidences" happened again, I wondered if the witch had passed something evil on to me. Or maybe I'd caught it, like catching a cold from a grocery clerk who picks up your milk carton with the hand that she just used to wipe her nose.

I knew I had *something* when I actually killed my neighbor. I did. Really. Not with a weapon. Merely by thinking it. I thought I'd try it, just to see. The guy had instructed his lawyer to drive up the legal fees by bombarding my lawyer with paperwork, and in a fit of temper, I'd wished him dead. Then I heard he'd had a massive stroke on the same day I'd mentally cursed him. They'd found him on the floor of his bathroom. And that was the end of the lawsuit.

Oh yes, I felt relief, even satisfaction. I loved that I had such power. I felt *expansive,* and I wanted to see what else I could do. But it wasn't long before the ramifications hit.

I was having a fight with my fiancée when I realized with a start that I might actually harm her. I stopped, frustrated, but unwilling to take it any further. It hit me then that I had no idea how to control this power. Suppose I got angry with my boss? Or someone cutting me off on the road? I could see myself randomly hurting or killing people merely by having normal human reactions. And if I'd caught this thing like a common cold, I wondered if I was passing it along to someone. Might I inadvertently create serial killers merely by pressing against people in a crowded elevator?

I needed more information, so I asked Kimm for the witch's phone number. She looked at me without comprehension.

"Come on, Kimm," I said. "The guy we interviewed. Where you thought I acted like a jerk. I took some pictures of the house, remember? It was right before Halloween. You wrote the story and it ran."

"I really don't know what you're talking about," she insisted. "I did a story on a guy who drinks his girlfriend's blood. I didn't do anything on witches. Besides, a male witch is a warlock, you know."

I couldn't believe it. I pressed again, she resisted, so I pulled the Halloween issue of the paper and had a look. I was astonished. Kimm was right. There was no story about a male witch, no photo by me. But I remembered it. Recalled developing the film and looking at the dark outlines of the house. I was getting sick. When I went to retrieve the film, I couldn't find it. There was no evidence that I'd taken any pictures at all.

Next thing, I got in my car and tried to find the road we had taken to get to the guy's house. I just started driving, but nothing came back. It was as if it had all been a dream. Except that my neighbor was really dead and I really could hurt someone else.

I thought I got a break when I saw the witch—or whatever. I spotted him on the street one day. I know it was him and I know he recognized me. He even smiled before he ducked into a building. I quickly followed, shoving people aside to gain ground. I could see his head bobbing over the other folks and I rushed toward him. I was only a few feet away when he turned and looked directly at me.

But to my surprise, it wasn't him. It wasn't his face or eyes. I stopped dead in my tracks and let him turn and walk away. Dead end. Zip.

So then I got the idea to visit the woman who had claimed she killed men just by being angry. Same problem I had. Kindred souls. I was surprised when she responded to my call and invited me over. I needed help, but her willingness made me hesitate.

I remembered her as a sort of fuzzy-minded kook with long black hair that needed attention. Her house had smelled of animals that had been inside too long, and she had eaten out of a box of Cheerios the whole time we were there. She had also rambled off the point a lot and made odd pronouncements, as if she were trying to prove she was psychic. I recalled how annoying she'd been. Still, I had nowhere else to turn.

The woman and her house were just as I remembered, only worse, and I had to breathe through my mouth to keep from retching. Invited to sit at her kitchen table, I explained myself as best I could and she nodded the whole time, like she understood me. When I was finished, I felt a little better, and I waited for her response.

"You hate children," she said.

My mouth dropped open. "What?"

"Oh, just an observation. You talk like you don't interact much with children."

"I don't hate them."

"So what can I do for you?"

It took me a moment to recover. I had to remind myself this woman was strange. "I don't really know if you can do anything," I said. "But you seem to understand this power. I want to be free of it."

She laughed. "Free? You *are* free."

"No I'm not. I didn't chose this. I 'caught' it, like I told you."

"Your mother was a victim of incest, wasn't she?"

"No! What does my mother have to do with this?"

"Just an observation. Then it must have been your sister."

"I don't have a sister. Now can you help me or not?"

She looked at me coyly through a jagged row of greasy bangs, then said. "If you think it's a virus, why don't you go to a witch doctor?"

"What?"

"You know. Get an antibiotic."

This woman was obviously amused and I had to curb my anger lest I burst a blood vessel in her brain or something.

"It's just a metaphor," I said. "The guy touched me, like he was passing something on to me, and I acquired it somehow. Now I can't find him."

"It's no wonder. A virus is a shapeshifter, you know. It mutates and survives changes in form. It no doubt made him appear different when you saw him later and even had the effect of erasing your partner's memory. It looks after its own interests."

"Which are . . . ?"

"To replicate. It either has to be passed on or it continually reproduces itself in its host body. Unfortunately, it eventually explodes the body. I've seen it happen."

I swallowed. I couldn't believe she was saying this with such a cavalier attitude.

"Are you telling me," I asked slowly, "that if I don't pass this on to others like he did to me, it'll kill me?"

"It may. This thing is very ancient, you know. It's been penetrating the human species for a long time, and it's spread all over the place. It's not really a virus, but your metaphor is apt. At some point, because of your power, you may wish your own death, and of course, it will occur. You were a math teacher once, weren't you?"

"No."

"A geologist, then."

"No! Can we get focused, please? This is scaring me. So this thing can make me want to die? How?"

"It will eventually transform you into itself."

"What? What does that mean?"

"It's all motive without a brain; you have to give it opportunities to jump to someone else or it will devour you."

"And that's what *you* do? You lure unsuspecting people—"

"No. I pass it to my disciples. Those who want it and learn how to handle it. That's what a coven is, you know. Protectors of the power. It's a gift. It can be quite valuable when handled properly. Perhaps you'd like to join us."

A dark gray cat jumped into her lap and she shifted to receive it. "I have it," she said with triumph in her eyes. "You wanted to be a psychotherapist. That's what you studied in college, right?"

"Wrong." I breathed against the rising lump of my increasing irritation. I knew I had to keep my cool. "I don't remember you telling us all this stuff last year when we interviewed you," I said. "Why not?"

She smiled. "You weren't one of us last year. And you weren't vulnerable then. There wasn't any point in explaining the true nature of this thing. Besides, it's not what gets said that counts; it's getting someone to write the story. Then the vulnerable ones who read it seek me out. They come. They don't know why exactly, but they come."

I didn't quite understand that at first but now I know what she means.

"So the witch I encountered was irresponsible," I pressed. "He shouldn't have just handed it off to the first person he could find."

"Or he was desperate. Perhaps he'd gone too long without shedding. You just happened to be there. But you can't just give it to anyone, you know. The new host has to be vulnerable. No doubt he spotted something in you."

"What do you mean? Are you saying that my immune system against the supernatural was somehow weak?"

She laughed, and with her right hand scratched the cat under its neck as its yellow eyes stared at me. When it became obvious she wasn't going to answer, I took a different angle.

"So how do I decontaminate?" I asked.

"You can't. You've got it now for good."

"But I don't want this thing."

"Oh, honey, you wanted it. You wouldn't have gotten it if you didn't want it."

That was the first thing she said that interested me. It meant that maybe I couldn't pass this on to just anyone. (Although when you think about the type of people who want this kind of power, it's scary. I just had to hope I wouldn't inadvertently brush against them.)

So I've learned to "read" people well enough to know who can handle it. And I know now why witches like me take opportunities like this to be interviewed. Someone might come along to help me shed the power. And we have to shed some of it, like she said, so it won't turn on us. Remember that.

So that's how I became one of those weird people who describes his experiences every Halloween to anyone who asks. And that's why I described it to you.

Heartbeat

NANCY KILPATRICK

I t was the beat that got to him. Now, looking back, Greg tried to reconstruct what had happened, to analyze events. He realized he'd never heard rhythms like that before, not within conscious memory anyway.

It made sense. His roots, at least on his mom's side, were Haitian. But his mother had moved with his Irish father to Canada before Greg was born, and the ties to her culture and history were out of place in the lonely, yellow land of Saskatchewan.

Why they chose the dry, desolate, sparsely populated prairies, Greg did not know. Growing up in the tiny town of Tisdale, 150 miles north of Saskatoon, the small city where he had gone to university, Greg had not encountered music like this, even on the radio. Music that pounded through him as naturally as his heartbeat.

That morning at the harbor, Greg remembered turning to glance at the glass-and-chrome skyscrapers behind him. This was his first time in a large city. He came to Toronto a month early for purely practical reasons: to find a place to live, to learn how the streets were laid out, to get organized with the university before starting on his Ph.D. thesis. After breakfast, he'd decided to walk along the flagstoned shore of Lake Ontario at the south end of the city. Out on the water he saw a long island, with an airport at one end. Expensive cruisers and historic schooners sailed the harbor; he snapped pictures of the tall ships on display, with the gulls circling their masts.

Suddenly he realized that over the hours the lakeshore had become crowded. Droves of people headed in the same direction, seemingly drawn by a tinny-sounding music. He could see the parade route two blocks away, something colorful swaying above the heads of the throngs in the distance.

Women, gorgeous women, of all skin colors and ethnic origins, passed him, laughing, dancing to the rhythm of this sound, their long colorful skirts swinging as their hips moved so naturally. Some wore tight jeans or spandex, others shorts. Feet sandaled, midriffs bare, heads decorated with big straw hats or multicolored bandannas. The men surrounding him seemed relaxed beneath the brilliant summer sun. Black-skinned and white-skinned walked together like brothers. There were Asians, East Indians, South Americans, and even a few North American Natives, all talking and grinning as though the United Nations had declared a day of world peace. It was astonishing to see so many people getting along well, and he decided to walk a little toward the sound to investigate what this parade was all about.

Of course, being a member of the only mixed-race family in Tisdale, a tiny, isolated community, Greg hadn't been aware of much prejudice. He had met with some in Saskatoon, but he'd been virtually cloistered there, living on-campus. Still, he read the papers and subscribed to magazines. He watched the news on TV, and caught the gist of the larger world in movies. By the time he'd acquired his M.A. in quantum physics, he considered himself worldly. But nothing had prepared him for this.

"You a visitor, yes?"

He turned, startled. A short woman with very black skin walked in step beside him. Her midnight hair held fiery red highlights, braided and beaded, and her eyes were an arresting green. *What an odd combination,* he thought. Intriguing. A bit unnerving. Her colorful cotton skirt hung to her thighs in front, and to her heels in back, and rustled around her as she moved so gracefully. A rope holding a carved gourd was slung across her chest—he suspected the gourd acted as a purse. A black, red, and yellow African cap perched at an angle on her head, and a low-cut top composed of several silk scarves, wrapped and knotted in a creative fashion, allowed her breasts natural movement. He found this attractive but disconcerting.

"I'm . . . I'm from Saskatchewan," he said, adding, "I'm going to school. Graduate school." He wondered why he felt as shy as a freshman. "What about you?" he managed.

"Me? I be a witch, doncha know?"

The exquisite woman beside him smiled up at him, her knowing green eyes shining, teeth brilliant. So white, the color temporarily blinded him.

Greg was aware of leaning against a wooden barrier, pressed in by people behind and on both sides. Across the street were more people, hundreds, thousands, eagerly waiting. Distant music wafted through the air like scent.

"*Caribana* is an annual event," he heard one woman explaining to someone. "Draws about a million people. Amazing lack of violence, considering the numbers."

He did not recall walking the last couple of blocks. How odd! Maybe it was this humid heat; he was accustomed to dry prairie summers. He shook his head to clear it and took a deep breath. Across the asphalt, behind a barrier directly in front of him, he saw the gorgeous woman. Their eyes locked. She waved and smiled, her emerald irises glittering in the brilliant sunlight.

He waved back, wondering if he should run across the street and join her. He'd like to. But they were together before; how did they get on opposite sides? Maybe she didn't want to be with him.

As a band rounded the corner to his right, the street exploded with sound and movement. Two skimpily clad women, one black, one white, carried a banner that read "MUSIC MAHN RECORDS PRESENTS:" and the name of their act: "TRINIDAD-TOBAGO—DRUMS OF FANTASY."

Three dozen dancers wore silver and gold costumes, both the men and women in short skirts, or string bikini bottoms that exposed quite a bit of flesh. Their tops were shaped like twinkling gold stars. The hats glittered with stars or moons. The lead dancer, encased in a kind of costumed cart on wheels, carried an enormous headdress—half a story high—composed of both stars and a giant new moon in the center. The entire costume was a sky of gold and silver sequins, beadwork, and feathers that sparkled and swayed beneath the hot sun.

They danced and thrust forward in the small-stepped style of Caribbean folk dance to the music of the steel band following on a flatbed.

Greg glanced across the street. The green-eyed woman's body gyrated so naturally to the beat. Suddenly she snapped her head in his direction and smiled. He could not help but grin.

As the band neared, the music became ear-splitting, and Greg had an urge to cover his ears. Sound pounded against his eardrums painfully. All around him people danced and strutted and clapped. He had never seen so many grinning fools! Not that he minded people having a good time. But exhibitionism bothered him. It lacked decorum.

He checked his watch. Nearly lunchtime. He had to find a store where he could rent a computer before Monday.

The sound swelled to nearly overwhelming. He felt pressure in his chest, as though the bass shoved against his heart and forced it to beat at a different rhythm. Greg began to feel afraid. He was not used to this much stimulation. He turned to make his way through the jiggling bodies before the fear could get too much of a grip.

"Don't go. It's not yet begun." She was behind him.

"How did you get across the street?" he blurted.

Her hand lightly touched his arm. The feel of her warm, moist skin on his flesh was electric current through water. Each of her fingernails— well over an inch long—had been filed almost to a point, and painted such a blood red he was not at all sure the color wasn't really black. His reaction to what his eyes saw was far different than to what his skin tasted.

When she took her hand away, he felt dismayed by the emptiness that hit in the pit of his stomach.

Her eyes brightened as she pointed one of those daggered fingers down the street. Another band approached the turnoff. The stars and moons band was almost past, and the sound had reached a level he could tolerate. He decided to wait a bit.

She leaned to the left, close up against him, her body both soft and firm. She smelled of exotic sweet flowers, and the scent filled his nostrils, cutting out the odors of ginger beer, meat patties, sunscreen. Two heads taller, he looked down at her hair flying from beneath the cap that could not restrain it, streaking her smooth dark shoulders. He wondered at the red strands. Of course, women color their hair. The red highlights were probably from a bottle.

She snapped her head around and up. Those green eyes narrowed, and her full lips pressed together tightly. "My mama, she Irish, my father Haiti. I know the pagan practices from both lands. It make me special. Like you, mahn."

He could only dwell briefly on the fact that she seemed to have read his mind. And that she was going on about this witch nonsense. What startled him was her ancestry, the same ethnic mix as his.

Before he could say or do anything more, she gripped his arm, sending more shocks through his skin that left him speechless. "This band for you," she cried through the increasing sound surrounding them, gesticulating lavishly at the approaching dancers.

As the band turned the corner, the crowd roared. More than with the previous group, these costumes were spectacular on an entirely new level. The dancers, in black and white, each wore a thin, two-toned mask, nearly obscured by a hood attached to a long cape. Only the feet shuffling forward to the beat betrayed race, and again it was a mix. Greg wondered how they could stand to wear capes in this heat.

The lead's headdress draped behind in a long train carried on two carts with wheels. It reached higher than the other, at least one story of a building. The crowd went wild, screaming, clapping, cheering, bodies swaying. As the band neared, Greg saw that this masterpiece of a headdress was dotted with many small masks, made from sequins and beads, duplicating the obscured faces the caped dancers wore. Long black and white plumes alternated, and movement let these feathers sway and bend like the leaves of a palm tree, or fingers beckoning. Black and white, black and white, black and white. Each mask depicted a different emotion. The opposites glittered and sparkled, the satin shimmered, all of it blended together to weave a hazy world between light and dark, one that had the crowd ecstatic.

The flatbed truck pulled up; steel drums sang and horns blared through ten enormous speakers. "Haitian Drums—Synergize."

As the music swelled, Greg felt almost knocked off his feet. The vibration pounded in his head, his chest. He lost track of his hearbeat, which capitulated to this intense beat. The relentless sun, the scent of exotic flowers, the volume of sound like a tidal wave . . . Greg felt himself slipping down, slipping away. . . .

Warm flesh curled around his bare arm like five strips of fire. He glanced down and saw the blood-red claws press against his skin. The woman with the green eyes smiled in the most seductive way, a smile that visually represented the sound that made his body quake. As sunlight hit those emerald orbs, the dark dots in the center shrank to pinpoints that transfixed him.

Before he could stop her, she pulled him beyond the barrier and into the midst of the dancers.

She faced him, shoulders rotating, hips swaying, head bobbing, her smile luscious. Her body began to undulate. He could not feel his body moving. He could not feel his body at all. But when he looked down, he saw his feet step forward one at a time, imitating the slow shuffle happening all around him.

The music controlled him, turning him into only sound. Around him, the crowd had moved into the street and the line between observer and observed vanished. People of all skin tones trembled violently, as if throwing a fit. Several couples did an erotic dance, a kind of hopping close together, the woman in front, the man behind, their faces joyous as they melded with the music. Before he realized it, he was doing this dance with the green-eyed woman.

Her dark hair with the beaded red plaits whipped his chest as her head snapped back and forth to the beat. The sultry scent of her permeated every pore of his body. He felt her body meet his, from head to toe, as if they were one flesh, not two. It was no longer just the music. He was losing himself, blending, disappearing. . . .

Greg broke and ran!

The music of steel drums dogged him. He tripped and fell, got up and raced down the street, fighting unconsciousness. Another band was turning the corner. He saw the sign "JAMAICA—BLACK/WHITE MAHN/ WOMAHN REGGAE" and felt desperate.

People barely parted as he rammed between them, stumbling over curbs, running into traffic to blaring horns, falling onto the grass, getting up, running against the curious faces coming toward him, until finally the crowd thinned.

The sun pressed him down. The air felt dense and he could not breathe easily. He gulped in breaths and felt sweat trickle down his face, sticking his clothes to his body. He looked around—he was at the spot along the harbor where he had begun. A semblance of normalcy was returning. But the music that had invaded his chest still beat where his heartbeat should be. And the ringing in his ears cut off the outer world.

He slowed, gasping, wiping sweat from his eyes. His heart did not slow. The steel drums felt imbedded in there, pounding a tinny rhythm that was too voluminous and too fast. This was too much life for him to contain.

A thought gripped him—he needed to get to a hospital. Maybe he was having a heart attack. Or a seizure.

The next few hours were a blur, like a nightmare that leaves a taste of terror afterward. He remembered hailing a taxi. Sitting in the emergency room. Undergoing an EKG. A young resident, an Asian woman with ancient eyes, telling him nothing was wrong, handing him a prescription for Adivan. Greg heard the words "Heat stroke" and "Call your doctor."

The drug helped some. But in the middle of the night, the pounding of his heart kept him from sleeping. His body vibrated and throbbed. But when he looked at his hands, they were not shaking. In the mirror he could see his body was not trembling, although it felt that way. His eyes looked desperate, frightened, and he had never felt so alone.

By instinct, with no plan to guide him, Greg made his way to the lakeshore, to the parade route. Traffic gone, the street was eerily silent. Sanitation workers had removed all but the odd sequin and feather. The barriers had disappeared.

Greg did not know why he had come here. Above, the moon shone full and expectant. It was quiet enough to hear water lapping against the dock when a boat passed in the harbor, although the ringing in his ears continued. The air was hot and heavy for this late at night, and a mist rolled in off the lake. He caught the scent of flowers and turned.

"What have you done to me?" he cried.

The green-eyed woman moved and swayed toward him like a shadow in the night. When she reached him, she raised her arms, as if to caress him, but he pulled back.

"You fear me, you fear you, doncha know?" she said.

He watched, paralyzed, as if what was happening occurred in slow motion. She unbuttoned his shirt. She laid her black palm against his bare chest. He watched her sharp fingernails press against his skin. And enter his body.

His heart beat wildly, erratically. Her touch exaggerated the pulse of the muscle on which his very life hinged. Suddenly, the beat of the steel drums settled in again, as strong as it had been in the afternoon.

"Make it stop!" he cried, his chest heaving. Tears spilled over his eyelids; he could not recall the last time he had cried.

"It not stop now, mahn. No, never," she said, backing away just a little. "You grow used to it. This drumbeat, it be your heartbeat, and these tears you weep so sadly, they will seal them beats together. Oh, you get used to it!" Her eyes danced, sparkling like green stars, like the Caribbean ocean, like the Emerald Isle. Like the color of his steel-drum heart.

Blood of the Rose

Karen E. Taylor

The first time Adam saw Marie she was seated by the side of her husband's casket. She made an oddly composed widow, dressed all in black, complete with hat and gossamer veil that did not quite hide her somber smile and the predatory gleam in her eyes. Her hands rested, smooth and reassuring, along her gently expanded abdomen and she held court with visiting relatives and friends like a queen.

He knew all about her, of course, her age, her address, even her credit rating. But the neatly completed information form she had given the funeral director days before had not prepared him for the utter shock of her menacing beauty, the black eyes and perfect olive complexion that seemed to shine through her veil. The sharpness of her gaze was like the cold whisper of a scalpel against his skin and slashed him where he stood in his obsequious pose in the far doorway.

"Maintain the distance," his boss, Louis Bowe, owner of the Bowe Funeral Home, always said. "Think of yourself as a highly paid and valued servant, because that is what you are. Comfort should be offered, but with dignity and grace. We are the detached, sympathetic voice of reason in an insane world."

But Marie's eyes beckoned him into her insanity and he fell, moving across the distance of the outer room, propelled through the inner room, almost as if dragged through the crowd of mourners and the overwhelming display of funeral roses to a suddenly vacated space at her side. "Mrs. Zenos?" His ordinarily composed, detached voice cracked slightly to his embarrassment. "I'm Adam Rose. Allow me to express my sincerest condolences on your bereavement."

She held her hand out and he touched it briefly. Her skin was smooth, hot. "Mr. Rose." Her voice was a rich deep contralto with a faint touch of a Greek accent. "Thank you. I understand that you did the work on my Stephen."

So much meaning was encompassed by her words, "my Stephen,"

492

a love and devotion almost beyond his comprehension. But the eyes that considered him through the veil were dry and eager. He cleared his throat. "Yes, I hope you are satisfied with our results, Mrs. Zenos."

"Indeed, I am, most pleased." She reached over and tenderly stroked the cold arm of her husband. "We have all been saying that he looks so well, so alive." Her hand lingered caressingly on the corpse and Adam blushed, thinking suddenly and unavoidably of that hot skin pressed against his own. "You have done well."

He nodded briefly. "I'll be here for the remaining days of viewing, and of course for the funeral service. And if there's any other way I can be of assistance, please ask for me."

Marie smiled at him, exposing perfect, tiny white teeth. "You may be sure I will do that, Adam."

The next two days of viewing Stephen Zenos's body seemed to Adam to fly by in a feverish rush. Surrounded by a throng of mourners, swathed in black, and shrouded in the heavy scent of the flowers, Marie watched him as he tended to his duties. Her black eyes continually followed him, as he played escort to elderly women and men, steering them to vacant chairs and whispering dignified words of comfort; her eyes studied him as he pressed endless glasses of cool water into reaching hands and sought him out as he delivered and rearranged the continual onslaught of bouquets.

The flowers were all roses; he'd thought that a coincidence on the first day, but with each new arrangement an odd and ominous symmetry was being established. The other attendants laughed about "The Rose Funeral" in hushed but irreverent tones, speculating on Marie's apparent interest in Adam. "Maybe we should put you into a vase, too, Adam, and deliver you to her."

And he would blush and they would laugh even harder. But he didn't laugh, couldn't laugh. Everywhere Adam went, she was there, her rich voice rising over the other voices, her hands either caressing the dead skin of the corpse, or clasped possessively over her stomach, where Stephen's child rested. Over those two days, he grew to hate the corpse and then even the child, jealous for the touch of those hands.

The last night of viewing he lingered in the office, waiting for the mourners and family to depart. Mr. Bowe was present that night and Adam had made himself as unobtrusive as possible, fearing his fascination with the widow might be noticed. When Bowe finally entered the office, he smiled at Adam. "Good job, son. I'm going home now. Close up for me, will you?"

Adam nodded, "Yes, sir." The front door opened, then shut, and the faint sound of Bowe's car faded as it pulled out of the parking lot. Silence descended on the rooms; Adam shuffled some papers, then put them aside and stood up, stretching and yawning slightly. Turning out the light, he closed the office door and started down the hall to the viewing rooms, to put them in order before the morning.

He gasped when he entered the room where Stephen Zenos's body lay. Marie stared up at him from where she sat, cross-legged in the middle of the floor, her dress billowing around her, surrounded by a circle of flickering votive candles. She had removed her hat and veil and was reaching into the basket positioned next to her, pulling out several dark round objects and lining them up carefully in front of her. "Adam," her smile sent an anticipatory thrill through him, "I know this is most likely a little unorthodox, but it is an old family tradition. Humor me. In fact," she smiled deeper, her eyes boring into his, her small hands beckoning, "do more than that. Join me, Adam."

"But," he hesitated at the edge of the candles' circle, "I shouldn't, or you shouldn't . . . be here, I mean."

Marie laughed, "Ah, but it is only you and I and Stephen here now, and he won't tell a soul. Join me, Adam."

He stepped into the circle and sat down, overwhelmed by the aroma of the roses, the candles, and her. "It is a beautiful scent, isn't it, Adam? Stephen loved my candles. I mold them myself, mixing the wax and the essences according to very old customs. My mother taught me when I was just a girl." Shepicked up one of the objects in front of her, held it up to her face and inhaled, then handed it to him. It was a plum, the outer skin so dark it seemed black in the candlelight. "Stephen's favorite fruit." Her eyes, no longer hidden by the veil, were beautiful and reflected the flicker of the flames. "Eat," she urged him, selecting a plum for herself and biting into it. The juice ran over her chin and she wiped it away with the back of her hand, laughing.

Adam sat on the floor and stared at her, light-headed from the scented air. The plum rested in his palm, forgotten and uneaten, until she gave another laugh and guided his hand to his mouth, pressing the cool skin of the fruit to his lips. "Eat, Adam."

His teeth burst through the surface of the plum; the skin was tart and crisp, but the center so sweet it brought tears to his eyes. He rolled the fruit in his mouth, savoring its texture, its flavor. He saw as he pulled his hand away that the plum's flesh was colored a deep red, as red as the roses, as red as blood, as red as Marie's lips as she urged him to eat more. Adam finished, sucking the last shreds from the pit, embarrassed by the sticky juice that now coated his fingers and his lips.

Marie laughed again, and pulled his hand to her mouth, licking the fingertips, then leaned into Adam and kissed him. His head reeled with that kiss, with the heady scent of the candles, the roses, and Marie, with the cloying taste of the plum and her tongue. And when the kiss was done, she held his head between her palms. "Ah, my dear, do you know how long I had to search for you? How many funeral homes I had to call to find a Rose like you?"

He shook his head; he felt drunk, drugged with her presence. She smiled, stood up within the circle of the candles, and slowly began to unbutton her black widow's dress. Adam could only stare as she slid it from her shoulders, as she shed her bra, her hose, her black satin panties. When she stood naked in front of him she reached her hands down to pull him up to her. He rose on unsteady legs, his eyes still fastened to her, admiring the swollen breasts, the soft curve of her stomach where the child rested. She was beautiful, the most beautiful woman he had ever seen, and she wanted him, she said; she'd been searching for him.

He opened his mouth to speak, to say that he loved her, but could only produce a strange garbled sound. "No, don't try to talk," she reached down into her basket again, pulling out something long and shiny, "it won't help. Old family traditions, Adam, are so important. So very important. The candles, the roses, the plums, all prepared especially for you. My mother was a powerful woman, and bequeathed that power to me. Power over life and death," Marie laughed as she brought the knife to his throat, "yes, even power enough to bring back the dead. All is ready now, but for the final step. To bathe my Stephen's body in the blood of a rose."

Louis Bowe was surprised early the next morning to discover Marie Zenos waiting for him by the locked doors. "Mr. Bowe," she smiled sadly and touched his hand, "I have decided that I do not wish a final viewing this morning. All my goodbyes were said last night and I do not want the coffin open again. Let him rest now, safe from prying eyes."

"Whatever you'd like, Mrs. Zenos; we are here to serve your needs."

"And that you have, Mr. Bowe. I have been satisfied." Marie's voice dropped lower. "Most satisfied."

Bowe shook his head slightly when a man emerged from the Zenos car and came to stand next to Marie, gently cupping her elbow in his hand. Such an uncanny resemblance to her late husband, he thought briefly as he unlocked the doors and escorted them inside. But he didn't give it much consideration, thinking only how glad he'd be to see the end of this funeral; the smell of the roses was stronger this morning, made his eyes water and his head ache. He hoped that Adam would arrive soon. It was not like him to be late.

Predator's Moon

MEL ODOM

I swear to God, Tryx, she's a real witch. Took a tattoo off Hairball last night slicker 'n birdshit on a pump handle, and didn't leave no scars behind."

Still astride the Harley-Davidson, my road leathers covered in red Oklahoma dust, I looked at the Weasel and asked, "And she's inside?"

"Yeah." The Weasel was so pale and thin he looked like a bearded ghost. He stood in the graveled parking lot in front of the Jade Cock Tavern only a few miles off I-40 near the Muskogee turnoff on Highway 69.

I got off the scooter, took a smoke from the Marlboro pack inside my jacket, and lit up. "She been here long?"

"Couple days. That's her rig over there."

Looking past the line of sleds owned by the Scorpions Club and the handful of dust-covered beaters driven by the tavern's clientele who hadn't been frightened off by the sudden descent of bikers, I saw a jumped-up Dodge Ram pickup hauling a short, silver Airstream trailer parked at the back end of the lot. "She looks kinda up-scale," I said.

"Only cost Hairball twenty bucks to lose the tattoo."

"What brought you guys here?" The front of the tavern was scarred and weather-beaten, and a green neon fighting cock swooped in one window while a blinking red and blue Coors sign filled the other. The main sign advertised happy hour, which was over, and dancers, which—judging from the basso thump of music coming from inside the building —were still grinding away. Night had drawn long and lean shadows around the tavern, and the light coming from inside made it seem bigger than it was. I didn't think I'd ever been there before, but I knew a thousand places like it, and they'd all been good places to while away an evening. This was the first one I'd ever seen with a witch.

"You know John Thomas," the Weasel said. "Guy still likes all that *Twilight Zone* shit. Somebody up in Tulsa told him about the witch, he figured he'd come see for himself."

I *did* know John Thomas. *Twilight Zone* I'd seen a couple times in hotels late-night during cross-country runs. I'd been away for a while during the show's original run. Missed a lot of things during that time. Still catching up.

"So what brings you out this way?" the Weasel asked.

I took another drag on the cigarette and let the wind rip the smoke from my lips. "Running from an APB down in Dallas for a disagreement with the Colombians. Missouri sounded good for a time, maybe Florida after that."

He jerked a thumb at the coyote head on the back of my jacket. "Maybe it's time you thought about changing from the Lone Wolves to the Scorpions. We can protect you."

I grinned, let him know I meant no disrespect. "I belong to a good club. Got no reason to change."

"I never seen no Lone Wolves around here, Tryx."

"We're kind of exclusive."

"Yeah, well think about it. John Thomas would put you up for membership." The Weasel unzipped his pants and loosed a few beers, not caring that it splashed his boots.

"I will." I flipped the butt into the pool at his feet and it hissed and went out. I walked into the tavern. I didn't know exactly what had brought me to the Jade Cock, but I'd followed a dark wind into Oklahoma. The Dallas APB was a fact too, and I knew the Weasel would check on it even though the Scorpions knew me. A club like the Scorpions didn't trust. They ran meth and crack across the Southwest. John Thomas was cagey and smart, and genuine entertainment for somebody like me. The witch increased the ante.

The interior of the tavern smelled of beer and piss and reefer. It cloyed my lungs. I'd been on the open road a lot lately and it was hard adjusting to civilization again. Overhead, the dim lighting offered only token resistance to the shadows draped across the gathering of mismatched tables and chairs, saving its strength for the small dance stage where two nude women gyrated to the hooted encouragement of the assembled Scorpions.

John Thomas held court in the back. Three dancers in Victoria's Secret underthings and four bikers sat with him. A fortyish woman with classic Cherokee features and coal-black hair, dressed in a turquoise Rockies, Ropers, and a fringed leather jacket, sat beside him. A feathered braid pulled her hair back on the left and lent a piercing gaze to her slate-gray eyes.

I nodded to John Thomas and snagged a chair from a table I passed. The jukebox started up with an Elvis rockabilly tune that had been new the last time I'd heard it. John Thomas was a confirmed Elvis freak.

He stood six-five in socks and looked like he'd been pressed out in 4x4 timbers. His long hair hung across the black leather jacket stretched tight across his shoulders. Despite the gloom in the club, he wore mirror sunglasses.

One of the new bikers started to stand in a defensive posture but John Thomas waved him away. "At ease, Snakebite. This here's a friend." He grinned at me. "How's Tryx?"

"I'm fine, JT." I signaled for a beer and took it from an anorexic waitress in a black MegaDeath T-shirt. "This the witch?"

A cold light flashed through her eyes that didn't match the smile. She studied me more closely, but I knew she wouldn't know me.

"This here's Rita Ninehawks," John Thomas said. "She's about to tell me my fortune." He indicated the shallow ceramic dish on the tabletop that looked a couple hundred years old. "She's Cherokee. What they call a skinwalker. Supposed to be able to take the shape of animals, cast spells, and such."

"That a fact." I looked at her and saw the carved soapstone coyote held covetously in her slim-fingered hands.

"Yes," she said in a snake's hiss, low and lasting.

"What animals?" I gazed at the soapstone figurine. I felt the electricity in it.

"Tell me this man's name," the witch said.

"Hell, this here's Tryx," John Thomas said. "An outlaw among outlaws. Don't let that little boy face fool you none, Rita. Man's a stone killer. I seen him do it about a year ago in Hobbs, New Mexico."

That was when we'd first met, though I'd known bikers for years.

"Tryx," she said, as if testing it. "That's your name?"

"One of several," I said.

"And your true name?"

"Nobody's business but mine."

She leaned back in her chair and regarded me. Her hand closed over the figurine and I felt her draw on the power inside her and it. I set up wards of my own. Now I understood the black wind I'd followed.

"You're insolent," she declared.

I regarded her, keeping my sunglasses dark so she couldn't see in. "It's a practiced art."

"Hey, Tryx," John Thomas said, "ease up. We're here just to have a little fun. Don't go and spoil it." He uncrinkled two twenties and a ten and smoothed them on the tabletop, looking at the witch. "What about that fortune?"

She nodded but kept a wary eye on me. Casually, she poured beer into the ceramic dish, enough to cover the bottom. "Spit," she told John Thomas, "into the dish."

The Scorpions' captain sipped beer, then spat into the dish. The spittle ran across the alcohol's surface, breaking into a squid-shaped formation.

The witch leaned in slowly, drawing everyone around the table in with her. Except me. I lit another Marlboro and watched the flare of the match wink in the dish's contents. She ignored me as she waved her hands and mouthed Cherokee words that dated back almost two hundred years. She mispronounced some of them. She should have known them because it was an old prayer, handed down through generations, bastardized in the telling. Once it had opened gates to other worlds, now it merely petitioned for mercy.

I did know it.

"What do you wish to know?" the witch asked in a quiet voice that captured the attention of most around the table. In the background, the DJ put on a Billy Joel tune and a fiery redhead took the stage.

"The future," John Thomas answered.

I felt the witch's exasperation as I turned to watch the redheaded dancer. Everyone says they want to know the future, but they fail to

499

realize they don't even have the questions to ask about it. The dancer was compelling, and I caught her eye several times as she whirled.

In the end, the witch expertly guided John Thomas through a series of questions that she answered easily and in mild extrapolation. Most of them she got right, though she didn't mention the fact that John Thomas would be dead, shotgunned by one of his own in seventeen months while in Atlanta. I figured she didn't mention it out of politeness, because there was no way to miss it.

I filed the double-cross away for further reference. If it was worthwhile and looked like fun, if I was in Atlanta in seventeen months, and —mostly—if I remembered, I might save John Thomas. Unless he grew boring.

Promised health and wealth and fame, John Thomas leaned back in his chair and bought the house a round. Bikers only, of course. The redheaded dancer gathered her clothing and approached me. Within minutes she was giggling and breathing in my ear while sitting on my leg. I didn't forget about the witch, and she didn't forget about me.

"Isn't there anything you want?" she asked me. She held Skullcrusher's arm in her hand and looked at the new skin where a tattoo had been only moments ago. Her magic was real. But then, after seeing her, I'd had no doubts.

I captured the redhead's wrists in one of my hands and made her stop playing for the moment. She pouted, but I knew her feelings weren't hurt. With my other hand, I took out a hundred-dollar bill and let it flutter to the tabletop.

"Your fortune?" she asked, picking the bill up.

"Yours," I told her.

She froze. Conversation died around the table for a moment, then Snakebite broke it with his raucous laughter, saying that was rich and how he'd never heard a fortune teller being asked to tell her own fortune.

With cool anger, the witch emptied the dish, wiped it clean with a napkin, then poured beer and spat. She studied the surface for long moments while everyone waited. Then she started her lies. I knew she could only see uncertain blackness there.

When she finished, I laid another hundred on the table.

"What?" she asked. She left the money there.

"The figurine," I said, pointing. "Tell me about it."

For a moment, the silence hung between us.

"Go on, Rita," a dancer at the table urged. She was blonde and baby-faced, probably no more than eighteen. She'd gazed in wonderment during the fortune-telling.

The witch gazed at the dancer, then reluctantly faced me again. Then I knew what she was really there for. She opened her hand and the soapstone coyote stood on her palm. "This is a powerful talisman of the coyote god of my people. He was lecherous and tricky and knew no loyalty. Coyote only looked out for himself. But sometimes he fell in love. My ancestor was one of the women he loved. He gave her this figurine as a symbol of his love and protection. But being Coyote, he grew tired one day and wandered away. Gods take their immortality for granted and he was surprised when he came back to the village to find that the woman he'd loved had died of old age. My family chose to keep the figurine to remind us never to take any promises from Coyote."

I smiled at her, glad my sunglasses could hide the hurt. "I heard it another way."

She stared hard at me. "You are Indian?"

"No," I said truthfully. "But I am a collector of stories. One of the old men in Talequah told me about a statue like that one."

She said nothing, but John Thomas told me, "Well, tell the damn story, man."

"The figurine was called Coyote's Promise," I said, "and it was given to one of his many loves because Coyote doesn't have an aptitude for monogamy." All of the bikers laughed because they knew the feeling. All of the dancers commented sarcastically on the fickleness of men. "He gave her the figurine as a token of his love and did wander away. But he wasn't gone all that long. When he returned from his journey— one that he didn't want to undertake but that was necessary—he came home to find his love murdered at the hands of a jealous friend. He went after the murderess, but didn't know she was a witch, and she managed to bind him from the mortal world with the power of the figurine while he was still blind with grief. It's said that Coyote's Promise also extended the life of the one who possessed it." I paused. "But that's just a story. Hell, there's probably a million soapstone coyotes out there."

The witch regarded me with evil intent while the redhead demanded my attention. I gave it to her. Then more money dropped on the table and the bikers continued their requests. The redhead pulled me away to a table by ourselves, telling me her shift was over. I let myself be swayed by her charms and my lips caressed hers while my hands roamed.

But my attention was on the blonde dancer who seemed enthralled by the witch. Despite the redhead's natural dislike of talking about other women while she was concentrating on seducing me, she told me about the dancer. Her name was Clarice, and she'd always loved magic and wasn't particularly fond of the management of the Jade Cock.

By midnight I was sweaty and naked in the back of a 1971 Oldsmobile Cutlass and wasn't minding the cramped quarters I was sharing with the redhead at all. She was nibbling my ear, hoping for reignition, when I saw the witch come out the back of the tavern with the blonde dancer in tow. I glanced up through the moonlight-splashed back glass of the Olds and saw the moon, fat and round and gleaming. A predator's moon.

The witch led the blonde into the Airstream trailer.

The redhead started to protest, but I put her to sleep with a gesture, covered her with the afghan we'd found there, and pulled on my jeans, hurrying now. Time is almost alien to my nature and has cost me dearly in the past.

With the trailer chilling my back, I peered in through the window. The witch wasted no time in throwing a glamour over the dancer and robbing her of conscious thought. The figurine did offer an increased life-span, but in the absence of Coyote's love, the cost was hellish.

Rita Ninehawks seemed to melt like the witch in *The Wizard of Oz*. I'd seen the movie when it had first been released and had found it diverting. When the woman finished changing, a hawk's grim visage peered out beneath the thick mop of black hair, the eyes black over a cruel beak that hinged into a still-human jawline. Small pinfeathers covered the arms, and talons took the place of hands. She was taller now, more fearsome and totally without mercy as she advanced on the dancer.

The lock shattered in my hand when I tried the knob. I swung the door open and confronted the witch.

Her plumed head swiveled toward me. "You!"

"You murdered Dani Leaping Panther a hundred years ago," I accused. "I didn't know you were still alive. But that won't last." I smiled, gathering my power.

"Who are you?" she demanded, whirling to face me.

"You know my name."

"Coyote! But I bound you! Forty years ago!"

"You can't bind a god forever," I told her.

"You're no god," she snarled.

"But I'm much more than you'll ever be," I said. "And this time I won't be taken by surprise." I'd nourished my grief and my anger, forged it into a remorseless tool that had lain fallow for the last two years. Now I drew it from its sheath and held it, bright and hard in my mind.

The witch tried to use the figurine's power, tapping it like a child, but with brute force. The impact slammed into me and knocked me back against the wall. Flames spread out across the interior of the trailer as I repelled the wild magic.

Out of the witch's glamour, the dancer woke and shrieked, and ran from the trailer. The witch wouldn't be able to steal her youth now, leaving a drying husk of a corpse behind. For that to happen, the victim must willingly go with the witch.

She fought me, burnt my skin in places, and ripped it with her talons in others. The fire raged around us, but didn't consume us. Her black eyes blazed in fury as I reached out and seized her neck. She tried to bite me, and her cruel beak scored my cheek, drawing blood. Mostly, I'm immortal, but death is still to be avoided. There are limits, even for me.

I broke her spells and wards with magic of my own. When she reached for the figurine, I melted it in the flames I held cupped in my fist. Then I tightened my hold on her neck and snapped her spine. Even with the fire raging around us, the light died from her black eyes.

I jumped through a back window that had shattered from the heat and dragged her corpse after me. Although the Scorpions had gathered on the other side of the Airstream trailer, no one saw me. The bikers cleared off in minutes, long before the fire trucks arrived.

By then I was deep into the broken countryside. I hung the witch from a tree, her body now having returned to that of an old woman, shrunken and gray. Sitting cross-legged before the corpse, I called the night feasters, the coyotes, owls, and rodents, and bade them eat. I watched them in silence as they stripped the flesh from her bones. Although I couldn't return Dani's life that had been stolen, I could avenge her death.

Years ago, I had given my love my promise, Coyote's promise. Tonight I gave Dani my tears and my thoughts, remembering. Although it took hours, and though Coyote is known for his impatience and wanderlust, and for the cruel sense of humor that also names him Trickster, I sat there until the witch's bones were picked clean, and the final marrow had been crunched and claimed. With the coming of the dawn, I stole quietly and unseen back to the tavern, recovered my Harley, and followed the wind out of there.

Djinneyah & Co.

BLYTHE AYNE

I was still in my office in the social science complex at eleven o'clock one night working on a paper that hated me, when I succumbed to the call of a dark chocolate Milky Way. I headed downstairs to the vending machines. There stood E.J., drinking a soda.

I hadn't expected to see any other living thing. I thought about how awful I must look and considered making my escape, but in the moment I hesitated he turned and looked at me. I ran my fingers through my standing-on-end hair, and fed the candy machine fifty-five cents.

"Are you in archaeology?" He had an accent I couldn't place, faintly Mediterranean I thought, but his pale coloring didn't match.

I shook my head, intent while the machine dropped my chocolate fix. "Anthropology." I grabbed the Milky Way. Even with my mouth watering, I demurred from ripping it open in front of the blond, blue-eyed stranger.

The ugly fluorescent lighting made E.J.'s face flat and sallow, and the dark circles under his eyes looked like bruises, taking the life out of his eyes.

I hoped I looked at least as well and half as good.

"I have to get a paper done by Friday, but it's not going very well," he said.

"Yeah. Same here. Exactly. Paper. Friday. Not good." I fingered my candy bar.

He extended his hand. "I'm Elias, but everyone calls me E.J."

I took his hand. Firm, thin, nice. "Ashley. Everyone calls me— Ashley."

E.J. smiled. "You're cute."

"Really?" I thought. 'Cute? Ick. . . .'"

"I mean," E.J. went on, "if you're like me, you're very tired, but still, you're friendly. I've seen you in the halls and you seemed so serious. By the way, you're not only cute, you're beautiful."

"Thank you." I liked this appraisal much better. I thought of myself as serious, and who didn't like to be called beautiful once in a while? Particularly when feeling like a rag, a bone, and a hank of hair. "Well, I suppose I'd better get back to work. I only have one more night I can abuse myself with that wretched paper." I moved toward the stairs.

"What's your office phone number?" he asked.

"Twelve thirty-three." Hey, why be coy?

He called on Monday, after I, for one, had slept away the better part of the weekend.

We were married five months later.

I didn't realize until after we were married that what had infatuated me about him was not "him," because in that five months of eighteen-hour days working at our graduate degrees I never really found out who "he" was. I was intrigued by his ethnographic stories—which for him were simply talking about his family, his life. I was fascinated by his ethnographic mix, a blue-eyed blond with an Israeli passport, Arabian blood, and Christian religion. Mostly, I was infatuated with his infatuation with me.

But after we were married, it didn't take me long to learn that love was not infatuation, fascination, or intrigue.

I found out that E.J., as a person, liked to sleep on the same side of the bed as I did, that the fact that he never ate what I ate in restaurants was more of a problem when he didn't want to eat what I cooked. I found out that although E.J. was Christian, he took his religion far more seriously and to much greater lengths of ritual and commitment than my live-and-let-live doctrine. Conversely, I couldn't stir him to political fervor—he said American politics were magnificent in concept and pathetic in practice. I discovered I didn't like his friends and he couldn't stand mine.

I'd never been taught what married love was, not in the way I visualize people in tribal lives sitting down with their young people and imparting the wisdom and art of living with someone and loving them, whether the two of you agree or disagree. The only socialization I'd been given about marriage was to watch my parents fight, become silent, and divorce.

No wonder I was going through an internal litany of ambivalence as I packed in preparation for the semester dig E.J. and I were going on in his homeland. It was because he'd been chosen to go on the dig that we decided to get married right away. We didn't want to be apart for four months, and people on the dig were allowed to take spouses. This was a fabulous career and education opportunity, I told myself. I'd be able to do anthropology *and* archaeology. Who'd pass that up?

When we first arrived in Israel we spent a few days with E.J.'s mother and two unmarried adult sisters. The sisters pinched me and stared at me when I laughed. E.J. told me they thought I was too skinny to bear children, and they wanted to be sure I had most of my own teeth. They fed me to the gills six times a day. I was relieved when we left.

E.J. said I met with family approval, even if I was "one of those American women." I restrained myself from saying approval went two ways. I dreaded the thought of future pinching sessions with in-laws. I didn't say anything critical about his family, but I could see E.J. was hurt by my lack of enthusiasm. Problem number one.

Problem number two cropped up that night after we'd arrived at the dig site. We were provided with our own two-room tent, which I found charming and romantic. And there were actual American fiberglass Porta Pottis off at a distance. I'd done my share of camping, so this was a great adventure. But much to my surprise, E.J. started complaining as soon as he saw the bevy of tents in one place and the Porta Pottis in another.

"I can't believe they expect people to go hiking, just to relieve themselves."

"A little fresh air won't hurt you." I was unpacking, trying to make the best use of limited space.

"Why couldn't they put one of those facilities by each tent?"

"That'd smell great in a day or two." I started to put things away. I stopped unpacking. "You've been on digs before."

"Two summers in Colorado. We stayed in a motel."

"Jeez," I said, awed by his inexperience. "Better get used to it, Mr. Archaeologist. Anyway, this is a dream come true, a dig in your own country. Real Indiana Jones stuff."

"Humph."

About three A.M. E.J. woke me up with a whispered urgency.

"Wh-what's wrong?" I was disoriented, frightened by his tone of voice.

"Nothing. I just wondered if you have to go to the bathroom."

"Given how soundly I was sleeping, I don't think so, no."

"Are you sure? I thought if you needed to, I'd walk with you."

"No. Don't need to." I closed my eyes. E.J. didn't leave. I kept my eyes closed.

"I . . . I want some company."

"Come on, E.J., let me sleep." Then I replayed the tone of his voice, which had something in it I'd never heard before. Fear.

I lugged myself out of the comfort of the sway-bottomed cot and stuck my feet into my thongs. "Let's go."

We didn't say anything on the way. The night was clean-edged as a new knife. The sky seemed different—the stars looked larger, whiter, sharper, and the velveteen of the sky appeared unusually far away and touchable at the same time. One could have heard a pin drop at two miles. There was no wind, no sound, and only the faintest odor of something like dryness, and I thought of the sand.

I was full of feelings. I was peeved and mystified by E.J.'s fear. How was it possible I'd married a man afraid of the dark? I was awed by the bigness of the sky, the sharpness of the stars. And I had creepy-flesh. I couldn't understand it. Was I catching E.J.'s fear?

There was something about the poised, heavy stillness, as if some gigantic being had taken a step and was just about to put the other foot down when we came out of our tent—as if that huge, unseeable foot was hovering, waiting for us to return to our tent so it could continue its restless night meandering.

We walked back to the tent, still not speaking, but the moment we got inside, I made E.J. pull his cot up alongside mine and talk to me.

"Didn't you feel anything out there?" he asked.

"You mean, besides the beauty and the peace and the quiet?"

"Beauty and quiet, yes. Peace, no. The night belongs to creatures of the dark, especially in this part of the world. Didn't you feel like someone or something was waiting for us to get out of its way?"

I remained silent, refusing to add fuel to the fire of his fantasy. "Why did you go into archaeology if you believe in this stuff?"

"Because I have to take on the fear, although I didn't think I'd have to face it so soon. I have to find out about the Djinneyah, and arm myself against . . ."

"Who?"

"Beings created of smokeless fire."

"That's Islamic myth, E.J., I thought you were Christian." Now *I*

507

began to feel fear. Never mind folkloric Djinneyah, I was with a real live madman.

"I've seen one. Or *not* seen her."

"Uh-huh.' I tried to sound agreeable. "Well, I've not seen her either—too."

"When I was twelve," he went on, "my friends dared me to walk on an ancient road that was a trade route before the time of Christ. At the time I was afraid of nothing and didn't believe in supernatural forces. I went to the spot where folklore says she's stolen men for millennia. She's particularly fond of men. I felt spooky, but I wasn't frightened.

"Then she came. I remember noise and odors and I remember her yelling, 'This is just a boy! But he will make a good man for me one day.' My eyes used to be hazel, before that night. She marked me by taking the color from my eyes."

"My folklore is a bit rusty," I argued as I fell back to sleep, "but isn't it impossible for a mere mortal to take on the disembodied dark forces?"

"Not impossible, no. There's tremendous power in being physical. We're dense matter, which Djinneyah loves to consume, but she can't if you're not afraid. Fear is vulnerability, and vulnerability is an open door to the spark of life."

"Can't wait to hear more. . . ." I mumbled as I tumbled into sleep. I'd be lying if I said I had no dreams.

When I woke in the morning, E.J. was already a member of the breakfast-making crew. He kissed my forehead as if no weirdness had transpired between us in the night.

Everyone raved about his pancakes. Everyone liked him. He was the translator, made great pancakes, and was a nice guy. There wasn't anyone I could walk up to and say, "Excuse me, but last night I discovered I've married a madman."

The whole crew struggled to stay awake so that the following day we'd be more or less on local time. The payoff was that E.J. stayed asleep through the night, and so did I.

But the first night's events lingered, and by the third day I felt I couldn't go on with my confused feelings toward my new husband.

"E.J., about this Djinneyah thing . . . am I right in guessing it's your intention to face it—that that's why you're here?"

He sat on the edge of his cot and watched as I brushed my hair.

"Before we left the states, yes. But now it seems enough just to be here and do the work I'm doing."

I nodded. "You know I don't believe in that stuff, and I'm wondering how you expect to lead a scientific life if you do. I love folklore, but it's just stories."

E.J. shrugged and said nothing more.

I thought the next day that he'd forgotten our conversation, but after supper he told me he'd arranged to borrow one of the jeeps.

"Why?"

"To meet the Djinneyah. I guess I'll never be more ready. You've shown me these last couple days that you'll never respect me again, that we'll never be close, unless I prove to you her existence."

I was game to go because I was equally determined that he see her nonexistence—although I kept the thought to myself.

We drove almost an hour on the hard-packed, rib-crunching dirt road. The sun sat on the great, straight line of horizon directly behind us and, as much as I wanted to feel like I was on an adventure, a lark, there was an uncomfortable silence between us. I was wondering what E.J. would do when he saw there were no Djinneyah.

We came to scrubby vegetation along the roadside and E.J. suddenly turned the headlights and the engine off and drove off the road. The sun was gone and night wrapped around us as if we'd been shoved into a black closet. E.J. coasted around behind the scrub. I heard him get out and walk around to my side of the jeep. Silently, he took my hand and led me into the scrub.

He pulled me to the ground. My eyes were becoming adjusted to the dark—I could make out the shape of the scraggly bushes around us, I could see the stars, the hard-packed blackness of the road, the outline of E.J.'s body stretched on the ground. Suddenly a ragged edge of moon came into the sky with a wobbly, flickering light. Even the wan light made everything stand out in unrelenting bas-relief. Something stirred, there was an odd swirl of wind, laced with the redolence of cardamom. I breathed deeply, heady and dizzy with the fragrance on the breeze. The night colors distinguished themselves—the *zaffer* blue sand, the purple sky, the ebony branches and black bisque leaves of the scrub, and E.J.'s pale hair, pale eyes glowing with a silver-blue hue.

How strange he looked!

That was when the raucous noise began. Coming toward us on the road were the sounds of a band of Gypsies—tribal entertainment. It was the tambourines I heard first, and the high piercing tinkle of ankle bells. Then laughter—cheerful, infectious. A donkey brayed and was answered by two or three others. There was a drumbeat pounding with a deep-to-the-feet thrum. Then a *nye* and *muzmar* joined in with a provocative melody. A camel coughed and another bellowed out over the flat land. Several voices rose in song, while a child's giggle could be heard above the urgent melody.

What luck! I thought, what a coincidence, to come to *nowhere* in the middle of the night, to lie prostrate on the earth for no reason, and to be treated to a wandering band of Gypsies. I couldn't wait to see their bright, swirling fabrics, the gaudily dressed donkeys and camels, the madly painted homes on wheels, the dark eyes and gold jewelry and long black hair.

I jumped up in anticipation. E.J. reached for me quick as a snake and slammed me back to the ground.

"What's the matter with you?" I snarled.

"What's the matter with *you?*" he whispered back, not letting go of my arm.

Then I had second thoughts. This was his homeland, he surely knew more about it than I. A band of Gypsies on an abandoned road in the middle of the night—they'd probably steal me and sell me into white slavery.

"Are the Gypsies dangerous?"

"Gypsies?" E.J. hissed. "It's not Gypsies, it's the Djinneyah and her demons."

"Still with the Djinneyah thing!" I hissed back. Then I stopped whispering. "For God's sake, Elias, give it a rest!" I shouted, angry beyond reason.

All the myriad sounds of the oncoming troupe stopped instantly— a metronome count of four—then started up again. I wrenched myself from E.J.'s grasp, stood, and stumbled away from him. Pushing aside the brush, I peered at the road.

From the sounds, the troupe must have been fast upon me, but I saw nothing. I glanced at E.J. to see if he'd try to grab at me again, but he was cowering in the sand, looking frightened to death. I found myself feeling intense disgust for such a paltry excuse of a man.

The singing drew my attention back to the road. What melody, what sound! Could any human voice produce such clarion perfection? I fell in love with the song, the sound of that music, that singing, those drums, as if altogether it was a creature I longed to hold. The music was right *there* as I stared at the road, glowing black in the wilted moonlight. Where were they?

Then I saw the sharp-edged print of hooves appear in the dirt road and long thin trails, the marks of wagon wheels. The singing and the tambourines and the ankle bells were directly before me, but there was nothing other than the legion of hoof prints materializing before my eyes.

I was drawn to the music as the *nye* and *muzmar* and the big drum passed directly in front of me, with only more hoof prints appearing. I couldn't stand it! I stepped through the brush and onto the road, right into the arms of a tall, beautiful, amber-eyed woman. She smiled and I saw that her teeth were too large, quite literally looking like pearls. She began to speak, but, even though her mouth moved, the sound of her speech came from the night and from the earth. She spoke in a pre-Koranic Arabic, and yet I understood every word, although I knew modern Arabic marginally.

"I'm pleased by your appreciation of my music," she said, "and it's good that you please me. It's also good that you bring Elias back to me now that he is a man." The red of her cloak swirled around me like an alien dawn. "Since you've pleased me, I will not make of you a bodiless creature, haunting the desert until the end of time. I'll simply take your mortal life."

E.J. came flying through the brush as if he'd become a demon himself. I was unaware that the Djinneyah had folded me to her, but when E.J. flung her cloak away from me, I tripped backward and sat flat on the ground.

Like a child, I watched.

"Withdraw yourself from my beloved and from me!" E.J. commanded with a frightening authority in that ancient language. "In the name of the Lord of the Mystery of Heaven and Earth, the Lord of the Two Easts and the Two Wests, the Lord of Dawn, I command you! Remove your impudent and malapert spirit, and all your attending consorts and legions." His body shook with fury and his voice cut through the din of the unseen like a lighthouse beam.

The music swelled and wailed, the Djinneyah's laughter poured from every grain of sand, every leaf, every branch, the odor of burning rose water built to a crescendo with the music. Then, instantly, it was gone. As the Djinneyah disappeared in a swirl of red, my eyes were drawn to her two furry black fetlocks and shiny black hooves that were before me and then were gone.

All that was left were the prints of the mad trampling of cloven hooves.

E.J. pulled me up from the dirt, dusted me off, put his arm around me, and walked me back to the jeep. I held on to him all the way back to the camp, without uttering a word.

The most interesting thing about life is not the things that happen in it, as much as what one learns from living it. Although that night was amazing, and although I came to believe in things I previously couldn't have imagined, nothing made a greater impression on me than seeing how much my husband loved me—more than I loved him. More than he loved himself. That's when I began to truly love my hazel-eyed husband. I learned to love how he's different from me even more than how he's the same.

And this is the wisdom I intend to pass on to our children.

The Mudang

WILL MURRAY

An understandable oversight had brought Metallus Duende, sorcerer, extradimensional traveler, and collector of arcane skulls to Seoul, South Korea.

Now the skulls Metallus Duende collected were outré indeed. They filled an entire room of his Boston brownstone. Some were human; most were not. Vampire and werewolf and mummy skulls occupied certain niches, as did the braincases of beings far more exotic.

Of witch skulls, the collection abounded. Romany witches. Brazilian *brujas*. Innuit *angakoks*. Even a rare seventeenth-century New England witch skull, unearthed from the cellar hole in Dogtown, Massachusetts, and said to have encased the brain of Granny Looncraft, whose codfish, turnip, and periwinkle stew was supposed to cure all ailments of the flesh, and who died in 1775 of a bullet fashioned from a revengeful redcoat soldier's brass button.

But no *mudang*. Metallus Duende had never heard of mudangs until the Korean population of the United States mushroomed and he began to overhear tantalizing whispers at the greengrocers.

Those whispers were compelling. Duende had to possess the skull of a mudang if his witch niche was to be complete. And no immigrant mudang would do. Thus, he had come to Seoul.

Mudangs, Duende knew, held forth as storefront fortune-tellers, and since anyone could pretend to read sticky rice grains on glass or effect the voices of the dead, there were many who claimed the distinction, but few who practiced the ancient woman's art that had inexplicably risen in all cultures the world over.

A day in prowling more disreputable back alleys near Namdaemun Market proved this to his satisfaction. Duende had had his fortune read by many a stiff-faced *mansin,* none of whom had recognized him as a fellow being of power and one of which he had shrunk to the size of a squeaking toad for poisoning his persimmon tea as the most direct path to his wallet. He must venture into the countryside, after all. This was good, for Duende preferred a country witch, not a city witch, a mudang, not a *mansin.*

The village lay outside the old fortress city of Suwon, nestled at the foot of a piney hill that reminded Duende of New England, in a green glade pink with thistle.

A bent-backed farmer, seeing him approach, bowed and inquired, *"Pam-mo-go-sso-yo?"*

And the electrum amulet around his neck told Duende the man had asked, "Have you had rice today?" It was a traditional countryside greeting, and not an invitation to break bread.

"Yes," Duende said, and thanks to the amulet the words coming out were couched in perfect Korean. "I seek a mudang."

"You are troubled?"

"Only a mudang can end my troubles," Duende said truthfully.

The old man leaned on a willow staff and pointed north. "In the next valley sits the hut of Chong-gi, the mudang. If you ail, or have spirit troubles, Chong-gi will appease the gods or demons who vex you. Although she has been known to eat travelers."

And the old farmer laughed in the Asian way that said he might be joking, but then again, might not.

"Ko-map-sup-ni-da," Metallus Duende said by way of thanks, skirting the hill and plunging into the valley beyond, where yellow for-

sythia trembled under a wind Duende did not feel. Gimlet eyes peered from behind the forsythia, but he pretended not to see them. It was always wiser not to disturb unseen lurkers.

It had been called a hut, but it resembled a jade-roofed pavilion with the four upswept roofbeams that legend had it were the favorite roosting places of the mischievous horned goblins of Korea, the *tokkaebi*. Peach trees were flowering in the front yard. And off to one side leaned a garish spirit totem.

Geese honked and flapped as Duende stepped up to the door. The decapitated head of a horse hung over the entrance. It was fresh. Blood still dripped from its slack mouth. Duende stood off to one side as he knocked.

"Go away, tokkaebi!" a woman called from within. "Can you not see the head of a horse over my door?"

"I am no tokkaebi, but a white man come seeking the boon of your wisdom," Duende called back.

A knothole withdrew and an oblique eye regarded him briefly before the door opened.

The first thing Duende noticed were two tight eyes that resembled the seams of two walnuts. In the exact center of the forehead bulged a cyst or subcutaneous tumor. It did not matter, any more than nose warts would have. Bone was bone.

The mudang wore peasant costume—a cinnabar red *han-bok* dress over black pants tied at the ankles. Her black-brimmed hat rose to a scarlet peak. Stiff white hair sprouted from her scrunched chin, but for all that she was a woman. She beckoned Duende into her home, which was spotless and filled with gaudy costumes and odd musical instruments.

Over *maggoli* wine, into which Duende surreptitiously dropped a niter pellet that fizzed briefly as proof it was not poisoned, he told the mudang his troubles.

"I have an enemy I wish cursed with evil spirits," he said simply.

"It is worth gold to inflict bad spirits," Chong-gi said after a pause and a sip, sealing her own fate, for Metallus Duende did not pluck the skulls of those who practiced the good arts, only those who perpetrated evil.

"I have no gold, only won," Duende said.

And the mudang pointed to the pig's head that stood on a low taboret. Duende placed three hundred won in the tusked mouth, and that seemed to satisfy the mudang.

"Tell me of this enemy, ghost face," said the mudang.

As he explained his needs, Duende examined as best he could the prize dwelling behind the animated fleshy mask before him. High cheekbones dominated. This was as expected. Koreans were more Turkic than Asian. The mandibles appeared to work well despite the advancing years. Teeth were more absent than not, which was considered a defect in a werewolf skull, disaster if the prize were vampiric, but for a witch, a judicious sprinkling of gaps lent a certain authenticity. All in all, it was a sturdy specimen. Osteoporosis seldom wasted the skull bones.

The question remained how best to extract the skull from the mudang's head.

"I will perform a *kut* for you," she was saying. "But I must have an object once worn by the one you seek to curse."

Duende removed a silver signet ring and laid it on the taboret. The Old English initial D would mean nothing to the mudang, who knew only hangul characters.

Chong-gi regarded it solemnly and asked, "Ten thousand spirits are at my command. Which would you have me summon?" Her walnut eyes regarded him with bland wisdom.

Those eyes grew round when Duende said, "I have always feared the Lightning-bolt General, although the Fire General is very powerful, too."

And the mudang threw her head back and howled jeering delight at the white foreigner who knew the names of the spirit generals of the old Silla Kingdom.

"Hee-hee-hee," she tittered. "I can raise MacArthur, if you would prefer. I have spoken with his mighty spirit often."

"I would prefer a Korean general," Duende said simply.

And swallowing her mirth, Chong-gi flung herself up from the floor and rooted among her costumes, choosing a yellow and white uniform that suggested the Lightning-bolt General. She wore the signet ring that had been in Metallus Duende's family since the Moorish occupation of Spain. For there was no enemy, only Duende, his quest, and great personal danger.

Duende leaned back as the *kut* began. Squatting astride an hourglass-shaped drum, Chong-gi banged on each end, crying, "Out! Out!" to chase away unwanted spirits in preparation for the séance to come.

She began to sing, her face and voice taut. Rising, she stepped around, capering, head twisting this way and that as if something were trying to wrench her head off her wattled turkey neck. Her witchy hat fell to the floor, where entranced sandals crushed it flat.

Duende had seen this many times. In Haiti, in Africa, and once in a Navajo hogan. Different behaviors, but the identical phenomenon. The mudang was genuine.

And the Chill That Knows made the short blond hairs on the back of Metallus Duende's neck hackle. For the Lightning-bolt General was nigh.

All at once cymbals clashed like thunder. The mudang had not touched them but they crashed and clashed as her head rotated back and forth until her walnut eyes focused on Duende's own violet ones.

"Ghost-faced liar!" she hissed in an electric voice not her own. "I know your secret! I know the designs you have upon the skull of the flesh that enwraps me. For this ring belongs to your ancestors."

And the ring bearing the Duende family crest was flung at his impassive face. It dipped in flight, slipping perfectly over the beckoning finger to which it belonged.

Duende rose to his feet.

"Are you ready to fight to protect your host?" he asked the Lightning-bolt General.

And in response, bony fingers flung forward, spitting cracking yellow bolts white at the core.

Duende stood his ground. Five talons of crackling light snapped and sparked around him. The two that disappeared into his chest came out again when Duende lifted his arms in return.

Chong-gi—the Lightning-bolt General now—screamed back in inarticulate fury, dodging the spitting electrical magic. A copper gong in a teak frame melted into bubbling slag. Outside, geese set up a fearful honking.

Duende unbuckled his snakeskin belt and, whipping it to its full length, muttered an ancient Nahuatl chant. The flat skin swelled, the wedge-shaped head snapped open and green membranous wings sprouted.

Undulating, the serpent beat across the room to wrap itself around the thin neck of the mudang. Screaming, the Korean witch clawed and ripped at its hide. Her cracked nails clicked and scritched on irridescent scales to no avail. Around and around the room she wheeled, fighting and gasping until the fire of the Lightning-bolt General in her eyes abated like dying sparks.

"You tricked me! It is unfair! You tricked me!" she shrieked over and over again. And from her eyes glared a venomous hate. She was a country mudang once more.

"How many have suffered because you exchanged sorcery for won?" Duende shot back.

Chong-gi spat a pungent curse, villifying Duende's ancestors all the way back to protoplasm. Lurching, she stamped her feet as her face darkened to lavender and the wheezing of her lungs whispered of the final rattle of death.

In those last moments, she drew upon her last reserves of strength and croaked, "I have something you prize more than my skull."

"There is nothing I prize more than your skull," Duende said coldly. Then added, "Today."

"Today, tomorrow, in the century to come," the old mudang shrieked, "the treasure I am thinking of is more valuable than my poor old skull."

"Name it then," Duende said.

"Grant me the air to speak the words."

"This is a trick."

"The air, or you will always wonder."

Duende snapped both fingers in unison and the green-winged serpent about the mudang's throat relented. Air flowed into the straining lungs and good color returned to her ivory-yellow face.

"Have you the skull of a tokkaebi?" she asked thinly, one thin eye on the serpent circling her head.

Duende hesitated. He owned elfin skulls, kobold skulls—even the delicate skull of a bottle imp.

"No," he admitted grudgingly.

"Tokkaebi have vexed me for years. For I once slew one of their number for a meal. Only the bleeding head of a horse keeps them at bay, for horse blood frightens tiny tokkaebi."

"Tell me how to capture a tokkaebi and I will relinquish all claim to the skull within your head."

"Remove the horse head from my door and you may select the tokkaebi you most admire, when they enter," Chong-gi spat.

"Done," said Duende. For while mudang were uncommon, tokkaebi were exceedingly rare.

517

"You must promise not to cheat or evade this bargain with sorcery," the mudang insisted.

"Agreed." And hearing a snap of Duende's fingers, the orbiting Quetzalcoatl dropped to the floor, a mere snakeskin belt once more.

When Duende went to retrieve it, Chong-gi flung a gall-powder irritant at his eyes. He blew it back into her face, and as she fell weeping and cursing to her bony knees, Duende stood over her, weaving luminous sarabands of blue vapor with his splayed fingers. The Korean witch subsided into a bitter muttering.

Leaving the mudang under a Spell of Stillness, Duende removed the horse head, burying it at the foot of the spirit totem. The blood he washed away with a wet rag. After that, he repaired to the hut to await the night, leaving every window open.

No tokkaebi came at sunset. None when the cold calcium moon rose. By midnight there was still no sign of them.

Duende sat in a lotus position in the center of the hut, all eight senses alert, for he had never beheld a living tokkaebi, much less owned its skull.

In the evilest hour of the night, they began to clamber over the window sills, dropping to the hardwood floor like fat round spiders.

Duende had seen elves and other wee folk. These were unlike them. Wearing the snarling faces of Asian gargoyles, they sported short horns peeping from black moplike hair. Leather belts cinched rude tigerskin garments about squat ugly bodies. And they carried small clubs studded with spines harvested from hardy sea urchins.

Like miniature cavemen, they fell to hammering the floor with their clubs in the dark.

"Show yourself, mudang!" one challenged.

"Let us see you, devourer of tokkaebi," rasped another.

And Metallus Duende lifted a finger that flared with a sourceless yellow light.

The tokkaebi snarled, recoiling from the eerie light.

"You are not the mudang who lives here," one accused from behind shielding fingers.

Saying nothing, Duende let the tokkaebi drink in his pale skin, his round violet eyes, and—by Asian standards—exaggeratedly pronounced features.

"Do you bury your dead?" he asked coolly.

"Why do you ask?" a tokkaebi grunted, surly of voice.

"The skull of a dead tokkaebi appeals to me as much as that of a living tokkaebi," Duende said simply.

The tokkaebis flinched as one. Their green-gold eyes narrowed with a cold understanding.

"What will you trade for the skull of one of our dead?" one asked Duende.

"Why should I trade when my wizardry enables me to take what I covet?"

"You do not know tokkaebis, then. We trade. We do not give up what belongs to us. Not without battle." And a dozen spiny clubs waved in definance.

"Yes," another challenged. "What will you trade?"

And Duende lifted his burning digit so its radiance consumed the shadows in the far corners of the room.

And in the farthest corner, squatting and helpless, glowered the old mudang, Chong-gi.

"This mudang has offered me the tokkaebi skull I covet most in return for forsaking her own," Duende explained.

A tokkaebi pounded the floor with his club. "We will trade a dead skull for her live body!" he cried. Others took up the pounding. The roofbeams shook with their eager fury.

When the commotion abated, Duende asked, "What do you want with a live mudang?"

Snaggletoothed grins came. "One of us filled her cruel belly one night. All of her will satiate us for a week."

Duende considered. "Done," he said.

And in the corner the mudang tried to wail and protest but a sorcery greater than her own had welded her teeth together. Only a silibant hissing escaped from between the gaps.

The spiky clubs put an abrupt stop to that and Duende held the door open as in unison the tokkaebis lifted Chong-gi's lax-limbed form off the floor and carried her out into the cool Korean night.

In a glade where a horned owl stood sentinel in a juniper tree, Duende received the freshly disinterred skull of a not-long-dead tokkaebi, which, he was delighted to see, still had its blunt horn firmly socketed.

Bowing his gratitude, Duende accepted the little tokkaebis' impatient bows to him in return. He declined their half-hearted invitation to feast, and expressing his regrets, bade them farewell. The long journey home beckoned and there was still the problem of getting two skulls—one human and the other not—past customs officials.

For during the rendering ceremony—in which he watched but did not participate—Duende scavenged the very fresh skull of the treacherous mudang, Chong-gi, from the red bone pile. It bore some slight tokkaebi club dents, true, but these added a certain character, he felt.

Metallus Duende departed the forsythia-sprinkled valley well satisfied. After all, he had traded one skull for another, yet retained the one relinquished for the one received. And he had kept his promise to refrain from sorcery to accomplish all this.

If such a feat was not exactly sorcery, it was certainly a kind of legerdemain.

Agnes Across the Swamp

RICH POWELL

Agnes lived alone for nearly one hundred years. Although there was a brief time when she did not, those scant recollections were bitter, and suppressed. There wasn't much anyway. Her mother had not returned from fishing the swamp. "Some don't float," was all her old, bootlegger father had said about it.

After that, chores and abuse increased with repulsive regularity. The only respite for the child came when "White Lightnin' " called and she'd be alone. In time, she found herself hoping the drunken trips would be more frequent. Then she wished for longer duration. Finally, one dark and green moon night, she lit a candle, and prayed he'd not return at all! When the deep snows melted in the spring, and she found his battered, empty truck near the remote whiskey still, Agnes knew that her entreaty had somehow been granted. So from that day forward, with gratitude for her new freedom and seclusion, she existed absolutely and utterly alone.

Ordinarily, isolation for any immature creature would have been an ordeal, a brief episode owing to innate desires or societal intrusions, but not for Agnes. Internal fear of her kind negated the one, her locale, deep within a remote tract of woodlands many miles from human habitat, the other. Eventually, and as though protecting, the twisted rutted road leading to her became swallowed up by the forest, and much like her mostly forgotten creators, disappeared from view.

And so Agnes began her solitary life. Naturally bright, she taught herself to read by the one treasure her mother had successfully hidden, a thick book filled with drawings of creatures, symbols, and words. The contents fascinated! Additionally, and while the battery lasted, she listened to the dead truck's radio reports of an alien civilization somewhere beyond her woods. It had little appeal. For companionship, she preferred her forest friends. There were many forms. Even some that had never been seen since their primordial emergence. Yet Agnes communicated with them all in her own special way. So unnoticed and content, this then was how her years passed.

Quite unexpectedly one sunny morning, her old ears detected the silent wails of trees as they fell. It was distant, but their pain was clear. She poled the old, flat-bottomed boat across the weed-choked swamp to where it entered the lake. From a cluster of low, moss-covered water stumps, she saw humans for the first time in nearly a century, and something deep within her stirred.

Each day she observed from her shadowy place across the lake, as the wooden planks and logs were shaped into a dock, then amazingly, an immense double-tiered lodge. When the roaring waterbird deposited and retrieved more humans at regular intervals, the old woman wondered as to the purpose. Her answer came with the crack of rifles deep in the surrounding woods. When the wounded animals came to her for help, she talked, soothed, applied herbs, and recited incantations from the book. When the lodge inhabitants continued their actions, she decided it was time to visit.

So on that fateful day, she drifted from her secret watching place, tied her boat to the dock, and slowly walked toward the shiny new lodge to introduce herself to her first neighbors. Now, Agnes wanted to create a good impression, so she had put on her mother's black dress, and washed her long white hair for the occasion as well. Being a weekday, the guests were few, and Agnes negotiated the steps to the wide porch door unnoticed. She was quite proud of herself as she ambled her hunched form softly across the lobby carpet to the lone man at the front desk.

The shadow fell across his ledgers, and Tennessee Jimmy began to look up from his paper work. He smiled automatically in expectation of a familiar guest's face. What he saw, of course, was Agnes. Now inches away, she had straightened from her stoop by leaning heavily upon the countertop. She returned his frozen smile as best she could, albeit quite toothlessly.

"Howdy, I be Agnes . . . across the swamp," she said amiably.

The evening before, while the fireplace crackled, the few guests had been regaled with fabricated tales of hideously deformed swamp creatures. With the first glimpse of the wart-covered, toothless, white-haired crone nearly upon him, it all came back, and Tennessee Jimmy shrieked.

This abrupt action also startled Agnes, and the short cob pipe slipped from the corner of her mouth and fell. She snatched it up, keeping her eyes on the first human face she had seen in decades, and wondering if this form of greeting was indeed commonplace.

"My God!" Tennessee Jimmy finally managed.

Agnes shook her head. "No, I be Agnes, like I told you." She narrowed her eyes, nodded perfunctorily, and jutted out her hair-covered chin.

Jimmy spoke fearfully. "What is it . . ." Then he quickly added, ". . . that you want?'

He watched her clublike cane carefully as it pointed, and waved menacingly, and he listened intently as the croaking voice explained. Moments later, elated to discover it was a thing beyond his meager capacity to fulfill, he scurried to the manager.

As he knocked on the suite door, he reassured himself that his fear was well founded. For Jimmy had seen "Ancients" like her in the deep woods of Tennessee, and knew what they could do.

Suddenly, Fat Frank's door yanked open. "What?" barked the round man.

"Frank, there's a—a lady here to see you."

"Lady? Did somebody just fly in today? We dint have any ladies as guests up to yesterday."

The words "fly in" triggered something in Tennessee Jimmy's mind. He immediately saw a picture of Agnes on a broom. He saw her high in the black night, white hair trailing, as she zoomed and cackled.

"Well?" asked Fat Frank. "Where'd she come from?"

The image vanished for Jimmy as quickly as it had come. "No, boss, she didn't just arrive, she's been here all along. Believe it or not, we have a neighbor."

The words struck like a lightning bolt. The syndicate had purchased the acreage for miles. Remote, a retreat for the various high-ranking "family" members across the country. It had been a vital point to have the isolation. No roads, no way to get in, no intrusions, no people. A place to hunt, fish, and relax. Of course, business animosities cropped up during the uneasy truce, but they were brief, and prohibited like six-shooters in a well-marshaled town of the Old West.

"Neighbor?" said Fat Frank, with an astonished look. He had convinced them of the idea, been responsible for selecting the site. No one lived here! Not for over twenty miles. There had to be a mistake. If there wasn't . . .

Moments later Fat Frank, still in his morning robe, walked up to Agnes in the lobby. She was examining the Indian design on the rug as he strode angrily over. He had been prepared to say, "You realize you're living on OUR property," but when the old woman looked up and fixed her piercing green eyes on him, he relented and merely introduced himself.

"I'm Frank Anunziatta. I understand you wanna see me?"

Sensing his hostility, she came right to the point. "I be Agnes. Live alone across the swamp. You folks been hurtin' the animals 'round here. You got a reason?"

"Hurtin'? We call it huntin', but yeah, I guess you could call it that," said Frank with a smirk. "And we do it 'cause we want to. For fun! What business is it of yours?"

She examined his eyes; they were cold, like the fishes. "They come all torn up. I be alone, they be my friends, and you got to stop!"

Fat Frank frowned. "What you, their momma? Stop?" He wanted to laugh, but again, her eyes made him hold back. "I tole you this is a private huntin' lodge. Guests come here for that purpose. If they coont shoot there'd be no reason to come, no reason to have the lodge here." He shook his head. "No, lady, we ain't gonna stop."

"Never heerd of such a thing. You just have to clear out then!"

Frank's face tightened. "Good you brought that up. You're on private land. We own all the land for miles. The lake, swamp, everyting! I dunno exactly where you live, but you're the one to leave, and you better get to it now!" He let a smile come. "I ain't responsible for any stray shots, you unnerstand?"

Agnes nodded. "It be you who don't. I been here long afore you," she said succinctly.

Fat Frank narrowed his eyes at her. "Then yer lucky we ain't charged you rent for all that time. Be out today, lady!"

Agnes turned without speaking. She walked slowly to the door, then stopped and looked back. She waved a bony finger as she finally spoke. "There's things a body don't see. Sounds that ain't fer hearin'. Animals understand when they's taken for food. It be when they's just hurt and left to suffer that makes no sense. You just kills for no reason, and that be wrong. I warn ye if it happens again afore you move out, retribution will come down upon ye."

Frank started to speak, but she had turned again and moved through the door. He was muttering to himself as Tennessee Jimmy came up.

"Well, boss, looks like we got a neighbor."

"Not for long."

Jimmy knew the look in Fat Frank's eyes. He'd seen it in wild animals before they attacked their prey. "Boss, I got somethin' to tell you."

"No, I got somethin' to tell you. Somethin' we gotta do quick! That old hag might have a claim, a land claim."

Tennessee Jimmy leaned close as though telling a secret. "Please, boss. I seen her kind before. I think she's one of the old ones, got the magic," he whispered.

Fat Frank studied Jimmy a moment, then shook his head disdainfully. "You country boys is all the same. She's just a old broad who's lived too long. Listen, we don't tell nobody about her. This is my business. She's alone, all alone. This evening after the plane picks up, we eliminate the problem, bada-bing!"

It was afternoon when old Agnes arrived back at her cabin. She immediately went to her mother's trunk and took the book out. After she lit the ceremonial candles, she began reading. The section was new to her. It told of the transformation. By evening, she knew it by heart. Still, she sat hunched over the thick black book looking for another way. When her eyes began to fail, she undressed and went to bed. The decision had to be made, and she agonized over the consequences. If she did nothing, innocents would be slaughtered. If she took the step, only she would be affected, but she would be damned! The life she had known for nearly a century would be gone forever! She would never be able to return to it throughout eternity. Agnes felt warm tears and closed her eyes tightly to stop them, and for the first time in her long life, she found herself asking for help. She silently willed the words forth, then finished aloud. "Please, Ma! Can you send me a sign?"

She lay there a long time drifting in the soft darkness. She began to think she saw a face. It seemed to be smiling at her, then she felt the wind, and lost concentration. Agnes opened her eyes. The heavy feeling of sadness seemed to have lifted somewhat, but she wasn't sure. The wind she had felt, gusted and the tattered curtains moved straight out from the force of it. She watched as the candles were snuffed out, then heard the sound. It came from the porch. Something brushing softly against the door. Agnes struggled from the bed and opened the door. Soulful eyes looked up. Agnes fell to her knees and threw her arms around the gentle creature. Then she felt the blood, and knew the sign had been sent.

Suddenly, she felt a shock, as though lightning had struck. She was on her back. The doe bolted away. Agnes blinked, then the pain started, and she closed her eyes.

From behind the bushes, two men watched anxiously, then ran back the way they had come. "Ain't movin'. Nailed the old broad good!" puffed Fat Frank.

Later, the doe returned, looked down, then tilted its head quizzically as Agnes's lips began to move. It listened a moment. The strange words were barely audible, but the incantation had begun. The doe's friend would be no more.

In the morning Frank was having his breakfast on the porch, and Jimmy was serving. He looked out across the lake as he sipped his coffee. The early mist hovered above the water, creating eerie, white vapor shapes.

"You think we should have buried her?" asked Jimmy as he re-filled Frank's cup.

Frank dismissed the comment with a wave of his meaty hand, and continued to watch the odd fog forms rising from the depths.

Suddenly, a flock of blackbirds came screaming out of the shadowed woods on the far side of the lake. His tiny, sunken pig eyes followed them as they zoomed across, then squawked to a stop on the roof of the lodge.

"What you think got into them?" asked Frank.

Jimmy shook his head. "Could be a sign. I wish we hadn't a done it."

Frank stared at him angrily. "They just want food. Sign? You country weirdos. What the hell you think woulda happen if she caused trouble? S'pose she come up with some old paper that showed she had a claim? I'll tell ya. After the boys kicked my ass in, they'd leave the joint. What they don't need is publicity. They still ain't too keen on this. If anything was to happen, they'd drop the place like a hot potato, and me with it. Where you think that'd leave you, country boy?"

Tennessee Jimmy nodded, then looked out toward the lake. One of the swirling, ghostlike puffs seemed to be coming closer, moving toward them rapidly. He pointed. "Look at that, boss."

They focused on the shape now in the middle of the lake. As it continued to drift toward them, they realized someone was standing in an old flat-bottomed boat. The relic was approaching relentlessly, yet nothing seemed to propel it. As it neared, they saw a woman in a black dress. A young woman, and she was smiling at them. She was beautiful, and her green eyes invited them to come. They complied. As they moved trancelike toward her, the flock of blackbirds fluttered down, and lined up on both sides of the dock railings. When the two men passed mechanically between them, the birds screeched their approval.

Frank and Jimmy ignored the ceremony. They had reached the end of the dock. Below them smiled the striking, silver-haired young woman. She extended her arms gracefully, and they assisted her up.

"Hello, boys. Isn't there something you want to do for me?" she asked in a sultry voice.

Frank felt the irresistible desire to please her. His hand moved to his eye, and he plucked it out. It plopped wetly to the dock boards, and a glossy, iridescent bird seized it, then flew off to eat.

Jimmy knew he had to do better.

It was evening when she returned to the small cabin. She looked back the way she had come. Thin smoke wisps from the charred ruins drifted above the tree line into the darkening sky. It had felt so good to do it! She inhaled the night air in satisfaction, then she smelled them. They were all around, but would no longer come near. She laughed evilly as she made a tree fall, and heard them scurry away. There were other things, night things, that she would learn to summon.

Inside, she removed her clothes and admired herself in the cracked mirror. Her hands moved over the white, supple flesh. The faint scar high on her chest was all that remained of the gunshot wound. The book lay open where Agnes had left it. She picked it up and pressed it against her full breasts.

"Mine, all mine!" she laughed.

Now she knew the intoxicating power! She would learn all, then leave. Be forever young as long as she followed the ways of the black witches. The white witches were fools! The part of her that had been Agnes was a fool. Tending and healing. They could never know the satisfaction that came with lust, self-interest, and bloodletting. How delicious to hurt, to selfishly deceive. There was much work to do. She put the book down. No hurry, tomorrow and tomorrow, and all the tomorrows to come were hers. Before she allowed sleep, she decided to call herself Senga. It was the reverse name.

In the morning Senga realized that she hadn't slept well. Many voices with confusing messages had come. She got off the bed stiffly. *Must have slept wrong,* she thought. As she moved to the well for water, she noticed the rabbit nearby. She glared at him, but he didn't hop off. Back in the cabin she put the pail down, and went to the mirror. Beautiful Senga smiled back. She noticed something in the reflection, and looked closer. A line? No, it was a wrinkle! She touched it and then saw the liver spots on her arm. The skin beginning to sag. She took both her hands and felt her face. As she did, a voice came.

"Good you don't read well, darlin'. It was an unselfish act. You didn't qualify. Welcome back, Agnes honey."

Hunger Gulag

MARTIN MUNDT

I knotted Dinker's tail tight, tighter than necessary, and the suppression spell was complete. Now kitty's free will was clogged like a drain with hairballs, and she would thrash in my whims like a kite in a storm. I unwrapped her from the pink blanket that had absorbed her clawing struggles, and scooped her up onto the mantle. She blinked twice and didn't move.

The house was quiet, as if made of cloud.

The Mommy and Daddy who lived here lapped calmly at their

bowls of dreams in the bedroom, twin slices of white bread sopping up bland illusions. Their thoughts lay beneath my morphia-spell, minds chilled to absolute zero, the trip-wires of their wariness cut, peace-doves cooing in their ears, mirrors inside their eyelids.

The house was soundless.

But the baby, safe in crib, wrapped in love, the unkneaded white-bread baby breathed innocence and teetered and tottered on the knife edge of my plan.

The house was still.

HE was coming. This night for sure, to bring an excess of virtue to the virtuous. To bring an infant soul, a new-minted, holy quarter to drop into the baby-slot and start her mystic life ratcheting and clanking along. He carried the soul, swaddled in fresh-made light, filled with subservience. He brought the soul, but it would be mine to eat when he arrived, mine to swallow whole, and mine to fatten on.

The cat was the last warning that there could possibly be. All the windows and doors were nailed shut, sealed with black wax and un-passable but for one left open in the attic, leading right to my trap. He will come and find just one entrance open to him, and he will enter straight into my grasp.

Everything was arranged sweet and beautiful for the angel, warm and happy. Soothing spells draped the attic window and hung like tapes-tries from the rafters. All the house was ready to submit and serve. There was nothing for an angel to fear.

Dinker blinked. I took one more look around the downstairs, but there was nothing there to hurt or hinder me, nothing to clash with my plans. I gathered myself together and took no counsel of my fears. Nerves was all, so close to feasting I was nervous. I was hungry, concen-tration being fragile with the smell of marinating souls lying close in bed, even thin-gruel souls steamed tasteless with age. The whole house reeked like a cooking pot. I could almost eat the air, the aroma was so thick and heady.

I ignored it with effort and left. My work was upstairs.

The rafters creaked. Cold, still air huddled beneath the peaked roof. It was a beautiful place for bats and monkeys. A snug and safe place to thrill at the moonrise. A place that could mellow like an old ghost in the smokes of spell-pots and incense. But everything was subur-ban clean, neat as a maiden. Time was the only useful thing there.

Time to wait.

My brooding warped the rafters; my mood chilled the air even more. I stared at the window, hours' worth of slow waiting, and the window like a wooden eye stared back. Stars passed. And then, outside, deep in the sky, at the black capstone of the night, I heard wings.

I smiled, running my hands over the smooth, crooked length of Broom, my companion, a hard and heavy yew-stick to bash in the brains of a heavenly messenger and so liberate the tasty baby soul, like cracking a nut for the meat.

Hungry. My own soul long ago devoured and passed like a stone, and only twenty or forty delectable babies boiled and braised and savored since. Hungry almost to death.

Wings. Close by, circling, hovering. A comforting sound for those still able to grasp for the crutches of comfort. A cooing of peace-doves. I'd heard it before, the better to pour it like poisonous maggots into the ears of the unwary.

I made myself smaller, burrowed backward into shadows, leaving only my eyes uncovered. The wings rustled outside the house, brushing bricks and windows, scratching sills in failed attempts to enter, clutching at doorknobs I'd slickened with hexes of failure. The house was mine, beam and floorboard, brick and glass, all stretched out from me like the silken whisker senses of a cat.

I clutched the shadows thicker around me, smiling still, to make myself invisible, more than invisible, to make myself unbelievable, a fairy tale or fiction. The vile wings grazed the baby's window, shedding angel-light and love on the cradle. Shedding warmth into the sleeping, soulless room. No doubt he watched the empty vessel breathe, but he could not reach the flesh. No doubt he grew frantic because he could not reach it, the burden of duty to deliver the soul weighing heavier.

The wings lifted, and finally the attic window began to glow with flickering light like a rack of candles.

I hid deeper, quieter than a corpse, quiet as bones, harmless and suburban. I whispered spells to pile a façade of images around me in a dark jumble: locked trunks, lamps without shades, a cardboard box spilling colored Christmas lights like entrails, and myself as Grandma's treasured rocker, peaceful and revered, rocking a teddy bear.

I wished blindness on the angel. I wished him to be no more curious than a stone and see no threat in a teddy bear.

He came to rest on the sill, a seed from the sun. He reached his long stork legs to the floor. My shadow-spell nearly buckled like a dam under the torrents of light. I sandbagged with hunger, envy, bitterness, and rage. I whispered encouragement to Broom, hardening it, letting it suck up the hunger, envy, bitterness, and rage. Broom squirmed with pain in my hands.

Vicious greedy stork, hoarding souls. His light burned my skin. The smell of innocence choked me. Pass by, pass by.

He hesitated. I laughed to my silent self, even under the burning, braying light. Perhaps he could feel me, but he didn't know for sure, did he? Noxious stork.

He started for the stairs. The light pushed me like a current, and I had to concentrate to stand my ground, not to close my eyes on my pain and just drift away. But even if he burned out my eyes, I could still grope for the soul he carried by scent alone; it roared like a bonfire of succulent delicacies.

He turned and stepped for the stairs, the sterile drone.

He turned his back on me.

I swung Broom and felt the gratifying thud on holy flesh. I swung again and again with an oiled stroke. The long, pious neck collapsed around the wood. My spells edged Broom like knives to cleave incorruptible flesh, hexes like clubs to bludgeon his will. He fell, and I hit him, beat him, lashed him, crushed his wings, snapped his neck. I grunted the blows. My senses blossomed with the beating, the whip-slash of air that followed each stroke, the shivering thrill of cracking venerated bones.

It was as happy as even eating could ever be. I hit him a few more times while he was down, until his light pooled like blood.

I stopped. I didn't want to batter the soul, my meal. My shadows surged back from the corners to fill the room, trailing from the ceiling, rising up the walls like a fast sunset.

I knelt at the fallen angel, tossing Broom aside. I reached my hands into his light and it burned like lime. I hissed. I thought about clubbing him into the floor and the pain lessened. I smiled.

I lifted a smashed wing and uncovered the soul, touched it with my fingertips, stroked it. My fingers smoked. I bent my face down to bite it, to gorge myself on it.

That's when he backstabbed me, skunked me, stole my only food. The stork stirred. I grabbed for his neck, miserable scrawny thing.

He turned his face on me, and the light exploded. I thought my eyes had melted. My skin peeled. The angel's flood tore away my shadows. That flash, that gush of light filled the room. My sight is dimmed still.

That meek and mindless stork blew me out the attic window with the force of his revealed self.

Poor me, hungry wretch, just hoping for a morsel, a bite to ease my fiery belly, I was allowed nothing by the wise and reverend angel.

I smoked and hissed in the snow where I landed. The stars spun around me. Thrown out of my own house, my own house filched fair and square. I looked up. The light left the attic window.

He was heading downstairs, to give my meal to someone else. My head reeled. Everything was gone. I hadn't clubbed him to his core. I hadn't stamped out his living heart, the lump of God that drove him on. And so I would lose everything.

I picked myself up, singed and soaked with melted snow, and left behind my depression in the snow. The hun-angel had torched my fields and pillaged my house; he took my Broom, whom I'd withered and hardened all these years like my very own son. He took everything. I hate angels.

I decided. I was hollow and empty and barren, the better to consume everything in my path, angels not excepted.

I climbed back to the window, driving handholds into the clapboards with my unsheathed nails, each two inches of blackened iron. I hauled myself hand over hand to the attic.

My soothing spells hung in rags; my shadow-spells puffed underfoot like ashes. The whole room was warm as a comforter. I shivered, nearly vomited. It was a sad sight, all my hard work smashed like padlocks. I oozed through the room, careful as oil. My eyes reddened and watered; I sneezed, a reaction to heaven-pollen or angel toxins.

I stopped at the stairs, hearing the choir of his breathing and the steady praise of his heartbeat fill the house below.

I grew angrier.

He had left a trail down the stairs, an afterimage of light, a blessing, like slime from a snail. I followed down to the second floor, the baby floor, but the trail continued straight to the ground floor.

Strange! But now there was still a chance to escape the hunger gulag. The soul had gone downstairs. I followed and found him in front of the fireplace.

Holding Broom. Precious Broom, devoted Broom. Broom squirmed and whimpered in his hands. I was fluent in ambush. I netted my hands with clutching-spells; I honed my teeth with ripping-spells.

Broom whined.

I wound grinding-spells between my thighs and took aim for the angel's head.

He snapped Broom, with his hands, like a match.

Broom screamed and died, and I flung myself into flight.

The angel turned, and I saw his sleek, well-fed eyes, bright as filaments raging in the current of faith, just as I struck. We both went into the fireplace. Brick cracked. Soot whooshed. House shook. I clinched his head; I seized his hair; I throttled his neck. I was heroic, but he revealed himself naked to me. His light burned and blistered; my spells melted.

I fought fire and crushed fire to my breasts. I bit fire and spat it out, snapping my jaws at the soul. I tasted gingerbread, or fire. I didn't know. Fire tinged everything right then.

He hadn't expected my attack, or maybe he had. It hardly made any difference to the outcome. One doesn't ambush an angel easily. I should have learned that while lying in the snow outside. But fury filled me at Broom's snapping. And hunger too had a part.

I didn't last much longer. Spells overthrown. No retreat. Tired. Hungry. Overmatched. I lost my strength. My arms and legs failed. My voice burned to ashes. My eyes were blinded by the heaven-beast. My body and Broom were burned up completely in that accursed fireplace, billowing smoke.

But he did not consume my mind and will. Not yet. I rode the smoke of my body and hovered against the ceiling. I could not keep myself from drifting and dissipating for long. My thoughts grew fragile, hazy, random-floating. My will thinned. The edges of myself faded. I saw only one chance.

The angel went upstairs.

From the top of the dresser, I watched baby, pink and glowing, soul absorbed and beyond my reach. The stork had disappeared after delivery. The house went quiet of choir and praise and as dark as three A.M. I blinked and licked my teeth. I turned to look at my tail and easily untied the knot of the suppression-spell, releasing it.

My senses flew open. I felt movement in the house, a mouse some-where. I heard the baby's heartbeat. I smelled the final wisp of smoke of

Dinker's disappearance. Dinker had coughed when I entered her, but
not for long. I am fluent in entering. I am smooth as whiskey when I want
to be. When Dinker disappeared, there was a yowl and a hiss and that
was that.

The baby smelled strongly of tantalizing gingerbread, warm and
soft from the oven, gooey with frosting, and with tasty raisins for eyes.

I peered over the edge of the crib and judged the distance to be
about three feet. Easy enough. That's what cats are made for. If I can't
have the soul, then no one will, but at least the cat will have a full
stomach tonight.

I cocked my head at the crib.

Such a tiny, helpless, cute, helpless baby.

I jumped.

Young Goodwife Doten

ROBERT M. PRICE

A crowd stood gathered just outside the iron fence of the Duxbury churchyard. They watched closely as John Doten shov-
eled the last spadeful of graveyard dirt back into the small
plot and tamped it down. Then the young man, bowed with the effort of
the task but more with the need for it, stooped and brushed away bits of
flying dirt that had clung to the new marker, a somber stone tablet
engraved with the familiar winged skull design. His young wife stood
only a few feet distant and wept quietly, as did some in the uninvited
multitude beyond. Others in that band, however, seemed to be shuddering more from fright.

All alike swiftly dispersed at the approach of the bereaved couple.
The man had recovered his threadbare black coat and had his shovel
slung over his shoulder like a musket. His other powerful arm rested
tenderly about the still-heaving shoulders of his wife, Prudence. One or
two from the crowd extended a word of sympathy, knowing such to be a
seed that never reached its mark to sprout. For what words can comfort
the parents whose infant the Grim Reaper has claimed?

But others in the crowd sought comfort for themselves as they secretly traced the sign of the cross over gray- and black-clad breasts. And it was their eyes that followed the slow progress of the couple down the street to their small, wood-frame house just off the town commons. So slowly and gravely did they move that almost they seemed a funeral procession in their own right.

The afternoon had grown late, and storm clouds encroached, as they did so often in the season. Before long not a soul lingered in the streets of Duxbury of the region of New Dunnich. All alike soon drew close around blazing hearths, some offering up prayers for the grief of their neighbors, others thanking the Good Lord that misfortune had passed them by this time. And others still clinging close to the light as if they feared the shadows. For all of New Dunnich was in the grip of the witch-fright that had now spread all over the Massachussetts Bay colony, the contagion having spread outward from Salem and Arkham.

Few misfortunes did not cause the fear either that the witchcraft had caused them or else that the Almighty had levied punishment for deviltry. And thus were the townsfolk divided in their regard for young Goodwife Doten and her husband. Had some witchdame foully hexed her? Or was she herself another secret trafficker with Satan? For this was not the first instance of her losing a baby, whether before or during birth. Surely these misfortunes could be no accidents, and many pious village tongues had decided that her womb must be poisoned with the devil's gall.

Goodwife Doten had herself heard such whispers and paid them no mind, save that she bemoaned lost friends who durst not be seen with her. Indeed, few remained to comfort her in her latest hour of sorrow, only her fine husband. And John Doten contemned those whom he called old hens and vultures, the gossips of the town. His attendance at the meetinghouse was not frequent because his faith was not great, and he liked not to play the hypocrite, no matter the ill-will this might earn him from some quarters. He sat now before the raging fire alone, Prudence having retired to the bed. The day had been long and a heavy burden to bear. And besides, she was still weak from the ordeal of childbirth. John gazed into the leaping tongues of fire and let his mind drift into thoughts and dreams of the future that looked so far away.

Scant moments later, he was roused by his reverie by a firm knock at the door. Rising, he hastened to open the door and offer hospitality to whomever might wait upon his step. It had begun to rain, and he would be as good a host as Abraham had been.

The open door revealed the imposing form of the parson, the Reverend Abijah Hoadley. His impassive features did not relax as he entered, removing both tall broad-brim hat and heavy woolen cloak. These John took as the clergyman began to offer his sympathies for their loss, his stern visage belying the tenderness implied in his words.

"How I regret not being able to stand at your side in the hour past, but I fear the great number of ill congregants required my attention till late in the day." Thus he spake as he took a proferred seat before the fireplace. Of a sudden Goodwife Doten appeared from the bedroom, pale of cheek, and both men rose to acknowledge her. All sat as the somber Mr. Hoadley addressed her.

"My child, you have my heartfelt condolences. And my prayers as well, for I would not that the want of God's blessing should cause men to doubt your sincere love for the Almighty."

"Then, good parson, you do naught but echo both mine own hopes and prayers," replied Prudence Doten. "For 'tis true that I love God, and it taxes me to think why He may see fit to try me in this manner."

The parson rose, saying, "It is good to hear such pious sentiments from a pure heart. And sure am I that our Lord shall in due course reward such faith as he did the faith of Job. Now I must beg your pardon, as I have many rounds to make, even in such weather as this."

As he closed the door behind the belling cape of the Reverend Hoadley, John Doten could not hide his indignation. "His deceit is rank and fools me not. I doubt not that it is the Reverend Hoadley himself who is the chief rumormonger! Note how his artful words ill conceal his own belief that you bear the barrenness of Sodom's ground, cursed of God!"

Prudence rose to return to bed and made no reply. She hoped her husband erred but feared he did not. "True, he preaches of a Sabbath little else than the judgment of heaven against the wizard and the witch. Nor does he suffer a witch to live, and in his zeal, I am persuaded, the innocent suffer. They fall not before the wrath of the Reverend Hoadley's God, but of the Reverend Hoadley himself. And I like not the thought of incurring his wrath in my own case. But what is to be done?"

John Doten sat down upon the side of her thin mattress and took her pale hand in his own. "Beloved Prudence, we dare not wait any longer upon the grace of God. Nay, but let me speak," quoth he, motioning her to silence. Mayhap there is a path open to us, and seeing the danger that looms, I say we must take it. And it is in no wise perilous, I feel sure."

She shaded her eyes with her hand. "You speak of old Goody Watkins, out by Briggs' Hill. Think not I have not ofttimes considered her. It seems to smack of heathenism and is more than a little redolent of Sarah's unbelief when she made Abraham go in and beget by Hagar. But it may profit us to consider her ministrations. It is said she is one of the Wise Women of old, and that she has knowledge of herb and root for healing. When my strength is restored, I will betake myself to her cottage. It may be that the Lord helps those who help themselves. But we must take care that none knows of it."

"Aye," agreed John, refreshed by new hope, "for it is naught but her keeping her distance from Duxbury that has spared her the zeal of the mob ere now."

Weeks passed before Goodwife Doten felt sufficient vigor return to make the trek out beyond the village limits. But she felt hale and hopeful as John made her comfortable in their small wagon and prodded the horses forward onto the Briggs' Hill road. They had taken care that all knew their feigned plan that Prudence should visit her cousin Elspeth in Zoar for a fortnight. John should return once he had seen to her safe arrival. As innocent as this might sound, suspicion, having once been kindled, feeds on any available fuel. So their wagon, as it drove out of sight, was followed by doubtful eyes.

The road out this way was not well kept up, as few traveled it. Their progress over the rocky and weed-grown lane was bumpy but as swift as one might ask under the circumstances. At length the time came to tether the horses, leave them munching a reward of carrots, and scale the steep incline leading to an almost hidden cottage resting against the face of Briggs' Hill.

John sought to gain a glimpse through the grimy window set into the oak-board door before knocking. This effort proved futile, but even as he raised a fist to rap upon the wood, the great door opened with surprising ease. Before the startled pair stood a wizened, stooped form, chirping in a brittle but loud voice, "What business have ye w' Goody Watkins, she who but seeks to serve the Lord in silent retreat?"

"Old Mother," John began, unable to suppress a quaver in his voice, "we come to you for aid, for medicaments of a type. We . . ."

For the first time in their married life, Prudence Doten dared to interrupt her husband. Taking his arm, she stepped between John and the remarkable tiny figure and said, "Mother, my womb bears no fruit but thorns and thistles, children who do not live outside me. It is said you are able to help women such as I."

Old Goody Watkins appraised her with a calculating eye. "Surely you know what the Governor has done, how he has cut off the witches and the wizards from the land . . . not that I am one of them, mind you! Why would you lay a snare to bring about my death?"

"Aye," cried John Doten as he stepped again to the fore, "we know well what the Governor has wrought, a plague that rages and that threatens to take my good wife if she bear not a child! The fools charge her with diabolical trafficking, believing her misfortune the result of divine misfavor! Lady, we humbly crave your help, else there be no help for us at all. We await your mercy."

The old lady remained silent for a moment, during which time Prudence thought she heard the noise of scampering within the cottage. In these woods, that should afford no surprise.

"Very well. You shall have my help. Missy, you will share my modest accommodations for a few days. I see by your baggage you are prepared for that. Good. But no man may cross my poor threshold." Withal she placed her fragile arm about the younger woman's shoulder and led her into the cottage. John Doten could see his wife's furrowed brow as she gave him one last look before the closing door took her out of his sight.

He returned to the wagon, not without a sense of foreboding, yet not at all regretting their decision. He took the reins and turned the obedient horses about where they would head for a shaded creek. He would do some fishing to fill the time before heading back, so that none should mark a premature return for one making the trip to Zoar and back.

Goody Watkins proved an amenable host to her young charge. She bade her take her own rough bed, which was yet softer than that Prudence slept in at home in Duxbury. Old Goody would daily retrieve and grind certain dried roots and other substances hard to identify. These she would mix into foul-smelling broths and teas which Prudence dutifully drank up, trying to conceal her distaste. Once or twice she remained alone while her caretaker journeyed into the woods or the fields to procure some ingredient of which she had run short, or which could not be kept in powdered form.

A week passed speedily before Goody announced, "Now ye be

prepared right well. It is a toilsome affair. But one step remains. Dearie, I vow ye know those tales in the Scriptures where the barren conceive?"

"Oh yes, Mother Watkins, I have read them often and treasure them in my heart. They are the stories of Sarah, of Hannah, of Manoah's wife, of Elizabeth, and of Mary the mother of our Lord."

Goody Watkins tittered, "Well do ye know them of a certainty! A pious lass. Tell me, then, if you can, how the Good Lord did answer their prayers to open their closed wombs."

Prudence felt as if she were back in catechism class, but she was sure she had the answer ready to hand. "It was a miracle of the Lord whereby his Spirit did overshadow the holy women."

The arthritic finger wagged in mock rebuke. "I think ye hasten through the inspired text like a lass too eager to run from the school-house and play! Think again, missy. Did not Jehovah send his angel to do the deed?"

Prudence paused in puzzlement. True, an angel had appeared from heaven to announce the birth in every case. But she had never taken the meaning old Goody now suggested. It seemed to her faintly blasphemous. . . . But she had resolved to put herself into the kind old woman's hands, and so far she had seen no reason to regret her decision.

"You will understand better when midnight strikes. I will betake myself elsewhere. And you may expect a visitor who will complete what we have begun. Now, dearie, it were best you try to sleep." So saying, her strange benefactor gently closed Prudence Doten's eyes. At once she began to feel drowsy. Perhaps it was the effect of one of the herbs Goody had administered that afternoon. . . .

She awoke abruptly in deepest darkness. The interior of the cottage seemed filled with rushing, airy presences. Had the window come open? No, in the dim moonlight she could see it was still securely fastened. And now she believed the cloud-dimmed rays of the moon faintly silouetted a figure standing before her, at the foot of the bed. As clouds swept past the moon outside, the room grew a modicum brighter, and she could see it was not after all Goody Watkins, as she had momentarily assumed, but rather the tall figure of a man. And she could swear it was the form of a Caribbean slave who stood silently before her, his jetty skin of a piece with the enfolding midnight. But, no, as the room grew lighter still, she rejoiced to behold the familiar smiling face of her husband, John!

He came to her and she welcomed his embrace. John Doten was a passionate man, and never more so than tonight, and yet she marked a certain coldess of member. But this she quickly dismissed as she felt herself yield to a thrill she had never before, as a Christian woman, dared to feel.

Goodwife Doten awoke the next morning under the watchful gaze of Goody Watkins, who sat and knitted. "Ah, my lass, I believe that now you understand Goody's exegesis of the Scripture, do you not? Was it not the rapture of heaven that visited you last night?"

Prudence Doten blushed crimson at the tittering of the old woman whose discretion should have withheld such a remark. At this, old Goody only laughed with greater vigor and shook her head.

"Where is John?" the younger woman asked, sweeping the small space of the cottage with wide eyes. "He must still be here, surely?"

"He will be here soon enough, my girl. My friends in the woods have told me so. Even now he approaches. But look."

Here came her husband up the hill, almost losing his footing as he squinted to see if he might catch some sight of her. Dizzily she arose, gathered her sleeping clothes, and opened the door to greet him.

The big man crushed his wife to him with an enthusiasm she found surprising given their reunion of only scant hours before, but she was ill-inclined to complain. The two of them thanked their smiling benefactor, and without a word John placed a jingling pouch in her clawlike hand. They departed, and Prudence did not like to admit the relief she felt at being away from the old crone.

Weeks passed, and husband and wife felt both joy and fear when it was discovered that Prudence was again with child. Would all turn out well this time? The village gossips speculated freely, but Prudence tried not to listen. She had other matters to consider and there was much planning to be done. The conviction grew in her, even as the baby did, that she would indeed bear a living, healthy child. Oft she would pray, "My soul magnifies the Lord, and my spirit rejoices in God my Savior, for he has done great things for me, having taken away my reproach among women."

John came to feel more confident as well, though he could not keep calm on the day when it came time to summon the midwife. The distant baying of Squire Weston's hunting dogs hardly helped the state of his wrought nerves, and he paced nervously to and fro as the moment neared. How he wished he might somehow ease the pains of his dear wife, whose moaning was loud enough for the neighbors to hear. He doubted not that most of the village waited without, fully as anxious as he. And then the loud moaning seemed to grow yet louder. Something must be amiss.

In the bedroom his wife emitted a throat-skinning shriek. He rushed in. Blood was everywhere. The screaming continued, and the midwife came close to knocking him off his feet as she bolted from the room. In shocked confusion he surveyed the close quarters of the room and his eye registered the tiny form of the new baby squirming on the bed, stained by a tangle of umbilical cord and thick blood. He stooped to grasp the little bundle, his eye still half on his distraught wife. When he focused on the little one now cradled in his arms, he recoiled, slipped on the bloody floor, and involuntarily threw the small form back onto the bed, where its flapping, membranous wings and coiling tail spattered blood droplets in every direction.

For the first time in many a year Goody Watkins dared a stealthy entry into the village of Duxbury. She had heard of the unfortunate sentence passed against John and Prudence Doten, and now she had to see for herself their abandonment to the flames. All eyes in the commons were focused on the two smoking forms, though through the curtain of flames one could no longer determine which was which. With the crowd thus preoccupied she feared no danger for herself, albeit she kept an eye open for the Reverend Hoadley, whose vigilance one might never safely discount. He himself had lit the fire that had consumed the Doten baby with the full blessing of the High Sheriff only an hour before.

"It was all too bad," she had confided to her own son later that night, as she rocked him before the blazing hearth. "In his own way, I thought he was rather cute." As if to agree, her boy turned over on her lap and motioned with one rodentine paw for her to scratch his belly.

Newcomer

Tim Waggoner

Yuli crouched in a corner of the cabin and watched as his mistress rocked by the fireplace, chanting softly beneath her breath as she worked on a charm, pausing now and again to gently stroke her swollen belly.

The firelight didn't reflect off the tiny imp's flat black eyes as he peered at the bundle of cloth, herbs, bone, and twine in her hands. He didn't recognize the charm she was making. Once, she would have needed his help with the charm, would've sent him into the forest to fetch herbs for her, perhaps asked him to stir the cookpot while she spoke the Dark Words. What else was a familiar for? But ever since her belly had begun to grow large, she'd taken to working her spells by herself, leaving Yuli with nothing to do but watch and worry.

Yuli took his gray-scaled tail in his mouth and gnawed on it. He was concerned about his mistress, was afraid she was sick. One time a farmer had bought a fertility potion for his cows from her and promised to pay with three calves come spring. The potion worked, but the farmer refused to pay what he owed. In return, Yuli's mistress had cast a spell on the man's cattle, causing their stomachs to swell with obscene growths until finally they burst and the animals died. Yuli was afraid something similar was happening to his mistress now. But she didn't seem frightened. Instead, she appeared quite happy. It was too much for the little imp to understand.

Yuli left his corner and scuttled across the dirt floor to his mistress and crouched at her bare feet. At six inches in height, he reached only a little higher than her ankle. Yuli looked up at his mistress, and his tiny black heart was filled with love for her. Although she was quite old as he understood humans reckoned time, she still possessed the aspect of a young, beautiful woman. Her hair was a thick and lustrous ebony and fell down the back of the rocking chair almost all the way to the floor. She was wrapped in a diaphanous gown of silky green, which stirred as if caught in some sourceless breeze.

Yuli tugged at his mistress's foot, trying to get her attention. When she didn't look down, he went behind the rocker and gripped her hair with two tiny paws and climbed quickly and dexterously to the top of her head, where he perched like a miniature gargoyle. He looked down at the charm that busied his mistress's hands and made a soft, querying bleat.

"It's just a bit of magic, Yuli," Amaia said in her warm honey voice. "For the baby."

Ba-bee. Yuli did not know this word. He decided it must be the name of the sickness that had infected his mistress. Ba-bee. It had a sinister sound. He was glad Amaia was working on a cure.

His mistress had first taken ill after the dark man left. The dark man had come to her one night last summer, and they had spent much time together, walking, talking, and lying together in his mistress's bed. Yuli hadn't liked the dark man's intrusion into his and Amaia's world, but his mistress was happy and so he tolerated the interloper.

Then one day the dark man left, on *biz-ness,* whatever that was, for the Fell Ones, and he hadn't returned, which suited Yuli just fine. Soon after, his mistress took sick with the growth. Yuli thought the dark man had really been a warlock who, before leaving, had cursed Amaia with this strange sickness, this Ba-bee. It didn't matter, though. No matter how strong the warlock's magic was, Yuli knew his mistress's was stronger.

He leaned down over her forehead, holding onto a handful of hair for balance, and sent forth a stream of mocking chatter directed at the horrid growth, gloating over its imminent demise.

"Hush, now, Yuli. You'll give me a headache."

Yuli hastened to obey. He curled up atop his mistress's head, snuggled into her soft-soft hair, and closed his eyes, content. Soon she would be well again and everything would be back to normal.

But as the days went by and turned into weeks, Yuli was forced to face a fact that would have once been unthinkable to him: his mistress's power had failed. The growth, instead of getting smaller, seemed to swell even faster. It had grown so large that Yuli feared Amaia's stomach might burst at any moment. But still she sang softly to herself, still she rubbed the growth, almost lovingly. Yuli remembered a time—it seemed so long ago—when he had felt that loving touch.

Yuli thought and thought, bringing all the resources of his simple imp mind to bear on the problem, until he finally came to an inescapable conclusion. This sickness, this growth had driven his mistress mad. Why else would she sing while this terrible thing was happening to her?

No wonder her magic had failed. She hadn't been fully in her right mind while constructing the charm to kill this awful Ba-bee. And it seemed her madness had increased along with the size of her belly, for now she wasn't even trying to get rid of the Ba-bee.

She would surely die. Unless Yuli did something.

That night, Amaia brewed a hearty stew for herself. Its tantalizing homey smell filled the cabin, making Yuli's stomach growl. But he would not beg any food from his mistress this evening, oh no. Instead of taking from the pot tonight, he was going to give to it.

He hid behind one of the table legs while his mistress sat on the stool before the fire and stirred her dinner. In his clawed hands Yuli held a tiny ball of herbs and mud. He watched Amaia taste the stew thoughtfully, and then nod in satisfaction. She hauled herself to her feet awkwardly and with great effort—how it hurt Yuli to see his proud, beautiful mistress so impaired—and go over to the cupboard to fetch a wooden bowl and spoon.

As soon as her back was turned, Yuli made his move. He ran across the dirt floor toward the cookfire, clawed feet slapping almost soundless against packed earth, clutching the herb-ball to his scaled chest. When he reached the hearth, he jumped as high as he could, his small but powerful muscles springing him into the air. At the apex of his leap, he hurled the ball up and toward the pot. He wasn't able to jump quite as high as the lip of the pot, but he got high enough. The herb-ball arced up and down and fell into the stew with a tiny plap! almost at the same time as Yuli landed on the floor.

The imp whirled immediately to check on his mistress, terrified he would be discovered and his plan undone. But Amaia was just placing the spoon on the table and hadn't seen a thing. As she came toward the fire with her bowl, Yuli looked up at her, unable to keep from trembling.

"Cold, Yuli? Well, you have the right idea; the fire will warm you soon enough." She ladled some stew into her bowl and waddled back over to the table to sit and eat.

Yuli knew his herb-ball hadn't had time to dissolve yet. None of the medicine he had prepared—the recipe for which he'd cobbled together from half-forgotten memories of helping his mistress mix this powder, prepare that poultice—was in her bowl. But he knew she would go back for a second helping. Ever since she'd gotten sick, she had taken to eating more and more. And he knew the foul thing inside her would demand its share of stew tonight.

He wasn't disappointed. Before long, Amaia had emptied her bowl and returned to the fire to fill it again.

After three spoonfuls, she doubled over in pain.

Yuli chewed anxiously on his tail as his mistress cried out and a gush of bloody water poured out from between her legs. He prayed to the Fell Ones that he hadn't put too much medicine into the stew.

His mistress's cries of agony echoed throughout the night.

By the next evening, the sickness had been expelled and Yuli—who had expected to see a fleshy, tumorous mass—instead saw a small being with arms and legs, wrinkled pink skin, and a loud, squalling voice. So this Ba-bee was not a tumor, then, but rather some sort of parasitic creature that had been preying on his mistress. Yuli was doubly glad that he'd snuck the medicine into the stew then. Sickness was bad, but a parasite was even worse. Didn't his mistress reserve such horrible spells for only the worst of her enemies?

When the thing was out and lying wrapped in a blanket on the bed, Yuli wanted to go to his mistress and comfort her, but when he tried, she rebuffed him. Instead, amazingly, she fretted over the crying creature her body had fought for so long to be rid of.

"Too early, it's too early," she kept saying to herself, and she hobbled about the cabin, opening and closing cupboards, gathering ingredients, preparing charms and potions, chanting in the Dark Tongue all the while. She laid the charms around the creature's body, poured some potions on its flesh, others in its mouth. And then she knelt before the table, head bowed toward the Lower Places, and prayed.

Yuli knew it was only the lingering madness induced by the thing that made his mistress work so hard to save its disgusting little life. He hoped the Fell Ones would understand and deny her prayers.

But whether his medicine had been too weak, his mistress's powers too strong, or the Fell Ones in a capricious mood, the wailing parasite did not die.

When Amaia realized the thing was safe, she clapped her hands in joy and hugged the creature to her breast. Yuli put his face in his hands and wished he were able to cry.

As time went by, the thing, the Ba-bee, grew stronger. And if it had been a parasite while inside his mistress, it was far worse now that it was out. It seemed whenever she put it down, it howled to be picked up. Whenever she went to sleep, it cried to wake her. It soiled itself regularly, often immediately—and perversely—after Amaia had changed its bottom cloth. And how did his mistress react to all this? Did she scream in fury and hurl the accursed thing out into the night? No, she rocked it, cooed to it, sang to it.

Yuli remembered when she used to sing to *him*.

Worst of all, the thing constantly demanded to be fed. But it didn't eat the fare from the cookfire; instead it fastened itself to Amaia's breast and suckled, draining forth her very life! Yuli thought it no wonder that she was always so haggard looking. So pale, the flesh beneath her eyes dark and puffy. Having failed to kill her from the inside, the creature was now killing her from without!

Yuli had failed to end the wretched Ba-bee's life once before. He wouldn't fail again.

One night, after his poor exhausted mistress put the Ba-bee into its tiny wooden bed—it's *kra-dul*—and finally took to sleep, Yuli made ready. He retrieved a scrap of cloth from where he had hidden it beneath one of the cupboards. He then paused and listened to his mistress's breathing. When it deepened, he stole across the cabin toward the kra-dul where the parasite—for this moment at least—slept.

Yuli climbed into the kra-dul cautiously, knowing that the slightest noise might wake the creature and set it to squalling. The imp perched on the edge of the kra-dul and examined the Ba-bee up close for the first time. It wore a small white nightshirt that his mistress had sewn with her own hands. Yuli felt a wave of jealousy. His mistress had never made anything for him.

The creature's skin was smooth, its face fat. Its hair was as thin as a corpse's, and its breath was a sweet-sour stink. Yuli had never seen anything so revolting since Amaia had summoned him from the Lower Places—and perhaps not even before.

Yuli's last plan for dealing with the parasite had been too complicated; he hadn't had the skill to mix the medicine properly. But this time his plan was simple: he would steal into the kra-dul and smother the horrid little beast. And Yuli knew he could do it, too. He might only be six inches tall, but he was stronger than he looked.

He placed a tentative foot on the creature's rising and falling chest, then paused, waiting to see if the Ba-bee would stir. It did not.

Yuli brought his other foot onto the creature, and, when it still remained asleep, he started toward the thing's head, wad of cloth held out before him.

When he reached the Ba-bee's neck, Yuli paused and stared at the creature's face in the dim light of the dying fire, and wondered at the exact nature of its power, a power that could hold even a being as strong as his mistress in thrall. Well, whatever the parasite's magic, its influence over Amaia would end tonight.

Yuli pressed the cloth hard against the Ba-bee's face, covering its nose and mouth. The thing's eyes flew open—Yuli saw they were a deep, rich brown—and it started to squirm. Yuli gripped the creature's night-shirt with his toe claws to keep from being dislodged and held the cloth tight. Soon . . . soon it would be over and his mistress would at last be free.

But then Yuli felt one of the Ba-bee's hands close around his arm, its pudgy fingers clamping down with a strength far greater than such a small body should possess. Yuli struggled to maintain the cloth's seal as a second tiny hand grabbed him around the waist. And even though the imp struggled with all his might, he was unable to break the Ba-bee's grip.

He found himself being lifted away from the thing's face and held in the air. The cloth fell away from its mouth and Yuli fully expected the Ba-bee to begin wailing, but it did not. Instead, it looked at him with those brown eyes. Eyes that started to glow red.

And then the monster that had plagued Yuli's mistress for so long opened its mouth and there, thrusting downward from its pink gum, were two tiny incisors.

The Ba-bee brought Yuli to its mouth and the imp squealed in pain as it began to feed.

Amaia stood over the cradle, beside her a tall, thin man garbed in black.

"I found them like that," she said, scratching through her night-gown at the healing scabs on her breast.

546

The tall man, who had finally finished his dark business and re-turned, nodded. "Did you try to take the imp away?"

"Yes, but I couldn't. The little devil is too strong."

The baby cooed and waved his new toy—the desiccated body of an imp—in the air.

The man in black laughed, displaying long, razor-sharp fangs. "Of course he is. After all, he takes after his father."

Just the Two of Us

HUGH B. CAVE

Again they were alone together, and the old man's heart flut-tered in his chest like a frightened bird in a box. It terrified him now to be left alone with his grandson. Side by side they stood at the picture window in the living room watching the car, with the boy's parents in it, go down the road to town.

"What time will they be back, Grandpa?" In the boy's eyes was the strange, frightening glitter that had appeared soon after old Mrs. Kempfer moved into the long-vacant house next door. Danny and Mrs. Kempfer, who lived alone there, had quickly become friends, and the boy called on her almost daily.

"What time will they be back?" Grandpa echoed. "About twelve, your dad said. But you can't stay up till then."

"Why can't I?"

"You're only eight, Danny. Eight-year-olds don't—"

"I'm eight and a half."

"All the same, you can't—"

"I'm going to, though." Danny turned a cherub's face toward him, grinning. But the grin was not a cherub's grin, the old man realized with a feeling of panic. Nothing about the boy was the same as it had been before Mrs. Kempfer's coming to this formerly peaceful neighborhood. Kempfer the Witch, people were calling her.

"Do you want to play a few games of checkers?" the old man asked in an effort to sidetrack the boy's train of thought.

"Sure, Grandpa."

They always played checkers at the long, glass-topped coffee table in front of the sofa, Grandpa sitting on the sofa, the boy on the floor. As the old man set up the board now, Danny trotted across the room and turned on the TV.

"Do we have to have that on, Danny?"

"There's a good movie coming up, Grandpa."

"I can't watch a movie and play checkers at the same time."

"I can."

The old man sighed. But it didn't matter, he told himself. His job was to keep the boy occupied and out of mischief. Whether they played checkers or watched television was not important, so long as *something* kept Danny from unleashing the Jovian thunderbolts born of all that pent-up energy. A boy his age who could move an ashtray over a table without even touching it was dangerous.

That, really, was why Phil and Evelyn didn't go out so often now, and to be honest about it, it was also why he, Phil's father, had been invited to come live here when his wife died. "Face it, Dad," Phil had said with his usual bluntness. "After being married to Mother all these years, you'll die of loneliness in no time if you try living alone. And *we* need someone we can leave Danny with, or we're going to be prisoners in *our* home. Since he's become friendly with old Mrs. Kempfer we've run out of babysitters. Even the ones who haven't sat with him have heard about him from those who have. We call a sitter up, they won't even talk to us."

So here he was, living with his son and his son's wife—a thing he had told Mary all through her long, last illness he would never do. And tonight, left alone with Danny again, he would give almost anything to be *able* to live alone in the house he had shared with Mary.

That bridge had been burned behind him, though. Under pressure from Phil and Evelyn he had sold the old place. Home was here now, and would be until the end. Here with them and Danny.

He tried to concentrate on the checkerboard and, for a change, was in a good position to win when Danny distracted him by laughing loudly at something on the television. He looked up to see what was so funny. When he returned his atention to the board, a scowl creased his face and he peered at his grandson.

"Wait just a second now. You moved my king!"

"Uh-uh." Danny solemnly wagged his head. "I never touched it."

"That isn't where it was! It was right here, and I looked over at the TV—like this—when you laughed, and then—"

This time when his gaze dropped to the board again, something like a lot of small, cold legs ran up his back. The boy hadn't touched the board this time, he was certain. There hadn't been time. But the king had moved again.

"How did you do that, Danny?" The words came out in a whisper.

The boy laughed gaily. "I've been practicing. Watch." Rising to his knees, he focused his gaze on the board with such intensity that Grandpa thought it might burst into flames. And suddenly *all* the pieces were in motion, slowly gliding over the red and black squares as though made of iron and being manipulated by an arrangement of magnets below. It was like watching a slow-motion movie of skaters on a frozen pond, Grandpa thought. Mary and he had been great for skating when they were young.

"I can't believe it." The old man clenched his hands on his knees to stop their trembling. "I just can't believe what I think I'm seeing!"

"That was easy," the boy countered with a grin. "Watch me now!"

This was a summer evening in a Massachusetts town once notorious for its witchcraft trials, and the old man wore slippers and slacks and a multicolored sport shirt. Clipped to the shirt's pocket was a ballpoint pen, in case the phone rang and he might have to take a message. Now suddenly he felt a gentle tugging at the pocket, and the pen was out of there, floating in space a few inches in front of him. He could feel his eyes bulging half out of their sockets as his gaze followed the pen to the big table in the dining alcove at the far end of the room.

His son Phil, an accountant, had worked there after dinner on some tax forms, while waiting for Evelyn to finish dressing. Stacks of papers were still there. The pen hovered over them for a few seconds like a helicopter preparing to land; then it descended point first and began a furious scribbling.

"Danny, don't!" For a moment the old man was more apprehensive than awestruck. In this house, he had learned, to his chagrin, no one was ever allowed to touch Phil's work. Though Phil left it in everyone's way at times, even his wife did not dare move it without his permission. More than once, since coming here to live, Grandpa had been forced to admit to himself that Mary and he had not done a good job of bringing up their son. He was selfish, morose, and ill tempered.

But the boy did not make the pen cease scribbling. Instead, he leaped to his feet beside the coffee table, where the checkers had now stopped their *danse macabre* on the board, and began jumping up and down in glee, excitedly clapping his hands.

"See? See, Grandpa? I told you!"

Reaching out, the old man caught him by an arm. "Danny, please. Your dad will be furious." A tear trickled down one eye. *"Please,* Danny? Give back my pen?"

"Sure, Grandpa!" The pen stopped its insane squiggling and floated gracefully upward. It circled above the cluttered table for a few seconds like a homing pigeon getting its bearings, then—zip!—it was suddenly back in the old man's shirt pocket. So suddenly, in fact, that he found himself wondering whether it had ever really left him.

He got up from the sofa. Frowning at the boy, he walked the length of the room to the dining table and peered down at the papers his son had left there.

The pen had been there, all right. Like an industrious hen scratching in a farmyard, it had left its mark on the top sheet in every stack. Some of those sheets looked as though Phil had spent much time peparing them, too; under the scratchings were columns of calculations. Someone was going to be very angry about this. Very angry indeed.

The old man returned to the sofa. Seating himself, he gazed solemnly at the boy and shook his head. "Danny, why did you do that?"

"Because I *can!*"

You climb a mountain beause it's there, Grandpa thought with a mental sigh. All right, the lad had this power, no doubt due to the teachings of his friend the witch-lady. He must be especially gifted, of course—if gifted was the word—but then, he had always been precocious, hadn't he? And always defiant. And always a bit terrifying. *My own grandson,* the old man thought, *and I'm scared to death of him.*

"Danny, let's just watch the movie?"

"No."

"But you said—"

"No!" The boy went to the set and emphatically turned it off. When he swung himself around, the glitter in his eyes was even more startling than it had been, and there was a wicked promise in his grin. "You'll like this better, Grandpa. Watch!"

Slowly raising his right arm, he aimed his extended forefinger at the bookcase. The case was an old-fashioned one that Evelyn had picked up at a garage sale; she loved garage sales and was an avid collector of antiques. Behind its glass doors were perhaps a hundred books. Most of those too had come from garage sales, and very few, the old man guessed, had ever been read in this house. Phil never read fiction of any kind, and his wife was not the sort who would stay long with Shakespeare or Mark Twain or Thomas Hardy.

Suddenly the bookcase behaved as though the floor beneath it were being shaken by an earthquake. It clattered against the wall as though alive and shivering. Its twin glass doors flew open and began flapping as though the case were about to take off and go soaring. Books cascaded out of it onto the carpet, every which way.

At this point the old man was beyond being shocked. All he could think was *Oh my God, I'll have to put them all back. All that bending. It will take forever.*

Some of the volumes had landed shut, others open. Many of the shut ones opened now of their own accord, their pages fluttering as though turned by a gale. Some slid over the carpet as far as the center of the living room. Others rose from the floor and flew through the air until walls or furniture stopped them with a series of thuds that could have been the old man's heart pounding. The boy remained by the television —he had not moved from there after turning it off—and jumped up and down and clapped his hands and gleefully cried, "I told you! Didn't I tell you?"

"Danny." Tears filled the old man's eyes and found their way into his voice. "Please put them back."

The boy shook his head. "That wouldn't be any fun."

"Are you going to make me do it? Don't you know I'm an old man with a bad back?"

But Danny was not interested in a dialogue, it seemed. Only in making a statement. "I can move *anything*," he boasted. "Anything at all! Try me!"

"No," Grandpa whispered.

"*Try* me! Anything! I can move that sofa you're sitting on. Or you, even. I can move you!"

"Danny, please. I don't feel good tonight. All I want is to—" The old man heard something and stopped talking. He turned his head. A car had come into the driveway.

Thank God.

"It's your mom and dad, Danny. They're home early."

551

"I don't want them to be home." The boy looked pouty at first, then quickly angry. "I want us to be alone together."

But I don't, the old man thought, limp now with relief as he heard the automatic garage door swing up and the car come in and go silent. The books, he thought then. *There's no way I can restore Phil's papers, but these books all over the room . . .*

But there wasn't time to put the books back. He had to face the fact that Phil would blame him for letting it happen.

Full of apprehension, he waited. And he was right. Entering the living room from the kitchen, Phil and Evelyn saw the violated bookcase, the scattered volumes, and reacted as he had known they would. Evelyn put her right hand to her mouth and voiced a gasp of dismay. Phil lurched to a halt, spread his feet wide, jabbed his clenched hands against his body, and let out a roar.

"What the hell's going on here?"

Not knowing what to say, Grandpa only pushed himself up from the sofa and backed away in silence.

"What *happened*, God damn it?" The shout was an accusation—if not blaming him for the hurricane that had swept the room, at least holding him responsible for having let it in.

"Ask Danny," was the best Grandpa could do.

"All right, I will! Danny! What happened here?"

"I got even," the boy said. He stood very still, close to his grandfather. Only his eyes moved. They were like flecks of fire, though, as his gaze traveled from the bookcase to the table and back to his father's contorted face.

Phil said furiously, "What do you mean, you got even? Even with who?"

"You and Mom. You told the doctor I was crazy."

"We told him no such thing," Evelyn weakly protested. "We only told him you've been acting strange since you became friends with that awful Kempfer woman."

"Big difference," Danny said.

"So for that," Phil growled, "you had to take all the books out of the bookcase and throw them around the room? What are you, anyway? Some kind of monster?"

"I didn't move them," Danny said. "I just told them to move."

"What?"

"I told Grandpa's pen to write on your papers, too. Go look."

His face paling to blend with the off-white woodwork, Phil turned like a store-window dummy to peer at the table—as though he didn't want to but knew he had to. Having looked, he walked stiffly to the table and examined the piles of papers more closely. His face lost its pallor and slowly turned fiery red.

He glared then at the old man. "Dad, were you here when the little monster did this?"

Grandpa nodded.

"Why in hell didn't you stop him, then?"

"I didn't know what was happening."

"He said he did it with your pen!"

"So he did. But neither he nor I went near the table."

Phil began to shake. He was a tall man with wide shoulders and fat hands. He shook all over. He shook so violently he could scarcely unbuckle his belt and pull it through the loops on his pants. It was a leather belt. He ran it through his fingers as though it were a whip to train tigers with.

Taking the first of the six or seven steps that would carry him to his target, he bellowed, "This time you're going to get it!"

"Wait, Dad," Danny said quietly.

Phil stopped. "Oh, no you don't! I've let you get away with this crazy stuff for the last time. Now I'm thrashing you!"

"I don't mean that. I just want to ask Mom something." Danny turned to look at his mother. "Are you going to let him whip me, Mom?"

"I certainly am," Evelyn said.

"Just stand there and let him do it? With his *belt*?"

"Yes. Tonight you deserve it. This is the worst you've ever been."

"All right." Danny seemed saddened by her decision. "I just wanted to know if it should be only him or both of you." Folding his slender arms on his chest, he gazed at both parents—first at his father, again advancing implacably with the belt, then at his equally unforgiving mother.

This time the boy's eyes did not glitter; he squeezed them shut as though concentrating with all his might on the thunderbolt he sought to hurl.

What happened then couldn't be happening, Grandpa decided. But it *was* happening. First the man with the belt faded slowly from view, then the staring woman, exactly as though they were figures on a motion-picture screen being dissolved to end a movie. One moment they were there, then they were not.

The boy opened his eyes and looked around the room. Rubbing his eyes, he walked to the sofa. He looked like a very tired little boy who wanted nothing more than to lie down and go to sleep now. But he sat there gazing at his grandfather, waiting for the old man to speak.

After a struggle to find his voice, the old man did speak. "My God, Danny . . . what did you do to them?"

"I moved them."

"You *moved* them?"

"Of course. I told you I can move things."

"But where *are* they, Danny?" Grandpa whispered.

"*I* don't know, Grandpa. There wasn't time to think about that." Danny shrugged. Then he smiled at the old man and patted the divan with one small hand. "Come sit beside me, Grandpa. There's just the two of us now, you know."

A Bluegrass Reunion

BEN P. INDICK

Paw and I was setting on the porch in late June, him jes chawin and me with my old cob. I got off a good booger onto a post maybe ten foot away.

"I got off a good one, Paw," I told him.

"That ye did, Maw, that ye did," he said, and took a good bite of chaw, and chewed fer a while. Then he let go and covered that old post good.

"Right fine spittin, Paw," I acknowledged proudly, and he nodded and patted my freckled old arm. So we set fer a while, rockin and spittin, and me thinkin of somethin I had in my mind, which was makin me feel kinder low.

"Paw," I said at last, "it's been grievin me that we ain't had a nice family reunion in too many years."

"That's right, Maw," he allowed, and he painted that post again.

"But you have ter reckamember our meetin time always was Christmas, and since this be near July, we're only halfway there."

"That be true, Paw," I agreed, and I chawed my cob fer a time. "But all the same I sure misses my Aunt Gertrudie. That woman were a peck of fun, Paw."

"She sure were indeed that," Paw said, gettin his words out between chaws. "But, of course, Gert's been laid away up in Hog Waller Hill these three year now, Maw."

"I misses her all the same, Paw. And there's Nephew Oscar, what a caution he was! Afore he took sick from the smallpox."

Paw nodded. "Uh huh, died lookin like that polky-dot dress you bought down at Honest Luke's General Store. From the catylog."

I laughed out loud. "Heck, Paw, I didn't bought that from that cheatin Luke. I bought it when I was a bride with foolish notions. I don't have no truck with store-boughtens. You know that, Paw! Anyway, what about Nephew Oscar's maw, my oldest sister, Irmie. We ain't seen her in a long time neither, Paw."

Paw didn't say nothin fer a space, and I thought maybe he didn't reckamember Irmie. Which was peculiar seein he always had an eye fer Irmie. But he was savin up his cud and he let out a blast and caught a squirrl right on his bushy tail. "That talkytive female is jes as daid as her son, Maw," he said, "as I am certain you recollect."

"I do, Paw," I said. "She shore were indeed a talkytive person. Say, Paw, what do you reckon's been happenin to our family, so many of our beloved kin dyin off like that? Paw, it sometime seem like there ain't no one ter talk with no more. And that bein the case, how could we have our Christmas party? Anyway, you recolleck last time we called the family together, five year back it were, fer a nice comin-together, why it were so cold nobody could come. Heck, they couldn't even open the doors offen their houses, they was froze so solid and buried in snow."

"That were one cold winter, Maw," Paw said.

"So I been thinkin we shouldn't have ter wait fer Christmas, Paw, ter have our family Christmas party. We should have it now, when it be nice and warm. Can't nobody not come when it's so all-fired and heart-pleasurin summertime."

Paw considered this, rockin and gettin off two or three good ones. "I don't know butten you're right, Maw. Still, it'd be mighty diffycult. Half of em is buried up on the hill, and t'other half is moved ter where it be warm, down in Toothpick Holler cross the river. And what about my half-brother Jedadiah, the bastard, he lives up in the North on Park Avenoo in Noo York City. I don't know iffen they'd any of them keer ter come."

I was workin on a notion, howsomever. "They'll come, Paw, iffen you spell them." Paw always knew a heap about spellin. When my fifth cousin Zachariah, who helps Paw and me out in the field, was gored by that old boar, and he was lyin thar in the woods with all his innards spilled out, Paw tucked him back together, and he spelled him right good. Zachariah don't talk none no more, but he does his work. He never talked much anyhow.

Paw nodded his head. "I guess I kin, Maw, but it won't feel like Christmas."

"It only lacks scarce more'n six days till the Fourth of July, Paw," I responded, "and that seems like a good nacheral holiday ter celebrate with one's near and dear kin. Wouldn't it be nice ter have Maw, and little Jabeth, and even maybe our own Ruthannamae, whose purty face I ain't seen in thirty year! Not since we put her in her little pine box!" Thinkin about Ruthannamae made me sad and I could feel my eyes grow wet and softlike. "We oughter had this party years ago, Paw, instead of complainin about the cold."

Paw thought about it and I could see he was right touched by the memory of our little Ruthannamae. He even stopped chawin. "Well," he said, at last, "the full moon be an absolute necessity, but now I think on it, it comes round this year. Maw," he said, "iffen you have yer heart set, by gum, I'll do it!"

I was so happy I hugged him, and he had ter shake me off, cause he don't like fer me to show my love. But Paw's a good man, and he keers about family like I do, so he got busy.

Lands, the things that man brought in the house, some of them bein herbs and flowers smellin pretty as my bridal bokay which I still have all squashed flat in my big bible here. And some stinkin like that outhouse back there on a hot day. But Paw didn't pay no mind ter smells; he just got everthing tergether, all the while hummin and ooh-ooh-ooh-in them funny songs he larned from old Widow Zenobie Watson, the hex woman, which make my back crawl. He stirred the concoction up in pots and pans, strainin the boilin mess and sometimes mumblin some right peculiar words too. They made me feel crawly too, but it ain't my business ter listen. Paw's the one knows spellin.

556

"Okay, Maw," he said at last a few days later, "I'm ready. Now let's decide who ter invite."

Well, them brothers and sisters and cousins of mine who packed off ter the Holler and never try to see us or find out iffen we is still alive, thinkin they be so good now, some of them is even wearin shoes, I hear, I fergive them fer their sin of Persumption, so I told Paw ter invite them all. They anyhow should come fer a special holiday like the Fourth of July, but it don't matter, cause if Paw spells them, they got ter come. So I wrote down all their names on a piece of paper and Paw did his work on that with that stuff in his boilin pot.

"How bout them on the hill in Hog Waller, Maw?" Paw inquired when he was finished. "You ain't goin ter bring your paw, I trust." He frowned bad. "You recolleck iffen he puts too much moonshine in that big gut of his, he's a caution!"

I agreed with Paw about my paw, but still, what kind of party would my maw have if I left him out, even though it were likely he would start in bashin her round like always. And my aunts and uncles up there, well, it made a good list, and Paw had ter whittle it down jes a mite because he was runnin out of spellin soup ter mark against their names.

He got everthing done in right good time, and we could set back and wait fer that full moon. It give us jes enough time to get plenty of vittles together and smoke up extra supplies of possum and skunk. And weren't we lucky when Zachariah come in draggin a big black bear which had holt of his leg! I know how fond my kin are of bear steak! I'll bet Jedadiah don't find no steak like that in none of them fancy eatin places in Noo York City!

Next day we made up tables and set them full of all them delicacies and Paw even tried spellin the weather, although he allowed as how nobody, not old Widow Zenobie or even them master spellers on the T and V could do much about that! Paw's spellin must have helped anyway, because the Fourth of July dawned like the picture in my bible of the Great Redemption Day, with a blue sky, and white clouds all glowin rosy and pink. And soon a clatter of horses and wagons and old tin lizzies come chuggin up, and danged iffen all our kin in Toothpick Holler aren't comin up, men and wives and children, old folks too, all full of smiles, and huggin and squeezin us, and not even put out none cause they was forced by Paw's spell ter come or else.

"We shoulda thought of it ourselves," they kep saying, and by gosh, they even brought us gifts! A nice old coat fer the winter fer me, which will be perfect once I sew in some sleeves. And although Paw snickered and his face got red as a cow's behind, Jedediah, who come flyin in by airplane from Park Avenoo in Noo York City, give him some shoes fer his feet, all nice and wore in already. When Paw tried them om, they wasn't hardly too tight at all, jes a mite, but his feet nacherly split them open enough and then he liked them a deal, and strutted around in them, like he was a shoe-wearin man, and kep sayin as how he couldn't imagine why he never went in fer shoes afore.

The ladies got busy in the house settin out more vittles and the men did a lot of stump-clearin, and then somebody hollered out, "They're comin!"

I looked up and my heart near bust with joy when I spied a regilar parade comin down the hill from the Waller. Tramp, tramp, tramp! That's how they was marchin smartly along, men and ladies and behind them I could spy the little ones. There was my maw! Oh, didn't Maw look purty in that nice white winding sheet! And my paw, shovin her behind him like always, and her smilin ter see as how he loved her like before! And there! There was my Ruthannamae! I run ter her first and hugged and hugged her and she didn't look surprised how old I become. She just hugged right back!

They all come on and soon here they was, and such embracin and old-time talk like I ain't heard in years since I was a girl myself.

Oh, it were a glory day! Eatin and drinkin and game-playin and time jes flew by. Everbody were happy and praisin Paw fer his spellin and him tellin them all it were my idea too, and he could share the credit. Paw always were a generous soul.

The sun jes wore itself clear across the sky, and the clouds puffed on along, and the evenin whipporwills begun their singin, and then the shadows begun gettin longer and we knew it were time fer the fireworks. It couldn't nohow be a real Fourth of July withouten no fireworks, and the boys had taken care of that. They made big piles of splinters from all them trunks they chopped up, and smeared bear fat around them and then they started firin them.

Did they ever spark and sputter and shoot off little lights! It minded me of them little fairy folk I used ter see hidin in the woods when I was jes a little tyke, it were that pretty. When all the explodin were done, Maw took her seat on the old rocker which has been mine since she died amd was put up on the hill, amd she allowed as how she could not reckamember such a grand day. Even my old paw put down his jug of sour mash, which Paw had special distilled fer him that week, and he told Maw fer a change she were right, and danged iffen he didn't lean over and give her a real nice hug. I think maybe bein in that box fer so long makes a soul gentle. How we all clapped and cheered at that, and he blushed and did it one more time, until Maw shooed him off.

All too quick it were time fer everone ter go back home, and there was lots of huggin and squeezin and tears too. All opinioned that they had enjoyed themselves so much we should do it again. Then off went them wagons and lizzies back to the Holler, the folks wavin and cheerin and singin. And then our hill folk, Maw and Paw, and little Ruthannamae too, marched on back ter their places too, not sayin a word no more, jes trampin slow and sadlike on back up there ter sleep.

The next day Mr. Hoskins, the caretaker from Hog Waller, come ter see us and he was right angered and fussin, sayin as how the hill was a mess, all them stones turned over and lots of holes to be filled in. Paw said quietlike that they didn't make hardly no mess ter speak of, and he would come hisself with Zachariah and fix it all up. That caretaker kep on fussin, so finally Paw stood up tall in his new shoes and said real slow and lookin Mr. Hoskins right in the eye, he didn't reckon it were such a turrible thing at all. So that little man thought it over and he agreed Paw was right, specially when Paw started fingerin his old shotgun. He began stutterin and asked Paw iffen at least he wouldn't spell no more, but Paw just slid a shell into the gun and that caretaker lit right out.

We sat back on the porch after that, chawed and did some good spittin, and we felt the warm peace after a good busy day. Real comfortable-like. Finally Paw said, "Maw, what are you thinkin?"

I said, "I'm thinkin we should do it again next year, on the Fourth of July again!"

"Jus what I was thinkin," said Paw, and he took my arm.

Tarnation take that old caretaker!

Poppet

KATHRYN PTACEK

The fourteen-year-old kid across the street plays the trumpet. He plays every day and sometimes at night, always rather enthusiastically, if not particularly well, although he's much better now than four years ago.

Right this moment he is belting out "Louie, Louie." I've never heard that song performed with a solitary brass instrument, and I hope I never hear that rendition again. Some things just aren't meant to be.

He debuted with "When the Saints Go Marching In," got stuck on "Heart and Soul" for a year or two, and has just recently progressed to the Russian folk song "Meadowland" and some old rock classics, among them "Blue Suede Shoes" and "Peggy Sue." It is to his credit, though, that I do recognize all these tunes.

Each day he intrudes into my life a little with that golden trumpet. Even in the winter with our windows closed and his windows shut we can hear the music faintly, as if from a great distance. If only we were that lucky. But we're not, and the kid and his folks still live close by, and when it comes springtime, their windows fly up at the first hint of good weather, as do ours, to catch those wonderfully warm and fragrant spring breezes, and it's time once more for young John Philip Sousa to perform before his captive audience. The kid has even been known to play the trumpet at night—after eleven, and sometimes after midnight on weekends. Never for very long, though, and no one except me seems to comment on it.

Sometimes when the kid sees that I'm home or sees me passing the window either upstairs or downstairs, he whips out the ol' trumpet and starts in. Sometimes he hangs out his window and toots it in our direction, and I have wondered what would happen if he slipped just the tiniest. Sometimes he stands in their kitchen, which faces our house, or on the back porch and practices those songs. Sometimes I wish I were Artemis, the Divine Archer, with a conveniently handy bow, and a magic arrow to shoot that way.

The kid sees me, and somehow senses that I hate that, that I hate to be watched in my very own house, and he smiles, and I realize then how very small and close and piglike are his dark eyes. And again he raises the trumpet to his lips.

Sometimes when I lie down in the bedroom for a nap, I think he must be telepathic, because the instant I curl up on the bed, the trumpet begins. And I imagine those piglike eyes with their dark intent.

I complain a lot about young JPS to my husband, who smiles rather patiently. He doesn't have to listen to the kid all day long in the summer. My husband works at an office and commutes those long hours from our small northwestern New Jersey town to the city, New York City, that is, and often he's traveling in other states on company business.

I, on the other hand, don't work, or that's the opinion of those who are forever calling me during the day or dropping by "just to chat." Just because the women and men in this neighborhood aren't sure about me, doesn't mean they avoid me—after all, gossip can't operate in a vacuum, and they have to have something to fuel their talk.

Of course I work, although not in an office. I have many important things to do. I have this wonderful house—a large Victorian with ten rooms, all of which exude dust constantly—which always needs cleaning, no matter how hard I work at it—and a truly immense yard with numerous azaleas and rhododendrons and honeysuckle and lilacs and wisteria, and over a dozen flowering trees as well as those that bear fruit.

And I have a huge garden—with rosemary and rhubarb, sunflowers and sage, larkspur and lily of the valley, hensbane and hemlock, mint and marigolds, leeks and lavender (both English and French), borage and basil and bay leaves, daisies and dill and daffodils, cabbage and carnations, poppies and potatoes, three kinds of lettuce, as well as endive, radishes and roses, carrots and caraway, sweet peas and spinach, string beans and bush beans, Halloween pumpkins and colorful squash —and all these plants need to be attended to on a daily basis.

Some people garden; I GARDEN. In some ways it is my life, and I guess my neighbors think I'm a little dotty on the subject. They tend to their little patches and are quite complacent about the matter. On the other hand, I yell at the kids who look like they might even be thinking about approaching my garden, and I have been known to turn the hose on a dog or two.

I'm sure the moment any new people move into the neighborhood, one of the older residents self-righteously takes it upon him- or herself to scurry on over there to alert the newcomers to just what sort of place they've gotten themselves into.

It's all a matter of coincidence, of course, but no resident of the house on our immediate right stays there longer than a year or two.

Sheer happenstance.

And it's true that the crows and marauding squirrels and gophers leave my garden alone. Not even the bunnies are so bold as to nibble there.

Happenstance again, I tell you.

On our left is a narrow street, hardly more than a car-and-a-half-wide lane. The house where the boy with the trumpet lives is on the other side of that road.

It's not that far away; not more than a stone's throw, not more than the blast of a trumpet.

So, I listen to the trumpet as I trot from room to room, and not even the growl of the vacuum cleaner, not even the blaring of the CD player, not even my own off-key humming can totally shut out the efforts of our young would-be musician. Not even earplugs work one hundred percent. I know because one day I tried them out of desperation. Somehow, the trumpet always manages to wheeze its way pass them.

So I do my work—the many chores about the house—and then it's time for the fun stuff, the labors of love out in my yard. I open the backdoor and go past the twigs of ash hanging over the doorpost and walk outside. I like to prune my dozen roses and admire the tender blossoms as they unfold from tiny tight buds; I like to watch a small seedling grow minutely each day, unfolding bit by bit so that it finally stands straight and tall in the nurturing sun and starts to bear fruit. I even like to weed, although I don't have many stragglers to pull from the soil. I really enjoy this. I thrive on my gardening. I talk to my plants and sing to them, and not even the trumpet music seems to deter them.

I know the kid's piggy eyes are upon me as I stoop and stand, then bend down to inspect my long-stemmed flowers. I know he watches, and I do not like that. He has altogether too much free time. He needs to be kept busy, I tell myself, and wish his mother would send him to camp. Boot camp, perhaps.

But of course she doesn't, and he continues to watch me each day as I wander through my garden, picking the sugar snap beans or strawberries, harvesting the zucchini that flourishes so well, or snipping off a dead leaf here and there, or admiring my berry bushes.

He watches, and I wait, and within moments he begins playing.

I glance up at his window, and he is looking down at me, his eyes unreadable from this distance. He continues to play, the music somehow louder than a moment before. Such strong lungs, I think.

I pick up my basket filled with the harvest and go back inside to wash the produce.

In the evening I return to the garden to examine the herbal portion of my garden. They are so pretty, these plants, with their lavender flowers and white spikes, tiny crimson and emerald petals and silver striations. I like to touch them, stroke the soft stems. In a way, they are my friends.

I look up, and even though it is dusk, I see the kid staring at me. Doesn't he ever read, or watch TV, or play video games like the other kids around here? It's not healthy for a boy of his age always to be looking out the window at his neighbor. I wait, but he doesn't play the trumpet. I shrug, take out my shears and clip off a handful of herbs, and head for the house. I am no sooner in the kitchen than the trumpet begins.

The curious thing about the kid—one point, that is—is I've never heard him play the scales. And I always thought that was such a significant part of learning to play any musical instrument. My mistake, I suppose. And he never really plays anything long enough—he flits from song to song, day in, day out. He should concentrate on one song at a time, I think, but then I'm no musician.

I hum to myself as I wash the herbs, and realize the tune is "Stars and Stripes Forever," which the kid has just recently been learning. I know because whenever he plays it, I briskly snap my fingers, trying to get him to quicken the timing. He doesn't count very well, does the kid. What a shame. That's the true mark of a good musician. Ah well, I never said he was good, not yet anyway.

I dry the herbs carefully and spread them on a clean linen towel in the sunshine. How pretty are the leaves. In one cupboard I reach past the jar of alfalfa—it's supposed to keep the home safe from poverty and hunger—to get the other jars with the beans in them, and the one with the dried material well behind those.

I take out a handful of the castor beans from the glass jar on my counter and admire them. So pretty in their shiny casings, and such a dreadful oil that comes from them. I shake my head over that mystery.

The mix from the cupboard is a combination of dried leaves and flowers of datura, also known as Jimsonweed, the Ghost Flower (no doubt because of its white trumpetlike blossom), or Witches' Thimble. Datura doesn't grow here, but I have a friend in the Southwest, who has the same interests as mine, and we exchange various plants that don't fare well in our own particular states.

The periwinkle I wash carefully, because I don't want to harm the delicate light blue flower. Its folk names are Devil's Eye or Sorcerer's Violet; I prefer the nickname of Joy on the Ground.

I take the anise leaves and inhale their fragrance, even before I crush them. I love anise-flavored candies and cookies. Its Latin name is *Pimpinella anisum,* but that sounds so silly. I use anise a lot at Christmas, when I make dozens of cookies for various charities.

Then I take out the mortar and pestle—a beautiful gray-and-black swirled marble so cool to my fingertips even in the summer—and place them on the counter, then reach for the large wooden bowl needed for enchanting the herbs. I like the pattern in this wood and sometimes I take it in my hands and stroke the whorls, almost like those of a fingerprint. Perhaps it matches my own.

I go into the living room to collect a few items, and I see him standing on their kitchen stoop and he is staring across at the house, at me. There is only one faint light on in my living room, yet I know he can see me as plainly as if it were daytime. I cannot see his expression, because it is dark and there is a light on in the kitchen behind him. But I know that he is smiling. For a moment neither one of us moves, then he raises the trumpet to his lips. "Taps" this time.

Next I sit at the dining room table and spread out the plain white paper and the expensive colored pens I brought in from the other room and begin drawing. I hear the kid switch over to "Meadowland." Its such a nice song, and one of my favorites, and I can almost forgive him anything for that. Almost. He doesn't seem to have quite the soul for it, but I imagine that will come in time. He's still rather young.

The outline takes form quickly, and then I pay special attention to the trumpet in its hand. That's very important, you know. I draw in the features as best I can, making those eyes particularly piggy.

With my gardening shears, the green liquid of the herbs still on the blades, I cut out the shape.

It's a poppet, what some make from roots, potatoes, lead, bark, or cloth. I prefer to make mine out of paper; I have more artistic adroitness than sewing ability, and when sewing I somehow always manage to stab myself with the needle, and then the blood gets onto the material and spoils the poppet. No, far easier to use paper.

I smile at the poppet, satisfied with its resemblance, and go back into the kitchen. I grind the castor beans with my pestle, and sprinkle in some dried datura and pulverize that. Next comes the anise to join in the mixture.

Carefully I wind the periwinkle around the poppet's neck; what a pretty necklace it makes.

I pour the dried mixture into my wooden bowl, and take from the refrigerator a fresh lime. I don't grow them—it's not tropical enough here, so those just purchased from the local supermarket will have to suffice—and I slice it in half, then squeeze some of its juice into the mixture. I follow that with garlic buds in the garlic press, and watch as the smelly liquid drips into the bowl.

Again, I hum as I mash the ingredients together. I lean back because the odor rising from the bowl chokes me a bit and makes my eyes smart.

I'm not a violent sort, anyone will tell you that. After all, I live in a small town amidst the peaceful countryside, not in the large city with its rage and pain and brutality and stupidity. There are quite reasonable solutions to everyday problems, ends other than death, and God knows I've been tolerant enough so far. But there does come a time when you can only take so much.

He's playing "The Battle Hymn of the Republic." I hum along.

Then I retrieve a small artist's brush of natural camel hair and dip it into my rank brew, and smear the dark-colored matter onto the poppet's face.

I hear the trumpet stop abruptly, and the kid across the street screams. And then his mother is screaming.

I smile.

I don't much like the trumpet playing, but I know I'll get used to it, and he is improving, after all. But it's those damned piglike eyes that disturb me the most.

I hear the rise and fall of the ambulance's wail as it rushes toward our street.

The mixture is drying, and now I hold a lit match to it, and watch as the paper browns and curls and ignites.

The ambulance arrives; the attendants scurry inside the unlocked door.

I pour the remaining mixture down the sink and wash the bowl and mortar and pestle and put them back until I need them again.

The ambulance attendants bring a writhing form out on a stretcher; I am constantly amazed at how quickly these local volunteers can respond to an emergency. It's very encouraging.

The kid's mother is sobbing, and climbs into the ambulance with the others.

The poppet is now just ash, and I wipe it off the counter and into the trash bag. I wipe the counter clean; my kitchen bright and spotless, no doubt the envy of every suburbanite on the block.

I watch as the ambulance wails away into the early evening. The hospital is not far from us, not more than a mile or two, so I know the kid will get fast, if not effective, treatment.

And after all, blind musicians, I've heard, can be very successful. Just as long as the kid continues to practice.

The Robbery

CYNTHIA WARD

Sarah Martin unlocked the front door of her tract house and stood staring: the kitchen door had been broken open. She'd been burglarized. Again. A month after she'd bought this house in a "safe suburban neighborhood," someone had broken in when she'd gone to Chicago for the weekend. They hadn't taken anything except the coins on her nightstand, but still she had felt furious and violated.

This time Sarah had told no one she was going away except her neighbors, the Armstrongs: a friendly, nervous blonde housewife named Trisha and her pompous lawyer husband, Carmichael. They'd known about her previous break-in, and they'd agreed not to tell anyone she was going away. They wouldn't have told anyone. Except, Sarah suddenly realized, their son.

She'd never met the boy, but when she'd invited the Armstrongs to dinner, Carmichael had boasted at length about his only son, Thomas. About what a great athlete and terrific quarterback, what an overachieving student and well-behaved Christian his son was. Because Thomas was so good, Carmichael Armstrong had bought his son a Corvette and, if Thomas didn't get a full scholarship, he would pay his son's way through college and law school. "I had to drive a dangerous junk car and pay for my education with lousy back-breaking labor," Carmichael had told Sarah over dinner. "Why should my son suffer through some low-paying menial job when he doesn't have to?" Sarah had said nothing, though she'd been angry at Carmichael's scornful dismissal of labor. All her relatives back East worked hard jobs—lobstering, logging, driving trucks, waiting tables—and they deserved respect. Sarah had held her tongue and, remembering the brawny, sullen youth she'd seen working on the sports car in the Armstrongs' driveway, she had thought that Thomas would benefit enormously from working like every college-bound teenager she'd ever known.

But they seemed to do things differently in the Midwest. Especially when the kid was the star quarterback of the high school football team.

She'd lived here a year now, and Sarah still couldn't believe how *big* football was in the Midwest. God, the high school teams played in stadiums of NFL dimensions! Schools in eastern Maine couldn't even afford football. The boys played soccer, and often the spectators didn't have a bench to sit on.

Sarah Martin realized she was still standing in her doorway, staring into space. Shaking off her stunned reverie, she reached down and picked up the rope that had lain alongside the inner sill of her front door. The rope was slightly longer than the doorsill, and tied along its length in four complex knots. Sarah stepped into the house, closed the door, and untied every knot in the rope. She went to each window, removing the rope from the sill and undoing its four knots. Then she went to the half-open kitchen door, which opened into her tiny backyard. The doorjamb had been splintered by blows to the latch and deadbolt. Hammered open by someone strong, just like last time. Sarah looked down. The knotted rope had been slightly disturbed. She picked up the rope but did not touch the four knots.

The utility drawer was open and in disarray, but nothing appeared to be missing. Sarah dropped the lengths of rope in the drawer. *Did it work?*

She called the police.

While moving through the house she'd noticed that she hadn't lost any big-ticket items; she still had the stereo, the TV and VCR, the CDs and videocassettes, the computer and printer. When she hung up the phone, she checked her medicine cabinet and her yanked-open closets and drawers. The thief had gone through her jewelry box but taken nothing—had busted open her strongbox but ignored her stock certificate for the private medical clinic where she worked; however, he had taken the silver dollar her father had given to her before he'd died.

Sarah's fists clenched with rage.

He'd gone through her underwear drawer. He hadn't done anything except search for money, but she still couldn't bear the knowledge that he'd fingered her panties and bras. She emptied the drawer in the laundry basket.

Two officers and one detective arrived in response to her call. The uniforms dusted for fingerprints. The plainclothesman asked questions and Sarah answered.

Then she said, "Detective Adams, can I tell you something in private?"

"Pete," he said. "Sure."

She stepped into her home office and Pete Adams followed. She closed the door and spoke softly: "I've only been gone two nights. And I'm a doctor, so I keep weird hours. Someone who knows my movements did this. It was a neighborhood kid."

"Definitely," Adams said. "This has all the earmarks of a juvenile perpetrator. Ninety percent of these crude B-and-E's are committed by kids looking for money."

"I'll bet," Sarah said. "Pete, I know my neighbors' son broke in here—"

"He's under eighteen?" Adams asked. Sarah nodded. "A juvenile. If he has a record, we can bring him in."

"*What?*" Sarah cried. "Under those conditions, no juvenile thief could *get* a record!"

"I'm sorry, I was unclear. If we lift fingerprints that match a convicted juvenile's prints, we can make an arrest. But we can't go and fingerprint a juvenile without a record purely on your say-so. We'll question your neighbors—if someone else witnessed the crime and recognized the perpetrator, or gives a description matching your neighbor's kid, then we can bring him in. But a hunch isn't enough, Dr. Martin."

"Christ!" Sarah said. "I *know* it's the son of my neighbors across the street. I asked them to keep an eye on my place and not to tell anyone I was gone. I *know* their son did it! I know he did *both* break-ins here! The thief is Thomas Armstrong."

"Thomas Armstrong!" Adams exclaimed. "The star quarterback of the Lincolnville Eagles. Ma'am, no one will believe the biggest celebrity in town broke into your place."

Sarah's eyes narrowed and her mouth opened.

"Oh, I believe you, Dr. Martin," Adams said. "Thomas is a spoiled, swell-headed brat. I think he's broken into some other houses on this street. But you keep your suspicion to yourself. Telling anyone else won't do anything but make you enemies. Anyway, it is possible Thomas didn't break into your house this time. Yesterday he woke up in such terrible pain he could hardly move. His parents took him to the hospital. He's developed such a bad case of arthritis the doctors can't *believe* it. They can't do anything except give him tests and pills and a wheelchair. They can't even figure out how it happened so fast."

"My God," Sarah said. "I've never heard of such a thing!"

"No? And you're a GP. Jesus!"

When the police left, Sarah went across the street. Carmichael Armstrong was at the law office where he was a junior partner, but his wife Trisha was home, taking care of their son. Sarah told Trisha how sorry she was to hear about Thomas's illness, and asked if she could speak to him; she was a general practitioner, maybe she could think of something that might help. It was a long shot, but surely worth trying. . . .

"Of course!" Trisha said, nodding several times. She looked more nervous than ever, and seemed brittle; Sarah guessed another blow would shatter her. Sarah suppressed a sigh. She liked Trisha. "Please, Sarah, come in—this way—"

The Armstrongs' house was laid out exactly like Sarah's. Sarah hated suburban housing, but she couldn't afford anything old enough to possess individuality.

"His room . . ." Trisha pointed to an open door. One of the two bedrooms, Sarah knew from her own tract house.

"I think it would be best if I spoke to Thomas alone."

"Oh, of course . . ." Trisha drifted away.

Sarah closed the door and turned to a riot of color; the bedroom walls were covered with glossy posters of NFL stars. Sarah didn't know their names, but she recognized the logos of the Chicago Bears, the Denver Broncos, the San Francisco 49ers.

Thomas wore a Minnesota Vikings jersey. He sat rigidly in a wheelchair. His face was as sullen as Sarah remembered.

"What do you want?" he demanded. "Did you come to *pity* me? You can't help me, Dr. Martin. The experts said *nobody* can help me." His voice rose, harsh with rage. "You doctors are all useless bastards!"

"I understand your frustration," Sarah said, glancing over the powerfully built, utterly motionless body. "But sometimes a clear conscience can work wonders, Thomas." She kept her voice calm. "While I was away, you broke into my house. If you apologize and return the silver dollar you stole, I will forgive you and you may feel better."

"You lying bitch!" Thomas's tone was furious, but his voice was soft. "I didn't break into your house!" His voice rose: "Get *out!*"

Sarah stepped out of his bedroom and softly closed the door. She saw Trisha rushing toward her. She apologized for disturbing Thomas, and said, "If there's anything I can do, Trisha, please don't hesitate to ask."

"You're so kind, Sarah," Trisha said.

Back in her house, Sarah took the knotted rope out of the utility drawer. She'd learned how to tie a knot practically in infancy; her father and grandfather had been fishermen, in the days when fishermen made their own nets. But the foreign trawlers stripped New England's ocean waters, and most of Maine's fishermen were driven ashore, or turned, like her father and grandfather, to lobstering. Sarah heard tales of the old days on Dad's or Grampa's knee, and she heard that there was power in the knots a fisherman tied: power to summon the fish, to summon a wind fair or foul, to summon trouble for a troublemaker. When she grew older, Sarah realized no amount of knots could regenerate the schools of fish captured in miles-long nets and eaten by foreigners; she realized her father and grandfather were superstitious old men embroidering tales of past glory.

She studied science, she was going to be a doctor; she knew better.

But when someone broke into her new house, Dr. Martin found herself feeling vulnerable, and unable to afford installation of an alarm system on top of her mortgage and medical school bills; she thought about buying a dog, but she worked such long, odd hours, it would be cruel neglect. So she found herself thinking about what her father and grandfather had told her. Dad and Grampa were dead. She called her grandmother, said she was just curious about it—couldn't quite remember what she'd heard when she was a kid. "You know how that goes, Gram. . . ."

"Oh, ayuh, there's power in knots," Grandma said in her age-weakened voice. "If someone's troubling you, granddaughter—"

"That's just it, Gram," Sarah had said, dropping the pretense of idle curiosity, and she'd listened carefully to everything her grandmother had told her.

Sarah looked at the rope in her hand, the rope that had caught the unwelcome intruder without his noticing; she looked at the four knots, one for each of the intruder's limbs. If she untied the knots, she would unbind the intruder's arms and legs, free them from crippling agony.

Her grandmother had told her the best thing to do would be to tie a slipknot. Make a noose. But Sarah was a doctor. She worked to save lives, not end them. All she wanted to do was stop the thief from breaking in.

The idea of causing such pain was disturbing enough. But this pain could be stopped. Death could not be reversed.

But if this crippling pain were stopped, it was clear Sarah would be right back where she started.

Sarah took her trowel out of the utility drawer and went through the broken door into her backyard. She struck the earth of her tiny flowerbed with angry blows of the trowel. She buried the rope. The hemp would rot, the knots dissolve without unbinding; Thomas Armstrong would remain crippled for as long as he lived.

Patience Serves

DAVID C. SMITH

With Areil were perhaps twenty others in the wide hall, each waiting patiently for his or her name to be called, each looking up expectantly when the heavy bronze doors were pulled open and the latest visitant led out. Looking up expectantly and listening carefully as the seneschal announced another name and took that one by the arm into the farther chamber, all gloomy and quiet as it was, and hazy with incense and candle smoke, dark with prayers, abode of the dead.

"Lady Tristania of Oll."

Areil rose gracefully to her feet and glided forward. Whispers and eyes, all around. Her rich robes unfolded smoothly behind her and rippled over the marble floor. The seneschal fixed her with his stare and declared before allowing her entrance:

"Our lord is sinking. Each penitent can be allowed only a few moments to be near his Honor and whisper a prayer for him. If you expect a miracle—"

"I do not come as a penitent."

"What, then?"

"I knew his Honor long ago. Before he was ever a lord. Remind him of that, and tell him that we were lovers."

Through all the morning and the long afternoon the seneschal had admitted into the dying man's sanctum all ranks of local potentates and suppliants, businessmen, councillors, the wise of the cloth: and here came this dowager, a heartflame from his youth, to collect one last kiss or to remind him of some lingering, kind memory. The seneschal was not so much touched by sentimentality as he was intrigued; into the chamber he led Areil and with a gesture summoned a servant to him. He spoke low into the old man's ear, and the servant moved then to the right-hand side of Lord Mors's bed to lean close and inform.

On the other side of the room, in the shadows and in the light of great candles taller than men, stood physicians watching with darting eyes every labored breath, twitch, nod. And Mors's family, his sons and their wives and children, bored and restless.

The servant returned. "His Honor will see Lady Tristania."

"Quickly, then. Others wait."

Areil approached on the left, her back to the physicians and the family. She looked down upon the dying man, studying him. Lean and frail, now. Areil remembered him robust and arrogant. Mouth agape, now. Clenched, shivering fists netted with veins. Perspiration shimmering in the hollow gray cheeks. Surely all flesh decays according to the same law.

Areil sat in the chair that was there and leaned close. "We were once lovers, my Lord."

He tried to reach with a faltering hand, turned his damp face

572

toward her. Pain. "I cannot." Barely audible. "Hear on. This side." He closed his eyes, opened them with a moist sound. "Who. Are you?"

"Who indeed?" Areil smiled but did not raise her voice. "We were . . . lovers."

The faintest of nods, perhaps only a trembling, and no expression.

The odor of him was the stink of the dead, not sweet. "I was introduced to you as Lady Tristania. By that name I have lived in this city for three years. But my name was Areil."

He closed his eyes.

"Areil, Lord Mors. You do not recall?" Her whisper took an edge. "We were . . . children, really. You thought you loved me, but I was to marry—I know you'll remember the name—I was to marry Arin. Your father's stableboy? Ah, you remember."

The throat clenched, moving to force down a swallow, and did not succeed. The eyes remained closed, the lips open for air, the head shivering.

"Two nights before the wedding? You and four others?"

The nostrils flared.

"You ruined my life, Mors." Areil spoke quickly but kept her voice carefully low. "Arin and his family canceled the marriage, of course, when they learned of it. My family was shamed. My father didn't ask me to go—he wouldn't have done that—but my family was shamed." She waited, but Mors lay still, offered her nothing. "When I was healed, I left of my own accord. And you, your Honor . . . you and your four. For you, it was jealousy and drunkenness and evil done to appease your pride. Foul, Mors. You are foul. You, the five of you—ruined my life. Can you know what that means? I was unable to bear children. Physicians tried to help, but what could they do? What could *I* do? I prayed to the gods. 'Make what happened unhappen. Turn back the world, return me in time.' But that's not possible, is it? So . . . revenge? Hurt those who had hurt me? Revenge?"

The eyes opened.

"Revenge, yes, Mors."

The working chest. The stiffened hands, hurting skin. The pain. His eyes.

"We become what others make us, don't we? I've learned that; it is as certain as the stars. We're still ourselves, but not who we intended to be. In a moment, one person steers the entire direction of someone else's life, and we all live in each other's shadows."

The eyes closed.

"Essel was the first, when I returned. Not for my family, but for him. He didn't even remember me. Were you all so drunk that night that you didn't *see* me? With these hands . . . These hands, I learned, could accomplish anything. I castrated him in his own bed when he lured me there. It was bloody, and he screamed. I didn't enjoy it, Mors. And a little while later, a year, I think—Uveros. I had some money by that time so I hired a man to kill him for me."

He didn't look, didn't respond. A wave of pain took him for a moment and Mors fought it, suffered it, and Areil waited until it had passed, leaving him breathless and washed in new sweat.

"I can't say that my heart went out of it after two bloody crimes, but I began to think about life and the future. I should build, I thought, as well as destroy. I had learned that life didn't have to happen to me; I could happen to life. Patience, I told myself. What's the old saying? 'Patience serves vengeance best.' I went to Osad and began a business enterprise. Halas was in Osad by that time. I spent six years there. I even met him occasionally at social functions. He didn't recall me, either. I had another name, of course. But I did what many would envy: I destroyed his business. Revenge comes in as many colors as the rainbow. Halas took his own life because of his failure. Or perhaps because I told him at last my true name and why I had ruined him."

Areil moved closer. "Many colors." She felt the pulse of life in him, ebbing life that yet held on. Mors opened his eyes suddenly to shock her, but Areil met his stare without flinching.

"Twenty years passed, Mors. Long years. I sold my business. To make peace with my conscience, I sought faith and lived for a time in an abbey, and I came to think there that I had actually salvaged my soul. But the solace did not last; the abbey was on the coast, it was attacked, and I witnessed more violence. By some fate I was not touched by this violence myself, and I've often wondered why. But when I stood in the wreckage and looked at the burned bodies and listened to the wailing of a few who, like me, had survived, I felt the old feeling awaken in me again like a dark flower that had slept for a long time only to blossom afresh in the shadows of that violated place. I sought other answers and followed my awakened heart, and it led me to the dark arts."

Mors watched her.

"I learned many things from proud, powerful people, strong as only the willful and damned are strong. Are they evil? I think them wise in ways that others do not contemplate and can't imagine. All the signs, all the prayers, all the works they taught me. When I left them, I was old in years but made young again by my purpose, and when I slew Odis, it was by a secret means with these hands." She held them up. "I learned where he lived and I went there. Every evening he stepped onto the balcony of his tower to view the sunset. I fashioned a doll in the image of Odis and on the last night that he came out to his balcony, I mimicked his movements with the doll, then forced him over the wall. He screamed for help as he climbed the stones against his will. I twisted the doll's head so that Odis would look to see me standing in the garden below, then dropped the doll to my feet. Odis's eyes were upon me as he fell, and in the last moment he understood who I was. Four," Areil said. "With these." her hands, old yet delicate, finely formed.

Mors moved his lips with difficulty. His body, resisting him, made weak, bending sounds as he turned his own head to face Areil. "And now. Me."

"Yes."

He smiled.

"My patience is ended, Mors. You are in great pain, aren't you?"

He bared his teeth, his grin, sharing his sophisticated appreciation of her story and of the old woman's achievements. But: "You come. Too late. Witch. Death. Reaches. I em. Brace this. Cold. Black. Ghost. I. Cheat you."

"Mors." Areil leaned very close, now. "Who do you think brought this disease upon you? The pain, the numb limbs, the black, dying flesh?"

He stared, he could not speak, he did not fear death but now he stared at Areil with fear in his eyes, fear. "Your. Curse?"

She bared her teeth, her grin.

Mors tried to laugh, but his pain was too great.

She rose then, erect, proud, a stately white-haired woman in regal dress, and surveyed a last time the frightened Mors, lean and thin and frail, every breath a challenge, his body but a vessel for his pain. The pain. To live with such undying pain.

Glaring at her, Mors moaned, "You come. Witch. To wit. Ness. Your. Work?"

Behind her, Areil heard the approaching footsteps of the returning seneschal.

"See. Me. Suffer?"

575

The footsteps stopped.

"No," Areil whispered.

"My lady," said the seneschal.

"No." She bent over Mors, moved her face close to his, and said softly into his good ear, "I come to complete my work."

"My lady, please."

"My curse," Areil whispered. "Why I waited until now for you." Mors stared at her.

"You will remain as you are, Mors. Forever."

His eyes showed his fear.

"Please, my lady!" urged the seneschal.

She turned to him and begged, "Another moment only. A last prayer?" then leaned over Mors again, smiled into his frightened eyes, pressed her hands, *those hands,* upon his laboring chest, and so quietly that only his Honor could hear her, hissed at him as though murmuring devoutly, "You wish so strongly to live, my lord—"

The eyes. The clenched fists. The pain, the pain.

"—then, by all the gods I worship, live! Stay and do not leave us, Lord Mors! *Live!*"

This House

YVONNE NAVARRO

I wish I were back in the city, amid the noise of the traffic and people, the screams of dangerous children and the midnight gunfire. It is not really as quiet out here as people claim; there are small, insidious sounds that creep around doorways and wind their way into the ears of a woman alone in a big, dark house. The alone part doesn't bother me; this house does. It is not an old one, it is new. Barely a year old and cheap of construction, it moves with every ridiculous breeze and the creaks and moans it makes are only the pretentious lies of a character it does not have.

The house where I was born was two hundred years old and full of the family and its magic. My mother is a white magic witch; I am a black magic one. Where she simpers and squeezes a living out of little potions of luck and love teas, I kill without hesitation. We have been apart for many years, our differences having finally sent me on my own after a nasty confrontation in the front parlor. I remember it grudgingly: it involved some trivial cheerleader who'd met an untimely and quite ugly death due to some rotted wood in the stands of the school's football stadium. There was a boy somewhere in the situation, too, and my mind's eye can still see the sunwheat strands of his hair and the color of his eyes—that same incredible turquoise that television uses to tout tropical seas in vacation commercials.

But that's all old history, and life went on without the boy and his ladykiller smile and beachbum tan, and even without my mother. I found a new home and a job that, while it wasn't the most interesting, at least put food in my mouth and gave me the means to build a modest side living. At first, of course, it was nowhere near the grandiose lifestyle at which my mother had always hinted, but it was also without the slavish service and pseudo-smiles she gave her rich clients as she made stupid little spells and poultices to cure their petty ills. It took me a long time to cultivate it, but now mine is a life not only well funded but rich in details and darkness, intrigue, and the passion that comes with the receipt of an envelope of hundred-dollar bills in exchange for a packet of carefully disguised hemlock meant for the espresso of an unfaithful spouse's lover.

But it is not without its own annoyances. I've had to move four times for one reason or another and have become too well known to use the family name. I've yet to invent a spell that could rid me of my own reputation, though I've managed a number of cloaking concoctions to buy me the time to relocate—after a while, I just get too tired to take on everyone. This house is a first for me and a kind of bitter surrender, a rental under a false name rather than a purchase of my own. Cheap prefab, like a new and flimsy cloak thrown carelessly over the shoulders in disregard of a familiar and snug-fitting coat. I am as lost here as I was two decades ago when I stalked out of my mother's house and into the dusk of a Saturday Sabbath, as awkward in these freshly painted rooms as I was when I spun in indecision at the crossroads that offered me three different avenues of freedom and one path of return shame. Where would my life have led had I taken either of the other two?

More of the past, best left alone in favor of the here and now. This house moves again, laughing at me in a silent voice not unlike the shrill, uncontrolled pitch of a ghostbaby. No character, no maturity, no *empa-*

thy. That same phantom toddler, emitting peal after peal of vicious laughter, all the more grating for its empty, evil innocence. I never could abide children.

It's time to bring the house some character.

Every dwelling has a spirit of its own, though most are silent and shy pulses, the metaphoric equivalent of the stars in another galaxy that are impossible for the human eye to detect without proper equipment. Like a newborn human, a dwelling has a soul and exists within the arms of its caretaker—the surrounding wood, brick, and plaster—totally dependent on the decision of the outside forces as to whether it lives or dies. Most are "fed" and ultimately rooted by the energy of their occupants and live in harmonious anonymity, symbiotic human flesh and inert matter. Occasionally something richer rises from the house's depths, a presence that is vibrant and dark . . . and to me, so very preferable to the empty-headed, chuckling echoes that fill my tacky rental.

Despite my resolve, the loneliness has been getting to me the last few years. I've only been here for six months, yet counting the times I'd found myself staring into the space of one of the unfurnished rooms would be impossible, and there's no urge to decorate, or shop, or do any of the homey things that usually commandeer a woman's life when she relocates. I lied when I said I'd left the loss of my mother and the surrounding family, as well as the memory of the boy with the wheat-blond hair and turquoise eyes, in the past. The pain of those partings still burns, even tonight as I light the seven dozen candles surrounding the pentagram I've drawn in blood on the inexpensive linoleum floor in the kitchen. If anyone misses the scrawny wirehair terrier I caught digging into my trash last night . . . well, they should have had a collar and ID tag on it. Then I would've let it be. Mixed with the dog's blood is a good portion of my own, drawn from a deep gash across my left wrist using the thorns of a rosebush that hasn't bloomed. The one at the side of the house did quite nicely—stupid landscapers, how could they have thought the thing would flower, placed as it was on the north side and only fifteen feet from the shading wall of another house? Scrawny stalks still boasting quarter-inch barbs, a witch's choice of knives.

It took some long, hard thought to come to this decision. There were many angles to consider, not the least of which was that the house is a rental. The original dwelling spirit will stay with it for as long as the house exists; it can't *ever* be moved, and the only way to kill the spirit is to destroy—not to be confused with renovate—the house itself. Actually, calling it a dwelling spirit and saying it's bound to the house isn't really accurate; as it matures, the spirit binds more to the ground on which the home is built—hence the seemingly spiritless multiresidence and office buildings that pepper the civilized world. One spirit divided by so many rooms is seldom felt, and only rarely will a phantom choose a particular room or group of rooms in which to brood. In truth, I don't care about the dwelling spirit of this place anyway. What really interests me is the possibility of *adding* a spirit.

I wrestled with so many questions! A human spirit—but whose? Dead? Or alive? Not such an impossibility, though it requires considerably more effort to accomplish. There was the trade-off to think about, too; I couldn't just snatch someone's spirit—or soul, if you prefer—and leave an empty body somewhere, sitting and drooling but still very much alive. It would be too easy for another to use the empty body as a tool for retribution. If I wanted a spirit from somewhere else, a living person in my vicinity would have to die so that the soul stolen from the original body could be replaced. All *very* tricky.

Oh, I do so love a challenge.

Despite my line of work, I don't relish slashing the throat of some dippy suburban housewife in the rear of Stratford Square Mall, or even giving some cheating husband what he really deserves for trying to pick me up at Carrington's bar. I'm just not into the bloody stuff that much, at least not in volume, and besides, those kinds of tricks are too easily traceable. I'm not so hard to spot or remember, with my nearly brick-colored mass of curls and dark emerald eyes. A stereotypical witch if ever there was one—bluebloods always look like that—and definitely the kind of looks the women in town found suspect from the moment I pushed my first grocery cart into Gorski's Food Store. I've gone for the plain look in this new town, a loose bun and no makeup, and have started to prefer it to the siren visage of previous years; besides, romantic relationships have proven disastrous for me time and time again, and I have no urge to try it here. Despite the passage of time and our differences, I've kept a quiet surveillance on the rest of my family. At forty, I've become at peace with the idea that the family's bloodline will have to be carried on by one of my sisters and my brother—a tall and randy double for Pierce Brosnan who'll have no trouble finding a willing bride once he settles down. I'm sure my mother will be pleased at the ensuing horde of grandchildren.

It's truly amazing how Father Time can gentle the most rebellious of attitudes. Even me—I'm not the same vehement and proud teenager who once screamed vile things at my mother and in return was told in no uncertain terms to choose between the light and dark ways. I chose the dark, which obviously has nothing to do with the slow erosion of the stubbornness in my spirit; as a woman—any woman—grows older, she learns to flex. After all, you can't fight the whole world, no matter how strong or right you are.

Pride, however . . . well, that can be a little tougher.

I'd give nearly anything to see my mother again in person, to hold her hand—now softened by twenty-some-odd years—and smell the scent of her beloved violet candy on each calm breath she exhales. Witches don't live forever, no matter what people think; maybe a little longer than ordinary humans, but certainly not the hundreds of years that foolish so-called experts prattle on about. Witching families are very close and my siblings will always eventually follow where my mother goes, myself having been something of an anomaly when I got the bright idea of self-banishment all those years ago. Now instinct compels me to return . . . yet I cannot. My sense of self, my *me*, has been built from strands woven through the long and twisted genealogy of my family tree, a span traceable backward some eight hundred years. In each generation can be found the great-grandfather, aunt, or third cousin with that barely noticed smidgen of stubbornness and pride—all of which seemingly coalesced in my own unsuspecting personality as a child.

As I gather the things I need to complete the spell that will bring a bit of life and love to this house, the realization that it is not my fault is comforting. A witch is physically like anyone else, and I had no more control over the RNA and DNA that structured my cells as an embryo than did the poor old drunk who scrounges in the dumpster behind the McDonald's at the intersection of Maple and Route 19—the grizzled unfortunate who will be my sacrifice. While bits of my character were formed as I grew and learned from the family, I did not *choose* to be obstinate, nor did I sit down and plan to be the sole, too-proud black sheep revolutionist in our family tree. To have done so would have been akin to my own premeditated emotional murder. It is grossly unfair that I should have to spend my life as a punished outcast because of a ludicrous quirk of Mother Nature.

I try not to be bitter, but I cannot help the mirthless smile that slides across my lips and transforms them into a thin line. My mother, so forgiving of others, so *lenient*—why couldn't she have accepted me and the calling that was my somber inheritance? I could no more have mixed a salve to make someone's bored lover return than she could have conjured the spell that sent that conniving little cheerleader to her splintery —and I still believe well deserved—death. I've spent countless hours brooding about it, and can only assume that it was the *dead* part that Mother couldn't deal with, the actual taking of another's life. After all, she'd certainly turned a blind eye to my often less-than-savory learning process as I grew. I'd started as a toddler who turned frogs and garden snakes inside out to satisfy her curiosity, then grown to a young girl with a reputation for making . . . *odd* things happen to the school bullies when they stole her lunch or candy money. Not once did mother try to stop me or offer any of the white magic alternatives that came as second nature to her and the rest of the family. At times, I think she rather *liked* the idea of having a dark witch in the family line—as far as I know, I was the first—and presumed us therefore protected against the minor jealousies of other white magic families. Perhaps she dreamed of seeing me married to someone in a more powerful darkside family. Reflection makes me wonder if that, too, had something to do with our final blowup —not only had I . . . *eliminated* was the word she used . . . a human being, I'd done it over a teenaged boy she'd never met, a worthless mortal who had no powers or potential.

The shaking drunkard is easy to entice into the backdoors of my van with a bottle of sweet strawberry wine and the promise of more if he will just do a few simple odd jobs. He trusts me so readily—why in the world would I want to harm a drunkard? I am a woman besides, and though I am bigger, younger, and stronger, he hauls himself into the vehicle without the slightest hesitation, that same old assumption of superiority with which all men seem to be born.

Killing him will be another easy task, and bloodless. The liquor he had already imbibed made him cooperative, and within a quarter hour of sending him into the basement to sweep out the old coal bin, the paralyzing herbs I'd shaken into the bottle of wine left him incapable of speech or resistance. I won't give a second thought to slipping a sheet of plastic from the dry cleaners over his head—*This Is Not a Toy!*—and suffocating him at the appropriate time; he won't be able even to twitch. As they track my steps around the basement, his eyes still move and are wide with fear and a clarity of thought he probably hasn't enjoyed in years. Odd how the optic muscles never seem to be affected by paralysis of the rest of the body. In any case, disposing of him will not be difficult; there are centuries-old secrets that work much better than quicklime or burying and won't leave enough for even the most sophisticated forensics team to find. He should count himself blessed; ripping a soul free is a painful thing that my herbs will spare him, and he will not feel anything as he dies.

I am almost ready. The ingredients are gathered—after all these years I can find even the most elusive items—and the drunkard awaits within the dried-blood pentagram. The soul I steal from another and replace with the drunkard's will soon be slipping through the walls and rooms of my rental house; it is a simple transfer spell, really, and the soul I bring here will look for the body of the drunkard, but in the short time span of transference, the flow of oxygen to the man who is bound upright to an old wooden chair and whose stubble-rimmed mouth gapes at me will cease forever. Without a vessel within which to settle itself, a short quarter hour will see the new soul bound to this house—or rather, to me. Unlike the original dwelling spirit, the new spirit can be moved again and again, although as the conjurer, only I can do so—a fact that keeps me from the physical or spiritual revenge that might otherwise be inevitable. Eventual discovery is a certainty, but it doesn't matter; I will change what I have done only if *I* move, and then only to take the soul with me.

The vagrant's soul will be deposited in the body of the other, but his spirit is a weak and incompetent thing, fleeting and sickly, and I don't expect the other's body will survive the shock of transference for more than a few hours.

It will be a sad time, but my pride will finally no longer matter and will truly become a thing of the past. I can go to my mother's funeral with my head held high, then return to the house and the sweetness of her company.

Saunder's Little Friend

AUGUST DERLETH

For almost twenty years, Raneleigh Saunder had kept up a progressive feud with his one remaining relative, Aunt Agatha, who lived in a small house in Stepney to which he repaired from time to time from his furnished room near the Inner Temple, where he had a law office. Their feud was primarily about money, which Raneleigh seldom had, and Aunt Agatha did; and which Raneleigh felt he ought to share, being the only surviving relative in the Saunder line. It was somewhat disconcerting, therefore, to receive a note by the hand of a messenger from his aunt's only servant informing him that Aunt Agatha was very ill, was, in fact, dying—though not so much so as to preclude the possibility of his fleeting regret that there would not be time perhaps for a parting shot at her parsimonious habits.

Nor was there. When he got to the house in Stepney, the blinds were drawn, and the house wore that patient, resigned air of death which instinctively caused him to assume a somewhat similar attitude of appropriate dolefulness. The old servant was alone, and was in the act of packing her things. Aunt Agatha had died and her body had been duly called for; by her own directions, she was to lie at the undertaker's only twenty-four hours, and then be buried. She had left a will, and there was no harm in telling Raneleigh what was in it; so the woman told him. He had been left his aunt's tidy little fortune, and only one condition attached to it; he was not to disturb her favorite room so much as displacing a chair—which was tantamount to telling him that he must keep out of it altogether.

Nevertheless, however goaded he was, he maintained that air of obsequiousness so common to his profession in need.

"Poor Aunt Agatha," he said. "Her death was very sudden, then?"

"Yes, quite," said the woman. "As you might say, struck all of a heap. She was at work makin' something when I heard her call out. So I went to her, and there she lay. I got her up and on the couch in there, and she told me a few things—like to send for you—and that was all.

When I came from the boy I gave the note for you to, she was dead. So I sent for the undertaker, and he took her off just before you came."

"I understand you've been taken care of," he said, though he understood nothing of the sort and would have been hard put to it if she had asked him to pay her wages, little as they were.

"Yes, sir, thank you," she replied. She gave him a slip of paper, explaining, "This here's my address if you should need to know about anything in the house."

"There's really no need to hurry off so," he protested.

"Miss Saunder's wishes, sir. I'm paid up, and I'm off, just exactly as she wished it."

He went through the house, very much aware, with that mixture of regret and relief which is all too human, of the absence of the old lady's acidulous voice. Much as he had hated it, often as he had cringed under the lash of it, he missed it now that it was no longer here to be heard; indeed, he would not have minded hearing it a few times more, provided, of course, that he had had foreknowledge of her imminent end. He went through the house primarily to take a look at Aunt Agatha's room, and noticed with angry disgust that she *would* have chosen the best room in the house to leave behind untouched. It was the only room with a view, opening out upon a little walled garden, certainly not a common sight in this part of London; it was also the most agreeably lighted room, with old-fashioned windows in a kind of semicircle at the far end of the room, just over the garden. And right there, at the windows, stood a table with what looked to have some kind of waxwork or cyla-modeling on it—at which his aunt had no doubt been at work when she was stricken. What a mess! Last wish or no last wish, he had no intention of obeying Aunt Agatha's directive—unless, of course, he mentally reserved, she had the matter secured in her will.

Aunt Agatha went to her grave in due course, and Raneleigh Saunder heard his Aunt Agatha's will read. It sounded very much like her; he could almost hear her tongue clack from time to time, though the illusion was spoiled by the droning voice of the ancient barrister who had had her will in safe-keeping. Raneleigh, who had manifestly some knowledge of legal matters himself, studied the will carefully and ascertained that no one would be likely to step forward and challenge his inheritance of her property if he chose ultimately to make such changes as he saw fit in his aunt's room.

"I shall have to come round every little while and look at the room, I suppose," said the barrister, Mr. Cumberland.

"Have you seen it since her death?"

"I'm sorry, but I've not had time to go over."

Saunder needed to know no more. He lost no time in going to his new house in Stepney; at least he could clear the table at the windows and put the room in something like order before Cumberland came to examine it. There would be nothing to show that it had not been the way he, Saunder, would like it at the time of his aunt's death.

The table at the windows, however, arrested him.

It was covered with objects decidedly alien to his preconceived notions of his aunt's character. Clearly, the old lady had been modeling in clay. Some kind of figure lay partially completed near an ancient Latin tome, directions in which his aunt had apparently been following. The book, he determined at a hasty glance, was quite clearly a kind of work which he might expect to be utilized chiefly by crystal-gazers, professional magicians, and sleight-of-hand artists, to say nothing of those highly dubious old ladies who set up shop in tents at fairs and carnivals and pretended to tell fortunes and interpret dreams.

Just the same, the clay figure fascinated him.

He could not explain that fascination. Even though Cumberland had plainly indicated that he was in no hurry to come around and look the place over, Saunder did not want to waste any time in putting the room to rights; therefore, the fascination so instantly exercised by this incomplete clay figure was something for which it was not possible to account. It was so strong, in fact, that he found himself sitting down to it and actually taking it up, fingering it.

Oddly enough, the clay seemed still fresh; it was malleable under his fingers. He pressed and prodded it experimentally. Quite against his reason, he took up a crude ball of clay and added it to the incomplete figure, pushing at it and shaping it, not at all certain that he was adding to his aunt's conception, though he had an uneasy conviction that he *was* following whatever concept had been in her mind, and, a little later, he had the most extraordinary belief that he should not have touched the clay figure at all, that he should have followed the instructions Aunt Agatha had left him to the letter.

He worked with increasing swiftness, though he was now no longer conscious of Cumberland's impending visit. Under his fingers the figure began to shape up and assume an identity, though he could not put a name to it. When he looked at it at last, he was properly horrified. It was a repulsive thing—a cross between something not quite human, and something completely out of this world, but on the anthropoid side of creation, with a brushy tail and long, gangling, almost serpentine arms, and possessed, moreover, of a wickedly toothy mouth, inordinately wide, an ugly, flat head, one Cyclopean eye, and unusually large, elfin ears.

Saunder gazed at it incredulously for a long minute, his disgust mounting; then he dropped it to the table and fled precipitately, out of the room and down the narrow hall, ending up, unaccountably, in the kitchen, where he paused and pulled himself together.

"What an extraordinary thing!" he exclaimed.

It was almost as if the house had put a spell upon him! He shook himself, much in the manner of an animal, hawked once or twice, as if to be reassured by the noise, and then went back to the room with the view.

There he began methodically putting it in order, arranging things in the way he felt he might like to see them, which was not, after all, too far out of the pattern his aunt had left—except for the table at the windows. This definitely had to come out of that place, and a comfortable chair put here instead, one which would enable him to enjoy the view when he chose to take his leisure—and this, thank Aunt Agatha for dying!—he could now do just about as often as he pleased. He left the table until last, however, so that his very real repugnance should have ample opportunity to subside.

But at last he returned to it.

His repugnance vanished before the discovery that the figure was nowhere in evidence. Apparently, in his haste to escape the aura of malevolence he had fancied he felt about it, he had dropped it and it had broken among the balls and crumbs of clay still lying there. He was too relieved to make any really careful examination of the tabletop, but just swept everything together into the little chest his aunt had used for storage, put the chest away, folded up the table, and moved in a chair— and his rearrangement was complete. Now let Cumberland come!

That night in the house in Stepney was not his first.

It was, however, the first night he was to experience that extraordinary sensation of being not quite alone. It was, in fact, the beginning of a series of quite inexplicable events. That night by itself was extraordinary enough. He woke shortly after midnight, convinced that something had passed over his face. As he lay awake in the darkness, his room just faintly illuminated by a street-lamp not too far away, he fancied that he heard something rustling about not far from his bed, the sound diminishing toward the door, which stood open to the hall—only a small sound, so that in a short time he was able to rationalize it and pigeonhole the entire episode as the work of mice. He resolved to obtain some traps and end this kind of nocturnal disturbance once and for all.

On the following day, he found it necessary to go to the Inner Temple. As he was coming up King's Bench Walk, a colleague in robes on his way to court, hailed him jovially.

They exchanged greetings.

"And who's your little friend?" asked Mentone.

At this point they came up to each other. "Eh? What friend?" asked Saunder, somewhat irritably.

"By Jove! I could have sworn you had a dog or a cat or a squirrel or something trailing you along. Pattern of sun and shadows, no doubt."

"Or old age," thought Saunder, grimacing and going on.

Poor Saunder! This was unfortunately only the beginning. When he went into a restaurant that noon, he was astounded to be accosted by the head-waiter who informed him with the air of proper severity so readily assumed by head-waiters who must go home every evening to be brow-beaten by wives, mothers, mothers-in-law, and/or landladies, that animals were not permitted inside.

"What animals!" exclaimed Saunder angrily.

"Sir, you had an animal—a creature," said the head-waiter stoutly.

"Have a care, sir! I am in law. You accuse me of bringing an animal into the restaurant. I own none. Produce it, if you please."

The head-waiter looked haughtily around, but in a moment his hauteur crumpled, and a kind of exasperated desperation took its place. He mumbled something about "its" having got away "under a table," and finally excused himself and took himself off muttering sullenly under his breath that Saunder did indeed have an animal trailing him into the restaurant.

Throughout Saunder's meal, he saw the head-waiter watching him with studied intentness, and once he saw him making his way purposefully over toward his table, only to stop halfway there, bewildered, and turn around again. "What a peculiar fellow!" thought Saunder. "He ought to be committed." He made a mental note to look into the matter, time permitting, with that comfortable sense of security which arises in the knowledge that time would never permit that sort of excursion.

Thenceforth, Saunder was badgered at virtually every occasion.

Wherever he went, he was accosted by inquiries about his "pet," or his "little friend," or that "stray dog" which was following him around; he was tormented by wits who made jokes at the expense of creatures which were manifestly born wholly within that strange, unreal world of delirium tremens—which, for a reasonably abstemious man, was very trying; and, worst of all, he got so that he actually began to share the unbelievable fancies which seemed to obsess all his friends and acquaintances with such fiendish persistence and such remarkable unanimity. He reached that point in his existence approximately eight days after his meeting with Mentone at the Inner Temple.

It was in the evening, just as a yellow fog was beginning to haunt the streets near his home, that he thought he saw something following him on the rim of a streetlamp's glow. He turned at once, somewhat more quickly than he might otherwise have moved, had he not been goaded almost beyond endurance by the singular conspiracy against him manifested by the torment imposed upon him by his acquaintances. There was nothing, of course. Yet he could have sworn that he had seen something. Since there was nothing, however, it was clearly the result of all the jibes and insults he had taken acting upon his imagination.

Unfortunately, ever since that first night he had heard the mice in his bedroom, he had kept on hearing them. Though he had set traps in every conceivable place, he had not caught one. Nor had there shown any evidence of anything at all getting at the bait he had set out. More than just hearing the mice, he had felt them about his neck once or twice, and this was doubly disagreeable because, instead of something soft and warm and furry, they had been strangely cold and somewhat moist and not at all furry.

Saunder, who was not overly endowed with imagination, nevertheless was not so stupid as to decide at the end of ten days that his Aunt Agatha had left him a very dubious legacy indeed. He was loath to give up his house, but he had already begun to shun his acquaintances, even to the extent of avoiding his club; yet he could not forever endure the sport of those he met on familiar terms, nor could he long stand the peculiar hallucinations which afflicted him from time to time—among which those of seeing pursuing animals were not the least disturbing.

Quite by chance, he unearthed his aunt's claywork chest one morning and discovered that someone had evidently been tampering with it. The clasp he had very distinctly pushed shut stood open. He took the chest up and lifted the cover, somewhat apprehensively.

Inside lay the ancient book of lore and legend which his aunt had used. With a prickling of his scalp, he saw that something more lay there —certainly something more than he remembered having put there. The clay, which he had put into the chest in loose crumbs and crude balls, had somehow shaped itself into a vague semblance of a human being. He stared at it for some time, incredulous. He thought at first that the clay had somehow rolled together, but no, the clay was compact, quite as if it had been molded.

Somewhat gingerly, he brought the chest closer to his eyes, so that he might the better examine the strange, unaccountable sculpture. All over the tiny figure were such marks as might have been made by very small fingers and hands. A little shaken, he put the chest down and took out the book.

He opened it at random, read a little, and tried again.

After dipping into it here and there, he was more mystified than ever. The book was a compendium of all manner of superstitions, lore, legend, omens, and the like; there was apparently also ancient Druidic runes, curious recipes (calling for the "blood of a newborn babe," of all things!), and similar outlandish things. Saunder was not sure, but he suspected that quite possibly this ancient tome was proscribed by canon law.

A further examination indicated that it had been bought at Mr. Chandos's shop in Soho, and, after mulling over the chest and its contents, it was to this shop that Saunder ultimately repaired, late that afternoon.

Mr. Chandos was, just as Saunder had suspected he might be, an Oriental, very probably from India, though Saunder was not sufficiently versed in the nationalities to be sure. He was very old, and not particularly communicative, though he was affable enough.

Yes, he had sold to an elderly lady such a book as Saunder described.

"I am unable to understand the purpose of the book," said Saunder, discarding his initial plan to make a frontal attack by representing himself as a barrister on the track of law-breaking.

Mr. Chandos shrugged. The book was nothing, he explained. Only a harmless collection. "Curiosa," he said.

"Yes, indeed, it is curious," admitted Saunder. "But what would an elderly lady such as my late aunt be doing with clay figures in connection with it?"

Mr. Chandos's eyes twinkled. He hissed politely. Perhaps the lady was attempting to make a wax image for the purpose of bewitching someone, Mr. Chandos explained. The clay very probably contained some portion of the body of her intended victim, and was intended to be destroyed in some manner. Such destruction would then inevitably—if one were to believe in such a rigmarole—result in the death of the victim. Mr. Chandos shrugged eloquently, as much as to say that, of course, if one were so medieval as to believe in this sort of thing, there was no good in saying more.

Saunder was therefore nimbly put off, half-informed. Nevertheless, he had his suspicions. He had long suspected that Aunt Agatha would not have minded in the least if he had shuffled off this mortal coil before her; indeed, she had even included such a provision in her will, indicating that if he predeceased her, her small fortune was to go to a home for homeless animals.

As he went out, Saunder was unpleasantly stopped short by Mr. Chandos's calling after him not to leave his "pet" behind.

Saunder swallowed determinedly and came back to the much cluttered counter. "Would you be so kind as to describe my pet?" he asked.

Mr. Chandos looked at him for a moment with intent blandness. "A small creature—like a monkey, with long arms, pointed ears, and a brushy tail. The head, I think, is flat."

Saunder turned on his heel and went out. He went home growing more upset with every step.

He sat for some time that evening turning Mr. Chandos's description of his pet over and over in his mind. There was no possible way of escaping recognition of the fact that Mr. Chandos's description precisely fitted that repulsive clay image he had so strangely fashioned when he had sat down at his aunt's table before the windows!

But such a thing manifestly could not be. Saunder had progressed beyond the point of turning to his law books for confirmation of his beliefs, but he had not yet got to that stage at which he could readily accept something beyond the pale of both the probable and the possible. That a clay image could somehow be imbued with life at his hands was inconceivable—particularly such a ghastly travesty as the thing which had so repelled him.

Just the same, Saunder did not propose to take any chances. He began systematically to watch for things out of the corners of his eyes. The result of this was that he had more hallucinations than ever.

Or were they hallucinations?

Saunder wondered. Saunder lost weight. More than once, Saunder reminded himself that he ought to have heeded his aunt's admonitions regarding the room with the view.

He bethought himself finally of the "mice" he had heard, and of that feeling of "mice" at his neck which was so much more like the feeling of a clay image than like that of mice.

Accordingly he lost sleep. In the confusion of his thoughts, he reasoned that somehow, inexplicably, his Aunt Agatha had set a trap for him. He had fallen into it, according to plan. He had not the faintest idea of what might happen next, but, knowing how the old lady had been in her bad moments, he could not view his future with much hope.

Three nights after his visit to Mr. Chandos's strange shop in Soho, Saunder heard the scampering sound he had previously associated with mice. He had been lying on his bed, trying vainly to sleep, and, hearing those padding footsteps scuttling past, he got up at once, lit the lamp, and held it high.

Nothing in sight. Nothing to be heard.

But wait—the sound continued, not from within the room.

Saunder stepped into the hall. He paused. The sound came from nearby. He went along the hall, down the stairs. The sound diminished, rose up, diminished again. He traced it, finally, to the room with the view—Aunt Agatha's room, which he had better never have entered.

Now, resolute and angrily determined despite the chill apprehension he felt, Saunder stood in the middle of the room and listened. There were still coals in the fireplace; he threw on more fuel, so that the flames danced brightly to add their light to that of his lamp.

The sound of tiny hands or feet, of a dragging brush, continued unabated from somewhere within the room. He began to turn over chairs in a feverish heat to find the clay image, not forgetting to close the door so that whatever was in the room with him could not escape.

In the midst of his search, he thought of the chest.

He went directly to it, and with each step he took it seemed to him that the scraping and patting sounds grew more pronounced. He picked up the chest, observing that the hasp had once again become undone. Swallowing hard, he lifted the cover.

And there it was—that ghastly clay thing his own hands had fashioned under a compulsion certainly not his own—crouched there in the recess of that chest animated by an unholy force, working rapidly over another image wrought out of what remained of that clay!

Saunder stood for one shocked moment looking at something his senses recognized but his mind denied. He saw that horrible creature's animation, he recognized the figure being shaped so unbelievably by those awkward clay hands at the end of those gangling clay arms as that of a man—then, with a cry of revulsion, he seized both the clay things in the chest and hurled them into the flames on the hearth.

It was unfortunate that Saunder did not take the time to examine the figure of the man more closely; he might then have recognized that it was, however crude, an image of himself.

The flames licked up and enveloped the clay figures.

Saunder dropped the chest and clawed at his throat. He fell back against the table and collapsed on the floor, completely oblivious of the lamp he knocked over. He felt for one cataclysmic moment as if all the coals on the hearth had come alive inside him.

The house was partially destroyed before what was left of Saunder was dragged out of it. At that, commented the coroner at the inquest, he had not been too badly burned. It was, however, entirely extraordinary that he should have burned so badly *on the inside*.

In the Chimney

SIMON MACCULLOCH

Remember the evening when you heard the first faint stirring of Mother's death in the chimney?

Remembering was the warp and the woof, the ebb and the flow of your long firelit talks with her, a tapestry of experience woven afresh between your drowsing minds, or a warm sea in which your younger selves splashed and swam sleek as dolphins. Watching the shadows dapple the wrinkles of Mother's face, hearing her voice meandering down from the springs of sudden recollection to lose itself in the ocean of a lifetime's musings, you breathed only in the past. Her spell kept the present closed as firmly as the old dark books on the mantelshelf, which waited like footmen upon your conversations, but which you were never allowed to touch.

That evening, you were recalling a holiday at the seaside—how many years ago? You had been nine, Mother assured you; a small quiet boy who took each new pleasure as solemnly and attentively as he took her warnings about not wandering far among the crowds on the beach, or keeping his voice down at breakfast in the guest house's sunny dining room. Did you remember being so frightened of the landlady's dog—an old Alsatian you'd never even seen walking, let alone offering any menace—that you couldn't bear to go into the television room where it lay in state, not even for "Thunderbirds," which you'd never missed once since it started? You did. And being so fond of the stripy tropical fish in a local pet shop that you had to go there every day to watch them wiggling through their blue-green fern jungle, and couldn't leave until each had been greeted by name? That too. Then there was that funny museum you had gone to, an hour's bus ride outside the town. A poky little place . . .

Somehow the books above the fire seemed to you to be part of the museum memory, as if they had come from that jumbled corner of history and folklore, or as if the visit had been no more than a story read from their hidden pages, a fragment stolen from someone else's life. But you could almost smell the sour dampness of the building's cramped entrance hall as it tried to mingle with the warm smeary sweetness of the chocolate bar you had left to melt in your pocket and were trying to finish eating so that you could look through the rack of paperbacks and pamphlets by the reception desk before you went in. There had been a book of stories with a picture of a gigantic snail on the cover; the rest had been too dull to remember.

Inside you saw the expected glass cases, so dusty it seemed the thick air had congealed on them. At first sight they made you think of fish tanks drained long ago of life and movement. Things that might once have floated or swum lay dry and dead on shelves shared with insect husks. Colour had leaked away long since.

No wonder the torture tools looked so bloodthirsty. The brittle identification notes assured visitors that they had last been used in sixteen-something. The iron claw ("heated red-hot, for tearing flesh") was black, spindly, and arthritic. The iron boot and thumbscrews must be rusted fast. The cat-o'-nine-tails could have passed for dead seaweed. This made them more horrible, of course; clean, well-oiled implements of destruction would have been as neutrally functional as scalpels or stethoscopes. These executioner's hand-me-downs were wise as old snake's fangs in the ways of pain. Their crusts of rust spoke of long red memories; you thought they must still dream of grinding and burning. The grip of a leather-gloved hand was all it would take to wake them. . . .

That was when the fire popped, drawing your eyes back to where the shadows fluttered round the spines of books. You found yourself trying to pick out the only one from which Mother had ever read to you. *Malleus Maleficarum*, Hexenhammer, Hammer of the Witches. There it was, the unholy bible from which you had been catechised, the fear it inspired not of God but of man. Its lesson was the same as the museum's: Never forget.

That was the connection, of course. The museum had drawn heavily on local witch trials, and you had always taken the one from among Mother's books with which you had been allowed to become familiar as representative of them all, a conclusion to which their leaden inviolability had added its weight. Now, as Mother's talk trickled away into sleepy mumbles, and the fire burned low, you felt the room and the past drawing in around the featureless huddle that the books had become. And when the silence grew sludgy, something broke its surface from behind them, in the chimney's throat.

Your first thought was that a bird was caught in the chimney. The noise was soft-edged and somehow panicky, although free of squawking or scratching. You pictured a clawless, beakless bird squirming in a paper bag, trying to stretch bruised wings. You felt that you should get up, put out the fire, use Mother's broom to coax down whatever was struggling in the hot sooty darkness. But as always when the conversation had seeped away, a torpor had crept over you, and you could scarcely shift your gaze, let alone your body.

Perhaps it was this that made you feel as if it was you stuck in the black cavity behind the books. The light from the dwindling flames, now so feeble that you could hardly see, contributed to the impression. When you tried to dispel your claustrophobia by thinking of the beaches and cliff walks that had filled your mind minutes before, you could recapture none of those vistas or the breezes that blew through them. The memories had evaporated, leaving a clogged heat in the core of which you wormed blindly.

Then the crumpled puppet that Mother had become jerked to life again. The chimney sound, releasing you like a last pent-in breath, died. And although you didn't realise it until much later, you began the wait for the time when those two mutually dependent events would be reversed.

You remembered that at the age of five, you had seen part of an educational programme about Victorian England. It had come after your customary half hour at lunchtime with "Andy Pandy." Usually Mother was on hand to switch off the television before the "For Schools" section started, but that time she had been busy in the kitchen and you had sat rapt as the strange territory that had hitherto been hidden by the drab green blind of the dead screen rolled past.

Until then, "Victorian" had meant only top hats on Christmas cards. Afterwards, the word would be invested permanently with the image of a boy's face, a profile tilted upwards with eyes and mouth wide as if he was finally close enough to death to see it falling on him. The boy was made of ash and soot, or so the grainy black and white of the picture suggested. The narrator told you with atrocious calm that it had been commonplace for boys as young as five to be apprenticed to chimney sweeps, who would use them to penetrate the remote crannies where adults couldn't reach. Here they might well become wedged beyond extraction, and die of suffocation, swallowed whole by the maw of a hungry old house and shut away forever with the bird and mouse bones of its earlier feedings.

The narrator had not used such a fanciful image, of course. That had been left to grow in your mind after the voice-over had been replaced by a sudden silence in which the screen held the boy's blackened face as remorselessly as the stone and brick that were supposed to be gripping him. When it seemed that the scream he was drawing breath for must break the spell, there came instead a muffled thudding, flat and echoless in the close quarters. Presumably this had been intended to represent the last sound the boy would hear, that of his straining heart; at the time, it sounded to you like nothing so much as the heartbeat of the chimney itself, audible only in the innermost depths of its gullet. The scream was never released.

If it had been, perhaps a part of your imagination would not have stayed trapped in a twisted black tunnel as the programme moved on to other topics, eventually to be extinguished casually when Mother bustled in. And perhaps it would not have started to find itself, when Mother seemed to be increasingly absent in mind if not in body as she prepared to leave you for good, back in the darkness of your earliest fear whenever she was gone.

After that first evening, the image of the sweep began to supplant that of the bird on those occasions when the talk would run down, and the air seemed to curdle, and you would try to speak, or look away from the guttering fire, and fail. No doubt the fact that the chimney sound was getting larger, stronger, was the reason—or was it the other way round? I'm sure you wondered more than once what you might hear if your mind could picture something to match your fear in stealthily growing bulk. You were never able to get to grips with the question, because the sound always swallowed your thoughts as it came, and when it had gone it was as ungraspable as the music of another person's dream. But you decided soon enough that if the thing that made the sound ever escaped, it would be because it had changed places with you.

"Mother, do you hear that?" you asked on the third or fourth occasion of the sound's emergence. But your croak didn't wake her. It was as if she had abandoned you as carelessly as when she had allowed the television's unwinking eye to remain open past its bedtime, seeing things for you that you hadn't wanted to watch. Now you were feeling the dreadful confinement of the screamless prisoner from a more intimate perspective.

"Mother, do you remember when I used to watch the children's programmes at lunchtime, how after one time when I'd accidentally seen the next programme I used to cry if you didn't switch it off for me right away? I never told you why that was, did I? Well, it was because one day I saw . . . I saw . . ." You couldn't continue. When you pictured a begrimed child with white eyes staring into endless black, your mind yielded no words, only a soft thudding that the years had neither amplified nor extinguished. Yes, that one memory was to be yours alone forever. Or was it that you belonged to it, your soul orphaned in those longago few minutes of your first abandonment, claimed by the starved eyes of the chimney's prey, and now being gradually reclaimed as the final abandonment shuffled towards you out of dim evenings' ends?

You became convinced that the answer to the mystery was somewhere in the books. Yet Mother's injunction had never been lifted, and you couldn't bring yourself to break the time-honoured taboo in her presence. Still, if the problem had begun when she had left you alone, it seemed fair that it should be solved in the same circumstance. You couldn't wait until she went to bed—somehow she always outlasted your wakefulness—and she no longer left the house. But often you would sit quietly in the parlour while she made herself supper or visited the bathroom. It was on one of these occasions that you first drew down Hexenhammer's neighbour and turned to the title page.

There wasn't one. You didn't know what you had expected; the book's spine had been dumb with age or wear. At any rate, the text began on the very first page, a solid block of tiny print under the word *Obi*. The *O* was a snake eating itself; otherwise the book was unillustrated. You tried to read, but lost yourself in the first sentence, which like the snake seemed determined not to have an ending. The words swarmed from page to musty page, forgetful of chapter breaks and paragraphs, like lemmings eager for the cliff edge of the book's ending, which they duly plunged off. You wondered if there had been other pages since removed, or if the book had simply shut itself gasping on as much as its covers could hold of an overwhelming word horde, like a Venus flytrap caught in a storm of locusts.

From then on, each time Mother left the room you would drift ghostlike to the mantelshelf, and a book would select itself for you. Some were in Latin, and other languages unknown to you. Dead languages, you thought, and the phrase struck you as ominous. Some were unremarkable: a dictionary, a cookery manual, a prayerbook given Mother as a school prize and, you guessed, unopened since. It was as you were looking at this that you realised that Mother never reminisced about her own childhood, always yours. It was as if your talks together were a kind of prayer themselves, an endless incantation whose purpose was to keep alive the child she no longer had. And the child would never grow up; the sentence would simply stop with the book's end, unfinished.

You got the same sense from the photograph album when you found that. The boy she was always reminding you about frolicked from page to page, age to age—John at two, stubby legs just learning to carry him; at seven, skinny arms stretching for the football floating mid-bounce in front of him; at twelve, brandishing a paperback as if the skull on its cover were freshly plucked from an enemy's shoulders. Then the photographs stopped; the sheenless black of the album's later pages sat dead as charcoal in a cold grate. And however hard you thought, you couldn't strike a spark of recollection from that inert mass. What had you done with your life since then, other than try to relive it? The unfilled pages gaped at you. When you turned back to the occupied ones, the spaces between the photographs seemed to have grown, and you realised you couldn't fill them either. The various incarnations of a boy called John flickering in and out of existence against the void were all you had to give you a sense of continuity.

You realised that it was the same with your days now, didn't you? The intervals between the talks with Mother that framed your being were lengthening as she spent more time in bed, or dozed unaware of you in her chair, and you might as well have been asleep yourself for all that you could make sense of your experience during those times. They were blanks in your self-awareness filled only by the glimpses stolen from Mother's books—or by the sound in the chimney, whose heartbeat by then felt more real than your own. Mother's voice was the only thing you could rely on to keep you separate from the twisted wretch whose hourly convulsions threatened to burst the chimney breast. And her voice and memory were failing together, each snapshot of the past they delivered more blurred than the last. Soon you would hardly be able to recognise yourself in them at all. Perhaps that would be a relief—you could slip outside them forever and see what was in the darkness they had been pasted on.

Mother confirmed all this for you when she caught you with the album. By that time you were uncertain enough about everything you had assumed in the past to ask if the photographs were really of you. She trembled, shouted, snatched the book from you, said that they *were* you, that they and the memories they might summon were all that remained of you. Then she wept, saying that she had forgotten so much already, and knew that she would go on forgetting until she lost you completely. Then you would both be nothing.

You knew otherwise by then. Her absences left you not in oblivion, but in the chimney, where you were beginning to suspect you always had been and would be. Its heartbeat was getting louder as she weakened. You found yourself there almost instantaneously whenever she slept, and its interior now seemed less like brick, more like the rubbery stomach of a living creature. Your squirmings seemed only to trap you more completely. Soon there was only one question that mattered to you: If Mother's dying was bringing this strangling entrapment, would her death bring release?

* * *

And now here I am to answer your question. She died last night, "peacefully in her sleep," as they say. I think you guessed when you opened your eyes and saw me squatting here in the empty grate like a carrion crow. It's me who's been released.

If you haven't recognised me yet—I know it's not easy with all this soot—I'll introduce myself. I'm John. That's right, John from the photographs, John who went to the seaside and the witch museum, John who was scared by a silly television programme fifty years ago. John who died in a burning car wreck at thirteen.

Now that's one memory of mine you can be glad she chose not to give you. The choking, the heat like a giant gloved hand closing into a fist around me—I have to admit this stupid chimney dream of ours is as good a representation of the only bit of my life you didn't steal as it is of the only bit of yours that was ever real.

I mean, of course, the time when Mother was carrying you. She was pregnant with you when Father and I died, and I suppose it's understandable that she became obsessed with not losing you too, and came to think of you as a substitute for me. Perhaps if she hadn't been so secretive by nature and nurture, so convinced by the hard-learned tradition of her ancestors that dealings with "outsiders" would bring rack and rope, or the modern equivalent, she could have got the help she needed.

Instead she came to believe that you would be taken from her at birth, perhaps to be raised in a good Christian family while she was consigned to the flames. You're not in a position to have heard of survivor guilt. You'll never really understand how a combination of an immediate personal taste of that bitter potion with an ingrained historical version—her ancestors fled the worst of the purges in Germany, you know—drove her almost mad.

So she was alone when you tried to come into the world, and failed. She barely survived the birth herself. That, of course, was the final weight in her psychological strappado, the last grinding notch on the lever that broke her on the rack, and made her turn to the books she had sworn never to use.

You've looked at them. Most are innocent, a few are noble, and one or two are as filthy in what they tell you to do to a human being as the last part of Hexenhammer. But you've never heard of homunculi, and can't imagine what it takes to turn the fresh corpse of a baby into one, and endow it with the memories of its dead brother.

I'll spare you the details. Suffice to say, Mother renounced whatever hope there might have been for her of rejoining sane society when she remade you in my image. And what did she get in return? A boy-sized doll reciting a soundtrack of the past, a lump of flesh that could talk, and move short distances, and might eventually achieve a rudimentary self-awareness and independence of thought after years of being told it was a person, but which would revert to dead meat whenever her mind was off it. Yes, that's all you are, little brother—a windup toy, something she could play "let's pretend" with through all the endless lonely evenings of her too-long life, until her own memory got too weak to turn your key.

That's when you began to glimpse what was left of that unnamed infant who died struggling to make it out of the womb. That's your one true memory, the one *I've* been stuck in ever since she dragged me back from . . . where I'd gone to . . . and stripped me of my past to clothe you. Now the old bitch is gone, and the spell's broken, and I can have my soul back. God, it's been such a wait. People use the idea of dying and being born all at once to suggest some kind of transcendence, but it's just the pain and the mess of the two sordid events doubled.

Maybe you haven't fully remembered yet; you will now. It's time for us to trade places again. I'll be packing up my thirteen years and heading off to where the rivers of memory end. You, I'm sorry to say, were stopped from going there when you should have done, and I'm afraid latecomers aren't welcome. That's the really nasty part of it. She took your death as well as your life. There's only one place left for you, and it's back where you began. So you really are all hers, forever.

And now you know whose heartbeat you heard, in the chimney.

Wall of Darkness

BASIL WELLS

The wall of the south room on the first floor of the house caught my attention that first day. The faded floral design of the paper that covered its blankness was lumpy with underlying layers of older paper, squares of cloth, and inexpertly applied patches of plaster.

Elderly Mrs. Gaspee, who had died a few months before, had used the room for nothing but storage—why, I couldn't imagine. It was the old half of the house; tiny panes of glass, exposed varnished beams of walnut and oak, and narrow deep shelves built into the east and west walls.

I called it to the real estate agent's attention, and he laughed, rather too heartily I thought, at my curiosity.

"Mrs. Gaspee was a peculiar person," he said. "She never used this room and permitted no one to enter it. Said it was unhealthy."

He showed a mechanically perfect set of uppers in what was supposed to be a winning smile, and cleared his throat.

"A little plaster, Mr. Borton," he said, "or a new partition of plasterboard. Yes, I would advise a partition. A wonderful room. Yes, wonderful!"

Half an hour later, despite the real estate agent, we had purchased the quaint little house. One of the peculiar things about it was the fact that one half of it was purely New England—out here in Ohio—and the other half was a substantial but poor copy of the other section.

It was three months after we moved the twelve miles from Kennard Junction before I found a man willing to plaster and paint the front room. The village of Enselm had lost all its handymen and carpenters to nearby warplants, and as yet, although the war was ended, none of them had returned.

Only by chance had I learned that a farmer named Renwood Peters, a wrinkled, short, skinny-limbed man with a surprisingly big stomach, spent his rainy days plastering and papering for his neighbors.

So the first rainy day in late May, on a Thursday, Peters' Model A sedan grunted into the yard and stalled a couple of feet from our front porch. Peters dumped his plastering trowels, stepladders, and other gear on the freshly painted porch—Vivian had applied the final coat just four days before—and pushed open the front door.

"Where at am I to work?" he asked.

I showed him the south room. "I intend to make this our library and my workroom," I told him. "I'm getting tired of pounding a typewriter on the kitchen table."

"Igad," snorted Renwood Peters, rubbing his protruding middle, "you ain't gettin' me to work on that wall. No sir. Not me. Mrs. Gaspee never done no more than stick more paper on the wall."

"But," I said, puzzled, "I'm not Mrs. Gaspee. I want the wall restored—smoothed up and patched where it requires repair."

"Heh," grunted Peters shortly. "She had reasons for not messin' around with that wall. Last man tried patchin' a hole in it died. Died right by that window a-clawin' panes of glass loose. His skin was raw as steak, and his clothes was like dust."

"And how long ago was this?" I asked, fighting back the impulse to laugh. "You remember it?"

"Igad no! 'Twas after the war of 1812. Old Herrod Enselm had built this big place . . . Herrod was a devil—his folks was all like that—witches and such so they was kicked out of New England years before. . . .

"Fired off all his help. They was green lights and blue lights back of the shutters and ungodly screechin's. Then one mornin' Herrod didn't come out to the barn for his milk jug. And they found him—so!"

"That happened right here?" I inquired, scratching down a few notes. Maybe *Werewolf Tales* would be interested.

"Igad no! Maybe a mile down the pike. Past the Ransom house, that's the stone place, on top of a knoll. Won't no grass grow there, only toadstools and such."

I laughed. "Then this room couldn't be part of that place." I tucked my notebook away.

Renwood Peters' lined old face twisted as he ventured a dry chuckle.

"Igad yes it could. Herrod's niece, what married a Todd, had the house broke up in four chunks. . . . Nobody'd rent the big place or go near it. And so this's one of the wings moved here."

I shrugged. "Then you won't repair the wall for me?"

"Get me some two-by-twos," Peters told me, "and some lath or plasterboard. I'll put another wall up there for you."

"And cover up the grain of those two beams?" I argued. "They're walnut and they're flush with the plaster as it is now. A partition would hide them."

Renwood Peters shrugged bent shoulders beneath the faded blue paleness of his wamus. He set to work reloading his equipment in the car's backseat. Having finished this he turned to me, his dried apple of a face serious.

"Now don't you go tearin' at that wall," he warned. "Paste on some cloth strips and put on paper. But don't be rippin' off no plaster."

And with that he drove off.

The next Sunday afternoon was warm and sunny. I had told Vivian of the old farmer's wild story about our house being haunted or accursed and we had even drafted a tentative plot, between us, that used the death of Herrod as its central macabre theme.

And so we drove out past Ransom's stone-walled farmhouse to the knoll where Herrod Enselm's old dwelling had once stood.

We found the depression that had once been a cellar about a hundred feet back from the highway. I was puzzled at the absence of grass around the rim of the hole and in its uneven bottom. There were fungi, unhealthy-looking colored growths: red, brown, tan, and a foul shade of corpselike white. And there was also a scattering of sickly brown-leaved growth, a snaky, waxen vine with dull red tendrils rooting from each meager leafy joint.

"It is foul!" gasped Vivian, pressing her handkerchief to her nostrils. "Like a—forgotten grave!"

And, despite the sunlight and the fresh spring breeze, I too felt a giddiness stealing over my senses as the full impact of the acrid stench of the shallow pit reached me. I laughed, hollowly, and, since I had come here to explore the ruins, jumped down into the ancient hollow of the Enselm cellar.

A powdery dark dust, feathery as ashes and yet heavier, covered the pit. I tore up a length of the strange vine with the brown leaves, thinking to discover what manner of ugly growth it was, and as quickly dropped it again. A thousand minute thorny needles projected almost invisibly from the snaking vine's sleek length.

And as I stepped back my leg brushed the edge of a small pile of recently cut brush that someone had thrown into the depression. The leaves were yet attached, though withered, to the branches.

I felt the contact and then I saw, with a fraction of my vision, that the little heap of brush was dissolving—crumbling into a powdery dark dust like that already coating the old cellar's depths!

Hurriedly I scrambled out of the place, my breath strangely tight and my heart hammering. That there was some explanation for the strange appearance of the depression I felt sure—poisonous fumes from some underground rift perhaps—but I had lost my desire to probe more into the possibly deadly nature of them.

We drove glumly back to our home and I smeared the throbbing little pinpricks of the vine with iodine. As for the smears of the dark powdery dust, they clung like tar to my flesh and only a liberal dosing with kerosene carried them away.

My trousers were ruined too; apparently a thousand moths had been working on them. More and more I was convinced that some sort of acid, probably in suspension in the air, was responsible.

"Vivian," I told my wife angrily, "I'm not going to let this get under my skin! Even if those fumes once killed a man out there on the knoll they'll be harmless here.

"I'm going to lay the ghost of old Herrod Enselm by tearing off that paper and patching the wall!"

Vivian's dark blue eyes widened in her heart-shaped fair-skinned face. She put her arms around me and when she kissed me her long dark hair blotted out the sunlight momentarily.

"Not today, dear," she chided. "This is Sunday. You know how it is in a small town. The neighbors will talk."

I stood up abruptly, almost letting Vivian tumble from my lap.

"Right now," I insisted. "Forget the neighbors for once. I'm not waiting any longer to get that room finished."

The table knives that we were using to strip away the loose sections of wallpaper were old bone-handled ones we had found in a forgotten nailed-up cupboard. We tore away great sections of paper, eight— ten—twelve layers of flowered, spotted, and striped paper. The floor was littered with it.

"Must be getting along toward night," I said once, frowning at the increasing dusk. "I was hoping we'd be finished by seven."

Vivian held up her wristwatch. It was only five o'clock and outside the small-paned windows the sunlight was bright as ever.

An unusually thick lump of paper resisted my dull blade. I pried at it . . . and it came away with a triangular chunk of plaster, at least a square foot in all, attached to it.

Vivian screamed and started to run from the room.

Pouring from the opening was a flood of inky, formless blackness. Out into the room it rolled slowly but steadily. It built into a dense wall of moving black blankness that slowly expanded itself.

I backed away. The same acrid evil stench that I had scented at the site of Herrod's old homestead was growing stronger with every passing second. And there was a muttered vibrant humming of all-but-inaudible sound that proceeded from the heart of the outward-spreading pall. The sound steadily grew louder.

I pushed out into the other room, a growing sense of helplessness oppressing my senses. I was beginning to realize that I was face-to-face with something that high school or college physics was unable to explain. Somehow old Herrod Enselm had come across an evil force or a hellish living substance—perhaps from another dimensional plane or another world—and this wall had been his sealed gateway between. Apparently only plaster, or the lime in the plaster, served to hold this weird darkness at bay.

The rattle of loose metal and the final chug of an engine from the driveway made me turn from my stunned inspection of the expanding night that was swallowing the room's interior. It was Renwood Peters, his prominent middle bulging through the unbuttoned front of his vest.

"Got worryin' about that wall," he began. I pulled him inside.

"Igad!" he said explosively, peering into the room, "you done it all right, son! Yep. That's what Herrod was sealing off that time, only enough of it got through to finish him off. Then it brisked out the window maybe."

"You mean that hole has to be closed again?" I said. "Why not knock out the window and let it escape?"

Renwood Peters wrinkled up his withered forehead and his sharp old eyes snapped. His old bow tie came off.

"If that hole ain't closed," he said, "no tellin' what's comin'. Maybe they ain't no end to that black. Wouldn't take many years to roof off the sunshine. Then where'd we be?" He was taking off his coat, folding it carefully across the back of our big chair.

"And the stuff eats skin and cloth and wood. Old Herrod Enselm's clothes fell right off him. Igad, we can't let it go loose!"

He ran out the door to his car. His tools were in the backseat and he hurriedly got them out. I ran for the pail to get water for him to mix with the dry plaster. He worked hastily, making a stiff mixture of moist whiteness in his coated metal mixing tray.

Then he dipped his shirt in the pail of water and tied it over his face. I did the same. He took his tools and I carried the prepared dough of plaster. We plunged into the room.

Darkness was complete. We groped across to the wall and I put down the loaded panful of plaster. I fumbled for the electric switch, found it, but there was no glimmer of light in the inky blackness. Light could not penetrate that oily thickening absence of anything but substance!

I became conscious of the intensified prickling of my body. I knew what it was, the devilish material sucking the very flesh from my body. I could hear nothing, but my fingers found Renwood Peters's arm and I could feel him slapping plaster madly against the cavity in the wall.

He slumped down at last. My own lungs were burning and my throat was raw. Every breath was torment. I ran my hand over the damp triangle in the wall. Closed completely!

I dragged Peters from the room, out into the blessed sunlight of the Sunday afternoon. I saw his clothes were falling from his bent old body as though they were rotten, and through the tattered garments his flesh showed raw and red as though it were sunburned or blasted by a desert sandstorm.

Nor was I in any better case. . . .

That is why, today, there are no exposed polished beams of native wood in my study. Instead there are two sturdy partitions of wood and plaster, one built before the other, and next to the old wall a third layer of plasterboard makes yet more secure the gateway barred against the darkness.

Mankind and the darkness must never meet again. . . .

Acknowledgments

"Gramma Grunt" by Donald R. Burleson. Copyright 1995 by Donald R. Burleson.

"By the Hair of the Head" by Joe R. Lansdale. Copyright 1983 by Joe R. Lansdale for *Shadows 6*. Reprinted by permission of the author.

"The Hunt" by James S. Dorr. Copyright 1995 by James S. Dorr.

"The Fit" by Ramsey Campbell. Copyright 1980 by Ramsey Campbell for *New Terrors 1*. Reprinted by permission of the author.

"Witches in the Cornfield" by Carl Jacobi. Copyright 1954 by Greenleaf Publishing Co. as "The Dangerous Scarecrow" for *Imagination*. Reprinted by permission of R. Dixon Smith, literary agent for Carl Jacobi.

"Somewhere My Love" by Stephen Mark Rainey. Copyright 1995 by Stephen Mark Rainey.

"Burning in the Light" by Juleen Brantingham. Copyright 1995 by Juleen Brantingham.

"The Scream" by Mike Ashley. Copyright 1995 by Mike Ashley.

"The Mandrakes" by Clark Ashton Smith. Copyright 1933 by the Popular Fiction Publishing Co. for *Weird Tales*. Reprinted by permission of Scott Meredith Literary Agency, Inc., 845 Third Avenue, New York, NY 10022.

"Next-Door Neighbor" by Don D'Ammassa. Copyright 1995 by Don D'Ammassa.

"Witch Hunt" by Christie Golden. Copyright 1995 by Christie Golden.

"The Laurel Lake Laser" by Aimee Kratts. Copyright 1995 by Aimee Kratts.

"The Only Way to Fly" by Nancy Holder. Copyright 1995 by Nancy Holder.

"The Princess and the Frog" by Tina L. Jens. Copyright 1995 by Tina L. Jens.

"There'll Be Witches" by Joe Meno. Copyright 1995 by Joe Meno.

"Alan's Mother" by Steve Rasnic Tem. Copyright 1982 by TZ Publications for *The Twilight Zone*. Reprinted by permission of the author.

"Blood Mary" by Simon McCaffery. Copyright 1995 by Simon McCaffery.

"Mobile Home" by Michael Skeet. Copyright 1995 by Michael Skeet.

"Of Time and Space" by Hugh B. Cave. Copyright 1985 by Hugh B. Cave for *Borderlands*. Reprinted by permission of the author.

"A Matter of Honor" by R. K. Partain. Copyright 1995 by R. K. Partain.

"Hair Apparent" by Don D'Ammassa. Copyright 1995 by Don D'Ammassa.